The Legend of Jig Dragonslayer

DAW Books presents these delightful fantasy novels
by Jim C. Hines

The Tales of Jig Dragonslayer

GOBLIN QUEST
GOBLIN HERO
GOBLIN WAR

Magic Ex Libris

LIBRIOMANCER

The Princess Series

THE STEPSISTER SCHEME
THE MERMAID'S MADNESS
RED HOOD'S REVENGE
THE SNOW QUEEN'S SHADOW

The Legend of Jig Dragonslayer

GOBLIN QUEST

GOBLIN HERO

GOBLIN WAR

JIM C. HINES

DAW BOOKS, INC.
DONALD A. WOLLHEIM, FOUNDER
375 Hudson Street, New York, NY 10014
ELIZABETH R. WOLLHEIM
SHEILA E. GILBERT
PUBLISHERS
http://www.dawbooks.com

Cover art by Mel Grant.

DAW Book Collectors No. 1592.

DAW Books are distributed by Penguin Group (USA) Inc.

First Printing, July 2012
1 2 3 4 5 6 7 8 9

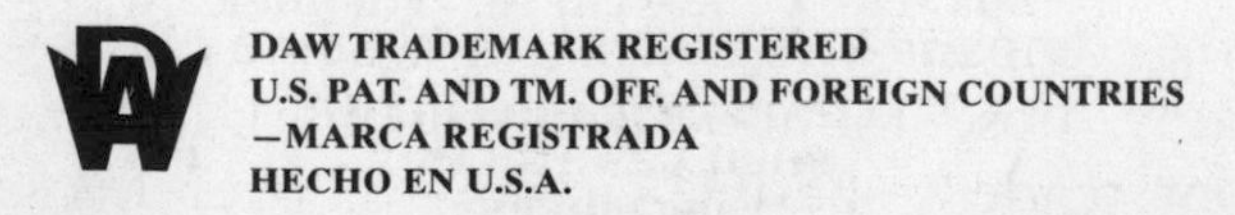

PRINTED IN THE U.S.A.

THE LEGEND OF JIG DRAGONSLAYER – INTRODUCTION

IT'S DISCONCERTING TO realize Jig and Smudge have been a part of my life longer than my children.

I've never been the kind of writer who believes his books are his babies. (Given how hard we work to *sell* our books, or the fact that unsold paperbacks are stripped and pulped, that strikes me as a highly disturbing metaphor.) But there's no denying that Jig is special. I love that little goblin and his companions.

Jig, on the other hand, likely despises me. If given the chance, I have no doubt he'd stab me in my sleep for everything I've put him through. Three novels and four short stories, setting him against everything from dragons to zombies to his fellow goblins. All he wants is to be left alone with Smudge to live in relative peace.

Small chance of that.

Jig is the only character I can remember who sprang fully-formed from my head. When I sat down in September of 2000, I knew *exactly* who Jig was. Contrast this with when I was trying to write *Goblin Hero* a few years afterward. The character of Grell was originally a sleek, deadly goblin warrior, dangerous enough to take on any hobgoblin. She didn't become an Elderly Goblin with Attitude™ until much later. That's not unusual for me. Characters change and evolve from one draft to another. With that first book, Rana became Riana, Fraum became Straum . . . but from the start, Jig was always Jig: smart, scrawny, and unapologetically goblin.

I love that the goblins never apologize for who or what they are.

It's now 2012, and the adventures of Jig and his companions have been translated into five other languages. A gaming miniatures company sculpted and sold a line of goblin miniatures (sadly, those are no longer available). I've received e-mail from readers sharing pictures of everything from a crocheted stuffed Jig to a tattoo of Smudge the fire-spider.

And the last time I checked, *Goblin Quest* was in its sixth printing from DAW.

Not bad for a goblin runt who's just trying to stay alive.

There really is something special about that little guy. One reader wrote an essay describing Jig as everyman, and while it entertains me to no end to read an academic-style analysis of the goblins, I think there's some truth to her claim. We all know what it's like to feel afraid, to feel bullied and alone. We know what it's like to be in so far over our heads that we don't believe we'll ever get out, and sometimes we all just wish we could shove that one annoying person into the tunnel-cat pit.

Or maybe that last part is just me . . .

Though I didn't know it when I was writing the book, in many ways, Jig marked the beginning of my career as a writer. This was the book that helped me to find my agent and landed me my first deal with a major publisher. Since the mass market release of *Goblin Quest* back in 2006, I've completed two series and will be launching a third this year with *Libriomancer*, a book I'm delighted to say features the return of a certain fire-spider.

But no matter how many new books and stories I write, I suspect that there will always be people who think of me as "that goblin guy." And you know what? I'm all right with that.

In fact, I'm proud.

Jim C. Hines
February 2012

The Legend of Jig Dragonslayer

Goblin Quest

"We may be outnumbered. They may have magic and muscle on their side. But we're goblins! We're tough, we're mean, and we're more than a match for a few so-called heroes. Some of us will die, but for the survivors, this will be a victory to live forever in goblin memories."

—Goblin captain (name unknown), shortly before his death by multiple stab wounds to the back.

CHAPTER 1

Muck Duty

JIG HATED MUCK DUTY.

He didn't mind the actual work. He liked the metallic smell of the distillation room, where week-old blood and toadstool residue dried in their trays. He never complained about having to scrape the pans as clean as possible and mix the residue with boiled fat, spiderwebs, and a dark green broth that smelled of rotting plants. He liked the way it all went from a lumpy soup to a smooth, gelatinous slime as he forced his stirring stick around and around in the giant bowl.

Walking around with the muck pot hanging awkwardly from his shoulder as he doled out gobs of the slow-burning stuff wasn't so bad either. True, if he got careless, it would be easy to splatter a bit of muck onto his skin. Even when it wasn't lit, the mixture could raise blisters in a matter of seconds. When burning, the yellow and green flames were almost impossible to extinguish, which was why they used muck to light the lair. But Jig was careful, and unlike most muck workers, he had survived for several years with all his fingers intact.

Jig would have been perfectly happy if he weren't the only goblin his age who still got stuck with muck duty. It was a job for children. Goblins Jig's age were supposed to be warriors, but the few times Jig had gone on patrol had only sealed his reputation as the clumsy runt of his generation.

He adjusted the thin handle on his shoulder. The goblin lair held forty-six fire bowls. Each one was little more than a hole in the dark red obsidian of the walls, with a palm-size depression at the bottom to hold two days' worth of muck. Jig squinted at the fourth fire bowl, the last in the corridor that led out of the distillation room and into the main cavern.

To Jig the flame was nothing but a blur. He could bring the fire into better focus by squinting, but that required him to put his face closer to the fire than he liked. The triangle of flame flickered as his breath touched it. The bowl was nearly empty. Whoever made the rounds yesterday had been lazy, and Jig would have to relight many of the bowls before he was done.

"Lazy children," he muttered angrily. He dipped a metal spatula into the muck pot and carefully scooped out a large blob. This he scraped into the dying fire bowl, where the flame whooshed and grew as it touched new fuel. He scraped as much muck from the spatula as he could, then extinguished it in the sack of sand on his belt. It wouldn't do to return a still-burning spatula to his pot.

He passed into the main cavern, a roughly circular, high-ceilinged cave of hard obsidian. The walls felt greasy to the touch, the polish of the rock hidden beneath years of grime. While the muck fires gave off very little smoke, several centuries of "very little" had led to a blackened, soot-covered ceiling. The sweaty odor of five hundred goblins mixed with the powerful scent of Golaka's cooking. Jig's mouth began to water as he smelled a batch of pickled toadstools boiling in Golaka's great cauldron.

Jig kept close to the wall as he worked. The faster he could finish his duties, the sooner he could eat.

But the other goblins weren't going to make things easy. Five or six large goblins stood bunched around the closest fire bowl, watching him. Jig's pointed ears twitched. He was too nearsighted to make out who was waiting there, but he could hear their amused whispers. Porak and his friends. This was going to hurt.

He thought about starting with the other side of the cavern. If he worked his way around to Porak's spot, which would take at least an hour, maybe they would get bored and go away.

"And maybe Porak will make me honorary captain of his patrol," Jig muttered. More likely they would circle around to meet him, and whatever they planned would be worse for having to make the effort.

Jig hunched lower and walked toward the group. Most of them were still eating, he noticed, and he tried to ignore his hunger. Porak grinned as Jig approached. Long fangs curved up toward his eyes, and his ears quivered with amusement. Several of his friends chuckled. Nobody moved out of the way.

"Cousin Jig. Muck duty, is it?" Porak asked. He scratched his bulbous nose with a clawed finger. "How long before you're ready for *real* work?"

"Real work?" He kept out of their reach, ready at any moment to continue the long goblin tradition of running away.

"Glory, fighting, and bloodshed." The goblins puffed up like rock lizards competing for a mate. Porak smiled, a warning sign if ever there was one. "We want you to come along on patrol."

"I can't." He held up the muck bucket. "I've barely started."

Porak laughed. "That can wait until they mix up a new batch of muck, one that hasn't been contaminated."

Jig watched Porak closely, trying to guess what that laugh meant. "The muck is fine," he said cautiously.

Fingers seized Jig's arms from behind. He squealed and twisted, but that only made the claws dig deeper. Stupid! He had been so intent on Porak that he ignored the others. "What are you doing?"

Porak held up a black rat by the tail. "Look at that," he said. "I don't know who's more frightened, the rat or the runt."

The goblins laughed as the rat flipped and jumped, trying to free itself. Jig forced himself to relax. They wanted him to struggle like the rat.

Porak stepped closer. "Everyone knows rat fur makes the fire bowls smell awful. A shame someone let this one into the mix."

The rat struggled harder, prompting more laughter. The hands holding Jig relaxed. As fast as he could, Jig grabbed his spatula and flicked muck over his shoulder. A few drops landed on his arm, and he cringed as the skin blistered. But the goblin behind him took a far worse splash in the face. He howled and tried to wipe the muck off.

Had Jig been in a better mood, he would have reminded his captor that wiping would only spread the muck around. A louder howl told him the goblin had figured that out for himself.

The laughter of the others had only grown at this display. Jig glanced around for the easiest escape route, but before he could flee, Porak lunged forward.

"Not so fast, cousin." He dropped the panicked rat into the muck pot. "Meet us for duty in two hours. Don't make me come find you."

The rat clawed toward the edge of the pot. Half its body was trapped in the muck, and its squeals grew higher as the muck burned through the fur. Jig couldn't have saved it if he wanted to. Even if the pain-crazed rat escaped, all it took was one open flame and Jig would have a frantic, flaming rat on his hands.

"Sorry about this." He put the spatula into the pot and grabbed his weapon, an old kitchen knife with a loose blade. Not much, but enough to put the rat out of its misery.

He cleaned off the blade, being extra careful to make sure no muck remained, then tucked it back into the sheath on his rope belt.

Well, at least he wasn't on muck duty anymore. This was what he wanted, right? He was going on patrol. A clear step up in the world. So why wasn't he happier? Goblins spent years waiting for the day they could go from lighting fire bowls to helping protect the lair from adventurers.

Maybe that was it. Odds were, if you spent long enough looking for adventurers, sooner or later you were going to find some. Adventurers didn't fight fair. They brought magic swords and rings, wizards and spells, and warriors who cut through goblin patrols as quickly as Golaka's spicy rat dumplings passed through the old chief.

Which reminded him, he still had a rat to dispose of. He headed for the kitchens.

Golaka herself was gone, but one of her helpers was there, chopping up an unidentifiable animal who had made the mistake of snooping around in the tunnels. Jig tossed the muck-soaked rat onto a nearby table.

"What are you doing with that slimy thing?"

Jig projected innocence as hard as he could. With a shrug, he said, "One of the others stole it from the kitchen. They wanted me to give it back before you noticed, so they wouldn't get in trouble."

The goblin poked at the greasy, shiny rat with a fork. "That's muck! We can't eat that." His eyes narrowed. "Who was snooping around the kitchen, anyway?"

Jig shook his head. "Porak said he'd kill me if I told." He covered his mouth and tried to look stupid. "Oops."

"Porak, was it? Golaka will want to get her hands on that one."

"Can I go now?" Jig slipped out of the kitchen without waiting for an answer. As he crossed the main cavern, he allowed himself to smile.

Surface-dwellers had an expression about the wrath of the gods. Since goblins didn't really care for gods, they had an alternate expression—they called it the wrath of the chef.

" 'Rat or the runt' indeed," Jig said with satisfaction.

Jig stopped by the privies on his way to meet Porak and the others. Waiting until nobody was looking, he knelt and grabbed a red-spotted spider the size of his hand. The spider crawled up his arm and onto his head. It gave one of Jig's ears a sharp nip before settling into his hair.

"Ow." Jig rubbed his ear. "Stupid fire-spider."

Smudge, the stupid fire-spider in question, ignored Jig's complaint. He was probably upset that Jig had neglected him all day. But since taking Smudge along on muck duty would have been unwise, Jig refused to feel guilty. The last thing he had needed was a spider who grew hot when he sensed danger. If Smudge had been around when that goblin surprised Jig from behind, they all could have gone up in flames.

Jig met the others near the cavern exit. Of the twelve goblins, Jig was easily the smallest, and he tried to avoid the worst of the shoulder-punching and mock fighting.

"Ah, Jig, there you are." Porak grinned. "Jig's going to be joining us tonight."

Unfriendly laughter spread through the group, and Jig forced himself not to cringe. Everything was going to be fine. He just had to prove himself. He could do this.

"Should we grab something to eat first?" someone asked.

"No." Porak's smile slipped, and Jig kept his face still to hide his amusement. "I think we'll avoid the kitchens tonight."

Jig wondered if anyone else guessed the origin of Porak's black eye. Not that he was going to tell them.

"Let's go," Porak ordered, cutting off any protests.

They passed through a long tunnel until they reached an old glass statue of a goblin, the marker that defined the edge of goblin territory. It had stood there for generations, and was probably as old as the mountain itself. Nobody knew who had carved the statue. Being goblins, nobody particularly cared, either. A big rock would have marked the spot equally well.

Two large goblins stood guard, if boasting about their latest sexual conquests could be considered standing guard.

Jig shivered as they passed into neutral territory. He hoped nobody had seen, but he couldn't help it. The underground inhabitants divided these tunnels among themselves. The goblins held the southern warrens. The larger hobgoblins took the warmer caverns to the west, farther from the entrance. Past the hobgoblins was the cold lake of the lizard-fish.

The lizard-fish were the worst, and goblins avoided them if they could. When food grew scarce, the chief would occasionally send goblins to the lake to hunt. This served two purposes. While the white-eyed creatures weren't pretty to look at, they *were* edible, and food was food. Since several of the hunting party usually managed to prick themselves on the lizard-fish's poisonous spines, these hunting parties also resulted in fewer mouths to feed.

Fortunately, the lizard-fish couldn't leave the lake, and an uneasy truce kept the hobgoblins out of goblin territory. Simple fear kept the goblins from trespassing in hobgoblin territory.

Jig glanced back at the statue. *That* was a true goblin warrior, one who had supposedly killed no less than three humans before an angry mage turned him into a green stain on the wall. Made of molded, and in many places chipped, black glass, he was as tall as most humans, with huge fangs that nearly touched his eyes. The nose was round like a lakestone, and his single eye was narrow and mean. A glass rag covered the other eye, which stories said had been lost to a human's sling stone. His ears were perked and wide, alert to the slightest sound. He was a *real* goblin, and even Porak paled in comparison.

Jig barely came to the statue's shoulder. His only scar was a torn ear, and that "battle" had been with another goblin who wanted to rip off Smudge's legs for fun. Jig's arms and legs were like thin sticks, and his constant squint was nothing like the mean glare most goblins wore. On top of that, his voice was too high, and he had some sort of fungus growing on his toenails.

"Torches," Porak ordered.

"This is dumb," Jig grumbled as one of the others handed out torches. "Why not run ahead to warn any intruders that we're coming? Maybe we should sing, too, in case they're blind."

Yellow nails closed on the blue-green skin of Jig's shoulder, and he yelped. Smudge grew warm and scampered to Jig's other shoulder.

"Because, young Jig, we're going to send a scout ahead to make sure everything is clear." Porak wasn't smiling. "That's called tactics." He raised his voice so the others could hear.

"You have to be smart to stay alive down here. Look at our cousin Jig, talking to himself and so distracted that I walked right up without him noticing. If I were a human, I could have killed our scout while he babbled. Then where would we be?"

Jig cringed as the others laughed and nodded. So much for proving himself.

"We have to be alert. We have to be strong. We have to be tough." With each pronouncement, Porak's grip tightened, so that by the end, Jig squirmed to get away.

"You hear me?" Porak glared at Jig. "You have to be tough." He shoved Jig into the wall.

With a harsh laugh, he added, "But even the weak have their uses. This one's going to run ahead to flush out any game. Our own little hunting dog."

Porak pulled out a set of dice, which brought cheers from the others. "We'll stay here, to protect the lair. If you find anything, we'll be along to do the fighting. All you have to do is stay alive long enough for us to rescue you. Go get 'em, dog."

The other goblins quickly picked up the chant, some barking while others punched and kicked at him. Jig covered his head and ran, Porak's loud voice following after.

"If you see anyone, make sure you scream before they kill you."

Jig's bare feet slapped against the tunnel floor. His ears burned as he put distance between himself and the others, but their jeers seemed to follow on his heels.

"Do we really want to send a runt to do a dog's job?"

"Scrawny bitch, isn't it?"

At least now Jig understood what was going on. He knew why he had been chosen to go with the patrol tonight. They wanted him to check the tunnels so they could play their games. This way they could carouse through the night without, technically, ignoring their duty.

Actually it wasn't a bad idea, which made Jig suspect someone other than Porak had come up with it. Porak was tough and mean, but he would lose a battle of wits with his own shadow.

Jig reached up to make sure Smudge was still there. He scratched one of the spider's legs as he walked. "Too bad I can't teach you to burn on command. I'd love to slip you into Porak's trousers one of these nights."

He reconsidered. Some things were too evil even for a goblin. He couldn't do that to poor Smudge.

"If Porak were smart, he would have brought me in on his plan. How does he know I won't tell the chief what he's up to?" Jig stopped to rest for a minute. "No, even Porak isn't that stupid. If he gets in trouble, he'll know who told. Next time he'll put *me* into the muck pot."

He extinguished his torch on the floor and started walking again, taking a left at the first fork, then two rights. He let his ears and his memory guide him through the dark tunnels.

"Maybe I could blackmail him instead. Threaten to tell the chief if Porak doesn't do what I want." He grinned. Porak was big and important. If Jig could get Porak on his side, life would get a lot nicer. No more sleeping by the entrance, where the draft froze his feet every night. No more waiting at the end of the food line so that his meal was nothing but bones, gristle, and the occasional lump of fat.

"No more getting sent ahead on patrol while the others gamble."

Maybe he'd even get a real sword instead of the stupid kitchen knife he carried now. He pulled the knife out of his belt and swung at an imaginary foe. He could almost hear the hiss of the broadsword. He ducked, thrust, and attacked again.

"Help me," Porak would say as two adventurers backed him into a corner. Jig grinned and crossed the tunnel to rescue his captain. He took one adventurer from behind. The other was meaner. He put up quite a fight before Jig's sword caught him in the chest. Jig raised his weapon in triumph as the adventurer gasped and died. Back in the lair, everyone would talk about his heroic battle. They would ask him to lead patrols of his own, and say things like—

"Be patient, lad. You've gone and made me lose count. I'll have to start again."

Jig jumped. The reality of his small kitchen knife replaced his daydreams of battle and luxury. He pressed himself against the wall and swiveled his ears forward to better hear the voices ahead.

"By all the gods, do not allow me to interfere, oh wise one. Perhaps you'd like to wait while I summon a calligrapher to assist you. And you'll want an artist to paint another scene of old Earthmaker."

"Enough. We're not going anywhere until I finish my map, and I'll not be able to do that until you get out of my way."

Jig clutched his knife in both hands. Two voices. The first one sounded old and gravelly. The second was definitely human.

So what should he do? Screaming was out of the question, despite Porak's orders. Sure, it would alert the others about the intruders. It would also alert the intruders about Jig. That was a problem. Humans had longer legs, and therefore longer strides, so Jig's chances of making it back to the other goblins were slim.

He knew how long he would last against real warriors. About as long as the average fly lasted once Smudge trapped it in his web.

Speaking of Smudge, Jig didn't know if the fire-spider could sense Jig's own anxiety, or if he had heard the intruders down the tunnel, but the top of Jig's head was growing uncomfortably warm.

"It's okay. Don't worry." Jig backed away from the voices as quietly as he could. His free hand went up to pet the spider.

That turned out to be a mistake. Smudge apparently didn't see Jig's hand coming, and when his fingers touched the spider's fuzzy thorax, Smudge curled into a frightened ball. With an audible whoosh, Jig's hair lit up like oil-soaked rags.

The knife clattered to the floor. Smudge leaped away. Jig yelped and tried to beat out the flames. Crazy shadows danced on the walls and floor, and he spotted Smudge racing toward the opposite wall. "Stupid spider," he shouted. He wasn't worried about the intruders anymore. Not with his hair ablaze. If they caught him, maybe they'd at least extinguish his head before they killed him.

"Ow, ow, ow." He smacked at the flames, trying not to burn his hands. The fire had died down when Smudge fled, and Jig soon managed to put himself out. Unfortunately the blaze had taken most of his hair with it. His scalp was tender and blistered, but he didn't seem to be bleeding.

Jig leaned against the wall and closed his eyes, trying to block out the pain. "What's the matter with you?" he whispered in Smudge's general direction. "You have eight eyes. Eight! How could you not see my hand? I'm the blind one.

What were you doing up there, daydreaming? I should let Golaka make a pot pie out of you."

Smudge skittered back and climbed up his leg. As he reached Jig's waist, Jig snagged him and lifted him to eye level. The spider waved his legs and pincers, almost like he had understood Jig's halfhearted threat. Which was possible, Jig admitted. The spider was at least as smart as Porak. "That's the last time I bring you along on patrol."

Smudge's head and legs drooped.

With a disgusted sigh, Jig set the spider on his shoulder. "Just try not to set me on fire again, okay?"

Only then did it occur to Jig to wonder why he could see everything so well. His own aborted blaze had lit the tunnel well enough, but it should have ruined his dark-vision. In fact, if it weren't for the torchlight behind him, he would be completely blind.

His first theory was that Porak and the others had come to see what was wrong. But they would have started laughing at Jig's misfortune. Since Jig heard no laughter, whoever had come up behind him wasn't a goblin. What was the expression surface-dwellers used at times like this?

"Oh, dung." He turned around.

It was the human he had heard earlier. In one hand the human held a blazing torch. The other pointed a long sword at Jig. A long, gleaming, very sharp sword. Jig bet the blade didn't wobble in its handle either.

"Draw a weapon or cry out for aid and you'll never draw breath again."

Jig blinked. What was he going to do, scramble for his kitchen knife? He should probably call for help though. Porak's orders. He had to warn the others. It was his duty.

It was an awfully big sword.

"A wise choice. Turn around, and walk into that room up there."

The human followed him to the room Jig had always thought of as the shiny room. Tiny glass tiles, no larger than his fingernails, covered the entire ceiling in sparkles of color. The ceiling domed upward, and the swirls of blue, green, and red all merged into a spectacular fireburst at the center.

Even with a sword at his back, Jig couldn't help but look up as he entered. The adventurers had a small fire going, and the reflected firelight danced on the tiles, turning them into a thousand jewels.

"What's this?" It was the gravelly voice Jig had heard earlier, and it came from a four-foot tall mountain of muscle, armor, and tangled black hair. In other words, a dwarf.

"I found him snooping up yonder passage." The human sheathed his sword. "Not much of a spy. He set himself aflame in his panic."

The dwarf laughed. In barely understandable Goblin, he asked "You lived here long?" Without waiting for an answer, he jumped to his feet and waved a large sheet of parchment in Jig's face. "We've got ourselves a room here that's thirteen and a half paces by twelve paces with a door in each wall. I don't suppose you'd be knowing which of those doors will take us to the deep tunnels?"

Jig shook his head and backed into a corner. "I was lost myself," he lied.

The human laughed again. "Probably true, Darnak. Even for a goblin, he has the look of a kitchen drudge. Perhaps a bit thick in the head as well."

Darnak shook his head. "I've thought the same of you from time to time, Barius Wendelson. That doesn't make you any less dangerous."

"How dare you speak to me in such tones?" All traces of mirth vanished from Barius's face. He started to take a step forward, but Darnak beat him to it, leaving him with one foot in the air and no place to put it if he didn't want to step on the dwarf.

"I've known you since you were a stripling," Darnak said, grabbing an iron-banded club and waving it under Barius's nose. "Prince or no, I'll still crack your skull if need be."

While they bickered, Jig took the opportunity to look around. He had no doubt that their quarrel would end instantly if he tried to run, but at least he could get a better idea what he was up against.

The human was . . . polished was the best word Jig could come up with. His chain mail gleamed silver, every link a mirrored ring. The jeweled hilt of his sword was wrapped in gold wire, and the pommel had been molded into the shape of a lion's head. His knee-high boots were soft black leather, and the purple velvet tights looked as expensive as the rest of the outfit. They also looked ridiculous and uncomfortable, but who was Jig to criticize human fashion?

Barius was strong, broad in the shoulders and trim around the waist. What Jig had first taken to be a black hat was actually his hair, cut in a perfectly straight circle around his head. His goatee was trimmed into a point so sharp you could use it for a weapon.

The dwarf looked the meaner of the two. The scale mail he wore under his white robe appeared battered but well cared for. Jig could see where many of the scales had been replaced over time. Likewise, his war club was nicked in several places, as though it had turned aside sword blades or crushed more than a few skulls. As for Darnak himself, a black tangle of hair hid most of his face. His skin was a leathery brown color. A crooked nose, almost as large as a goblin's, poked over a bushy mustache and beard. Jig could see two piggish eyes hidden beneath caterpillar brows.

Jig saw a third member to their party as he looked around. A skinny elf sat by the fire with his knees to his chest. He ignored the argument, the goblin, everything but the flames. His old trousers and torn shirt were as poor as Barius's clothes were fine, and his red hair was cut short and ragged. His face was odd, and it took several seconds for Jig to figure out why. Surface types insisted on wearing at least eight layers of clothing, which made Jig wonder how many hours they spent dressing themselves. All those clothes made it harder to tell, but if he wasn't mistaken, "he" was actually a "she."

What her role in the group was, Jig hadn't a clue. She was clearly the least threatening, but she could still be dangerous. She looked nothing like the graceful, slender elves of legend. For a second, he wondered if she might be some subrace he had never heard of. He knew there were different types of elves: forest elves, mountain elves, and so on. But urchin elves?

"So what do we do with him, Your Majesty?" Darnak asked.

That caught Jig's full attention. Since the elf was a she, there was only one "him" they could be talking about.

"Safest to slay him," Barius said slowly. "Though perhaps he could be of use to us. Idiot or no, he knows more of these tunnels than we do. At worst, he can precede us to lull the suspicions of any creatures we encounter. Still, I dislike the idea of a goblin in our group."

Jig crossed his arms and clung to hope. As long as he was alive, there was still a chance. Porak and the others might still find him. The other goblins were armed, and they outnumbered the intruders four to one. Even goblins might triumph at those odds. All they had to do was come looking. If they bothered to notice Jig hadn't come back. If they weren't too caught up in their games. If they had the brains to figure out what was going on.

Jig groaned and sat down on the floor. He was, without a doubt, a dead goblin.

CHAPTER 2

Barius's Vital Weakness

JIG HAD ENDURED MANY UNPLEASANT THINGS, from cleaning up after drunk goblins who didn't make it to the privy in time to those nights when Golaka decided to sing as she cooked. None of it had prepared Jig to sit helpless while his captors debated whether or not to kill him.

"He could help us," Darnak said. "Look at Riana. She picked the lock on that gate just as neat as you could ask. Rumor has it the path we want is 'cloaked in watery darkness'—maybe he knows where it is."

"Perhaps he does. But a world of difference exists between an elf, even one of her status, and a goblin." Barius glanced at Riana, who listened to the conversation as intently as Jig. "You should be watching for other monsters, girl."

Other monsters. That they thought of Jig as a monster cheered him up a little. Monster was a step up from "nuisance," which was how most adventurers categorized Jig's kind.

"To invite a goblin to join us is to invite treachery, cowardice, and deceit into our beds," Barius pronounced. "What help he could provide does not justify the risk."

"Ha. As if you've ever gotten anyone into your bed without flashing around your gold and your title."

Jig tried to bite back a laugh and wound up choking instead. Barius whirled while Jig coughed and fought for breath. The human's pale lips thinned, but then he shrugged and turned back to the dwarf. *He doesn't know I understand their language,* Jig realized, thankful for the days when the older goblins would sit around and test the younger ones' use of Human, the dominant language of the surface-dwellers. Each misspoken word earned a kick to the behind.

"Knowing what your enemy says could keep you alive," one goblin had said as Jig lay sprawled on the floor. With a hard laugh, he added, "But it probably won't."

More to protect his bruised body than to gain an advantage over his future enemies, Jig had learned quickly.

Before Prince Barius could resume his argument, Darnak held up a meaty hand and said, "I'd just as soon send him to hell, Your Majesty, as I would a snake who slipped into the palace. But even a snake has its uses. You've always been quick to throw things away without thinking. This is no game, and we could get killed down here faster than you can piss yourself."

"Granted," Barius said, sounding like he wanted to hit something. "But perhaps you've not heard your own words? That is precisely the reason I feel we should eliminate the goblin."

"Aye. Kill the snake if you want, but then tell me how you plan to find its hole?"

Barius started to answer, then stopped himself as the dwarf's words sank in.

"That's right," Darnak said. "Damn me if I'm not starting to chip through that granite skull of yours. Who knows how many of them are hiding up these tunnels? For myself, I'd rather know a bit more about what we're walking into. Otherwise you're likely to find yourself stepping in something unpleasant."

Jig kept his face still as they glanced at him. They wanted to use him as . . . what? A guide? If so, they would likely be disappointed.

He knew some of the tunnels, of course. Every goblin did. Every goblin who survived past their twelfth year, that was.

That was the age when each goblin was taken up to neutral territory and abandoned. It was a trial to see who had learned the layout of the tunnels and corridors that twisted and branched back on one another. Many spent days wandering in the darkness. Jig himself had taken nearly eight hours to find his way back to the lair. But he had been smart. A few weeks before, he had bribed several of the older goblins with food swiped from Golaka's kitchen. In return, they told him the tricks of the tunnels. He learned how to feel the slope of the ground and to listen for the echoes that told of open caverns. He learned the general layout well enough to avoid the hobgoblins or the lizard-fish and their lake.

He also heard many stories of the horrors that guarded the hidden tunnel to the lower caverns, and the gruesome death that waited for any goblin foolish enough to wander alone and lost through the tunnels.

"Worse than lizard-fish?" he had asked, trying not to tremble.

The older goblins laughed. "When your skin shrivels up and your bones tear out of your flesh, you'll wish you'd died a pleasant death among the lizard-fish."

Forty-one goblins, including Jig, went into the darkness that day. Nineteen made it back. Those with torches died first, since torchlight served as a beacon for hobgoblins and other creatures. Patrols found the bodies of a few, some killed by hobgoblin swords, others by arrows or the occasional beast that roamed the deeper tunnels. But the ugliness of those deaths was nothing compared to Jig's nightmares about the others, the ones who were never found. There were many stories about the inhabitants of the lower tunnels. Not a single one ended happily, and most made murder by hobgoblins sound like a pleasant way to spend an afternoon.

Jig had memorized everything he could learn about these tunnels, and he could find his way blind and deaf. He had moved through the darkness, one hand always on the wall, relying only on his memory. That day, memory had proven stronger than fear and confusion, and Jig had made it home.

But the adventurers wanted him to lead them beyond

goblin territory and the neutral tunnels. Once he crossed those borders, he would be as lost as any surface-dweller.

What could he do? He wouldn't lead them back to the goblin lair. His job was to *protect* the lair. Even if Porak and the others had sent him off on his own, he still had to try to stop the adventurers.

Unless he could trick them. He rubbed the tip of one fang as he considered an idea. If he lured the adventurers to the lair without saying where they were going, it wouldn't matter how powerful or strong they were. The goblins would overwhelm them with sheer force of numbers. Many goblins would die, of course. Goblins always died. That was a defining trait of goblinhood.

Wait—maybe he didn't have to risk goblins at all. What if he led them west, toward the hobgoblins? Hobgoblins were bigger, stronger, and better fighters. Jig could escape in the confusion and run back to the lair. By then Porak would have returned as well. He'd probably be laughing about how Jig had run off and gotten himself lost. Jig could imagine the look of shock on Porak's face when Jig not only turned up alive, but told them all how he had single-handedly led *three* adventurers to their deaths. Not even Porak had that kind of victory to his name.

What was the best way to lure them into hobgoblin territory? He needed to find out what they wanted. Treasure, obviously. Every adventurer wanted treasure. They seemed to want it more than food or water or air to breathe. But what else? From the gems on Barius's sword, this lot was already wealthier than the average adventurers. What reward would fuel their greed so they would rush to their deaths without a thought?

His ears shot straight up. Finding out what the adventurers wanted would have to wait. If he wasn't mistaken, those faint voices he heard from the tunnel were coming closer, and they sounded like goblins. His heart sank. They sounded like *drunk* goblins. Soon the others noticed as well.

"So what's this, then?" Darnak asked, turning toward Jig. "More of you? Planning to wait until your friends come along to take us on, were you?"

"We should slay him now, before he can warn his comrades," Barius said.

"No!" Jig cried before he could stop himself.

Their eyes widened. "The little bugger speaks our tongue." Darnak laughed. "Thought you'd sit there and spy on us?"

Jig knew what a real hero would do. A hero would scream something defiant, wrestle Darnak's club away, and use it against the dwarf and the human. A hero might even slay them both before making his escape. Of course, Jig knew all the goblin songs, so he knew what happened to goblin heroes. While he was busy going for Darnak's club, Barius would stab him from behind, and that would be the end of Jig. Unless he was lucky enough to make it into a song.

He had no desire to be a hero. He only wanted to go home, curl up with a hot bowl of lizard-egg soup, and feed dead cockroaches to Smudge.

The spider had resumed his perch on Jig's head, where he grew uncomfortably nervous. Jig didn't worry too much about the heat. Goblin skin was thick, and now that his hair was gone, he should be a bit more fireproof. Still he stroked the fire-spider with one finger to calm him.

"Well? Have you anything to say in your defense?" Barius strode across the room and looked down at Jig, a sneer of disgust wrinkling his aristocratic features like a prune.

A real hero would muster up something clever on which to spend his last breath. He would face death like a man, with courage. He certainly would *not* kick the young prince square in the vitals.

Jig was no hero. As Barius tumbled to the ground, Jig whirled and sprinted up the corridor as fast as he could. Behind him the dwarf swore, the prince moaned, and the elf giggled.

He had to catch the others. If he could reach Porak in time, they might have a chance. Because these were the tunnels Jig knew. Three of the doorways in the shiny room led down passageways that eventually merged into one. The fourth led to the surface.

From what Darnak said, they hadn't explored the other three passages yet. They would expect Jig to return with help, but they'd expect that help to come as a single mad rush.

Twelve goblins. Three passageways. That meant four goblins through each doorway. If they timed things right, the adventurers would face an attack from three directions at once. Even goblins couldn't mess up a plan of such beauty.

He wished Porak and the others would stop singing. They would call their deaths down upon their heads if they didn't shut up.

"Quiet!" Jig shouted as he neared the group. "Intruders. Adventurers, three of them behind me. We need to head back to the junction." He stopped to catch his breath.

The song broke off in midchorus. "Who's that? Jig? Running back with his tail between his legs already?"

"Jig! We thought an ogre had gotten you," someone said, giggling.

"No, I thought a bat had mistaken him for a bug."

A deeper voice said, "But it couldn't be Jig. Jig would never be foolish enough to tell me what to do."

Jig saw orange torchlight on the tunnel walls up ahead. "Porak, you don't understand. There are intruders back there!"

As Porak came into view, Jig bit back everything else he was going to say and retreated toward the wall. He had forgotten how mean Porak got when he was drunk. He was mean sober, too, but alcohol made him even worse. Bottle in one hand, Porak stomped up the tunnel and grabbed Jig's throat.

"Intruders or not, you don't command here. Not unless you want to fight me for it." He squeezed. "Well?"

Jig shook his head, feeling stupid. What had he been thinking? That Porak would be grateful for his help? That everyone would thank him for his advice and follow his plan? That wasn't the goblin way. The goblin way was to charge in like idiots, following whoever was biggest and loudest, and in this case, drunkest. Being this close to Porak meant his every breath filled Jig's nostrils with the scent of fungus-distilled klak beer.

"Come on," Porak shouted. "Most likely our little pup got

too close to the entrance and was frightened by his shadow. But we'll check it out anyway. Weapons ready."

Porak's hand moved to Jig's shoulder. He shoved the smaller goblin so hard that Jig nearly fell. "And you can lead us, pup. Take us to these intruders of yours."

He considered trying to explain his plan again, but one look at Porak's angry, bloodshot eyes killed that idea. There would be no clever ambush. No, they would fight like goblins and die like goblins, the latter being the inevitable result of the former.

He looked at Smudge, who still emitted dry waves of heat from Jig's shoulder. He thought about tossing the fire-spider into the shadows. No sense letting him get squished in the upcoming massacre. But he changed his mind.

"After all, if it weren't for you, I wouldn't be in this mess," he muttered. Smudge lifted his head as if to protest, then turned so he could see where they were going.

"Come on," Jig said wearily. "They're up this way." This was turning into a very bad day.

Where were they? Jig had almost reached the shiny room, and still no sign of the adventurers. Some of the more intoxicated goblins had begun to snicker, and a few were even singing again. Jig's heart beat so fast it was like a buzz in his chest. On top of that, he was going to have eight heat blisters on his shoulder, each the size of a certain spider's foot. This wasn't right. Something should have happened by now.

Behind him, the goblins started in on the chorus for the third time. Jig folded his ears forward, trying to block out the sounds of "101 Deaths for a Goblin Hero," but it didn't help. What kind of stupid song was that, anyway? He bet dwarven songs didn't all end with the dwarves getting their heads cut off or being trampled by horses or catching a poisoned arrow in the eye. "Only goblins," he grumbled.

The tunnel ahead was dark. "They must have put out their fire."

Porak shook his head. "Hear that? Jig's invisible friends are hiding. Maybe he frightened them off."

The laughter of the goblins briefly interrupted the song, and Jig flushed so hot he felt like a fire-spider himself. Trying to ignore Porak and the others, he found himself singing along as he crept up the tunnel.

He can run into battle and fall upon a spear.
He can peek around a corner, catch an arrow in the ear,
Or be chewed up by a dragon he just happened to offend,
There are oh so many ways a goblin hero meets his end.

His mouth dried out from fear. Every step he took was torture. What was their plan? Whatever it was, Jig guessed it would result in a lot of dead goblins. As "101 Deaths" continued, Jig found himself thinking of new lyrics.

The human's shining sword could slice off my poor head,
Or the dwarf could use his club; either way I end up dead.
Only a few more steps and every one of us is doomed.
Why oh why oh why did I go into that room?

"What's the matter Jig, afraid of the dark?" Porak raised a torch and shoved past Jig. "Nothing to worry about. Let a real goblin go first to show you that—"

Jig didn't get to hear what Porak wanted to show him. With a loud grunt, Porak spun and fell. The shadows flickered as his torch dropped to the ground. Suddenly the others were rushing forward, swords and clubs waving in the air as they charged. Porak himself had an arrow sticking out of his shoulder as he pulled himself up and stumbled toward the room ahead. Jig tried not to think about how close he had been standing to the goblin captain. A foot to one side, and that arrow could have hit him. He backed into the wall and waited for the rest of the goblins to pass by. If they were the "real goblins," let them be first to the slaughter.

But only four or five goblins made it into the room. Where were the rest? Jig looked back, confused.

He saw one of the drunker goblins stumble to the ground, not an unusual thing by itself, but at least half of the group had fallen, and nobody was getting back up. He couldn't see well enough to figure out what was causing their collective loss of balance, though.

Hurrying back, he grabbed a fallen goblin and shook him hard. His fingers touched warm blood on the goblin's back. Slowly, Jig released his grip. He could shake and prod all he wanted, but this goblin wouldn't be joining the fight. Jig had never been in battle before, but he was fairly certain this was one dead goblin. The arrow sticking out of his back like a roasting spit provided all the evidence Jig needed.

Sticking out of the back . . . Jig flattened himself to the floor as that sank in. Something buzzed over his head, and another goblin fell. The few who had survived long enough to enter the room weren't doing too well either. Jig heard Darnak the dwarf shouting merrily, stopping only to punctuate his war cries with the crunch of wood against bone. He also heard Barius yelling, "Back, you unwashed creatures, you monstrous cowards of the dark. Back, I say!"

Even if Jig hadn't recognized the prince's voice, he doubted anyone else could sound that pretentious and swing a sword at the same time. But if the prince and the dwarf were both up ahead, who was behind them in the dark? The elf? Elves were supposed to be fearsome archers, but the girl hadn't carried a bow.

Another arrow shot past, and Jig decided perhaps this wasn't the best time to ponder such mysteries. He dropped to the ground and crawled toward Porak's dropped torch. His ears were useless with all the shouting and dying going on, and he could barely see a thing in this blasted darkness. Not that he'd be able to see much better in the light, but maybe he would at least know which way to run.

He crawled past several more bodies to get to the room. Every time an arrow shot past, he cringed and stopped moving. Just a little farther. Once he made it to the doorway, whoever was back there would have to stop shooting, or else risk hitting their own party. *Unless they're a really good shot.* He tried not to think about that.

After an eternity of crawling through blood, bodies, and the occasional squishy thing he didn't want to identify, Jig finally made it. He pulled himself into the room and rolled away from the doorway.

Of the goblins who had made it this far, most lay senseless on the floor. Senseless, and in several cases handless, armless, or headless. A few groaned and swore in the general direction of the adventurers.

To Jig's shock, three goblins were still up and fighting. One sounded like Porak, still attacking and shouting despite the arrow in his shoulder. The other two were too busy with the dwarf to say much.

Jig wondered how long it would take for the last few goblins to die. When Barius slipped in a puddle of blood, Darnak moved close to protect him. The dwarf knocked Porak's sword aside, deflecting a blow that could have split the prince's head. Before Porak could recover, Darnak dropped his club, caught Porak's arms, and flung him into the other goblin, knocking them both off balance and giving Barius time to regain his footing.

Before the fight could continue, Jig heard two sharp twangs, and both goblins fell. One thrashed about on the floor, but Porak groaned and tried to rise. Two arrows stuck out of his body, but he still lived. As Jig cowered in the corner, all he could think was that being a "real warrior" seemed to involve a great deal of pain and blood loss. Darnak kicked Porak's sword away, then walked over to greet the archer in the doorway.

This wasn't the elven girl. Jig couldn't tell exactly what the shimmering form was, but it was too large to be Riana. He stared, rubbed his eyes, and tried again to focus. The outline of the archer ran and shifted like water, blurring into the shadows. No wonder none of the goblins had noticed him. If he was this hard to see in torchlight, he would have been all but invisible in the dark tunnels.

As he entered the room, the shadow-shimmer vanished as

if a curtain had been drawn back, revealing a slender human. He looked around, nodded curtly at Darnak and Barius, and set about unstringing his bow.

"Nice shooting, Ryslind," said Darnak.

Barius sniffed. "Though as always, brother, your approach to battle leaves much to be desired in the way of honor."

The one called Ryslind began to examine the fallen goblins. Those few who were still alive he dragged into the center of the room. The rest he left as they were. "If you prefer, I will let you seek the rod by yourself. Don't worry, when I see our father again, I'll be sure to tell him you died with your precious *honor*."

His voice was similar to Barius's. Both spoke in a clear, polished baritone, both had the same slight sneer—though that sneer was much more pronounced when they spoke to each other. But there was something more in Ryslind's voice . . . more power, a presence and self-assurance Barius lacked. It was that same dangerous edge Porak had always tried to project. But for all Porak's bullying and threatening, Ryslind made him look like a harmless kitten.

Ryslind's hand shot out and grabbed Jig's ear. As he was jerked to his feet, he had the unwanted opportunity to study the newcomer up close.

He smelled of strange spices, and Jig tried not to sneeze. Ryslind was as tall as his brother, but of a more slender build. He wore a loose black robe, tied at the waist with a simple white rope. A short sword hung from one hip, a quiver of arrows from the other. Green tattoos covered the backs of his hands and vanished into his sleeves. They looked like writing, but the spiking, angular characters were no language Jig had ever seen. Not that Jig was much of a scholar. Ryslind was completely bald, lacking even eyebrows or eyelashes. Jig wondered if he owned a fire-spider.

Ryslind's eyes ran the length of Jig's body, and the goblin stiffened. His fear grew stronger, if that was possible, for those eyes glowed with a soft red light. Taken with the robes and the tattoos, those eyes meant Jig was standing far closer to a living wizard than he wanted to. He wondered if he could subtly put a bit of space between himself and Ryslind. A hundred miles or so should suffice.

"No wounds on this one." Barius shoved Jig into the middle of the room. On his shoulder, Smudge flared again, and Jig thought he smelled burning skin. "Probably lost his weapon and spent the whole fight hiding in the corner."

"This goblin shows more sense than yourself, brother." Ryslind clasped his hands together. "Had the one who escaped you before been armed, you would have far worse than bruises to show for your carelessness. As is, you are fortunate I was in place before he led his fellows to attack."

"Here now, we won and that's the only thing that matters when you get down to it," Darnak interrupted. "Let me tie these three up before they try anything else. Barius, why don't you go find out where Riana's hiding herself?"

"Find her yourself, friend dwarf." Barius strode over to face the surviving goblins. "One of these creatures will pay for his assault on my . . . dignity."

"So that's what they're naming it these days," Darnak muttered.

Beside Jig, Porak groaned. "What's he talking about?" The third goblin shrugged, then groaned as the movement aggravated the arrow wound in his gut. Jig tried to look invisible. The prince was close enough for Jig to see the hatred in his eyes, and he wondered what sort of revenge Barius had in mind. Knowing humans, it probably involved sharp knives, hot coals, and a great deal of pain and unpleasantness. Pain for Jig, that was. Barius would no doubt enjoy himself immensely.

"Stupid coward," Porak grumbled. "You led us into a trap. An ambush. Why didn't you warn us about the archer?"

"I didn't know," Jig protested.

"You didn't know. Most of my patrol wiped out, and you didn't know." He snorted in disgust.

"Silence," Barius snapped.

"Silence yourself, human," Porak said.

Jig groaned. He didn't think the prince spoke Goblin—he probably considered it beneath him to learn such a "primitive" language—but there was no way he could have missed the contempt in Porak's voice.

Barius's jeweled sword moved slowly through the air to point at the goblins. Behind him, Ryslind sighed. "You haven't lost your penchant for melodrama."

Melodramatic or not, that sword dripped blue-black goblin blood, and Jig wasn't about to laugh.

"Answer me one question, goblins." Barius paced back and forth, studying each of their faces. "Which of you assaulted me in your cowardly attempt to escape?"

Without thinking about the consequences, without seeing anything but the tip of that blood-soaked sword, Jig's hand raised as if of its own will. Raised, and pointed at Porak.

"What?" Enraged, Porak lunged at Jig.

Jig squealed. Smudge leaped from his shoulder and scurried into the corner. But Porak never finished his attack.

Barius's gloved hand caught Porak by the belt and flung him back onto the floor. He landed next to one of the bodies. Dazed, he clutched his head, and his eyes fell upon the hatchet the dead goblin had dropped. Snatching up his new weapon, Porak charged.

Jig scooped up his fire-spider and set him on his unburned shoulder as he watched Barius take one step back, then another, flicking his sword out of the way of Porak's mad swings. On the third step, that sword dipped beneath the axe, then snapped back up to throat level. Porak either didn't see it or was moving to fast to stop. Either way, the result was the same, and even with Jig's poor vision, he could see blue blood spray the prince's tunic.

The other surviving goblin yelled in panic and fled. Jig started to follow, but movement to one side made him hesitate. The wizard walked with grim purpose after the goblin.

"Stop him!" Barius yelled.

Glowing eyes glanced at Jig in passing, saw that he wasn't moving, and snapped back to the retreating goblin. One hand flicked lazily at his quiver. An arrow floated into the air, rotated to point down the tunnel, and shot off after the goblin. Loud cursing signaled the accuracy of Ryslind's magic.

Jig wondered why Ryslind even bothered with the bow. Perhaps killing people with magic took more energy. Or maybe the bow was simply more fun.

"What are you waiting for?" Barius demanded. "Finish him off. Slay him before he can warn his fellows."

Ryslind shook his head. "Mage-shot such as this has a limited range." He held up his hand before Barius could answer. "And before you protest, dear brother, I suggest you try to fling an arrow three hundred yards up a tunnel that takes at least two sharp turns, and see what you can hit."

"But he'll tell the others," Barius said, his polished voice turning nasal, almost whiny. "Within the hour, we'll face a swarm of the vile things."

"Not bloody likely," Darnak said from the tunnel. He stepped back into the room, dragging the elven girl by her thin wrist. "Not after the pasting we gave 'em. Ryslind just handed them one more reason to avoid us." He surveyed the carnage, counting corpses on his fingers. "No, they won't likely bother us again. My thinking is that we'd best be getting ready for the real monsters."

He scowled when he saw the prince standing over Porak's body. "And what might have happened to that one while I was gone, Barius?"

" 'Twas an honorable fight. The prisoner grabbed an axe and attacked. I had no choice but to defend myself."

"True," Ryslind said. "A fair fight, despite the fact that the goblin had been shot twice. Likewise, I expect it was pure chance that my brother flung the prisoner within arm's reach of a weapon. Most noble indeed."

Barius whirled. "What about you? Sending magicked arrows after fleeing prisoners?"

"Simply following orders. You are the elder, after all." His voice was flat, but Jig sensed more menace in those easy words than anything else the wizard had said so far.

Darnak sat down and stared at the ceiling. "Earthmaker, if you wanted penance out of me, why couldn't it be something simple? Send me to move the Serpent River or chase the orcs out of the northlands. How did I offend you so that you led me here with these two louts?"

That quick prayer finished, he grabbed a leather knapsack and rummaged through the contents. Jig saw rations, clothes, a whetstone, a bedroll, a large hammer . . . the dwarf carried an entire shop on his back. "Aha." Darnak plunged a hand into the pack and seized a length of rope. He cut off about ten feet or so, which he tossed to Barius.

"Tie that last one up before he runs after his friends." With that, he began the momentous task of cramming everything back into his pack.

Jig's hands were jerked behind his back and bound tightly enough to scrape skin from his wrists. When Barius was done, six feet of rope stretched out behind Jig like a leash. The prince grabbed the other end and dragged Jig toward the rest of the adventurers.

In passing, he kicked the body of Captain Porak. "That's the last goblin who tried to flee from me. Keep that in mind if you're harboring thoughts of escape."

Jig noticed that Barius didn't say anything about *how* his prisoner had escaped. He still couldn't believe his luck at the adventurers' mistake. If they had recognized Jig as the goblin who had escaped before, nothing would have stopped Barius from killing him.

On further thought, their mistake wasn't as surprising as it appeared. After all, Jig wouldn't have been able to tell the two humans apart if they weren't dressed so differently. And to them, goblins were little more than pests. If a bug bit you, you slapped it. You didn't stop to see whether *this* was the bug with the torn ear, or if it was bigger than the other bug who had been buzzing around your ear an hour before.

"Easy there," Darnak said. "He's a prisoner now, and the gods expect civilized treatment from folks such as us."

"I doubt very much that they would treat us with the same courtesy," Barius said.

Jig thought he heard the girl snort, but he wasn't sure. Still Barius was right. If the situation had been reversed, there would have been none of this tying of the wrists or honorable combat. Goblins didn't waste time on that nonsense. Especially when they were hungry.

"Your friend spoke Human, goblin," said Darnak. "Do you?"

Jig nodded.

"Excellent. I'm called Brother Darnak Stonesplitter, tutor and scribe to their majesties Barius and Ryslind Wendelson, seventh and eighth sons of King Wendel and Queen Jeneve of Adenkar." With a nod at the girl, he said, "That's Riana.

"You try to betray us, we'll kill you. Same holds true if you try to escape. I don't like it, but we can't have you running loose, telling everyone we're here. But if you cooperate, I'll do my best to see you're still breathing at the end of the day."

"Enough of this," Barius said. "We should get moving. The rod would be in our hands already if you hadn't been so determined to map out every inch of this underground tomb."

"Never underestimate the usefulness of a good map," Darnak snapped. "Try walking through the iron mines of the northern peninsula and you'll quickly come to appreciate my quill. If you ever find your way back out, that is."

Very tentatively, Jig asked, "Will you let me go when you find whatever it is you want?"

"Of course."

Jig nodded as if he believed it. If it were just Darnak, he might have taken the dwarf's word. He seemed to take this honor stuff seriously, and so far, he had argued for keeping Jig alive. Of the four adventurers, that made him Jig's favorite. But the others clearly didn't want a goblin around. Not that Jig blamed them. Were he in charge, his first move after the battle would have been to kill the prisoners. Much simpler that way.

Still, how hard would it be to wait until the dwarf went off on another errand? Then it was a matter of letting Jig "accidentally" get his hands on a weapon, just like Porak.

"So what is it you're looking for?" He hoped they would say gold and treasure, but he didn't expect anything that simple. Treasure would be so much easier to find. Jig knew where at least one goblin hid his collected coins, and there had to be more tucked throughout the tunnels. Of all the adventuring parties who came into the mountain, most were satisfied with stealing the treasure their fallen predecessors had left behind. He could lead them to a few stashes and maybe they would let him go.

But there were a few groups for whom treasure wasn't enough. Barius had said something about a rod. Jig had a very bad feeling that he knew what they wanted.

In a voice so respectful that Jig didn't recognize it, Barius said, "We seek the Rod of Creation."

CHAPTER 3

History and Harmony

"THE ROD OF CREATION," JIG REPEATED. EVERY goblin knew of it, but no goblin knew anything *about* it. Or rather, they all knew the same three things. First, the rod was ancient, powerful magic. Second, it had been hidden in this mountain ages ago to keep it safe. Finally, trying to steal the rod was an elaborate but foolproof way to commit suicide.

"Surely you've heard the song," Darnak said. He had been attempting to sketch the ceiling's design onto his map. Setting quill and parchment aside, he coughed to clear his throat, took a drink from his wineskin, and began to sing in a low, rumbling voice.

There was a mage named Ellnorein
Who lived in times long past.
A merrier man was rarely seen,
For he made magic last.

One day he met a lonely queen,
A lass as pure as gold.
His eye for beauty was quite keen,
So he said in this bold:

A wizard am I, whom many dread,
With power like a God.
So come with me to yonder bed
And see my mighty rod.

"Darnak, please," shouted Barius, drowning out the dwarf's song. "What is this dwarven nonsense of which you sing?"

"It demeans the very memory of the wizard Ellnorein," added Ryslind.

Jig blinked. Truth be told, he had been looking forward to the next verse. Maybe he could convince Darnak to sing the rest of the song later, when the humans weren't listening. Goblins would like this kind of song. Assuming he ever made it home to share it with them.

"Allow me," Barius said. His voice was pure and perfect, a silver bell to Darnak's hunting horn.

Ages past, the high gods clashed,
The skies turned black and lightning flashed.
We men were naught but pawns who fought
And oh the terror that was wrought
As war swept o'er this world so vast.

The gods chose nine from all mankind
To be wizards of the blackest kind.
They pooled their might, from darkest night
They summoned dragons to roam and fight,
And in their wake the widows pined.

The gods' war ended, their quarrel they mended,
And mankind their victims tended.
But wizards' greed had fed their need,
For power greater than dragon steeds.
And so another war portended.

But in that age of the bloody mage,
There came an old and tired sage,
Who raised his eyes toward blackened skies,
And spoke a spell to terrorize
Those butchers born of gods' own rage.

The dragons fled, the nine fell dead,
The power from their broken bodies bled
Into a wand, which he had planned
To bury deep in a faraway land,
That it would stay safe once he lay dead.

Barius let his voice trail off on the final note, and his eyes closed, as if overwhelmed by the beauty of his own voice. Ryslind immediately broke in, saying, "First of all, as any tome will tell you, there were *twelve* Mage-Gods, not nine. You're confusing Ellnorein with a completely different tale. Furthermore, that last stanza should begin, 'The spell was spoke, their powers broke, the mages died in sickly smoke.' "

"Nonsense," Barius snapped. " 'The spell was *spoke*?' What bard would dare set such a clumsy rhyme to song?"

"Pah. Neither has the gut-ripping style of the dwarf version."

Jig looked from Barius to Darnak, then to Ryslind. "So what you're saying is that Ellnorein was a wizard?"

They stared at him.

"Did you not hear my song? The *Epic of Ellnorein* is famous. Surely even here you've heard of the great mage who healed the world after the God-Wars."

Jig didn't know what to say, so he just stood there.

Barius started to protest further, but Darnak interrupted. "The gist is this. Ellnorein was a mighty wizard, but he's dead now. Before he went, he trapped a goodly bit of power in his wand."

"Rod," Ryslind corrected. "The bards said 'wand' to make the rhyme work. But it was a rod, about three feet long and made of simple wood."

Darnak rolled his eyes. "So he put that power into a rod. The Rod of Creation. The power in that thing was the same magic the gods used to bring dragons into the world. According to legend, Ellnorein used it to make this whole mountain out of nothing. Pulled it out of the ground in a single day, then carved out these here tunnels to protect the rod after he was gone. Didn't want anyone else to get their hands on it, you see. Earthmaker only knows what guards the rod today."

"A dragon," Jig said.

Silence.

"What . . . what did you say?" Darnak asked softly.

"A dragon," said Ryslind. "Ironic, yet there's a certain logic to Ellnorein's choice. The magic used to create dragonkind could also destroy them, so what creature would have greater cause to keep the rod safe?"

Not everyone reacted to Jig's revelation with Ryslind's cool appreciation. Riana's wide eyes stared at Jig in disbelief, and Darnak whistled softly.

"We knew we faced an opponent of some power," Barius said.

"An opponent of some power?" Darnak glanced heavenward. "Lad, you've either got the greatest gift of understatement ever seen in a human, or else you've not the slightest idea what you're talking about. You'll be lucky if your precious sword doesn't snap like a twig against a dragon's scales. As for Ryslind, he may know how to toss magic about, but a dragon *is* magic. Throwing spells at one is like pissing on a forest fire. Either way, you're going to burn. We'll need Earthmaker's blessing to steal the rod from one of those beasts."

There was that name again. "Is Earthmaker another adventurer?" Jig asked.

This time it was Darnak's turn to stare at Jig. "Is that a joke? For if so, it's in poor taste."

"Silas Earthmaker is his god," Riana explained.

"Will he help you fight Straum?" When nobody answered, Jig added, "That's the dragon's name."

Darnak shook his head. "Earthmaker expects every man to prove himself. He'll not interfere in a fight, even when the odds are against us."

"Oh. He doesn't sound like much help." He saw Riana cringe.

His hand resting on the handle of his club, Darnak asked, "What would you be knowing of gods, goblin?"

Jig started to answer, but closed his mouth when he saw Riana shake her head. "Nothing," he said meekly. That seemed to satisfy the dwarf. Darnak turned back to the humans, leaving Jig to study Riana and wonder again what she was doing here. To judge by the way the others ignored her, she wasn't a friend. She had done nothing during the fight, so she wasn't here to help during combat. In fact, the only thing she *had* done was hide and stay out of the way. Which wasn't a bad example for Jig to follow.

So he sat down against the wall and tried to wrap his brain around exactly what this party wanted to do. To steal the rod from Straum's own hoard was unthinkable. As Darnak had said, their best efforts would do little more than annoy the great beast, and the most they could hope for was a swift death by flame, tooth, or talon. If the dragon was in a bad mood, he had other ways to dispose of those who annoyed him. Jig knew of tales wherein Straum had stolen the very souls of his enemies. Others he simply turned over to the Necromancer, the sorcerous master of the dead who some said dwelled beneath these very tunnels.

This would make a marvelous song: "The Raiders of Straum's Lair and Their Long, Painful Deaths." Goblins everywhere would sing about this quest as they ate their evening meals. Insanity. Jig had wondered about Barius's state of mind from the moment he heard the prince speak. As for the wizard, well, all wizards were a bit crazy. That much was common knowledge. So Jig understood how these two might believe they could successfully raid Straum's lair. But the dwarf looked sane. For a dwarf, at least. And what could have convinced an elf to throw away the virtual immortality of their race for such a futile—no, such a *stupid*—quest?

"Ellnorein placed the rod here to keep it safe?" Jig asked.

"Now you're getting it," Darnak answered.

"And Ellnorein was a smart man?"

"The wisest mage of his time," Barius said. "Indeed, perhaps the wisest man in all of human history."

"And you want to take the rod away, even though Ellnorein went to such lengths to keep you from doing that?"

"Er . . ." The dwarf glanced away.

"That is precisely our intention," Barius said. "To rescue the rod is my quest. Tradition and honor require me to prove myself to my father the king, as well as to his subjects. My six brothers before me each undertook such a quest, but by retrieving the Rod of Creation, I shall prove myself a man of more courage and strength than the best of them."

Jig tried to understand this. Less than half of all goblin children survived into adulthood. Scavengers claimed many, and others died the first time they ventured out of their territory. The rite of adulthood claimed plenty as well, but that tradition was a matter of survival. The goblin who couldn't find his way through the tunnels was a danger to everyone, and bound to get himself killed sooner or later. Better sooner, so he wouldn't take anyone else with him. But the tradition Barius described was like teaching a child to swim by throwing him into a lake full of lizard-fish.

"How many of your brothers survived these quests?" he asked.

"Four."

"Three," Ryslind corrected.

"Untrue. Thar survived."

"Thar believed himself to be the god of the sea. He fought a master mage to the east," Ryslind explained. "The mage died, but he took Thar's mind with him. So our brother lived, but he developed the unfortunate habit of running nude through the palace, searching for his giant starfish. He drowned in the moat six months later. It seems that our god of the sea never learned to swim."

"Enough," Darnak said. He tucked his map into a long leather tube, which he slid into his belt. "We get no closer to the rod by standing here telling old tales. Goblin, which way leads to the deeper tunnels?"

Jig stopped himself before he could answer truthfully. As the saying went, truth caused more trouble than humans and hobgoblins combined. The last thing he wanted to admit was that he knew no more than they did. They wanted a guide, and a guide they would have. Anything to keep himself breathing a bit longer.

"This way," he said, trying to sound decisive. He would have said more, but he didn't know if he could keep his voice steady. Besides, it didn't matter which of the three doorways they took, since all three tunnels merged anyway. Maybe this would give him time to figure out where to go once they reached hobgoblin territory.

The dwarf had said the way was cloaked in watery darkness. The only water Jig knew of was the underground lake, where the lizard-fish lived. He hoped that wasn't where they needed to go, but considering his luck, he wouldn't be surprised. Glancing at Smudge to make sure the fire-spider was still safe on his shoulder, Jig marched toward the doorway where he and the others had entered . . . only to be jerked short when Barius grabbed his rope and wrenched him back.

"Your enthusiasm is admirable," Barius said wryly. "But we prefer to be prepared before charging into the shadowy bowels of the earth."

Jig sat down and tried not to think about that image.

Darnak grabbed a lantern out of his seemingly bottomless pack and handed it to Barius. Jig stared, fascinated by the device. The lantern was a small metal box with four hinged flaps that could be left open or closed, allowing Barius to shutter the lantern completely when necessary. Or, by leaving only one flap open, the lantern could send a beam of light into the tunnels without being as obvious as a torch.

"I shall go first, accompanied by our goblin guide. Darnak will follow behind me, that he may continue to draw his map by the light of the lantern. Brother, I trust you are able to guard the rear? As well as keep an eye on our young elf, of course."

A few scrapes of flint against steel sent sparks into the lantern to light the wick, and a yellow glow spread throughout the room. Darnak stomped out the few smoldering torches the goblins had brought with them.

"Be wary, my friends." Barius's brown eyes gleamed with imagined glory as he stared into the tunnel. "We have beaten the enemy's first attack, but their resistance will only grow as we venture deeper into their nests. No doubt we will need every bit of courage, every ounce of strength, to survive."

Jig guessed he would have gone on that way for the rest of the day if Ryslind hadn't interrupted. "Either lead the way or hand the lantern to someone who will."

Barius blinked. With an offended sniff, he tugged Jig along and set off into the tunnel.

* * *

Progress was much slower than Jig had expected. After an hour, they still hadn't reached the junction of the three tunnels. Goblins in a hurry could run the distance in under ten minutes.

But goblins weren't accompanied by a dwarven scribe, one who insisted on mapping every twist and turn, often retracing his steps so he could get a more accurate sense of the distance. By the time they finally reached the junction point, Jig wanted to scream. Bad enough to be a prisoner whose only hope at this point was to die quickly before they reached the lake. Listening to Darnak mumble to himself, "Twenty-four, twenty-five, twenty-six . . . no wait, there's a turn here, better pace off the inside and outside walls . . . wonder if the tunnel narrows at all . . . nope, still six paces wide . . ." was pure torture.

Worse, as a dwarf and a teacher, Darnak apparently thought it his duty to critique the stonework as they went, and he was eager to share his observations with the others. "Mahogany obsidian, definitely magic. Someone sent enough heat through this place to melt the rock itself. Even the ceilings have a layer of the stuff. Molten rock is denser, see, so Ellnorein basically burned this place into the mountain. The dark red color comes from impurities in the rock, iron and other elements."

He stopped to hit a small hammer against the wall. Jig jumped.

"Look there, not even a scratch. Normal obsidian flakes away and leaves a nasty edge. I'm guessing that's magic at work again. Good thing, too. If the floor were chipped and rough like normal obsidian, it would shred your feet right through those boots."

"Wait," Ryslind said suddenly. He held up a hand, cutting off Darnak's insights on the buildup of dirt and dust by generations of goblins. Taking the lantern, he shone a light back down the tunnel. "There should be bodies here. I shot at least six goblins before joining you."

"You only now noticed their absence, brother?" Barius grabbed his sword. "Your powers of observation continue to astound me."

Darnak knelt to study the ground. No trace of blood showed on the floor.

"Could we have passed the corpses without noticing?" Barius asked skeptically.

"Nah. I'd have drawn them on the map."

"I can understand coming back to collect the bodies," Ryslind said, looking at Jig. "But would your people have cleaned the blood from the floors?"

"Why would we return for goblin dead?" Jig asked. "We've eaten well these past days."

Only Riana seemed to catch the implications of Jig's words. She turned slightly green and clutched her hands tightly to her stomach.

"To give them a proper burial," Barius said.

"You bury your dead?" Jig stared, trying to understand. Well, the surface was probably easier to dig than the impenetrable rock of the mountain. Still that sounded like so much more work than leaving the bodies for the carrion-worms.

"Not always," Darnak said. "At times they're burned on a funeral pyre so their sparks can rise to the heavens."

"That's disgusting," Jig said without thinking.

Darnak stiffened, and the humans wore matching expressions of anger, their eyes narrowed and their lips tight.

"Those who want to keep breathing know it's not a wise thing to be mocking dwarven rituals, goblin."

Jig swallowed. "I only meant . . . well, the *smell*. Burning hair and skin." His own hair had been bad enough when Smudge vaporized it. The idea of burning an entire body was enough to turn his stomach.

The dwarf's eyes were wide with shock. "And how do goblins honor the dead? What, did your friends throw the bodies into a pit somewhere to rot?"

"They're only bodies," Jig said quietly. He wanted to shrink into the shadows, like Riana was doing. With everyone's attention squarely on him, that was impossible. He didn't know what he had said to anger everyone, but he knew he had better calm them down quickly. "We leave them for the carrion-worms."

"For the worms," Darnak repeated quietly. " 'Tis an offense against the gods, even for goblins."

Jig wanted to argue, but that would only fuel their anger. Better to stare at the floor and hope they didn't decide to punish him for whatever offense it was that goblins had committed. The gods had never complained, so why should these adventurers? It wasn't like goblins left human and dwarven bodies for the worms. Dead adventurers were things to be valued and treasured. Especially warriors, who often carried enough muscle to make an entire meal by themselves.

He started to explain, then noticed Riana, who still looked a bit nauseated. Maybe they wouldn't take kindly to hearing that, if they died, they would end up in Golaka's cauldron. But if they didn't want to be left for the worms and they didn't want to fill goblin bellies, they should go somewhere else to die.

The thought of Golaka reminded him of the smells of the kitchen, and in that instant he felt a wash of homesickness stronger than anything he had ever experienced. He would have given anything to be back in the lair, stealing just one sip from Golaka's huge stirring spoon, tasting the tender meat and tangy broth. He eyed Darnak and tried not to think about the last time he had tasted fresh dwarf.

"The tunnel splits," Barius said, raising his lantern so they could see the dark openings up ahead. "Which way, guide?"

Thankful for the change of subject, Jig hurried to the front and stared at the two tunnels. The right branch was one he knew well. Depending on the turns they took, that tunnel would take them back to goblin territory. Other branchings led to the hobgoblins, an abandoned storeroom now infested with giant rats, and eventually to the lake. The left path could go anywhere.

Older goblins had a saying: *Go with the danger you know, for that's easier to run away from.*

"To the right," Jig said, hoping he sounded confident. That tunnel wasn't exactly safe, either. If the other survivor of Porak's patrol had made it back, the goblins might have sent another patrol into the tunnels. That wouldn't cause much trouble for the adventurers, since the second patrol would likely follow the same thick-headed tactics as Captain Porak. If Jig were lucky, he wouldn't survive their suicidal attack. If not, the adventurers would probably believe that he had led them into a trap. Barius in particular would love an excuse to cut Jig's throat.

But goblins were a practical bunch. If the adventurers had killed one patrol, they might decide not to waste a second. Let the hobgoblins finish 'em off.

Which led him to the other danger. Hobgoblins were an angry, vicious, territorial lot. They wouldn't let anyone pass without a fight. Still better to go with the danger you know. . . .

Ahead, Darnak jumped. "By Earthmaker's hammer, what manner of beast is that?"

Jig looked where Darnak was pointing. "Oh. Carrion-worm. Old one, from the looks of it."

"You permit *that* to consume your dead?" Barius said.

Jig shrugged, not wanting to continue that discussion. Carrion-worms resembled oversize white caterpillars. This one was about five feet long, and most of its round segments were bloated, probably with the remains of Porak's patrol. Each segment had a circular mouth on the underside and four black feet, two of which the worm used to shovel food into its mouth while keeping the other two on the floor for balance. When they grew too long, the worms would reproduce by breaking apart, sometimes into as many as six or seven shorter worms. At other times, when food was scarce, they turned on each other, and many starving worms became a single, well-fed carrion-worm. An elegant cycle, and one which kept the tunnels clean.

Carrion-worms were blind, but their senses of smell and hearing were uncanny. They could sense a battle from the other side of the mountain, and they never left so much as a drop of blood.

This one had been munching on a splinter of bone, probably a bit of goblin it had dragged here to enjoy. At the sound of the adventurers' voices, it clutched the bone with the feet of its middle segments and ran into the darkness, moving like an overgrown inchworm.

"It eats even the weapons and clothing?" Barius asked.

"The clothing, yes," Jig said. "Weapons they take back to their nests. They like the feel of metal."

"What's that?" Riana pointed to a thin trail of liquid on the floor.

"Worm piss," Jig said. Her nose wrinkled. "They use it to mark their path. They can find their way back by following the smell, even in the dark."

Ryslind was the only one not disgusted by the worm. His eyes glowed red with excitement and he licked his thin lips as he stared after it. "That was a created creature. Like dragons were born of common lizards, that worm originated from its simpler cousins in the earth. The rod *is* here."

Jig's shoulders ached, and the rope had already scraped his wrists raw. He didn't care about created creatures or Ellnorein's rod. He was hungry and frustrated, and his fear had begun to wear off. There was only so long he could sustain that level of terror. After a while impatience took the place of fear. Sure, Death was going to find him sooner or later, but it seemed as though Death were taking the scenic route to get there.

Darnak dipped his quill in ink. He had secured the inkpot to the strap of his backpack in a tiny harness. A leather thong around the neck of the pot kept it from falling free.

Darnak scratched a few new lines on his parchment, presumably marking the spot they had found the worms. Though why that information was useful, Jig had no idea.

Perhaps Death delayed because he had decided to make a map along the way. If that were the case, Jig might live as long as an elf.

"Let us be on our way." Barius tugged Jig's rope, forcing him forward and wrenching his shoulder.

Fortunately, they encountered no goblins. Perhaps the other survivor of Porak's patrol hadn't made it back to the lair. More likely they waited safe in goblin territory, listening for the sounds of battle. They might even be wagering on how long the adventurers would last against the hobgoblins. Jig wondered who would be sent out at the end of the fight to count corpses. Often he got chosen for that thankless duty, earning a few coins from the goblins who won their bets and a few bruises from the losers. As a change of pace, this time Jig would be one of the corpses instead.

They passed the tall crack that led back to the goblin lair. A slight draft carried the smell of sizzling meat into the tunnel.

"What's up that way?" Darnak asked. "What's that awful stench?"

Jig looked longingly at the ragged crack. His mouth had watered so much that a trickle of drool ran down his chin. To think he had complained about muck duty. He would cheerfully keep the fire bowls lit for the rest of his days if it meant he could go home. He would do anything to be safe again. As Barius tugged at his rope, he added to that thought. He would also do anything if he could just free his hands and scratch the tip of his left ear.

"There's nothing down there," Jig said. "It's a crack in the rock, a hundred-foot chimney to the hobgoblin kitchens below."

After waiting for Darnak to sketch the dark crack and label it HUNDRED-FOOT CHIMNEY TO HOBGOBLIN KITCHENS, they moved on. The tunnels slanted upward here, and Jig instinctively leaned forward to compensate. After a while the muscles in the back of his legs began to complain. He wasn't used to hiking for so long, and even the slight incline was enough to tire him. Sweat dripped down his face and into his eyes, blurring his already poor vision. He stopped trying to watch where they were going and concentrated on walking. One foot in front of the next, careful not to stumble. He had already fallen once, and with his hands bound, that fall had given him a nasty bruise on the side of his face.

"Halt," Barius said suddenly. "What manner of statue is this?"

To the right, an archway of dark red stone led down another tunnel, this one narrow and low. The humans would have to duck to keep from scraping their heads.

Barius aimed the lantern beam at the wall of the side tunnel, lighting up a detailed statue of a hobgoblin whose glass head nearly touched the ceiling.

Jig blinked to clear his eyes. He could see a wicked double-headed axe in the hobgoblin's hand. A pointed helmet covered most of the head. Muscles bulged along the bare arms and legs, and a round, spiked shield hid most of the hobgoblin's torso.

"Nasty-looking fellow," Darnak commented.

"We should keep going," Jig said. "That's hobgoblin territory. We shouldn't pass the marker."

"Hobgoblin, is it?" Darnak squinted at the statue. "Looks like an oversized goblin, to me."

Jig bit his tongue. Of all the blind, ignorant, stupid things to say. Comparing a hobgoblin to a real goblin. Hobgoblins were big, clumsy, ugly brutes, and goblins were, well, smaller. And weaker. But anyone who had ever tasted hobgoblin cooking knew goblins were the superior species. The differences were endless. If they lingered here for too long, the worst of those differences might quickly become apparent.

Among other things, hobgoblins liked to use nasty traps and ambushes. When they caught a goblin alone in their territory, they had been known to torture it for hours, then send the crippled wretch back to the goblins as a warning.

True, goblins did the same thing if they managed to catch a hobgoblin, but that was simple justice.

"Come," Jig said. In his nervousness, he actually tugged the rope that tied him to Barius.

Barius pulled him back, but with far more force. Jig stumbled closer to the archway, barely managing not to crash into the human.

"Why so afraid? Have you never explored the depths of this tunnel?"

Jig shook his head. "I'm still alive, aren't I?"

Barius grinned and looked at the others. "Then how do we know there isn't some faster way to our goal? Our vaunted guide tells us we cannot go a certain way. But what path should we explore, if not those forbidden even to the monsters? Does it not follow that those forbidden paths should be the ones to lead to the greatest treasures?"

Ryslind frowned. "As a boy, we were forbidden to explore the torture chamber. I seem to remember you following similar logic when you snuck down after father."

"Aye," Darnak said. "You had nightmares for months and kept your brothers awake with your screaming until they moved you to *my* chambers. As much to keep them from killing you in your sleep as to comfort you. Not that I wasn't tempted to shut you up a time or two myself."

Barius flushed so darkly that even Jig could see it. "May I remind you that this is my quest, and the two of you are here at my sufferance? I will be the one to decide our path, and I choose to explore a bit of this hobgoblin lair. Worry not. What is terrible to a goblin is hardly an annoyance to a true warrior."

"You can't," Jig whispered. It was the wrong thing to say.

"Can't, is it?" Barius tightened his grip on the rope and pulled Jig forward. "Come, and we shall teach this goblin what a prince can and cannot do."

The others looked reluctant, but they followed. Darnak had just begun to draw the hobgoblin statue onto his map when a quiet click sounded beneath Barius's boot.

Jig swore in Goblin as the floor fell away and they plummeted into darkness.

CHAPTER 4

Jig's Bright Idea

THE LANTERN DIED AS IT HIT THE GROUND, AND Jig counted himself lucky to avoid the same fate. He couldn't tell how far they dropped, but he landed on his heels with a jolt that threatened to crack everything from his ankles up to his shoulders and sent him tumbling onto the rock-littered ground. With his arms still tied, he kicked like an upended spider before getting back to his feet.

Still, he couldn't complain. Darnak, yanked backward by the weight of his pack, had landed hard on his backside. If that weren't enough, he wound up with Ryslind's knee square in his gut. At least that was how Jig interpreted the grunting and swearing from that side of the pit.

"Where are we? What happened?" Barius sounded close to panic. So much for the fearless prince. Even children knew better than to openly barge into hobgoblin territory. Barius was beginning to remind Jig of a very young goblin he had once known. Upon being told not to touch the fire in the fire bowls, this goblin had not only raced to the nearest flame, she had attempted to *taste* it. She hadn't survived childhood, and Jig wondered how Barius had managed to do so. *Darnak probably had to follow him everywhere, telling him not to eat the pretty fire.*

"What happened is we fell into a damned trap," Darnak snapped.

"How was I to know?"

"The goblin tried to warn you," Riana said angrily.

"The goblin wanted nothing more than to flee," Barius argued. "He said nothing of any trap."

I didn't tell you not to hold your sword by the pointy end, either. Jig held his tongue and scooted away from the others. Barius had let go of Jig's rope in the fall, and right now the last thing Jig wanted was to let the prince get his hands on Jig's throat.

Ryslind ignored the others. "If this rock is magically strong, Ellnorein himself must have created this pit five thousand years ago," he said reverently.

Riana spat. "Smells like piss and mud down here."

Jig's fingers touched metal, and he froze. Slowly he traced the outline of a pitted, broken sword. If it still had any edge to it, he might be able to free himself from this rope. A quick rub of the blade told Jig luck was with him. Ignoring his now-bleeding finger, he began to saw the knot against the sword's edge.

The awkward angle sent new cramps through his arms, and twice the sword slipped away. The others were arguing too loudly to notice the noise. Another accidental cut told him the edge was sharper near the hilt. With that knowledge, Jig eventually managed to free himself.

He had to clamp both hands over his mouth to keep from screaming. Blood pounded into his limbs like hot acid. He gripped his fangs and rocked back and forth, trying not to cry. The pain was so great he didn't immediately notice when Smudge found him and crawled up his leg. The fire-spider made it to Jig's thigh before he felt the tiny, burning footsteps.

What was Smudge afraid of? He couldn't see, but he looked in the direction of the broken sword. As the pain receded, his brain started to work again. What had happened to the owner of that sword? The fall wasn't enough to kill. Even Jig had survived the drop. Surely a hobgoblin trap would be more than a simple pit.

"Where's the lantern?" he asked softly.

Barius and the dwarf were still arguing. He didn't want to interrupt and draw their anger toward him, but. . . .

"Shut up," Riana yelled.

Their voices stopped, and for a moment the pit was so quiet Jig could hear them all breathing. His ears swiveled, searching. There was something else. A clicking, scraping sound.

"The lantern?" Riana asked.

"It slipped free in the fall," Barius said.

At the same instant, Jig whispered, "Something else is down here."

This time everyone heard him.

"And here we sit, arguing like children. Earthmaker help us, we've been waiting like lambs at slaughter."

On their hands and knees, they began to scour the dirt. Jig's cut fingers stung, and he jabbed himself in the palm with what felt like a splinter of bone. The owner of the sword? It did nothing to help his fear. Smudge had grown so hot Jig had to set him on the ground.

"Stay close," Jig whispered. The waves of heat beside his leg told him the spider had obeyed.

"I have the lantern," Barius said triumphantly. Jig could hear him scrounging for something. Sparks flew, surprisingly bright, as the prince scraped flint against the steel guard of his dagger.

The sounds Jig heard were growing louder. There were dozens of them, whatever they were.

"I hear it too," Riana said.

Barius paused. "I hear nothing."

Jig wasn't surprised. The monsters would be cracking Barius's bones for marrow by the time those puny human ears heard anything unusual.

"Light the lantern, boy," Darnak snapped.

"I'm trying." The sparks continued, but with no effect.

In those brief flashes, Jig thought he saw movement at the far side of the pit, but he couldn't be sure. He moved toward the others. The creatures were closing in from both sides. In the blackness, his imagination conjured up one horror after another. How soon before huge insects closed their pincers around Jig's throat or giant lizards dripping with black goo sank their fangs into his exposed skin?

He pulled his legs to his chest and wrapped his arms

around his knees, trying to present as small a target as possible. They were so close. A squeak of fear slipped past his throat. What was taking so long? Lighting fires was a child's duty, so why couldn't a full-grown human manage it? Panic ripped away common sense, and he lunged at the prince.

"Give me that!" He kicked someone in the process, but by following the source of the sparks, he managed to snatch the lantern into his own lap. One of the shutters was open, and the glass pane was slid to one side. Jig squeezed his fingers through the opening and felt the wick. It had slipped down through the crack into the oil supply, and only one corner still protruded. No wonder Barius hadn't been able to light the thing. He could shoot sparks all day without hitting that slim corner of wick, and Jig's fingers weren't small enough to pull the wick back out.

Something touched his leg. Jig screamed and barely stopped himself from squashing Smudge. He stroked Smudge for reassurance, and the fire-spider's head immediately set fire to the film of oil on Jig's fingers. He jammed his fingers into his mouth. The fire died, though Jig would have a blister on his tongue. Not to mention the awful taste of lantern oil.

What if he deliberately set his fingers on fire and used them to light the lantern? If it weren't for the intense pain, it would have been a perfect plan. Having had more than his share of pain lately, Jig doubted he could do it. But his smarting fingers had given him another idea.

"Sorry about this," he muttered, scooping Smudge up with his uninjured hand. He stuffed the fire-spider into the lantern and snapped the glass pane back into place.

The wick blazed to life, and Jig got one glimpse of Smudge tapping indignantly at the glass before he was forced to look away. The afterimage of the lantern obscured the center of his vision. They had light, and he *still* couldn't see.

"What are they?" he yelled.

"By Earthmaker's Black Anvil," Darnak swore. Behind him, Jig heard Ryslind muttering a spell.

Jig set the lantern on the ground and rubbed his eyes. When he looked again, he saw what had frightened the others. "I didn't know they grew that big," he said.

Two carrion-worms circled the party. They could be nothing else, but Jig had never seen worms of such length. Their bodies were at least twenty feet long, and each segment was the size of a goblin's head. The mouths were big enough to take a chunk of flesh large as Jig's two fists together, and black, curved teeth surrounded each mouth. If these were normal worms, they would have a second, sharper row tucked inside and out of sight.

Strangely, Jig seemed the least afraid. This was something familiar, albeit much larger than he was used to. "They're only carrion-worms," he said. "They don't attack living things."

Almost before he had finished speaking, one of the worms lunged toward Darnak, who scrambled backward. "And mighty glad I am to be knowing that," he shouted angrily. He backed himself against a wall and stood with his war club ready. Barius joined him there, guarding his left side.

The worm that had attacked began to circle, long antennae flicking at the dwarf. The other hesitated, then turned toward Riana, who backed away as quickly as she could.

The second worm reared, displaying six mouths in its bellies. The undulating teeth pointed outward, ready to rip the elf apart. Jig couldn't understand it. These were carrion-worms. They wouldn't eat anything live unless they were starving, and even then they limited themselves to rats and bugs.

Normal worms limited themselves, Jig corrected. A twenty-foot worm with about a thousand teeth didn't qualify as normal. Jig and the others might be nothing but rats to these beasts. It was not a comforting thought.

As Jig watched, the worm facing Riana went still. The teeth around one mouth folded inward.

"Look out!" Jig lunged across the floor and knocked Riana down. A thin black tongue shot over their heads. With a loud snap, it returned to the worm's mouth, and the worm lowered itself to the ground.

Ryslind finished his spell. Glowing yellow fire floated from the tips of his fingers to the first segment of the worm menacing Jig and Riana. The fire clung to the worm's pale flesh, and it reared up again, waving back and forth in pain. Slowly the fire spread to the second segment.

The worm lashed more frantically, smashing into the walls of the pit and bloodying the burning segments. The smell was horrid, like charred meat. The worm began to scream, a high-pitched whistle of agony. Jig hadn't known they were capable of sound.

"Get off of me," Riana snapped.

Without taking his eyes away from the dying carrion-worm, Jig rolled off the elf and slowly stood. Ryslind had already turned his attention to the other worm. Darnak and Barius had managed to keep it at bay with their weapons, but neither had done any real damage. The wizard raised his hands again and began another spell.

He didn't finish. There was no warning as the second worm convulsed with such force that it left the ground. The burned, dead half of its body flopped back to the earth, but the less damaged part crashed against Ryslind's back and knocked him into the wall. The wizard fell like a stone.

"Ryslind!" Darnak knocked his worm aside with a powerful two-handed blow, then rushed to the fallen human's side.

The worm turned to track his movement, giving Barius the opening he needed. Even as Jig shouted, "No," Barius raised his sword and sliced down, cutting the worm in two. Both ends fell still.

"No?" Barius asked, one eyebrow raised as he wiped gore from his sword. "You'll forgive me, I hope, if I fail to heed the advice of a goblin on matters of battle."

Jig didn't bother to answer. Already the split worm was beginning to heal. Each piece ended with an oozing half-segment where Barius's sword had struck. As Jig watched, those damaged segments dropped off, leaving two healthy, hungry carrion-worms. Each was half the size of the original, but that just made them faster. And hungrier. Carrion-worms were always hungry after they reproduced.

Jig needed a distraction. Something to keep the worms busy while Darnak revived the wizard. His eyes lingered wistfully on Barius. No, the others probably wouldn't like it if Jig fed their prince to the carrion-worms. He snatched up the broken sword he had used to cut his ropes and tried to think.

"To me," Darnak shouted. Riana and Barius raced toward

the dwarf. Jig started to follow. He didn't know if Darnak's rallying cry had been intended to include him, but he wasn't about to face those monsters alone. Halfway there, he stopped.

Carrion-worms preferred dead flesh. At least, normal ones did. He stared at the dying worm, now almost completely charred. That definitely qualified as dead, and the worms had no qualms about cannibalism. The only question was whether or not they would eat their meat cooked.

He used his rusty blade to hack and tear a chunk of the worm free. The meat was tough, and Jig had to cut through several stubborn, stringlike bits before he had a piece he could throw. He flung the meat at the nearest of the two living worms, which reared to catch it in midair. Meat clutched in its teeth, the worm dropped to the ground to feed.

"This is *the* most disgusting thing I've ever done," Jig muttered as he renewed his attack on the dead worm. Something wet splashed onto his forearms. "Even worse than privy duty after one of Porak's drinking binges."

A second chunk of flesh distracted the other worm.

As it turned out, the giant carrion-worms were not only large and deadly, they were also stupid. Fatally so. As long as Jig kept them fed, they were perfectly content to sit and eat. Even as Darnak ran around smashing one worm-segment after another with his war club, the worms continued to feed on bits of their fellow. At last the dwarf called out, "S'okay, you can stop. The beasts are dead."

The blood-slick blade fell from Jig's numb fingers, and he tried very hard not to look at the carnage in front of him. "This is *not* the kind of battle they sing songs about," he grumbled. He hadn't expected anyone to hear, but Darnak laughed.

"I don't know. I could imagine a nice little ditty about it." He raised his voice. "First verse should explain how we got stuck down here. Help me out, your highness. What rhymes with 'mule-headed stubbornness'?"

Barius scowled. "The goblin probably did this deliberately, hoping the worms would finish us off."

"Right," Riana said. "Except that the worms would have eaten him as fast as the rest of us."

"Silence." Barius's hand went to his sword. "He hasn't the foresight to consider such an end. And I warn you to keep that tone from your voice when addressing your betters."

Riana started to reply, but Darnak interrupted, which was probably all that saved the girl from a beating. Barius looked angry enough to loose his temper on anyone who got in his way.

"So how are we to be getting out of this little hole?" Darnak asked. He took the lantern and unshuttered all four sides. He couldn't aim the light upward without spilling the oil, but this was enough for them to see the dark shadow of the ceiling. "Looks a good fifteen feet to me. Lucky the ground is softer here."

"Lucky I landed on your belly and not your hard head, Darnak." Ryslind grimaced. "I'd have broken bones for certain."

Darnak grinned. "Aye. Though there's something to be said for the thickness of human skulls as well. They say it's the only substance harder than diamond."

"Enough of your banter," Barius said. "Brother, can your arts release us from this prison?"

Ryslind took a deep breath. "Give me a moment. Magic requires a clear head, and mine still spins."

While they waited, Riana walked over to Jig. She studied him with obvious distaste, but when she spoke, her voice was quiet, even respectful. "Thanks."

"Eh?" Jig blinked, unsure what she meant. He was still a bit dazed by everything that had happened. Worse yet, he had the nagging sense he had forgotten something. The worms were all dead, but still. . . .

"For knocking me out of the way back there."

"Oh. I saw a carrion-worm catch a rat like that once." He sighed. Giblet the rat had been a good pet. To this day, he suspected that Porak had deliberately turned Giblet loose by the worm's nest.

He scowled. Something about pets . . . oh no.

"Smudge!"

He ran at Darnak and tried to pull the lantern away. The dwarf swatted him with his free hand. "Here now, what's this?"

"My fire-spider's in there."

"What?" Darnak held the lantern higher and peered inside. "Ha. So he is. So that's how you were lighting this thing."

Very gently, he set the lantern on the ground and slid the glass back. Smudge scurried out, apparently unharmed. He raced away from the lantern like he was fleeing Straum himself. Halfway to the far wall, he stopped and rubbed his legs together, one pair at a time.

"Probably trying to clean off the lantern oil," Jig said. He knelt and held out one hand for the spider.

Smudge glanced at him. Then, very deliberately, he turned away and continued to groom himself.

"I am ready," Ryslind announced. He had taken another coil of rope from Darnak's pack. As the others watched, he sprinkled a bit of blue powder on the rope and began to chant. One end of the rope rose, reminding Jig of the way the carrion-worms had reared up to attack. The rope climbed steadily higher until it reached the ceiling.

"I don't suppose that magic rope of yours can punch through the trapdoor?" Darnak asked.

Ryslind frowned. "Do not disturb my focus. I need to channel more power." His voice was deeper than usual. His brow wrinkled, and the end of the rope curled into a tight ball. Ryslind's eyes flashed red, and the rope slammed against the trapdoor.

A shower of dust fell from the ceiling, making Jig's eyes water. Ryslind said the word again, this time with a wave of his hand for emphasis.

On the third try, a large square of rock swung down. Jig leaped back, afraid the stone would crash onto their heads. But it scraped to a halt, spraying them all with another layer of dirt and grit.

"Quickly," Ryslind ordered. "The longer I hold it open, the more it drains me."

Barius was already climbing. Darnak sent Riana up next, then looked back at Jig. "Your turn, goblin."

"My name is Jig," he grumbled. Climbing out of the pit was difficult. Jig had never been strong, and his hands and arms weren't used to this sort of work. But he eventually reached the top. Barius, who had reached down to help Riana out of the pit, didn't even look at Jig as he struggled to hook his ankle over the edge. Darnak followed a minute later, and then Ryslind, pulling the rope up behind him.

Stone grated loudly as the trapdoor sealed itself. Jig sat on the floor, trying to catch his breath, when he noticed Smudge clinging to his leg.

"Decided to forgive me after all, then?" Or maybe the spider had simply decided that coming with Jig was better than being left alone in the pit. It didn't matter. Jig felt better for Smudge's company. At least, he felt better until he spotted the hobgoblins coming down the corridor.

This was the first time Jig had really seen the adventurers in battle. During that first attack, he had been too busy hiding to watch much of the fight. He only saw the end, when Darnak and Barius beat the last few goblins. And the fight in the pit would have been too chaotic to follow even if he hadn't been elbow-deep in worm guts at the time.

But now, watching the others draw weapons and prepare for the hobgoblins' attack, Jig began to understand why surface-dwellers slaughtered goblins time after time.

Ryslind slipped his bow from his shoulder and nocked an arrow in one smooth motion. Barius and Darnak each took a step forward, leaving room for Ryslind to fire while at the same time shielding him from attack. Two hobgoblins fell before they even reached the adventurers. A third stumbled over the bodies of his fellows, and Barius's sword licked out to slice deep into the side of his neck.

Three hobgoblins down before the fight had even begun. Jig stared in disbelief.

All the hobgoblins wore armor they had cobbled together. Bits of plate mail strapped over leather and chain, and several had shields of varying designs as well. All used swords or axes. No kitchen knives here. This was a force that could overrun a goblin patrol in a matter of minutes.

Despite their strength and numbers, the hobgoblins didn't stand a chance. Jig wouldn't have recognized the adventurers as the same people who had, minutes before, shouted and snapped at one another like children. They were a team, working *with* one another, whereas the hobgoblins struggled as much among themselves as with the enemy.

That was the key, Jig realized. That ability to trust and work together in battle. Barius didn't bother to protect his vulnerable left side, trusting Darnak to smash anyone who tried to attack him there. Neither faltered at all when Ryslind fired his arrows between them, and each of those arrows took a hobgoblin in the throat or chest. Were these goblins, they never would have trusted one of their number to stay behind with a bow. The temptation to "accidentally" shoot someone who might have stolen your rations, insulted your family, or stepped on your foot at last night's dinner was too great.

The hobgoblins suffered from the same lack of trust. They tripped over one another, yelled and fought their way to the front, and seemed to have no plan beyond this straight charge. Jig watched as one hobgoblin pushed another out of the way. The one being pushed stumbled forward, and Darnak smashed his skull with a twirl of his club. The adventurers hardly needed to work at all. The hobgoblins were killing *themselves*.

And then it was over. Jig heard the survivors retreat back up the tunnel. Bodies covered the ground in front of the three adventurers. The carrion-worms would eat well tonight.

As he watched them clean their weapons and armor, Jig began to think he had been lucky when Porak sent him ahead as a scout. Had he remained with the patrol, he would have been cut down as easily as these hobgoblins. Easier, since he had been unarmored and practically unarmed. It made him embarrassed to be a goblin.

One unexpected blessing was that victory had improved Barius's temper. He didn't even insist on retying Jig's bonds. Instead he seemed to glow with pride as he checked to be sure the others were uninjured.

"Three victories in a single night," he gloated. "Surely the gods smile upon my quest. We shall find the rod, for nothing beneath this mountain has the strength to stop us." He didn't wait for an answer. "Come, let us find the entrance to the lower tunnels. We will rest there before descending, to give my brother time to renew his strength. Lead on, goblin."

Lead he did, guiding them away from the hobgoblins and through the slowly descending tunnel that led to the lake. He didn't even worry about what they faced there. Jig was too confused by what he had just seen and by what it meant.

All his life Jig had believed surface-dwellers killed goblins through trickery. They used enchanted weapons, spells to call fire and death, and fine armor the likes of which no goblin could make. Certainly some of that was true. That spell Ryslind had used to sneak up on their patrol, the one that made him appear to be a part of the rock, was magic no goblin could hope to fight. Nor was Jig's knife a match for Barius's sword or Darnak's club.

But there was more. In their fight with the hobgoblins, the adventurers had used no magic. Their weapons, while of good quality, were no more magical than those of their foe. There had been no time for trickery or ruses. And still *they had wiped out three times their number without losing a single one of their party.* Barius struck like a serpent, fast and deadly. He knocked hobgoblin swords aside with ease, because he *knew how to fight.* His sword was a part of him, and it twisted and dodged past his enemy's guard like a living thing. How many hours had he trained to be able to do that?

Jig flushed when he thought back to his poor kitchen knife, and how much he had secretly longed for a sword, thinking that all it took was a bit of steel to make him the equal of these adventurers.

The dwarven follower of Silas Earthmaker had stood like a god himself, unmovable and untouchable as his club lashed out to break swords and bones alike. He too must have worked hard to develop such strength of arm. Sure, dwarves were tougher than most races, but Darnak had taken that toughness and strengthened it further. Jig looked again at the dwarf's pack, remembering how much equipment had been stuffed into that bulging leather pack. Jig would be hard-pressed just to lift what Darnak carried around as though it were nothing.

Ryslind was the worst of them all. As a wizard, he was the one enemy no goblin would expect to defeat. But he had used no magic just now. Instead, he had sent one arrow after another safely past his companions. Jig had watched him more closely than the others, and the wizard had not missed a single shot. That cold precision terrified Jig.

Could it be that what the surface-dwellers said about goblins was true? Could goblins be the clumsy, stupid creatures Barius and the others assumed them to be? If so, what did that mean for the fate of Jig's people? They would never accomplish anything, not if the smallest group of surface-dwellers could slaughter them with such ease. It meant goblins were nothing but a nuisance, existing only to die at the hands of adventurers like this.

No, that wasn't it. The problem wasn't the adventurers, but the goblins themselves. They were incapable of working together, of planning or growing. All they could do was charge into battle and get themselves killed. Or in Jig's case, they could hide and watch from the shadows while the others died.

His people, his entire race, were no more than a joke. Jig had betrayed his captain, letting Porak die for an insult Jig had committed. He was nothing but a worthless coward, the same as every other goblin.

Jig perked his left ear as he heard the faint sound of water lapping the stone shore. His right ear continued to listen for sounds of pursuit. Despite all he had seen, a part of him still couldn't believe the dreaded hobgoblins wouldn't come back to finish them off. Depressed or not, he had no desire to let the hobgoblins get their claws on him.

The air was cooler here. A thin green film of moss covered the walls and ceiling, even the edges of the floor. The air smelled like dead fish as they neared the lake.

"How far to this lake?" Barius asked. "I feel as though we've passed through half the mountain. 'Twouldn't surprise me if we found ourselves emerging from the far side."

"Up ahead," Jig said, reminding himself that they couldn't yet hear the water. "Not far."

"Excellent. Then let us rest here for the night. Assuming it is still night, that is. Who can tell this far underground?"

"It's nigh about an hour past midnight," Darnak said without looking up from his map.

"Who but a dwarf, that is?" Barius said, still in high spirits.

"We will take turns watching for danger. I shall watch first. Each man takes a shift of one hour. No longer, or you will begin to lose your focus. Darnak, I will awaken you when my shift is up."

Jig knew without being told that he would not be asked to take a watch. Trust a goblin to protect them in their sleep? Ridiculous. Might as well ask a carrion-worm to stand guard.

He curled into a tight knot, back against the wall, and tried to pretend he was back in his lair. Safe and well-fed, with nothing more to worry about than the jibes of the other goblins. But the waves in the distance slipped into his weary thoughts. In his dreams he found himself in the water, trying to swim away but unable to move his arms while the lizard-fish surrounded him, coming closer and closer with those poisonous spines. . . .

CHAPTER 5

A Day at the Beach

SLENDER HANDS SHOOK JIG AWAKE. HIS VISION was always worst when he woke up, and at first he could only stare dumbly at the red-haired blur above his face. Darnak had shuttered the lantern for the night, and the cracks of light that escaped were barely enough to let him make out slender, pointed ears and a narrow nose.

"You sleep *hard*," Riana whispered when she saw he was awake. "Don't speak." She held a hand over his mouth, ignoring the fangs that could have torn through her palm.

"The others are asleep. If you go quietly, they won't be able to catch you."

Jig blinked, trying to clear his head of a dream in which he had been flung into a flaming pit while a huge, eight-eyed face watched from above. Who wouldn't be able to catch him? Where was he supposed to go? How had Riana taken the place of the giant fire-spider of his dreams?

He looked at the others, but saw only three mounded bedrolls, like giant cocoons. The dwarf snored like an earthquake, but Jig could hear the others as well, both drawing the slow breaths of sleep. Riana wasn't lying about that.

Could this be a trap? Maybe once he started to run, she planned to awaken the others and accuse him of trying to escape. That would give Barius all the excuse he needed to finish off the lowly goblin. But why would she go to such trouble to finish off a single goblin?

"Why?" he asked hoarsely. His mouth was dry, as it always was after sleeping. For a goblin, with teeth like miniature stalagmites, it was impossible to sleep with his mouth closed as the other party members did.

"They know I won't run off," she said bitterly. "I wouldn't make it past the hobgoblins, let alone survive long enough to see the surface. But you could escape."

"You're a prisoner?" He stared stupidly, trying to understand. "But you're an elf."

She laughed at him. "So?"

Jig didn't know how to explain. He only knew that elves were supposed to be graceful and powerful. Elven warriors slipped past their enemies like the wind, but when they fought, their slender arms lashed out with the strength of multitudes. Elven wizards were masters of the elements, forcing fire, lightning, water, and wind to obey their will with the flick of their fingers. He couldn't reconcile those images with this helpless girl who claimed to be a prisoner.

"I thought all elves were strong and powerful," he said at last.

"Yeah, and I thought all goblins were selfish, backstabbing cowards."

"But we are."

Riana rolled her eyes. "Never mind. Before they came here, they stopped at an inn to rest. Ryslind caught me trying to pick his pocket. I thought I could earn a coin or two off those pretty pouches he carries. Instead he dragged me to his room and offered me a choice. I could either come along and help them on their stupid quest, or he could kill me on the spot. He said he would prefer not to kill me, since a dead elf might cause diplomatic problems for his father."

She turned away, hiding her face. "I didn't believe him. I think he *wanted* to kill me. He's as bad as his brother. Those eyes . . . I felt like I was staring into my own funeral fire."

"Why would Ryslind want to kill you?" Barius was the bloodthirsty one. Ryslind was merely cold and distant. He didn't take pleasure out of fighting the way his brother did.

He was cold and efficient when he killed, and he didn't strut about for hours afterward like a goblin fresh from the mating bed.

"He's a wizard," Riana whispered. "Remember that powder he used to enchant the rope? What do you think that was made from? I heard them talking earlier tonight. He got that powder by grinding up the skeletons of two unhatched griffons. What sort of ingredients do you think he'd get from an elf? We're magical creatures too. Not as strongly magical as griffons, but I'm sure he could find uses for an elf girl."

"Are goblins magical?" he asked. He didn't want to end up in one of Ryslind's pouches.

"Of course not."

She needn't have answered quite so quickly, Jig thought. "Do all wizards use that sort of thing for their spells?"

"How should I know? Everyone does magic differently, I think. Even the dwarf can do a little when he prays hard enough. I saw him do it before we came here. He prayed over the two humans to make them stronger and faster. After that, they both looked larger, more dangerous." She laughed again, and this time Jig heard the deep bitterness behind it. "They didn't bother to give *me* Earthmaker's blessing, of course."

"I still don't understand why they brought you along. Isn't it dangerous for them to kidnap an elf? Won't the other elves be angry?" Even as he asked, his thoughts wandered back to the goblin lair. Goblins vanished all the time, and nobody thought twice about it. To mount a rescue for a lost goblin would be ridiculous. But he had believed that elves and the other surface-dwellers were different. Maybe he was wrong.

Riana shook her head. "My parents died in a border war when I was a child. A human family brought me up and set me to work as a kitchen drudge. They had a large family: aunts, uncles, grandparents, and a herd of kids. I scrubbed pots and cooked for them for ten years before I ran away.

"I thought I could go back and be with my real family. Even if my parents were dead, at least I could live with other elves. But I couldn't even speak the language. They were terribly kind, of course. They fed and sheltered me, all the while treating me like I was slow in the head. I was more of a pet than anything. So I ran away from them, too."

She was crying, Jig realized. Her shoulders shook, but her voice remained steady. "They were so proud and confident and graceful. Even a crippled elf could make me feel like a clumsy fool. Their attitude didn't help matters, either. They talked about me behind my back, called me a half-breed even though I was as elven as they were. But I wasn't. I didn't *feel* like an elf. I hadn't grown up with elves. The simplest rituals of daily life left me confused and angry. Soon I was stealing from the other elves. I didn't *need* to steal. I did it because I was so angry.

"I think everyone was happy when I left. Being on my own was no better, though. I robbed travelers so I would have enough money to eat. I slept in the streets. I thought about buying passage on a ship. Didn't know where I'd go, but anywhere had to be an improvement. Only it wouldn't have been. I think that's why I never really tried. I could have stowed away, but I knew there was no place I belonged."

Her voice trailed into silence. Jig waited, confused. Why was she telling him all of this? He felt like he should say something.

"You don't belong here, either." He ignored her disgusted glare and went on to ask his real question. "What did Ryslind want you to do for them? Down here, I mean."

She wiped her nose and eyes. "I've picked a lock or two in my time. They thought that might be useful. They wanted me to look for traps as well, but I've no more chance of spotting a trap than you would. Barius is furious that I didn't warn him about the hobgoblins' pit. They think that because I'm a thief, I'm a good hand at traps and knives and sneaking around in the darkness. Maybe some thieves do all of that, but I just cut purses and break into the occasional inn room. And it's a rare merchant who plants a trap on his purse."

Darnak's steady snores broke suddenly as the dwarf rolled over. He mumbled, "Earthmaker take you all, villains," kicked his leg twice, and began to snore again.

"Go," Riana said. "You saved my life. I owe you. And it will be good to thwart them in this one small thing."

Jig wondered if he was still dreaming. Before tonight, Riana had spoken only a handful of words. He understood how those elves in her homeland might have assumed something was wrong with her. He had begun to think the same thing. Could that quiet, withdrawn, angry girl be the same Riana who sat here telling him about her past and offering him his freedom all in the same sitting?

Freedom. The word had a bittersweet taste as he thought about what his freedom could mean. Only hours before, he had wanted nothing but to return to his lair. Riana had handed him his chance. All he had to do was take it. Grab Smudge and run. His bare feet would make no noise to wake the others, and if he was careful, he could probably make it past the hobgoblins.

He could go home. But to what end? To live as a coward among cowards? To watch his people die time and again, and for nothing?

Worse, one goblin from Porak's patrol had escaped. If he made it back to the lair, he would have spread the tale of Jig's cowardice. He might even have blamed Jig for Porak's death. If so, they would kill him as soon as he returned to goblin territory. Because killing Porak made Jig a goblin to be reckoned with. Others would want to prove themselves by killing Jig, preferably as painfully as they could.

A hollowness came over him as he realized he had no place to return to. His home was no longer safe. He was as lost as Riana.

"I can't go back," he whispered, more to himself than to the elf.

"You can." She looked about frantically. "They only let me stand watch because elves need less sleep than dwarves or humans, and they were exhausted from all the fighting. You won't have another chance to get away."

Jig shook his head.

"You goblins are as stubborn as . . . as that dwarf." With that pronouncement, she turned her back on him and stared into the tunnel.

Jig sat there confused, and eventually decided goblins simply weren't meant to understand the minds of surface-dwellers. He had almost fallen back to sleep when he heard her ask, "Do you think we'll make it?"

"Not really," Jig mumbled, and then he was asleep.

When Jig next awoke, he found Darnak's face hovering over him.

"Argh," Jig muttered, trying not to cringe. Waking from a dream to see Riana had been startling. Darnak was a nightmare all by himself. The dwarf had pulled his hair and beard into numerous ropelike braids, and Jig felt like he was under attack by a floating monster with black tentacles and a crooked nose.

"Get up. You've had yourself a better night's sleep than the rest of us, and it's time we were moving." He tossed a chunk of something round and brown onto Jig's lap, followed by a few strips of dried meat. "You're lucky to be getting any meat at all. His majesty wanted you to have nothing but bread. He said you'd be sharing Riana's waterskin. Don't get greedy—I don't know when we'll find fresh water, and Earthmaker's a busy god who doesn't like to waste time on water purification magic."

Jig nodded. He tore the meat with his teeth, and his mouth watered instantly. How long had it been since he last ate? His stomach protested that it had been weeks. Could it have been only yesterday that he was back in the lair, suffering through muck duty?

A few seconds later, the meat was gone, and Jig stared warily at the bread. He had heard of this crusted stuff from Golaka, but had never encountered it himself. Golaka said adventurers often carried it as a part of their rations, but that it was unsuitable for goblin palates. Studying the bread, Jig was inclined to agree with her. A dark brown shell covered a lighter interior of dry foam, visible where Darnak had torn the chunk from a larger loaf. He touched it to the tip of his tongue, but the bread had no taste. Like licking a rock.

He tried a nibble. Like chewing a rock, too. But the others were eating it, and those two strips of meat weren't going to keep his stomach happy. Jig shrugged to himself and smashed the crusted side of the bread onto one of his fangs. He swiftly tore it into manageable chunks, and soon the bread joined the meat in his belly.

Bread didn't taste like rock after all, Jig decided. Didn't taste like much of anything, really. He noticed that the humans had spread some sort of yellow grease over theirs. Though whether that was to improve the flavor or to make it easier to swallow, Jig didn't know.

"Water?" Riana handed him a bloated skin, then walked away without ever meeting his eyes. Was she angry with him for not running away last night? Or had she simply reverted to her usual cold self?

Not that it mattered. Jig was more comfortable when they treated him like a prisoner, or at best an untrustworthy guide. He wasn't used to kindness or consideration from anyone, let alone his captors.

So he didn't know what to say when Riana returned a few minutes later and handed him a long sheathed dagger. Jig stared in disbelief. "Where did this come from?"

She pointed. Down the tunnel, two hobgoblins lay facing the ceiling, one atop the other. Each had a black-fletched arrow jutting from his neck. He looked at Ryslind. "Oh."

He started to draw the knife. More of a short sword, really. The blade stretched the length of his elbow to fingertip, and it was heavy. The pommel and crossguard were simple brass, and the hilt was bare wood, but this was still the grandest weapon Jig had ever held. He shoved the blade back into its sheath, then drew it completely free.

"Are you mad?" Barius loomed over them both, his sword ready. "Let this creature have a blade of his own, and you'll soon find that blade plunged into your back."

"What if we're attacked again?" Riana countered. "Where would we be if Jig hadn't found that old sword when we were in the hobgoblin pit?"

"You'd trust a goblin to defend your person?" Barius shook his head in disbelief, but his sword remained level with Jig's throat. "I could understand if you secured a knife for your own safety, but to hand it over to this blue-skinned monster is absurd."

Riana spat on the floor by Barius's feet. He looked down,

momentarily speechless, and when he looked back up Riana had a knife in her hand. "What made you think I didn't secure one for myself?"

"Enough," Darnak snapped loudly. "Put them away before I crack all your skulls. Barius, let them have their pigstickers. They know well enough what will happen if they cause trouble."

The prince's sword hissed back into its scabbard. In a low voice, so Darnak wouldn't hear, he said, "Do not cross me again, elf."

As Jig tucked his new sword through his belt, he glanced at Riana. Whereas his sword was plain and well-used, hers was trimmed in gold, and even sported a blue gem in the pommel. She grinned at him as she slid it back up her sleeve.

"That blade looks as fine as Barius's sword."

"It should." She glared at the prince's back. "It's his."

Feeling bolder now that he was armed, Jig walked back to the corpses and took a large belt pouch for himself. Dumping a few corroded coins on the floor, he tied the pouch at his waist, then dropped Smudge inside. "Only until my shoulders have a chance to heal," he promised.

Once everything was repacked, new oil poured into the lantern, a few last touches made to Darnak's map, and everyone had eaten enough to take the edge off their hunger, they proceeded to sit around for another hour while Ryslind meditated. The life of an adventurer appeared to consist of roughly six parts boredom to one part stark terror, or so it seemed to Jig.

"What are we waiting for?" he asked.

"Silence," Barius hissed.

"He's needing to clear his mind and renew his focus," Darnak said softly. "Those tattoos on his arms are a spell, one that keeps him ever open to the power he uses for magic. Far better than books or scrolls, but a permanent spell is a permanent burden, and if he doesn't stop to rest, the spell could snap, leaving him powerless when he needs it most."

"What about his eyes?" Jig asked. "Is that a part of his magic?"

Darnak grinned. "Nah. He did that to himself a year or so

back. Thought it would make him look scarier or some nonsense like that. Turns out he got the spell wrong, and he hasn't figured out how to make it go away. The glow gets worse when he's pushed himself."

When Ryslind's eyes shot open, they looked almost human, with only the faintest trace of red. "I am ready."

Barius and Jig again took the lead as they neared the lake. They passed several side passageways, but Jig was out of his territory now, and when asked where the tunnels led, could only shrug and say, "The lake is this way."

He didn't like leaving unexplored tunnels behind them, but better to hurry past than to go sticking his nose in places where a large paw might rip it from his face.

The rush of water grew louder. Their cautious whispers became shouts, as anything less was drowned out by the noise from the lake. A fine mist coated Jig's face and tickled his ears. Soon he was constantly flicking his ears in protest.

The tunnel widened, and then the walls peeled back completely to reveal an enormous cavern. Dark red obsidian gleamed as if polished, the water having renewed the rock's shine. The walls stretched out of sight to either side.

"What are those?" Riana pointed to the ceiling.

Jig could barely make out the clumps of green, but he knew what they were. "They're just rocks."

A long time ago, malachite formations had striped the walls and ceiling near the entrance as well, but hobgoblins and goblins had taken the green needles of rock for jewelry and decoration. They still existed over the lake, beyond easy reach. Some were as long as Jig's sword, though malachite made a poor weapon.

"They look like green porcupines."

Jig nodded rather than admit he didn't know what a porcupine might be.

The lake itself was black, with white foam cresting the waves that crashed against the shore. In the distance, toward the center of the lake, the water rushed with even greater violence. To Jig, it was no more than a blur of waves and whitecaps, but the others stared worriedly at whatever it was they saw.

"That's a bloody whirlpool," Darnak shouted.

"The way to the lower tunnels is through *that*?" Barius yelled at Jig.

Jig nodded, trying to project confidence and calm. In truth, he hadn't a clue how to get to the lower tunnels. *They* were the ones who had mentioned going through the lake. A sense of self-preservation kept goblins from even trying to venture into the water.

"I sense power here," Ryslind said. Though he alone didn't shout, somehow his voice pierced the roar of the water. "No natural lake could sustain a whirlpool for long. If the lake bed itself were cracked, the water would soon drain into the tunnels beneath."

"Wager the way through is at the bottom of that twister?" Darnak asked.

Jig wanted to laugh. All this way, past goblins, hobgoblins, and carrion-worms, to face a dead end. But would the adventurers face reality and turn back the way they had come? He doubted it. More likely they would continue on, stubbornness pushing them all to their deaths. The only question was whether they would drown first, or if the whirlpool would batter them to a bloody pulp.

Something slipped out of the water and began to crawl toward them. Oh yes, that was the third possibility. They could all die from lizard-fish poison before they even made it to the lake.

"Lizard-fish," Jig yelled, hopping and pointing and scanning the shore for others.

"Ugly things, aren't they?" Darnak drew his club and calmly waited while the lizard-fish crawled closer.

Jig had never seen a living lizard-fish before. This one was as long as his arm, with clawed front feet and webbed rear feet that dragged behind in the sand. The round head had slits for a nose and a wide mouth filled with needle-sharp teeth that could rip flesh from the body so cleanly you wouldn't even notice. The eyes bulged like white bubbles that had been stuck to the skull as an afterthought. Most dangerous, Jig knew, was the line of two-inch spines that started at the back of the skull and ran all the way to the tip of the lizard-fish's long tail.

"The spines are poison!"

Darnak ignored him. The dwarf watched as the lizard-fish drew nearer. When it was only a few feet away from the dwarf, it raised its head and hissed. The blue tongue flicked out, and the spines lifted threateningly.

Threatening or not, Darnak didn't appear to care. He waited for the lizard-fish to finish hissing, then calmly stomped its skull into the rock. "Stupid little beasts, too."

Stupid they might be, Jig thought, but there were a lot more lizard-fish than there were adventurers. Even as he watched, several more emerged from the water and crawled toward the dwarf. Barius stepped forward to join him. His sword impaled one of the creatures and flipped it back into the water. Another attacked with a sudden burst of speed, only to die beneath Darnak's heavy boot. Even as Darnak wiped lizard-fish guts from his boot, however, more were racing forward to attack.

"Back," Barius shouted. Jig rolled his eyes. He and Riana had already retreated to safety.

The others joined them farther up the tunnel. Nothing followed. The lizard-fish wouldn't come this far from the water, it appeared.

"We could stand there until we were hip-deep in the things," Darnak grumbled. "They'd still keep coming. Not a brain in the lot of 'em."

Like goblins, Jig thought suddenly. Swarming to their death and hoping to overwhelm the enemy with sheer numbers. But he said nothing.

"All it takes is one slip, one moment of carelessness, and those spines would be the end of us," said Barius.

"Then I guess we'd better stay on our toes, eh boys?" Darnak grinned.

I was right, Jig realized. *They won't turn back. They probably don't know* how *to retreat.* As they continued to discuss how to get past the lizard-fish, Jig walked to the end of the tunnel and stared at the beach. The lizard-fish had returned to the water, leaving the dead bodies behind to rot. Something else would no doubt come along to feast on the remains. Carrion-worms, perhaps. Or maybe some other creature scavenged the lakeshore. That was how the cycle worked.

At least that was the way things were back home. Who knew what life might be like lower down? No goblins had ever explored much beyond their own territory. Nor had anything from the lower depths ever emerged into Jig's world. Which was probably a good thing. In fact, for all Jig knew, the lizard-fish might be there as much to keep the monsters of the lower caverns trapped below as to keep those from the surface out.

Still, he wondered if things would be different there. Jig's world was a constant battle for territory between goblins, hobgoblins, and the other creatures. But the world below belonged to the Necromancer. Maybe he would keep the creatures under his control from charging off to be senselessly slaughtered every time something came through the entrance. The monsters there might actually win battles from time to time. Jig's imagination conjured an image of a patrol all his own, returning to the lair with the bodies of the adventurers dragging behind them. There was cheering and shouting and singing. Songs that *weren't* about goblins getting themselves killed.

He didn't care if he was the one leading the patrol. Even to be a part of such a group, to work with other goblins to *win* battles, would be a thing worth all the treasure in Straum's lair.

Reality intruded as Jig remembered the sound of Porak's last gurgling breaths, right after Barius's sword poked out of his back. Jig shook his head, angry at himself for his silly fantasies. Goblins were nothing. The natural hierarchy meant the deeper you went, the stronger the monsters. That was why goblins lived here, closer to the entrance than any other monsters. Things had always been that way, probably since the day Ellnorein made this place.

"Goblin, get in here," Darnak yelled.

He joined the others. Ryslind held out five vials of a dark green liquid. "This is an antitoxin," he said. "I had hoped to save it for emergencies, but I see no other way to survive the lizard-fish."

Jig took one of the small vials and stared at it with suspicion. *What had died to create these potions?* he wondered, remembering what Riana had told him about the blue powder. And how had Ryslind known to bring antitoxin? Was this common practice among mages? Maybe so. If Ryslind was a normal mage, Jig could understand why people would try to poison them.

The others drank it down, even Riana. If anyone had reason to doubt the mage, it was her. Jig shrugged and swallowed his own potion in one gulp. After all, it couldn't be worse than bread.

The potion tasted salty, and it was thicker than he expected. A thin, slimy coating clung to the roof of his mouth and the back of his throat. This would save him from the sting of the lizard-fish? He didn't understand how, but what did he know about magic? If Ryslind said this would work, who was he to question? Nobody else seemed to have any doubts.

"We have a half hour. Maybe more for the goblin and the elf, as they're smaller. Come." Ryslind rose and strode back toward the lake. Darnak hurriedly finished drawing a small lizard-fish on the map, marked it DANGEROUS, then rolled the whole thing up and tucked it into a hard leather tube. As they walked, he used a block of sealing wax to waterproof the seams. By the time they reached the shore, Darnak's precious map was safely tucked into his pack.

"Follow," Ryslind commanded. He walked straight toward the water, ignoring the lizard-fish that scurried up the beach. Darnak and Barius killed them as they approached, but Ryslind appeared oblivious.

What was he planning to do, just swim out to the whirlpool? The wizard's hands began to move in small circles, fingers pointed toward the surface of the lake. Jig waited for a flash of lightning to kill the lizard-fish, or a magical bridge to suddenly appear over the water. As he stared, a lizard-fish ran up and jabbed Jig with the spines of its tail.

Cursing, Jig grabbed his knife and stabbed at the lizard-fish, which dodged to the side and ran off. Lizard-fish weren't terribly bright, however, and it ran straight into the path of Darnak's club. *I guess I'll find out whether or not this potion works.*

He looked back toward Ryslind, and his eyes widened. Ryslind had begun to walk across the surface of the lake. As Jig stared, Barius followed his brother. Jig hurried after them, not wanting to be the last target for swarms of angry lizard-fish.

He and Riana reached the edge together, and only then did he see what Ryslind had done. "It's frozen," he whispered. A path of ice several yards wide led straight toward the center of the lake. "Incredible."

"But at what cost?" Riana asked. At Jig's confused look, she said, "Where does he get all that power?"

Jig shrugged. Magic was beyond him. All he knew about wizards was that you were smart to get out of their way, and lucky to do so with your skin intact. He was more interested in knowing how he was supposed to walk along the ice path without slipping.

Several of the lizard-fish started to follow, but Ryslind's spell had an added bonus: lizard-fish didn't like ice. Some of them took a step, then backed onto the shore shaking their claws. Others, apparently more stubborn than the rest, tried to run after the party. Their legs danced like marionettes as they tried to minimize contact with the ice, and eventually they slipped out of control and splashed back into the water.

Halfway to the whirlpool, something cold touched the back of Jig's neck. He turned to protect himself, but saw only Riana. He stared, suspicious, until it happened again. This time the water dripped onto the top of his head and rolled down the side of his face.

He looked up and caught a third drop in his left eye.

"Stupid lake."

As he walked, he wondered if the entire lake was nothing but water droplets that had collected over the years. Had this all begun as a few puddles? How long would it take for a few scattered drops to become a lake this size? Trying to comprehend time on that scale made his head hurt.

At the whirlpool, Ryslind stopped. The water wasn't as violent as before. Jig wondered if the ice went deep enough to blunt the whirlpool's power. He still had no desire to leap into that funnel of death. The water splashed them all as it passed Ryslind's path of ice, and Jig shivered. Whether because of the ice, or because the water itself was colder here, the air carried a bitter chill. Jig longed for something more than his old loincloth.

"There *is* something below," Ryslind said, his voice tight. "I sense a buildup of power beneath us, and none of the creatures have come near this place."

Of course not, Jig thought. Lizard-fish might be stupid, but no monster was *that* stupid. Except, perhaps, for the occasional goblin. And adventurers, naturally.

"Hold your breath. As you pass, I will cast a charm to strengthen your lungs, but you must fight the urge to breathe. Water is a powerful element, and it will throw all its power against you. If you fail, you will die."

With that pronouncement, he rested his fingertips on Darnak's shoulder. The dwarf waited for the wizard to finish. Shooting a dark look toward the roof of the cavern, he shouted, "Earthmaker watch over me." In a slightly lower tone, he added, "But if you had told me what I'd have to endure to keep these two safe, I'd have told you to send a bloody merman in my place."

He checked to be certain his club was lashed to his belt, tightened the straps of his pack, and leaped into the water. Jig tried to follow his progress. Several times, he saw the dwarf bob past, hair flattened to his head, arms waving madly. Once a pair of booted feet rushed by. Then the water dragged him down, and Jig saw nothing.

Barius went next, followed by a reluctant Riana. When Jig's turn arrived, he couldn't help looking back at the shore. He wished now that he had seized the chance to escape last night. Maybe he *could* have snuck past the hobgoblins. If he made it back to the lair, he could have figured something out to explain Porak's death. There had to be a way. Why hadn't he run when he had the chance?

His heart was racing, and Jig realized he was terrified. His heart was pounding, and he was on the verge of soiling his loincloth. When Ryslind's fingers brushed his forehead, he yelped in fright.

The wizard's touch was cold, almost skeletal. Jig's skin crawled, and his head felt stuffy. Between one breath and the next, it was as though he had come down with the worst head cold of his life. His eyes watered.

"Remember to hold your breath," Ryslind said.

Jig stared at the whirlpool. The ice actually extended a few inches past its edge, so he would fall several feet into the freezing water. All he had to do was jump. The others had done it.

Another look back told him he had no choice. He could see unbroken waves behind them. The bridge of ice had begun to melt. He couldn't go back.

But he couldn't go forward, either. Not into that. The whirlpool was a giant mouth, waiting to devour him. The lake had swallowed the others in seconds. He had seen Riana's face, white with fear as she flailed about, trying to keep her head above water. None of her struggles had made the slightest difference to the lake. As Ryslind had said, water was a powerful element. Why should Jig be sacrificed to the lake's hunger?

Tears slipped down his cheeks. He wiped them on his shoulder. Jig had expected to die since he first saw the adventurers. But death by sword was one thing. This was fear on an entirely different scale. At least in combat, you didn't have time to watch death approach. The whirlpool watched Jig in return. It taunted him. In the center of the cone, the water's surface was glassy and clear, and only the whitecaps at the edge hinted at the pool's true might.

At that point, Jig's frightened thoughts were interrupted by the foot that kicked him headfirst into the whirlpool. He barely remembered to hold his breath.

The whirlpool jerked him sideways and plunged him deeper into the water. Jig reached out for the surface, but which way was it? He spun faster and faster, and finally he gave up on reaching the surface. He clutched his knees to his chest, closed his eyes, and waited for the lake to decide whether he would live or die.

Without warning, when he was spinning so fast he thought his stomach would explode, the water spat Jig out like a quarrel from a crossbow. He flew through the air and collided with something hard.

As the world flashed white, he had time to realize that Smudge was still tucked into his belt pouch. He hoped the fire-spider had survived.

He hoped that he survived as well.

CHAPTER 6

More Needling

JIG HURT. HIS HEAD FELT LIKE ONE ENORMOUS bruise, his muscles ached, and his waterlogged loincloth gave him a chill he couldn't ignore. But to squeeze out the excess water would require him to move, which didn't seem like a good idea yet. Not to mention that modesty prevented him from stripping down in front of the adventurers.

While he waited for the throbbing in his head to die down, he cracked his eyes and took his first look at the Necromancer's territory.

As Ryslind had predicted, the whirlpool flowed through a large crack in the ceiling and into this room. The spinning cylinder of water stood like a pillar as wide as Jig's outstretched arms. The surface was smooth as glass, and only the bubbles rushing around in quick circles broke the illusion. Jig wondered how he had passed through the barrier that kept the water in place. Was it a part of Ryslind's spell, or the nature of the pillar itself? Neither answer brought much comfort. Especially given the force of the water trapped behind that invisible barrier.

I fell through *that. As if I didn't have enough fodder for my nightmares.*

Everyone else had made it through more or less intact. Ryslind was checking on the dwarf, who looked as though he was still unconscious. Riana bled from a cut on her head, and her cheek sported an angry bruise. Barius slumped against a far wall, barely awake. All of them, Jig noticed, sat in the center of large puddles. At least he wasn't alone in his discomfort.

Moving slowly so as not to aggravate his headache, Jig fumbled with the wet ties on his belt pouch. Eventually he managed to undo the knot so he could check on Smudge.

A blast of steam caught him in the face like a miniature geyser. Smudge leaped a good foot into the air, trailing steam beneath him. He turned to run away from Jig, spotted the tail of the whirlpool, and raced right back to the goblin's side. Jig searched the room for something to feed the battered fire-spider. A few bugs, an old rat, anything would do. Smudge had been through a lot, and he deserved some reward. But the room was as clean as any he had seen.

The walls were black marble, polished to reflect the lantern light. Someone must have relit the lamp, since Jig doubted the flame could have survived the trip. The floor was the same black marble, and up close, Jig could see that red lines ran jaggedly through the marble like tiny veins. As for the ceiling . . . Jig stared. Before when he glanced at the crack in the ceiling, his mind hadn't registered the glass tiles and swirls of color. This was another mosaic, the same as in the shiny room up above.

The same style, but not identical. The colors were brighter. Perhaps the maker had used different types of glass, or perhaps the Necromancer's minions weren't as dirty as the goblins and hobgoblins. The column of water interrupted the image. Rather, the picture had been created around the pillar. Whorls of color came together around the column, where flecks of blue glass gave the impression of splashing water.

"Ach." Darnak spat weakly into the puddle that surrounded him. "Feels like I took a nap on Earthmaker's anvil and woke up with his hammer pounding my bones." He reached back and pulled off his pack. His movements showed the same stiffness Jig felt. The dwarf grumbled a bit more as he sorted through his belongings, eventually pulling out a large blue wineskin. A few long swallows, and he sat back again.

"Much better," he said contentedly. "Nothing like dwarven ale to take the edge off a bad day." He took another drink before glancing around. "Everyone got a bit banged up, it seems."

He used his club to push himself up. With a nod of thanks to Ryslind, who had cleaned a cut on Darnak's scalp, he hobbled over to check on Barius.

"I'll get him fixed up, and then we can see about paying a visit to this Necromancer of yours."

"Um, Darnak?" Jig searched the room again, hoping his poor eyes had betrayed him.

"What is it?"

"How are we going to find the Necromancer?" When the dwarf didn't appear to understand, Jig said, "There are no doors. How are we supposed to get out of the room?"

Darnak stared at the walls. "Damn me." He took another long drink from his wineskin. "Check around for hidden doors. I won't believe I let myself be flushed through *that* for nothing. As I'm not looking to go back through anytime soon, there must be another way out."

Leaving Jig to cock his head at the questionable logic, Darnak knelt next to Barius and took the prince's head in his hands. He studied Barius's eyes for several minutes before reaching inside his armor and pulling out a small silver hammer on a chain. He clasped both hands around the hammer, as if to pray.

"Go on then," Darnak snapped. "Get the elf to help search."

Jig pushed himself to his feet. Riana joined him, limping slightly. One hand pressed a large, raw scrape on her elbow.

"I feel like I swallowed half that lake on the way down," she complained.

Jig didn't answer. He studied the walls closely, wondering how he should go about searching for hidden doors. Dwarf logic aside, what made Darnak think there was a door here? Wouldn't it make more sense to drop adventurers through the whirlpool into a room with no way out? Let them starve. That way the intruders died without a struggle. It would be easier and more effective than sending wave after wave of monsters to fight and die each time someone snuck through the lake.

The marble was smooth and cold to the touch. Jig shivered and wished for a fire to dry himself. Even Smudge's warmth would have helped, but for once the fire-spider was uncooperatively cool, having steamed any trace of water from his small body.

Already he hated this place. He distrusted the magic that kept the lake from pouring in on them. If Jig and the others could pass through that barrier, how long before the lake broke free? The room itself was equally disorienting. At home the walls *flowed* into the floor, like liquid rock frozen in place. Which, if he were to believe Darnak's crazy explanation, was exactly the case. The sharp corners of this room were alien, and they emphasized Jig's sense that he didn't belong.

Jig saw Riana rap her knuckles against the wall. She was listening for hollow areas, he realized. Knocking on a door would produce a different sound than knocking on a wall. How clever of her.

Jig followed the wall in the opposite direction, tapping and running his hands over the marble as he walked. He heard nothing unusual, and his knuckles swiftly began to complain. He took out his new sword and used the pommel to tap the wall instead. Still nothing.

By the time he ran into Riana on the opposite side of the room, Barius was up and pacing impatiently. Darnak's prayers had apparently done wonders for the prince. Jig wished he could have seen exactly how this magic healing worked, but the dwarf had already pulled out fresh parchment to begin his new map.

"Have you found nothing?" Barius demanded.

Neither Jig nor Riana bothered to answer. *The least you could do is help us search.* But Jig knew enough to keep that thought to himself.

"The fool goblin has led us to a dead-end." Barius glared at Jig, ignoring the fact that the fool goblin was just as trapped as the rest of them.

He was like Porak in that way. If things went wrong, he searched for a scapegoat. He had to first find someone to blame before he could try to solve the problem. Porak used to beat up the younger goblins every time he lost at Rakachak. Jig wondered if this was something all leaders did.

"Brother, use your art to find a way out of this trap."

Ryslind's face was as cold as the marble walls, but his eyes burned brighter than Jig had ever seen. On Jig's shoulder, Smudge grew warmer, echoing his unease. Jig tried to move Smudge back into the pouch, but the spider would have none of it. He wriggled free and ran back up Jig's arm. After what they had gone through, Jig couldn't really blame him. He simply didn't want to burn his other shoulder. Besides, tucking Smudge into the pouch would put the spider's heat closer to Jig's dripping loincloth, and if he didn't get dry soon, he would start to chafe.

But he couldn't pay attention to Smudge, not without taking his eyes off of Ryslind. Jig knew Smudge well enough to heed his warnings, and at that moment, Smudge thought the wizard was dangerous.

"Yes," Ryslind said softly. "Let me use my art once more. As if it were no more than a tool to be used at your convenience."

Nobody missed the fury in Ryslind's normally calm voice. Even Darnak froze, his quill leaking black ink onto his thumb and fingers.

"Easy lad," Darnak said. "Barius meant nothing by it." Jig wondered if anyone else saw the warning glare the dwarf shot at Barius.

"No need to apologize," Ryslind said. "Indeed, without my power, we could spend the rest of our lives in this room."

"Without your brother, we wouldn't have come after the rod in the first place," Darnak pointed out. "Without the elf, we'd have had a rough time getting through that first gate. And without me, you two would have killed one another before we ever made it to the mountain. We're all needed here, and nobody's questioning your importance."

Jig didn't find that reassuring. Nor did Smudge, if the waves of heat on his shoulder were any indication. He also noted that Darnak's argument had ignored anything the goblin might have done for the group. Not that this came as a surprise.

Jig watched closely as Ryslind strode to one wall and raised his head. He studied the unbroken marble and frowned, as though insulted by its presence. The green tattoos on his hands began to glow. Once Jig thought he saw them move, like luminescent worms crawling beneath white skin.

Hands still at his side, Ryslind began to circle the room. Jig hurriedly got out of the way. So did the others, though Barius tried hard to make the move appear casual.

A few paces past Riana, the wizard stopped. "Here." He raised one hand and pointed. Green light spread out from his finger to form a rectangle on the wall. His hand closed into a fist.

Nothing changed. Ryslind squinted at the door. "Ah." Another beam of light struck the center of the door, revealing a narrow keyhole.

"This is the elf's responsibility, I believe. Will there be anything more, my brother?" The light died as Ryslind walked away, but the door remained visible behind him.

Jig's eyes widened, and his ears flattened against his head as he realized why he was suddenly so afraid of Ryslind. Ever since they came through the whirlpool, the wizard's voice had been different. The difference was so subtle Jig hadn't noticed at first, and he doubted any of the others could hear it at all. But each time Ryslind spoke, it was as though a second voice spoke the same words along with him.

He stroked Smudge's head and body, trying to calm the agitated spider. Was he imagining things? Slamming into the ground on the way out of the whirlpool could have affected his hearing. Yet if that were the case, why wasn't he hearing the same distortion when the others spoke?

Besides, he wasn't the only one afraid of Ryslind. Even Barius regarded his brother with wary eyes, and one hand rested on his belt, close to the hilt of his sword. Whether they heard the change or not, they knew enough to be watchful.

"I will be fine," Ryslind said wearily. "I have simply . . . overexerted myself. By the time you open the lock, I shall be myself again."

Nobody relaxed, but Barius did wave Riana toward the

door. She rolled her eyes and pulled several thin metal tools from a pack at her belt. She grabbed the lantern in passing, leaving the rest of them in shadows.

Jig heard her curse as she dried her tools. The scratch of metal against metal told him she had begun to work on the lock. But he didn't watch. He couldn't look away from Ryslind's struggle.

For the human was obviously at war within himself. His fists clenched into knots, and his neck had tightened to the point where the muscles formed raised lines of skin between the neck and shoulders. Each deep, ragged breath sounded like that of a dying man.

Barius had gone to watch Riana work on the lock, but Darnak remained close by the wizard. He kept saying Ryslind's name over and over. One hand went to the small hammer around his neck. His other reached toward Ryslind.

Ryslind's fist shot out, and the dwarf caught it in his free hand. Between the darkness and his own poor vision, Jig couldn't be certain, but he thought he saw the dwarf flinch. *What kind of strength did it take to do that to Darnak?* He decided he would rather not find out.

"I am . . . all right," Ryslind whispered.

"Almost lost it there, did you?"

Ryslind didn't answer. He turned around, and his eyes narrowed when he saw Jig watching.

Jig tried to swallow, but fear stuck in his throat like an oversize chunk of meat. He couldn't apologize for watching. He couldn't even break away from Ryslind's angry gaze. The faint red lights of those eyes seemed to call to him. Even blinking had become difficult, and his eyes began to water. This was something beyond fear. His body was no longer under his control. What was Ryslind doing to him? His eyes grew dry. He could barely breathe. Was this his punishment for daring to see Ryslind's moment of weakness?

Behind him, Riana yelped.

Ryslind looked away, and Jig gasped for breath.

"What happened?" Darnak asked.

"The silly girl triggered a trap," Barius said angrily.

A trap? Jig followed the dwarf to the door. Riana sat on

the floor, clutching her index finger with an expression of shock. A tiny bead of blood glistened at her fingertip.

"A needle trap," Barius said. "Probably poisoned."

His words chipped away at Riana's hard facade. She shot a pleading look at Darnak. "It was an accident."

"Wait," Jig said. "What about the potions we took, to protect us from the lizard-fish poison? Will they be enough to protect her?"

Hope and gratitude flashed in Riana's eyes as she looked to Ryslind for the answer.

The wizard shrugged. "The potion was a short-acting one. I don't know if it will still be effective. Nor, without knowing what poison was used, can I be certain that even a full dose would have protected her. Were I to create such a trap, the types of poison I might choose would still kill her."

Jig stepped closer to the door. A tiny needle protruded from the lock. It reminded him of the way the lizard-fish had flicked their tongues as they attacked. "Is this sort of thing common where you come from? Hidden doors, trapped locks . . . how do you people survive from day to day?"

Barius shrugged. "Only a fool would put his faith in a simple lock."

He wondered how many accidents came from trying to build such intricate traps. It was a strange world where the job of the locksmith could be more dangerous than that of a soldier.

Riana whimpered suddenly. Darnak gasped. "Earthmaker help us."

Her finger had begun to shrivel, and the skin turned gray as they watched. The nail yellowed and cracked at the tip. She touched the dying flesh with her other hand. "It's cold."

"The Necromancer's work, no doubt," Barius said.

That much Jig could have figured out without the prince's dramatic pronouncement. What he didn't know was how to stop whatever was happening to Riana. Would this poison spread throughout her body, or would the potion be strong enough to stop it before she died? Worse, if the poison took her, what would happen to her then? The fingertip still moved like living flesh. Would she be truly dead, or would she become something worse, some kind of toy for the Necromancer? If this was a taste of the Necromancer's power, Jig would happily stay up above with the hobgoblins and the lizard-fish.

"Can you heal her?" Jig asked.

But Darnak was already shaking his head. "It's in the gods' hands now."

Jig turned to Ryslind, but words caught in his throat. Could the wizard save Riana? He had made potions to counteract the lizard-fish, after all. Seeing the shadows beneath Ryslind's eyes, and the sweat still shining on his bald scalp, Jig decided against asking. If the overuse of Ryslind's art had caused the fit Jig saw, the last thing he wanted to do was ask the wizard to exert himself further.

The decay spread toward the second knuckle. Riana held her hand away from her, clutching the wrist with her good hand.

"Broken bones, bloody cuts, and other wounds of honest battle, those I can heal with Earthmaker's blessing. Poison and magic, though . . ." Darnak shook his head. "Those are beyond me."

"Your counsel, old teacher," Barius said. He drew the dwarf to the other side of the room and began to speak in a low whisper.

Jig perked his ears. No doubt their voices were too quiet for Ryslind to overhear, and Riana was too distraught to listen. Goblin ears were another matter. With everything he had seen in the past hour, Jig wasn't about to let *anyone* start plotting behind his back.

"How long before the poison slays her?" Barius asked.

"It's not the slaying that worries me. You saw her finger. Dead, but still moving. I fear what she'll become."

Jig nodded. He had seen the same thing. Good to know Darnak agreed with him.

"If the poison takes her, she could turn upon us. That cannot be permitted."

"And what would you have me do about it?" Darnak sounded suspicious.

"I will distract the girl. Make her end quick and painless."

Barius was so calm that it took Jig several heartbeats to

understand what he was saying. He wanted to kill Riana! No, that wasn't true. He wanted Darnak to do it.

" 'Tis not in me to murder an innocent girl in cold blood," Darnak said sternly. "Nor is it a worthy thought for a prince. I'd have expected such from the goblin, but not you."

Jig scowled. Why would he have made such a suggestion? They didn't listen to him anyway. Nor would he have proposed murdering Riana even if they did listen. Running away before she finished her transformation, maybe, but not murder.

"She's no innocent," Barius snapped. "She's a thief. By law, she should have been imprisoned the moment she tried to rob us."

"Imprisoned, aye." He took another swig from his wineskin. "But not executed. Your father would have my head if—"

"My father is not here with us. In his absence, my word is as law."

Darnak fell silent. Jig risked a glance back to see what was happening. Both had their arms crossed, and Darnak was shaking his head.

Jig also noticed Ryslind leaning against the wall, looking bored. His lips curled slightly, hinting at amusement. He probably couldn't hear what was being discussed as well as Jig, but that didn't matter. He knew Darnak and his brother, and he must have deduced what Barius wanted to do. He only waited to hear who would win the argument.

"I'll not do it," Darnak said finally. "I'll not kill a girl in cold blood. Not even for you."

Jig nodded with satisfaction. Only an instant passed, though, before he realized what the dwarf had not said. He'd not kill Riana, but he wouldn't stop Barius from doing so, either. Jig looked again, and saw Barius walking toward Riana. His hands were empty, but his face was carefully expressionless. Ryslind fell into step behind his brother.

"Riana, give me your hand," Jig whispered. She obeyed, too scared to argue.

Jig rolled his eyes. "The other one."

Trembling, she held out her poisoned hand. The decay had

taken over most of the finger, with only a thin ring of healthy skin above the knuckle. Jig studied it closely, folding her other fingers back so he could see better.

"What's going to happen?" Fresh tears dripped down her cheek, making her look like a young child.

"How old are you?" Jig asked absently.

"Sixteen."

He stared. "But I thought elves lived to be hundreds of years. Even thousands."

That earned a small, brave grin. "You think we're born with centuries already behind us? That'd be hell on the mother."

He shook his head, confused. Of course there were young elves. It was only that none of the songs or stories ever mentioned them, so Jig had never stopped to imagine an elf less than a century old. Elves were ancient beings who had lived through events other races only knew of as distant history. That was what made them so hard to kill. How did you beat someone with that much experience?

"Riana," Barius called. "We must speak of your injury."

"They're going to let me die, aren't they?"

"No," he said. An honest, if misleading answer. They wouldn't *let* her die. All that remained to be seen was whether Barius or his brother would do the actual killing. Jig wagered it would be Ryslind.

When Riana started to move toward the humans, Jig tightened his grip and pulled her off balance. With his other hand, he drew his sword and placed it at the base of her wounded finger. She looked back, eyes wide with fear and betrayal.

Jig didn't have time to explain. Before she could speak, he pulled the blade toward himself as hard as he could.

Which was harder than necessary, as it turned out. The poison must have weakened the bone, or else the blade was sharper than Jig was used to. His sword sliced through the finger, then continued on to slash Jig's own forearm.

Riana stared, shocked, at the blood leaking from the stump of her finger.

Jig watched his own blood drip from the long cut in his arm. All of his strength drained away. His legs threatened to give out, and the sword slipped from his fingers. Pain and shock spread from his arm throughout his body. He looked to Riana, mouth open to speak, but words failed him.

Her eyes narrowed, and with her good hand, she punched him in the nose. As he staggered back into the wall, Jig realized that at least one of the legends was true: Elves were much stronger than they appeared.

Jig probed his throbbing nose. Blood dripped from both nostrils, but the nose itself didn't feel broken. "Gak," he said as blood ran down the back of his throat. "Disgusting." Even worse than Ryslind's potion. He sat down and rested his head between his knees, using one hand to pinch his nose shut.

Hot footsteps on his back brought him back to alertness. What was Smudge running away from?

He looked up, and when his eyes focused, he found himself staring at the tip of Barius's sword. As he had noted earlier, it was a masterful work of weaponscraft. The blade was perfectly straight, and three narrow grooves ran the length of the sword. To make it lighter, Jig guessed. Which no doubt made it easier for Barius to keep it leveled at Jig's heart.

"We should have slain you from the outset, goblin."

"Me?" Jig asked. *Stupid question. How many other goblins do you see down here?*

"I turn my back but for a few brief moments, and you draw steel against your own companions."

The quiet outrage in Barius's voice was so perfect that, for a heartbeat, Jig felt guilty. Only for a heartbeat, though. Then he remembered *why* he had done it.

"Me?" he said again, dumbfounded. "I heard you talking to Darnak. Better to cut off her finger than—"

The prince stepped forward and punched Jig in the jaw, knocking him to the floor. As he lay there staring at the beauty of the ceiling, he wondered if there was any reason to stand again. Not if people were going to keep hitting him, he decided. No, he would stay right here. If the gods were just, Barius would at least chip his sword on the floor when he finished Jig off.

His eyes traced one of the blue whirls toward the center of the ceiling, where it vanished into the water. *Yes, this is much better. As long as I don't move, nothing hurts. I should have thought of this from the beginning. They could have killed me and been done with it. At least I would have died comfortable.*

He wondered what was taking Barius so long. *Maybe he doesn't want to chip his sword.* Jig grinned. The prince would be so offended if he damaged his weapon on a mere goblin. Smiling turned out to be a mistake. The prince's blow had split his upper lip, and his amusement vanished with a hiss of pain.

He closed his eyes and tried to relax as he waited. *This is why goblins make such poor adventurers*, he concluded. A few blows to the head, and Jig was out of commission. Well, to be fair, he had also been flung out of a whirlpool into a stone room. That cut on his arm hadn't helped, either. And he'd be in better shape if he had eaten a real meal in the past day and a half. Still real heroes were the men who shrugged off a half-dozen arrows and continued to fight. Goblins tended to run and scream if they stubbed their toe on a rock.

A strong hand grabbed his injured arm. Until that moment, Jig had thought he was ready to die. He had been expecting it all along, ever since Porak sent him off alone. Death should have been a relief. But as powerful fingers pulled him into a sitting position, Jig realized the waiting wasn't so bad after all. Perhaps he could stand to put things off for a mite longer. He raised his other arm to protect his head and kicked blindly.

"Here now, none of that," Darnak grumbled.

The alcohol on Darnak's breath was enough to knock Jig backward, even with his nostrils half-clogged by blood. His eyes snapped open. "What?" Where was Barius? Why wasn't Jig dead yet?

"I know what you did," Darnak said in a low voice. "True, she hates you now. And that wouldn't have helped her against normal poison, but you may have saved her life."

"I did?"

"Not a word about it, I warn ye." The dwarf wouldn't meet his gaze. "He's got a temper, Barius does, and he's throwing a right fit about you. I persuaded him to let you keep breathing for a while yet, but you're to lose the sword. And it's back to the rope."

"Riana?" Jig asked.

"I stopped the bleeding. Earthmaker should kick me for not thinking of that myself. A bit of magic, and the skin healed over as smooth as an egg. She's a little put out, mind you, but she should live." He grabbed his hammer on its thong and closed his eyes. "Now let me see what I can do about that arm."

This time, Jig watched closely as Darnak called upon his god to work his healing magic. With the hammer hidden in his thick fist, he began to mumble. Jig listened closely, but the words were foreign. Dwarvish, he guessed. The language sounded like a mixture of coughing, spitting, and gnashing of teeth. A bit like Goblin, really, but not close enough for him to understand.

So intent was Jig on watching the dwarf, he didn't notice when the pain in his arm began to recede. What had been a sharp tearing pain became a dull burn, unpleasant but less intense. He could feel his blood pound with each beat of his heart. The rhythm grew louder, booming in his ears until he expected to see his very skin throb. The heat in his arm grew.

Like a blacksmith, Jig thought suddenly. Each pulse was a hammer blow that forged the flesh whole again. Fitting, coming from a dwarven god.

When Darnak pulled his hand away, a dark blue scar ran the length of Jig's forearm. Blood still smeared the skin, but it was dark and crusted. He brushed his arm, marveling at the new scar. His battle scar. Not, he admitted, that he had come by it in the normal way. But he doubted any goblin would ever learn he had inflicted the wound with his own hand.

"Best I can do, lad. Dwarven magic doesn't work so well on goblins, it seems."

Jig ignored him. He flexed his arm, watching the way his new scar moved with the muscles beneath. Bits of blood flaked away as he moved. He wondered if the scar would fade with time. If only he had been allowed to keep the short sword as well. But Barius had already taken the weapon and tucked it into his own belt. The exuberance of his scar faded as he realized what it had cost him.

He had lost the first good weapon he had ever owned, and for what? To protect an elf girl's life? These were the people he was supposed to kill. Porak would have taken the sword from Riana and buried it in her back as soon as she turned. Not Jig. No, he had tried to *help*. See where that misguided effort had landed him. Unarmed, and soon to be tied up again like a slave.

Jig tried to tell himself it would have made no difference, that had he used his sword against the adventurers, he would have died instantly. He had seen them fight, and he knew he had no chance. But still the guilt and confusion warred. What was wrong with him?

His only consolation was that the Necromancer would soon make it right. Already one of the party had almost died, and they hadn't even left the first room. What would they face beyond that door, and how many of them would wish they had drowned in the lake above?

CHAPTER 7

The Heat of Battle

BARIUS WAS NOT HAPPY. "WE HAVE STILL ACCOMplished nothing! The door remains sealed both to my brother's art and the elf's tools."

And the party is short by one finger, Jig added silently. He watched as Riana examined the lock. She struggled to grasp her tools with her crippled hand, a task made harder by fear. Her hands trembled as they approached the door, and she had yet to actually touch the lock.

Not that Jig blamed her. If he had been in her place, the last thing he'd want to do is poke around the trap a second time. But the ache in his jaw and the rope around his wrists made it hard to feel any sympathy. As Riana tried again to examine the lock, he commented, "I wonder if the Necromancer was clever enough to put a second trap on the lock."

She leaped away from the door so fast that she tripped and fell. Her tools jingled as they hit the floor. Jig grinned at his mischief. The enemy might be stronger and better armed, but he could still cause trouble.

"Enough," Barius shouted. He stomped toward Jig. "*You* will probe the lock for further traps."

Wordlessly, Jig held up his bound wrists. Barius turned a deeper shade of red, and Jig wondered if he had pushed too far.

The prince grabbed the end of Jig's rope and yanked him upright. He untied the knot and jerked the rope away so quickly Jig lost a layer of skin. Jig started for the door, but Barius caught his ear and held him in place.

Jig stopped, indignant. Didn't he know you only grabbed *children* that way? No adult goblin would allow himself to be dragged about by the ear. He should bite off Barius's hand for this. He should plant a lizard-fish in Barius's bedroll!

Glimpsing the prince's face, he decided that he should do nothing at all. Barius tied a quick loop in the rope and tightened it about Jig's neck. Still, the freedom to use his hands was a victory, if a small one. Jig was a small goblin. Perhaps his triumphs were better taken in small bites.

With an impudent grin, Jig headed for the door. Darnak knelt with Riana to one side, trying to boost her spirits. He had given her a bit of his ale, a kind gesture which may have been a mistake. To judge from the way her head wobbled, elves didn't handle dwarven ale very well.

"Don't worry about a lost finger," Darnak said gently. "Many an adventurer has lost a finger, or worse, and still gone on to accomplish great things. Have you heard the song of . . . I forget his name. The little guy with nine fingers, from the middle continent. The one involved with that ring business a while back."

Jig hovered over them both, clicking his toenails against the floor until Darnak acknowledged him.

"I need a bit of twine." He held his hands a foot apart to indicate how long.

Darnak said nothing. He still seemed a bit uncomfortable with Jig. Did he feel guilty for almost letting Riana die? Jig didn't care. In fact, the more uncomfortable they felt, the happier he would be.

Riana wouldn't look at him at all, but it was harder for Jig to feel pleasure at that. Still, what did Jig care for an elf's goodwill? If they hated him, he would hate them right back. That was his job. He was a monster and they were adventurers.

As he had hoped, among the endless junk the dwarf carried upon his back, Darnak managed to find a ball of twine, tangled up like an abandoned nest. He ripped a piece free and handed it to Jig.

He seized his trophy and moved to the front of the door, humming quietly under his breath. For once he knew exactly what to do. Better still, none of the others had thought of it. He scooped up one of Riana's discarded tools, a thin steel rod as long as his hand with several diamond-shaped ridges near one end. He also grabbed her severed finger.

As he lashed the rod to the end of the finger, he began to sing. In Goblin, of course. The song sounded ridiculous in Human.

Oh, down came the humans into the dark.
Up raced the goblins, ready for a lark.
The humans were weary, much had they drunk that day.
The goblins found them sleeping, said, "Come on, let's play."

First they stripped the humans bare, then they painted 'em all blue,
Said one goblin to his mate, "This one looks a bit like you."
From a fighter's leather shield, they carved ears with points so keen,
And moldy old potatoes made noses large and green.

When the humans all awoke, they were in for quite a fright.
The goblin-looking fools instantly began to fight.
The wizard who survived called upon his magic flame
To slaughter the real goblins, then he killed himself from shame.
For if you fall in battle, all your friends and family mourn,
But to fall against the goblins is a thing that can't be borne.

As he sang, he jabbed the metal rod into the keyhole and wiggled it around. The finger itself felt strangely stiff, more like leather-wrapped wood than flesh. No trace of blood showed at the severed end, and a bit of bone protruded a half inch past the shrunken skin, giving Jig a convenient handle. The poisoned needle jabbed the fingertip repeatedly as he worked, but nothing else happened. He tried for several more minutes, not knowing what exactly might trigger the traps. He could feel the rod scrape the inner workings of the lock, and he poked those as well. Still nothing.

"I guess there are no more traps," Jig said. He dropped the finger, still tied to the lockpick, and walked back to sit against the wall. If he had built this room, he definitely would have put a second trap there.

Riana stood. Her face was stone as she walked determinedly, if a little unsteadily, to the door. Pale as she was, she didn't flinch when she picked up the finger and tugged her lockpick free. She used her knife to bend the needle aside, then began to work on the lock itself.

While she worked, Jig went over to claim the discarded twine. He returned to his spot by the wall, where he took his belt pouch and chewed at the leather cord, trying to remove it without damaging the pouch itself. After a few minutes, the old cord lost its fight against goblin teeth, and he slipped it free.

He used the cord to tie the pouch over his right shoulder. Bringing the end of the pouch to his mouth, he used his fangs to bore two holes in the bottom. The twine secured that end to his upper arm. Smudge still refused to crawl into the pouch, and Jig couldn't blame him. But this would provide a perch where the fire-spider could sit without burning Jig whenever they walked into danger. Which seemed to happen every time Jig took a breath.

"Prepare yourselves," Barius said. "We've dallied here long enough, and the gods only know what waits behind that door." He grabbed the end of Jig's rope, looped it once around his wrist, and tugged.

Jig gagged and scrambled to his feet. Riana still hadn't picked the lock, but Barius's patience had run out.

Darnak drew his club and moved to stand behind Riana. Ryslind remained where he was, resting against the far wall.

His eyes were alert though, Jig noticed. He watched, not the door, but the other adventurers. Jig looked away.

Three bodies peering over Riana's shoulder did nothing to help her concentration. Her pick slipped, and she turned to glare at the dwarf. "Bad enough that my head pounds from your ale. I don't need your breath adding to my drunkenness."

"Your pardon," Darnak said, taking a step back.

Only Jig heard her mutter to herself, "This would be easier if I wasn't seeing double. Hard enough to pick one lock, let alone two."

Something clicked. Riana grabbed a second tool, a thicker, angled rod which she jabbed into the keyhole. Keeping the first pick in place, she turned the larger rod, and the door popped inward.

Riana scrambled back to avoid the door and fell with a loud "Oof." Darnak stepped over her body, club held high.

"Nothing," he said.

The others moved toward the doorway as Darnak raised the lantern, shining a beam of light down the corridor.

Where the goblin tunnels had been smooth obsidian, this hall shone with the same black marble as the room behind them. Large panels of marble covered floor, walls, even the ceiling. Only the threads of red in the marble and thin stripes of glittering silver mortar gave the passage any color.

The labor that must have gone into building these tunnels didn't impress Jig as much as the fact that they were so *clean*. Not a trace of dust marred the gleaming tiles. After all these years, he would have expected the floor to lose its polish. Either the Necromancer used magic to maintain his domain, or else nobody ever walked these tunnels. Jig decided to believe the first explanation.

"Nice," Darnak commented.

"Dangerous," said Barius.

Jig looked up, confused.

"Each panel is wide enough to cover a pit, like the one we encountered above," the prince explained. "We must be cautious."

Cautious meant sending the goblin ahead to trigger any traps. As Jig moved to the front of the party, he consoled himself with the fact that Barius kept a firm grip on the rope trailing from his neck. If the floor did fall away, at least the human would be able to haul his choking body back out. Assuming, of course, that Jig didn't break his neck in the fall.

Once again they made slow progress as a result of Darnak's compulsiveness. The dwarf had taken it upon himself to draw each individual tile on his map. "If one of these squares hides a trap," he explained, "we'll be wanting to know which one."

This time, Jig had no complaints. The sluggish pace meant that he could test each tile before putting his full weight on it. He would press his back against the wall for balance and extend his toes to tap the next tile up the hall. If that felt safe, he ran to the opposite wall and did the same on that side. As the corridor was three tiles wide, this procedure eliminated all but one. The middle tile he simply tested with the ball of his foot. If something happened, he would be off-balance, but without a convenient wall to lean against, he had no choice in the matter.

Naturally it was a middle tile that turned out to be trapped. The corner sank a half inch, and Jig leaped back, flailing his arms for balance.

"Which tile?" shouted Darnak. He hurried to Jig's side, counting as he went. "Ten, eleven, twelve . . . the thirteenth tile. Center one, right?"

Jig nodded. That had been too close. He could have easily fallen forward instead of back, and who knows what would have happened had he landed on the loose tile. *But I didn't.* That was the important thing. He glanced to either side, waiting for the trap to spring.

Darnak's quill scratched furiously as he penned a warning about the tile. Barius stepped closer, shoving Jig to one side. With his sword, Barius prodded the corner Jig had stepped on. Another click, but nothing else happened.

He tried again, harder this time. "Perhaps it's stuck," he mused. "The mechanism grown tired from disuse? A clumsy oversight by whomever maintains these tunnels. What could be more useless than a trapdoor that refuses to open when triggered by its prey?"

"Behind us," Riana yelled. At the same instant, Smudge flashed red-hot.

Darnak whirled, blinding Jig as the lantern's beam passed over his eyes. The rope tugged Jig forward, then went slack. Jig crashed into the wall and stayed there, out of the way. Whatever was coming, Barius had decided to keep both hands free to deal with it.

Jig blinked and squinted. Riana had stayed behind, next to him. He could make out the shapes of Darnak and the humans moving back up the tunnel. Beyond, more humanoid figures moved in silence. Jig saw the glint of weapons from the newcomers. What were they? His vision was bad enough without the party blocking his view.

Riana had drawn her stolen knife, and her chest moved rapidly as her breathing quickened. She and Jig both jumped at the first clang of steel against steel.

But what was it they fought? Where had they come from? He suspected it was something to do with the trapped panel, but he didn't understand what.

As if in response, the wall Jig had been leaning against vanished. It didn't slide or fall away, as Jig would have expected. One moment it was there, and the next Jig was falling back into a small alcove. He looked up. A pale, dead face looked down at him. Nothing but an old corpse, Jig thought at first.

The corpse raised a spiked mace to strike.

Jig squealed and rolled aside as the mace cracked into the floor beside him. The thing's decayed arm was little more than bone and a thin layer of dried flesh, but the strength behind that blow was a match for Darnak.

Smudge sprang free and hid behind the creature, out of sight. Lucky spider. Before the thing could attack again, Jig scrambled out of the alcove and collided with Riana.

The panel had disappeared from the opposite wall as well. Unlike the first creature, however, the inhabitant of this alcove was truly dead. The skin had decayed and flaked away, and one skeletal arm lay on the floor. Dust mingled with the smell of preservatives, and Jig had to grab his nose to keep from sneezing.

"There's another behind me," Jig yelled.

Whatever it was, it had begun life as a human, to judge from the rounded ears. Like the rest of its flesh, those ears were white and shrunken, but still recognizable. Rusted chain mail hung loosely from its shoulders, reinforced with metal plates at the knees and elbows. The hair was gone, making the head look like a skull covered in white mud except for the slight bulge of a nose and the clouded eyes that moved to track Jig's movements.

The mace came up again. Riana fled farther up the corridor, and Jig started to follow, only to slip on the smooth marble. He rolled out of the way of another attack, but this moved him into the thing's legs. It kicked Jig in the stomach, knocking him to the other side of the hall.

Jig gasped for breath. Doubled over, he could still see from the corner of his eye as the creature closed in.

But it stopped a few paces away. The skull-head turned to the right, then the left. Jig swore he saw the skin of the forehead wrinkle, as if in confusion. As the creature turned around, he saw why.

Beneath its armor, the creature wore tattered rags that had no doubt been magnificent finery, back when it was alive. Over time, decay had turned them to dry scraps. No color remained, and bits of thread hung down like the roots of a plant. Somehow those scraps had begun to burn, and nothing made better tinder than dry rags. Orange tendrils of flame danced beneath the armor, slowly climbing up the creature's body while the threads blackened and shriveled.

As the fire grew, the creature began to slap the flames, but to no effect. Its own skin began to burn as it tried without success to extinguish itself.

Whether it was truly dead, or if some spark of life remained to guide it, Jig didn't know. But the creature was apparently able to make decisions. Having realized it couldn't stop the fire, it turned again toward Jig. A few more minutes and it would be consumed, but that was plenty of time to dispose of one little goblin.

So instead of the walking dead, Jig found himself facing a warrior of fire. Who still carried a big mace. This was not good.

At least there was more light to see by, though. *I guess there's a bright side to every flaming corpse.*

Jig grinned. That would make a good proverb, assuming he survived to tell it to anyone.

He scooted backward until he bumped into the bones that had fallen out of the far alcove. In his desperation, he grabbed the arm bone and flung it at the approaching creature.

It ducked out of the way, and the bone clattered into the far alcove. The far panel reappeared.

Jig stared. The panel was really back. He could see the flames reflected in the polished marble. *That's how they seal the alcoves after they kill off the intruders. That way they can go back and wait for the next adventurers.*

"In here," he shouted. Riana looked confused, so he grabbed her arm and threw her into the open alcove behind him. Even as she collided with the skeleton, her weight triggered the magic, and the marble panel began to shimmer into existence.

The creature swung as Jig leaped. He felt the wind and heat pass his head, and if Smudge hadn't already burned his hair off, the creature probably would have ignited him. Passing through the shadowy panel was like swimming against a strong current. Or struggling against a whirlpool. His head and arms were already inside. He tried to push against the panel to help him through, but his hands sank uselessly into the half-formed marble.

What would happen if the panel finished appearing before he was inside? Would it fling Jig back into the creature's grasp? Would it form around him, leaving his legs sticking out in the hallway?

Probably not, he decided. A better trap would simply cut him in half. Which would at least save him from a slower death by fire and mace.

Jig reached out blindly, caught Riana's arm, and pulled as hard as he could.

He made it through. Old bones snapped as he landed on the now ruined skeleton, and Riana grunted with pain. In the sudden darkness, Jig couldn't tell what part of Riana his knee had landed on, but she swore at him as she wriggled away.

Blackness. Not even a sliver of light passed through the panel. At first, Jig didn't even want to breathe. He could hear sounds of combat in the hall. If he pressed an ear to the panel, he could even make out the cracking and popping of flames. A clatter of bones told him the fire had overcome whatever black art held the creature together.

"I hate this," Riana said.

Jig didn't bother to respond. He wasn't too happy with the situation either, but at this point he didn't know what he could do about it. At least they were safe. So he continued to listen to the fighting, wondering which side would come out alive. So to speak.

Only then did it occur to him that he didn't know how to open the alcove from the inside. The dead warriors probably didn't mind being trapped here for years at a time, but Jig did. Even ignoring the stench, he would quickly starve to death. With Riana here, he might last an extra week or so before hunger killed him.

If the adventurers lost, would the creatures leave him here to die? Or would they be intelligent enough to open the panel and finish him off? Of the two possibilities, Jig didn't know which one frightened him more. A quick death was always better, that was a goblin truism. But whoever made up that truism hadn't been fighting animated corpses. The idea of dying at the hands of those creatures left him queasy.

Riana spoke again, distracting him from what was happening outside. "I would have ended up like that."

Remembering the hard, tight feel of her severed finger, Jig thought she was right. Those things had the same shriveled look to them. Were they adventurers who had fallen prey to the same trap that had caught Riana? Or did the Necromancer have other ways to collect his soldiers? This whole place could be nothing more than a trap, one designed to provide new corpses for the Necromancer.

"I hate this," she said again. "Can't we make a light?"

Jig threw up his hands, forgetting that she couldn't see. "Barius neglected to give me a lantern of my own. And Ryslind hasn't taken the time to teach me magic. So I'm afraid we're stuck in the darkness."

"Don't push me, goblin," she snapped. "I'd wager my knife can find your heart even in the dark." The anger drained from her voice at the end, though. Jig heard her shift position. It sounded like she had backed into the corner.

"I've never known darkness like this. Outside there were always the stars. When I scraped together enough gold for a night indoors, or when some innkeeper took me in out of the snow for a night, I always slept in the common rooms, with a fire blazing."

"I've never seen the stars myself," Jig said. The idea of such openness made him nervous. Worse, he had once heard stories about *snow*. Water and ice falling from the sky, with nothing overhead but a thin wooden roof for protection? How could they live like that?

Jig tried to stretch out, but the end of his rope was still looped around his arm, and the movement tightened the noose.

"What's that?" Riana said loudly.

"Me," Jig said, once he finished choking. He quickly unwound the rope from his arm. The noose was too tight for his fingers to pry loose. He felt around for a thin bone to use as a lever. Barius would be furious if he freed himself, but Barius might also be dead, and Jig was tired of being tied up.

He found two long bones that might work. One was too thin, but the other had a broken end with a jagged point. This could make a passable weapon. Not as nice as his sword, but better than nothing. As he felt along the other end of the dry, scaly bones, his fingers touched a loop of cold metal.

A bracelet? It was wide enough. The oval ring was as wide as his upper arm, but might fit snugly about a human's wrist. He could feel hammer marks on the metal, and a bit of engraving on the inside. That was odd. Who engraved jewelry on the inside, leaving the outside bare and ugly?

Still maybe he could swap it to Barius for his sword. He slid the bracelet onto his arm, above the elbow, then snorted. Sure, and after Barius returned his sword, Jig would get Ryslind to teach him that fire-shooting spell. Maybe he'd follow it all up by asking Darnak for his wineskin.

He grabbed the bone and shoved it through the noose,

close to the knot. The point scratched his neck, and he couldn't pry the knot too hard without choking himself. He tried again, giving up only when blue spots of light began to float across his vision. Had the knot loosened at all? He couldn't tell. Gasping, he fell back against the wall.

"What are you doing?"

Jig felt his neck. The touch stung, and his fingers came away sticky. "Cutting my throat."

"What?"

He ignored her confused question. Tossing the bone away, he went back to searching the floor. Whoever this was, he had died wearing that bracelet. The other creatures still bore weapons and armor. What else might this one have with him? Jig hadn't had time to look at things very closely before flinging himself into the alcove.

"If anyone cuts your throat, it should be me," Riana muttered.

He often brushed against her foot or hand as he searched. Each time she slapped him away. It was too easy to get turned about in here. Time after time, Jig fixed Riana's position in his mind, only to run into her in another corner. Bad as his vision might be, he wished for even that poor sight to return. Worse than his disorientation, Jig was beginning to hallucinate. Movements to either side, colors that vanished when he blinked. But Jig had lived his whole life underground. Darkness was not uncommon. While not a welcome thing, anyone who couldn't cope with the dark tended to die an early death.

Jig closed his eyes and straightened his ears. The most difficult part was letting yourself ignore the lies your eyes told. Eyes were like children. If they had nothing to say, they made things up. Focusing on Riana's breathing, he continued to search through the bones.

His search turned up a few small coins, an old belt, and a pair of boots that came all the way to Jig's knees, but no knife or sword. Nothing he could use to free himself from Barius's noose.

The boots he kept, even though they were a bit too large. Their hard soles would be too loud on the floor, so he tore them off. The threads were loose and broke easily. In the process, he ripped the seams by the toes of one boot, but that didn't matter. They were still better than bare feet, especially down here, where he didn't know what he might be stepping on.

More importantly, they gave him a way to hide his bracelet. Goblins had large feet, but skinny limbs, and with a bit of force, Jig shoved the bracelet around his ankle. It might pinch a bit when he walked, but this way Barius wouldn't take it from him.

The belt tore apart when he tried to use it. The leather had rotted too badly to be worth anything.

"What are you doing, Jig?"

"Trying to find a knife." Failing to find a knife would be more honest. Wasn't it Jig's luck to end up trapped with the only unarmed corpse in the place? If he couldn't find a weapon, he would have to go back to the bone.

"Why? Didn't you already cut your throat?" She snorted. "Or are goblins as clumsy at suicide as with everything else?"

"For this noose. I want it off!" Where was the bone he had used before? There were so many. Could all of these bones really fit into one person? Even a human? And what were all of the tiny ones for? There must be hundreds scattered across the floor.

Before he could find one to use, Jig was jerked sideways by the noose. His head smacked into the wall. His fingers clawed at the rope as he tried to gain himself another breath. He could hear Riana next to him. She had the rope in her hand. What was she doing?

"This noose?"

Jig gagged something close to, "Yes."

Riana stood, pulling Jig with her. "If you had been tied up back there, I'd still have two working hands."

Or you'd have been one of those creatures. Even if he wanted to say it, he couldn't. The noose was too tight, and he couldn't pull it away. He needed air.

Wait, it wasn't the noose he had to fight. It was Riana.

"They were coming back to heal me. Barius told me Darnak had prayed for a spell that would cure the poison."

That made sense. They couldn't have told her the truth,

after all. Not if the prince didn't want to wake up one morning with a knife in his belly. They knew Riana's temper as well as Jig did.

Jig squirmed and reached behind his head. He didn't know if she would really kill him or not, but he couldn't take the chance. His fingers found Riana's wrists. He squeezed, but she was too strong. He couldn't pry her grip loose.

That was okay. He hadn't planned to do this by brute strength.

His hand slipped past her wrist and up her sleeve. She figured out what he was doing and pulled back, but he had already grabbed the hilt of her knife, the one she had stolen from Barius. As she leaped away, the knife stayed with Jig. Seconds later, he was free of the noose and gagging on the floor.

"I can still kill you," Riana warned. "For all you know, I could have a dozen more daggers stashed away."

But she didn't attack. She was afraid, Jig realized. Afraid of him! They had fought, and Jig had won. And he was too tired and sore to give one whit about his victory. He only wanted to curl up and rest.

So he did. He kept one ear aimed at the corridor so he could hear what was happening outside. The other remained pointed at Riana. He thought she was bluffing about the knife, but there were plenty of sharp bones in here. He wouldn't let her surprise him again. Which was why he couldn't allow himself to sleep. Even though he was so tired that the bone-littered floor felt almost comfortable.

The fighting couldn't go on for much longer. If the adventurers won and came back for Jig and Riana, they would be free soon. Otherwise, it didn't matter if Riana killed him or not.

The noise in the corridor stopped a little while later. Despite Jig's vigilance, Riana noticed first. "They've stopped."

Jig had listened as the clash of battle died, but he hadn't really heard it. Dealing with all of these people trying to kill him must have left him more tired than he realized.

"Should we call for help?" Riana asked.

"I don't know. If those corpses won, they might not be too

eager to help us. Especially after we burned one of them up like that."

"What happened to him anyway? Where did the fire come from?"

Knowing she couldn't see, Jig grinned at her. "My guess is that Smudge got hungry. I haven't fed him since yesterday." When she didn't say anything, he explained. "Fire-spiders like their meat cooked. Not much meat on those things, but I guess he decided it was better than starving."

He felt bad when he thought about it. Usually Jig took much better care of Smudge. Things had been too hectic lately, that was all. He hoped he'd be able to find something better than ancient human corpses to feed to the spider.

Since he couldn't do that from in here, Jig pounded against the marble panel with his dagger. The noise echoed in the small alcove, and Riana yelped.

"What are you doing? You said yourself that those things might still be out there."

Jig hit the panel again. "Either something lets us out, or else you get to stay in here with me until we both die."

A few seconds later, Riana grabbed a bone and joined him.

CHAPTER 8

Armed to the Teeth

THE PANEL FADED TO SHADOW. JIG SQUINTED AS light pierced the blackness of the alcove. Outside he saw Darnak's stocky silhouette waiting, club held high.

Before the panel could vanish entirely, Jig moved his stolen knife behind his back, handle toward Riana. Darnak probably wouldn't complain that Jig had, once again, freed himself of the rope. Coming out with knife in hand would be a different thing entirely. Darnak could get a bit club-happy after a fight, and Jig had been abused enough today without adding a whack from the dwarf.

"Take it," Jig whispered as the panel disappeared entirely. He stepped forward, placing himself in front of Riana so she could grab her knife unseen.

Which she did. Jig's relieved grin tightened with pain as she sliced his fingers in the process.

"Thanks," she said sweetly, too low for Darnak to hear. She slipped past Jig and smiled in passing.

Elves. They could be as bad as goblins sometimes. Jig clenched his fist to close the cut and hoped nobody would notice.

"Come on," Darnak said. Sweat streaked his face and plastered curls of hair to his forehead, and he sported a stained red bandage on his arm. "We've regrouped back this way to catch our breath. Undead bastards gave us quite a fight."

Jig could see that for himself. Of the creature Smudge had burned, nothing remained but a skeleton that lay in the middle of a man-shaped pile of ash. Jig felt thankful for his new boots, since he had to walk through those remains to catch up with the others. He tried to ignore the crunch of his footsteps as he followed Darnak.

Smudge scurried over and climbed Jig's leg.

"Good spider," Jig whispered, reaching down to scratch Smudge's head. "*Very* good spider. A warrior-spider." He glanced back at the bones and ash. "And still a hungry spider, I suspect. I doubt you found much meat on that thing. Don't you worry, I'll get something for you to eat."

The remains of the other creatures cluttered the corridor. One had been hacked to pieces, probably by Barius's sword. Another still jerked and twitched, as if trying to continue the attack. It might have succeeded, had its head not been lying upside down farther up the corridor. Darnak gave the body a lazy smack in passing, and the thing fell still.

As for the rest, even Jig could figure out how they had died. Only Ryslind's magic killed with such *finality*. These bodies were the least damaged, but each showed a large, blackened hole where the hearts would have been. Was there any limit to what Ryslind could do? Jig counted four who had fallen to the wizard's fire.

The smell was terrible, and he tried not to breathe through his nose until he had joined Darnak and the others in the room where they had first come through the whirlpool. Even there the charred scent of Ryslind's work followed him.

He braced himself for Barius's outburst as he passed through the door. No doubt the prince would yell and threaten and demand to know how Jig could have been so stupid as to trigger the trap. But Barius was in no shape to yell.

The prince lay in the middle of the room, next to the water pillar. His shirt and armor were piled to one side, and his white skin was pale even for a human. Bandages covered his stomach; another bound his left shoulder. Both were wet with blood.

"Is he dead?" Jig asked, trying to keep his hopefulness from showing.

"Pah." Darnak spat on the pillar. Jig stared, fascinated, as the spittle shrank and vanished, somehow passing through the barrier and into the waters of the whirlpool.

"He's not dead. He just tried a riposte when he should have parried in four."

Jig nodded as though he understood.

"Don't worry, he'll be his charming self soon enough. Earthmaker won't allow us to fail, not from a few scratches like that."

"Earthmaker sounds like a useful person to have around," Jig said.

"Aye. He's one who rewards his followers. Over a hundred years I've offered up my sacrifices and prayed to him for guidance. Far be it from me to guess the mind of a god, but I'm thinking he'll not repay a century of service by letting us all die here."

Ryslind strolled to the dwarf's side. "Yet for all of your devotion, your magic is still limited to those powers your god grants you. To be so dependent on the whim of a deity would be disturbing, to say the least."

"It's called faith," Darnak snapped. "And it's a far cry safer than your wizardry. When's the last time you heard about a priest blowing himself up after trying a new spell and waving three fingers instead of four?"

They glared at each other, the dwarf's tiny eyes not leaving Ryslind's glowing ones. They might have continued for hours had Barius not stirred.

"Forgive my interruption," the prince said, "but could your time not be better spent by aiding one who still bleeds from his wounds?"

"Aye," answered Darnak. He knelt next to Barius and began praying. One hand covered the stomach wound, which looked like the more serious injury. Between his prayers, so low that even Jig could barely hear, Darnak muttered, "I'd love to see your high and mighty wizardry cure this."

After a while, he leaned back and said, "He'll need a few hours of rest. Earthmaker has closed the cuts, but it'll take a bit of Barius's strength to finish the job."

"Perhaps your god is busy with other matters," Ryslind said.

"Aye," Darnak answered agreeably. His easygoing nod contrasted sharply with his earlier grumbling. Perhaps relief at Barius's recovery had put him in a better mood. "A whole world of prayers, and you think he can spend all his time on one dwarf?"

Jig ignored the rest of the discussion. Several times now, Darnak had healed wounds that would have crippled a goblin. What would it be like to have that kind of power available all the time? To know that, no matter how grave the injury, a journey to the closest priest could fix you in a matter of hours?

At first the idea seemed wondrous, and Jig had to fight off a surge of jealousy. The more he thought about it, though, the more he began to question if that sort of power would necessarily be a good thing. What would bullies like Porak do if they knew their victims could recover from almost anything? Instead of tossing rodents into the muck pot, why not set Jig himself on fire? Wouldn't it be far more entertaining to spend the afternoon playing flame-the-goblin? Especially if the victim could come back the next day, good as new and ready to play the game all over again.

But maybe gods were smarter than that. The fact that the gods had always ignored goblinkind might be a sign that they understood how much trouble a magic-wielding goblin could cause.

Darnak dug into his pack for food and came up with a new loaf of bread, which he passed around to the party. He also found several more strips of meat, as well as a small wheel of cheese. This he dusted off and cut into five pieces.

The cheese was good, if a bit strong. As before, Jig received only two pieces of the meat. He would have to endure bread again if he wanted to fill his belly.

Riana, he noticed, had taken some of her bread and tucked it into her shirt, along with a little meat. Saving something for later? That was probably a good idea. He waited until nobody was looking, then slipped one strip of meat into his boot.

The other he tore into with relish, eating half with one bite. As he swallowed, he noticed Smudge. The fire-spider quivered on Jig's knee, and all eight eyes followed the meat in his hand.

"I don't suppose I could interest you in some bread?" he asked, holding out a piece. Smudge actually heated up a bit as he scooted away, confirming Jig's impression of the so-called food. "Right," he sighed.

Resigning himself to a meal of cheese and bread, he tossed the remaining meat onto the floor. Smudge sprang. His legs landed to either side of the meat like a cage. Seconds later, the smell of burning meat drifted through the air as Smudge cooked his food.

"Enjoy it." Jig brushed a bit of dirt off the cheese and took another bite. By alternating cheese and bread and drinking a fair amount of water, he managed to finish off the meal. But he would have given so much for just one cup of Golaka's stew. Even day-old stew, the kind you had to skin before you ate, would have been heaven-sent.

"If I had the Rod of Creation, I'd use it to make some real food," he decided.

"Another attack like that, and we won't even make it to the dragon's lair," Darnak told him. "Let alone find the rod."

"Will there be more traps?" Riana asked quietly. She tried to sound casual, but Jig could see the way she kept looking at the stump of her finger.

Barius coughed and rolled onto his side. "You're the burglar of this party. What say you?"

She glared at him. "All those dead things couldn't have come from one little trapped lock. The Necromancer could have traps everywhere. He could have armies waiting to pour out of the walls next time. Or maybe he set spells to turn us all into creatures like that. Even if we found every trick panel and poison needle, how are we going to find those traps hidden by magic?"

Her eyes kept going to the whirlpool. Jig knew what she was thinking about. She wanted to escape, to find a way back up to the surface. But she was doing everything she could to hide her fear.

As far as he could tell, nobody else had noticed. None of them showed any sign of fear, so they probably didn't see it in others. They were adventurers, after all. Jig, on the other hand, had enough fear for the entire party.

Maybe that was what made Riana seem smarter than the others. She was no more a hero than Jig was. Of course, she was a young girl, barely more than a baby for her race, whereas Jig was a grown goblin. Why was *he* so afraid?

He didn't bother to answer that question. He could have spent the next three hours listing reasons to be afraid, and all it would do was make him even more frightened.

"Our elven thief has a point," Barius said. "Perhaps she begins to learn wisdom. No doubt the Necromancer's traps litter this place like horse dung on the highway."

"A beautiful image, prince," Ryslind said.

Barius nodded, completely missing the sarcasm. "Brother, I think we must call upon your art once more. Can you guide us through this maze of traps and death?"

"Perhaps we should rest a mite longer," Darnak said quickly.

Remembering the wizard's fit after they came through the whirlpool, Jig was inclined to agree.

"There must be another way to find the Necromancer and the path to Straum's domain. Would anyone be knowing a song, a story, even a rumor about this place?" Darnak looked around hopefully. "Anything at all, no matter how strange or confusing."

Jig spoke up hesitantly. "I know one, but it wouldn't help."

"Let us decide what is helpful," Barius said. "Perhaps we can intuit some vital fact that you never stopped to consider."

He wished he had kept quiet. "I don't think so. It's not much of a song."

"Enough protests. Goblins haven't the intellect to find those kernels of truth hidden within the old songs."

Jig shrugged and began to sing.

Ten little goblins walked off to drink their wine.
Up came the Necromancer, then there were nine.
They screamed and they hid and they ran away,
But those goblins came back the very next day.

Nine little goblins went looking for a mate,
Up came the Necromancer, then there were eight.
They screamed and they hid and they ran away,
But those goblins came back the very next day.

Eight little goblins—

"Enough," Barius shouted.

Jig shifted uncomfortably. "It's more of a children's song, really."

"That is the extent of your knowledge regarding our foe?" Barius had apparently recovered from his injuries, for he pushed himself up and walked over to glare at Jig. "You've lived here your entire life, and the best you can do is 'Ten little goblins'?"

"What about you?" Jig shot back. He had warned the prince it was a stupid song. Why did everyone keep blaming Jig for their stupid mistakes? "You knew what you'd be facing down here. Did you bring anything to help you against the Necromancer?"

The prince's eyes widened. One hand dropped to his belt, closer to the hilt of his sword than Jig was comfortable with. "I . . . I brought him." Barius pointed to his brother.

"A good thing for us all that you did, too." What was he doing? Jig couldn't believe the words coming out of his own mouth. He had seen the prince's temper. Why was he so eager for Barius to finish him off?

"I saw the bodies in the hall," he continued. "Your brother killed four of those things. If he weren't here, they would have killed you as easily as you killed my patrol. If you ask me, *Ryslind* should start leading this party before you lead us into another trap."

Nobody moved. Over the course of Jig's rant, Barius's face had turned red, then purple. Jig watched him curiously. He hadn't realized humans could change color. Perhaps they were part lizard.

Jig had never seen Barius, or any human for that matter, get this mad. Still angry people all seemed to react in the same way. Jig braced himself. Yes, here it came. Barius's open hand caught Jig on the side of his face and knocked him to the ground. *This is growing old*, he thought as he lay on the floor, staring upward. Still, he would be an expert on ceilings by the time he was through.

"What are you doing, lad?" Darnak asked. "He's unarmed."

"I'm challenging this goblin to a duel," Barius said.

"A what?" Jig turned his head toward the prince. "What's a duel?"

Darnak raised his hands in disgust. "Have your wits deserted you, man? We're in the home of the Necromancer, and you want to stand around fighting duels?"

"A duel," Barius explained, ignoring the dwarf, "is a battle of honor. To the death. As the challenged party, you have the choice of weapons."

Jig blinked. "What? Darnak, is he serious?"

"You've insulted my honor. Choose your weapon. Knives, swords, clubs, even quarterstaves. I saw a pair of spears we could use." His hawkish nose wrinkled in a sneer. "Your presence has plagued this party long enough, goblin."

Jig looked around for help. Him, fight Barius? Why not execute him outright and be done with it?

Ryslind looked bored with it all, and Darnak was shaking his head in disbelief. Riana rolled her eyes. "Men," she muttered disgustedly. Nobody moved to intervene.

"Enough dallying," Barius said. "Choose your weapon." He waved his arms in large circles, presumably some sort of warm-up ritual, then practiced a few lunges against an imaginary foe.

What should he choose? As if it made a difference. The only weapon Jig had ever held more than once was a kitchen knife, and he suspected Barius was as skilled with knives as he was with the sword. Either way, Jig would soon be bleeding his life all over the nice, polished marble.

"Choose."

He can't just kill me. Not with everyone watching. That means he has to play by the rules. Jig glared at him. "If I win, will you let me carry a weapon again? And no more of your stupid ropes, either."

Barius laughed. "Anything you like. Ask for my future barony or my firstborn child, it matters not. But ask and let us done with it."

What would Jig do with a human newborn? Even goblins didn't eat babies. Too little meat. Did humans typically go around swapping their children? He shook his head and decided he was better off not knowing. "Freedom and my sword. I don't want anything else."

"Very well." Barius appeared close to losing his temper. His cheek twitched, and each word shot out through gritted teeth. "Select your weapon."

"Fangs."

Barius blinked. "What? You can't choose fangs."

"Why not? It's a game goblin children play. We call it Rakachak. You bite one another on the arms and legs, and the winner is the one who goes the longest without crying." He smiled and fingered the three-inch fangs on his lower jaw. "If you want, you can go first."

Jig patted the short sword at his side, reassured by its weight. Not that it would be much use if they were attacked again. Darnak had told him about the fight, how Barius had cut down his first opponent, only to have it rise again and slash Barius's shoulder from behind. Stabbing the creature in the throat hadn't even inconvenienced it. Whatever these things were, they needed to be hacked apart, bludgeoned to a pulp, or dealt with by magic. *Or by a hungry fire-spider,* Jig had added silently.

Ahead, Ryslind raised his hand and brought the party to a halt. He gestured at the right wall. "Another passageway . . . here." He spoke in the same dual-toned voice Jig had heard before.

Jig didn't like it. He didn't like any of it. Well, he had liked watching Barius sputter and curse after Jig named his weapon for the duel. Darnak had to physically stop Barius from slicing Jig's head from his body. Seeing the haughty prince back out of his "duel" and formally ask Jig's forgiveness was worth almost all the pain and indignity he had endured on this quest.

Afterward, they still faced the same problem. Amidst

whatever traps and tricks filled this place, how could they find the Necromancer without dying in the process? In the end, they turned again to Ryslind.

The wizard hadn't said a word. He pulled a blue vial from his cloak and drained the contents in one swallow. A coughing fit took him, and the vial shattered on the floor. Jig watched as he doubled over and fell. He wondered if Ryslind had grabbed the wrong potion, taken something deadly instead of the potion he wanted.

Ryslind's eyes glowed brighter than ever when he struggled back to his feet. He blinked and squinted, and finally said, "Too much magic in here. I can't see anything. Someone lead me to the corridor."

Darnak had taken it upon himself to grab the wizard's arm and guide him over the corpses and into the corridor. Once there, Ryslind had begun to walk at a slow, steady pace. He stopped before the trapped tile, gestured at it with one hand, and muttered, "Don't step here."

"I think we're already knowing that much," Darnak said.

Ryslind ignored him. He pointed out two more tiles before reaching the first fork in the corridor. Without hesitation, he took the left turn. Jig wondered if Ryslind even noticed the other hallway, or if he saw anything but the path his magic showed him. He didn't seem to see or hear the rest of the party, much to Darnak's dismay.

"How can I make a good map if you're racing about like a tomcat on the prowl?" He sketched as fast as he could, but Jig could see that his careful map was devolving into a few lines and arrows. "Can't even keep track of which tiles we're to avoid. Probably trigger every one if we have to come back this way in a hurry."

In addition to the traps, there were a number of secret passages, like the one Ryslind had just found. Everything was constructed of the same marble panels, and from time to time Ryslind would point one out at random. Nobody knew how they were *supposed* to open, for the wizard's magic allowed him to bypass the normal mechanism. Even as he pointed, his eyes would flash, and the panel would crash onto the ground, often breaking into thick shards from the impact.

Jig got down and crawled through the hole into the secret passageway. "They could at least make the doors taller," he grumbled.

"You should mention that to the Necromancer when we find him," Riana said as she followed. "I'm sure he'd love to hear architectural suggestions from a goblin."

She hadn't been quite as mean to him since his aborted duel. In fact, she had laughed harder than Jig had ever seen, which only added to Barius's fury. But that didn't mean she had forgiven him, either. She merely flipped back and forth as to whom she hated more, Jig or Barius. With Barius up ahead, following his brother, that left Jig as a target for her frustrations.

At least the corridor beyond opened up to let him walk upright and put a few more feet between himself and her barbs.

"Another trap," Ryslind said. This time it was a thin wire stretched across the floor. Jig's poor vision meant that he couldn't see it at all, and he felt like a fool as Darnak guided his legs in an exaggerated motion over the wire. Better this than another attack, though. He wondered how much power it took for Ryslind to sense the traps and the hidden passages. Even tracking the Necromancer at all must take an enormous effort. Jig knew nothing of magic, but he assumed a powerful wizard would have ways to hide himself.

"Do you think this is what the Necromancer wants?" he wondered.

"What's that?" Darnak snapped. He scowled at his map and drew a quick turn, then made a line to indicate the tripwire. "Do I think what?"

"Well, he has to know we're here. And he probably knows we've got a wizard. So wouldn't it make sense to force the wizard to use up his power before we actually face the Necromancer? That way, when we finally get through this maze, the Necromancer will be able to kill Ryslind like a bug." Not to mention what the search might be doing to Ryslind's already questionable sanity. Those dual voices sent creepy tingles down Jig's back every time the wizard spoke.

"Aye, it's possible." Darnak hurried ahead, forcing Jig and

Riana to jog to keep up. When they were closer to the humans and their lantern, he slowed his pace again to draw. As he sketched, he explained. "That's why we all have to be ready to strike. Only two ways for the likes of us to deal with wizards of the Necromancer's caliber. Run away, or hit him with a rock."

"I don't have a rock," Jig said worriedly. There were no rocks down here. Had he known, he would have taken one from the lakeshore above.

Darnak's eyes came up to glare at Jig. "Figure of speech. Your sword there'll do the job. The trick is to take him out before he can use his magic. Hard and fast, and no hesitation. Let him get a spell off, and it's your death. I'm afraid you're right about Ryslind being at the end of his rope, so if you wait for him to save your blue hide, you'll not last long."

Jig had no illusions about his skill with a sword. A day ago, he would have taken the dwarf's advice and thought himself a match for any wizard. Like Porak, he had believed that a good weapon made a good warrior. But Porak now resided in the belly of a carrion-worm. Jig had seen Barius and Darnak in combat, and next to them, he was nothing. Even Ryslind was a more skilled fighter, and he was a wizard. What hope did Jig have, sword or no sword?

"What about your magic?" he asked, searching for another option. "Won't Earthmaker help you beat the Necromancer?"

"Doesn't work that way. Earthmaker wants us to choose our own path. He can guide us and give us strength, but where mortals come into conflict, he'll not interfere." Darnak stopped and cocked his head. His face wrinkled like a raisin. "Something's not right. The tunnel changes up ahead."

"How can you tell?"

"He's a dwarf," Riana answered, as if that explained everything. She hurried up to tell the others.

They soon found that Darnak was right. Barius and his brother stopped, lantern held in front of them. When Jig caught up and saw why they had paused, it was all he could do to keep from throwing up.

Not only did the tunnel change, it ended completely. The walls and ceiling stopped, and the cramped passage opened into a huge cavern. The top was too far to see, and the bottom . . . Jig's stomach knotted just thinking about it. At the far side, he could just see a glimmer of reflected light, presumably from the marble paneling the Necromancer seemed to like so much. All they had to do was cross.

"Bottomless pit, you think?" Darnak asked.

Barius nodded. " 'Twould be my guess."

That was when Jig decided they were both as mad as the wizard. They talked about this chasm as if they crossed bottomless pits every day before breakfast. Worse, as he looked at the others, he had no doubt what they were about to say.

"Let us be on our way," Barius said, right on cue.

"Over *that*?" Riana demanded.

Good to know that Jig wasn't the only one who had problems with this. True, the paneled floor continued across the pit, creating a sort of bridge. The problem was that *only* the panels continued. As far as he could see, they rested on nothing but air. Only thin lines of silver mortar held the panels together. Although Jig knew nothing about bridges, he guessed this wasn't how they were supposed to look.

Each panel was no thicker than Jig's thumb. While the others planned the safest way to cross, Jig dropped to his hands and knees and crawled to the tunnel's edge. Peering over the edge, he saw nothing but blackness beneath the bridge. Wind brushed past his face and pushed his ears back. The walls of the pit were smooth black stone. Not polished like the marble, but still too smooth to climb. *What were you expecting? A nice ladder and a sign saying "Here's the* safe *bridge for goblins only"?*

Something landed on Jig's back. He shouted and rolled away, kicking wildly at his attacker. Smudge slipped off his shoulder and started to fall, and Jig barely managed to grab one of the spider's suddenly hot legs. Once he was back in the tunnel, Smudge scurried a good six feet away from the edge and cowered there.

The attacker turned out to be the end of a rope. Darnak and Riana both laughed at him, while Barius muttered something about "stupid, cowardly creatures." Jig noticed they had each wrapped a loop of rope about their waists.

"Best to be safe when crossing these things," Darnak explained. He helped Jig up and tied the rope around his waist with a sure hand. "Earthmaker willing, we'll not be needing this. But I've not yet seen a bottomless pit that didn't have some nastiness hidden away, waiting to knock you to your doom."

"You've crossed these before?" Jig asked.

"Oh, aye. Back when I was a lad, there wasn't a wizard around who didn't conjure up his own bottomless pit. They're less common these days, but you still find 'em lying about in older labyrinths and lairs. They're useful things. If you can cut a shaft through the entire place, you've got some ventilation. Otherwise the air gets stale and things start to die. Not to mention the stink."

He lowered his voice, as if sharing a secret. "Truth is, they're not really bottomless. You'll fall for a while, no doubt, but sooner or later you find the bottom. A real bottomless pit takes too much magic."

Perhaps that was supposed to reassure him, Jig didn't know. He saw Darnak take another drink of ale, and decided that strong drink would have been far more comforting. Strong drink he could enjoy back in the goblin lair would be even better.

"Onward," said Barius. He walked close behind Ryslind, lantern held high to light up the bridge. Riana followed, then Darnak, still scribbling at his map, and Jig brought up the rear. That meant he would be the last one to step onto those floating tiles.

He watched as each member of the group stepped onto the bridge, and each time he expected the tiles to crumble away at the touch of their feet. The tiles didn't even wiggle.

The rope went taut, tugging Jig closer to the edge. Another three steps and he'd be on the bridge. What if he fell? What if the wind got stronger and blew him over the edge? Would the others try to pull him up? More likely they would cut the rope and let him fall. Why else would they put him last? This way they could cut him loose without sacrificing themselves.

Two more steps. Maybe the bridge only worked for certain

races. Would it support a goblin as well as a human? Magic was funny that way, and he had a sudden, vivid memory of the marble panels that had hidden their dead attackers. Those had felt solid enough, up until they vanished. Was there a trigger to make these panels disappear as well?

One step. Of course. The spell must be designed to wait until the last person stepped out of the tunnel. Only *then* would it vanish. He was the last one. As soon as he took that next step, they would all fall to their deaths. He was the only one who could save them. He had to get this knot undone. His fingers clawed at the rope, but the dwarf had tied a good knot, and it wouldn't budge.

"Wait," he whispered. "Please wait."

The rope jerked him forward, and he fell onto the bridge. The solid, unmoving bridge. Jig froze. Ahead the others glanced back impatiently. The tiles hadn't faded. He wasn't falling. *He wasn't falling!* He was trembling so much he couldn't stand up, but he wasn't falling.

"You planning to walk, or were you expecting us to drag you across?" Darnak yelled. His voice echoed in the chasm.

Jig tried to rise. The bridge was wide enough. Three tiles wide, which was more than twice the length of a goblin. He would be okay. All he had to do was stand up and walk after the others.

"I'm coming," he yelled back. He rose to his knees, glanced over the edge, and promptly dropped back to the floor. Crawling would be just fine, he decided. Smudge crawled everywhere, and he never lost his balance. At that moment, Jig would have been happier with eight legs, but he'd be all right with four. He hoped.

About thirty feet ahead, Ryslind pointed to a tile in the center. "Illusion," he said.

What a nasty trick. Jig chewed his lip as he neared the false tile. He would have to go around. The tile looked as solid as the rest. He touched a finger to the marble surface and watched it pass right through, so it looked like his finger had been severed at the knuckle. Like Riana's. If Ryslind hadn't seen the trap, they would have fallen.

"Watch us, not the bottom," Darnak snapped.

Right. *Watch them. Don't look over the edge. Don't even think about it. Don't imagine the wind rushing past your ears or tumbling helplessly out of control.* Would he see the ground rushing up? Would he feel the impact, or would death be too quick? His head began to spin from breathing so fast. *No, don't get dizzy. Not now. Relax. Be calm. Anything to distract yourself.*

He crawled forward a few inches and began to sing in a strained voice. "Ten little goblins walked off to drink their wine. . . ."

He curled his fingers around the edges of the tile for stability, but that only reminded him that a single tile hung between him and the abyss. To his right was the false tile, to his left, nothing. He hoped the magic and the mortar were strong enough. In his imagination, he could see one side of the tile break free, see himself dangling helplessly as the tile dropped away like the hobgoblins' trapdoor.

A few more steps. He could do this. Everyone else had done it. If the bridge could support Darnak's weight, it would surely hold Jig. It would hold a half-dozen goblins. He clenched his teeth and continued to sing.

By the time he reached the third verse, he had passed the false tile and was back in the center of the bridge where it was safe. Relatively speaking, at least.

"Good job," Darnak said. "Now let's be on."

Jig nodded. He could do this. He could make it. They were going to be okay.

That was when the attack started.

CHAPTER 9

Torment of the Gods

AT FIRST JIG THOUGHT THE FLUTTERING WAS A figment of his frightened imagination. A trick of the wind, perhaps. He certainly couldn't see anything when he looked around.

The first squeal, so loud Jig grabbed his ears and folded them flat to his head, told him this was no trick. Something really was out there in the blackness.

More squeals followed, causing Jig to change his conclusion. Some *things*.

"Don't stop, but keep your eyes open," Darnak yelled. He pointed his dripping quill at the other side of the bridge. "We're halfway there. If we can make it to the other side, we'll be safer."

"Keep your eyes open," Jig mimicked. "As if I'd do this sort of thing blindfolded." He started to crawl, only to stop when the next squeal deafened him. He couldn't crawl and cover his ears at the same time.

"Why do they have to be so loud?" He couldn't hear his own voice. Clasping his hands to his ears, he stood up and hurried after the others.

They had gone another twenty yards when something large and black swooped toward Darnak. Huge, leathery wings batted the dwarf's head, pushing him backward.

Darnak dropped his quill and struck out with his fist, knocking the thing away and letting Jig see it clearly in the lantern light.

They were bats. Bigger than any bat Jig had seen, but they could be nothing else. Their bodies were almost as big as Darnak himself, and the wings stretched at least ten feet to either side. Another swooped down behind Jig, giving him a close look at their bristled, piglike faces, and a row of needle-sharp teeth. The only redeeming features were their brown ears, even bigger than a goblin's.

Jig grabbed his sword and swung wildly. More by luck than any skill, the tip grazed the bat's wing and sent it spinning out of sight beneath the bridge.

Darnak yelled something else, but Jig couldn't hear. More bats were coming down behind him. He ran to join the others.

Only to drop through another illusionary tile. He didn't have time to panic. One second he was running, the next he was dropping his sword and scrambling for a handhold. His fingers slipped, and then the rope jerked him to a halt. Jig clutched the rope with both hands and hoped Darnak wouldn't follow him through. If the dwarf and all that equipment fell through the hole, Jig doubted the others would be able to support the weight.

The rope tore skin from Jig's armpits as he dangled helplessly. Smudge flattened himself to Jig's shoulder, legs clinging to the leather pad, and Jig could feel the heat on his cheek. "Don't touch the rope," he warned. The last thing he needed was for the stupid fire-spider to crawl around and set the rope on fire. Fortunately, Smudge appeared to be stiff with fear.

Something moved nearby. He couldn't see very well since the bridge blocked most of the light, but the shifting shadows in front of him took on the ugly form of a bat, only a few feet away. Even if his sword weren't lying useless on the bridge above, he wouldn't have dared release his grip on the rope long enough to use it.

So the next time the bat came near, he kicked as hard as he could. His boot caught the bat's snout, and it looped away.

The movement started him twisting. Another bat flew at him and clobbered his head with a wing. The bat's small claws reached out but missed. Now he was spinning the other direction. Much more of this, and he'd lose what little food he had eaten. He imagined the undigested bread dropping endlessly through the darkness and wondered what the bats would make of it.

More squeals ripped at Jig's ears. What he wouldn't have given for another alcove to hide in. He twisted his head, trying to see where the next attack would come from.

Nothing but blackness. Which, between his own poor vision and the fact that he was looking for brown and black bats in the dark, meant very little. Wind buffeted Jig's body as a bat flew up to land on the edge of the bridge. The smell of guano was so strong he could practically taste it.

There was a crunch, and a huge, senseless body plunged past Jig's left side. That would be Darnak, teaching the bats the futility of a ground-based attack.

He wondered if the others would be able to pull him back. Would they even bother? With so many bats to fend off, why lower their guard long enough to rescue one goblin?

Darnak's head poked through the illusionary tile. To Jig, it looked as if the marble had sprouted a small, hairy face. Darnak's braided tangles hung upside down, like black moss. His mouth moved silently, and he grinned at the goblin.

Jig grinned back. He was too deaf to hear what had been said, but what did it matter? Probably boasting about the bat he had just slain.

The rope jerked up a foot, costing Jig another strip of skin. *Or maybe he was telling me to hold on.* Jig's fingers tightened on the rope as he lurched closer toward the bridge. Another bat came at him from behind, and Jig kicked again. He missed, but it was enough to make the thing change course. Then thick fingers grabbed his wrist and yanked him onto the bridge.

Darnak nodded sharply, said something Jig couldn't hear, and then he was off to whack another bat. Riana stood close behind Barius. The bats had apparently learned to avoid the human's flashing sword. Ryslind waited a little way beyond, arms folded. One bat flew down behind him, only to bounce off an invisible wall. It landed on the bridge, took a few stunned steps, then teetered over the edge.

Another bat gone, but it made little difference. Jig spotted his sword sitting close to the side of the bridge. He grabbed it and turned to join the others, for all the good he could do. Bats were everywhere. The adventurers were doing a good job defending themselves, but the bats could wear them out with sheer numbers. Eventually they would all be knocked into the bottomless pit.

Jig grimaced as he recalled Darnak's assurances. The pit wasn't truly bottomless. So maybe if they killed enough bats, the bodies would pile up at the bottom and provide a softer landing. Not that being trapped at the bottom of a pit up to his neck in giant bat bodies was much of an improvement.

They were close to the end of the bridge. If they could make it across, they could hide in the tunnels. The bats' wings were too wide for them to follow. The group would be safe. Safe from the bats, at least. If the Necromancer's personal labyrinth could ever be considered *safe*.

Jig began to walk, testing the tiles as he went. He made it about ten feet before the rope grew taut. Darnak was still behind him, merrily crushing bat skulls and breaking bat wings. Jig could no more pull the dwarf along than drag the mountain itself.

"Come on," Jig shouted.

Darnak yelled something back.

Jig rolled his eyes. *He can't hear me any better than I hear him.* He grabbed the rope and pulled. Darnak tilted his head, and Jig pointed toward the tunnel.

Darnak frowned, then shook his head as understanding came. He waved his club at the bats, as if to say he wasn't finished yet. Ignoring Jig's pleas, he spun and leaped into the air after another bat.

Between his own bulk and that of his pack, the dwarf's tremendous leap took him nearly six inches into the air. High enough to break a bat's foot, but no more. As Darnak landed, the bridge vibrated beneath their feet. Jig fought the urge to go back to all fours.

So Darnak wanted to stay until the fighting was done. That could take a while. The bats showed no sign of slowing. Jig was half tempted to cut the rope and cross to the far tunnel himself. Let the adventurers enjoy the battle; *he* would enjoy some peace and quiet. Only two things stopped him. One was the knowledge that, were he to cut the rope, the next illusionary tile would send him to his death below. The other was that he didn't know what waited for them beyond that dark opening in the far wall. With Jig's luck, he would escape the bats but find himself surrounded by more of those fighting corpses.

Jig tugged the rope again. When he had Darnak's attention, he pointed to Ryslind, who still waited motionlessly as bat after bat bounced off his magical shield. The dwarf didn't understand, so Jig did his best to pantomime Ryslind's fit from earlier. He clutched his head and walked in tight circles. One hand fluttered as if he were casting spells. Didn't he understand? How long before Ryslind overexerted himself again? The only thing worse than another of Ryslind's seizures would be another seizure in the middle of a fight.

This approach appeared to work. Darnak glanced at Ryslind. He grabbed a hank of his beard and worriedly twisted it around his index finger. A bat came at him from the side. Darnak knocked it senseless, but this time his heart wasn't in it. Jig had guessed right. No matter how much Darnak enjoyed battle, his loyalty to the humans took precedence.

That was a good thing to remember. A very different attitude than goblins, most of whom would have simply cut the rope and shoved Ryslind over the edge.

Darnak nodded. He kicked the unconscious bat he had just bludgeoned off the side of the bridge and headed toward the others.

Jig glanced over to watch it fall out of sight. He shivered and hurried back to the middle of the bridge. Darnak had his map out again in his off-weapon hand. Had he been able to mark most of the trapped tiles? Jig hoped so, because he was following the dwarf's steps as closely as he could.

They reached Barius and Riana. Darnak went through the same hand-waving that Jig had done, pausing from time to time to help them kill more bats. Barius needed less convincing than Darnak.

Moving slowly, Darnak and Barius escorted the others toward Ryslind. From there, they inched their way to the other side. The bats launched a desperate attack near the end. They flew as a group, no longer bothering with claws as they tried to physically knock the party off the bridge. It might have worked if they hadn't picked Ryslind as their first target.

Bats bounced in all directions, like water splashing from a boulder. Jig saw Ryslind smirk as one bat spun off and crashed into the chasm wall.

A few more steps, and they were through. Once they passed into the tunnel, the bats gave up and returned to whatever they did when they weren't attacking innocent adventurers. Well, maybe "innocent" was too strong a word.

Still, Jig wondered what sort of life there was for giant bats trapped in an endless chasm. Did they spend their days trying to find enough bugs to keep from starving? If so, no wonder they were so desperate to attack the party. This could have been their first real meal in months, or even years. Whose cruel idea had it been to trap bats in the chasm anyway? Was that part of Ellnorein's design when he created this place? Or perhaps Straum the dragon had brought them.

How long had the bats lived here, knowing nothing beyond the walls of their pit? Then again, the same could be said of the goblins. For thousands of years, goblins had lived in their small lair, and those few who left for the outside world tended not to return. He wondered what that kind of isolation had done to them over the centuries.

As he followed the others, Jig decided he was just as happy the bats couldn't escape their pit. He had seen enough of those black-eyed, flat-nosed faces to last a lifetime.

A lifetime, or at least until Jig and the others came back on their way out and had to cross the bridge again. The thought didn't bother him as much as it might have. What were the odds that they would survive to make it past both the Necromancer and the dragon? His chances of seeing the bridge again were slim, so why worry about the bats?

His hearing returned slowly, bringing with it a splitting headache, as if Smudge had crawled into his ear and set his brain afire. Maybe there was an advantage to the humans' tiny ears after all. Neither they nor the dwarf seemed to suffer any aftereffects of the deafening shrieks that still occasionally echoed up the tunnel after them. Even Riana's slender ears would have been considered small and malformed by any goblin.

Darnak had healed him before, Jig remembered. Would he and Silas Earthmaker be able to do anything for this headache? More importantly, would they bother? Probably not, he decided. *What kind of god is going to waste his time and power on a goblin?*

Another shriek fanned the fire in Jig's head to a white-hot blaze, and he reconsidered. *What's the worst the gods could do? Strike me down for asking? At least that would make the pain stop.*

Jig hurried up to Darnak. His hand was out to tug the dwarf's sleeve when, up ahead, Ryslind stumbled.

The wizard dropped to his knees and pressed the palms of his hands against his ears. The tattoos on his hands writhed in the light.

A strange pressure filled the air, and Jig's skin tingled.

"Get back and leave me alone," Ryslind yelled.

Barius, who had been hurrying to his brother's side, stopped at once. Riana backed off until she had put Barius between herself and Ryslind.

"Get away!" Ryslind ordered.

Personally, Jig thought that was the wisest suggestion either of the humans had made so far. So naturally Barius began to argue.

"What's that? Abandon my quest? Surely you jest, brother." Barius folded his arms. His foot tapped impatiently on the marble floor. "If this is no more than a feeble ploy to frighten me off and allow *you* to seize the rod, I shall be most incensed."

Ryslind snarled, a sound more animal than human. His red eyes fixed on his brother.

"Not good," Darnak mumbled. His pack slid to the ground, nearly smashing Jig's foot. He noticed the goblin standing there and handed him the lantern. "Hold this and stay out of the way."

"What can we do?" Jig asked, headache forgotten. He

didn't know what was going on, but he sensed that it was bad. Darnak looked grim, his mouth tight. As the dwarf had displayed nothing but merriment at an onslaught of giant bats, that was enough to worry Jig a great deal.

"You can shut your flap and let me work," said Darnak. He grabbed his holy amulet and dropped to one knee. "Come on, Earthmaker. I know I've asked a lot lately, but if you'd be giving us a hand again, I'd be mighty grateful."

He was praying, Jig realized. He listened closer. Goblins didn't pray. They had no use for gods, a disinterest matched only by the gods' disdain for goblins. If they cared for us, goblins figured, they'd help us win a fight or two from time to time. Since the only time the goblins won a fight was when they outnumbered the enemy by at least five to one, they assumed that the gods, like everything else, were the enemy.

On those few occasions that goblins got the upper hand, their victims had been known to pray for help or mercy from their gods. Generally this was taken as a weakness, an opportunity to slip in and stab them in the back. But having seen Darnak work his magic before, Jig perked his ears as the dwarf talked to his god. He sounded almost like he was having a normal conversation, albeit a one-sided one. Did the god respond? Jig moved closer, hoping that maybe if he listened hard enough, he might hear Earthmaker answer.

"The idiot boy strained himself again," Darnak said quietly. "If 'twere up to me, I'd say he dug his own tunnel, so let him find his own way out. But you know I can't be doing that. I'm sworn to protect them, and he'd kill us all in his madness."

He sniffed in what could have been amusement. "You wouldn't let your humble servant die of dark magic, would you? Give me an honest fight, at good odds, not this invisible art that slips past an honest blade like smoke."

Jig swallowed. Darnak worried that Ryslind was going to kill them? Maybe he was exaggerating in order to persuade the god. Jig used to say he was starving to try to con a bit more food from Golaka. Somehow, though, he doubted Darnak would do that. And since Golaka had never believed Jig, why would a god be any more gullible?

Darnak stopped breathing. Jig wouldn't have noticed if he

hadn't been standing with his ear practically at the dwarf's mouth. What kind of god would suffocate his own followers? Maybe Darnak *had* been trying to deceive the god, and this was his punishment. Jig vowed at that moment that, were he ever in a situation to talk with a god, he would stick to the unadorned truth.

"Darnak?" Dare he touch the immobile dwarf? Would it make any difference? He looked around, but the others were with Ryslind. Darnak's face and lips had taken on a bluish tinge. *How long could dwarves hold their breath?* he wondered.

A terrible thought hit him. If Darnak died, the others would find Jig standing over his body. How was he going to explain *that*?

"Darnak, wake up." He grabbed the dwarf's shoulder and shook him. Rather, he tried to shake him. It was like trying to move a wall. Darnak's muscles were hard as rock.

"Wow," Jig whispered. Growing braver, he poked Darnak's chest and arms. No wonder he hadn't worried about a few bats.

Jig's stomach growled, turning his thoughts down another path. A dwarf like this could keep the entire lair fed for a day and a half.

He shook his head. *I couldn't eat Darnak any more than I could eat Smudge.* Still after a day and a half with nothing but dried meat and bread, the idea was tempting.

"Come on, Darnak. Breathe!"

Darnak gasped. Jig's heart scrambled up into his throat with fright. Even as Jig tried to get his own breathing under control, he turned toward Ryslind. For his ears had noticed something none of the others could possibly have heard. Ryslind had gasped for breath at the exact same moment as Darnak.

What does that mean? What is it that connected them?

"Go see if he's all right," Darnak said. He took a long drink from his wineskin. A line of dark ale trickled from the corner of his mouth and into his beard, a tiny stream through a black forest. "Go on now."

Jig hurried up the hallway. Ryslind stood with one hand on

the wall for support. Jig's attention had been on Darnak, so he didn't know what had happened. That was a shame, for he would have loved to know how Barius had ended up on the floor with a puffed lip. Ryslind didn't usually rely on his fists, but maybe in his madness, he had made an exception.

"Brother?" Barius asked.

Ryslind nodded. "I am ready to go on." With that, the mage straightened his robes, used his sleeve to mop his sweaty face, and walked up the corridor as though nothing had happened. Whatever he had done to Barius was enough to stifle the prince's imperious manner, and he fell in next to Ryslind in silence.

Jig slowed until he and Darnak were walking side by side. "Is this a common thing with wizards?" he asked nervously.

Darnak kept his eyes on his map. At first, Jig didn't think he was going to answer. He scribbled another row of tiles, extended the tunnel another few inches, then dipped the quill in his inkpot.

"No, it's not," he said at last. He counted tiles and continued to draw as he spoke. "Never seen anything like it, truth be told. Mind you, Ryslind's always been a queer one. But he never warred with himself like that. Makes me wonder if he hasn't taken on more than he can handle with this quest."

They walked in silence down the right-most of a three-way fork. If Darnak was right, could they trust Ryslind to lead them in the right direction? Without the dwarf's help, would he have even made it this far?

"What did you do back there?" Jig asked.

"Eh?"

"When you prayed. You and Ryslind were connected somehow, and you stopped breathing." At the dwarf's scowl, he quickly said, "I didn't mean to listen in. But you were distracted, so I thought someone should watch for more of those creatures." Jig almost smiled as he thought up the lie. No goblin would have believed it. But Jig didn't want to admit he had been eavesdropping. Fortunately, Darnak didn't know goblins well enough to understand that rather than try to protect the others, the average goblin would have simply cut the dwarf's throat and fled.

"Something's been draining his strength," Darnak said quietly. "Felt it when we first reached the mountain two days ago. Been growing ever since. Earthmaker can't help him directly. Wizards don't get along with gods, never have. But through Earthmaker, I can lend him a bit of power and will."

He shook his head. "There's some who'll be telling you that dwarves have the thickest, hardest heads of any race in this world, and I'll not argue with them. And a good thing for Ryslind, too, for without my help, I've no doubt he'd have lost himself when we came through that whirlpool. My help and that of the god, that is," he amended hastily.

Jig bit off his next question as Darnak stopped to note another trap Ryslind had pointed out. When he finished, Jig asked, "How long until you can't help him anymore?"

Darnak didn't answer.

Despite Ryslind's magic, they still triggered another trap. At least this time it wasn't Jig's fault. So intent was Darnak on mapping every detail of the tunnel that he stepped squarely on a trapped tile, even as he drew that same tile on the map.

Like before, a panel in the wall flickered and vanished. Another of the corpselike creatures looked up and raised his sword. Darnak dropped his quill and raised his club, screaming a battle cry.

Before he could attack, something flew by and hit the wall of the alcove. This triggered the magic again, and the panel reappeared seconds later. As the marble solidified, Jig imagined he saw a look of annoyance on the creature's sunken face.

Darnak stood there, club still raised, mouth still open, as if he didn't know what to do now that his opponent had been taken away. After a few seconds, he lowered his club and glanced back at Riana. "I guess that'll work too."

Riana had thrown a piece of the bread she kept hidden in her shirt. Hard as stone, the bread had been more than enough to activate the magic of the alcove. She smiled sweetly. "But it cost me the remains of my lunch."

Wordlessly, Darnak dug through his pack and handed her a small loaf. Jig grinned, happy to know that bread did indeed serve *some* useful purpose.

They stopped to rest in a small chamber, empty save for a black crystal fountain in the center. A wide pillar rose to Jig's waist. Atop the pillar sat a wide bowl, guarded by four carved dragons perched on the rim. Each one looked almost lifelike, every scale glistening in the light. Their eyes were smooth blue jewels, and their teeth clear glass.

"Interesting," Darnak said. Riana smirked.

He referred not to the carvings, but to the actual plumbing of the fountain. For each of the dragons stood with a leg cocked, and the water arced from between their legs into the pool at the center.

Jig knelt beneath it, staring through the black crystal to learn if it was pure enough to see light from the other side. He could, though the light was faint and diffused. He had never encountered anything like this. The bowl itself was ridged on the underside, cut so perfectly that Jig sliced his finger on the crystal. The wide rim formed the impression of a dirt trail with rocks and roots and even small plants. "It's beautiful," he whispered.

Barius sniffed. "Created, no doubt, by goblin artisans."

Jig ignored him. The water in the bowl moved in a gentle swirl, propelled by the four streams. But how did the water get from there up into the dragons? It must drain through the pillar, then flow up through the sides of the fountain. He knelt again, trying to find where the water went.

What wonderful magic, to be able to move water about so easily. But why was it wasted here, where nobody could appreciate it? If Jig could build something like this, he would move water from the few pools around the goblin lair into the kitchens, so nobody would have to toil back and forth with the buckets. He could create fountains where goblins could go for drinking water, fountains that constantly replenished themselves. And washing down the privies would become at least a little less disgusting.

"Don't be drinking that, mind you." Darnak sighed. "A strange day, when I find myself warning a goblin not to drink dragon piss."

"It's only water," Jig said.

"First rule of adventuring," Darnak answered, voice muffled as he chewed his bread. "Never drink from strange fountains. Half the time it'll turn you to stone, or shrink you to the size of a roach, or kill you on the spot."

"I imagine you would more likely suffer the same fate as those wretched corpses," Barius said. "Worry not, goblin. You can rest assured I would strike you dead at the first sign of such a transformation, rather than permit you to suffer such horrors."

He took a small sip from his waterskin. " 'Ware the dragons themselves as well, lest they come to life and tear out your throat when you turn your back."

Darnak laughed. "Getting a mite paranoid, aren't you?"

"Cautious, friend dwarf," Barius corrected. "In a place such as this, who knows what magic lurks in seemingly innocent things."

That did it. Jig was tired of magic. Dead people coming through vanishing walls, giant bats, floating bridges, Ryslind talking with two voices, Darnak talking to his hammer, it was enough to make a goblin mad. How was he, with no more than a short sword and his wits, to deal with all this magic?

He would have to get some magic of his own. That was the goblin way. If your enemy had a knife, you got a sword. If he had two friends, you brought twelve. From what Jig had learned about magic, he had two choices. He could try to be like the wizard or the dwarf. Both of them had magic of a sort. Jig only had to figure out which kind of magic he wanted on his side.

Tough choice. Learn to talk to the gods, or become a freak of a man with tattoos and robes, fighting a losing battle with his own mind. Jig's bald head, courtesy of Smudge, already gave him more in common with the wizard than he liked. He left the fountain and went to sit with Darnak. Better the lesser of two oddities.

"Tell me of the gods," Jig said. A simple enough request, or so he thought. Barius cringed and moved to the other side of the room. Riana followed a few minutes later. Even Ryslind walked away until he had positioned the fountain between himself and the dwarf.

For it turned out that Darnak considered himself a bit of

a historian, as well as an expert on the gods. A huge grin split his face. He finished off another wineskin and launched into a detailed saga, starting with the creation of the universe. Jig tried to listen, he truly did. But after a few minutes, he found himself wondering if Ryslind's brand of magic was really as bad as it looked.

"To start with, you had the Two Gods of the beginning. All they did was fight. Spend an eternity with someone, you're bound to get a bit tired of their company. They hurled magic back and forth, trying to get the upper hand, even though they couldn't actually kill each other. The universe was young, and they were dumb as newborns. But powerful. They had all the power in the universe to themselves, you see. But some of it began to leak. And sooner or later this loose magic came together to form the Twenty-One Lower Gods. They were the ones who actually went about making the world and all the creatures on it."

He ticked off their names, one after another, counting on his fingers and toes as he went. That only took him to twenty gods, but Jig didn't bother to ask about the twenty-first. He didn't try to remember all the names. Not one had fewer than five syllables, and they all had some sort of fetish about hyphenation and apostrophes. Really, what kind of a name was Korama Al-vensk'ak Sitheckt, anyway? When Darnak first mentioned that one, Jig thought he was hacking up yesterday's dinner.

"What about Earthmaker?" Jig asked. "If the Twenty-One made the world, why didn't you mention him?"

He looked embarrassed. "Well, Earthmaker didn't actually make the world, as such. He came along a bit later, and he was after helping those blessed races who lived *in* the earth. Dwarves, gnomes, and the like. But he didn't appear until after the Year of Darkness."

"The Year of Darkness?" he asked before he could think better of it. As Darnak started in again, Jig looked longingly at the others across the room who sat safe from this endless storytelling. What had he started? And how could he steer the dwarf toward something useful, something that would help Jig?

Jig tried to understand the difference between the Lower Gods and the Gods of the Beginning and the Gods of the Elements, but then Darnak would mention something new, like the Gods of Men, and Jig was back to being confused. He began to wonder if the others would hold it against him if he stabbed Darnak to shut him up. Or perhaps it would be easier to turn his sword on himself.

Jig interrupted, desperately trying to break the endless flow of words. "How many Gods of Men?" From the other side of the room, his sharp ears caught a very unprincely groan from Barius.

"Nine hundred fifty-four," Darnak said happily. "Starting with Abriana the Gray, Goddess of Storms and Sailors. She was born of a union betwixt Taras of the Oak—he's a tree god—and a human woman named. . . ." Darnak frowned.

"Well, her name's not important. Taras appeared to her in the form of a three-hundred-pound tortoise and propositioned her. Gods were always doing strange things back in those days. A right kinky lot, if you ask me. But like any good lass, this girl grabbed the nearest hammer and cracked that tortoise on the back. Split Taras's shell right in two. Did I mention she was a dwarven girl?"

He hadn't, but Jig wasn't terribly surprised. He had only met one dwarf in his life, but he could imagine Darnak doing something like that. As for the rest of the story, Jig tried not to think about it. He didn't know much about mating rituals, but he did know that all this changing into tortoises and other shapeshifting was a bit peculiar. Though maybe this explained why surface-dwellers were so fascinated by religion.

"Anyway, out sprang Abriana the Gray in a flash of thunder. She was twin to Wodock the Black, God of the Deep Ocean."

"If they were twins, did he come out of the tortoise too?" Jig asked, trying to keep up.

"Nah. He came later. Had something to do with a mortal who fell in love with an acorn." Darnak frowned. "Human, naturally. Wouldn't catch a dwarf pining over an acorn." He burst into laughter and punched Jig on the arm. "Pining. Get it?"

Jig got back up and rubbed his arm. He didn't get the joke, and he didn't want to. His arm hurt, his head hurt, and he still hadn't learned anything useful. Over nine hundred gods. How was Jig to choose which one would be best suited for him? All he knew was that he didn't want any god who turned into an acorn or a turtle to have sex, fell in love with a campfire, trapped mortals with bits of dandelion fluff, or any of this other nonsense. Which seemed to eliminate almost all of those nine hundred gods. "Are there gods for goblins?"

Darnak snorted. "Nah. Gods aren't much for the dark races—goblins, orcs, ogres, kobolds, and the like."

The dark races. Jig liked the sound of that. Intimidating and mysterious. But it didn't help his problem.

He listened with one ear as Darnak droned on and on. The dwarf must have studied for years to memorize all of this information. He knew the stories of origin for almost every god. How he managed to keep the divine family trees straight in his head was beyond Jig. Or perhaps family vines would be a better term for the way the relationships twisted and intertwined and looped back on themselves, as gods mated with their mothers' sisters, and so on. Jig twisted his ears, trying to filter out the worst of it.

There was something Darnak had said before, back when he was healing Barius. Something about Earthmaker being busy with the prayers of an entire world. Too busy to spend all his time on one dwarf.

Jig chewed on his bread without tasting it. Not that there was much to taste. But his mind was elsewhere. He could see two ways to use the power of the gods to his advantage. One would be to become a follower of the most powerful god, one who could hurl thunderbolts and destroy worlds without breaking a sweat. Did gods sweat? It didn't matter.

The problem was that such a god wouldn't have much of a use for a mere goblin. Which brought Jig to the other option. He could follow a god who had grown unpopular. One with few worshipers, who wouldn't be busy answering other prayers. One who could devote his full attention to people like Jig. One who might be grateful even for a goblin follower.

His ears shot up as a phrase caught his attention. "What was that?"

Darnak blinked. "Eh? Oh, the Fifteen Forgotten Gods of the War of Shadows?"

Forgotten Gods. That sounded perfect, if a bit misleading. If they really were forgotten, how would Darnak know about them?

"Who were they?"

The dwarf played with his beard. "Let me think . . . they fell out of favor for going up against the Two. You can't kill a god, of course, but the Two showed them all that you *can* beat one within an inch of his or her life. Take the Shadowstar. They stripped his mind, flayed his body with blades of lightning, and cast him loose in the desert. May have turned him into a lizard for a while, I'm not sure. He wandered there for two hundred years, all but forgotten."

"Tell me about him," Jig said eagerly.

"Well, Tymalous Shadowstar was God of the Autumn Star. When his lady brought the snows of winter, Shadowstar lengthened the nights and danced in the darkness."

There was more, but Jig had heard enough. A forgotten god, one with power over the darkness. He didn't understand this idea of longer nights, and he knew nothing of the seasons, but it didn't matter.

Jig the goblin would be a follower of Tymalous Shadowstar.

CHAPTER 10

Falling Short of Expectations

THEY MIGHT HAVE STAYED THERE FOREVER, LIS-tening to Darnak's endless recitation of divine history. He was determined to tell Jig about every wart on the frog-god's back and every copper coin claimed by the god of gamblers. No matter how often Jig cleared his throat or glanced at the others, Darnak kept on talking. Jig could have done without this demonstration of dwarven stamina.

Finally Barius strolled around the fountain and tapped his boot for attention.

Darnak hesitated.

"You have not yet completed your map of this room, friend dwarf?" He waved at the fountain. "Such a creation deserves to be noted, would you not agree?"

"Aye." He looked torn. "But I've not yet told the goblin of the godless years."

The goblin had already taken the opportunity to scoot away, and now hid on the other side of the fountain. He wondered why Barius hadn't intervened an hour ago. *Probably this was one more way to punish me*. If so, Jig hoped the prince would go back to hitting him next time. Still, he felt a strange sense of gratitude to Barius for having rescued him at all.

He remained hidden until Darnak finished his map. They

moved on, again following Ryslind as he used his magic to track the Necromancer. While they walked, Jig pondered a new problem. How, precisely, did one go about worshiping a god? Maybe he would need a necklace like Darnak's. Something with the starburst and lightning of Tymalous Shadowstar instead of Earthmaker's hammer. But what else?

In his tale, Darnak had mentioned mortals who made sacrifices to the gods in exchange for divine help. Jig tried to remember the details. There had been something about giving up one's firstborn son, and another who killed "lambs," whatever they were. Jig had no son, no lamb, and he wasn't about to try to sacrifice one of the adventurers. The best he could do was Smudge, and the little fire-spider wouldn't make much of a sacrifice. Not that Jig would have given him up. Except for right after Smudge had burned off Jig's hair, maybe.

That left prayers. What did you say when you prayed? How did you strike up a chat with a god? Jig wasn't even very good at starting a conversation with other goblins. Did you have to say the words out loud, or would the god hear you in your head?

He decided that gods could hear your thoughts. If he had to speak the words, he'd be too embarrassed to try. He could already hear Barius's reaction. "What god would tolerate a follower of your ilk?" he would say. And he might be right. To be honest, Jig didn't expect much. Goblins and gods were like . . . well, like goblins and every other race. There wasn't much in the way of mingling.

Still it couldn't hurt. All things considered, it would be difficult for Jig's situation to be any worse. So he began to talk in his mind as they crept through the corridors.

Tymalous Shadowstar? What a clunky name. He wondered if he could get away with calling a god "Tym." Probably not. *My name is Jig. Can you hear me?*

He paused, but there was no answer. Then again, Darnak's conversations with Earthmaker seemed pretty one-sided as well, so it might not mean anything.

I'm wandering around lost with a dwarf, an elven child, an arrogant prince, and a wizard teetering on the edge of madness.

Well, not so much teetering. More bouncing back and forth between mad and really *mad. I wondered if you could help keep me alive long enough to get home in one piece?*

Still nothing. Jig sighed and started to hurry after the others when inspiration hit. No goblin helped another without getting something in return. Why should gods be any different?

I don't know how worship works or anything, but if there's anything you need, I'll try to help out.

That felt better. A fair deal, just like a human would make. Jig would help Tymalous Shadowstar, and the god would help Jig. He wondered what kind of favors a god might need. He hoped it would be nothing like that acorn story Darnak had told.

"Hold," Barius said in a low voice. "A door. Thief, check for traps and locks and such."

Riana grimaced. Remembering what had happened the last time, Jig couldn't blame her. A few more traps, and she would have no fingers left.

"Wait," he called.

He hurried up to the door with her, to Barius's annoyance. There, he reached into his boot and retrieved the strip of meat he had been saving for later. He brushed off the dust and fuzz and tried to ignore the rumbling of his stomach.

"Tie your tools to this." He handed the meat to Riana.

She nodded, apparently remembering how Jig had checked the other door. With a bit of Darnak's twine, she secured her pick to the meat and probed at the keyhole. As before, there was a click, and a silver needle lodged in the meat. Dry and stiff the meat might be, but Jig swore he saw its color fade.

"Why do you delay?" Barius asked. "Disarm the trap and open the door."

Riana muttered, "Disarm it yourself, you overdressed sheep-lover."

She pulled out her knife and used the blade to bend the needle out of the way. That left only the lock itself. She stared angrily at her hands.

"I wasn't very good at this even before I lost my finger,"

she snapped. Jig took a step back, hoping she wouldn't decide to punish the one who cost her that finger. She slid the lock-pick into the keyhole and probed the mechanism of the lock. Her eyes narrowed with concentration, and her tongue tip stuck out of the corner of her mouth as she worked. "Come on, damn you."

The pick slipped from her fingers. With an icy glare at Jig, she tried again. Then a third time. She tried using the pick in her left hand, but it was no use. "I can't do it."

"You did it before," Barius said.

"That was an easier lock. This has two tumblers instead of one, and I think there's some kind of button in the back that needs to be pressed."

"Try again," Barius said. He shook his head. "We've dragged you through half this accursed place, and on the two occasions we require your help, you fail us."

"I'm sorry to interfere with your great quest. Next time bring a key instead." She punctuated every third word with a vicious jab at the lock. When that still didn't work, she grabbed Jig's wrist. "Hold this."

She pressed the stronger rod into his hand, keeping the slender pick for herself. "Place the bent end into the lock and twist toward me. There are two tumblers in there, and I can't get both of them at once. I'm going to try to rip the lock."

"What?" He had an image of Riana tearing the door loose with her bare hands. Darnak might be able to do it, but he couldn't see Riana succeeding, no matter how strong elves might be.

"It's a thieving trick. I'm going to yank the pick past the tumblers and hope it knocks them both up long enough for you to turn the lock." She adjusted the rod in Jig's hand. "There, like it's a key. I've got the end pressed against the button in the lock. Hold it still, and keep pressing sideways. If this works, the tumblers will bounce up, and you need to turn the lock before they fall."

He squinted, trying to bring the lock into focus in the dim light. The least Barius could do was bring the lantern closer.

"Not that tight," Riana said. "Didn't you see how I held it before?"

"I don't see very well," Jig muttered.

"Oh." She grabbed another lockpick from her kit, this one with a smoother bump on the end. "The elves make lenses that would help. Jewelers use them a lot. Sometimes they sell them to old rich humans whose eyes are starting to fail."

"Sure," Jig said. "I'll remember that the next time I pass through an elven jewelry shop."

Riana ignored him. She slid the pick in past Jig's fingers, took a deep breath, and jerked it free. Nothing happened. "Too hard," she muttered. She tried again, and again.

The fourth time, it worked. The rod in Jig's hand turned, surprising him so much he dropped it. He winced, waiting for Riana's explosion. But that first quarter-turn was enough. She picked up her tools and finished opening the lock.

"Back up," she said. Once Jig was clear, she yanked the door open and shot Barius a look comprised of equal smugness and annoyance. Blinking innocently, she asked, "Will there be anything more, Your Majesty?"

Barius didn't answer. He stared in shock through the door into the room beyond. His lips moved without speaking. This from a man who had faced hobgoblins, lizard-fish, and even the Necromancer's warriors.

Jig peeked around the door, half afraid to see what monster awaited them. But better to see what it was, so as to know if he had any hope of running away. His eyes widened.

The door opened into a large, empty room. The floor and walls were made of the same black marble they had seen all along, but the ceiling was a familiar mosaic of tiled glass. In case Jig had any doubts about where they were, a pillar of whirling water stood at the center of the room.

Of everyone in the party, Darnak appeared the most distraught. He shoved his way into the room and stared at the pillar, as if sheer indignation would make it disappear. He counted the tiles of the floor and walls and compared his figures to the notes on his map. He studied the patterns in the ceiling, trying to persuade himself that they hadn't in fact come back to the very room where they first arrived.

"One forty-seven, one forty-eight, one forty-nine." He

spat on the final tile as he finished his second recount. "How could I have been so far off?"

He had spread his map on the floor to better study their path. Jig peered over his shoulder, looking at the winding tunnels that led from the center of the map—this room—through various tunnels and over what must be the bridge, to judge by the small bats Darnak had drawn, and finally to a door in the upper right corner of the map. Jig didn't know much about maps, but he knew that the door in the corner shouldn't have led them into the room in the center.

"There's no way we got turned about that badly." Darnak chewed the tip of one dark braid as he paced tight circles around the map, nearly colliding with Jig. "Even if I were off four or five degrees on those turns. A right rotten trick that would be, using eighty-five-degree turns instead of solid right angles. I'll have to remember that when I get home. I could design a nasty maze that way. But we didn't even pass over the chasm a second time.

"And what happened to get your magic so clogged up?" he demanded of Ryslind. "You said you were taking us to the Necromancer. Unless he's a wee fish swimming about in that column, I'm not seeing any Necromancer here."

"As I said before, this room was blocked to me." Ryslind's eyes were cracks of red light as he studied the walls. "I thought it was the magic of the water that overwhelmed my spell, so I commanded my power to ignore this room and take me to the Necromancer."

Darnak glanced down at his map once more. "Ah, hell." So saying, he grabbed the map, crumpled it into a ball, and tossed it into the corner. "Getting cramps in my fingers anyway."

"Is that all you have to offer me?" Barius threw up his arms. "One hundred and thirty-two years of age, Silas Earthmaker at your side, and all you can do is complain of cramped fingers."

He whirled on Ryslind. "As for you, my brother, what are we to make of your vaunted powers? Where is your otherworldly wisdom, great one? I was wrong to doubt you. How great your art must be, that it led us back to the very spot from which we left."

"What if he's right?" Jig asked. The room felt much colder to him. Colder and darker. "What if the Necromancer *is* here?"

"Ridiculous." Barius waved one hand. "He must be hidden away, down some tunnel we neglected to explore. Only after defeating the minions do we face the master. Else what point to having minions at all?"

Jig frowned. That was a good question. Maybe this was a good time to ask for help again. *Shadowstar, am I right? Why would the Necromancer play with us like that?* He blinked as a thought occurred to him.

"Maybe . . ." It sounded ridiculous now that he started to say it out loud. Too late, though. Everyone waited for him to finish.

"Well the Necromancer isn't a very nice person, right?" Barius rolled his eyes, and Jig hurried to finish. "Maybe he's doing this just to be mean. Teasing us, like animals, before he kills us. He probably doesn't get much company here, you know. He probably gets lonely."

"A master of the dark arts lonely?" Ryslind raised both eyebrows.

Is that the answer? But if so, that would mean the Necromancer was here*, watching us even as we argue. He probably laughed when we found ourselves back here, like it was the greatest joke in the world. But where is he watching from?*

Jig's gut tightened, and sweat ran down his back as he looked around. The room was empty, as before. Nothing but the water. No place to hide. Even with magic, it would be difficult to hide in here, with the way the light bounced off the marble panels, illuminating every corner of the room.

The panels. Jig stared. Like the panels in the hall that disappeared when those creatures had attacked.

Riana sat by one wall, gnawing on her bread and looking bored. Ryslind looked like he was trying to use his art to find the Necromancer again, but Barius kept interrupting. Darnak had flattened his map and begun again to retrace their path. Aside from a few chuckles and Ryslind's raised brows, they thought Jig's idea was a waste of time. What could a goblin know? But he was right. He knew it.

"He's behind the panels."

Only Riana heard. Her eyes widened, and her cheeks went pale. "Are you sure?"

Before he could answer, a booming laugh came from the walls. Ryslind raised his hands, fingers twisted to hurl a spell, but he could find no target. Barius's sword hissed free, and Darnak grabbed his club. From Jig's shoulder came the smell of singed leather as Smudge branded eight dots onto his shoulder pad.

"Very good, little goblin." The voice came from every part of the room at once. Not even Jig's ears could pinpoint the speaker.

"Show yourself, Necromancer," Barius said calmly. "Face us with honor and die like a man."

Even Darnak sighed at that. Jig didn't know a lot about adventuring or quests, but even he knew that "honor" wasn't a word that went with "necromancy." But if Barius insisted on playing the noble hero, Jig had no complaints. Barius's posturing made him the center of attention, as he no doubt intended. It also meant that he, not Jig, was the obvious target.

"You've all done very well," the voice went on. "I thought my warriors would finish you off in the hallway. But your wizard had more power than I expected. He's a fool, but a powerful one."

Ryslind's eyes burned a deeper red at that; he said nothing.

"Come, wizard. Find me if you can. I'm here, right beyond your grasp. Waiting and laughing."

"Can you find this villain?" Barius demanded. At Ryslind's angry nod, he snapped, "Why then do you delay?"

No, that's what he wants! Jig didn't know where the thought came from, and it was too late anyway. Ryslind's fingers straightened. He turned toward one of the panels, and fire shot from his hands.

Jig cringed and turned away as orange light brightened the room. Black smoke stung his nose, and even from behind the pillar he felt the heat against his skin. How Ryslind could touch that fire, hold it in his fingers, and control it was beyond Jig.

The flames stopped. Ryslind's fingers curved and straightened again, and this time water shot forth, freezing instantly when it touched the wall. Flakes of snow fell from the stream as he shot more water at the icy wall.

Smudge hid behind Jig's neck, making Jig wish he had something more substantial to hide behind. He had seen evidence of Ryslind's power before, but never in such a raw display. Those two spells alone would wipe out a goblin patrol before they could even grab weapons.

A thick layer of white ice covered the marble panel. Ryslind sent a second line of fire into its center. As soon as the flames touched the marble, a loud crack shot through the room. The panel fell to the floor in a dozen triangular pieces that shattered upon impact. Behind the steam and smoke, one of the dead warriors drew a sword and stepped forward.

Ryslind's lip curled into a sneer, and another blast of fire incinerated the corpse. Seconds later, only ashes remained.

"You might try toning it down a little," Darnak said nervously. "Better to keep a bit of power in reserve, just in case."

Ryslind either didn't hear or didn't care. The flames that had destroyed the corpse moved to the next panel.

How many were there? Jig counted as fast as he could. Twenty-eight panels. He didn't know much about magic, but he doubted Ryslind could keep up this kind of magic long enough to destroy them all. Darnak appeared to have the same idea, for he was tugging Ryslind's robe, trying to make him stop.

The wizard brushed him away with a gesture that left Darnak angrily patting wisps of flame from his beard. One hand fell to his club, and Jig watched as Darnak fought the urge to club the wizard unconscious. Jig didn't know if that would be an improvement or not, but in the end, the dwarf decided against it. Instead, he grabbed his amulet and began to pray. *Probably trying to lend Ryslind more strength,* Jig guessed.

Ryslind made it through two more panels and destroyed two more of the creatures before collapsing in pain. This time, as Ryslind fell, so did Darnak. But where the dwarf remained on the floor clutching his head, Ryslind stood back up as swiftly as he had fallen.

"Excellent," came the Necromancer's voice. The rest of

the marble panels vanished, and two dozen dead soldiers stepped into the room. "You proved stronger than I had guessed, wizard."

With the panels gone, the Necromancer's voice no longer echoed from all directions. Nor was it the deep, threatening voice they had heard before.

To Jig's left, guarded by two well armored corpses, stood a throne. Jig had never seen a real throne before, but this could be nothing else. No gold or gems decorated this chair. It had been carved from a single piece of stone, so black that even the marble looked bright by comparison. Light vanished into the throne, sucked into shadow. The legs formed claws, and the arms ended in small animal heads. Jig couldn't see well enough to identify them. The back of the throne rose to the top of the alcove, nearly ten feet. The Necromancer himself sat cross-legged upon purple cushions of velvet. In one hand, he held a long silver wand.

Jig smirked. He couldn't help it. After all his fear, all the legends and songs about the terrible Necromancer, this was not what he had imagined in his nightmares. For starters, Jig had expected him to be, well, taller. For another, a dark wizard shouldn't have large, gossamer wings. And didn't wizards wear robes? Granted, the Necromancer's loose trousers and vest were both black, and his bare arms did have a pale, deathlike pallor, but the effect was spoiled by the mop of brilliant blue hair that topped it all off.

"He's a mere fairy," Barius whispered, an uncharacteristic grin tugging his lips.

That was the wrong thing to say. The Necromancer stood up in the chair, pulling himself to his full height. Had he been on the floor, he would have been at eye-level with the prince's knee. He waved his wand about like a sword. "A mere fairy, eh? And what's to keep this mere fairy from mastering the dark arts? I'll show you what real power is. I killed the old Necromancer, you know."

He hopped down and ran at Barius. His dead bodyguards flanked him, weapons ready. Barius slipped back and raised his sword in a defensive stance, but the Necromancer slid to a halt a few feet out of range.

"This was his domain, but I took it away from him. Me! By myself. The others all died, but I lived long enough to cast a spell of dancing on him." He giggled. "He couldn't stop long enough to cast a spell, and that gave me time to put a knife in his eye. Horrid mess. Eye gook everywhere. Disgusting."

"Ryslind, destroy this pest," Barius said.

"Destroy him yourself, brother."

Jig froze, not even breathing. No longer did Ryslind speak with two voices. The voice that remained was not Ryslind's. Whatever had happened to the wizard when he overexerted himself, he was now as dangerous as the Necromancer. Jig hoped the others realized it, because the last thing he was going to do was face either mage himself.

"Take them," the Necromancer said, pointing absently with his wand. The other creatures stepped out of their alcoves.

Barius's head snapped one way, then another as they closed in. Even human arrogance had limits. With Darnak unconscious and his brother as great a danger as the Necromancer, Barius had no choice. His sword slipped through limp fingers, and he raised his hands in surrender. Two creatures grabbed his arms and forced him to his knees. Others did the same with Riana and Jig. They even grabbed Darnak's limp body and held him in a kneeling position.

"Very good." The Necromancer strutted before them. He still had to look up to meet their eyes. "You see, prince, your brother is . . . well, not himself today." He giggled. "If you're nice, I might even tell you who he *is*."

"What do you want?" Barius sounded tired and beaten. Maybe reality had finally tunneled through his skull, and the prince realized he was going to die. Jig wanted to reassure him that he'd get used to the thought after a while, but decided it would be better to remain silent.

"It's not about what I want. It's what *he* wants." The Necromancer nodded at Ryslind. Then he smirked again. "Still, nobody could complain if I kept one or two, to replace a few of my toy soldiers. The dwarf, I think. He'll make a good warrior. And one other." He rubbed his tiny chin.

His eyes looked from Riana to Jig and back. To Jig's

shame, all he could think was, *Take the elf. Elves are stronger than goblins. They're smarter. You don't want me.*

"The elf could be useful for the task ahead of you, but I see no reason for you to take the goblin. Leave him for me."

"Dung!" Jig shouted. "Why me? Why not her? Why does it always have to be the goblin?" His voice trailed off as he realized what he was doing. He had shouted at the Necromancer. "Uh . . . sir," he added quietly.

The Necromancer didn't take offense. "You intrigue me, goblin. You were the one to figure out my little game. You were quite right, you know. Dreadfully lonely down here. Sometimes I summon one of my bats and play with it, but they die so quickly. With the lizard-fish guarding the vortex, I rarely get to talk to anyone from above. I've even snuck into Straum's domain a time or two, just for the company.

"You should be honored, little goblin. You'll be the first of your race to become one of my servants." He gestured toward the corpses. "I've humans and dwarves and even an elf or two." He lowered his voice and looked at the others, as if sharing a deep secret. "Though elves don't take too well to being dead."

"Neither do I," Jig said.

The Necromancer grinned, revealing blackened gums. Seeing Jig's stare, he explained, "Nothing much to eat down here. Had to make do on what I could conjure, and I'm afraid it wasn't all that healthy. Rotted the teeth right out of my head. What I wouldn't give for a crisp, juicy apple. Some days I think I'd trade all my power for one apple."

Jig stared. "But without teeth, how would you eat it?"

"Shut up!" The little fairy flew into the air and shouted. Spit sprayed Jig's face. "You know nothing of the sacrifices I've made. Stupid goblin. Within an hour, I'll give you a few sips from my beautiful fountain, and you'll never worry about anything again. But for me, there's always something to worry about. What if the magic wears off? What if a stronger mage comes after me?" He looked around fearfully. "What if Straum comes to take my beautiful lair?"

"I don't think he'd fit," Jig pointed out. "And doesn't Straum already have a lair of his own?"

The Necromancer blinked. "I suppose so. See, that's why I chose you. You're a smart one." He waved at one of the creatures. "Take the dwarf and the goblin to the fountain and drown them."

He winked at Jig. "That way you'll be sure to swallow some of the potion as you die. I've tried a lot of ways, and trust me, this is the best. Why, once I even changed a man into a fish and dropped him into the fountain. It worked, but I wound up with an undead bass. It's no good, you know. You can't kill an undead bass. I took him out of the water, and he flopped about for hours and hours until I finally had one of my warriors stomp on the poor thing. Laughed for days about that one, I did."

"What are you going to do with me?" Barius asked. "With us?"

The Necromancer's eyes sparkled merrily. "It's a surprise."

Unfair, Jig thought. Barius and the others would probably be taken prisoner, left in a dungeon somewhere until Riana helped them break out. That's what always happened. No matter how secure the dungeon, the heroes always managed to escape. Luck favored adventurers, while goblins got dragged off to be drowned. Why him?

The question burned in Jig's brain. Why was he the one to be kicked around by the prince? Why, when he tried to help Riana, did he get threatened and punched and end up with everyone hating him? How had he ended up with this doomed party, fighting dead warriors and eating *bread*? Bread which, as it turned out, gave him terrible gas in addition to having no taste. He hadn't seen a proper privy in a day and a half, and this pissing in corners was a thing for beasts. Why had he been born a goblin at all? Sure, he was smart for a goblin. Look where it had brought him. Had he died with Porak and the others, at least it would have been a fast death. Why in Shadowstar's name couldn't things go right for him, just this once?

Why, in my name, don't you quit whining and do something for yourself, just this once?

Jig froze. "Who said that?"

The Necromancer frowned. "What?"

Smart for a goblin. That's what the little blue-haired one said, right? The voice in Jig's head sighed. *I see this is a relative thing.*

Jig's eyes went wide. *Tymalous Shadowstar?*

Well done. Perhaps there's hope after all. Jig got the sense that the god was shaking his head. *Still, a goblin follower. Have I really fallen this far? Well, what are you waiting for, goblin?*

"Jig," he said.

"What are you talking about, little goblin?" the Necromancer asked.

"My name is Jig." He heard Shadowstar laughing in his head. "Jig! Why does everyone call me 'goblin'? I'm Jig!"

He squirmed and bit and kicked and tried to wiggle free, but the dead hands held him fast. His arms hurt where their fingers dug into his skin, and his shoulder was beginning to burn even through Smudge's leather pad.

"Smudge!" Jig turned and pushed Smudge with his nose. It hurt terribly. He would have a blister on his nose, and Smudge clung to the pad even tighter when he realized what Jig was doing.

"Please," Jig said. He pushed again, harder, and Smudge came free and dropped onto the creature's arm. The Necromancer didn't notice, and without orders, it continued to hold Jig even as its skin blackened and burned.

"What's the problem, goblin?" the Necromancer snapped. He raised his wand.

"My name is Jig!" he screamed. He bit down on the second corpse's hand and used his fangs to pry the fingers free. By now the muscles of the first creature were on fire, and it was a simple matter to bend the hand back. Jig was loose. He whirled on the Necromancer and drew his sword. "Jig, Jig, Jig!"

The fairy raised his wand. A line of yellow smoke shot out, and Jig's vision sparkled. The smoke smelled fruity and sweet. Jig's ankle flashed in pain, but nothing else happened.

The Necromancer stared at his wand. So did Jig, but only for a second. Then he leaped into the air, screaming incoherently as he flailed about with his sword.

The Necromancer started to take to the air, but Jig's blade

slashed through one wing. As he fell, he raised his wand, and fire rushed into Jig's face.

Again Jig's ankle felt like it had exploded, but the fire didn't harm him. No worse than Smudge had done on many occasions, at least. But he couldn't see with all that fire in his face. Where had the Necromancer been?

He lunged blindly, felt his blade sink into something soft, and the flames disappeared.

On the ground in front of him, the Necromancer stared in disbelief at the sword sticking out of his belly. He had dropped his wand, and both hands gingerly touched the blade, as if he couldn't believe it was real. Only Jig was close enough to hear the Necromancer's final tormented words.

"By a goblin?" And then he died.

Jig stepped on the fairy's chest and pulled his sword free. He wondered briefly if fairy would taste as good as elf, but decided he wasn't hungry enough to find out. Not when the fairy had also been a Necromancer. Who knew what potions and preservatives might be mixed in with that flesh? Besides, the fairy was a little thing, scrawny as well as short. Hardly any meat at all.

Jig turned to face the others. The Necromancer was dead. That left only two dozen dead warriors and a possessed wizard.

Jig grinned like a madman and waved his sword. "Who's first?"

CHAPTER 11

Between Death and a Dark Pit

TWO DOZEN DEAD FACES STARED AT HIM. Riana's mouth hung open in shock, and Barius looked every which way as he tried to comprehend what had happened. Ryslind's red eyes swept over the Necromancer's body, then locked onto Jig. He did not look happy.

Jig could think of only one thing to do. He prayed. *That worked great! Thank you so much. What next?*

The answer, when it came, sounded a bit put out. *I don't know. I didn't expect you to live through it.*

Oh. Some of Jig's elation drained off at that. Some, but not all. What had Shadowstar said? Quit whining and do something for yourself for once. And he had. He had slain the Necromancer. A deed worthy of song! A song about him, Jig the goblin. Sure, the Necromancer looked harmless now, a dead fairy bleeding a puddle onto the floor. But that fairy had been the Necromancer, a two-foot-tall master of death with hideous blue hair.

The point was, Jig had done it. He had been stronger than the Necromancer's magic. His sword had ended the Necromancer's life. *He* had done it, not Barius or Darnak. It was all he could do not to giggle. He spun to face Ryslind. The dead creatures hadn't moved, which made Ryslind the next threat to be faced.

The wizard smiled, and the ground beneath Jig fell away. No, he was floating! Even as he watched, the room start to spin, his ankle throbbed, and he fell onto his backside. He stood back up with a grimace, rubbing his bruised posterior. *So much for the dramatic hero.*

"What have you done?" Ryslind demanded. He tried another spell, but nothing happened. "Where did you find this protection?"

Protection? Jig remembered the pain that had come as each of the Necromancer's spells failed. He looked down at his ankle. Inside his boot he saw the bracelet he had taken from the skeleton in the hallway. That bracelet must protect him from magic. That was why the Necromancer hadn't been able to stop him.

That must be why the skeleton had stayed dead, while all the others had come back to fight. The bracelet couldn't stop all magic—the stinging burns on Jig's face told him that much. The Necromancer must have turned the bracelet's former owner into another dead guard, and there had been just enough magic for him to walk to his alcove. There the spell had worn off, and he had died for real.

What a marvelous find. Jig was safe from magic. He looked up. Safe from magic, but not from his own foolishness. While he had been figuring out how the bracelet worked, Ryslind had strung his bow. He had an arrow nocked to the string, pointed at Jig's chest. His eyes fell on Jig's boot. "What have you got there, goblin?"

"Jig," he muttered with an echo of his earlier rage. Ryslind's fingers tightened on the bowstring, and Jig decided against another mad rush. "It's a bracelet I found."

"Let me have it."

Jig saw movement behind Ryslind. If he could keep the wizard distracted, maybe someone would help him. He sat down and pulled at the boot.

"I see you, brother, so please do not try anything foolhardy." Ryslind nodded over his shoulder, and Barius flew through the air and into the wall.

Jig started to go for his sword, but even though Ryslind

wasn't looking, the bow followed his movements. "That's a dangerous idea, goblin."

That wasn't Ryslind. His body, yes, but not *him*. Jig could hear the difference, even if nobody else could. "Who are you?"

The wizard's smile widened. "One who searches for the rod, the same as all of you. Now give me that bracelet."

Jig sighed and went back to wrestling with his boot. He could have slipped it off easily, but he wanted time to think, and as long as Ryslind hadn't noticed how overlarge the boots were, Jig could continue to stall. What should he do? Barius was helpless, pinned against the wall. Which wouldn't have bothered Jig in the slightest, except that Barius had been on his way to stop Ryslind. Riana was still free, but as soon as she moved, she'd join Barius.

At least the creatures hadn't attacked. *They had no minds of their own.* He remembered the one who had burned to a crisp rather than take the initiative to push Smudge off of its arm. They would stand there and wait for instructions forever, at least until the magic wore off.

Jig's eyes fell upon the Necromancer's silver wand. Could he use that to fight Ryslind? Sure he could, if he knew anything at all about magic. He wondered how much power remained in the wand. Maybe he could bluff. If he could get his hands on the wand, could he convince Ryslind to let him go?

Probably not. Ryslind hadn't been afraid of the *real* Necromancer. What were the odds he would surrender to a goblin?

"You're delaying," Ryslind said.

"I'm trying!"

"Perhaps you need help." He didn't appear to do anything, but suddenly the Necromancer's guards were closing around him.

Jig's eyes widened. Ryslind wasn't supposed to be able to control them. These were the Necromancer's creatures. How much more unfair could things get?

"I've got it." He hastily ripped off his boot and grabbed the bracelet. The skin of his ankle was a bit blackened. The bracelet had probably burned him when it tried to absorb too much magic. Still, better another burn than to end up like those mindless corpses.

"Throw it here," Ryslind ordered.

Jig obeyed. He threw as hard as he could. And as he dove out of the way, he thought, *Is it my fault Ryslind didn't specify what to throw?*

Ryslind ducked as Jig's boot flew past his face. The creatures walked closer. Jig snatched the Necromancer's wand and scampered back. Something buzzed past his face. Probably an arrow.

Trying not to think about how close that shot had come, he thrust the wand through the center of the bracelet.

The creatures collapsed. Jig tried to smile, but his teeth were clenched too tightly from fear. *Another victory for Jig.*

Ryslind's next arrow slammed into Jig's shoulder like a fist, spinning him in a complete circle before he fell. His eyes wide, he tried to push himself back up, but his arms wouldn't work. His cheek was wet and sticky. What was that blue stuff on the floor? Oh, right. That was his blood.

He lay there and waited for Ryslind to finish him. Would it be magic? The fire and ice he had used to blast away the walls? Or maybe he would settle for cutting Jig's throat. Either way, Jig hoped it would be quick. The floor was cold, and the longer he waited, the more his shoulder hurt.

A hand rolled him over, and he found himself looking into Darnak's bushy face. He tried to say something, but at that moment the pain increased tenfold. The dwarf had rolled him onto the arrow. Jig felt like someone had twisted a knife in his shoulder. He heard himself mutter something like, "Grargh."

"Hold on, lad," Darnak said. "The arrow was barbed, so I'm needing to break off the end. This is going to hurt."

Going to hurt? Through teary eyes, Jig tried to see what was happening. He saw Darnak's hand close around the back of the arrow. The shaft snapped, and the world went white for an instant. "Aach," he whimpered.

Darnak placed a hand over Jig's shoulder while someone else pulled the broken arrow through his back. Jig felt nauseous as he realized that he had a hole passing all the way through his body. And how much blood did he have left? That warm puddle all over the floor, that was *him!* He needed that stuff to stay inside his skin, not be spreading across the marble and soaking into his loincloth.

"What happened?" He had to ask three times before someone understood his pain-slurred speech.

"Darnak clubbed Ryslind on the head," Riana said. "With all of those creatures falling, he got so angry that he stopped paying attention to the rest of us. He's tied and gagged, so we should be safe when he wakes up."

"Oh. That's good." Jig's head felt tingly. Was this what happened when you lost too much blood? Darnak was praying and working on the wound, but Jig still hurt. Maybe that was a good thing. Maybe he shouldn't worry until the shoulder *stopped* hurting.

"Have him drink this." Darnak handed a waterskin to Riana, who put it to Jig's lips. His mouth felt parched, and he sucked eagerly.

Only to spit and cough a moment later. That wasn't water; Darnak had passed over his wineskin. In other circumstances, Jig would have been stunned by the gesture.

"Here now, don't be wasting it. That's good stuff, and I can't get more until my cousin returns from down south." Darnak grabbed the skin and took a swig for himself. "Care to take another shot at it?"

This time, Jig forced himself to swallow, even though it made his throat burn and his eyes water even harder. He felt vapor rise into his sinuses, making his head light. The pain in his shoulder was still there, but somehow it didn't matter quite as much. He took another few swallows.

Darnak grinned. "Dwarven ale," he said, a note of pride in his voice. "Made in the finest underground breweries in the land."

"Tastes like klak beer," Jig said.

"Watch your tongue," Darnak snapped. "This is fine dwarven drink. No race in the world can match it, least of all goblins. You can't even make this stuff without knowing where to find the best Blue-spotted Mushrooms, the oldest Nightblooms. . . ."

"And a lot of Ruffled Lichen root," Jig added. He considered the taste. "This needs to age more, though."

Darnak scowled at him and snatched his wineskin back. "You need to rest."

Jig smiled as the dwarf worked on his shoulder. This was more like it. Riana was watching him with, well not exactly respect, but at least without her usual loathing. Darnak was healing him, just like he had done for Barius. And for the first time in Jig's recollection, probably the first time since the world was born, a dwarf had shared a drink with a goblin.

Riana pressed something into Jig's mouth, and he chewed automatically. "Ptah," he muttered. He should have known it was too good to be true. First they treated him like a friend, then they tried to feed him *bread*.

"Eat it," Darnak said firmly. "You'll need your strength."

What else could he do? He didn't want to offend the one who was closing the hole in his shoulder. So he forced himself to chew and swallow. He took small bites. That way he didn't have to chew as much, and the dusty aftertaste didn't linger as long. He hoped Riana might take the hint, but she kept shoving bread at him until the whole thing was gone. She even seemed to enjoy his disgust there at the end.

"Where's Barius?" Jig asked.

"With his brother." Darnak shook his head. "They hate each other, but neither wants to see the other die. Not unless it's by their own hand, that is. Strange and tragic, but true."

The dwarf sat up. "Best I can do, but a mite better than I'd hoped. You'll have an ugly scar, and a matching one on back. Don't strain that left arm anytime soon, either. But you'll live." He laughed. "At least until the next time you go picking fights with two wizards in one day."

He helped Jig to sit up. Smudge had rejoined him at some point, and now scooted to his normal spot on Jig's shoulder. "Good spider," he muttered.

Jig tried to stand, but his head spun, and he decided maybe it would be better to stay on the floor and not move for a while. Yes, that would be for the best. He perked his ears—even his *ears* hurt—and listened as Darnak joined Barius.

"So how's his wizardness doing?"

"My brother will survive," Barius said angrily. "A fortunate thing for you, Darnak. Even striking a prince is an offense worthy of death. Had you killed him, you would have left me no choice but to execute you."

Darnak grunted. "Aye, and you'd have left me no choice but to box your ears. Would you rather I let him kill us all then?" He didn't give the prince time to answer. "Come on, we've got to be finding a way out of here. Maybe if we get him back home, your father's advisers will have some ideas for restoring his mind."

"What do you mean, leave? Our quest is unfinished, Darnak."

"Aye, and your brother the wizard has lost his mind, or were you forgetting that? He's beyond my power to help, Your Majesty. How were you planning to finish your quest without Ryslind?"

"It is *my* quest," Barius said coldly. "My brother has experienced these fits of weakness before. He shall recover in time."

"Fits of weakness, are they?" Darnak laughed. "This is the first time he's been shooting members of his own party. And he wasn't too weak to toss you about, was he?"

"That goblin is no member of my party."

Darnak's eyes widened. "Oh, is that so? Then I suppose he should have left the Necromancer alive for you to kill."

"Your tone borders dangerously close to treason, Darnak."

The dwarf snorted. He looked ready to speak, but paused when he saw the fury in Barius's bulging eyes and white lips. "Perhaps, Majesty," he said. "I'm only trying to do my job and keep you alive."

Barius smiled at this concession. "You are my tutor no longer. You were brought for your skill at arms, your experience in the bowels of the mountains, and your gift for cartography. If you find yourself unable to restrict yourself to these duties, you may wait here for my return." He turned his back on the dwarf and ran his hands over the arms of the throne.

"Where are you going?" Jig asked. "And what's a cartographer?" He couldn't figure out what carts had to do with anything. Unless they planned to build a cart to carry the treasure out with them. That made sense.

"I am departing this accursed place," Barius said. He tugged the top of the throne. Nothing happened, so he ripped out the cushions and began to poke and prod at the seat. "There may be a concealed passageway by the throne."

"And how would you know that?" Riana asked.

Barius gave her a tolerant smile. "Common sense. At any time a ruler could find himself in need of a quick escape route. That truth is even more common for black-hearted lords such as this Necromancer, whose enemies are many. What better place to make your escape than through the throne itself?"

Jig's brow wrinkled. "Is there a hidden door behind your father's throne?"

"Of course not," Barius said quickly. "My father is beloved by his subjects, and has no need to plan for escape."

Perhaps Barius is adopted. For if the father were anything at all like the son, Jig couldn't understand how he had survived long enough to walk upright, let alone to rule a country.

"Behold," Barius said. His chest swelled with triumph. "The throne itself moves. Darnak, help me to shift it back."

The dwarf lent his bulk to the task. Slowly the great throne scraped back a few inches, screeching like a tortured animal. Jig pinched his ears shut. Apparently Barius had been correct this time. Though if this was meant to be a quick escape route, why was it so hard to move the throne? Jig had a hard time imagining the diminutive Necromancer shoving the throne aside when Darnak and Barius together could barely move it.

The floor around the throne vanished. Darnak and Barius tried to cling to the now-floating throne, but couldn't find handholds. Jig had one glimpse of Riana's face before she fell. She had come over to watch the prince search, and thanks to her curiosity, she now tumbled after the others.

That made more sense, Jig decided as he crawled to the edge of the hole. So it had been a trap, not an escape route. Yes, that was more in keeping with the Necromancer's style.

Darnak had set the lantern on the floor next to the throne.

When the floor vanished, the lantern had followed the others into the pit, leaving Jig blind. He moved slowly and tested every inch of the floor as he went. A muted chuckle drew Jig's attention away from the pit. Ryslind was awake and laughing, though the rag Darnak had tied into his mouth muffled the sound. The light from his eyes gave his face a demonic red tinge.

They're going to die down there.

Ryslind's voice spoke in his head. No, not Ryslind, but the second voice, the voice of whatever had taken control of the wizard.

Fools and children. Straum will slaughter you all like insects.

Jig walked over and kicked the wizard in the stomach. Why was everyone suddenly speaking in his mind? Bad enough when Shadowstar did it. Jig had nearly wet himself that time. Was he now to endure Ryslind's babble as well?

Not for much longer, little goblin.

Jig's eyes narrowed. Moving by the faint light from Ryslind's eyes, he grabbed the ropes around the wizard's ankles and dragged him over to the pit. His shoulder ached, but Darnak had done a good job, and his wound remained closed. Jig looked into Ryslind's glowing eyes, and for the first time, he didn't flinch away from that dark red light.

The only escape is to fall on that sword of yours.

Jig shoved him into the pit. Then he sat down with his legs dangling over the edge and tried to figure out what he should do.

"Which tile was it?" Jig slid his sword along the floor until it hit the slight dip that marked the edge of a tile. He tapped the next one with his sword. One of these had opened the walls. They had killed most of the creatures here the first time they triggered the trap, so if Jig set it off again, he should be safe. He hoped. Besides, the Necromancer's wand was destroyed. This was probably the safest place in the whole mountain.

What frightened Jig was knowing that it was also the emptiest place. Aside from the bats and whatever else inhabited that chasm, he and Smudge were the only living things down here. He could survive for a few days if he stayed, but he would eventually go mad from hunger and thirst.

So he had to get out of here. He couldn't go up, not unless he had a way to swim through the whirlpool and avoid the lizard-fish. Even if Tymalous Shadowstar decided to help him again, Jig doubted he could manage that much. Which left down. He would have to follow the others.

He had shouted into the black pit for a while, but nobody answered. The pit absorbed his voice, making him sound small and scared. Which he was, but he didn't like having the fact thrown in his face.

After putting his boots back on, he had felt around for his bracelet, but the metal had melted into the wand. There was no way for Jig to wear it anymore, even if it still had any power, which he doubted. He tucked the glob of metal into his belt as a souvenir, in case he ever got home. The other goblins would never believe it was the Necromancer's wand. But it would be a good keepsake nonetheless.

The other thing he wanted was light. A lantern, a torch, even a candle would be a godsend. Jig held his breath at that thought, thinking Shadowstar might take the hint, but no candle appeared in his hand. He sighed and kept walking. No light, no bracelet, and no food.

The thirteenth tile shifted beneath his sword. The faint whiff of preservative and dust drifting into the air told him the alcoves had opened again. Logically, Jig knew he was safe. Logic, however, had only a single small voice, and was easily overwhelmed by panic. Jig shouted and waved his sword around his head as he waited for the attack to come.

Nothing happened. Jig lowered his weapon slowly. His chest pounded, and his palms were so sweaty he doubted he could have used the sword, even if something had attacked.

He stepped into the alcove where he had hidden with Riana. The noose should be to his right. Jig hoped he would be able to use the rope to lower himself into the pit. He was about to scour the ground when the god spoke to him again.

The panel, dummy.

Jig jerked up indignantly. What did he . . . the panel . . . oh no. Jig leaped for the hallway, hoping he was fast enough. He had only been in the alcove for a second or two. Was it too late? Had the panel already reappeared, trapping him inside? If so, he prayed he would hit it hard enough for the impact to kill him.

He made it through. He felt like he had leaped through an icy waterfall, but he was out. His legs were shaking so badly he had to sit down. That was stupid. Stupid! He could have died. After surviving the Necromancer and everything else, he could have starved to death because of a dumb mistake. Nobody would have come around to let him out of the alcove this time.

Once his hands no longer shook, he opened the panel again. This would be tricky even were he able to see. Snagging the rope and pulling it out in the darkness was next to impossible.

But Jig was in no great hurry. For the first time in several days, he didn't need to worry about anyone sneaking up on him or stabbing him from behind.

He experimented for a while to find out exactly how long he had before the panel closed. It would remain open for a little more than two breaths after he touched the floor or wall of the alcove. Plenty of time to reach in, holding his sword by the blade, and drag the crossguard across the floor toward him. All he had to do was catch the rope.

After cutting his hand twice, he stripped off his loincloth and wrapped it around the blade for protection. Everyone else was dead or gone, so he wasn't worried about modesty.

He pulled out at least half of the skeleton in assorted bits and pieces before he managed to snag the noose. Once he had rope in hand, he stood up and redid his loincloth. Feeling decently dressed once more, he hurried back to the Necromancer's throne room.

The rope measured seven feet once Jig untied the knot. It would have been longer, but he had sliced off the last few feet when he cut it from his neck. Jig sat down at the edge of the pit and began to work.

The rope consisted of three cords twisted together, and Jig guessed that any one of those cords would hold his weight. He wouldn't have wanted to haul Darnak around with one, but goblins were skinny and light. It took a while to get the cords unraveled. The rope acted almost alive, the way it twined about itself and tried to tangle into knots.

In the end, Jig held a thin rope about twenty feet long. He tugged on the two knots that bound the cords end to end. They didn't give. Satisfied, he tied a loop in one end and tried to toss it over the arm of the throne. Looping the arm of a floating throne in pitch blackness would have challenged even the most coordinated of heroes. Jig took close to an hour before the rope caught.

The plan would have worked, save for his cut hand. As he lowered himself into the pit, his hand flared with pain. His arms were already tired from throwing the rope so many times. With blood on one hand and sweat slicking the other, his hands slipped free, and Jig followed his companions into the darkness.

He landed on his backside on something springy and damp. The sudden light blinded him. After so long in silence, the noise greeted Jig like a long-lost friend. He heard a breeze blowing. A rustling sound surrounded him, and in the distance, he heard the whistling of birds. Birds, in Straum's lair? He shrugged. Sparrows and other birds flew into the tunnels from time to time. They made great snacks. Perhaps there was a crack leading to the surface, small enough for birds to fly in and out.

"Jig? Is that you? We were wondering if you'd be joining us."

"Darnak?" Jig turned toward the sound. Everything was still too bright, but he could make out the dwarf's stocky form a few feet away. "It was either follow you down or stay there and starve."

"Good choice." Darnak's hand clapped Jig on the shoulder. "Since you're here, mayhaps you can help us with a bit of a dilemma. See, this isn't exactly what we were expecting to find down here."

They waited for Jig's eyes to adjust. When they had, he looked around in amazement. He sat in a field of soft green grass. Trees ringed the field at a distance of roughly a hundred yards. Sunlight warmed his skin, and he could smell the soft sweetness of pollen in the breeze. He scraped at the damp ground, digging up a clump of grass to find, not cold stone, but moist, black soil.

"I'm outside," he whispered, not knowing whether to rejoice or cower at the news. He raised a hand and saw his shadow on the ground. It didn't waver, as it would have done in torchlight. Clear and sharp, his shadow-hand followed his real one perfectly. Slowly Jig looked up at the sky.

"Wow."

He even stopped breathing as he stared. He saw no sign of the rope he had used to climb down. Nothing but blue sky, and clouds like white clumps of fur drifting past. He reached out, but the clouds were too far away to touch. How high were they? They looked to be at least thirty or forty feet up, higher than anything Jig had ever seen.

And the sun! An orange circle that shone with warm, perfect light, like a thousand thousand torches all burning together. He squinted, trying to see if it burned like a normal fire.

"It's not real," Darnak said. "If 'twere, you'd be blind right about now."

Jig ignored him. Real or not, this was the most incredible thing he had ever seen. He didn't know how they had come here or even where "here" was, but none of that mattered. After spending his whole life underground, knowing nothing but the lair and a few dark tunnels, Jig had discovered a completely new world. Still gaping, he managed to tear his eyes away from the sun long enough to say, "It's so *big*."

CHAPTER 12

Big Prints, Mad Prince

"I TAKE IT THEN," DARNAK SAID DRYLY, "THAT you wouldn't be knowing how to find the dragon."

Jig shook his head. From time to time, he had fantasized about sneaking down and making off with some piece of Straum's treasure. Every goblin dreamed about it. A few of the older ones told stories about their search for the dragon's lair. Some even claimed to have made it past the Necromancer.

Nobody had ever described anything like this place. Jig had known they were lying, of course. Oh, he believed goblins tried to explore the deeper levels. What he didn't believe was that any of them survived to come back and tell stories about the experience.

Staring again at the world around him, he wondered if he would get the chance to share what he had seen. The grass tickled the backs of his knees when he moved, and he laughed with delight. He lay back and stared into the sky. So open and endless . . . after a lifetime of living beneath solid rock, he felt as though he could fall into that blue sea and float forever. A wave of vertigo made him gulp, and he gripped the grass with both hands.

"It's an illusion," Riana told him. She ripped out a clump of grass and sniffed the roots. "No smell. The sun's too orange, and I can only see one kind of tree."

"How many kinds are there?" Jig asked.

Riana laughed. For a second the anger vanished and she looked like a child. "Hundreds. Thousands. Oaks as proud as the gods, willows that sway and dance in the wind. There are trees with leaves as pointed as rapiers, and trees that need rain but once every six months to survive. I've even seen trees only a foot tall that mimic their larger cousins in every way." She laughed again at Jig's delighted expression.

"Elves and trees," Darnak grumbled. "Something unnatural about their love for plants. Besides, I thought you were a city type. Where'd you learn about trees?"

Riana's face hardened. "I spent a month hiding out in an arboretum, behind the Monastery of Batoth."

Darnak held up a hand. "Don't tell me the details. I'm still the prince's man, and I'd not like to be arresting you the second we leave this mountain." Turning to Jig, he asked, "How is it that you've never seen the outdoors?"

"I just haven't," Jig said. Goblins didn't go outside. They rarely ventured past the shiny room where he had first encountered the adventurers.

There was no reason for them to stay inside. No monster guarded the entrance, as far as he knew. The gate locked itself when closed, but it could be opened easily from within. Goblins simply felt no need to explore the surface. Everything they needed, the mountain provided.

Besides, goblins weren't welcome outside. Throughout history, every surface-dweller who came through that gate saw goblins as vermin to be wiped out. Bad enough that the occasional party came through on a killing rampage every few months. The outside world must be even worse, with thousands of people who would put an arrow into Jig as soon as they saw him. His ears would end up on a trophy necklace before he made it ten feet past the gate.

Still, it might be worth sneaking out some night if I could see all of this. That led to another thought. *I wonder if we'll see* stars *while we're down here.*

From a little way off, Barius stood and shouted, "Darnak, come and see this."

Darnak and the others hurried over to join the prince. On

the way, Jig noticed the tied and bruised body of the wizard stretched out in the grass. Ryslind glared at him as he passed, and Jig glanced away quickly. He hoped they wouldn't untie Ryslind anytime soon. A hundred years should be long enough.

Barius stood over the huge body of an ogre. Jig yelped and grabbed for his sword when he saw it. But the ogre wasn't moving. To judge by the deep slashes across its chest and throat, it would never move again.

He noticed that Darnak's hand had also gone to his weapon, which made him feel a little better.

"You did this, lad?" Darnak sounded impressed.

"Not I." Barius knelt and pointed to the cuts on the chest. "Three deep cuts, all in a row. A fourth scraped the skin here."

"Claws. Aye, I see it." Darnak chewed at his thumb. "But what beast could best an ogre?"

A good question, Jig thought as he stared at the body. He had never seen an ogre, and now he prayed he would never see a living example. It must have stood over eight feet high, with muscular arms as long as Jig was tall. Its callused green skin looked tough enough to serve as light armor. Ragged black hair topped a long, oval head. The teeth, while shorter than goblin teeth, still looked sharp enough to do serious damage. The huge mouth meant the ogre had a lot more of them, too.

Something shiny caught Jig's eye. A battle-axe, six feet long and double-headed, lay discarded in the grass to one side. Jig bent down and grabbed the handle to take it back to the others.

The axe didn't budge. Off-balance, Jig stumbled to the ground. *Maybe they should come here instead.* "I found something."

Darnak whistled when he saw the axe. The dwarf could lift it, but he needed both hands to raise it in the air, and Jig doubted even Darnak could swing such an axe in a fight.

"You think he was waiting for whoever fell through?" Darnak asked.

"If so, then whatever slew the beast has my gratitude," Barius said.

"Aye. So long as it's not coming back for dessert, that is."

The dwarf's wary tone made Jig see the distant trees in a different light. What creatures might be hiding in those shadows? This place was so open, with too many places for an enemy to hide. He knew nothing of surface monsters, but anything that could destroy an ogre was, in Jig's opinion, a good argument for staying in the tunnels.

"Strange, though." Barius peered more closely at the wounds. "Whatever killed the ogre wasn't interested in food. A kill such as this would feed an animal for days. Why then did it not at least drag the ogre off for safekeeping? Unless it was a territorial dispute, perhaps."

He pointed to a patch of grass behind Riana. "The tracks lead back to the center of the field."

Jig stared at the grass. It looked green, the same as everything else down here. Had madness now touched Barius, that he could communicate with plants?

"Spread out," Barius ordered. "Search for anything unusual."

As they retraced their path, Jig's sharp ears caught Darnak's grumbling comment. "A hundred feet underground, in a fake field beneath a fake sky, with an ogre slaughtered like no more than a rat to a cat, and he sends us to search for the unusual."

They found two more ogres. Together with the first corpse, the bodies formed a rough triangle around the spot where the adventurers had appeared.

"Ambush?" Darnak asked.

"Most likely. By the time we recovered from the fall and drew our weapons, they would have been upon us." Barius chewed his lip, one of the only times Jig had seen the prince show anxiety.

"Even if you and I could stand against such beasts, they still outnumbered us." He clearly didn't consider Riana or Jig worth counting.

The pit was a trap. Anyone who beat the Necromancer was supposed to die here. Sizing up the two-handed sword one ogre had dropped, Jig tried not to think about how long he would last in a fight against ogres, let alone whatever beast had killed them. Perhaps the party had arrived in the middle of a power struggle. Hobgoblins and goblins occasionally slaughtered each other when food ran short, when one group was caught stealing from the other, or when the younger warriors simply grew bored with bullying their own. Jig prayed that the creatures here would finish each other off before he had the poor luck to meet one.

Barius touched the wounds on the third ogre. "Whatever did this, it killed this one last." He crawled around the grass for a few minutes. "It left for the woods, in this direction. We should follow."

"What?" It came out more as a squeak, but Jig didn't care. He must have misheard.

But Barius only nodded, a determined glint in his eyes. "This way we are the hunters instead of the prey. Better this than to sit and wait for it to creep up on us in the night, wouldn't you say?"

"Maybe it only kills ogres?" Jig suggested weakly.

"It pains me to be saying it," Darnak said, "but his highness could be right. Until we know the dangers of this place, we'll be as children walking blindly into the bear's cave."

If we find those dangers, won't we be walking blindly into the bear's jaws? Jig didn't say anything aloud, however. He knew Barius and the others too well to expect them to change their minds.

"Know thy enemy, eh Darnak?" Barius said cheerfully.

He was enjoying this. Jig's mouth hung open in disbelief. He *wanted* to go chasing after this creature. "What about the rod?"

That made Barius pause, but only for a heartbeat. "We can't pursue the rod with this monster at our heels. Nor do we know in which direction the rod may lie. We could be here for days, so it behooves us to learn as much as we can about this land."

Jig pointed at Ryslind. "And him?" he started to ask. The words died when he saw the wizard's face. Though the gag hid his mouth, the corners of his eyes had wrinkled with amusement as he watched Barius's preparations.

"You know what it is, don't you?" Jig asked softly.

Ryslind heard. The wrinkles deepened. Red eyes beckoned Jig closer.

He crossed the clearing, one hand on his sword. With his other hand, he reached for the gag. He hesitated, hand outstretched. Was this another trick?

Of course it was a trick. Ryslind was a surface-dweller, and a wizard to boot. Smudge remained cool on his shoulder, which should mean it was safe to remove the gag. Still he hesitated.

"I'll kill you if you try any magic," he warned.

Ryslind dipped his head in amused acknowledgment.

"As will I," Darnak said from behind Jig. "I was coming to get him," he explained. "Heard you talking. So go ahead, remove the gag. He knows we'll brain him if it comes to that."

Feeling more confident with the dwarf beside him, Jig tugged the rope down around Ryslind's chin and pulled a balled rag out of his mouth. The wizard opened his mouth and inhaled deeply.

"Water," he said hoarsely. Darnak held a waterskin to his lips, and Ryslind took several deep swallows. When he spoke again, his voice was smoother. "You will die for what you did, goblin." He sounded cheerful about the prospect.

"Enough of that," Darnak said. "You were telling us about the thing that did this. Or was that all a ploy to get free of the gag?"

"No ploy." Ryslind smiled. "And there is no need to hunt for him. He will find you soon enough."

"He?" Jig asked.

Ryslind nodded. "He is one of Straum's . . . servants."

"How would you know this, brother?" Barius had returned. Arms crossed, he glared down at the wizard. "What reason do we have for trusting your word?"

Ryslind chuckled. "Believe me or not, it makes no difference."

The pit in Jig's stomach grew deeper. For despite everything Ryslind had done, Jig believed him.

They untied Ryslind's legs so he could walk with the party. At first, Barius had argued, preferring to build a travois to drag the wizard along.

"And how am I to fight if I'm lugging your brother behind me?" Darnak snapped. "I'm doubting the enemy will want to wait while I unstrap a blasted travois."

For once Jig agreed with the prince. Tie Ryslind up and leave him that way. They all knew the wizard was mad. What was to stop him from killing them all? He had promised to use no magic, but who could trust the mind behind those eyes? As soon as their guard dropped, he would attack. Starting, Jig guessed, with the goblin who had insulted him back in the Necromancer's throne room.

But as they reached the woods, it looked like Ryslind would keep his promise. He had not spoken a word, and his hands remained bound behind his back. Darnak walked at the end of their line, so he would see if Ryslind tried anything. So far, Ryslind had been content to follow along.

He still made Jig nervous. Especially the way he smiled at them. Like this was all a game, and only Ryslind knew the rules.

"The trail goes deeper into the woods," Barius said. He squatted by a patch of bare dirt. "See here, the creature has left a partial print."

Jig stared at the brown, scuffed dirt. He saw nothing, and wondered if Barius was hallucinating. To make his frustration worse, he had already become disoriented. He thought he could find his way back to the clearing if he had to, but he wasn't certain. Being lost made him feel uncomfortably dependent on the others.

"Clawed, as we guessed," Barius muttered. He stretched a hand out over the dirt. "Toes spread for balance. The print is deep, so I would guess we face a beast nearly as massive as the ogres. A lion, perhaps. But longer of toe."

He eventually tired of studying dirt and said, "Come, let us continue."

Jig waited for the others to pass by. He took an extra step back to let Ryslind go by, but the wizard only smiled at him. Falling into step beside Darnak, Jig whispered, "Are both of them mad? They prod one another like children. And the only reason we're chasing this beast is because Barius refuses to back down in front of his brother. What's wrong with them?"

Darnak sighed. "Earthmaker only knows what has happened to Ryslind. As for Barius, I'm afraid he sees the competition as being more important than the rest, even more important than his own life."

He shook his head. He had resumed his duty as mapmaker, and he sketched small, bushy trees as they walked. A jagged line marked their progress into the woods. At the center of the map, Jig saw three bodies labeled BIG, DEAD OGRES.

"Barius has competed all his life, and he's always lost. He's the seventh son of King Wendel. That means he's got no more chance to sit on that throne than you or I do, and he knows it. Even with three of his brothers dead on their manhood quests, he's no more than an extra mouth to feed around the palace. A noble mouth, mind you, but still a burden. Sooner or later they'll marry him off, give him a nice little plot of land somewhere out of the way, and forget he ever existed."

"He grew up with his parents?" Jig asked dubiously.

Darnak stopped to blot a smudge of ink on his map. "Aye. What of it?"

He had known that the surface races often built separate homes for every mated pair and their offspring, but it still seemed like a waste of space. Then again, if these woods were any indication of the size of the surface, maybe they could afford the waste. And only seven brothers? Jig had grown up with dozens of cousins, all raised by the entire lair. Jig didn't even know who his parents were. Nor did he care. That sort of thing simply didn't matter.

"Isn't that inefficient?" Jig asked. "To rely so much on the parents, I mean."

"For a dwarven family, 'twould make no difference. For us, family is everything. Parents, cousins, grandparents, brothers and sisters, all of 'em squeeze together in one home and look after one another. But for Prince Barius, his parents were always busy ruling Adenkar. He grew up surrounded by servants and tutors, none of whom saw him as anything but one more spoiled Wendelson to care for.

"He's quite a lonely boy, really. Most of the sons are. They began very early to compete for their parents' attention. Who would be the best fencer, the swiftest rider, the most accurate shot with a bow? Barius fought in tournaments from the time he was thirteen. Never won, mind you, and once he wrecked his knee so badly it took me a week to straighten everything back out.

"He learned the lute, studied every book he could get a hold of, and once stayed out three nights in a row to catch a wolf that had been stalking the stables. It was never enough."

Sighing, Darnak glanced up to make sure the brothers were too far away to hear. "There was always something more pressing, some treaty to negotiate or some ambassador to dine with. Even when Barius accomplished some grand feat, his older brothers were there to overshadow him. He hunted that wolf right after his oldest brother returned from slaying a rogue griffon to the south. I was proud of them both, but especially Barius. He stayed out in the rain and the cold, and killed that wolf with no more than a child's training bow, whereas his brother had gone out with a full regiment of guards and slept in a sturdy tent. But how could Barius compete with his brother's griffon?

"The quake that finally collapsed his tunnel was Ryslind. Ryslind set out one day and didn't come back for two months. All of Adenkar searched for the lost prince, but he had vanished like shadows at midday. Rumors spread and multiplied faster than fleas on a beggar. 'Ryslind had been abducted by elves, he had drowned in the Serpent River, he had run off to be with his spirit lover.' Everyone had a different tale.

"Barius didn't know what to believe, but he saw his chance for glory. He had always been a skilled hunter and tracker, and he declared that he would bring his brother back. Interrupted court to make his pronouncement, and made sure everyone heard. He spent a week in preparation, gathering horses and supplies and men and maps, everything he thought he would need.

"And then Ryslind returned. Walked into the throne room just as calm and confident as ever. He had completed his quest, he told us. To demonstrate, he sent tiny bolts of blue lightning racing across the ceiling. Levitated his eldest brother into the air and left him there, shrieking like a banshee. Before, he struggled even to learn simple tricks and sleight of hand. But somehow, in those two months, he had become a master of his art.

"Barius was devastated. His brother, two years his junior, had outshone him. His heroic preparations made him look even more the fool."

Darnak took a drink of ale to soothe his throat. "A year ago, that was. Then some idiot gave him the idea to go after the Rod of Creation. Wish I could get my hands on the fellow who suggested it. Everyone thought it suicide, but for Barius, it was the only thing that could surpass his brothers."

By this point Jig was listening with only one ear. Darnak's story simply confirmed his belief that the prince was mad. Given a place to live, food to eat, even people to wait on him and make sure his every wish was taken care of, Barius wanted more. He had to "prove himself."

What was the point? Admittedly, Jig wasn't sure he completely understood human motivation, even after Darnak's explanation. But this whole quest sounded like nothing more than a search for the most spectacular death. What good was attention and recognition if you had to be ripped apart by an ogre-killing monster to get it? All this for a magical rod that, as far as Jig knew, Barius didn't even want. He only wanted to be the one who found it. Or at least the one who died trying.

There was a reason "glory" rhymed with "gory," Jig thought. He grinned at his cleverness. Maybe he could make up a song about the prince. He worked out the first stanza as he walked.

Barius the human prince came down in search of glory.
Ran into a goblin horde and slew them all but one.
Dragged poor Jig along to face an end most gory,
All so Barius could prove himself the bravest son.

He glanced up to make sure nobody had heard his mumbling. He would have to finish his song later. Assuming they lived long enough.

His attention turned to the forest. Riana had complained that the trees weren't real, but Jig didn't care. He had never seen anything like them. Brown trunks, thick as his waist, rose a hundred feet into the air. The roots snaked through the dirt, tripping Jig time and again as his eyes wandered skyward.

This must be why surface-dwellers invented boots, he decided as he picked himself up for the fourth time. Even through the oversize boots, his toes throbbed from their encounters with the roots. Were he barefoot, he would no doubt be unable to walk by now.

Gradually Jig learned that this mock forest was less idyllic than he had assumed. For one thing, he had to walk differently. The ground sank beneath his feet, and he found himself stepping ridiculously high to try to avoid those blasted tree roots. Worse, the ground itself was soft and uneven! Soon the backs of Jig's legs burned from climbing small hills where the dirt constantly shifted.

He needed to rest. Sweat stung his eyes, and every step became a quest in itself. He could feel the blisters, each one the size of a small mountain. On his ankles, heels, toes . . . by now, his feet had a landscape to rival the woods around them. He also found that the boots that protected his toes had grown heavy as stones, and only the knowledge that he would be worse off barefoot kept him from flinging them into the woods.

Despite it all, he kept his mouth shut. If he complained, Barius would only hear it as a sign of weakness. He'd probably even increase their pace. Besides, nobody else was having any trouble. Even Riana, skinny as a snake, matched Barius's march without trouble.

Finally, as the sunlight faded to orange, then red, Barius called a halt. He pointed to a large pair of trees.

"We make camp here. Riana, you and the goblin will gather wood for a fire while Darnak and I discuss a plan for dispatching the dragon Straum."

He made Straum sound like nothing more than a nuisance. A carrion-worm to be chased out of the kitchens, rather than a creature of legend that could kill with a single breath.

Jig kept an ear cocked back as they searched for firewood. He couldn't hear well enough to make out what was being said, but he wanted to make sure he didn't get turned about and lose his way. As long as he could hear their voices, he could get back to the others. How did people get around without walls to guide them? Why, he could go in any direction he chose, turn left or right at random. The trees looked alike, the ground was the same everywhere, and were it not for the low voices behind him, Jig would have been lost already.

This must be why Darnak spends so much time on his map. If the others were as disoriented underground as Jig was here, no wonder they needed to note the way out.

He glanced into the sky and received another shock. *The sun had moved!* Before, it had been directly overhead, but in the past few hours it had traveled to the very edge of the sky. How could they find their way when even the sky shifted position?

Riana had stopped to watch a bird circle overhead. When she didn't move, Jig looked up as well. Following the wide flight made him dizzy, and he wondered if real birds ever felt nauseous. Did Jig and the others seem as small from up there as the bird did to him? Did the bird feel free, able to go anywhere it chose?

"I wonder what it's like."

He didn't realize he had spoken out loud until Riana spat. "I'm sure it's great. You can fly anywhere, right up until some hunter turns his trained falcon loose to break your back and bring you down."

She stomped off, Jig following close behind to make sure he didn't lose sight of her. So much for birds. When she began to gather wood, he picked a tree at random, drew his sword, and chopped at one of the lower branches. The impact jolted his fingers and forearm. Trees were tougher than he thought. He drew back for another swing.

"What are you doing?"

"Getting wood." He saw her expression and hesitated.

Riana shook her head with exasperation. "A fat lot of good that will do. You don't use green wood for a fire unless you want to make a smoke-tail."

"A what?"

"A smoke-tail. A signal humans use to let one another

know where they're at." Her lips tightened. "I don't think we want to announce ourselves to the dragon quite yet, do you?"

Jig stared at the tree. The leaves were green, but the wood itself was brown and rough. Wood was wood. Jig had never seen green wood, and he had no idea why the sticks Riana was picking off the ground were any better than this branch. Except, maybe, that he didn't know how many trees he could attack before his hand grew numb.

Seeing his indecision, Riana sighed and dropped her small pile of sticks. "Put that away," she said impatiently. When Jig's sword was safely back in its sheath, she pointed to the branch he had cut. "See the sap?"

Jig squinted. By putting his face three inches from the branch, he could make out a few drops of clear liquid oozing out of the cut.

"That's because the branch is still alive. It's wet inside, so it won't burn. Gather the branches that have died and fallen off. The dryer the better." She picked up one branch and broke it in half. "See? No sap. I'm amazed you goblins haven't suffocated yourselves if you don't know enough to use dry wood."

"There aren't many trees in the upper tunnels," Jig snapped. How was he supposed to know that brown wood wasn't always brown, and that clear tree blood turned wood green? He gave the tree a disgusted look and began to grab sticks from the ground.

"What do you burn for fuel?" Riana asked.

"Elves." He didn't want to admit that, for the most part, goblins couldn't scrounge enough fuel for fires. As for the muck, that was barely enough to keep the lair lit, let alone warm. It was all they could do to fuel a real cookfire, and even that required them to trade with the hobgoblins. Unlike goblins, hobgoblins would venture onto the surface. They took the weapons and coins the goblins had scavenged in exchange for a few bundles of wood. Just one more way to keep the goblins weak and the hobgoblins strong. Jig wondered why he had never seen it before. By taking most of the weapons, the hobgoblins kept the goblins from becoming a real threat.

A rustling from ahead made Jig start. He dropped his sticks and grabbed his sword. "Did you hear that?"

Riana shook her head. She did draw her dagger, though, and Jig saw fear in her eyes as she scanned the woods.

"We could get killed out here," Jig whispered. Why had Barius sent the two weakest people off on their own? He remembered the dead ogres. Was this another ogre, one who had avoided the creature that killed its fellows? Jig shivered. Or perhaps this was the creature itself. Having slain the ogres, was it hunting new prey?

The woods had grown quiet. The ever-present song of distant birds died out, and the occasional rustle of leaves sounded far too loud to Jig's ears.

"Barius probably *wants* us to get killed," Riana said, voice soft. "If we die, that's two problems he doesn't have to deal with anymore." Another noise, this time a grating sound, came from the right. Like someone rubbing two sticks together, only much louder. "It sounds big."

Jig felt naked and exposed with no walls around him. He backed toward a large tree. The tree was a poor substitute for hard stone, but at least it would guard his back. On his last step, his heel caught on a root. His head smacked the trunk, and his sword flipped end over end and stabbed into the ground.

The noise stopped for a second. Jig held his breath, hoping the thing hadn't heard. Riana didn't speak, but her eyes shot profanity that would have done a patrol captain proud.

The beast charged. Clomping footsteps tore through the dirt and the undergrowth toward them. Jig scrambled for his sword. Before he could find it, the thing leaped over a fallen tree, straight at Riana.

It was enormous. Sharp branched horns topped its narrow head. Rocklike hooves kicked the air with every bound.

"Dragon!" Jig yelled. He curled into a ball and covered his head.

Riana ducked, and the thing sprang right over her and disappeared. Jig tried to listen, to make sure it was really gone, but the pounding of his heart made it impossible to hear anything else.

"Are you okay?" he asked. She wasn't bleeding. Though she trembled with fear, she hadn't been wounded.

Jig looked closer. That wasn't fear after all.

The elf was *laughing* at him. Jig's face grew hot. It wasn't like he had intentionally fallen. "We should get back, in case there are more of those things."

"Jig, it was a deer," she gasped. "Not a dragon. And I hope there *are* more. I haven't eaten venison in years."

Jig blushed harder. He knew it wasn't a dragon. Dragons had scales, not fur, and he had never heard of a brown dragon. "I didn't see it that well," he said sheepishly. "I panicked."

Riana's eyes widened, and she laughed even harder. "Jig, don't worry. Deer are the biggest cowards out there, and they only eat *plants*. Not goblins."

She stood up and brushed dirt from her clothes. "Come on. He was probably rubbing the velvet off his antlers. I'll show you."

Jig gathered up his wood and followed. He ignored her giggles, as well as her warnings about flying squirrels and other terrible surface monsters. Sure enough, they found a tree whose bark showed long gouges. Other places had been polished smooth by the deer's antlers.

She smirked. "Alchemists sometimes collect deer velvet. They use it for an aphrodisiac."

He didn't bother to ask what an aphrodisiac was. "Riana, are deer stupid?"

"I don't think so," she said. "But I've never lived in the woods. Why?"

Jig frowned as he stared at the tree. "The deer couldn't have heard us at first. Otherwise, if they're as timid as you say, it would have fled. But when I fell, he came *toward* us. Which means something else must have scared it even more."

Riana's face went still. "You're right."

From behind them, a dry voice said, "Indeed you are."

CHAPTER 13

Pointing Fingers

JIG COULDN'T FLEE. HE WANTED TO, BUT SEVeral things kept him rooted in place. He could no longer hear the others back at camp, and since he had completely lost his bearings during the confusion with the deer, any attempt to run would probably lead him deeper into the woods. Also, he knew that voice.

Recognition strengthened his desire to escape, while at the same time making him realize that trying to do so would be pointless. No matter how quickly he moved, Ryslind's magic could strike him down. To run would only provide an easier shot at Jig's unguarded back.

"Ryslind?" he said, searching for the wizard's hiding spot.

"Did I startle you, little ones?" Ryslind asked as he stepped out from behind a large tree.

His bonds were gone, as was his bow. To anyone who hadn't seen the charred corpses left by Ryslind's magic, he looked like a harmless man with odd taste in tattoos. Jig didn't move. He still remembered Ryslind's threats, and whereas Barius's temper always warned Jig when to expect an attack, Ryslind would boil you in your skin without ever losing that thin smirk. Now was a time to remain very polite and nonthreatening.

"How did you escape?" Riana asked.

Ryslind smiled. "My brother ordered my hands and feet tied again after you left. I lay there in silence until their attention wandered." He folded his arms behind his back and began to pace. "Barius and Darnak are naïve. They know nothing of true magic or those who use it, so they believed I was helpless."

Ryslind reached into his robes and flourished a short knife. "All that work to prevent me from spellcasting, and they never searched for weapons."

The single-edged blade curved forward like a sickle, and the handle was black bone. Too short for combat, Jig decided. For humans, at least. It was still a far cry better than the kitchen knife Jig had carried at the beginning of this escapade.

Whatever Ryslind used it for, aside from cutting ropes, Jig didn't want to know. There was a sinister aura about it that made him hope Ryslind wouldn't need goblin parts for any of his spells.

"You killed them?" Riana's gaze didn't leave the knife.

"No," Ryslind said. Regretfully? Jig couldn't tell. "I considered it. But he is still my brother." The knife vanished into the shadows of his robe. "I put them both to sleep. They will rest safely until the spell wears off, sometime tomorrow afternoon, or until someone disturbs the glyphs."

"Safe?" Riana repeated. "What if another ogre comes?"

Ryslind smiled. His eyes searched the trees. "I imagine even the thick-skulled ogres have learned to leave us alone. If not, the lesson will be repeated."

Repeated by whom? Jig shivered, remembering the clawed corpses of the ogres back at the clearing. Did something watch over them even as they spoke? "You know what killed the other ogres."

"I know much more than you or my brother ever realized, little goblin."

Jig realized then why Ryslind hadn't killed him yet. It had nothing to do with Barius being his brother, or with any sort of loyalty. No, Ryslind—or whatever had taken control of Ryslind's mind—wanted an audience. He was like Porak, though stronger than the goblin captain had ever been. Both of them thrived on showing off their power and making others afraid.

Both of which, Jig admitted to himself, *he had accomplished quite nicely*. Ryslind was far better at it than Porak was. Especially the fear part. Ryslind sane was enough to twist Jig's stomach. Ryslind with this second, strange voice, and the glow of his eyes brighter than ever . . . if Jig had been a fire-spider, the entire forest would be aflame by now. Fortunately, Smudge had restrained himself to singeing his leather pad.

"You're going after the rod, aren't you?" Riana crossed her arms and cocked her head.

Ryslind nodded. "Barius would take the rod back to our father. Oh, he would receive everything he had ever hoped for. There would be a celebration, with dancing and musicians and all the glory Barius wanted. Until the next morning, when the people's attention turned elsewhere and left him more bitter and empty than before. In the meantime, the rod would be tucked into some vault and left to gather dust, locked away as if it were naught but a mere trinket.

"My brother is like a crow who steals a gold necklace for its pretty sparkle, with no understanding of its real value. Much as I hate to snatch the necklace from my brother's beak, I think I can find a better use for its power."

He pointed a finger at one of the trees. The tattoos on his hand pulsed once, and a thick branch began to twist like a serpent. Small twigs fell from the main branch, and the bark peeled away like dead skin. With a loud crack, the smooth branch tumbled free and flew to Ryslind's hand.

He brushed a few last flakes of bark off of the pale staff. "If you are wise, you will leave."

"How?" Riana demanded. She jerked her head toward the sky. "Are we supposed to fly out of here?"

Ryslind scowled. He grabbed one of the smaller sticks. "Watch." He threw the stick into the air. It whirled end over end for twenty feet, then shot back to earth. Jig heard nothing, but it appeared as though the stick had collided with something solid. It landed somewhere to their left.

Jig stared.

Seeing that they didn't understand, Ryslind sighed and picked up another stick. He repeated his demonstration. "What you see is the stick hitting the roof of the cavern."

"What cavern?" Jig asked.

"And *you* killed the Necromancer," Ryslind said in wonder. "Did you really believe an entire sky existed beneath the mountain? That those clouds are real? You fell less than thirty feet, yet you accept the existence of those birds soaring hundreds of feet in the air. It's illusion, all of it. A powerful illusion, but no more. Which means the pit we came through is still there, if you have the wit to find it again. If not. . . ." He stabbed the end of his staff into the dirt.

Before Jig could work up the courage to ask more questions, Ryslind walked off into the woods. Jig rubbed his eyes and wished for a set of those elven lenses Riana had mentioned. For it looked like Ryslind's feet passed *through* the roots that had snagged Jig's boots time after time. He wondered if Shadowstar could provide the same magic for Jig.

"We should stop him," Riana said. She had her dagger out, and she glared in the direction Ryslind had gone.

"Why?" Personally, Jig thought that going back home was a lovely idea. He thought about Golaka's famous peppered dwarf roast, finding a corner to himself where he could feed Smudge and where the only bullies were goblins, not wizards and princes and dwarves . . . he could almost smell the smoke of the cookfire. "I say we go find the way out."

Riana rolled her eyes. "So we make our way to the Necromancer's little throne room. What then?"

Jig started to answer, then his mouth clapped shut. Ryslind was the only one who could get them past the lizard-fish . . . which Ryslind knew perfectly well. "Okay, so he's still playing with us," Jig said slowly. "What's your plan for stopping him?"

Now it was Riana's turn to hesitate. "We could sneak up on him," she said. "Like Darnak told us, against a wizard, we just have to be fast enough to kill him before he can cast a spell."

"But this is Ryslind."

"Why are you so frightened of him? Everyone dies sooner

or later. If you stab him in the heart, he'll die like everything else."

"Not everyone dies," Jig muttered. "Some of them turn into walking corpses."

"Jig, stop being such a coward. You killed the Necromancer, right?"

"I was lucky."

She grabbed his shoulders and pushed him against a tree. "Lucky or not, you did it. There's two of us. If we don't kill him, who knows what he'll do. He's only human, right?"

"No," Jig said. He wiggled free and sat down. "Haven't you listened to his voice? Whatever he is, he's not like any human I've heard."

He told her how the second voice had taken control back in the Necromancer's chamber. "Even Barius was afraid of him."

Riana's jaw tightened. She took a few steps after Ryslind, then stopped. Slamming her knife into a tree trunk, she swore angrily. "I hate bullies. He and his brother both. They expect you to do everything they want, and if you don't, they threaten you."

Jig shrugged. That was the way it had been with every goblin captain he had ever known. What did she expect? Ryslind was too powerful. For all they knew, he could have turned himself invisible and waited to see if they chased after him.

"Besides, if we kill him, how are we supposed to get through the lake?" He didn't give her time to answer. "We should go back."

He listened to make sure Riana was coming. After a few paces, he heard her follow, kicking sticks and rocks with every third step.

Good. Now if they could find their way back, everything would be just great. He looked around nervously. The sunlight was mostly gone, and the stars had begun to appear in the sky. Jig had never seen stars, but he found them a disappointment. The songs described them as pretty, but all he saw were weak dots of white light. They provided little light, and in the darkness, the roots had begun to attack his feet with abandon. Stars might be fine for surface-dwellers, he decided, but he'd trade them all to have the sun back.

Riana wasn't having as much trouble. She eventually passed Jig, which was fine with him. If she could find the way back to their camp, he would happily let her lead the way.

"They're going to kill you, you know," she said casually.

Jig stopped. "Who are?" He grabbed his sword and looked around.

"Barius and Darnak. They'll kill you as soon as they don't need you anymore. If I'm lucky, they'll toss me in prison."

When he didn't answer, she said, "What did you expect? You're a goblin. I'm a thief. They're not going to let us go once they find the rod and escape."

He tried to think of a good argument. What reason did they have to kill him? He had helped them through the tunnels above. He had killed the Necromancer. But he suspected Riana was right. After all what reason did they have *not* to kill him?

"Darnak wouldn't," he said weakly. The dwarf wouldn't have bothered to heal Jig only to kill him later. Not that Darnak's help meant much. Barius was the leader, and he would be only too happy to put an end to Jig. Especially after that Rakachak incident.

"Everywhere I go, I meet men like him," Riana muttered. "Follow them into Straum's lair or let them toss me into the dungeons. They offer you a choice between hells and expect you to thank them for it."

"They were going to kill you," Jig blurted out. As long as they were discussing impending death, he thought she should know the truth.

"What?"

"Before, when you set off the Necromancer's trap. They were going to kill you to keep you from turning into one of those dead things."

She didn't say anything, but Jig could see her playing with her knife. The starlight glittered on the twirling blade. "He would have, too," she whispered. "Bastard."

Jig nodded agreement.

"We should let them sleep and hope the ogres *do* find them. Or kill them ourselves. They deserve it."

He wasn't about to argue that point. But as Riana pointed

out, they couldn't escape either. Killing the others would only leave them that much more vulnerable to attack.

"Maybe we can kick them around a bit before we break the spell," she said.

"I could use a knife and Darnak's ink to draw some rude tattoos," Jig offered. "What do you think Barius's father would say if he came home with 'Goblin-lover' scrawled across his forehead?"

She grinned. "Or we could steal their clothes. Make them face Straum naked." With a frown, she added, "Except that I don't really want to see that. I'm going to have enough nightmares about this place without those images haunting me."

"If we were back in goblin territory, we could rub their clothes in carrion-worm urine. That way they'd wake up surrounded by worms." He didn't mention that Porak had taught him this trick, nor that he had screamed loud enough to wake Straum himself when he felt the worms crawling over his legs.

Riana giggled. "And if we were on the surface, I'd boil some tea from poison ivy leaves and slip it into their waterskins."

Jig laughed even harder once she explained what poison ivy was.

A while later, she said, "You should have warned me before you cut off my finger." She didn't sound angry, though. At least not at Jig.

"Sorry. I'll say something next time."

She chuckled. "Next time I'll cut off something of yours in return, and it won't be a finger."

A few hours later, after backtracking twice, they managed to find Barius and Darnak. They lay as if dead, hands folded on their stomachs and their equipment placed to one side. The lantern, lit but shuttered, sat between them. Indeed it was the faint orange lantern light that Riana had spotted to guide them here.

Jig opened the lantern and sighed with relief as it lit up the woods around them. He could see again. As well as he ever did, at least.

"Ryslind's glyphs?" Riana pointed at Barius's face.

Two red lines traced a circular path around his forehead,

starting at the eyebrows and merging by the bridge of the nose. Darnak had the same character inked onto his brow, though they had to shove his hair out of the way to see it.

"Ryslind said we could wake them up by breaking the glyph," Riana said. Her eyes narrowed. "I'll do it. You take the lantern and make sure nothing's out there."

"Why me?" Jig asked, looking around at the dark woods. The last thing he wanted was to go wandering alone.

Riana's knife appeared in her hand. "Don't argue, Jig."

Right. He picked up the lantern and walked a few paces into the woods. "And she was complaining about bullies," he muttered as he shone the light around. Despite the stars, the darkness here felt somehow *bigger* than Jig was used to. Up above, the lantern would have revealed solid walls. Here, darkness engulfed the light like a predator. If anything crept near, it would have to step directly in front of the lantern for Jig to notice.

A loud scream came from behind, and Jig immediately dropped the lantern. He started to run, stopped, ran back, and grabbed the lantern. Seconds later, he shifted it to his other hand and stuck his burned fingers into his mouth.

"Grab the lantern by the *handle,* stupid," he muttered, voice muffled by his fingers.

Had he stopped to think, he might have run the other way, into the darkness. Instead he hurried back to the others, to find Darnak and Barius both awake and staring at something in the prince's hand. No, not *in* his hand.

Riana sat on the ground in front of them both. She sounded deeply forlorn as she explained what had happened. "Ryslind cast a spell on you and escaped. He wants the rod for himself. He said we should leave. We came back as soon as we could."

She shook her head sadly. "He said something about a spell that would let him look like you, Barius, to fool your father. I'm afraid that, for one of the spell ingredients, he had to cut off your finger."

Jig bit his lip and hoped that neither the prince nor the dwarf could hear the satisfaction beneath Riana's words.

* * *

"I'll slay him myself," Barius raged. He thrust the newly healed stump of his left ring finger in Darnak's face.

Jig and Riana had stayed out of the way ever since the prince began his tantrum. Seeing the fury on Barius's face, Jig took another step back, strategically putting a thick tree between himself and the prince.

"Once we're home, I'll take you to one of the healing temples. You've more than enough gold sitting around to buy a simple regeneration. Besides, if he was wanting to finish you off, he'd have slit your throat rather than lay you out with a magic lullaby." Darnak glanced at Riana and twirled a lock of his beard. "If it was your brother who was doing this, that is."

"Of course it was him," Barius snapped. "Fearful of my success, he seeks to steal the rod which is rightfully mine."

Jig didn't say anything. Darnak had so far kept his suspicions to himself, and Jig didn't want to draw any attention he could avoid. At least Riana had the foresight to dispose of the finger. She had flung it far into the woods, then wiped her knife on the prince's white shirt.

He found it peculiar the way these adventurers thought anything they found was "rightfully" theirs. Why couldn't they come out and admit they were stealing from the monsters? Nothing wrong with that. Goblins and hobgoblins did it all the time. True, it was mostly hobgoblins stealing from the goblins, but that was part of life. Why this nonsense about the rod really belonging to Barius? Did he think Straum should rush out and present the rod to him? Should the goblins have given over their meager treasure because it "rightfully" belonged to Barius?

No wonder the prince was so bitter and angry. All that treasure was rightfully his, and none of the current owners were considerate enough to realize it.

"We should be off," Barius snapped. "We've no time for slumber. If we are to catch my treacherous brother, we must leave at once."

Barius had taken four steps before Darnak raised his voice and said, "Before you're running too far, you might want to ask which way your brother was headed."

Jig pointed. Barius straightened his shoulders and, refusing to make eye contact with Jig, turned and walked back the way Jig had indicated.

Darnak grabbed the lantern in one hand, hoisted his pack with the other, and followed. "Come on, then. He'll be setting quite a trot until he burns off the worst of his temper."

"Are you sure we should go after Ryslind in the dark?" Jig asked as he half jogged alongside the dwarf. "If we wait until the sun comes back . . . it does come back, doesn't it?"

"Aye," Darnak said. "And I could do with a long, nonmagical nap myself. But yon hothead won't rest until he gets back at his brother, and if he has to, he'll rip off his own eyelids to keep from sleeping."

"Even though he knows Ryslind isn't right in the head?" Jig grimaced. That had come out a bit more bluntly than he meant. Ryslind was a prince, after all, and Darnak might not take too kindly to hearing him insulted.

But the dwarf only chuckled. "Madmen in the noble line are as common as rat turds in the grain shed. Barius couldn't care less about his brother's sanity. He doesn't care why Ryslind showed him up; he just knows he's been made to look the fool. If it happens again, Barius won't stop until one or the other is dead." In a more serious tone, he added, "I expect it will be Barius who finds himself wearing a funeral shroud. A good fighter, but too impetuous. And Ryslind's power is nothing to sneer at."

He dipped his quill into the inkpot. "Enough talk. How many paces since that forked tree?"

The prince's pace was not a good one for mapmaking, and Darnak valiantly tried to sketch their progress as he jogged. Ink had smeared his fingers up to the knuckles, and several drops of ink tracked across the map like tiny rivers. Even when the quill pierced the parchment, Darnak didn't give up. "Always map the way in," he said. "For it's a far cry harder to do so on the way out."

Jig didn't bother to point out how useless the map had been so far. He was too busy watching the ground. The lantern made it easier to avoid stumbling, but not by much. The light leaped and twisted with Darnak's every step, so the trees appeared to be moving. More than once, Jig gasped when his imagination turned a low branch into an arm reaching for his throat.

He still couldn't understand this competition between the two princes. If matters were so strained between them, why wouldn't they fight and finish the matter? Goblins would have exchanged insults, pounded one another with clubs or whatever was handy, and been done with it. Whoever walked away was in the right, and the loser, if he or she survived, would then acknowledge the other's superiority. Why drag things out?

Based on Barius's fury back at camp, he suspected things would finally be settled once they caught up with Ryslind. That too made Jig uncomfortable. For they needed Ryslind's help to get out of this place. That would be difficult if Barius killed him. If the fight went the other way, as Darnak predicted, would Ryslind bother with the rest of them? Either outcome seemed to leave Jig stranded in the lower levels.

Maybe they wouldn't fight at all. He hoped not, because he needed them both alive if he were to have any chance of escaping. If they did start to fight, maybe Jig would tell them it was Riana, not Ryslind, who took Barius's finger. He didn't want to betray Riana, but at least that scenario left a chance for Jig to get out alive. Riana would turn on Jig, Barius would turn on Riana, and all Jig would have to do was hope the prince was faster.

He thought Riana would understand. She would still try to kill him, but she would understand.

He hoped it wouldn't come to that. Of everyone in the party, Riana was the only one Jig could even remotely relate to. The prince was too greedy, the dwarf too interested in his maps and his gods, and as for the wizard, Jig could only pray he never understood Ryslind's mind.

"This is where you met the traitor?" Ever since they left camp, Barius had refused to call his brother by name.

Jig looked around. There was his firewood, scattered and forgotten. To the right, a pale round wound on a tree marked where Ryslind had torn his staff free. "Yes."

Barius dropped to one knee and examined the ground. "His sandals are smooth soled, harder to track, but I see that he stood here while talking to you. Darnak, bring the light closer."

Darnak drew a quick *X* and labeled it RYSLIND, then hurried over to Barius's side.

"There." Barius pointed. "That shallow dimple in the earth. That must be the indentation from his staff. Between his footprints and that staff, we can track him even in this black night." He laughed. "My poor brother. Strong in art, but weak in flesh. He could never outmarch me in the field, even with a staff to support his weight."

They continued through the woods until Jig lost track of time. His stomach grumbled angrily, and his vision narrowed to the patch of trail just ahead. His thoughts faded until he was aware of nothing more than the need to put one foot forward, then the other. His blisters were worse, and a painful dryness burned his eyes. All he wanted was to lie down. How long did the sun take to return? Surely they had been walking for days. Several days without food or water, and the only time they rested was when Darnak insisted on relieving himself, which he did frequently.

He probably drank too much dwarven ale, Jig thought. He had seen Darnak take several drinks as they hiked along. *It's probably the only thing that keeps him sane, living with humans all the time.*

"Strange," Barius mused as they walked. "The traitor fled in a different direction than the creature I had been tracking. Yet another indication that he knows something he refused to share."

Perhaps he knew that chasing a creature that could kill three ogres was a stupid idea. As usual, Jig kept his thoughts to himself.

"He divined the Necromancer's hiding place," Barius continued. "Could he be strong enough to discover the rod's location as well? The tales say it hides itself from magic, but why else would he go this way, if not to reach the rod before me?"

Wait, who *found the Necromancer?* No doubt Barius had already rewritten that incident in his memory, erasing Jig's role so he wouldn't have to admit to being upstaged by a goblin.

Near morning the forest began to thin. Jig only noticed

because he wasn't stumbling as often. The light had come so gradually he couldn't say when he first began to see the faint gray outlines of the trees. Overhead the stars had faded until only a few faint spots of light still showed.

Barius brought them to a halt at the edge of the woods. "Look."

Jig stumbled forward to see what Barius had pointed to. He tried to rub the sleepiness from his eyes. One part of him knew he wasn't imagining things, but another part knew equally well that he *couldn't* be seeing what he his eyes told him was there.

"Odd lair for a dragon," Darnak said. "And I've seen one or two in my time."

Jig hadn't. Maybe this was something other dragons did. Jig had never heard of such a thing, but his experience in the world was terribly limited. Tugging on Darnak's sleeve, he asked, "Do all dragons own flower gardens?"

"First I've run across."

It was an impressive garden, Jig admitted. He sat down and tried to take it all in.

The cavern ended about a quarter-mile away. The bowl-shaped wall rose about thirty feet to end at a tree-covered cliff. Large birds circled the cliff top, and even though Jig knew the sky, and therefore the birds, were all an illusion, he could still hear their harsh cries. Impressive as that magic was, it paled next to Straum's gardens.

Thin snakes of water flowed down the cavern wall. Midway down, they hit a magical barrier and flowed into the air, where they curved around one another and looped back to form an arched overhang. It was like fine lace, but formed entirely of water. Streams split apart and split again. The patterns changed gradually, a row of intricate diamonds fading into a series of interlinked ovals, all formed by those shifting rays of water.

Accenting the magical overhang were numerous vines that blanketed the wall. Their purple flowers hid the rock so well, Jig wouldn't have been surprised to learn that the cliff itself was nothing more than flower petals. The wind created waves of motion across the flowers, reminding Jig of the lake.

The true work of art was at ground level, where a huge flower mural stretched out for at least a hundred yards from the cliff. Jig couldn't see well enough to discern the finer details, but he could tell the pictures were laid out to tell a story. On the left, a large green dragon flew with wings outstretched. Orange and red flowers created flaming breath. Another area seemed to depict the outside of the mountain. Jig wondered where Straum had found gray and brown flowers for that part of the mural.

A narrow white trail wound through the center of the garden to the cavern wall. There, about ten feet up, a wide hole beckoned. Jig hadn't seen it at first, because some of the vines hung over the entrance like a curtain. That had to be the entrance to Straum's lair.

He took a deep breath, letting the sweet perfume of the flowers fill his nose. Immediately his eyes watered, and he sneezed three times.

"Sorry," he said meekly when Barius glared at him.

"The opening is off the ground, and wide enough for the dragon to fly through unimpeded." Barius thrust out his chest and chin as he faced the rest of them. "We should prepare ourselves."

The only preparation Jig wanted was a good, long nap. And maybe something to eat. Water would be nice, too. He wondered if it was safe to drink from one of those water streams.

"Come. Before the sun finishes rising." Drawing his sword, the prince hurried toward the garden.

Jig waited. He wanted to make sure nothing was waiting to leap out and kill whoever went first. Or if something did kill the prince, Jig wanted to be sure he was nowhere near when it happened. But Barius made it to the edge of the mural without incident, and then Darnak's club prodded Jig in the back, and he followed.

At the garden, Jig saw something he had missed before. A tiny wall of blue fire bordered the entire mural. In the red light of sunrise, the points of flame were almost invisible. The fire also segmented different portions of the mural. Over here, wizards dueled at the gates of a black tower. Another image showed a blue-scaled dragon flying through the clouds. He remembered Ryslind explaining the legend of Ellnorein, and wondered if the mural was supposed to depict a battle from those times.

Jig grinned when he spotted something tucked into one corner. In a tiny triangular panel, a squad of goblins fought a catlike creature. Naturally, the goblins were losing, but Jig didn't care. He felt a surge of pride at seeing his people in Straum's garden. It made him feel like he was a part of history.

Looking closer, Jig saw that there were even tiny dark blue flowers, each one with a ball-like tip, to represent all the goblin blood. He overbalanced and fell into the flowers. One hand crushed a troll's belly while the other flattened the end of a serpent's tail. More pollen floated up to trigger a second sneezing fit.

Darnak grabbed Jig's elbow and pulled him upright. "Come on. Once we reach Straum's hoard, you'll see something worth gawking at."

The path through the garden was actually a sort of white grass, so low and soft it felt like feathers beneath Jig's feet. As they neared the cave, Jig began to wonder why they hadn't been attacked yet. Surely if Straum's magic could create water sculpture and flower art like this, he would have no trouble adding a few spells to discourage intruders. Barius was so obsessed with his brother that he hadn't bothered to look for traps along the path. At least Barius was in the lead, so if anything did happen, Jig would have the satisfaction of seeing it happen to him first.

Despite his worries, they reached the wall of the cavern. There, Darnak took a rope from his pack and handed it to Riana, the lightest in the group. She raised both eyebrows and handed the rope right back.

"Stick my head up there and let Straum burn it off? I think not."

"My brother is up there, girl." Barius pointed to an indentation in the grass, one that could have been made by the end of a staff. "I've defeated every foe and every trap we have encountered, and I'll not be stopped by your stubbornness."

Jig cocked his head. *Barius* had defeated everything? From the sound of his voice, he believed that, too. And he'd likely kill Riana if she pushed him much further.

"I'll do it," Jig said. He grabbed the rope from Darnak. "Boost me up."

As he scrambled onto the dwarf's shoulders, Jig wondered what had possessed him. Goblins were cowards—that was what helped them survive. So what was he doing poking his head into a dragon's cave?

It's simple—I'm hungry, I'm tired, and I don't feel like waiting while they argue for the next hour. Perhaps courage was nothing more than impatience. Besides, the sooner he got away from the flowers, the quicker his eyes would stop watering.

His fingers caught the edge, and with some pushing from Darnak and Barius, he managed to swing one leg up. That, he decided, was a mistake. Pain tore through a very sensitive part of his anatomy. He pulled the other leg up quickly and rolled into the cave.

He tumbled over several of the flower vines, and spent the next minute untangling himself from a vine that had torn free and wrapped around his legs. Silence followed. The others waited below to see if he would die a hideous death. Looking around, Jig wondered the same thing.

Two trolls lay dead on the tunnel floor. Wisps of smoke rose from the holcs in their chests. Barius was right. His brother *had* been here.

CHAPTER 14

Straum Heads off a Possible Rebellion

IF ANYTHING, TROLLS WERE EVEN BIGGER THAN the ogres had been. Uglier, too. They looked like a cross between giant humans and spoiled apples. Their bald skin was wrinkled and rubbery, and they smelled like old eggs. They also smelled of charred flesh, but that was a result of Ryslind's magic.

Jig kicked them both to be sure they were dead. Not that most things could get back up with a hole in the chest big enough to crawl through, but Jig wanted to be safe. The trolls didn't respond, though a few flies buzzed up from the eyes of the closest one.

Smudge leaped off Jig's shoulder. His legs snapped out in midair, and when he landed on the troll's forehead, he held a buzzing fly between his forelegs.

Jig watched jealously as Smudge cooked his breakfast. Even flies were starting to sound good. His eyes went to the trolls. Traditionally, the first bite went to the victor, but Ryslind wasn't around to enjoy the rewards of his kill. His mouth began to water. He had no way to cook the bodies, and raw troll meat probably wasn't the healthiest thing in the world. Though the wounded area was nicely blackened, and the smell no worse than overcooked carrion-worm. . . .

"What's taking you so long up there?"

Jig perked his ears at the dwarf's whisper. Swallowing hastily, he called back, "I was looking for something to tie the rope to. I'm not big enough to pull you up by myself."

He wiped his mouth and scanned the entrance. No stalagmites, no rocks, nothing that would hold the rope. His gaze returned to the trolls. They *were* pretty big.

He wound the rope around both trolls' waists, thinking that dead trolls had turned out to be pretty useful things. He wondered if Golaka had ever cooked troll meat. He'd have to see about bringing some back for her cauldron. If he survived long enough.

Jig poked his head through the vine curtain. "Ready," he said. Pulling back, he braced himself against the trolls, adding his meager weight to theirs.

Barius came up first, then Riana, and finally Darnak. The dwarf in his armor was heavy enough that the trolls started to slide across the ground. If the others hadn't heard Jig squawk and grabbed the rope, Darnak would have pulled Jig over the edge and buried him beneath a pair of dead trolls.

"Now this is a proper dragon's lair," Darnak said. "Much more to my liking." He quickly lit the lantern and retrieved his mapmaking tools. As Jig retrieved the rope, Darnak was happily pacing off the width of the tunnel.

"Twenty-five paces exactly. Figure three or four paces for clearance, but that still means a pretty good wingspan on the beast."

The tunnel was wide, but the roof was only a few feet higher than Barius's head. If Straum decided to come out for an early-morning flight, there was no place for the group to hide. Indeed, they'd be lucky if the dragon didn't smash them on his way out.

"Quickly," Barius said. "My brother cannot be far. We've outmarched him, and soon he will be back within our grasp." With a tight smile, he added, "And he has kindly led me to Straum's hoard. For that boon, perhaps I shall be lenient."

Perhaps Straum would welcome them with open arms and present Barius with the Rod of Creation as a birthday gift, too, but Jig doubted it. He wondered if death by dragonfire would be quick. Fire was a painful way to go, but the stories said dragon breath was so hot the victim burned to ash in seconds.

"Should I stay here to watch the entrance?" Jig asked nervously. "To make sure nothing follows." *And to run like a frightened mouse once Straum kills the rest of you.* "It's not as though I'd be much use against the dragon," he added, trying to sound helpful.

"You will remain with us." The decisive tone of Barius's voice squished Jig's hope of survival. "If nothing else, perhaps the dragon will waste valuable seconds on you, giving us time to execute our attack. Therein lies your usefulness, goblin."

"Oh." After that he was too depressed to say anything else.

The tunnels grew warmer as they walked. What did a dragon's lair look like? A creature that breathed fire would probably want to keep its home as warm as possible. Would there be bonfires and torches? Dragons were supposed to have great piles of treasure that they used as nests. Uncomfortable as it sounded, it did make a kind of sense. Perhaps dragons followed the same logic Jig used when he slept with his few belongings clutched to his stomach. People had a harder time stealing something in your sleep if they had to roll you over to get it.

Not that this technique had ever made much difference for Jig. True, no goblin had taken Jig's possessions while he slept. They woke him up first. Being awakened and kicked out of the way by larger goblins wasn't much of an improvement, but it did mean he knew who to get back at later.

At least they were back on good, solid rock. Far easier to run away when the ground didn't shift beneath your feet and the roots weren't reaching out to catch your toes.

Jig's ears twitched. He heard something up ahead, too faint to identify. A whispery sort of sound. Too smooth and rhythmic to be voices. It was familiar, though. He fingered a fang nervously as he walked.

"I see something," Darnak said. He raised the lantern and aimed the beam forward.

Soon Jig could see it too, a faint blue glow from farther up the tunnel. At a nod from Barius, Darnak shuttered the lantern.

Jig's eyes were slow to adjust, but his ears made up for that. Over the past few days, he had learned to recognize every sound the group made. From the clop of Barius's boots to the quiet flap of Riana's soles to the ring of Darnak's studded boots against the stone, Jig knew them all. He knew exactly where Barius was simply by listening for the prince's nasal breath, whereas Darnak tended to grunt with every third or fourth exhalation. As they neared the source of the light, his vision improved as well.

A wide portcullis blocked the end of the tunnel. Black bars as thick as his wrist extended from the ceiling into holes in the floor. Flat iron bands ran across the bars, riveted to hold each bar in place. The bars ended in nasty-looking points, like oversize spearheads lodged several inches in the rock. Jig could envision being trapped beneath those points as the portcullis came crashing down. He winced.

"Behold," whispered Barius. "The very resting place of the beast."

Jig moved closer to peer through the bars. Beyond the portcullis, the tunnel opened into a large cavern, and he could see the source of the whispering noise he had heard. A glassy lake filled the far half of the cavern, and the water moved just enough to make small waves on the shore. The lake was small, more of a pond, especially compared to the lake of the lizard-fish. The waves were likewise softer, which was why Jig hadn't recognized the sound at first.

The shore itself was black sand that stretched almost to the tunnel. The sand sparkled like the night sky, illuminated by blue flames around the edge of the cavern, similar to the fire that had bordered the flower mosaic. Turning his attention to the cavern walls, Jig felt his mouth open in awe.

Shelves had been carved into every square inch of wall, and every shelf overflowed with . . . stuff. Jig had a hard time calling it treasure. True, many shelves glittered with gold and silver coins of all shapes and sizes, stacked into perfect cylinders. But there was far more to Straum's hoard than mere money.

Weapons played a prominent role in the décor. Swords hung between every shelf, some taller than Jig, others slender as a blade of grass. Jig saw jeweled swords, plain swords, swords with polished steel blades, and swords of hammered bronze. He even saw one that looked like it was made of glass. *No surprise that the owner of* that *sword didn't last long.*

Another shelf was devoted to footwear. Most came in pairs, but here and there Jig saw a lone boot or sandal. For the first time he understood a little of Barius's greed. If not for the portcullis, he would have run to the shelves and grabbed every pair he could find. Never again would he have to suffer bruised toes, blistered heels, or cracked toenails. Finding his current pair had been fortunate, but this was treasure indeed. He wondered if he would have time to search for at least one pair that fit better. Maybe those blue ones, with the furry white fringe at the top and red flames painted down the sides. That was the kind of dramatic style any goblin would kill for.

There were helmets and bows, books and gemstones, even a long shelf devoted to what Jig took to be feathers, but Darnak quickly recognized as writing quills.

"What a load of junk," Darnak muttered. "Aside from the gold, that is. And I could take a liking to that peacock quill there. Could make some fine maps with such a pen. Wonder what kind of nib she's got on her?"

"Find the rod," Barius said. "Once the rod is safely in our possession, you may help yourself to any booty you wish. But first, find the rod."

Riana cleared her throat. "What does it look like?"

Nobody answered.

Jig fought a sudden attack of giggles. He looked at Riana, whose incredulity was plain in her wide eyes.

"You don't know?" she asked.

"The rod was hidden here thousands of years ago. No man has seen it since, and the bards of old did not see fit to describe it in song." Was it Jig's imagination, or was Barius blushing? "I presumed my brother would be able to identify it through his art."

"I've spotted a mess of quarterstaves there, by the waterline." Darnak pointed. "Could your rod be mixed in with that bunch for camouflage?"

Barius rubbed his hands together like a man preparing for a feast. "Our course is simple. We must search the dragon's lair before it returns." He looked up and down at the portcullis, clearly offended that someone had dared impede his quest with such a mundane obstacle. As they waited for him to speak again, it became equally clear that he had no idea how to get past it.

Darnak grabbed one of the bars and gave it a tug. Pressing the side of his face to the gate, he stared up into the ceiling, where presumably the portcullis went when raised. "I'm not seeing any chains or gears up there. Mechanism must be on the other side."

Jig frowned. If the mechanism was on the other side, and the cavern was empty, who had closed the gate? Riana was apparently thinking the same thing, because she asked, "Are we sure there's nobody in there?" She and Jig glanced at each other and stepped backward.

"I will not be stopped by iron bars. Not when I am so close." Barius crossed his arms in princely determination. "Darnak, open the gate."

Darnak responded by grabbing his wineskin. He sized up the gate, but didn't appear willing to respond without a drink to bolster his courage. As he pulled the stopper free with his teeth, another voice came from beyond the portcullis.

"Perhaps I can assist you, brother."

"Traitor." Barius lunged at the gate as his brother stepped into view. "Not even Father will raise a hand against me for taking your life. Not after *this*." He shoved his crippled left hand through the bars.

Ryslind frowned. Mind-damaged or not, he had to know he wasn't responsible for his brother's injury. Jig tried to think of something to say, some way to distract them both.

Riana beat him to it. "He's *inside* the lair," she pointed out. "Ryslind must have been the one to lower the bars."

"Indeed, that makes sense." Barius withdrew his hand. "You may have beaten us to the treasure, but you'll not leave this place without defeating us. Hide behind this gate for as long as you want. You cannot wait forever."

"Such an abrasive manner, brother." Ryslind grabbed two

of the bars. "In truth, I did not close the gate. But I believe I can assist you nonetheless."

He closed his eyes and took several deep breaths. Jig could see the red glow of his eyes even through the lids. As though Ryslind's magic was a kind of polishing agent, the iron bars began to gleam. Small ripples spread along the two bars he held.

Ryslind released his grip. Smiling at the group, he reached between the center bars and tapped each one lightly. Like the streams of water outside, the bars turned fluid and moved toward the edge of the tunnel. The flat iron crossbeams trickled to the floor. Soon, instead of an impassible gate, only a ring of black liquid ran around the end of the tunnel.

"Illusion." He tucked his hands back into the sleeves of his robe. "To stop the weak-minded."

Barius's sword hissed free of its scabbard. "Steel, to stop the craven of heart."

"Oh, my brother." Ryslind shook his head in dismay. "So bold, yet so predictable." His eyes flashed, and the blade of Barius's sword vanished at the crossguard.

Barius dropped the useless hilt. "You've always been a coward."

"And you've never learned to compromise. It's why even the goblin beat you at your duel. Your 'honor' and 'nobility' are chains holding you back. Had the goblin offended me, I would have crushed him."

He smiled at Jig, a reminder that the goblin *had* offended him, and that Jig could look forward to a painful death at Ryslind's convenience. "The poor wretch would die as quickly as I would, were I to meet your challenge 'honorably,' sword against sword."

With a twisted sneer, he added, "But you seem to lack a sword, brother. Here, take this instead." He tossed a knife to Barius. Halfway between them, it twisted into a hissing snake.

Darnak's war club knocked it aside before it could strike. The snake bounced off the tunnel wall and fell to the ground, where it became a dagger again.

Barius grabbed for the dagger. "Darnak, help me fight his foul magic."

The dwarf looked at them both. The humans wore mirroring expressions, jaws tight and eyes narrow with determination. "No, I can't be doing that, Barius."

To the prince's outraged expression, he said, "I've served your father for longer than you've been alive. I'll not tell him how I was after killing one of his sons. And if you've any brains at all between the two of you, you'll stop this nonsense. We may have found the ore, but we've yet to haul it from the mine, as the saying goes."

Behind them, the sound of the waves changed. Something had disturbed their rhythm. Jig stared at the lake, noting the low shadow that broke up the reflections on the surface. It moved toward the shore, growing more distinct as it neared the sand. Ripples spread out from the disturbance. A head rose out of the water, and Jig felt a surge of fear streak from the tips of his ears down to his toes.

"Dragon," he said. Tried to, rather. His mouth was too dry to speak.

Barius, still searching for an opening against his brother, hadn't noticed yet. But Darnak did, and his head jerked up as he spotted the dragon sliding out of the water.

"Now there's something I can be pummeling on," he said. "Solve your problems quickly, boys. I'm off to tenderize myself some dragon steak."

Barius finally saw the dragon. "We shall resolve this at a later time. For now, there is a common foe to slay."

Twirling his club over his head, Darnak charged into the room toward the dripping dragon. Barius followed close behind, his knife looking like a joke before the dragon's bulk.

Jig glanced at Riana. Their eyes met, and they nodded in silent agreement. Leaving the humans and dwarf to meet their respective painful deaths, they ran back down the tunnel as fast as their feet could move.

"A common foe to slay," Riana gasped, mimicking the prince's crystalline enunciation. "Though maybe Straum will laugh himself to death when he sees Barius's weapon. I swear, it's a wonder there are any humans left."

Jig saved his energy for running, not talking. The tunnel

was wide enough; he only bumped the walls twice in the darkness, neither time losing more than a bit of skin against the rock. Riana had a harder time, being less accustomed to darkness. She fell several times, cursing like a dwarf every time she scrambled back to her feet.

I should help her. But another part of Jig's brain overruled that idea, the part that argued, *If she's behind me, that's one more thing between me and the dragon*. Not terribly noble, but he and Ryslind were in agreement on the usefulness of nobility. As Barius had so aptly demonstrated time after time, nobility was the first step toward suicide.

In this case, however, he might have been better off to wait for Riana after all, or even to let her go first. Yes, far better for *him* to have followed *her* out of the tunnel. That way she would be the one to face the large figure silhouetted against the mouth of the tunnel.

Jig clenched his teeth and ran faster, ignoring the cramps in his legs. He was short and skinny. Big creatures tended to be slow. If Jig was quick enough, maybe he could slip past the thing, whatever it was.

He wasn't quick enough. Nor was this big thing at all slow. A long arm snapped out and caught the back of his loincloth so fast that Jig never saw the movement. He grunted as his rope belt bent him double and took his breath away. The arm lifted him effortlessly into the air. Jig grabbed at the creature, but it was awfully hard to get a good grip on something behind his back. He scraped the thing's wrist and felt scales, but he couldn't break free.

Slowly he found himself turned around to face the creature. When he saw what held him, he stopped struggling and concentrated on looking small and harmless. For now he knew what had killed the ogres.

The thing stood a head shorter than an ogre, but Jig would have happily faced all three ogres by himself rather than fight this beast. Dark bronze scales the size of large coins covered most of its body, with lighter scales along the belly and chest. Its legs were jointed like an animal's, so it stood with its thighs hinged up close to the stomach. A long tail helped it balance. As Jig watched, the tail twitched back and forth, causing the barbs at the end to smash against the wall. The creature didn't seem to feel any pain from the impact.

The head was a miniature version of the dragon's that Jig had seen coming out of the water, and he would have been happier had he never gotten the chance to examine it so closely. Curved white teeth lined its long, flat jaws. The eyes were golden, with slitted pupils. Twin horns spiraled back from behind its small tufted ears.

Jig glanced at the nostrils, watching them widen and close as the thing breathed. *Could it breathe fire?* he wondered. Then he banished that thought, afraid one of the gods might hear him and decide to satisfy his curiosity.

Something tickled his back. Jig craned his head and saw Smudge hastening toward his belt pouch. Before, Smudge had fought like a cornered tunnel cat to avoid the pouch. Faced with this thing that had snagged Jig so easily, the fire-spider had obviously decided that maybe the pouch wasn't as bad as he thought.

"Don't struggle, little one," the dragon-thing said. The voice sounded male, though Jig saw no evidence either way on its naked body. But dragons were probably built differently than goblins, and Jig wasn't about to ask. "Once I have your friend, we'll be on our way back to Straum."

His breath smelled like rotting meat. Jig wondered what he ate, and again decided he was better off not knowing.

Riana's footsteps came closer, then faltered as she fell yet again. Jig could hear her saying, ". . . going to kill you, Jig. Leave me behind, will you? I'll take a strip of your skin for every one of these bruises. You owe me a finger anyway."

He almost wished she'd have the chance to take her revenge. Without thinking, he cupped his hands to his mouth and screamed, "Riana, run!"

One golden eye swiveled at Jig, and he wisely shut his mouth. "Very well," the thing said. "The hard way."

He pulled Jig close against his body, and Jig felt the spring of powerful muscles as his captor leaped into the air. Clawed feet scraped against the wall and launched them another twenty feet down the tunnel, where he bounced onto the opposite wall. Three more bounds took them to where Riana stood, torn as to which way to run.

Even had she fled as soon as she heard Jig's warning, it would have gained her only a few seconds. As easily as Smudge had caught the fly, the creature pounced and snagged Riana's tunic in his claws. He tucked Riana under his other arm and continued at a slower pace toward Straum's lair. As Jig fought to keep from throwing up and waited for the tunnels to stop spinning, he heard Riana mutter, "I *hate* this place."

The creature dropped Jig and Riana in the sand. He was so confident, he hadn't even bothered to take Jig's sword or Riana's knife. Not that it mattered. Riana had managed to squirm enough to slash at the creature's arm. Against those scales, she might as well have attacked the stone walls.

"Ah, your friends have returned." Straum's bronze body rested half-submerged in the lake. His front legs sank into the sand, and his long neck stretched just high enough to let him look down at his newest captives. "I was telling your friends about my collection of chamber pots. So many adventurers bring their own. That way they don't leave as much of a trail to follow. I have one hundred and thirteen. Fourteen, now that I've claimed Barius's pot as well. Ingenious, the way the lid twists into place so perfectly. I'd guess that elven craftsmanship went into this beauty."

Straum picked up the gold-trimmed chamber pot, which looked like a porcelain bead in his claws. "I'll have one of my children clean it out. The flowers can always use an extra bit of fertilizer." He tilted the pot. "Not terribly decorative, though. No artistic style. See that blue pot on the third shelf? That belonged to a barbarian lord named Terinor."

The indicated pot was covered in cloisonné images of huge muscular men and women, their hands raised high as if they were trying to raise the sky. The wide-rimmed top appeared to be cushioned in leather and trimmed with red jewels. It suddenly occurred to Jig that, were the owner to sit on the leather, the men and women would appear to hold him up.

The chamber pot was easily one of the tackiest things he had ever seen, and he felt a wash of pity for those poor bearers of barbarian buttocks.

"Very nice," Barius said sharply. "And now that our companion has been returned, perhaps you can get on with the matter of our deaths." He stood with Darnak on the other side of the dragon. Behind them, Ryslind had taken their weapons and watched the proceedings with a smile. Even Jig could see that, unlike the others, Ryslind was no prisoner.

"Oh, but I so rarely have company," Straum protested. His voice was like an earthquake, though his serpentine tongue gave him a bit of a lisp when he spoke Human. "Most people never make it past the Necromancer. If they even find him. I had such a good time watching you figure that out."

He tilted his head toward two small pools that Jig hadn't seen before. No more than puddles a little way from shore, a short wall of clear glass bricks surrounded and protected each one. The surfaces were so still it was like looking at a pair of mirrors. Instead of reflecting Straum's muscular bulk, Jig saw a whirling pillar of water at the center of an empty room when he studied the nearest pool. A small corpse lay to one side, next to an enormous throne. *The Necromancer's room.* He wondered how the magic could show so much detail when the throne room itself was dark.

Flecks of color sparkled across the both pools, and finally Jig understood the purpose for those two decorative ceilings in the shiny room and the Necromancer's throne room. Straum had been watching them, probably since that first confrontation where Jig betrayed his captain.

While Jig wrestled with a new wave of fear, Straum gestured to a wall full of lanterns. "See that one, with the handle shaped like a naked eight-armed woman? That belonged to Erik the Eunuch. Used to be a slave of some eastern emperor. Once he built a name for himself, he had everything he owned redesigned with a kind of 'melon-breasted naked woman motif.' Personally, I think it's a blatant example of overcompensating."

Lowering his head toward Barius, he asked, "Tell me, do women of such proportions truly exist among your people? If so, are they able to walk upright like the rest of your species?"

"And where in your fine collection do you keep the Rod of Creation, oh great worm?" Barius asked, ignoring the question.

Straum began to laugh. Whitecapped waves crossed the lake as the dragon's chest heaved, and Jig flattened his ears to block the worst of the sound. It was a terrible laugh, one that combined fury and bitterness with genuine mirth. Straum's head and neck slid through the sand until his mouth rested mere feet from the prince.

"Therein lies Ellnorein's greatest joke. 'Twas a joke played as much on you as on me." His voice dropped to a whisper, though a whisper from Straum's mouth still blew Barius's black hair backward. "I don't have it."

"No! You're the guardian," Barius protested. "You must have it. This is a trick! You seek to gull me." His head whipped around as he scanned the shelves.

"No trick, brother," Ryslind said. "Ellnorein had no choice, you see. The rod needed to be safe from even the most powerful adventurers, so his first step was to trap the most powerful creature he could find and imprison him here, at the heart of the mountain. In thousands of years, no party has survived an encounter with Straum.

"Ellnorein knew this would happen. He predicted the tales of wealth, the fame that would draw adventurers from around the world in search of the rod, all of them intent on battling their way here. Many die before they reach this point. Others flee after a few encounters. A fortunate few live long enough to again see the light of the sun."

Straum growled at that. "*They* see sunlight." His claws began to flex in the sand, and Jig could imagine those claws tearing thousands of years' worth of adventurers into scraps of meat. "*I* have been trapped here, alone, for so long that I cannot remember what it feels like to be free."

Clouds of hot smoke formed around his nostrils. "I can

create an entire world of illusion, but I can't break these walls. All the illusion in the world cannot change the fact that I am a prisoner. I could grind an ordinary mountain to dust and scatter it on the wind, but Ellnorein, damn him to the lowest pit in the Shadow-elves' icy hell, used the rod to form these caverns and tunnels. Rod-created rock resists lesser magic, including my own. Only the rod can free me."

Ryslind ducked past Straum's mouth, probably afraid that the dragon might loose a jet of fire in his fury. "That is why Ellnorein couldn't leave the rod here," he explained. "Straum, being a created creature, could not use it himself. But like all dragons, Straum collects followers. Ogres, trolls, and other creatures you haven't yet seen. One of them could have used the rod, either to free the dragon, or for their own use. It had to be hidden, but hidden so well that nobody would ever be able to use it."

"Why not encase it in the mountain?" Darnak asked. "Why all this nonsense with the tunnels and the monsters? He had to know that would bring adventurers like beggars converging on a feast."

"The rod's magic is like a living thing," Ryslind said. "Left alone, its magic would have seeped into the mountain itself, the effects could be . . . unfortunate. It had to be left somewhere those effects would go unnoticed."

Straum sighed, and smoke shot across the room. "If I had the rod, I would give it to you with my blessing and send you on your way. I would give you all of my gold, every treasure I own, if you only used the rod to release me. Do you know how bloody *bored* I've been? I tried talking to the other creatures for a while. But the ogres talk about nothing but fighting and food, and as for the trolls, they're a bit too clever. They kept trying to steal from me, and I grew tired of disintegrating them. The smell of burned troll is, by far, one of the most nauseating scents in the world."

Jig thought of privy duty and disagreed. The corpses at the mouth of the tunnel had been almost pleasant by comparison. But he kept his argument to himself.

"I taught myself magic from the spellbooks I collected.

The trick was to kill the wizards without damaging their books. A difficult trick, since your races use such flammable materials for books. Though there was one fellow, a bright young lad, who had his spells engraved on brass plates. Heavy book, but it survived just fine."

Another tuft of smoke floated from Straum's nostrils, and Jig tried not to wonder what had happened to the owner of that book.

"That killed a century or two. But all too soon, I was better at magic than the wizards who approached me, and the fun began to wane. And then I created my children."

The dragonlike creature that had captured Jig and Riana stepped forward. Head raised, it seemed to preen before Straum's proud gaze.

"Your children?" Darnak asked. "Don't tell me you've got a lady dragon hidden away in that lake."

"If only there were." Straum's eyes glazed. "I haven't flown a mating dance in five thousand two hundred and twelve years. While I may have forgotten most of the surface world, I still remember the scrape of scales against scales, the lashing of tails, the twining of necks."

He shivered, and his scales puffed out, turning him a darker bronze. Jig was thankful that the lake concealed the dragon's lower body. This adventure had given him nightmares enough already without the extra fuel of an aroused dragon.

"No, I used magic to create them. They're fairly intelligent, stronger than anything else down here, and excellent company. Their only flaws are arrogance and a powerful loyalty to one another that tends to override their common sense. You were tracking this one back to his lair, Barius. Had your brother not diverted your party, you would have been slaughtered the moment you threatened his offspring."

Which meant that by diverting them here, Ryslind had saved their lives. Jig glanced at Barius.

Taken aback, the prince said nothing. The stoniness of his face as he studied Ryslind was an expression Jig had come to recognize. It was the expression Barius wore when he had made a mistake, but wasn't yet willing to admit it.

"Yes, my children are a clear improvement over the low creatures Ellnorein abandoned me with," Straum said. He gave Jig a dismissive nod. "Goblins. Ogres. Trolls. Worthless creatures. But I'm afraid that even my children have their flaws."

Jig wasn't sure, but he thought he saw *this* dragonchild's eyes narrow with suspicion.

"See, in order to keep them interesting, I had to give them a bit of independence. Sadly, it goes to their heads from time to time. This one plans to bring me a poisoned deer and take my place as ruler."

Before anyone could move, his head shot toward the dragonchild, who had time for one shrill scream before Straum's jaws closed over its head with a loud crack. The headless body crumpled.

Jig began to shake. For all Straum's bulk, he had moved faster than any creature Jig had ever seen. He watched as Straum's tongue flicked out to clean dark blood from his teeth.

"He'll not get any more ideas into his head," Straum said. When nobody spoke, he added, "That was a joke."

Jig forced himself to smile. *Yes, that was a good joke. Please don't eat me.*

"I can read their minds, you see. I never mention that detail to them. I fear they might react badly."

"How did my brother know where that thing was going?" Barius asked. His toe nudged the headless body.

"There are many ways to grow in the magical arts," Ryslind said. He stepped forward to stand next to Straum's head. The dragon closed his eyes and pulled his lips back. Ryslind drew a dagger and began to clean between the huge teeth. Thankfully Jig couldn't see well enough to identify what that stringy bit used to be.

Ryslind continued to explain as he worked. "I went off alone to seek a teacher, someone who could show me *real* power. I sent my spirit questing for the most powerful wizard around. I found Straum."

"Thank you," Straum said. Ryslind nodded respectfully and retreated. "Novices do that from time to time. Foolish, really. There's a shock when two spirits touch. I understand they seek quick power, but to seek that power from me is like a small child who stands in front of a charging stallion hoping for a ride. Fortunately, this stallion decided not to trample your brother."

"My master had grown bored once again." Ryslind smiled. "He offered me a deal. He would give me magic that the most powerful warlock might envy."

"Magic, yes," Straum said. "But power was another matter. No matter how stubborn he might be, Ryslind's power was limited. Every time he overexerted himself, he drew on my strength to help him. I'm afraid it was too much for his poor mind. Like a weak branch beneath winter snow, it snapped. What could I do but replace it with my own? I locked him away in his own mind so he wouldn't cause any more harm. Otherwise he could have injured himself in his greed."

"You used him, you bloody oversized snake." Darnak kicked the corpse out of the way as he stormed toward Straum. "You killed him. Where's my club? Earthmaker help me, I'll crack you open like a walnut, you damned dragon."

"I warned him," Straum shrugged. His tongue flicked out and slapped Darnak in the face, knocking him to the sand. "But he accepted both the terms of my agreement and the risk it would involve."

Barius grabbed Darnak's arm before the dwarf could resume his charge. Darnak actually dragged him several yards before coming to a grudging halt.

"What were the terms?" Barius asked.

"I can't send anyone in search of the rod. Most are too stupid, and my own children might attempt to betray me. I've attempted to create mindless creatures I could use as puppets, but they lack the wit to find the rod. That was why I created the Necromancer's fountain. A simple warlock used to control those tunnels. I thought I could animate his corpse and use that in my search. I failed. The upper levels are too alien to me, and I could not find what I needed.

"I required someone who would give me control, but who retained a spark of intelligence. Someone who might discover where Ellnorein hid the rod. I found Ryslind. In exchange for my power, he offered to bring me a group of adventurers who could retrieve the Rod of Creation and set me free."

CHAPTER 15

Stirring Up Trouble

JIG HAD NEVER NOTICED THE SMELL OF HOME before. Like the smell of his own sweat, it was simply *there*. But as he crouched low against a wall, listening to the growls and curses up the tunnel, he found himself smiling at the familiar odors. The earthiness of the carrion-worm trails, the distant smoke of cooking meat, the moist, fishy smell of the lake . . . it all blended together to create *home*.

"Watch yourself, lads!" Darnak's shout was followed by the crack of wood against flesh. A tunnel cat yowled in pain.

"That's another one down," Riana commented. She sat opposite Jig, her back against the wall in an almost identical position of boredom.

"How long do you think it will take?" Jig asked.

She peeked around the bend. "Looks like at least five or six more cats. How many do the hobgoblins have?"

"I've never tried to count them." Jig leaned his head against the rock and closed his eyes. The tunnel split off past the tunnel cats, but there was no way to get to it until the adventurers took care of the cats. Or until the cats took care of the adventurers, he supposed. Funny, but after standing before Straum in the dragon's lair, the huge albino cats just weren't as frightening.

Jig crawled over to see the battle for himself. Another cat

pounced, only to die on Barius's sword. Over the generations, the cats' eyes had grown to the size of Jig's palm, letting them see perfectly in the faintest light. Their ears were better than his, and their noses were equally keen. Fortunately, the same inbreeding that left them mean-tempered and rapier-swift had given them weak hips. If you could avoid that first leap, as Barius had done, they tended to stumble.

Not that it mattered. The cats were silent as shadows, and few goblins ever noticed their presence before being seized by the neck, shaken, and dragged back to the cats' nest.

Still, tunnel cats or no, Jig would much rather be here, under siege by the hobgoblins' pets, than wandering the empty tunnels of the Necromancer's lair. For the past two days they had searched every alcove, room, and corridor. Darnak came up with the idea that the rod might be hidden within the fountain, so the group had smashed those beautiful crystalline dragons to dust. The Necromancer's throne had been similarly pulverized, thanks to a bit of Ryslind's magic. But the rod was nowhere to be found.

Claws scrabbled against stone. Barius yelled. A rushing sound and a squeal of pain signaled another of Ryslind's spells. Without a word, Jig and Riana moved a bit farther down the tunnel, trying to get away from the scent of burned fur and flesh.

"I almost feel sorry for them," Riana said.

"Why?" The more tunnel cats that died, the fewer there would be left to pounce on Jig in the darkness.

"Ryslind."

"Oh." The wizard hadn't spoken since they left Straum's lair, except to cast the occasional spell. He had used a bit of magic to help them find their way through the sky, into the Necromancer's throne room. A few bolts of fire had scared away the giant bats on the bridge. He had also incinerated a swarm of rats they found in one of the alcoves in the hallway. Jig didn't know how much power Ryslind had at his disposal, but if he could draw energy from a five-thousand-year-old dragon, he probably wouldn't dry up anytime soon.

"I say we charge," Darnak shouted, sounding winded but eager. "If we can scare 'em good enough, they'll turn tail and head straight back to their masters. We can follow them in and use the confusion to start bashing hobgoblins."

Jig crawled back to take another look. Four cats lay dead, two from Ryslind's magic, and the others from more mundane wounds. The corpses didn't seem to deter the other cats, which werc as stubborn as they were dangerous. Several more of the snarling beasts had joined their fellows and now waited for the chance to attack. Only a narrow bottleneck in the tunnel kept them from charging as a pack.

Riana scooted close to Jig's side. The instant she started to whisper, Jig knew what she was going to ask.

"Do you know where the rod is?"

Jig bit his lip to keep from sighing. In the past few days, everyone had pulled him aside to ask if he knew the rod's hiding place. Barius had threatened to torture him. Darnak hinted that helping to find the rod might be Jig's only hope of getting through this alive. As for Ryslind, when he asked about the rod, Jig had sensed Straum watching him from behind that glowing gaze. Jig hadn't been able to think of anything except Straum's terrible jaws closing over the helpless dragonchild.

"No," Jig answered. Didn't they realize he would happily give them the rod if he could only go home?

He watched as Darnak and Barius charged up the tunnel, the former shouting a dwarven battle cry. They returned a few seconds later, Darnak swatting furiously at the cat that had locked its jaws onto the dwarf's forearm. If not for his thick bracers, Darnak's arm would have been nothing but shredded meat. He managed to hurl the cat against the wall. It whined and crawled away, dragging its paralyzed hindquarters along the ground.

Jig closed his eyes and breathed deeply. He wasn't worried about the cats. The adventurers would win or else they wouldn't. Either way, there wasn't much Jig could do about it. He just wanted to be done with it.

Was he imagining things, or could he smell the faint spice of Golaka's ever-simmering cauldron? Thinking about food made his mouth water painfully. He reached up to his shoulder and stroked Smudge's head. The fire-spider evidently recognized home as well, for his head was high, and he kept turning around, as if searching for familiar landmarks.

Although it felt good to be home, everything seemed strange as well. Knowing his fellow goblins would likely kill him didn't help his comfort, but there was more. Like the smells. He never would have noticed them before. The tunnels themselves felt smaller, too. Was it only because he had been beyond them, because he knew how much more there was past goblin territory?

Yet he still knew so little. He hadn't seen all of Straum's lair, nor had he explored much of those woods. He didn't know where else the Necromancer's not-really-bottomless pit might lead. He didn't even know where the rod was. If Barius and the others were right and it was here, then Jig had lived his entire life within walking distance of one of the most powerful magical artifacts in history.

He inhaled again and remembered Straum's description of the rod. *A seemingly innocent wooden rod, wide as a human's thumb and a little over three feet long.* In other words, a stick. It could be anything from a piece of a door to the chief hobgoblin's favorite tool for scratching between his toes. Magic wouldn't detect it, and the emanations of power would appear natural to those around it, since their wills would shape the way that power manifested. Basically, the thing was next to invisible.

Barius and Darnak charged again. This time, Ryslind helped by sending several arrows past them and into the pack. Perhaps he used magic to augment his skill, for two cats whined in pain and fled. A huge male leaped at Darnak, only to fall as Barius lodged his sword between the cat's ribs. Its spasms wrenched the sword out of Barius's hands, and it wound up trapped beneath the cat's dying body. Fortunately, the rest of the pack had finally seen enough. As one, they turned and fled.

"Come on, then," Darnak yelled. "We'll rout the mangy furballs all the way back to their masters."

Barius had one foot on the dead tunnel cat and was trying to free his sword. His sword wouldn't budge, so he ended up on the floor, both feet against the cat, tugging with all his might. When the sword finally did come free, Jig shook his head at the prince's luck. At that angle, the blade had come within inches of turning the prince into a princess.

Barius didn't notice. He scrambled to his feet and raced after Darnak, his long stride helping him close the distance.

"Come on," Riana said wearily.

Jig hesitated as he thought about the plan Barius had shared as they left the Necromancer's lair. It was both simple and terrible. They intended to use Ryslind's magic and their own considerable fighting skill until every last hobgoblin died or surrendered. Which sounded fine to Jig. If the hobgoblins were out of the picture, that was one less thing for him to worry about. The only question was how long it would take. Hundreds of hobgoblins lived down that tunnel, and they wouldn't simply line up in a neat single-file line to die. In true hobgoblin style, they would set traps, attempt ambushes, and terrorize the tunnel cats into another attack. But in the end, whether by Barius's sword or Ryslind's mystic fire, they *would* die.

Like goblins, the hobgoblins always lost to the heroes. Unfair as it seemed to Jig, Barius and the others were the heroes.

Jig stopped. If the hobgoblins didn't have the rod, what would happen next?

Lantern light faded behind him as he moved toward the right branch of the tunnel, slipping into a jog, then an all-out run as he abandoned the others.

"Where are you going?" Riana yelled.

He ignored her. He knew what would happen if the adventurers didn't find the rod. Once they slaughtered the hobgoblins, the only place left to search would be the goblin lair.

Jig stopped to catch his breath. He heard Riana coming up behind him. She must have followed the sound of his footsteps. Was this the same girl who had cowered in darkness a few days ago? She had changed too, apparently.

He could see the red flicker of torches up ahead. A part of Jig wanted to run past the guards and into the main cavern, to curl up in his corner and forget about everything. He could lie about what had happened, say the surface-dwellers had used magic to make him betray his captain. The next time they chose him for patrol, he would think of some excuse to stay at home. So what if they branded him a coward. At least he could live the rest of his life without having to see another dragon or adventurer.

Except that he knew it wouldn't work that way. If he was lucky, one day might go by before Barius brought the others here.

Maybe Jig could convince the goblins to negotiate. If the goblins gave Barius permission to search for the rod, there would be no cause for bloodshed. But even as he tried to figure out a way to persuade the other goblins, he knew it wouldn't work. Barius *wanted* bloodshed as much as any goblin. He lived for combat and glory and victory, and every time he cut down an enemy, it made him feel stronger.

Nor would the goblins take kindly to surface-dwellers scrounging through their homes. Sooner or later, and Jig would wager on sooner, one of them would try to put a knife in someone's back.

On Jig's shoulder, Smudge waved his forelegs in excitement. He recognized these tunnels and knew they had come home. He couldn't understand that Jig might be killed as soon as one of the guards spotted him. Nor could he know that, even if they survived, it would only be to die as soon as the adventurers arrived.

So why had he come back? Why not stay with the others? At least that way, when they killed the goblins, they might have let Jig live. If Jig was here when Barius arrived, they would kill him without a second thought. They probably wouldn't even know it was him. All goblins looked alike, after all.

Shadowstar, I could use a little help down here. How am I supposed to survive what's coming?

The god's answer was brief and discouraging. *If I think of something, I'll let you know.*

Jig started to laugh. Not even a god could think up a way out of this. In the past few days, Jig had come within inches of being eaten, drowned, poisoned, zombiefied, ripped apart, and if you included having to live on bread, starving to death.

He could be an entire song all by himself. "The Hundred Deaths of Jig the Goblin." If he was going to die anyway, why not add a few more deaths to the song by storming back into the clan and trying to prepare for the inevitable battle?

"Keep going," Jig said when Riana caught up. He pointed down the tunnel. "You should reach the way out in a little under an hour."

"I can't." When Jig cocked his head in confusion, Riana explained, "I'd have to go through that room with the glass ceiling. Straum would see me. If he realized I was trying to escape, he might think I had the rod. And he can talk to Ryslind."

Jig nodded. She was right. Ryslind would be after her in a heartbeat. *They might already be after us. They probably think we know where the rod is, which means they won't bother with the hobgoblins. We don't have a day after all. They'll come as soon as they realize we're missing.*

"Come on." Straightening his shoulders, Jig walked past the goblin marker and into the tunnel. Riana followed, knife in hand.

"What are we doing?" Riana asked.

Jig didn't get to answer. Up ahead, he spotted the two guards. One carried an old spear, the other a club. After spending so much time with Darnak, Jig wasn't impressed with the club. It looked like an old table leg. Darnak would have knocked it into splinters, right before doing the same to the goblin's skull.

"What are you doing out there?" the one with the spear asked. Getting a better look, he said, "Jig? Is that you?"

"You're in trouble," said the other. "We hear you killed Porak."

Jig didn't break stride. They thought *he* had killed Porak? How marvelous! He wondered how much the story had grown in the past few days. Never mind . . . so long as they thought he was dangerous, maybe he had a chance.

The guards pointed their weapons at him. "Who's the elf?" one asked. "Did you bring her back as a gift for Porak's friends?"

"Wait," Jig said, more for Riana than the guards. Another comment like that, and the guard would find himself eating

Riana's knife for a snack. "She was with the surface-dwellers. We're going to see the chief."

"Uh . . ." The guards looked at each other uncertainly. "You can't."

Jig walked right past them, motioning for Riana to follow. He had counted on this. Goblins didn't go in for sneakiness. If Jig was the enemy, he should have attacked immediately. Instead Jig acted like nothing was wrong. Like he *belonged* here. He could imagine their confusion.

"Wait," one said. Jig glanced back to see the guard's spear leveled at his back. "I don't know if we should let her in there with you. She's got a knife, you know."

Jig spoke quickly. "She's with me. The other adventurers will be here soon. You should worry about them instead."

The one with the club looked nervous, but the other shook his head. "Porak's friends are mean, and they'll have my head if they find out I let you live. Besides we haven't had elf meat in months." He jabbed his spear in Riana's direction, forcing her to hop back.

Jig nodded. He should have known it wouldn't work. Maybe heroes and adventurers could get away with this sort of trick, but Jig obviously wasn't good enough to make it work. So he would have to do this the hard way.

He stepped closer to the guard, who frowned. Jig had again done something unexpected. *He's wondering why I don't run away,* Jig guessed. If goblins were better trained with their weapons, would this one have realized that the last thing he should do was allow Jig to get inside his guard? If Jig hadn't watched the way the others used their different weapons, would it even have occurred to him to try?

Probably not, he decided. He drew his sword and attacked. The guard snarled and tried to swing his spear, but Jig was too close. The shaft bounced off his shoulder, hard enough to hurt, but nothing more.

Remembering one of Barius's moves, Jig took a quick half-step and lunged. He overbalanced and almost fell, but his sword bit into the guard's stomach. Jig caught himself, pulled the sword free, and spun around before the other guard had figured out what was happening.

Jig pointed his sword at the other guard, ignoring the groaning goblin on the floor. Doing his best to mimic Barius in voice and posture, he said, "I told you we need to see the chief."

"But . . ." The guard glanced at his bleeding companion. He stared at the sword in Jig's hand, his eyes focusing on the blue smear of blood. He took a step back, and the tip of Jig's sword followed him.

"Right," he said meekly. "Sorry about that."

Jig nodded. He lowered his sword, hoping the guard hadn't noticed how his arm shook. Dramatic poses were *hard*! Even a short sword got heavy if you held it outstretched for very long.

"Come on," he said to Riana. He led them down the tunnel toward the main cavern. He hoped he hadn't killed the guard. He had come here to *help* the goblins. Though eliminating some of the stupider guards might be construed as helping. He would have to think about that later. For now, getting past the guards had been the easy part. Getting past the hundreds of goblins they were sure to encounter next would be a much larger challenge.

Apparently Riana was having similar thoughts. As they neared the jagged entrance, she whispered, "Do you have a plan, or was this just another way to commit suicide?"

"Suicide," Jig answered. Plans were for adventurers. He preferred the goblin approach. Blind panic might not work all the time, but at least it saved you the stress of planning.

He blinked. Panic might be exactly what he needed. His jaw jutted into a wide grin. "Come on," he said, grabbing Riana's arm.

"If this doesn't work, I'm going to make sure you die with me." But she sounded resigned, not angry.

"If this doesn't work, I'm sure I will."

A hundred goblin voices washed together in a low roar as they walked into the room. The noise died within seconds as the goblins stared at Jig and Riana, trying to understand what they were doing here, so obviously out of place. At any moment, someone would cry out and send the cavern into total chaos. Jig wanted to make sure that someone was him.

"Adventurers!" he screamed at top volume. He waved his bloody sword in the air, hoping nobody would remember that adventurers tended to bleed red, not blue. "They're attacking the guards! Where's the chief? I have a deserter from their party who can help."

Whispers spread like lice, and Jig heard his name mentioned a number of times. Nobody moved. Didn't they believe him? He waved his sword again. Riana swore at him and wiped off the dots of blood which had sprayed from his sword onto her sleeve.

"What did you say?" she asked.

He had forgotten she didn't speak Goblin. "I told them the adventurers were coming, and you were going to help us."

"Oh." She chewed her lip for a second, then shouted, "They've rallied the hobgoblins and their tunnel cats. They're coming to steal your women and children."

"And our food!" Jig added.

That earned a much stronger response, at least from those who understood Human. Goblins everywhere scrambled for weapons or ran deeper into the warrens to hide. More the latter than the former, but at least they were moving. More importantly, nobody had tried to kill him.

The chief had a large room behind the kitchen, so that he could eat whenever he felt like it. Jig's stomach grumbled at the thought.

"Come on." He struggled through the crowd of goblins, toward the far side of the cavern. Riana followed close behind.

Strong fingers grabbed Jig's wrist. The goblin's grip was weak compared to the dragonchild's, but it was still too powerful for Jig to break. "How do we know this isn't a trick?" the goblin demanded.

Jig felt a moment of bizarre relief. *At least we aren't* all *gullible*. The fact that it could cost him his life took some of the satisfaction away, though. The other goblin had Jig's sword arm, and his fangs were almost an inch longer than Jig's.

The goblin's eyes widened. He looked down. Following his gaze, Jig saw a dagger sticking out of his side. Silently the goblin fell.

"You blindsided him," Jig said, impressed.

"I'm a thief. We're sneaky that way."

A few other goblins had seen what happened, and Jig's stomach tightened as a crowd began to form around him and Riana. They were close to the kitchen. All he needed was a few minutes with the chief. After that Jig would probably die, and Riana would go into the pot, but at least he would have warned them about Barius and the others.

He pulled out his sword and screamed. Compared to Darnak's battle cry, Jig sounded more like a frightened rat than a warrior, but it worked. Goblins fell back, startled and uncertain. Jig dashed through the gap and into the kitchen, Riana stepping on his heels as she ran.

Golaka scowled at him as he entered. "What are you doing, barging in like that? It's another hour before dinner."

The noise dropped as he entered the kitchen. Nobody followed. Few goblins dared intrude when Golaka was cooking, which was most of the time.

Golaka the chef was the largest goblin Jig had ever known. While not quite as tall as the average hobgoblin, she easily surpassed them in terms of bulk. The goblins liked to joke that you wouldn't be able to tell Golaka from her cauldron if it weren't for the fact that she never stopped complaining.

Jig figured her size was an occupational hazard. How could you spend day after day manning the kitchen without snacking a bit? But Golaka was as much muscle as fat, and she pulled out her stirring spoon and shook it at Jig like a broadsword. "Jig, isn't it? Are you the one causing all that commotion? And what's this morsel here? She's a skinny one, isn't she? Couldn't find anyone with more meat on her bones, I suppose."

Jig gave quick thanks to Tymalous Shadowstar that Riana couldn't understand Goblin. "Golaka, where's the chief?"

"Dead. He went looking for those adventurers and ran into a hobgoblin ambush. Seems there's been all sorts of excitement these past few days. Means everyone will be all stirred up, no doubt. Fighting over who gets to be the new chief and all that nonsense."

Jig's body went numb. He dropped his sword. Dead? He

had fought through the entire goblin lair, only to learn that the chief was dead?

"Long as I can remember, it's always the same. Adventurers come in and cause trouble. Bunch of young goblins run out and get themselves killed. Another patrol goes out and ambushes the adventurers. I end up with a few more bodies for the pot and a dozen less mouths to feed.

"At least they'll bring in some wood for the fire. A few arrows, maybe an axe handle or something. Haven't had any new wood in almost a month, since that hobgoblin trader slipped and fell on my carving knife."

Jig ignored her. The shock was so great that his entire body tingled. He stared at the scraps of wood burning merrily beneath her pot. If Golaka was telling the truth, they had continued to burn for *an entire month* without any new fuel.

She snorted. "That'll teach those hobgoblins to get fresh with *me*. Of all the raw nerve. He's lucky I didn't make sausages out of his worthless guts. All for the best, though. Hobgoblin causes indigestion something fierce."

The emanations of the rod would appear natural, shaped by the wills of those around it. "Golaka," he said, voice hoarse. "Have you ever run out of wood for the fire or food for the cauldron?"

"Course not," she snapped. "Though why you young know-it-alls can't bring me a fresh human from time to time is beyond me."

Golaka had run the kitchen for as long as Jig could remember. Older goblins would sometimes tell stories about meals she had made when *they* were children. How long had she been alive? Could *anyone* remember a time when someone else cooked here?

Goblins rarely died of old age, a sad fact Jig had never before stopped to consider. So nobody really knew how long a goblin could expect to live. But surely Golaka had long ago exceeded her life span.

Jig stared at her with such intensity that she actually stopped in midrant, an occurrence unheard of in goblin history.

"What's the matter? I suddenly turn beautiful or something?" She laughed loudly. "Not nice to stare, Jig. And I'm afraid you're a bit too young for me." She took her stirring spoon and smacked him on the arm, splashing broth onto his stomach.

Jig ignored the burning broth as he stared at the spoon. The brass head topped a wooden handle. A simple, unadorned wooden handle, about a yard long.

"What is it, Jig?" Riana followed his stare, and her sudden gasp told him that she had reached the same conclusion.

They had found the Rod of Creation.

CHAPTER 16

Fetching the Rod

JIG SNATCHED FOR THE ROD. GOLAKA STEPPED back, and the heavy spoon crashed onto Jig's head as he stumbled past. He staggered, white spots floating across his vision.

"Stupid kid," Golaka said. "Get out of here and let me work. Nobody samples the food before mealtime, not even the chief."

"You said the chief was dead."

"That's right, and unless you want to join him, you'll keep your grimy claws to yourself."

Jig leaned against a wall. Maybe he didn't have to do anything more. Darnak had thought a dragon made a fearsome guardian. That was because he had never encountered an angry goblin cook.

Jig could leave Golaka and the rod in peace. When Barius and the others got here, she would pummel them with the rod, throw in a tongue-lashing to make them sorry they ever saw a goblin, and send them on their way. If they protested, well, Golaka could always use more meat for the pot. Yes, that would be much easier.

Riana slipped close to his side and whispered, "Jig, are you okay?"

What a stupid question. But he nodded anyway.

"Good." In a louder voice, she added, "Then let's kill her and get out of here." She leaped toward Golaka, sword flashing in the torchlight.

Jig slapped at his waist. That was *his* sword! Riana had stolen it.

His annoyance was nothing next to Golaka's reaction. Her eyes bulged like a lizard-fish's. Her ears flattened, and her broken fangs scraped against her upper teeth. "Pull a knife on *me*? Not in my kitchen, little elfling. You won't kill Golaka that easily."

She dodged backward and rushed for her butchering table. For all her bulk, she moved as fast as any adventurer. Grabbing a knife in each hand, she spun to face Riana. "You're too small for a meal, but I can make a mean dessert with elf liver and Sweetroot."

Dried blood and other things crusted the blades of her knives. Golaka didn't believe in cleaning her tools, claiming that the remnants of previous meals added flavor. They were still sharp enough to slice Riana into bite-size chunks, though. As a child, Jig used to come watch Golaka cook, so he knew those knives were a far cry from the discarded blades he and the others took to carry on patrol. These could fillet a dwarf in minutes, armor and all.

He didn't know what to do. For the first time, he understood Darnak's struggle when he watched Barius and Ryslind try to kill one another. Like Darnak, Jig didn't want either one of the combatants to die. He could probably grab another weapon and join the fight, but on which side? Stabbing Riana in the back didn't feel right somehow. Even if she *had* swiped his sword. And he certainly couldn't kill Golaka. Who would run the kitchen?

Riana scurried away from a vicious combination of thrusts and swipes. Having watched the others fight, Jig realized she wasn't a much better warrior than he was.

"Hurry, Jig."

Huh? She pointed past him, at the cauldron. That almost cost her a hand as Golaka chopped at her sword wrist. But Jig understood.

Sticking out at an angle from the top of the pot, the Rod

of Creation was unguarded. Jig grabbed the rod and pulled it out of the cauldron. The metal bowl on the end was heavier than he expected, but the rod itself felt like any other stick. Years of handling had smoothed and darkened the wood, turning it deep brown.

"Got it," he shouted. While Riana tried to retreat without taking a knife in the back, he traced a finger through the residue on the bowl and stuck it in his mouth. Delicious. After days of bread, cheese, and smoked meat, Jig was in heaven.

"My spoon!"

Seeing Golaka's rage, Jig changed his mind. He wasn't in heaven after all. Though if Golaka got her hands on him, she would no doubt send him there.

He ran back into the main cave, hoping Riana was behind him but not stopping to check. Not with Golaka swinging knives as if she were the goddess of cutlery. His panicked retreat took him halfway through the cavern before he noticed he was in more trouble than he thought.

"Oops." He should have expected this. He should have wondered why none of the other goblins had followed him into the kitchen. Thinking back, he had heard the tone of the cavern change from confusion and anger to pain and fear. He had simply been too busy to understand what that change meant. "Hello, Barius."

They stood at the entrance of the cavern, looking as though they had come straight out of a goblin's nightmares. Jig remembered the first time he had seen the adventurers and compared their appearance then to the worn, dirty apparitions who now blocked his escape.

Darnak's hair and beard were brown with dirt, and the tangles made him look like a walking nest for mice and other rodents. The fighting had cost him several scales from his armor, leaving bare patches of leather on his stomach, chest, and shoulder.

Prince Barius was even worse. His torn, bloodstained shirt, once immaculate, was little more than a rag. Black stubble covered his face, almost invisible under a layer of sweat-streaked dust. His boots were scuffed, his tights torn and dark with his own blood, and he favored his left leg when he moved. One of his eyes had puffed up with the beginning of a dark bruise.

The wizard showed the least wear. His robes were dirty but otherwise unscathed. His pouches were all in order, and his quiver, now almost empty of arrows, still hung at his side. Where the others looked worn and tired, Ryslind had only grown more dangerous. The emberlike glow of his eyes had intensified until they burned like angry flames, leaving Jig to wonder why the party bothered with the lantern anymore. They could send Ryslind ahead and light up entire tunnels. When Ryslind spoke, Jig could hear the overtones of Straum in his words.

"You found it."

Before Jig could answer, an enraged voice behind him called out, "No, it's mine!"

Golaka managed three steps before a wave of Ryslind's hand flattened her against the wall. Pinned like a child, she could still rail against Jig and Riana and everyone else who had conspired to steal her spoon.

"Wizard, is it? Golaka's not afraid of magic. Haven't seen a wizard yet who could cast a spell with a knife in his gullet. Soon as I get down from here, I'll give you a whipping to make you wish you died before you met me. As for you, little Jig, how funny do you think your little prank is now? You'd better hope the wizard and his friends kill you before I can get my hands on you. I'll twist those ears right off your head and feed them to you."

Darnak gave Jig a strange look that mixed weariness and sadness. "Ryslind saw you run off with the girl. He was thinking you had betrayed us. I told him, goblin or no, you wouldn't do such a thing. But perhaps I was mistaken."

Four dead goblins lay at their feet. The rest stood at a distance, weapons ready. Clearly nobody knew what to do. No, that wasn't right. Like Jig, everyone knew what they *should* do. But without someone to bully them, they simply couldn't work up the courage to do it. Nobody wanted to fling themselves onto Barius's sword or face Ryslind's magic. Who said goblins were entirely stupid?

"I didn't know for sure," Jig said quietly. In the large, silent cavern, his voice sounded tiny. Hearing Darnak's disappointment hurt more than he wanted to admit.

"It matters not." Barius sheathed his sword and stepped forward, hand outstretched. "Give me the rod, goblin."

Jig hesitated. "Will you leave once you have it?"

"Naturally," Barius said. "What more could we possibly desire from goblins?"

"Don't trust him." Riana spoke so softly that only Jig heard.

He glanced back, saw her young, thin face wrinkle with anger. *She's probably right, but what else can I do?* His gaze lowered, and he saw that the spoon had come loose. *Probably when Golaka whacked me on the head.*

Instead of a rivet to hold the spoon in place, a hammered cuff covered the last few inches of the rod. This had been pinched inward, with wire lashed around the upper part of the cuff for additional security. Placing the end on the ground, Jig stepped on the spoon and tugged the rod free.

Barius took another step. He moved like a hunter trying to close in on his prey without frightening it off. What would he do once he had the rod? Would he really depart in peace, leaving hundreds of angry goblins at his back? His honor might require him to wait until the first goblin came after him. But he would use that first attack as an excuse to kill every goblin without a second thought, since after all, the goblins would have been the ones who broke the peace.

Jig was starting to understand how this honor stuff worked. If the prince was allowed to leave in peace, his honor would force him to respect that peace. The problem was that goblins had no use for honor. Turning your back on an enemy was both an insult and an invitation for that enemy to stab you in the back. As soon as Barius appeared to retreat, the goblins would rediscover their courage and attack.

As far as he could see, there was only one way out. Jig would have to do something dumb again.

"Wait," Jig said. Barius hesitated. Speaking Goblin as fast as he could, Jig shouted, "Why are you all wasting your time with these so-called adventurers? They're nothing!"

All around him, goblins protested. Some pointed to Golaka as evidence of the intruders' powerful magic. Others shouted about how the dwarf had slain two goblins before they could even draw weapons. How could Jig say they were nothing? They had come into the lair and killed half a dozen without any apparent effort.

Jig waved the rod in the air and tried to be heard. "I've traveled with this lot for days, and I say they're nothing. Their leader is a frightened child, the dwarf a spineless lackey. The wizard is mindless."

The last point was true, if misleading.

The goblins were still talking. They hadn't made up their minds yet. They hadn't attacked, either, which was good, but Jig knew he still hadn't convinced them. What else could he say?

Barius's hand rested on his sword. He studied Jig, as if trying to determine what the goblin was up to. "What are you telling them?"

"I'm trying to convince them you're too strong," Jig answered, straight-faced. "I'm telling them of all your battles."

That was it. Jig turned back to the goblins. "They cowered in fear at the sight of a mere carrion-worm. They tumbled into the hobgoblins' most obvious traps. When they stood helplessly in the lower tunnels, who do you think was forced to save their worthless lives?"

"Who?" called a handful of goblins, starting to get caught up in Jig's taunts.

"Me," he yelled. "A goblin rescued the brave adventurers."

Sensing Barius's glare, Jig spun around.

"Why do they laugh?"

Jig shrugged. "I told them how you outwitted the hobgoblins. Give me a few more minutes. They're almost convinced."

He continued in Goblin. "Look at them! They dress like beggars, they smell worse than hobgoblin piss, and they eat food even a dog would ignore. That's all your so-called adventurers are, dogs running around in the darkness, searching for bones."

Raising the rod, he said, "I'll prove it. Watch them fetch."

Hard as he could, he hurled the rod over Barius's head and past the others. It whirled end over end through the cavern and into the tunnel beyond to clatter against the rock.

The laughter grew as Barius raced after it, followed closely by Darnak and Ryslind. Jig grinned at the jibes and jeers, for once aimed at someone other than him. It felt good.

"I'll kill them myself," Jig said as he hurried toward the tunnel. He took his sword back from Riana and waved it overhead. Trying to make his voice sound commanding, he said, "Wait here for my return. We'll have a feast tonight."

That reminded him of Golaka. Ryslind's spell had faded, and even as Jig watched, the huge chef slipped free from the magic's grip and fell to the ground.

Jig grabbed Riana's wrist. "Time to go," he said. Hopefully the goblins wouldn't follow, and he doubted Barius would bother to return now that he had the rod. Not for a few worthless goblins, at least.

So why am I going toward *him?* The answer came almost immediately. *Because I'm an idiot.*

Jig collided with Darnak. The impact bought a huff of breath from the dwarf, and sent Jig crashing into the wall.

"I think I convinced them to let us go," Jig said once he had recovered.

"Did you, now?" Darnak's thick brows lifted. "You know, it happens that I speak a smattering of Goblin myself. I couldn't make out everything, but I picked up a few words here and there."

Jig swallowed, but his mouth had gone dry. He had forgotten that detail.

"Spineless lackey, was it?" His fingers drummed the shaft of his club. "One of these days, I'll repay you for that. We dwarves hold a grudge for a long time, you know."

Fortunately, the two humans hadn't heard any of it. Barius stood to one side, clasping the rod to his chest as if it were a long-lost lover, while Ryslind caressed it with his eyes. It was a little disturbing to watch, truth be told. Jig cleared his throat.

"You have the rod. Shouldn't you be on your way? Back to the castle and the king and all that?" *Please,* he added silently.

Barius nodded slowly, but before he could speak, Ryslind's voice cracked like thunder. "No! We must free Straum from his prison."

"You dare to give me commands, brother?" Barius asked softly.

Jig pressed his back to the wall. He had hoped they would simply leave, but if they decided to kill one another, that would work too.

Sadly, things weren't going to be that simple. Ryslind's eyes flashed, but when he spoke again, he sounded calm and reasonable. "Think of the reward, brother. Five thousand years of gold and plunder. Straum will have no need of such things once he is free. You could have your pick of his hoard. Enough wealth to buy a kingdom of your own."

Barius's lips twitched into an involuntary grin as Ryslind went on. By the end, he was practically drooling. "A good point, brother. But why not use the rod to create whatever treasure I need?"

"The rod can only affect what already exists. Rock can be shifted, animals changed to other forms. You could turn a gold crown into a pile of coins, but you couldn't make a diamond out of nothing." Ryslind clasped his hands together. "Imagine our brothers' reactions when you return with wealth enough to make them look like paupers on the street."

"We did make a bargain with Straum," Barius said thoughtfully. "For the sake of our family's honor, we should fulfill that agreement and set him free."

Jig and Riana exchanged tired glances. She looked ready to strangle Barius, and Jig wanted to sit down and cry. Home was only a hundred feet away. He was so close. If only they had left, he could have returned to the cavern and joined the others for evening meal. He imagined the laughter as he told them all how he had driven the half-witted adventurers out of goblin territory. Would he ever be able to go home?

An angry shout echoed down the tunnel. "I'll have your head on my cutting board, you runt," Golaka yelled.

Jig hopped to his feet. "Right. Let's go free Straum then."

Ryslind led them back to the lake, walking like a man in a trance. Several times he had asked to carry the rod. "As a wizard, I know more of its powers than anyone."

Barius had refused, insisting that this was *his* quest, and he would not let the rod out of his hands until he was back at the palace. For once Jig agreed completely. Bad as Barius was, the idea of Ryslind carrying that kind of power was even worse.

But Barius had his own reasons. Jig had to strain his ears to hear the prince's whispered conversation with Darnak.

"He is not my brother," Barius was saying. "Straum controls him."

"If Straum truly controlled him, we'd all be dead, and he'd be taking the rod down himself. He's still struggling, though there's little enough he can do against the dragon. He surrendered to Straum's control all by himself. It was his own greed that did him in." In an angrier tone, Darnak went on. "It's greed that will be your end, too. You don't want to be turning a dragon loose on the countryside, lad, no matter how much treasure you carry away as a reward. You're too young to remember, but I was around the last time one of those beasts came around this way. That was a small one, and he gutted half the kingdom."

"I do not plan to release him," Barius said. "The dragon enslaved my brother, Darnak. Any deal they made is worthless. I will not let this go unavenged."

"You'll be the death of me yet." Darnak stopped for a moment to check his map. "Take the left tunnel up ahead," he said in a normal voice. Handing the lantern to Barius, he grabbed for his wineskin.

"So you're planning to use the rod, I take it?"

Jig thought he heard approval in the dwarf's question.

Barius nodded. "Dragons came from the Rod of Creation, all those years ago. Is it not fitting that the same rod be used to end Straum's existence?"

"Fitting, aye." Darnak took another drink. "I just hope you're not trying to mine more than you can haul. Dragons are a tricky lot, and a dragon with magic at his command is doubly dangerous."

"He must pay," he snapped. "You told me once that Earthmaker requires his followers to avenge themselves upon their enemies."

"Not precisely." Darnak picked his next words carefully. "Earthmaker teaches us to maintain balance and justice. In a case like this, where your brother went off in search of his own doom, I'd be hard pressed to lay the blame entirely at Straum's feet."

"My brother was a greedy, shortsighted fool." Jig shook his head at the blind irony as Barius continued. "But Straum will still pay for what he did."

Ryslind led them to the shore of the lake, where he killed several lizard-fish with bolts of fire. "Perhaps you will change your mind, brother? As a mage, I can use the rod far more easily than you, and its power will make our path easier."

Barius tightened his fingers until the knuckles went white. "I think not. Tell me what I must do to use it."

Ryslind absently sent another lizard-fish to a crispy, smoldering death, and said, "The user must impose his will on that of the rod. You must imagine precisely what you want, in perfect detail. If the rod works like most magical artifacts, you will feel a strong tug. The rod will seem to pull you forward as it tries to draw power from you. You must resist. Brace yourself and force the rod to draw on its own stored energy. Do not lose control, no matter how much it pains you."

"Very well." Barius stepped closer to the shore and raised the rod. "Be sure these creatures do not endanger me while I work."

Darnak and Ryslind took positions on either side, guarding him from the lizard-fish.

"I suggest a tunnel," Ryslind said. "The lake bed is obsidian. Envision the tunnel as a long bubble rising from that stone. Be certain it is waterproof, and large enough for us to move about."

Jig stood behind the prince and watched as he pointed the end of the rod at the ground. It was hard to split his concentration between the lizard-fish and Barius, but he wanted to see the rod work. They had all nearly died many times over to find this stick, after all. At last Jig would see Ellnorein's legendary artifact in action.

Compared to the other things he had seen in the past week, the rod was spectacularly boring. There was no burst of light, no sparks or smoke, nothing but a slight humming sound that any tone-deaf child could have duplicated.

"Be careful," Ryslind said. "Work slowly."

A tiny bulge appeared in the rock by the shore. As Jig watched, it grew taller and wider. A dark hole formed at the center.

"Jig," Riana snapped.

He glanced down to see a lizard-fish climbing over the toe of his boot. With a squawk of alarm, Jig kicked it back into the water. A few more steps, and it could have killed him. From then on he ignored the growing tunnel and worked on staying alive and poison-free.

The humming of the rod grew painfully shrill, then cut off. The instant the noise stopped, Barius gasped and clutched his head. "What did it do to me?"

Ryslind gazed into the newly formed tunnel. He tapped the stone, as if to insure its solidity. "I suspect your tunnel intersected the magic that held the whirlpool in place. The backlash will leave you with quite a headache for the next day or so."

"You should have warned me."

Ryslind smiled, a picture of innocence. "Magic comes with a cost, dear prince." Before Barius could answer, he ducked his head and entered the tunnel, vanishing in the darkness.

The tunnel was barely taller than Jig, and he hunched over as he walked. The walls and ceiling were damp and cool, but they didn't appear to leak. The cold air was eerily still, and their footsteps echoed down the tunnel. He almost refused to follow. The tunnel walls were only a few inches thick, and Jig didn't see how that could be strong enough to support the weight of an entire lake.

That was another facet of the rod's magic, of course. Those stone walls were probably stronger than the rest of the mountain. Still, Jig expected the tunnel to collapse at any second. He wondered if the water and rock would crush him before he drowned.

They reached the end. A perfectly round hole two feet across opened into blackness. The sides were smooth and damp. Darnak passed the lantern up to Ryslind, who slanted a beam of light into the room below.

The Necromancer's throne room was the same as when

they had left, empty and foreboding. The corpses were gone. Darnak had insisted on disposing of them when they came back from Straum's lair, saying it was disrespectful to leave bodies sprawled about like that. They had spent several hours dragging the corpses to what Jig had dubbed the "Pit of Big Bats" and tossing them over the edge. How that was more respectful than leaving the bodies to decay, Jig hadn't bothered to ask.

"Perhaps a ladder?" Ryslind suggested.

Barius frowned, but didn't argue. He pointed the rod at the hole, and a bit of stone dripped into the room to form a thin ladder. From the lines on his forehead and by his eyes, Jig guessed he was concentrating harder this time. Sweat dripped down his face by the time he finished.

"Excellent." Ryslind lowered himself into the room. Once the others had joined him, he said, "I suggest you do the same thing with the Necromancer's little trapdoor. Or do you require time to rest, to regain your strength?"

Even Jig could see the way Ryslind baited his brother, pushing him to admit that the magic was too strong for him. Every word the wizard spoke positively oozed compassion, as if it were all he could do to watch Barius shoulder this heavy burden by himself.

"We shall proceed," Barius said through gritted teeth. Again he used the rod, this time melting the throne itself into a ladder. Before he could finish, he cried out and fell. His hands pressed against his temples.

"Such pain," Ryslind muttered sorrowfully. "You must have triggered another backlash when your ladder pierced Straum's illusionary sky. A pity, for in most cases the rod's magic is easy to control. Only when it collides with other art does it cause this kind of anguish, and then only to the unskilled."

As Barius used the rod like a cane to push himself back up, Jig found that he actually felt *sorry* for the prince. Then he remembered being led around at the end of a rope, punched in the face, and threatened time and again for the past week. His sympathy faded.

Barius managed to finish the ladder without further problems. The rungs were a bit slippery, having taken on the glassy polish of the throne, but nobody fell off.

At the bottom, another of Straum's dragonchildren waited for them. "You have the rod," it said. This one was smaller and darker than the first. Female, Jig guessed. Or perhaps it was simply younger.

Barius drew himself up and forced the fatigue from his face. "I do."

He saw Darnak glance worriedly at their escort, and he could guess what the dwarf was thinking. Barius might, with luck and a great deal of help from the gods, be able to use the rod against Straum. But did the prince's plan include a way to deal with Straum's children? A lot of good it would do to kill the dragon if the dragonchild tore them apart a second later.

They couldn't retreat. The creature probably had orders to stop them if they tried. The only thing to do was march onward, through the gardens and into the cave, and hope Barius knew what he was doing.

When they arrived, they found that Straum had emerged from his lake. His body stretched across much of the cave, and rows of enormous wet footprints suggested that he had been pacing. His head perked up as Ryslind entered.

"You have it," Straum breathed. When he saw what Barius carried, he threw back his head and roared so loudly Jig thought his head would crack. The terrible sound went on and on, and when it stopped, the echoes continued inside his skull.

"I think he's happy to see us," Darnak said dryly.

Strong clawed hands nudged Jig into the room. He glanced back, wondering if Straum suspected something. Dragons were supposed to be the most dangerous creatures in the world, undisputed masters of trickery. When he thought about it, how could Straum *not* suspect something? With freedom so close, he wouldn't risk anything going wrong. Barius's plan would get them all killed.

Jig started to inch closer to Darnak. Maybe he would know what to do. Before he got close enough to speak, Ryslind walked up to the dragon's side.

"We have it, master," he said. "It was a close thing." His

thin finger pointed at Jig. "The goblin attempted to betray us and take the rod for himself."

Jig froze. Maybe his ears were still recovering from Straum's roar and he had misheard. "I gave the rod to you," he said meekly.

Ryslind smiled, a cold expression of triumph. The slitted glow of his eyes seemed to burn into Jig's chest. As he had done once before, Ryslind spoke directly into Jig's mind.

I warned you that you would pay for humiliating me, goblin. Jig suddenly understood. Whatever Straum had done to the wizard's mind, enough of Ryslind remained to want revenge. He hadn't forgotten his promise to punish Jig. He had simply waited for the best time to exact that punishment.

"It wasn't like that, exactly," Darnak protested.

"Silence," Barius hissed.

Jig glanced over. Barius had begun to edge away from his guard. He glanced at Darnak, who tilted his head slightly. They planned to use Jig's execution as a distraction. A good plan, Jig admitted. The only flaw involved the minor detail of Jig's painful death.

"Did he?" Straum asked. His neck twisted around until he stared down at Jig. "I've always thought goblins to be cowardly, stupid creatures. Betraying me took more boldness than I'd have expected from you. For a goblin, you're quite the brave fellow."

Jig didn't breathe. He couldn't look away from those huge, gold eyes. He could see himself reflected in the slitted pupils, his body distorted on the curved surface. He watched the mirror-Jig raise his hands, as if to explain. He saw the wide-eyed expression of fear, the frantic trembling in his jaw.

He never saw Straum's tail rush through the air to smash into Jig from the side.

The last thing Jig heard as his body crashed into a wall was Straum's amused voice saying, "Pity, really. Had you been as cowardly as the rest of your race, you might have survived."

CHAPTER 17

In the Blink of an Eye

"YOU LASTED LONGER THAN I THOUGHT YOU would, I'll grant you that much."

Jig opened an eye, closed it again. He peeked out through the other one, just to be certain. Nothing had changed in the interim.

"This isn't Straum's cave."

"You can do better than that, Jig. If you were really this thick, I can think of seven times in the past week alone when you would have died. Use your brain. Figure out where you are."

Jig scowled. He knew who he was talking to, if nothing else. Somehow, Tymalous Shadowstar sounded less impressive when his words weren't reverberating inside Jig's skull. As for *where* he was . . . he sat up and took a good look around.

He noticed the sky first. Straum's illusionary sky was nothing compared to this. There must have been hundreds of stars here. Thousands, even. He didn't try to count, since his vision would make the task impossible.

Except that it didn't. Instead of round blurs of light, each star was a clear pinpoint. He could even make out individual colors. Some sparkled with a blue tinge, others appeared yellow, and several flashed red as he watched. *He could see!*

He stared at his hands. For the first time, he could hold them at arm's length and still see the layer of grime beneath his nails. Everything had come into focus. This was wonderful! He looked back into the sky, noticing one star that stood out from the others. It was a large red star, which appeared to be a half-inch wide and shone brighter than the rest. In fact, that star provided the only illumination. The red light gave everything an angry, flamelike tinge. His own skin had turned purplish.

What had Darnak told him? Shadowstar was the God of the Autumn Star, so the Autumn Star was probably that big red one. He lowered his gaze to survey the more immediate surroundings. Whatever this place was, it needed to be torn apart and rebuilt from scratch. Crumbled walls traced a roughly rectangular outline. Scorch marks blackened parts of the walls and the floor. The floor itself was mostly dirt and clumps of yellowed grass, and only the occasional ceramic fragment gave any hint of what must have once been an impressive temple.

There was no smell. Even the stink of sweat and blood that had followed him for days was missing. Jig glanced down at himself.

His boots and loincloth were the same as before, only brighter, lacking any trace of grime. He didn't even try to remember when he had last washed the loincloth.

His body appeared whole. He couldn't remember what had happened right before he came here, but he had expected to find himself torn in two, or at least bent at a sharp angle. Instead, he was healthy as ever.

He tested his fingers, flexing each one individually to make sure the bones still worked. He checked the wrists and elbows next. *So far, so good*. As he pulled off his boots to check his toes, it occurred to him that he was stalling. Jig didn't really want to admit he was sitting here with a god. He might have grown used to the day-to-day oddities of traveling with adventurers, but this went beyond strange.

He cast a furtive glance at Shadowstar.

"You're not dead, so don't bore me by asking. Everyone always asks me that. Right after the 'Where am I?' bit. You'd think they could at least come up with something more original."

Jig straightened, confused, and so got his first clear view of Tymalous Shadowstar. His first impression was not a flattering one. *I thought gods were supposed to be . . . taller.*

"Not this god," Shadowstar said. "Big gods make better targets."

Jig absolutely refused to think about what it would take to threaten a god. Another god, presumably, but he didn't want to imagine fighting of that magnitude. Quarreling among the adventurers was more than enough for Jig. Instead, he took a closer look at Shadowstar.

He stood only a few inches taller than Jig. He could have passed for a short, skinny human, about thirty years of age. Assuming nobody looked him in the eyes, that was. The skin around the sockets appeared normal, but they contained a blackness as deep as the night sky. Red starbursts shone from the center, reminding Jig a little of Ryslind. But unlike the wizard, Shadowstar's eyes held no malice. As Jig stared, he felt as though he were falling into the sky itself, and his stomach gurgled in protest.

Jig forced himself to look away before he lost himself completely. As he took in the rest of the god's appearance, he deliberately avoided that face.

Shadowstar wore loose-fitting clothes of black silk. Strips of tiny silver bells ran down the outside of his pants and sleeves. The shirt was open at the chest, revealing a smooth, lean body. His skin wasn't quite white, but it was pastier than that of any other being Jig had seen. His silver hair flowed to waist-level, but the hairline appeared to have receded a bit over the years. A balding god? Even gods grew old, he supposed. At least Shadowstar hadn't acquired the swollen gut carried by most older goblins.

"Why am I here?"

Shadowstar grunted. "Another obvious question, but not quite as trite as it could have been." He chuckled. "Worship is a two-way deal. I'll help you out a bit, but it means I get first dibs on your soul when you and your body part ways. After the pounding you took from Straum, you came here."

"But you said I wasn't dead yet."

He ignored Jig's question. "Rule number one when dealing with dragons," he said, extending one gloved finger. "Never look them in the eye. It's distracting, to say the least. But seeing as how goblins don't usually go in for dragonslaying, I understand why you hadn't learned the rules.

"Unfortunately for you, ignorance makes a poor shield. At this moment, your body is upside down against the wall of Straum's lair. Your back snapped in two places when you hit, your ribs are gravel, and you're paralyzed from about here down." Shadowstar tapped his hand at the middle of his chest. "You also bruised your brain, which wouldn't make a difference to the average goblin, but you've shown yourself to be far from average, my friend.

"When faced with a choice between living in excruciating pain, albeit only from the nipples up, or getting a head start on death and avoiding that last bit of nastiness, you opted for the latter. This left your body in a coma and your mind and soul here with me."

"Oh." Jig's shoulders slumped. "What if Darnak heals me?" The dwarf had done it before. Maybe there was a chance Jig could still survive.

Not that this place was so terrible. At least he was safe. He had never thought much about an afterlife. Goblins believed that once you died, your body went to the carrion-worms, and that was the end of it. He didn't care what happened to him after he died, because he had never expected to see any of it. Goblins died, and then other goblins came along to steal their belongings and toss the body into the tunnels. He never imagined spending time with a forgotten god in the midst of a run-down temple.

Still, while Shadowstar might be good company, Jig wasn't ready to make this place a permanent home. Nor did he like the fact that Ryslind had beaten him. In a strange way, he had been having fun. Not that he enjoyed always hearing Death's footsteps follow him around, and he would have chosen different company if he could, and those dead warriors had been a bit much. But skipping between Death's fingers time after time gave him a strange, bubbling thrill in the middle of his chest. He had learned things, too. Things that could help the goblins hold their own against the other races. Or they would have, had he lived long enough to pass them on.

When Jig spoke, it was in a soft voice, full of wonder. "I want to go back."

He looked hopefully at Shadowstar, but the god was shaking his head. "You can't. Rather, you're already there. You've just taken a step sideways from reality, that's all. But I'm afraid Darnak can't help you. Things are about to get messy, and nobody is going to worry about a goblin they believe to be a corpse."

His starburst pupils bored into Jig's eyes. He was waiting for something. Jig didn't understand what Shadowstar expected him to do. That Darnak couldn't help him was hard to accept. Goblins, by nature, did not ask for help. To ask for help was to make yourself vulnerable. The closest word for "trust" in the goblin tongue was a word that meant either "gullible" or "dumb as dung," depending on context. So for Jig to admit he needed help was hard enough, even if Darnak would never know. To learn that Darnak couldn't help was worse, because Jig *knew* he would have tried to heal Jig's wounds if he could.

That was simply who Darnak was. He might not like Jig, but he would obey the rules of Silas Earthmaker. He would obey because he wanted to, not because he had to. If nothing else, Darnak was loyal. Loyal to the princes and their father the king, loyal to his god, and loyal to his fellow adventurers.

Jig grinned at that. He had thought of himself as an adventurer. At least he hadn't gotten tangled up with traditional hero traits like loyalty or nobility. Too much of that and he'd turn into another Barius.

His smile faded. He was still thinking like he was going to survive, and Shadowstar had made it pretty clear that wasn't the case. Though if he was slated to die, why did Shadowstar watch him with that patient expression? Why all of the games, if he was truly stuck here?

"You want me to live, don't you?" Jig asked. Shadowstar shrugged noncommittally, jingling the bells along his sleeves. But his eyes literally twinkled, and Jig knew he was right. Darnak couldn't help him, because he didn't know Jig needed help. But Jig was a goblin, and if a goblin wanted help, he had better help himself, 'cause nobody else was likely to do it.

"Silas Earthmaker gives Darnak magic to heal people. Can you do that for me?"

"Maybe," Shadowstar said, drawing the word into a long drawl. "I've helped my followers before, back in the days when I had any. As I mentioned, worship is a two-way thing. You haven't yet committed to me."

Before Jig could argue, he held up a hand and said, "You picked out a god who would help you because he had nothing better to do. Darnak wouldn't even have remembered my name if I hadn't jogged his mind a bit. You wanted someone you could use, correct?"

Jig nodded. No use lying to a god, he figured. Still, it hadn't sounded quite so calculated when he first decided to follow Shadowstar.

"If I help you this time, there are things you'll need to do for me. Rules to follow, like Darnak does for Silas Earthmaker. Can you do this?"

"Sure."

Apparently Jig answered too quickly. Shadowstar smiled. "Remember, you come to me when you die. Betray me, and we'll have a very long chat once you get here."

Jig had heard many threats over the past few days, but Shadowstar's cheerful warning made them sound like the work of clumsy amateurs. In a small voice, Jig said, "I can still lie to other people though, right? Telling the truth is a good way to get killed."

Shadowstar laughed. "Fair enough. Now, let us discuss the terms of our partnership."

Partnership. Awestruck, Jig watched as Tymalous Shadowstar walked toward him. *Him,* Jig the goblin. The runt who hid in corners and cringed when it came time to choose guards for patrol duty. This goblin was about to partner up with a god.

What *had* the universe come to?

Smudge jumped in shock when Jig turned his head. He had been peering into Jig's mouth, presumably seeking signs of life.

A good thing the spider had moved, because Jig bit his lip so hard he expected the fangs to pierce his cheeks. Shadowstar hadn't warned him how much this would *hurt!* As he surveyed the damage, he couldn't believe this was his body. This body had too many joints in the legs, and the chest was bumpier than it should have been. He didn't know how his skeleton worked, but he knew he shouldn't bend this way. To make matters worse, he was upside down, propped against the wall like a discarded doll. And why couldn't he feel anything from the chest down?

I told you, you're paralyzed.

Right. That was probably a blessing, all things considered. He had enough pain in the parts he could feel. Even moving his head made him want to vomit. Flopping onto his side was torture, and he had to lay there for over a minute before he could move again. His vision was worse than usual, too. Outlines wavered and shifted, and he thought he saw two dragons arguing with two Bariuses. That couldn't be right. Unless he had angered Shadowstar somehow and this was his punishment.

Relax. That's the bump to your brain, remember? You're going to feel a bit strange, even when we start to heal you. Especially when we start to heal you. I can give you the magic, but you have to use it. We'll begin as soon as you're ready.

Jig tried to relax. The tips of his fingers grew warm, as if he had dipped them into a bucket of water. Was this magic? He could feel the sensation move through his wrists and into his arms. He pulled back involuntarily when it reached his neck. This was too much like drowning.

Trust me.

Back to trust again. Was Jig gullible, or simply dumb as dung? Probably a bit of both, but he didn't have much of a choice. Shadowstar wouldn't help him out only to drown him. He tried to relax, but he couldn't get enough air. His chest felt tight, and he breathed faster, struggling to inhale. Why couldn't he breathe? He heard himself panting like an animal, but the sound was growing distant. He was dying again.

You're hyperventilating. Stop it. Think about . . . whatever it is goblins do to relax. Killing and eating, or something like that.

Jig tried to concentrate on what was happening on the other side of Straum's lair. He forced himself to inhale and hold it for a few seconds, breaking up the frantic rhythm of his breathing. He exhaled slowly, turned his head, and tried to put Shadowstar out of his mind.

Very little time had passed since Straum flung Jig into the wall. His conversation with the god must not have taken as long as he thought. Barius and the others still stood in front of the dragon, apparently stunned by the attack on Jig.

Jig twitched an ear, which didn't hurt as badly as the rest of him, and tried to listen.

"You shouldn't have gone and killed him, not after he found your precious rod." That was Darnak. His protests were feeble, though. Did he expect an apology from the dragon?

"There are things you have to learn if you're going to live to see your five-thousandth birthday. One of the first is that when someone betrays you, you kill him. Preferably in a way that teaches a lesson to his friends."

That was a warning, to make sure the rest of the group cooperated. Jig wondered if Barius had noticed it. Not that he would change his plans if he had. In his own way, Barius was as loyal as Darnak. He might hate his brother, but he would still die for the chance to avenge Ryslind's destruction.

Jig had no problem with Barius dying. Indeed, he would have been far happier if Straum had chosen to break Barius against the wall instead of him. Barius could die happy and alone, knowing his had been an honorable end, while the rest of them crept quietly out of the lair and back to somewhere safe.

Instead he expected Barius to get them all killed when he tried to attack Straum. Unless he managed to win. Was it possible? He was a prince and an experienced adventurer. He had the Rod of Creation.

But Straum was an experienced dragon, and he had really big claws and a tail, as well as one of his children to guard him. Not to mention Ryslind himself, standing over there with those glowing eyes and all of Straum's magic at his command. At one time those eyes had frightened Jig. After seeing Shadowstar, he found them an annoyance, no more. He wanted to run over and pull tiny curtains over Ryslind's face.

"The rock overhead is almost a quarter of a mile thick." Straum's wings flapped in a quick, small movement. A nervous twitch? The sound reminded Jig of rugs being shaken clean.

"I'll need enough room to flap my wings. At least thirty paces wide. Once I'm free, you may help yourselves to anything you like from these walls." He shifted his weight from one pair of legs to the other. "Begin."

Are you ready?

"Yes." The voice in his head had startled him into answering aloud. Luckily everyone's eyes were on Barius. Nobody noticed the discarded goblin in the corner.

I feel bloated, Jig complained. The magic had filled his body while he watched the others. *All stuffed up and constipated.*

Please stop. Shadowstar sounded disgusted. *You'll get used to it. For now, what you want to do is place your hands over the worst injury. That would be the place where your spine takes a right-angle turn, right below the sternum.*

I know, Jig thought, annoyed. He touched the part of his chest that bulged worst. As long as he didn't think of it as a part of his body, he could keep from throwing up.

You'll have to push the bones down as the magic works.

Gross. Why does healing have to be so disgusting?

Why do goblins have to be so fragile? Next time you'll know better than to stand in the way of a dragon's tail. Now when you press down, imagine the magic inside of you flowing through your hands and into the spine. You need to visualize the flow.

The only thing flowing out of Jig's hands was sweat. So he used that. He imagined the magic seeping through his sweat and oozing into his chest.

Strange, but it'll do, was Shadowstar's reaction.

Overhead, illuminated by the blue glow of the walls, a circular hole began to recede into the ceiling while the displaced stone formed a ring along the outside. Barius clutched the rod in both hands. His entire body had gone rigid with concentration. Everyone watched as the hole began to grow.

That was good, because it meant they still hadn't noticed Jig's struggle to put his bones back into place. The pain really wasn't too bad. True, Jig had never *felt* anything this excruciating, but he was sure there had to be something that could hurt more. He simply couldn't imagine what it might be.

Worse than the pain was the grinding sensation in his chest, like rocks scraping against one another. Sometimes he had to push with all of his strength, and then something would pop into place, and he felt a surge of magic seep through his skin to bind the bones together again. "Next time I'm going to stay dead."

Next time, you should try to duck. You think it's easy for me, trying to find all those bits of rib and put them back together?

Jig scowled and pushed another chunk of backbone into place. His toes had begun to tingle, which he took to be a good sign. He could even wiggle his feet again.

A heady rush of power distracted him from the pain. He was fixing himself! The same as Darnak had done. Jig the goblin was doing magic.

Concentrate, fang-face.

Jig snorted indignantly. But he paid more attention to the magic. Most of the bones were back in place, though he could still feel things shifting and moving inside his body. A bizarre sensation, really. He wondered if this was anything like being pregnant. Goblin women generally gave birth to anywhere from two to five babies at a time. And Jig could feel at least three distinct places where his guts were rearranging themselves.

True, but pregnancy lasts eight months for you goblins. And you don't have to squeeze the kids out of your—

"I'm trying to concentrate," Jig interrupted quickly.

At the center of the room, Barius had deepened the hole. Darkness hid the inside, so Jig couldn't tell how high it extended. Presumably he would know when Barius broke through to the surface. Jig expected a dramatic beam of sunlight if nothing else. So far there was nothing but blackness.

Straum peered into the growing hole, his tail shivering

with excitement. "Yes," he growled. "So close. To fly through real clouds again, to hunt real food. Faster, human."

Barius's attack came in silence. A huge spike of rock shot down from the black tunnel. He had used the rod to shape an enormous spear, one that he could release to impale Straum's skull. The interior of the hole was dark, and Straum shouldn't have seen the spear coming in time to protect himself.

Jig's eyes had reverted to their nearsighted state when he left Shadowstar's temple, so he saw nothing but a black streak heading toward the dragon's enormous skull. Halfway there, it broke into a cloud of dust and gravel. He twisted his face away as pebbles showered his body.

Barius lay on his back, clutching his head while his face twisted with pain. Ryslind bent down and plucked the rod from his brother's hands.

"You know, brother, if you had done as you were asked, we might have allowed you to live." Ryslind cradled the rod like an infant. "Naturally we both expected you to betray us. You never were the smart one, were you?"

"Keep the bloody rod," Darnak said. His hair and beard had turned gray from the dust. "You've got your freedom. Let me take his highness home, and we'll not be bothering you again."

"Ah, Darnak. Do you really think it's so simple? My brother would insist on hunting us down. You know it as well as I. He couldn't live with this humiliation and defeat. We'd have to kill him sooner or later. Isn't it more efficient to finish him now and be done with it?"

Straum hadn't yet spoken. He seemed content to let Ryslind do the talking. Or maybe he was speaking *through* Ryslind, Jig wasn't sure.

Jig pressed against the wall and pushed himself to his feet. His legs felt like water, and he didn't know if he'd fall down as soon as he took a step, but this was a far cry better than he had been a few minutes ago. Even as he waited to see Straum's legendary temper reduce Barius to ash, a part of Jig's mind couldn't let go of his awe at the magic he had used to heal himself.

"A pity the rod can't be used to slay you outright," Ryslind said. "One of its few weaknesses. Though I suppose I could transform you into one of Straum's children. That might be a fitting end, to serve the one you tried to murder. Not forever, of course. Only for a few centuries. Or less, if you found the strength to rebel against him. You saw what happens to those who try."

Jig looked past them, toward the exit. If they focused on Ryslind, he could probably sneak past without being noticed. Even Straum's dragonchild appeared distracted by Ryslind's last comment.

After escaping from Straum's lair, it would be a simple march through the tunnels, across the forest, and back up to his own home. Assuming his legs lasted more than two steps, he'd still have to face ogres, hobgoblins, and who knew what manner of creatures, but what did that matter? He had survived all of these things before.

He managed one shaky step before someone spotted him. Riana wasn't as enthralled by Ryslind's cat-and-mouse game as the rest. Her eyes constantly scanned the cave, probably waiting for the best moment to flee, just as Jig was. She jumped when she saw Jig alive and moving.

So much for that. Jig waited for her to cry out. The smartest thing would be for her to use Jig as a distraction to cover her own escape. He sighed. At least *someone* would make it out of here. She'd probably have a better chance at making it through the forest anyway.

The expected shout never came. Instead she watched the others to make sure they hadn't noticed, then began to nod at him.

Not at you, *dummy,* came the weary voice of Tymalous Shadowstar.

Jig looked over his shoulder. Nothing there but shelves bearing Straum's assorted junk. Some nice belt buckles, folded tabards in various stages of decay . . . oh. Jig stared at her. She couldn't mean for him to. . . .

But she nodded harder, both at Jig's comprehension and at the row of javelins lined up behind him.

Was she forgetting that Jig was a goblin? A half-blind one at that. He had never thrown a spear or javelin in his life.

Had he been a true adventurer, things might have been different. He could have leaped up, shouted a defiant battle cry, seized a javelin—probably that silver-tipped one with the finlike flanges—and hurled it at Straum with all his might. A true adventurer might even have wounded the dragon, assuming he managed to pierce those scales.

But Jig was a goblin, and goblins had a different approach to big, dangerous monsters. They ran away. If they were fortunate, someone else would take care of the heroism. That would either finish off the monster, or at least create enough of a commotion for the goblin to escape unscathed.

Wait a minute. Jig gave himself a mental shake. *The one thing adventurers and goblins share is their ability to get into deeper trouble. Forget about what goblins would do. Forget about what an adventurer would do. I need to figure out what* Jig *should do.*

Running away still sounded appealing. If he succeeded, that would mean leaving the others behind to die. Jig thought about each one, trying to decide if he could live with that.

Ryslind: Insane. Threatened to kill Jig numerous times. Responsible for Straum snapping Jig's spine. Okay, he could stay here to die or live as Straum's puppet. No problems there.

Barius: Ultimately responsible for dragging Jig into this whole mess. General twit, to boot. He would probably kill Jig sooner or later on general principles. He was another one the world could do without.

Darnak: Decent fellow. Healed Jig's wounds. Still, he hadn't stopped either of the humans from trying to kill Jig. He had *refused to kill Riana after she triggered the Necromancer's trap, but he hadn't tried to stop Barius from doing so. In the end, he was still the prince's man.* Jig felt a twinge of guilt about Darnak. But, Darnak hadn't put his neck on the line when Ryslind betrayed Jig, so why should Jig risk himself for Darnak?

Riana: Dragged into this mess against her will, the same as Jig. Offered him the chance to escape, back in the beginning. He frowned. The others could stay here and die, but his conscience nagged him when he thought about leaving Riana behind. Sure, she hadn't been terribly nice to him all the time, but she had at least begun to treat him like an equal. Besides, Jig owed her something for that finger.

Still, she was one elf. Was she really worth risking his life for?

Shadowstar's voice whispered to him. *I expect better from you.*

"A lot of good it will do if I'm dead," Jig muttered. He glanced around. Ryslind was still toying with Barius. Darnak had turned his pleas from Ryslind to the dragon, who eyed the dwarf much as a tunnel cat might contemplate a plump mouse. Riana stood with her hands on her hips, watching Jig impatiently.

"Oh, hell." He pushed himself up and grabbed the javelin. *If you want me to try this noble stuff, you'd better help me out.* The god didn't answer. Jig shrugged. If this didn't work, he would have ample opportunity to complain in just a few minutes.

As he pulled back to throw, his movement attracted Ryslind's attention. The wizard opened his mouth to shout a warning. He needn't have bothered. His link to Straum carried the message faster than words.

Jig thought he could feel another hand over his own as he threw, one which guided his aim down and to the left. The javelin became a silver line, tracing a path from his hand to Straum's enormous eye.

Straum blinked.

The point hit the scaled eyelid and lodged there, quivering, as Straum snarled in fury.

Ryslind pointed at Jig and clenched a fist. Invisible fingers clamped around Jig's body, so tight he couldn't breathe.

"Wait." Straum's voice held no trace of pain, even with a javelin pinning his eye closed. "Hold him. I want to see this brave goblin who somehow survived my attack. I want to see how long his courage lasts." To the motionless dragonchild, he said, "Help me."

The dragonchild walked slowly to Straum's injured side, pausing only once when she passed the stained patch of sand where her fellow servant had died between the dragon's jaws. Jig wished she would hurry. His head pounded from lack of air, and his chest felt as if Straum had sat on him.

The creature placed both hands on the javelin. Straum's claws dug furrows in the sand. Jig looked to the others for help, but they hadn't moved. Maybe they were smarter than Jig had realized. Smart enough to stay away from an angry dragon, at least.

The dragonchild tightened her grip and *pushed,* forcing the length of the javelin through Straum's eye and into his head.

Ryslind screamed in pain. Straum's head dropped to the floor. His tail crashed into the wall, where it reduced several shelves to splinters and destroyed a five-thousand-year-old collection of oil lamps.

Then the dragon's body went still.

CHAPTER 18

A Fatal Misstep

JIG WAS NOT HAPPY. *STRAUM BLINKED. HE blinked! I could have died!*

Tymalous Shadowstar's answer sounded grumpy. *How was I supposed to know? Even I can't see the future. Besides, you're still alive, aren't you?*

Thanks to a dragonchild.

It was a good plan. The eye was the only vulnerable spot large enough for you to hit. If he hadn't *blinked, that shot would have gone right through the eye and pierced Straum's oversized brain. A weakness you'll never have to worry about, I'm glad to say.*

Good, Jig answered without thinking, thus proving the god's point.

Ryslind was curled into a ball and crying like an infant. Barius and Darnak both bent over him, while Riana watched Straum's newly orphaned child. The dragonchild hadn't moved at all since plunging the javelin into Straum's eye.

Jig grabbed another spear and used it as a staff to help him walk over to the others.

"Nice throw," Darnak said without looking up. "You might have had him, if Ryslind hadn't spotted you. I dare say I couldn't have done it better myself, though if you tell any dwarf I said that, I'll deny it to my dying breath."

He peeled Ryslind's eyelids back and said, "He's not dead. Don't know what it'll do to him though, losing Straum that sudden-like. Meaning no disrespect, but if he had any mind left, that might have broken it."

Riana grabbed Jig's elbow and pulled him a few steps away from the group. "You hesitated. That could have gotten you killed. What were you waiting for?" she said, her voice pitched for Jig's ears only.

In an equally soft voice, he said, "I only had one shot. I couldn't figure out if I should try to kill Straum or Barius."

Riana nodded in perfect understanding. "Tough choice. I think we need to get you away from these adventurers. Deciding to go after the dragon instead of your companion . . . you'd think some of their 'nobility' had rubbed off."

"Not really." He glanced at the prince. "Straum just made a bigger target."

The dragonchild straightened and walked toward Jig, who tightened his grip on his spear. Darnak rose behind him. The dwarf had lost his war club, but he held a large chunk of rock and looked ready to bash anything remotely threatening. On Jig's other side, Riana drew her knife and waited.

"What happened to the one who was here before me?" A long, clawed finger pointed to the blood-soaked sand.

"Straum killed him," Darnak answered. "Said he was getting ideas of his own, not wanting to follow his scaliness anymore."

The dragonchild's head drooped. "I assumed as much."

"Straum said something about being able to read your folks' minds," Darnak said slowly. "That's how he was knowing what your friend was up to."

"Of course. Straum was ever paranoid. We have wondered if he had some magic to sense our hearts."

Darnak frowned. "So tell us how it is that you killed him without his realizing what you had in mind?"

The dragonchild squatted down and grabbed a handful of sand. "When we were younger, a pair of ogres found our lair. The adults were hunting, and the ogres were confident in their ability to massacre mere children. They killed one of our cousins, as well as the old grandmother who had been left behind to watch for danger."

Wet clumps of sand fell to the ground. "We leaped on the nearest ogre. Our claws and teeth are sharpest when we're young. I doubt the beast felt anything as I tore open his stomach. The second fled, only to encounter the hunting party. He died . . . slowly."

Jig glanced at the creature's hands. Those claws might not be as sharp as they used to be, but they still looked powerful enough to rip a goblin in half.

"He and I were mated several years later." Glancing back at Straum's body, she said, "As you said, Straum knew our thoughts. But when I realized my mate was dead, I stopped thinking. I simply acted."

Her eyes turned back to Jig. "What should we do now?"

Jig blinked. She was asking *him*? The others looked as confused as Jig felt. Except for Barius. He looked angry.

"You ask this miserable coward for advice?" he said with a derogatory wave toward Jig.

Jig agreed completely with the sentiment, though he might not have said it in those words. "Me?" he squeaked.

"I lead this party," Barius said. "I brought us here to slay Straum."

The dragonchild's eyes narrowed. "You failed. Without this goblin, Straum would still live, and all of us would have died." With a flick of a black tongue, she turned back to Jig. "We . . . we don't know how to live on our own." Her head lowered, and that elongated, scale-covered face managed to convey a sense of embarrassment. "The others will be scared to go on without Straum."

Jig's ears picked up urgent whispers from either side.

"We can use them to help carry our treasure to the surface," Barius said. "Imagine returning home with a retinue of these creatures as an escort. Instruct them to begin gathering the gold and jewels."

At the same instant, Riana was saying, "Ask if they'll come with us. They could protect us." Jig didn't think "us" included the humans or the dwarf.

Darnak said nothing. A low groan from Ryslind had sent the dwarf running to his side like a worried mother.

What advice could Jig possibly give the dragonchildren?

Don't let a nervous fire-spider perch in your hair. If you're going to annoy a wizard, make sure you kill him when you're finished. Never steal a chef's spoon. He had nothing to offer Straum's orphans.

He tilted his head, hoping for divine help, but Shadowstar apparently thought Jig should figure this one out on his own. All he picked up was a faint sense of amusement.

"Go home," he said. "Go back to your family."

The creature cocked her head. "But we have no home, not without Straum."

"Don't throw this chance away, goblin," Barius said warningly. He took a step closer, menace plain in his balled fists. He didn't manage a second step. The dragonchild slipped between Jig and the prince. One hand seized Barius by the shirt and lifted him off the ground before anyone else could move.

Jig grinned. He could get used to this. But it wouldn't work. Even if he could persuade the dragonchildren to follow him around as guards, like Riana suggested, he didn't think he could ever learn to tolerate the musty smell of dragon.

"You should leave," he repeated. "Find another home. There's a ladder in the clearing at the center of the woods. Another ladder in the throne room above will take you to the upper tunnels. Darnak will give you a map to lead you out of the mountain. You'll have a whole world to choose from."

"You're wanting me to give up my map?" From Darnak's expression, Jig might as well have asked him to shave his beard. But a glance at Barius, still dangling helplessly, silenced any protests. "Ach. Take it. I can draw it again from memory when we return."

For a long time, the creature said nothing. Jig began to wonder if he had said the wrong thing. Maybe they wouldn't want to leave.

"An entire world, you say?"

"I've never seen it myself, but I hear it's pretty big."

The creature nodded, her long neck exaggerating the gesture. "Thank you."

She dropped the prince and walked over to Darnak, who handed over his map. A few minutes later, she was gone, leaving Jig to collapse as the excitement wore off and his legs gave out.

Barius didn't kill him, though it was a close thing. There was a limit to how much humiliation the prince could tolerate, and Jig had obviously pushed far beyond those limits. Being told that a goblin had done more to kill Straum than the prince himself had been the breaking point, and finding himself helpless in the dragonchild's strong grip had added humiliation to rage. As soon as the creature left, Barius lunged to his feet with murder in his eyes.

Thankfully, Darnak intervened. As the prince stormed toward Jig, the dwarf shouted at top volume, "Your brother's awake!"

Ryslind looked as bad as Jig felt. His pinched features were more sunken than usual, and dark smears underlined his eyes. His eyes no longer glowed. Strangely, Jig found Ryslind's beady brown eyes even more disconcerting. He had gotten used to those twin points of red.

After a bit more healing from Darnak, Ryslind managed to stand up under his own power. He could talk, though his voice was raw, and he sounded exhausted. He could remember nothing beyond their encounter with the Necromancer, a fact that made Jig infinitely grateful, as it meant he wouldn't remember his oath to kill Jig.

They decided to rest for a while. With the dragonchildren gone, hopefully for good, this was probably the safest place in the whole mountain. As Darnak pointed out, "Would *you* go poking around in a dragon's lair?"

When Riana pointed out that this was exactly what they had done, Darnak merely laughed and said most monsters had more sense.

So they rested. Darnak shared a bit of his ale, which helped immensely. Ryslind found that he could still cast small spells, but most of his power had vanished with Straum's death. This also contributed to Jig's cheerfulness.

Smudge sat happily on Jig's shoulder, munching a small chunk of dragon meat Jig had cut from Straum's body. He had considered trying a bit of dragon for himself, thinking it couldn't be worse than human food, but decided against it. Even retrieving this small chunk had nearly broken his sword. Those scales were tougher than they looked.

Hours later, Barius decided it was time to depart. "Everyone carry as much treasure as you can. We will need to make at least a dozen trips to retrieve our wealth, but we must take the most valuable items now, to insure their safety."

Fortunately, among the odds and ends Straum had collected over the ages were a wide variety of sacks, pouches, and backpacks. Jig found himself lugging a small sack full of gold coins. He had tried to carry a larger bag, but that nearly destroyed his newly repaired spine. Gold was *heavy*.

He knew Barius was angry at him for not carrying more, but goblins weren't known for their strength. Had the sack been any heavier, Jig would have ended up with his knees jammed through his shoulders. He did tuck a jeweled dagger into his belt, though, and he shoved a few rings onto his fingers.

"I hope nobody tries to stop us," he muttered. If they were attacked, he planned to throw his gold away and hope the enemy stopped to snatch up the coins. It should work, if Barius's greed was any example. Jig's life was a lot more important than gold. Besides, he could always come back for more.

They made it unscathed. They found occasional footprints, but nobody saw any other sign of Straum's children. Perhaps they had already left. Jig hoped so. They had saved his life, but he would still feel more comfortable if he never encountered another one.

Lugging their gold up the ladders was a chore, but with more of Darnak's rope, they eventually managed to pass the treasure up through the ceiling.

There they ran into two hobgoblin sentries. But the hobgoblins fled as soon as they spotted Darnak and Barius.

"Good to have a reputation, eh?" Darnak said.

The time they spent traveling gave Jig a chance to think. More than anything, he wanted to lie down and sleep for a week. A month would be better, but he'd settle for a week. That should be enough time for the aches and bruises to begin to heal. After that he wanted a real meal. A huge helping of stuffed lizard-fish, with those dumplings Golaka made from rats for dessert.

But thinking of home reminded him that, without the rod's magic, Golaka's cauldron would swiftly run dry. They could still manage. Probably. With Straum dead, there would be an influx of adventurers to prey upon. Enough to feed the entire lair? He hoped so.

Jig knew he was lying to himself. Barius would return, and he would bring an army to help him. They would march through the tunnels and kill anything that got in their way. They would gut Straum's lair, and Jig wouldn't put it past them to wipe out the goblins and the rest of the monsters out of sheer spite.

All for what? So Barius could prove himself? So his heroism would outshine that of his brothers? Was this the kind of hero all the songs celebrated? Barius's glory had come, not from his own courage and valor, but from the blood and sweat of the rest of the party. Ryslind's magic, Riana's nimble fingers, Darnak's strength of arm, and even Jig's blind, stubborn luck. Yet Barius would be the one about whom songs were sung. He would be the one who found the Rod of Creation, the one responsible for slaying the great dragon Straum, the one who discovered five thousand years' worth of treasure and claimed it for his own.

They stopped to rest in the shiny room before leaving the tunnels. Jig stared at the designs, losing himself in memories. Little more than a week had passed since he came to this room, clumsily trying to spy on the adventurers. Here he had lied to Barius, which had saved Jig's life but cost the life of his captain, which Jig considered to be a double blessing. Here they had debated whether or not to take Jig along, or to kill him and save themselves the effort. What would happen to him now?

"What are you going to do to me?" Riana asked. Apparently her mind had wandered the same trail as Jig's.

"I will permit you to assist us in retrieving the rest of the treasure," Barius said generously. "Afterward you will be turned over to the proper authorities. You are still a criminal, after all. Fret not, for I am certain they will take your cooperation into consideration."

Riana nodded glumly, as though she had expected nothing more. Jig, on the other hand, was stunned. After all this, they would throw her into prison?

"That's not fair! She helped us," he protested. "She picked the lock on the Necromancer's door. She showed me the javelins I used to try to kill Straum."

He shouldn't have brought that up. The prince whirled on him at the mention of how Jig, not Barius, had fought the dragon. "The old worm was weak and tired, and I would have killed him myself had you not interfered. As for that lock, if you will recall, she nearly died in the attempt."

Jig started to argue, then thought better of it. No dragonchild would stop Barius from killing him this time. He looked at Darnak, but the dwarf only shook his head and looked away.

This started him wondering. If Barius planned to throw Riana away once he had finished using her, what did he plan for Jig? With Straum dead, Jig had begun to relax. But Straum had never been Jig's enemy. If not for Barius and the others, Jig would have lived out his life and never once bothered the old dragon. Riana herself had warned that the humans would kill him when they had no further use for their so-called guide.

He started to make plans of his own as he ate. He held no illusions about the prince's feelings toward him. Given the chance, Barius would kill him. Darnak wouldn't stop him. Nobody would.

Could he run away? Abandon the treasure and return to the lair? It might work. But if Barius were angry enough, that could also bring the adventurers right back to the goblins' cavern. Jig didn't think he would be able to stop the slaughter a second time. The only other choice was to kill Barius now, before he had a chance to do the same to Jig.

He would have to be fast. An attack from behind. Barius was too good with a sword, so a fair fight was out of the question.

Smudge, picking up some hint of Jig's plans, hopped off his

shoulder and crawled into a corner of the room. There he began to build a web, which reinforced Jig's sense of danger. Fire-spiders used webs not only to capture prey, but also for defense. Smudge was building a place to hide.

If only he knew how Darnak would react. In combat, the dwarf would protect his prince. But would he still feel the need to kill Jig if the prince was already dead? Would he understand why Jig had to kill Barius?

He would have to kill Ryslind as well, he realized. An attack on one brother earned the wrath of both. Though the wizard was half-dead already. That should make things easier.

Jig doubted Darnak would forgive the death of one prince, even if he understood the reasons. If Jig killed them both, he knew what Darnak would do. But if Jig didn't act, the humans would eventually return, and goblins would die. Adventurers were like fleas. If you didn't kill them right away, soon the blasted things were leaping into everything.

Jig had to kill them both. But he couldn't be in two places at once, and Barius was clearly the more dangerous of the two brothers. He would have to kill Barius, then get to Ryslind before Darnak used the new club he had claimed from Straum's collection to smash Jig's skull. He had a feeling that this time Shadowstar wouldn't be able to help him if he failed.

Maybe Riana could help. But how could he get to her without making the others suspicious? Besides, she appeared to be lost in her own despair. Her food sat untouched on the floor, and her glazed eyes stared into nothingness.

Jig glanced longingly at Smudge. How nice it would be to create his own web and hide there until the worst was over.

His best chance would be when they prepared to move out. Barius insisted on leading, which meant his back would be unguarded. Darnak had been walking with Ryslind to help support the wizard, which would make things a bit trickier. If he could kill Barius, then get to Ryslind fast enough . . . if Darnak hesitated for just a few seconds. . . .

Jig forced himself to finish eating, though his appetite had fled like a frightened goblin. His palms were moist where they rested on his thighs, but he didn't wipe the sweat off. He didn't want to do anything that might betray his nervousness.

Anyone who grew up inside the tunnels would have known from one look at Smudge that something was up, but nobody here recognized that clue.

He waited while Darnak finished off his wine, while Barius chewed daintily on his meat, while Ryslind sipped at some water. Had they ever before taken this long to eat? Jig didn't think so. They knew he was planning something, and they intended to torture him by making him wait. How long could it take to finish a bit of bread and cheese? Were human teeth so feeble?

At last Barius rose to his feet. "Beyond this tunnel lies glory." He waved an arm at the tunnel. "At last I will be accorded my due respect."

Jig forced himself to wait. He stood with the others, tried to shake out the stiffness in his legs, and grabbed his bag of gold. He slipped into line behind Barius. Not his usual place, but it couldn't be helped. He had to act now. He shifted the sack to his left hand and slowly reached toward his sword. His fingers touched the hilt.

Had Darnak or Ryslind noticed? His body should hide the movement. He wanted to turn, to make sure they hadn't seen, but he didn't dare. If Darnak had seen, he would be raising his club to strike. He wondered if he would hear the damp thud of his own skull cracking, or if he would simply reappear in front of Tymalous Shadowstar, looking sheepish after his failure.

Would Shadowstar want me to do this? Jig hesitated. He had promised to follow the god's rules, but Shadowstar had been a bit vague as to exactly how those rules applied. *Respect the shadow and the light both, for both have their place in the world.* What was that supposed to mean? Was Barius the shadow or the light? Stupid metaphors. Still, Shadowstar had protested when Jig thought about abandoning Riana and the others to their deaths in Straum's lair. He seemed to think killing was something to be done only as a last resort. It was a strange philosophy, one that would take some getting used to.

With a silent sigh, Jig started to put the sword away.

The sound of the blade returning to its sheath caught Barius's attention. He whirled, and his eyes homed in on the half-bared sword. His lips tightened into a terrible grin.

"I knew one such as you could never be trusted," Barius said. He sounded merry. He finally had an excuse to kill Jig, something he had wanted to do from the beginning. He tucked the Rod of Creation through his belt and slashed the air a few times with his own sword. Not knowing what else to do, Jig pulled his sword back out.

Barius promptly knocked it across the room.

"Jig!" Riana took a step after him, but Darnak caught her arm.

"This is how it has to be, lass."

She struggled, but the dwarf's grip was iron. "Why? Because your noble prince can't stand the fact that Jig humiliated him time after time? Maybe Jig knows Barius means to kill him as soon as we reach the surface. Maybe he was afraid."

Yes, he had been afraid. Now he was terrified. His sword was gone, and as his back touched the wall, he realized he had nowhere else to run. Fangs and claws were no match for steel, and Jig had never been much of a fighter anyway.

He glanced over and saw Smudge's web right beside him, now waist high. Fire-spiders built quickly when they were frightened.

"I'm sorry," Jig said. He hadn't intended to lead Barius back to Smudge. He hoped Barius would ignore the spider. Was he so spiteful he would kill Jig's pet once Jig was already dead?

"A bit late for apologies," Barius said, misunderstanding. He raised his sword. "If it's any consolation, I will be merciful. A single stroke to sever your head from your shoulders. A painless execution, which is better than you deserve."

"If you want to be merciful, shut up and get it over with."

Barius's eyes widened. "Brave words from a goblin. Very well."

Jig watched Barius flex his strong arms. Posing for the others, Jig figured. Typical. Jig straightened, determined to be brave just this once. He might not make it into songs or stories, but at least when he saw Shadowstar, he could say that he hadn't flinched at the end. What would Shadowstar say when they met?

He remembered what the god had told him before. *Next time you should try to duck.*

Jig screamed and rolled out of the way as the sword whistled over his head. His legs kicked madly, knocking Barius back. He tried to get up, but Barius kicked him in the side. Jig rolled over, clutching his gut. Barius stepped away, and his boot brushed Smudge's web.

"Little runt," Barius gasped. He glanced down at his leg. "Disgusting." With his free hand, he reached down to brush the web free.

Any goblin would have known better. Even Barius might have known, had he stopped to think. Smudge's web, like that of any fire-spider, was highly flammable. With an angry human looming over him, Smudge reacted the way he always did in the face of danger.

Barius screamed as flames enveloped his leg. He swatted his burning clothes, then stomped at the web. Smudge scurried back, flattening his body to the floor. He darted one way, then the other. Jig could see his legs waving in fear as he tried to get away, but Barius was too fast. Snarling like an animal, Barius turned so his foot was parallel to the wall.

"No!" Jig lunged, but he was too slow. Barius's boot landed on the terrified Smudge. To Jig, the crunch of Smudge's body sounded as loud as a dragon's roar.

"No," he repeated in a whisper. Most of the flames had died, and Jig could see there was nothing he could do. Even if Shadowstar would have helped him heal a lowly fire-spider, it was too late. Smudge was dead.

Jig snarled as he attacked, leaping onto Barius and sinking his fangs into the prince's sword arm. The sword hit the floor with a ring. Jig's claws raked Barius's body. Barius punched Jig in the head, but he didn't even feel it. All he could see was Smudge's crushed body. Tears blurred his vision as he bit down harder. His nails struggled to reach the flesh beneath the prince's armor.

"Curse you," Barius yelled. He wedged a knee against Jig's chest and pushed. Jig scrambled for anything to hold on to. If Barius got free, it was over. One of Jig's hands grabbed the prince's shirt, the other clawed at his belt.

Barius broke away. Jig flew back, still clutching a piece of Barius's shirt in one hand and something hard in the other. His head cracked against the floor. He wiped his eyes, and only then did he see what he had grabbed.

He had the Rod of Creation.

Barius saw it at the same time Jig did. He lunged for his sword. Jig scrambled to his feet and pointed the rod at Barius. "Stop!"

Barius froze.

"Look out!" Riana shouted.

Jig aimed the rod at Ryslind and Darnak, who stopped moving.

"You don't even know how to use it," Ryslind said. "Goblins have neither the strength of will nor the depth of mind for true magic."

"Neither do you," Riana snapped.

Jig felt his lips pull back into a feral grin. "*You* taught us how to use it," he said. He turned on Barius, who had begun to reach toward his sword.

"You can't destroy us," Barius said. "The rod is incapable of taking life."

"No matter what you do to us, we will find a way to reverse the effects," Ryslind added. "I've enough art left to see to that."

"Put the rod down, lad," Darnak said. "You go your way, we'll go ours."

Jig didn't have to look to know how the princes were taking that suggestion. "For how long?" he asked. "How long before they come back looking for more gold, or to get revenge on the goblin? When they get greedy for more treasure, they're not going to *ask* us to let them through. You know what will happen."

Darnak didn't answer.

"It's not as though you have a choice, goblin," Barius said. He had begun to smile again, believing he had won. "My brother is correct. You cannot kill us, not with the rod, even if you could control its magic."

Jig wavered. But then he saw the smoking web in the corner, and his arm tightened. "*You* controlled it," he said. He bared his teeth. "I bet I can do better."

The magic felt similar to the power Shadowstar had given him, but much more powerful. Jig felt as though his entire body were being crushed into the end of the rod and squeezed out the other side. He saw the prince stumble. His vision wavered, and his head began to pound. He concentrated on keeping himself whole. The rod tried to pull him apart, but Jig pulled back. He could feel the magic begin to work. He sensed the instant Barius's body started to reshape itself.

"Barius!"

Ryslind's voice, angry and panicked. He was trying to cast a spell of his own. Jig turned and pointed the rod at the wizard. Again the magic poured through him, halting Ryslind in midstride. White ice pierced Jig's brain as the rod's power broke through Ryslind's hastily erected shields. *Backlash,* he thought, remembering what had happened when Barius used the rod.

But even as Jig fell, he saw that it had worked.

He had just enough strength left to point the rod at Darnak. He didn't think he had enough strength left to use it, but Darnak wouldn't know that. So the dwarf stood helpless, watching the two enormous trout that had been Ryslind and Barius flop about on the floor as they suffocated.

"Go away," Jig croaked at Darnak.

The dwarf shook his head. Tears dripped into his beard. "I'll not leave them."

"I don't want to kill you, too," Jig said. *I don't think I can, for that matter.* If the other goblins heard him now, they'd think his mind had slipped. How could he not want to kill a perfectly good dwarf?

"They are family to me," Darnak said. "How can I go back to Wendel and Jeneve and tell them I watched their sons die?"

"Their sons were greedy fools," Riana said. She didn't bother to hide her satisfaction as she watched the gills of the Barius-fish stop moving.

"Aye," Darnak agreed. "But they were still family." With that he drew his club and walked toward Jig. He moved slowly, deliberately giving Jig time to use the rod.

Those few minutes had been enough for Jig to catch his

breath. Was he strong enough to use the rod again? He didn't think so. But was he ready to die and rejoin Shadowstar?

Jig sighed and grabbed the rod with both hands. Once again magic ripped through his body. He struggled to control it. He didn't want to kill Darnak, and that made things harder. He figured out what he wanted to do and concentrated on a different shape.

Darnak fell. His body twisted and bulged. The walls spun, and Jig blacked out.

CHAPTER 19

Parting Gifts

JIG WOKE UP TO FIND RIANA'S GREEN EYES STARing down at him. "My head hurts."

He still had the rod in his hands. She hadn't taken it from him. He wondered why. "What happened to Darnak?"

"You turned him into a bird," she said. For once no trace of sarcasm tainted her voice. She sounded impressed. "He flew away a few minutes ago."

"Good." He grimaced. The room had begun to stink of fish. He glanced down the tunnel, wishing he could have seen what Darnak had looked like. "Was it a good bird?" he asked.

She giggled. "Ugliest thing I've ever seen. Brown, with a dirty black crest and sunken eyes. He could talk, too. Said to warn you there'd still be people coming after this place. Barius and Ryslind had other brothers, and they'll want revenge."

"I know." He managed to sit up. "What will you do?"

Her eyes darkened. "What can I do?"

There was the bitterness Jig was used to.

"Go back to being a thief?" She gestured at the treasure scattered around the room. "If I take any of this, someone will only kill me to get it."

"You could always be an adventurer."

She snorted. "I never want to go on another 'adventure' as long as I live. I hate the dark, I hate the cold, I hate all the monsters from those ugly worms to that great hulk of a dragon. No treasure is worth this. If that's all I have to look forward to, you might as well kill me here and now. It would be a kindness."

Jig grinned. Only when she cringed away did he remember that his fangs were probably still covered in Barius's blood. Nor was his a reassuring face to begin with, even for a goblin. He looked around for something he could use to clean his teeth, and his searching eyes fell on the ashen remains of Smudge's web. His eyes stung.

"Oh Smudge," he mumbled. "I'm sorry." He shouldn't have let Barius get that close. An entire room, and he had led the prince straight to Smudge's hiding spot.

He crawled over and picked up the crushed spider. He stroked the furry head, then tucked Smudge into his pouch. He would take care of the body later.

Using the Rod of Creation as a simple cane, Jig pushed himself up. He didn't want to be here anymore. He wanted to go home.

"Wait," Riana said. She bit her lip, then said, "What about me?"

Jig shrugged. Why should he care? He wondered if she had meant it, when she said it would be kinder to kill her.

"I don't want to go back to that life." She grabbed the lantern Darnak had dropped and hurried after Jig.

"You've changed. You're not like the other goblins. Otherwise you would have killed Darnak. Well, I've changed too. I don't want to be a thief anymore, but I don't know how to be anything else. At least you can go back to your people. I've got nothing. I'm scared, Jig."

He stopped. He knew how hard it must have been for Riana to say that. "I can give you all the gold in the world, but you said you don't want it. What do you want?"

She began to cry. Why was everyone crying so much all of the sudden? First Jig, when Barius killed Smudge. Then Darnak, and now Riana. If this continued, they'd soon flood the whole mountain.

"I want to stop being afraid," she said.

"Fine." Jig grabbed the rod and used it before Riana could

protest. A minute later, he was gasping for breath while Riana stared in amazement at her hands.

He had used Straum's children as a model, but made a few changes. Where the dragonchildren had been a dusky bronze, Riana's scales were pearly white. Her body was smaller, retaining her elven slenderness, but the muscles beneath those scales were as powerful as any dragonchild's. Anyone who tried to hurt her would be lucky to walk away with their limbs attached. The scales should turn most blades. Only her eyes remained the same. Jig hadn't wanted to change those wide green eyes. She glanced at her hands and laughed when she saw that Jig had restored her missing finger.

She craned her neck to see Jig's other addition. Two wide, white wings spread across the tunnel.

"Can I fly?" she asked. She spoke with the same lisp as the other dragonchildren.

"I think so. You'll probably want to practice, though." He took a deep breath. "If you want, I can change you back. But you have to decide now. You won't have another chance."

She nodded slowly. "You're going to seal the entrance?"

"Yes."

Riana studied the sleek lines of her arms. Faster than Jig could follow, she punched a fist into the wall. Her delighted laugh echoed up the hall. "It didn't even hurt. Jig, this is beautiful."

He felt himself blushing. "Better than the bird?"

"Much better. I can go anywhere I want." Her voice rose with excitement. "I can fly through the clouds, I could cross the oceans, and nobody can stop me."

"You'll be lonely," Jig warned her. How could she not be? She was a monster now, and Jig had firsthand experience of how surface-dwellers treated monsters.

"I'm used to being lonely," she said. "Besides, if a goblin and an elf can be friends, what's to stop me from finding someone else out there?"

Jig had no answer to that, and he didn't know how to respond to her claim of friendship. He couldn't argue, either. Who ever heard of a goblin being friends with an elf? Who ever heard of a goblin being friends with anyone? But they had saved each other's lives several times, which was also unheard of. He blushed. If he tried to say anything, he'd probably make a fool of himself. Still, it felt surprisingly good to have a friend.

"I, um, I should go," he said. He blushed harder. "I have things I need to do."

"I understand." She rushed forward and pulled him into a hug he couldn't have broken out of if his life depended on it. "Thanks, Jig."

Then she was gone.

Feeling a strange mix of happiness and loss, Jig headed down the tunnel to close the entrance for good.

He took care of a few other tasks before heading back to the lair. He had a promise to keep to Tymalous Shadowstar. He took some time to redesign the shiny room. First, he shifted the glass tiles to form a clear image of the Autumn Star shining down on the best likeness Jig could manage of the god himself.

My nose isn't that big, Shadowstar protested.

I did the best I could. You're lucky I didn't stick with my first try.

That would have been even better. "Tymalous Shadowstar, the Cross-Eyed God."

The room itself remained empty, save for a small altar against the wall. For a while, Jig would likely be the only one to leave tokens of respect and thanks on that altar for the god. But he hoped to convince other goblins to do the same. If he could tell them of the things he had seen and learned, who knew what might happen? Shadowstar hadn't exactly been thrilled at the idea of a whole horde of goblin followers, but it was, in his words, *A hell of a lot better than nothing.*

At the base of the altar, an eight-pointed star marked the spot where Smudge had died. The fire-spider's body was buried inside the floor. A fine web traced the outline of the star. Jig didn't think the god would mind, and he wanted Smudge to have some sort of marker.

He left the gold and treasure where it was. What good would it do to bring it along? You couldn't eat treasure.

But you *could* eat trout. Jig had to stop several times as he lugged the huge fish along behind him. He had strung a rope through their gills to make them easier to drag, but they still weighed the same as full-grown humans. By the time Jig reached the edge of goblin territory, his hands were sore and rope-burned.

"Who's there?" challenged one of the guards.

Jig's ears picked up the other one's whispered, "It's *him*."

He grinned. They were afraid of him. What a nice change. "I've got food," he shouted.

Not two, but four guards ran down the corridor. *Stupid move. I could have been the point man for an ambush.* He would have to see about improving the quality of the guards.

"What's that thing on your face?" one guard asked warily.

His grin widened. That thing was another of the rod's gifts. He had used the blade of Barius's sword for the frames, since the steel was harder than any other metal he could find. The lenses were made of amethyst. Jig had needed a long time to get the shapes right, but finally he had a set of elven lenses that worked. The bubblelike lenses covered his large eyes, the frames hooked lightly around his pointed ears, and for the first time in his life, he could *see*.

"Forget it," Jig said. "Someone help me with these fish."

Seeing the trout, the guards began to drool. Forgetting whatever their orders might have been concerning Jig, they ran forward and helped him carry the fish into the cavern.

"Golaka's gonna be happy to see *this*," one said.

"Yes." Jig bit his lip. Hopefully she wouldn't throw Jig into the pot along with the fish. He gave the rod a spin, admiring the way its gleaming new steel bowl caught the torchlight. After all, when he finished with his lenses, most of Barius's blade had remained. What better use than to repair Golaka's spoon? Maybe this would help calm some of her rage.

"Pickings have been pretty lean this past day or two," another guard grumbled.

"Don't worry," Jig said. "I have some ideas about that." He would have to talk to other goblins, but he thought everyone would agree with his plan. Especially if it meant finding more food.

Straum's forest had continued to exist after the dragon died. According to Ryslind, the trees, the animals, and most of what lived down there were real. Poor imitations of the genuine articles, perhaps, but still real. That meant they could be eaten! All Jig had to do was convince a group to go hunting with him. Once they brought back their first deer, there should be no more arguments. He looked forward to finding out if venison tasted as good as Riana had promised.

Something brushed against Jig's foot, and he stopped.

"What is it?" one of the guards said. Jig waved them away as he stooped over to investigate. A tiny spider, black with red spots, waved its front legs in the air at him.

"Smudge?" Jig said in disbelief. The spots were the same, though the spider itself was much smaller. This was Smudge as he had been two years ago, newly hatched. But it couldn't be Smudge. He had buried Smudge only a few hours ago.

Goblins . . . no faith whatsoever.

Jig glanced upward. If he took the rod back and opened up the stone in front of Shadowstar's altar, would he find Smudge's body gone? The god didn't give an answer, and Jig didn't really want one. He placed his hand on the floor and waited while the spider crawled onto his palm.

When the fire-spider went straight to the leather pad on Jig's shoulder, he began to giggle with delight. He scratched the spider's head, feeling that things were finally right with the world.

A shriek stabbed his ears. "What? He's *here*? Where is he? I'll teach him to mess with his betters. Boil him until his skin peels off, I will."

Jig sighed. "Come on, Smudge. Let's go give Golaka's spoon back." Together they walked down the tunnel toward home.

Goblin Hero

The Song of Jig
(to the tune of the wizard drinking song
"Sweet Tome of Ally Ba'ma")

Heroes entered the darkness,
A dwarf, an elf, and two men,
Seeking fame, seeking glory,
Slaying goblins as they went.

But one lone goblin dodged their blades and their bow.
That lone goblin, he survived.
They tied him up, to be their guide down below,
But Jig's the only one who came out alive.

Hail, Jig Dragonslayer.
His sword is strong, his aim is true.
Hail, Jig Dragonslayer.
Treat him well, or he might slay you too.

Jig led them down through the darkness,
To the realm of the dead,
Where corpses leaped from the shadows
And the heroes nearly lost their heads.

Jig the goblin did not cower.
His sword is strong, his aim is true.
No, Jig the goblin did not cower.
He drew his sword and ran the Necromancer through.

So Jig, he led those heroes deeper,
To the darkness where the dragon dwelled.
Steam was rising from his night black scales,
And his eyes were pits from hell.

Hail, Jig Dragonslayer.
His sword is strong, his aim is true.
Hail, Jig Dragonslayer.
While others fled, Jig grabbed a spear, and he threw.

Hail, Jig Dragonslayer.
His sword is strong, his aim is true.
Jig finished off that beast of hell.
Then he finished off those heroes too.
So treat him well, or else he might slay you.

CHAPTER 1

"How come goblins never live happily ever after?"

—Jig Dragonslayer

JIG THE GOBLIN WAS NO WARRIOR. HIS LIMBS were like blue sticks, his torn ear tended to flop to the side, and his fangs barely stretched up past his upper lips. As a child he had been relegated to muck duty, hauling caustic sludge through the goblin lair to fill the fire bowls that illuminated the cavern. The putrid, rotting-plant smell of muck would seep into his clothes, his hair, even his skin. And muck duty was far from the worst he had survived. He tried not to think about his time cleaning privies.

His grand quest a year ago hadn't changed him. Well, except for the nightmares about the dragon Straum coming back to eat him, or the Necromancer casting a spell to wither Jig's body until it crumbled to dust, or giant carrion-worms crawling into his bedroll and—

Jig shook his head, trying to banish those images. Suffice it to say, he was still the same nearsighted runt he had been before. But he had emerged from the dragon's lair with one potent gift: the ability to heal various injuries.

Given the nature of goblin life, this made Jig one of the busiest goblins in the lair.

His current patient, a muscular goblin named Braf, was everything a goblin warrior should be. Strong, tall, and dumb . . . even for a goblin. Somehow Braf had managed to wedge his own right fang deep inside his left nostril.

Jig shook his head. Braf raised stupidity to new heights, then threw it down to shatter on the earth below.

A dirty rag looped around Braf's jaw held the fang still. Blood and other fluids turned the rag dark blue. Braf gingerly wiped his nose on his wrist, momentarily halting the seepage. He stared at the goo on his hand, then wiped it on his too-tight leather vest.

"Can you fix it?" Braf said, his voice muffled and nasal.

"Don't talk," Jig said. He closed his eyes. *How much longer?*

Tymalous Shadowstar, forgotten god of the Autumn Star, stifled a giggle only Jig could hear. *I'm sorry, I'm doing the best—* The god's voice dissolved into jingling laughter.

Jig had discovered Tymalous Shadowstar during that adventure a year before. Or maybe Shadowstar had discovered Jig. Shadowstar was the one who gave Jig the power to heal the other goblins. What Shadowstar got out of the deal, Jig still wasn't sure. There were days he thought Shadowstar did it purely for his own amusement.

How did he do this to himself anyway? Shadowstar asked between giggles.

Braf's not exactly the sharpest blade in the armory, Jig said. *But I'm guessing he had help.* Someone had tied those bandages on to Braf's head. Had Braf tried to do it, he probably would have hanged himself.

Goblins. Why did it have to be goblins?

It was a complaint Jig had listened to ever since he discovered the forgotten god. Now was when Jig would traditionally try to defend his people, to point out the things they had accomplished in the past year. Things like achieving a shaky truce with the hobgoblins deeper in the mountain, and sealing off the outer tunnel to protect them from adventurers.

Yet when he looked at Braf, Jig couldn't find it in himself to speak up on behalf of the goblins.

I think I'm ready now, said Shadowstar.

"Good." Jig crossed the small temple, trying to ignore the mosaic on the ceiling. Bits of colored glass formed an image of the forgotten god, a tall, pale man dressed in black, with silver bells striping his arms and legs. Sour smoke from the muck lanterns floated around the image, never quite reaching the pale face. The face had a definite smirk, one that hadn't been there earlier in the day.

Jig placed his hand over Braf's nose and tried not to grimace. Goblins had never been known for their attractiveness, and Braf was a spectacular example of why. Old disease scars dotted his skin, and his misshapen nose looked a great deal like a pregnant frog that had settled in the center of his face.

Shadowstar started to snicker again. *Now it looks like a frog with a huge yellow fang up its—*

"Hold still," said Jig. He tilted Braf's head back and slipped one finger beneath the bandage as he waited for the magic to start. The flow of Shadowstar's power through Jig's body always made him feel bloated, and he shifted uncomfortably as the magic warmed his hands.

Before he could do anything more, a glowing orange insect landed on his arm and began to creep forward. Jig yanked his hand back. The last thing he needed was for a bug to crawl up Braf's nose. He swatted it, splattering glowing bug goo over his arm, even as two more of the pests buzzed around his head.

"What are they?" Braf asked.

"I don't know. They started showing up a few weeks ago." Jig waved his hands, trying to bat them toward the spiderweb in the corner of the temple. "And stop talking!"

The bugs drew back. Jig slapped his free hand over Braf's swollen nose.

Slowly, Shadowstar warned.

A hair's breadth at a time, Jig slid the offending fang out of the nostril. He tried very hard to ignore the fluids that followed, coating Jig's hands with blue slime. He also ignored the feel of the fang moving beneath the nostril, the way the tooth scraped against the bone.

Braf's eyes crossed. The warmth in Jig's hands increased.

His fingers felt like swollen tubers, and the orange bugs were circling Braf's head. Jig's arms tingled.

Got it, Shadowstar said.

Jig slid the tip of the fang free, and there was a loud popping sound as the jawbone slipped back into the socket. Jig swung one hand at the bugs. He missed, and the motion splattered blood across Shadowstar's mosaic.

Braf sneezed. He touched his nose, and a broad grin split his blood-crusted face. "Thanks, Jig!"

Blood, spit, and snot had misted Jig's spectacles. He slipped them off and wiped the lenses on his pants. "So how did you do this to yourself?"

"I was on guard duty," Braf said. "My partner bet me I couldn't touch my nose with my fang. When I won the bet, he punched me in the jaw."

A shining example of the goblin race, Shadowstar commented.

"I guess you showed him," Jig said.

Braf laughed. "Yeah." He scratched his chin and turned to go. As he stooped through the low doorway, he hesitated. "Hey, don't tell anyone I came to you. Some of the other goblins don't like you that much, and I don't want them to—"

"To think you've been coming to the runt for help?" Jig asked, his voice tight. Nearly every goblin had needed Jig's help at one time or another over the past year, but not one wanted to admit it.

"Yeah!" Braf beamed. "That's right. Thanks!" He disappeared down the tunnel before Jig could find anything to throw at him. Some things never changed. No matter how many goblins he healed, no matter how many quests he survived, he was still Jig the scrawny, half-blind runt.

Jig sat down on the altar. A dark, red-spotted fire-spider the size of Jig's hand crept up the side and scurried toward him. Jig straightened his arm so the spider could climb onto the singed leather pad Jig wore strapped to his right shoulder. Fire-spiders grew hot when threatened, and Jig had the burns to prove it. Despite the scars, Smudge still made a better companion than most goblins.

"It's not that bad," Jig said to Smudge. "They can't afford to kill me. Who would fix their wounds?"

He glanced at the blood on his trousers and sighed. Another improvement from a year ago was the quality of Jig's clothes. Jig had spent most of his adult life in a ratty old loincloth so stiff he could have used it for a shield. Now he wore soft gray trousers and a loose black shirt. His old sword hung at his side, and he had his favorite boots on. The leather was bright blue, with red flames painted down the side and white, furry fringe on top.

Most importantly, he had his spectacles. Large, amethyst lenses covered his eyes, letting him see the world as clearly as any goblin, except for his peripheral vision where the lenses didn't quite cover. Steel frames kept them hooked over his pointed ears. They weren't perfect, and the frames irritated his bad ear, which had been torn and scarred in a fight with another goblin. But being able to see the world around him was worth a little pain.

Recently Shadowstar had suggested another addition to his wardrobe: socks. It had taken a long time to persuade one of the children to weave a pair of cloth tubes, then sew them shut at one end, but the result was literally a gift from the gods. No more blisters, no more dark blue marks on his legs where the dye from his boots rubbed off, and best of all, his boots didn't smell quite so horrid when he took them off.

"Jig?"

The voice came from the darkness of the tunnels, but Jig recognized it. "What do you want, Veka?"

Veka stepped into the temple, drawing her long black cloak tight around her considerable bulk. Broad-shouldered and thick-limbed, she had sent more than one goblin to Jig with missing teeth or a broken nose.

Veka worked in the distillery, turning rotted fungus, smashed glowworms, and pungent mushrooms into muck. As a result, she always smelled like decomposing plants. Her hands were covered in greenish stains, and the fumes of the muck room had left her eyes bloodshot.

"You didn't cast a binding spell when you healed Braf's nose. How did you do that?" She rapped the end of her staff on the floor for emphasis. Glass beads, bits of metal, and what looked like a mummified finger all clattered against the staff, tied there with scraps of leather and braided hair.

The staff, like her cloak, was part of Veka's obsession with all things magical. An obsession that unfortunately included Jig.

"I don't even know what a binding spell is," Jig said, hopping down from the altar. He walked toward the tunnel and hoped she would move out of his way.

Veka didn't budge. She raised a tight fist and slowly spread her fingers. Faint threads of light formed a dim, fragile web between her fingers. "The binding is the way the wizard taps into the magical powers that surround her. It is the first step of the journey toward—"

At that point, one of the orange bugs landed on Veka's hand. The binding spell flickered out of existence. "Stupid bug!" She smooshed it flat.

"Veka, I can't—"

She didn't let him finish. Scowling, she set her staff against the wall and fished through her clothes. From a pocket within her cloak, she produced a stained brown book. The cover had been torn off and resewn, and many of the pages were coming loose from the binding. "Josca says in chapter two that the Hero will find a guide, a mentor to lead them to the path." She waved the book at Jig like a sword. "You're the only goblin who knows anything about magic, and you won't even—"

"Who is Josca?" Jig asked, stepping back.

Veka tapped the cover. Oversize silver letters read *The Path of the Hero (Wizard's ed.) by Josca*. "Josca says every Hero follows the same path. Only the details change. I need a mentor. By refusing to teach me magic, you're blocking my way."

Her teeth were bared, and the long lower fangs looked freshly sharpened. Jig took another step back. "Josca should write an edition for goblins. In the first chapter the hero sets out for adventure. In the second he dies a horrible, painful death."

"You survived." Her scowl turned the words into an accusation.

Heavy footsteps running up the tunnel saved Jig from having to answer. Braf shouldered his way past Veka and said, "I forgot. The chief said she wants to see you. It's about the ogre."

"What ogre?" Jig asked.

"The one who showed up right after my . . . problem," Braf said, with a quick glance at Veka. "He smashed up a few other guards. He said he was looking for the Dragonslayer. The chief said to go right away."

Jig covered one of the muck lanterns and scooped up the other by the handle. Green light reflected from the dark red obsidian of the walls as he followed Braf into the tunnels. The clomp of Veka's staff followed close behind.

"What do you think the ogre wants?" Braf asked.

"I'm more worried about what the chief will do to me for taking so long to answer her." Ever since Kralk took control of the goblins, she had been looking for a way to get rid of Jig. He frowned, thinking about the rest of Braf's story. "Why didn't the other guards come to me for healing?"

"What guards?"

"The ones the ogre injured."

Braf laughed. "When I left, the older goblins were scrubbing what was left of them off the walls."

Jig swallowed and began to run.

Two guards stood outside the entrance to the goblin cavern. Fire bowls provided a cheerful yellow-green light. Jig ignored the blue bloodstains on the wall and floor. He flattened his ears as he walked inside. He had been away most of the day, and even the subdued, nervous conversation of five hundred goblins was louder than he was used to.

Smudge shifted restlessly on Jig's shoulder. The heat from the fire-spider's body caused drops of sweat to trickle down Jig's neck. Not that Jig needed the warning.

The ogre was easy to spot. He sat near the back of the cavern, surrounded by armed goblins. Steel blades and long wooden spears trembled as the goblins fought to control their fear. For his part, the ogre didn't seem to notice.

Why should he? His leathery green skin was strong enough

to turn away most attacks, and his hands were as big as Jig's head. He sat on the floor . . . probably because if he stood, his head would scrape the ceiling. His teeth were smaller than goblin fangs, but still sharp enough to sever a limb. He could cut a swath through the cavern bare-handed. Shadowstar only knew what he could do with the huge, brass-studded club resting across his knees.

"Jig! It's about time you got your scrawny arse down here," shouted Kralk. The lanky goblin chief was smiling, which made Jig nervous. She wore a necklace of jagged malachite spikes and an ill-fitting dwarvish breastplate. Metal spikes adorned the shoulders and . . . chest area . . . of her armor. Kralk collected weapons, rarely carrying the same one two days in a row. Today a nasty-looking morningstar hung from her belt, clanking as she walked toward Jig.

Jig hadn't been around when the last chief died. At the time, he had been around the fifth or sixth stanza of "The Song of Jig," somewhere between fighting the Necromancer and cowering before the dragon. When Jig came back, many of the goblins had encouraged him to take over as chief, a prospect he found as appealing as dancing naked in front of tunnel cats.

Ultimately, three goblins had emerged as potential candidates, ready to fight for control of the lair. The morning of the fight, only one of those three showed up for breakfast. The other two were found curled up near the garbage pit with most of their blood on the outside of their bodies.

Kralk had been trying to get rid of Jig ever since. She never challenged him openly. No, it was always "Jig, could you slay that rock serpent that snuck into the distillery?" or "We need someone to lead a raiding party to steal food from the ogres," or "Golaka is experimenting with a new soup, and she wants someone to taste it."

Naturally, Jig always said no. Each refusal chipped away at his reputation, reinforcing Kralk's power over the goblins and making his life miserable. Why couldn't she see that he wasn't a threat?

The ogre's voice thundered through the cavern, making Jig jump. "This is the Dragonslayer?"

A path opened between Jig and the ogre. Goblins moved away like blood flowing from a wound. Jig reached up to stroke Smudge's head. The fire-spider was warm, but not hot enough to burn. They weren't in any immediate danger.

For an instant Jig considered lying. If he said Braf was Jig Dragonslayer, the ogre wouldn't know any better. One look at the grin on Kralk's face shattered that plan.

"I'm Jig," he said. His voice sounded like a child's squeak compared to the ogre's.

"You're the one who killed the dragon Straum?" The ogre picked up his club and made his way toward Jig, keeping his head and shoulders hunched.

Jig glanced at Kralk, then nodded.

"You put a spear through that monster's eye?"

He nodded again.

"You? You're the one they sing that song about, the one—"

"Yes, that's me!" Jig snapped. His momentary anger ebbed as quickly as it had begun, leaving his legs so weak he thought he was going to collapse. *Brilliant*, he thought. *Shout at the ogre. Why not kick him in the groin next?*

The ogre knelt, peering down at Jig, then back at Kralk. "He's like a little goblin doll!"

Jig's claws dug into his palms. Better a toy than a threat. "Braf said you wanted to talk to me."

"That's right." The ogre took another step, putting him almost within arm's reach. Almost within Jig's reach, at least. The ogre could have grabbed Jig by the head and bounced him off the nearest wall without stretching. His green scalp wrinkled into a frown. "We need . . ." His voice grew quiet, muffling the last word.

"What was that?" Jig asked.

The ogre's face turned a deeper green, almost exactly the same shade as the mold that grew on the privy walls. "Help. We need help."

Jig stared, trying to put the pieces together. He understood the words, but his mind struggled with the idea that ogres would come to goblins for help. What next? The Necromancer returning from the dead to start a flower garden?

"What kind of help?" Jig asked.

"A few months ago something showed up in Straum's cave and started hunting us. At first we thought it was those hobgoblin types, or maybe you goblins, so we came up and slaughtered a few of you." He gave a sheepish half shrug. "Sorry about that."

Kralk stepped closer. "You killed far more hobgoblins than goblins. We considered it a favor."

"Right. So you won't mind doing us a favor in return." The ogre stared at Jig. "Whatever they are, they've got magic on their side. Many of us have already died. Others have been enslaved. They're hunting down those who remain, the families who fled into the deeper tunnels."

Jig had met two wizards in his time. One had been a companion on his quest. The other was the dreaded Necromancer. Both had tried to kill him. To be fair, a number of nonwizards had also tried to kill him, but wizards tended to be much nastier about it.

"We've heard of you," the ogre said. "You've got magic of your own, right?"

Jig knew where this was going, and his mouth was too dry to answer. He managed a weak nod.

Kralk's smile grew. Smudge responded to that smile with enough heat to sear the leather shoulder pad. Tiny threads of smoke rose from beneath his feet. Interesting that the goblin chief frightened him more than the ogre. Jig had always known Smudge was smart.

"What do you say, Jig?" asked Kralk.

Jig took a step back. There had to be a way out of this. He whirled and pointed at Veka. "What about her? She can cast a binding spell, and she *wants* to be a Hero."

The closest goblins started to laugh, either at Jig's cowardice or at the idea of smelly, overweight Veka as a hero. As for Veka herself, she flashed a grin nearly as wicked as Kralk's own. "Sorry, Jig. If you had taught me magic, I might be powerful enough to help. But I guess you'll have to do this on your own."

"But—"

"This is your path, Jig Dragonslayer, not mine." Veka

tapped her staff on the floor, rattling the beads and bones. "A Hero must make her own path. To quote the valiant Duke Hoffman, who transformed himself to rescue the mermaid Liriara, 'I have chosen my way, and it is the way of the squid.' "

The ogre stared. "What's she talking about? What's a squid?"

Say yes. Shadowstar's voice was calm and firm.

Jig's was not. "What?" He closed his eyes, trying to shut out the rest of the cavern so he could concentrate on Tymalous Shadowstar. *You want me to say yes?*

I can't see everything that's happening, but I can tell you this much. Something about your ogre friend feels wrong. There's a residue of some sort, almost a magical shadow. Whatever's happening down there, it's dangerous. You have a choice, Jig Dragonslayer. You can go with the ogre and discover what's happening, or you can wait for the problem to come to you.

Waiting sounds good. Shadowstar didn't answer. Jig sighed. The god always meant business when he used Jig's full name. *What do you expect me to do? They're ogres! If they can't fight this thing, how am I—*

You've fought dragons and wizards and adventurers, and you survived. Veka is peculiar, even for a goblin, but she's also correct. A Hero is one who finds a way.

Kralk is trying to get me killed! She—

Or you can refuse. Tell the ogre no, and see how he reacts.

Right. Jig looked at the ogre. "I'll go," he muttered.

"Excellent!" The ogre slapped him on the shoulder, knocking him to the ground. "Whoops. Sorry about that. I forget how fragile you bugs are. Nothing broken, I hope?" He grabbed Jig's arm and hauled him upright.

Jig stepped back, testing his arm. Fortunately, the ogre hadn't struck the shoulder where Smudge was perched. The fire-spider was crouched into a hot ball, staring at the ogre. Smudge extended his legs. With a burst of speed, Smudge raced down Jig's chest and burrowed into a pouch on his belt, leaving a trail of smoking dots down Jig's shirt.

"Take Braf along for protection," said Kralk, sneering. "Whoever's hunting the ogres might not have heard 'The Song of Jig.' They might mistake you for a stunted coward and rip you apart before you have the chance to tell them of your great deeds."

Jig glanced at Braf, who was busy picking the scabs on his nose. He couldn't decide if bringing Braf would improve his chances of survival or make them worse. Braf grimaced and stretched his jaw, using the tip of his fang to scratch inside his freshly healed nostril. Definitely worse.

"Someone else volunteered to accompany you," Kralk added.

"I'm coming, I'm coming," said a goblin from the back of the cave, in a voice so old it creaked.

Kralk grinned again. "Jig will certainly need a nursemaid to look after him."

Goblins snickered as Grell made her way through the group to join Jig. If there was any goblin who would be of less use than Braf, it was Grell.

The canes she used to support her weight were smooth sticks, dyed dark yellow with hobgoblin blood. Grell was older than any goblin Jig knew, with the possible exception of Golaka the chef. But where Golaka had gotten bigger and meaner with age, Grell had shrunk until she was almost as small as Jig himself. Her face reminded Jig of wrinkled rotten fruit. Grell had worked in the nursery for as long as Jig could remember, and generations of teething goblin babies had covered her hands and forearms in scars. Dark stains covered her sleeveless shirt. Jig tried not to think about the origins of those stains.

"Are you sure?" Jig asked. "It will be dangerous. The ogres—"

"Ogres, ha!" Grell said. One whiff of her breath made the rotten fruit comparison much more apt. One of her yellowed fangs was broken near the gums, and the smell of decay made Jig want to gag. "Spend a week with twenty-three goblin babies and another nine toddlers, then we'll talk about danger."

"But—"

Grell jabbed the end of one cane into Jig's chest. "Listen, boy. If I spend one more day with those monsters, either I'm going to kill them or, more likely, they're going to kill me. I refuse to die buried in sniveling, crying brats. Kralk agreed to give me a break from nursery duty if I went with you and this green-skinned clod, so I'm going. Understand?"

"What about the nursery?" Jig asked desperately. "Who's going to take over?"

"Riva's still in there, but you're right. Without help, they'll probably overpower her pretty quickly." Grell turned toward the kitchens. "Hey, Golaka. Send one of your drudges over to help watch the brats!" To Jig, she added, "That should work. They can always threaten to barbecue the older ones if they get out of line."

Golaka peered out of the doorway. Sweat made her round face shine. She waved her stirring spoon in the air, spraying droplets of gravy over the nearest goblins. "My helpers are all busy mashing worms for dinner."

"I only want one. And your worm pudding tastes like week-old vomit anyway," Grell shouted back.

Jig cringed. He could see other goblins creeping out of the way, as far from Golaka as they could get. On the bright side, maybe he wouldn't have to take Grell along after all.

Golaka shook her spoon at Grell. "Last one who complained about my cooking got his tongue ripped out. The taste didn't bother him at all after that."

"Pah," said Grell. "Just send over whatever idiot overspiced the snake meat the other night. One day dealing with teething goblin babies, and they'll work twice as hard once they're back safe in your kitchen."

Golaka's spoon stopped in midshake. The rage on her face slowly melted away, and she began to chuckle. "I like that." She spun and headed back to the kitchen. "Hey, Pallik. Stop licking the hammer and get over here. I've got a new job for you!"

Jig turned to the ogre, who had watched the entire exchange with an increasingly skeptical expression.

"Come on," said Jig. *Before anyone else volunteers to "help."*

The laughter of the other goblins followed them out of the lair, stopping abruptly when the ogre spun around and snarled. The silence drew a faint smile from Jig. His goblin companions might be worse than useless, but he could get used to having an ogre along.

Jig studied the two goblins. "What is that supposed to be?" he asked, staring at the object in Braf's hand.

"A weapon, I think," said Braf. "I traded a hobgoblin for it a few days ago."

The so-called weapon was the length of Jig's leg. A thick wooden shaft ended in a brass hook, wide enough to catch someone's neck. The other end was barbed and pointed.

"Do you know how to use it?" Jig asked.

"I wanted to name it first. I was going to call it a hooker."

Jig cringed.

"But that didn't sound right," Braf went on, rotating the weapon and testing the point on his other hand. "I thought about calling it a goblin-stick, because I'm a goblin. But I think I'm going to name it a hook-tooth, because it's sharp like a tooth, only the other end is hooked, see?"

Standing behind Jig, the ogre snickered. He could probably snap Braf's hook-tooth with one hand.

"I wish I could remember where I put my shield though," Braf continued. "I had it at dinner last night because I used it as a plate, and I remember Mellok kept stealing my fried bat wings."

Grell's wrinkled face tightened with disgust. Shifting her balance, she raised her cane and slammed it into Braf's back, making a loud *thunk*.

Braf hardly budged, but his face lit up. He craned his neck and patted the edge of the shield, still strapped to his back. "Thanks, Grell!"

Jig turned to the ogre. "What's your name?"

"Walland Wallandson the Fourth."

"The fourth what?" asked Braf.

"The fourth Walland Wallandson."

Braf stared. "Couldn't the other ogres come up with enough names?" He seemed oblivious to the glare Grell shot him, so she slapped the back of his head.

"It's my father's name," said Walland. He flexed his fingers, and his knuckles popped with the sound of cracking bones. "He was Walland Wallandson the Third. His father was the Second, and my great-grandfather was Walland Wallandson the First. Your name is your legacy. Your family is everything. Anyone who mocks the Wallandson name had best prepare for a long, painful death." That last was said with a glare at Braf.

"Seems awfully inefficient," said Grell. "All those ogres taking care of their own offspring. How do you find time for anything else?"

Walland shrugged. "They don't stay young forever." He turned to Jig. "Well?"

"Well what?"

"Are we going?"

Jig had forgotten he was supposed to be in charge of the other goblins. "Right. Sorry." He raised his lantern, then hesitated. Going first meant leaving two goblins and an ogre at his back. Walland probably wouldn't do anything, not if he really wanted Jig's help. But the other two, well, they were goblins. Worse, Kralk must have talked to both of them before Jig even arrived.

"What's wrong?" Braf asked.

It wasn't that Jig didn't trust them. He trusted them to behave like goblins. "I'm wondering which one of you has orders to kill me."

He hoped his bluntness would startle the guilty one into confessing. Instead, Braf and Grell glanced at one another, then at the floor. Neither one would meet Jig's eyes.

Jig was in trouble. "Braf?"

Braf scratched his nose. "Kralk said she'd chop me up and toss me in Golaka's stewpot if you came back alive. She thinks you want to kill her and take her place."

"Why, so the entire lair can plot my death instead of just you two?" Jig asked, his voice pitched higher than normal. Borderline hysteria had that effect on him. "What about you?" he asked, turning to Grell. "What did she promise you?"

"She said if I killed you, she'd make sure I never have to work in that miserable, foul-smelling nursery again."

"You can't do that," Braf protested, raising his hook-tooth. "Kralk told *me* to kill him."

Jig's hand brushed the handle of his sword. From this angle, he could probably stab Grell in the back, but Braf was out of reach. Besides, Tymalous Shadowstar frowned on stabbing people in the back. Jig had never understood that, but he knew better than to argue the point.

Walland snorted and stepped past Jig, giving Braf a light shove that sent him bouncing off the wall. Braf landed on his backside, nearly impaling himself on his own weapon. "Trustworthy lot, you goblins," said Walland.

Jig didn't answer. Despite common belief, the goblin language did include a word for trust. It was derived from the word for trustworthy, which in the goblin tongue, was the same as the word for dead.

Jig stared at the ogre's leathery face, hoping he wasn't about to make a mistake. "Walland came to us for help," he said. "He asked for me. For Jig Dragonslayer." He narrowed his eyes and tried to look menacing as he turned to the other goblins. "I imagine he'd be very unhappy if something happened to me before we could help him."

Braf stood up, rubbing his behind. "I'm not afraid of some ogre," he said, lowering Jig's estimate of his intelligence even further. But he tucked his hook-tooth through the shield on his back and made no move to attack.

"Grell?" Jig asked.

Grell shrugged. "The way I figure it, there's a good chance you'll get yourself killed down there and save me the trouble."

"Fine." Knowing she was probably right gave Jig a sick feeling in his gut, as though he had eaten something that wasn't quite dead yet. His only consolation, as he raised the lantern and set off down the tunnel, was that whatever killed him would no doubt kill the other goblins as well.

CHAPTER 2

"The path to glory begins with a single step. Of course, so does the path to the headsman's block."

—Jasper the Godhunter
From *The Path of the Hero (Wizard's ed.)*

VEKA'S BOOKS BOUNCED AGAINST HER SIDES AS she hurried out of the goblin lair. She pulled her cloak tighter to minimize the jostling. She should have sewn more padding into the pockets.

She mumbled to herself, practicing the grand speech she had worked up to explain her departure to the guards. She would start by saying she had heard the call of destiny and had decided to set out on her own to fight the invasion of their mountain home. The path promised great danger and mighty trials which only the greatest of Heroes might survive.

She stopped when she reached the guards, who were in the middle of a game of Roaches. Both guards stomped their feet, each trying to scare the three roaches toward the other side of the tunnel. The goal was to gct them to flee past your opponent without touching either the roaches or the other goblin. The game usually ended with crushed bugs and broken toes.

Veka tapped her staff on the ground. Nothing happened. "Aren't you going to challenge me?"

They kept stomping. "Move, you stupid bug!" shouted one.

Veka cleared her throat. "I said—"

"I heard," said the guard. "Who do you think I was talking to?"

His partner laughed, and the first guard took the opportunity to jump in front of the closest roach, sending it racing back.

Veka hunched her shoulders and hurried past. She tried to comfort herself with the fact that many Heroes endured the mockery of their peers. Look at how the warriors used to treat Jig Dragonslayer, back before he had the luck to get himself captured by adventurers and dragged along to fight wizards and dragons and such.

Well, it was her turn now. She imagined returning with the power to cast a spell that would transpose the guards and the roaches, letting the goblins scurry about until they were crushed beneath giant roach feet. She had set out on the Hero's Path, and when she returned, she would have the power to punish all the goblins who had laughed and jeered over the years.

The first chapter of *The Path of the Hero* talked about The Refusal, when the Hero first sees the Path and turns away. Veka wasn't sure why the Hero did this, especially since they all ended up on the Path anyway, but Josca was adamant. All true Heroes began by turning their backs on the Path, just as Jig had done when he tried to get Veka to go with the ogre instead of him.

Fortunately, Jig had given her the perfect opportunity to announce her own refusal, and she got to make Jig look like a fool at the same time. Served him right for hoarding all that magic for himself. Veka had worked so hard to set Braf up, all so she could watch Jig perform his healing magic. Yet for all of her planning and spying, she had seen nothing new. Jig never used a spellbook. He never cast a binding charm. He didn't use a wand or a staff or any of the traditional wizarding tools. He grabbed the wounded goblins, and magic simply *happened*. "How am I supposed to learn anything from that?" Veka muttered.

The last trace of light disappeared behind her as the tunnel curved to the left. Veka moved to one side, brushing her fingers along the grime-covered wall as she walked. She had brought a small muck lantern from the distillery, but any light would make her far too visible.

The smell of the air changed as she walked, taking on the musty scent of animal droppings and hobgoblin cooking, both of which smelled equally foul to Veka's nose. She had come this way only twice in her life, both times sneaking through with other goblins to raid Straum's lair below. That was where she had found her spellbook, along with her copy of *The Path of the Hero*.

The harsh sound of hobgoblin laughter interrupted her thoughts. She hurried through the tunnel until she caught a glimpse of Jig arguing with the hobgoblin guards. Jig had left his companions behind, facing the guards alone, as a true Hero should. The twisting of the tunnel meant she couldn't see the hobgoblins, but she heard at least two different voices aside from Jig's own.

The other goblins and the ogre all waited before the bend as Jig said, "We need to get to the lower tunnels."

"Is that so? What did you bring for the nice tunnel guards?" said one of the hobgoblins.

"Fresh-cooked meat?" asked the other. "Maybe some of that spicy lizard tail your chef makes with fire-spider eggs."

"If you haven't got that, we could always settle for a few strips of your flesh." Both hobgoblins laughed.

Veka leaned forward, straining to hear how Jig would respond. Would he draw his sword and slay both guards, or would he use magic? She hoped for the latter.

Jig did neither. "We haven't got any food to spare, so you're going to have to settle for strips of flesh." Veka crept closer, hoping the other goblins wouldn't look back. Jig waved his hand at the ogre, who lumbered into the light. "Why don't you start with his?"

A disappointed sigh hissed through Veka's teeth. That was so typical of Jig, always finding ways to sneak out of anything heroic. It made her wonder again about "The Song of Jig." Had Jig really slain the Necromancer and the dragon? More likely he had skulked in the shadows while the adventurers did the real fighting, then stabbed them all from behind when they weren't expecting it. Though that was still pretty heroic for a goblin.

By now the hobgoblins were stammering and cutting each other off in their eagerness to let Jig pass. Veka waited for them to leave, moving only when she could no longer hear the tapping of Grell's cane.

Now it was her turn to face the hobgoblins. She had no ogre to protect her if the hobgoblins decided to punish her for their humiliation, which they almost certainly would. Veka had endured enough humiliation in her life to know what it was like.

So be it. This would be the First Obstacle. Just as the dwarven Hero Yilenti Beardburner had to overpower the nine-armed guardian of the black river, so would she, Veka the goblin, face these two hobgoblin guards.

Yilenti's First Obstacle sounded much more impressive.

She braced herself for the encounter. Aside from her books and staff, she had brought very little. Her muck lantern, currently hanging from her rope belt. Her wizard's staff. A skewer from last night's dinner, which she had swiped to use as a weapon. Bits of blackened rat meat still stuck to its length. At first she had tried to carry it up her sleeve, but after twice stabbing herself in the armpit, she settled for tucking it through her belt and hoping it didn't fall out.

Veka straightened, throwing her shoulders back and attempting to walk with the proper confidence and poise of a Hero. The hobgoblins watched from the junction of the tunnel. Both stood at least a head taller than Veka herself. One leaned his weight on a thick spear. A curved sword hung from the belt of the other, who was sipping what smelled like beer from a bloated skin.

A statue of a hobgoblin warrior stood beside the guards. Made of black glass, the statue marked the border of hobgoblin territory. A similar statue used to stand by the goblin lair, until one of the guards tried to climb it a few months back. Jig hadn't been able to save that one.

The statue towered over the guards, the spikes on its helmet nearly touching the ceiling. One ear had broken off, and the double-headed ax in its hands was heavily chipped. A burning lantern hung from the left fang, gleaming off the statue's angry scowl.

Structurally, hobgoblins resembled larger, uglier goblins. Their skin was yellower and their muscles stronger, but they had the same sharp fangs protruding from their lower jaws, and large, goblinesque ears topped the broad heads.

Between the guards and the statue, Veka felt like a child. For Veka, used to being the largest one in any group, it was an unpleasant feeling.

The one with the spear scratched a long scar cutting down the side of his face. He wore a hardened leather breastplate, and his pants were white tunnel cat fur. A small animal skull served as a belt buckle. His black hair was greased back in the style of a hobgoblin warrior. After a cautious glance down the tunnel, probably to make sure Jig and the ogre were really gone, he sneered and said, "Another rat-eater."

His companion punched him on the arm and said, "Forget rats. This one looks like she's eaten a whole tunnel cat."

Veka's nervousness disappeared. Bad enough her fellow goblins called her "Vast Veka" behind her back, and worse things to her face. She didn't have to take that kind of disdain from a couple of hobgoblins.

She slammed the end of her staff against the ground hard enough to make both hobgoblins jump. "I am Veka," she said. "I go to join the others in their quest."

She liked that, especially the quest part. It sounded very haughty and heroic.

"Is that so?" asked the one with the scar. Veka mentally dubbed him Slash. The scar nicked the outer edge of his eye, and that eye tended to look off in random directions. He glanced at the other guard. "Well if that's the case, go right ahead. If you hurry, you should be able to catch them before they reach the lake."

"Thank you," Veka said graciously as she passed. She saw a nasty grin spread across Slash's face, but before she could react, he yanked back with his free hand. In the dim light, she could barely see the line looped around his wrist, running to a small hook on the wall, then to the ceiling.

A wooden panel fastened to the roof gave way, showering her with sharp rocks. She stumbled forward, cursing and clutching her head.

"I told you," said the other hobgoblin. "Rocks don't do enough damage. We need to mount crossbows to the ceiling."

"You can't leave a cocked crossbow on the ceiling," Slash snapped. "They'll lose tension, and the strings will rot, especially with all the moisture from the lake."

"Look at the rat-eater. All your little rock shower did was make her cry."

"We need bigger rocks, that's all," said Slash.

Veka sniffed. One of the rocks had caught her on the nose. She reached for the skewer tucked through her belt.

Instantly both hobgoblins raised their own weapons. "Don't be foolish, little goblin."

Slash snickered. "Not so little, really."

Veka's hand shook, she was so angry. But there were two of them, both better armed than her. And no matter how badly they had humiliated her, they *had* allowed her to pass.

She straightened her robes, brushing away the dirt and pebbles. A true Hero shouldn't just scurry off into the darkness. A true Hero would make a disdainful remark about their personal hygiene, slay them both, and stuff their broken bodies into their own trap. She couldn't even think up a suitably scathing comment.

This was only the first step on the path, she reminded herself. Every Hero suffered setbacks and failures in the beginning. That's why the first part of Josca's book was subtitled "Stumbling Along the Path."

She rubbed a lump on her forehead as she hurried down the tunnel. Why did the stumbling have to sting so badly?

Veka moved fast enough to catch a glimpse of Jig and his companions as they reached the underground lake, the passage to the lower tunnels. A stone archway stood at the edge of the lake, a long tunnel stretching down beneath the water. A long swath of black sand covered the open stretch before the lake. No matter how quietly one moved, the scrape of that sand was more than enough to summon the guardians of the lake, the poisonous lizard-fish.

Jig and the other goblins used their weapons to knock swarming lizard-fish back into the water as they crossed the sand. The ogre didn't bother. His bare feet stomped lizard-fish into pale pink goo.

The lizard-fish kept coming. The white-skinned creatures were as long as Veka's arm, with clawed front feet to drag their bodies through the sand. Their bulging eyes swiveled independently, giving them addled expressions. Long white antennae flattened against their necks as they attacked. As she watched, another lizard-fish scurried up to the ogre and whipped its tail about, jabbing the needle-sharp spines of its tail into the ogre's leg.

The ogre kicked it across the cavern to slam against the wall.

Veka stared. Lizard-fish spines had enough poison to kill a full-grown goblin in the time it took to scream. The ogre had barely noticed.

And they needed help from Jig Dragonslayer?

"Come on, Walland," Jig shouted.

With one last stomp, the ogre followed them into the tunnel. From the look of it, he had been enjoying himself.

Veka untied her robe and grabbed an old grooved fire stone from the pocket of her apron. Setting her muck lantern on the ground, she felt the end of her staff until she found the metal striker dangling by its cord. She drew the striker through the groove in the rock, shooting sparks into the lantern. The muck whooshed to life, spreading green light through the cave.

Black sand covered the ground in front of her. The water was still, smooth as black glass, save for the occasional ripple or bubble where lizard-fish and other creatures surfaced in search of insects. Toward the back, water dripped from the rock overhead, too far away to see.

Bits of broken green malachite studded the roof of the

cavern, sparkling in the light of her lantern. The truly impressive formations were farther out, beyond the reach of greedy hobgoblin hands.

Veka could still hear the faint tapping of Grell's cane as they moved through the tunnel. Years ago the only way down had been through an enchanted whirlpool at the center of the lake, but generations of adventurers had left their marks throughout the mountain, blowing up bridges, smashing doors, triggering rockslides that blocked various tunnels, and generally making a mess of the place. At least the tunnel through the lake was a useful alteration. Veka grabbed her lantern and stepped onto the sand.

Instantly the lizard-fish returned, swarming from the water and spraying sand as they dragged their bodies toward her. Veka leaped back into the tunnel, and the lizard-fish slowed. Their claws couldn't find enough traction on the bare obsidian, so lizard-fish rarely left the sand of the beach. Unfortunately, the sand covered every bit of stone between Veka and the lake tunnel.

This wasn't fair. Jig hadn't done anything heroic to get past the lizard-fish. His ogre had done most of the work. All the goblins had to do was knock away the few lizard-fish the ogre didn't smush.

"I want an ogre of my own," Veka muttered. She tried again, moving as softly as she could, but it was no good. The instant the sand scraped beneath her feet, the lizard-fish returned. Veka's throat began to tighten.

"There has to be a way past," she said. There was always a way. She couldn't fail now, only a few steps into her journey. She sat down in the mouth of the tunnel and drew her spellbook from her cloak. The spellbook was in even worse shape than her copy of *The Path of the Hero*. At one time it must have been magnificent. Charred red leather covered engraved copper plates that formed the cover. The metal itself had survived the flames, but the pages within hadn't been so fortunate. Those few that weren't burned beyond legibility were incomplete and blackened around the edges. That was to be expected when you grabbed your spellbook from a dragon's lair, she supposed.

How many weeks had it taken her to decipher even the basic binding charm she had tried to show to Jig? The next page was a levitation charm, but no matter how many times she tried, she had yet to levitate even the hairs she plucked from her head for practice. All her long nights of concentrating had gotten her nothing more than aching eyes and a sore scalp.

The mocking laughter of the hobgoblins echoed in her memory. She started thinking about Jig, and how he had cowed the hobgoblins into submission. By the time she managed to follow him into the tunnel, Jig probably would have found whatever was hunting the ogres and destroyed it.

"This should be my quest. My path!" She brought the lantern over the spellbook and squinted. Her other hand clenched into a fist for the binding spell. Josca wrote that the true Hero would find new strength and power when her need was great. This time, the spell had to work. It had to!

Slowly she spread her fingers, imagining lines of power spreading from each fingertip to a point in the center of her palm. She moved her hand over her staff, forcing the magical star outward until it intersected the wood. According to her spellbook, her staff would help her control the magic. A wave of the staff would send her soaring gracefully into the air, and she would be able to slip past the lizard-fish unnoticed. She didn't need much power, only enough that her boots didn't touch the sand. Surely she could summon that much magic. She concentrated on the binding spell, staring so hard she almost believed she could see the silver lines wrapped around the end of the staff. Her hands trembled from her effort. If she could only—

A bit of muck spilled from the lantern, landing on the open spellbook. Veka yelped and flung the lantern away, slamming the book closed to smother the flames. Smoke continued to rise from the pages. She scrambled forward, scooping sand from the beach and dumping it over the book. She could see the tiny green flame burning through several more pages. She dumped more and more sand onto the book, covering the whole thing until at last the fire died.

Only then did she think to look up. Lizard-fish formed a

half ring around her. Slowly she backed away, into the mouth of the tunnel. Several of the lizard-fish tried to follow, only to hiss and retreat when they got too close to the muck that had spilled from her lantern. Whether it was the light, the heat, or the smell, they refused to pass the lantern to get to Veka.

Moving as slowly as she could, she picked up her spellbook and slipped it into her cloak pocket. She used her staff to right the lantern, then hooked the end of the staff through the handle. Keeping the lantern between her and the lizard-fish, she backed hastily into the tunnel. The spilled muck continued to burn on the sand.

Once she was safe on bare obsidian, she set the lantern down, grabbed her spellbook, and flipped to the levitation spell.

The muck had burned through most of the spell, searing the next ten or so pages for good measure. One of the few intact spells in the book, gone in an instant. She touched the browned edges of the hole, and flakes of burned paper stuck to her fingertip. She stared at the now-empty beach, wishing hatred alone was enough to destroy those hideous lizard-fish. "How am I supposed to become a Hero without a spellbook?"

She couldn't. Without magic, she was nothing but a fat, useless goblin who would probably spend the rest of her life working in the distillery until the fumes finally drove her mad.

She pulled out *The Path of the Hero* and set it down next to the spellbook. For a moment, she was tempted to throw both books onto the muck still burning in the sand. What kind of Hero lost her spellbook before she had even begun her journey?

She flipped to the beginning of the spellbook, cringing as more charred paper flaked loose and floated to the ground. The binding spell was still there, mostly legible, but that was only the first step in spellcasting. The binding was like her fire striker, providing the sparks to fuel true magic. Without those spells, her sparks simply fizzled and died.

Josca wrote that the Hero was supposed to overcome all obstacles, but he didn't explain how. Veka didn't have an ogre along to stomp lizard-fish. She didn't have anyone.

She blinked and wiped her eyes. Picking up *The Path of the Hero*, she flipped through the pages and began reading chapter nine, "The Sidekick."

"While not a prerequisite for true heroism, many legendary wizards have been known to take a companion. Whether it is the half-giant apprentice of the dwarven sorcerer Mog or the three-legged frog familiar that accompanied his master Skythe through the Bogs of Madness, the sidekick provides much-needed aide and support for the Hero's journey."

Veka's jaw tightened. She gathered her books and stood, brushing sand and ash from her robes. She might not have a three-legged frog, but a hobgoblin was the next best thing.

The hobgoblins were standing in the middle of the tunnel arguing. The wooden panel on the roof hung down, though the rocks had been swept to one side. Slash waved his hands and shouted, "There's not enough height for iron spikes to do any serious damage, not unless we add a lot of weight, and then the hinges won't hold it."

"So what's your idea?" snapped the other. "Nail rock serpents to the platform by their tails again?"

Slash's face darkened. "That would have worked if they hadn't turned on each other," he muttered. He started to say more, but stopped when he spotted Veka. He elbowed the other guard and pointed. "Speaking of more weight—"

They took in Veka's damp dirty robes and disheveled appearance in one glance and smirked.

Until now, Veka hadn't been sure how she would persuade of the hobgoblins to accompany her. Studying the creaking platform, she knew. The beads and trinkets on her staff made a nice dramatic rattling sound as she pointed it at Slash. "You. Come with me."

Slash stepped to one side and retrieved his spear, which had been leaning against the wall. "Much as I'd love to follow a rat-eating goblin around, I'm on duty."

Veka scowled, hoping it appeared menacing. Setting her staff and lantern on the floor, she loosened her belt and began fishing through the pockets of her apron until she found a small package folded inside several layers of smoky yellow cloth.

"What's that?" asked Slash.

"The last piece of your trap." She unfolded the cloth, revealing what looked like a pile of black dirt. Being careful not to touch the granules, she held it up for the hobgoblins to see. "This should solve your problems."

When they leaned closer, she blew the contents into their faces.

She leaped back, dodging a swipe of Slash's spear. The other hobgoblin was fumbling for his sword. "I'm going to cut you into strips and feed you to the tunnel cats!" he roared.

By now, the powder was already having an effect. Slash had dropped his spear and was scratching furiously at the tiny spots breaking out on his face. His friend had been hit with even more. His arms, neck, and face were all coated, and his eyes were watering so badly he couldn't see to stab her.

"Do you have any of that beer left?" Veka asked. They didn't answer, not that she expected them to. "Alcohol will neutralize the worst of the itching."

Both hobgoblins scrambled for the skin. Slash reached it first, pouring most of the contents over his face before handing it to his partner. He grabbed his spear.

"What do you think would happen if you coated the top of your platform with that powder?" Veka asked.

Slash hesitated. He glanced at the other hobgoblin, who was cursing and hopping about as he tried to shake the last few drops from the skin. "What is that stuff?"

"It's magic," Veka lied. "It's called turgog powder." She had been saving that packet to slip into the waterskin of a goblin warrior who had insulted her a few days back.

Slash was still pointing his spear at her. "How do you make it?"

Veka hesitated. Turgog was a by-product of corrupted muck. Rats would occasionally sneak into the distillery, and they had an insatiable appetite for the dried, treated mushrooms used halfway through the muck-making process. Their digestive systems processed the mushrooms into the highly irritating substance she had blown on Slash's skin. But she doubted Slash would want to know she had covered his face in powdered rat droppings. So she waved her hand and said, "It's a complicated magical formula."

Slash's eyes narrowed. "Magical?" He glanced at her staff. "What are you supposed to be, some kind of witch?"

"Wizard," Veka said. She pointed her staff at him. His companion had already fled into the hobgoblin lair, screaming for beer. "Come with me, and I'll provide you with enough turgog powder to douse a whole party of adventurers."

A smiling hobgoblin was an ugly sight, especially when that hobgoblin's face was still covered in an orange rash. "Let's go," he said.

"Grab one of those lanterns," Veka said. Hobgoblins used a different mixture of muck, one that burned with a bluish flame, but the basic formula was the same. "We'll need it." She stifled a grin as she turned and set off toward the lake. She had sent one hobgoblin fleeing, and convinced another to join her quest.

She was going to be a Hero after all!

The splashed muck on the beach still burned, giving them a clear view of the black sand. Veka stepped onto the beach and watched the lizard-fish crawl from the water, antennae waving.

"Why don't you use your magic on them?" Slash asked.

He wasn't as dumb as he appeared. "All power comes with a price," she said, quoting Josca's book. Unless you were Jig Dragonslayer. Then power was simply dropped in your lap through sheer stupid luck. "I see no reason to waste my magic on such low creatures as these lizard-fish, not when there is a simple alternative."

Before he could respond, she said, "We'll go together. They're afraid of the lanterns. Hook the handle over your spear and wave it behind us. I'll do the same with my staff to clear a path as we go. Once we reach the tunnel, they won't follow us."

At least she hoped they wouldn't. They hadn't followed Jig and the others into the tunnel.

Holding the lantern in front of her, she began walking. Slash didn't move. "This is your plan?" he snapped.

Veka scowled and hurried back onto the rock. She fished *The Path of the Hero* out of her cloak.

"What's that?" Slash asked.

"My spellbook," she said. She would have used the real spellbook, but *The Path of the Hero* looked much more impressive, plus it had better pictures. She thrust the book at him, keeping one finger on the illustration of an elf fighting what looked like a cross between a dragon and a dungheap. "And this is what I'm going to transform you into if you don't help me."

She slapped the book shut, nearly catching the tip of his nose. Without giving him time to think about her threat, she strode to the edge of the beach. "Well?"

To her amazement, Slash hurried to join her. "I'm coming, I'm coming."

"Good." Her heart thudded with excitement. He believed her. She had stood her ground, confident and in control. She should have been terrified. Slash was a hobgoblin, and everything about him screamed *danger!* Yet she wasn't afraid, and Slash didn't know how to handle it.

This time Slash followed close behind as she set out across the beach. As before, the lizard-fish hurried out of the water but stopped a short distance beyond the lanterns. Several tried to scurry around to attack from behind, but Slash swung his lantern back and forth, splashing drops of burning muck. One splashed a lizard-fish's tail.

With a high-pitched squeal, it raced back into the water. The still-burning flame was a blue glow disappearing into the depths of the lake.

"I didn't know they could make noise," Slash said. He shook his spear, trying to splash more lizard-fish. "Ha! Look at that. They run like scared goblins."

Veka glared but said nothing.

Slash shook his lantern again. The butt of his spear jabbed Veka in the side, not hard enough to draw blood, but enough to make her stumble. Her lantern dropped into the sand.

"Oops," said Slash.

Veka tried to get her staff through the handle, but the lantern had fallen on its side. Already the remaining muck oozed out through the broken panels of glass. By the time she got it upright, only a tiny bit of muck remained, emitting a feeble green flame.

The lizard-fish closed in around her. She smashed the lantern onto the nearest, then glanced back at the tunnel. The lizard-fish had closed in behind them, cutting her off. The edge of the lake was only a few paces away.

"Run," she said.

"What's that?" asked Slash.

Veka used her staff to fling the broken lantern forward, causing several lizard-fish to dodge out of the way. Slash sprayed a few more as he spun and ran after her.

Sand sank and shifted beneath Veka's feet as she fled. Shadows leaped crazily ahead of her as Slash swung his spear around, nearly setting Veka's hair and robes on fire. She couldn't tell if it was deliberate or not.

She was concentrating so hard on running, she nearly missed the tunnel. Only when her feet slapped solid rock did she realize they had made it. She turned around.

Outside, the lizard-fish waited, climbing atop one another in their eagerness, but never leaving the security of the sand.

Behind her, Slash was removing his lantern from the spear. He raised it high, examining the inside of the tunnel.

The rock was smooth and polished, far brighter than the grimy obsidian of the goblin tunnels. Puddles splashed beneath their feet with each step. She could see tiny snails in several of the puddles.

Slash's foot crunched three of them as he looked around. The sound echoed strangely.

The tunnel was too cramped, so she had to hold her staff parallel to the wall to keep from banging it. "Come on," she whispered.

She found herself hunching as she walked, and forced herself to lift her chin and straighten her spine. Heroes didn't slouch. They stood proud and tall.

But how often did Heroes travel through a lakebed tunnel, with all that water held back by nothing but a thin layer of rock? The silence was nearly as palpable as the moisture in the air.

Sweat dripped down her back. Cold water dripped onto her neck. She flattened her ears and kept walking. The tunnel sloped downward, following the bottom of the lakebed deeper and deeper.

The end of the tunnel was a black hole in the dark, glistening stone of the floor. A ladder made of the same magically shaped obsidian led down from the far edge.

"Give me the lantern." Moving the blue flame over the hole, she dropped her staff into the room below. The clatter sounded terribly loud after passing through the tunnel, but nothing happened. With the lantern heating her left arm, Veka climbed down into the throne room of the legendary Necromancer.

The walls and floor were black marble, thick with dust. She could see footprints where Jig and the others had come down. A glass mosaic covered the ceiling, reminding her a bit of the one in Jig's temple, though the images here were abstract and meaningless. The smell of preservatives and old bat guano made her sneeze.

Behind her, Slash was humming as he climbed down the ladder. Veka's jaw tightened as she recognized "The Song of Jig." She picked up her staff, horribly tempted to break it over Slash's head, but it was too late. The melody had already wormed its way into her mind. She thrust the lantern back into his hand, hoping the muck would splash his wrist, but no such luck.

How did that verse go? Something about corpses leaping from the shadows, until the noble, valiant, wonderful Jig managed to slay the Necromancer. She turned, searching the darkness for any hint of movement. There was none, of course. Goblins and hobgoblins alike had passed through here many times since Jig's little adventure, and not one had been torn apart by the animated dead.

Another pit on the opposite side of the room led down to the dragon's realm. Like the lake tunnel, this was a magical shortcut left by that same band of adventurers. They had used magic to carve their own path through the mountain, including the stone ladder on the far side of the pit. Veka's envy was so strong she could taste it, like the backwash of good slug tea. She stared, wondering what it would be like to have the power to reshape the stone itself.

She squinted and moved closer to the edge. "Cover the lantern."

The blue light diminished, and gradually Veka's vision adapted enough to see the faint silver light shimmering below. The ladder should have extended all the way to the ground below, but the rungs rippled and shimmered, and the bottom half didn't seem to exist at all.

"What is that?" asked Slash.

"I don't know. Whatever the ogres were afraid of, it's—"

"The ogres were *afraid*?" Slash asked. He stared at the pit, then at Veka.

"The ogres have been hunted down and wiped out," she said. "There are only a handful left. That's why this one came to us for help."

Slash was still staring, his spear hanging loosely in his hand. "And you want to go down there?"

"We should move quickly," Veka said. "I don't know what's happening to the ladder, but I don't trust—"

That was as far as she got before Slash's foot slammed into her backside, launching her headfirst into the pit.

CHAPTER 3

"No night is so dark, no situation so dire, that the intervention of the gods cannot make it worse."
—Brother Darnak Stonesplitter, Dwarven Priest

AS JIG CLIMBED DOWN INTO THE CAVERN WHERE the ogres made their home, the first thing he noticed was the cold. The wind made him shiver, especially where it slipped up his sleeves and down his back.

The second thing he noticed was that the last few rungs of the ladder were too insubstantial to support his weight. Unfortunately, he noticed this only when his feet slipped through the rungs, dropping him onto his backside.

He looked up to warn the others, then groaned. Braf had never been an attractive goblin, but from this angle . . .

"Something's wrong with the ladder," Jig said, turning away to retrieve his lantern. He scooped sand from a pouch on his belt to extinguish the flames. "The last three rungs aren't completely there."

"Like Braf," Grell said.

Jig ignored her. He was too busy trying to absorb the changes to this place. When the dragon Straum lived here, he had used his magic to recreate the outside world. Straum had been trapped, doomed to remain as a guardian for various treasures, so he had done everything in his power to make himself at home. Jig remembered blue skies overhead, the unnaturally bright light of a false sun, the rustling sound the trees made in the wind, like the slithering of a thousand snakes.

Some elements of Straum's world had been illusory, such as the sun that crossed the sky each day. Others were real, like the trees and plants Straum had spread throughout the cavern, feeding them with his own magic until his woods were a match for anything in the outside world.

Those trees were bare and skeletal now, encased in a thin layer of ice. The ice was everywhere. The whole place had a faint smoky smell, reminding him of the crude forge back at the goblin lair.

Jig knelt, and the grass crunched beneath his knees. He broke off a single blade and studied it. Was he only imagining the silver swirl of light trapped within the ice? Frigid water trickled down his palm as the ice melted. The grass inside was brown and brittle.

He blinked and squinted, flicking the grass aside to study his own hand. His skin appeared faded, having taken on a faint bronze pallor. Looking around, he saw the same metallic tinge everywhere. The ice sparkled silver, and the trees had the dull tarnish of old lead. The illusory sky had a dull gray glow, and there was no sign of Straum's false sun, which Jig appreciated. Even knowing it was an illusion, he had always half expected the sun to fall on him.

"Hideous, isn't it?" Walland said, dropping down beside Jig. "The change was slow at first. Cold winds coming from Straum's cave. Frost spreading over the grass each morning. The leaves withered and disappeared. And then there's the snow." He spread his arms to indicate the silver flakes floating down around them. Already they had begun to stick to the lenses of Jig's spectacles, blurring his vision.

Grunting and swearing marked the arrival of Braf, who either hadn't heard or had forgotten Jig's warning about the ladder. He got to his feet, brushing ice and snow from his clothes as he moved around behind Jig.

"Someone get me off this stupid thing," Grell shouted. Her canes were hooked over her belt, and she clung to the ladder with both hands. One foot gingerly poked the rung below. Black specks shot away from the rung as her sandal passed through it.

Wordlessly, Walland reached over and plucked her from the ladder.

"Where do we go?" asked Braf, making Jig jump. One of the first rules of survival was never to let another goblin get behind you, yet here he was, gaping at the trees and giving Braf a clear shot at his back.

They promised they wouldn't kill me until we dealt with the ogres. Not that a goblin promise was worth much, but fear of Walland's retribution might carry a bit more weight. And since whatever problems the ogres were having would probably kill them all, he really shouldn't have to worry about Braf.

A rustling at his waist made him glance down. Smudge was using his forelegs to push his way out of the small pouch on Jig's belt. Smudge's head appeared, took in the world around him, and promptly disappeared again. Jig wished he could do the same.

He started to tie the lantern to his belt, trying to find a place where the hot metal wouldn't burn his legs. Finally he hooked the handle over the hilt of the sword, so the metal rested against the scabbard. He ended up shifting several pouches to the other side of his belt to balance its weight.

Walland tilted his head and sniffed the air. He turned slowly, his eyes scouring the trees around the clearing. He took a step, paused, and turned again. Jig had no idea what he was looking for, but if possible, the ogre's behavior was making Jig even more anxious.

"You do know where you're going, don't you?" asked Grell.

Walland cupped one hand over his eyes and searched the sky, nearly bumping his head on the ladder as he circled.

Grell snorted. "He reminds me of a deranged rat the kids used to keep as a pet, until one of the older girls ate him."

"Just making sure we weren't seen," Walland said.

"Maybe we should go find the other ogres," Jig said. The longer they stayed in this clearing, the faster they would be caught and killed, and Jig preferred to postpone that as long as possible. "You told us there were some who had escaped whatever's been hunting you?"

To Jig's left, a small creature waddled out of the woods to stare. It resembled a cluster of icicles with a wrinkled pink face and a long snout. The icy spines glistened with color that changed from blue to green to purple with every movement. It seemed to be sneaking up on a pair of glowing orange bugs, the same kind that had been bothering Jig back in his temple. The bugs flew lower, circling the creature again and again. A bright spark leaped from one of the spines near its head, and the insect dropped dead. The creature pounced, shoving the bug into its mouth with both paws.

"What is that thing?" Jig asked.

"We've had all sorts of strange creatures creeping into our woods," Walland said. He scooped Grell up, holding her so she sat on his forearm with her canes dangling down and her heels kicking Walland's thighs. "Quickly. We don't have much time."

Soon Jig and Braf were running as fast as they could to keep up. Ice and grass crunched beneath their feet as they followed Walland into the woods. The ogre carried his club in his free hand. He didn't bother to stop for trees or low-hanging branches. Instead, that huge club smashed them out of his way, leaving Jig to wipe chunks of wood and ice from his face. Even if the falling snow hid their footprints, all an enemy would have to do was follow the path of destruction. But Jig was breathing too hard to say anything.

He could hear Grell swearing over the noise. Her voice shook with each step, giving her curses a choppy rhythm, almost a marching chant. An extremely vulgar and angry chant, but so were a good number of goblin songs.

As he ran, Jig occasionally saw movement to either side: a flash of white light that disappeared among the branches, a bit of snow shifting and crumbling, a shadow leaping away, brushing through bare shrubs as it fled. Nothing attacked them though. Not yet, at least.

Finally Walland slowed to a jog, momentarily stopping Grell's complaints until she could adjust to the slower rhythm. "Where are we going?" Jig asked, wiping sweat from his face.

Walland pointed. "That fallen tree over there." The tree appeared freshly toppled. The base of the trunk was wider than Braf's neck. Only a thin shell of ice coated the upper part of the tree. Given how hard the ice and snow were falling, Jig guessed the tree had been chopped down no more than a day before.

A closer look suggested "chopped" was the wrong word. Some of the trunk showed the toothy bite of an ax, but the rest was splintered, as if someone had grown impatient and simply shoved the tree down with his bare hands.

The branches shivered, sending bits of ice into the snow. Jig stopped in midstep. Behind the tree, partially concealed by broken branches, lay another ogre.

"You're being attacked by trees?" Braf asked.

Walland set Grell on the ground. She immediately walked over to slap Braf's head. To Jig, it wasn't a completely stupid question. This whole place had been created by magic. Who knew what was or wasn't possible? Though he doubted a sentient tree would have taken the time to tie the ogre's arms and legs to its trunk. Nor would it make much sense for the tree to lie there while the ogre struggled.

"My sister Sashi," said Walland, resting one hand on the broken tree. A rough hood was tied over the ogre's head. The muffled sounds coming from within suggested she was gagged. She appeared almost as large and muscular as Walland himself.

Grell limped closer, studying the knots. "That's good technique, tying her joints to the tree so she doesn't have the leverage to break free. There are a few kids I would have liked to use that with." She glared at Braf as she said this, but he didn't appear to notice.

"I told you we were being enslaved," Walland said. He held his club in both hands, twitching nervously every time the trees creaked in the wind or a bit of ice fell to the ground. "I led my family away from the others, hoping we could hide in safety. Sashi here disagreed. She wanted to go to Straum's cave and face this enemy head-on. She's always been the impulsive one in our family."

"What happened?" Jig asked.

Walland shrugged. "She found the cave. She returned a day later and nearly killed me."

"So you hit her with a tree?" Braf asked.

"Not right away. I pretended to lose consciousness. She didn't seem to want me dead. She started to tie me up, and I managed to get an arm around her throat." He rubbed his forearm, and Jig noticed dark scabs near the elbow. "Sashi always did fight mean," he muttered. "I tied her up and brought her here. That's when I went looking for Jig Dragonslayer."

"I thought you wanted us to help your people fight, to battle alongside ogre warriors . . ." Braf's voice trailed off as Walland gave him an incredulous look.

Jig looked at the bound ogre, then at Walland. He had an unpleasant feeling in his stomach that he knew where this was going.

Walland shook his head. "First you save my sister. Whatever spell they've put on her, I need you to break it."

"Whatever spell *who* put on her?" Grell asked.

"I don't know. Anyone who's gone to face them has either died or turned against us. We see lights in the sky sometimes, but never close enough to make out the shape of our tormentors. Ogres aren't what you'd call sneaky."

Sashi's muffled shouts had grown louder at the sound of Walland's voice. The tree shivered and creaked as she struggled to break free. She actually managed to lift the entire tree off the ground before collapsing again.

"Don't worry," said Walland. "I kept her blindfolded when I brought her here. Even if her masters are watching through her eyes, they won't know where we are."

This was why Shadowstar had sent him with Walland? Jig didn't have the slightest idea how to start. This wasn't a matter of broken bones or a pierced nostril. Jig took a tentative step toward Sashi, who had stopped moving. The roughspun bag over her head tilted to one side, as though she were listening to his approach.

What do I do?

Tymalous Shadowstar didn't answer.

Hello? A little help would be nice. Still nothing. It figured. There was never a god around when you needed one. Jig circled the tree, studying the ogre and stalling for time. She wore the same rough deerskins as her brother, though hers were damp and filthy. Her nails were broken, and several of her fingers bled where she had struggled to claw through the ropes. From the gouges in the wood, she had also tried to scrape the tree itself apart.

"Go on," said Grell. "Fix her up and let's get out of here. This place is cold enough to freeze snot."

Shadowstar? I don't think Walland is going to be happy if I can't help him, and I really don't want to be trapped down here with an unhappy ogre and his crazy sister.

"You can help her, right?" Walland said, giving his club an ominous twirl.

Jig nodded and stepped closer to the tree. "Um . . . I can't really get to her with all those branches in the way. Can you turn the tree over?" No doubt she had taken some scrapes and bruises in her fight with Walland. Maybe Jig could start with those while he tried to figure out what to do next. Though if Shadowstar had truly abandoned him, he wouldn't be able to heal so much as a hangnail.

Walland stomped over to the base of the tree, setting his club on the ground and gripping the trunk with both hands. Jig glanced around, trying to gauge his chances of escape if he started running now. He guessed he'd make it four, maybe five paces before Walland crushed his skull. Six if the ogre stopped to kill Grell and Braf first.

Walland grunted as he hoisted the end of the tree onto his shoulders, suspending his sister with her head toward the ground. More branches snapped as he gripped it with both hands and twisted, turning Sashi faceup on the tree, still secured by the ropes around her hands and legs.

That was the moment Sashi arched her body and slammed her back into the tree. At first Jig wasn't sure whether the horrible cracking sound had come from the tree or Sashi's spine. Then she was flexing again, using her legs to swing the lower half of the tree upward. This time the crack came from Walland's jaw as the broken tree smashed his face. He staggered back, blood dripping down his face. Sashi squirmed, twisting and flailing to free herself. She rolled away, dragging her wrists down past her ankles, then bringing them to her mouth. She tore the sack from her head, yanked the gag from her mouth, and bit through the rope. She glanced at the goblins. With an amused snort, she turned to her brother.

Walland had his club out and was circling around Sashi. She scooped up the lower half of the tree and flung it at him. He dove back, but it gave her time to loosen the ropes around her ankles.

"What now?" Braf asked. He had his hook-tooth out, and appeared perfectly willing to leap into the fight. How had he survived this long?

"We run," Jig said.

Grell was already hurrying through the trees as fast as she could. Jig passed her in the time it took Braf to say, "Does that mean you're not going to help Sashi?"

Glancing back, two thoughts crossed Jig's mind. The first was that there would be no way Grell could move fast enough to escape. No matter which ogre won, they would overtake her with ease. The second thought was that the time it would take the ogre to kill Grell was more time for Jig to get away.

He waited for the inevitable chastising from Tymalous Shadowstar, but the inside of his skull was silent. Shadowstar had such peculiar ideas about leaving one's companions to die. Even when those companions had orders to kill you.

Jig looked back again, trying to decide what to do, and ran straight into a tree. Ice and snow sprinkled down on him as he landed on his back, staring up at the dull gray sky. Hot blood trickled from his right nostril. He saw Braf and Grell running toward him. With her canes, Grell looked like a withered, four-legged bug. Jig scooped a handful of ice and snow and pressed it against his nose as he climbed to his feet. He could still see Walland and Sashi fighting in the distance. Walland was the larger and stronger of the two, but Sashi appeared to be winning. Maybe it was because Walland was still using his club, while Sashi was swinging half a tree.

Sashi's attacks were slow, but Walland didn't seem willing to kill her. Several times Jig saw openings where Walland could have smashed Sashi's skull while she recovered her balance, but he kept going after her hands and arms, trying to knock the tree away.

Walland tried again, and Sashi kicked him in the knee. Walland howled in pain. By the time the sound stopped, Jig and the others were fleeing again.

"We should fight," said Braf. "There are three of us."

Jig glanced at Grell. Sashi had snapped a tree in half. She would do the same to the old goblin without breaking stride. As for himself, he couldn't even run away without being knocked down by a tree. Braf was the closest thing they had to a warrior, and he was waving a weapon he had never used before.

"You killed the dragon," Braf said. "Why are you so afraid of a stupid ogre?"

The reasons would take far too long to list, so Jig didn't answer. Grell was watching him, waiting for his decision. They both were. What did they expect him to do, pull a dragon out of his pouch and turn it loose on the ogre?

Not that running away was doing much good. Already Sashi was closing the distance between them.

"Spread out," Jig said. His breath puffed from his mouth in silver clouds. He removed his spectacles and wiped the worst of the snow from the lenses.

Braf had his hook-tooth ready, though he kept changing his grip, first aiming the hook at the oncoming ogre, then the point. Grell leaned her canes against a tree and pulled a short curved knife from somewhere inside the blankets bundled around her.

Jig reached into one of his belt pouches and scooped Smudge free. The spotted fire-spider was already hot to the touch, and Jig swiftly set him on the ground. The ice began to melt, sending up clouds of steam as Smudge crawled toward the closest tree. As he climbed, he stopped several times to shake drops of water from his legs.

"Sorry about that," Jig said. "Trust me, you're better off there than with me." With that, he set his lantern on the ground, drew his sword, and turned to face the ogre.

A scream of rage startled him so badly he nearly dropped his sword. Weapon raised, Braf charged the ogre. As Jig stared in dumbfounded amazement, Braf thrust the sharp end of his hook-tooth toward Sashi's chest.

She dropped her tree as she twisted out of the way, then backhanded Braf to the ground. She glanced at Grell, raising one eyebrow as if daring her to attack. Grell shrugged, put her knife away, and stepped aside.

That left Jig. He raised his sword, holding the blade across his body in the guard position he had seen adventurers use. Sashi hadn't even bothered to retrieve her tree. She strode toward Jig, giving him his first good look at Walland's sister.

Her time tied to the tree had left her hair wet and tangled, like limp seaweed stuck to her skull. Dirt and bits of bark clung to her clothes. An enormous green bruise covered the upper part of her right arm. Apparently Walland had landed at least one good blow. She held that arm close to her body, but Jig had little doubt she could finish off a few goblins one-handed.

"So you're Jig Dragonslayer," she said.

Jig wiped more blood from his nose. If he ever learned who had come up with "The Song of Jig," he was going to push them into a fire-spider nest.

"Is it true what my brother said?" Sashi asked. "Can you use the magic of this world?"

Jig studied Sashi's face, trying to guess which answer would keep him alive the longest. If she thought magic was a threat, the truth would give her more incentive to kill him. On the other hand, what were the odds of an ogre seeing a goblin as a threat?

"Yes?" It was the wrong answer. Sashi lunged, her good arm outstretched to grab him by the face. Jig ducked, jabbing the point of his sword into her wrist. She howled and staggered away as blood the color of pine needles dripped onto the ice and snow. Braf tried to stab her with the tip of his hook-tooth, but it skidded off of her thick skin. Braf stared at his weapon, probably double-checking to make sure he had used the right end.

Sashi reached up and twisted a thick branch from the closest tree. Smaller branches rained ice as she swung at Braf. She attacked again, then yelped. Grell's little knife protruded from the side of her thigh.

They had gotten a few lucky shots, but it wouldn't be enough to kill an ogre. Jig knelt beside the cold lantern, jabbing the end of his sword through the panes and scooping as much muck onto the blade as he could. The muck was cold, and he had nothing to produce a spark. Well, almost nothing. He steadied the blade with his other hand as he brought it to the tree where Smudge was cowering.

One of the greatest challenges of Jig's life had been training Smudge to ignore muck. To fire-spiders, the caustic goo was like candy. When Jig was younger, a fire-spider had managed to sneak into the distillery, with disastrous results. Goblins passing by had never fully recovered their hearing, and Jig had been one of the unfortunate few assigned to clean what remained of the muckworkers inside.

He tried not to think about that as he brought the sword to Smudge. The fire-spider watched Jig closely as he took one step, then another. Jig had used Smudge's hatred of water to train him away from the muck. The only time fire-spiders went near water was to breed. He could tell Smudge fully expected to be spat upon the instant he went after the muck.

"Come on, you stupid spider," Jig said. Sashi was chasing Braf around a tree. Grell had produced another knife and held it ready to throw, but she didn't seem able to get a clear shot.

Smudge's training held. He turned around and began crawling away. Jig gritted his teeth, grabbed the spider, and dropped him onto the sword. Smudge was already terrified, as the burns on Jig's fingers proved. The muck burst into flames. Finally realizing Jig wasn't going to punish him, Smudge began scooping muck to his mouth with his forelegs.

It figured. Now that Jig needed his sword back, Smudge refused to leave. Jig stuck the tip of the sword back into the lantern and shook it until Smudge tumbled free. Leaving Smudge to gorge himself in the green flames, Jig turned back to Sashi. She had ended the ridiculous pursuit around the tree by ripping the tree from the ground. Now she stepped toward Braf, arms wide.

Jig rested his blade on his shoulder, grabbing the handle with both hands. Before his spectacles, he wouldn't have been able to aim well enough to do this. He swung the sword forward. Muck flew through the air like tiny green fireballs, splattering Sashi's back.

"Good spider," Jig whispered. Smudge didn't look up from his feast.

Grell threw her second knife. This one barely nicked Sashi's shoulder, but it was enough to distract her from Braf. She didn't even seem to notice the flames making their way up her back, into her hair. What was wrong with her? Smudge had given Jig a number of unintentional burns over the years, and he knew for a fact that fire *hurt*.

Jig charged, swinging his sword at Sashi's thigh. If they could take out her legs, they could run away. Also Jig was too short to aim much higher.

Sashi kicked him. The world flashed white, and Jig found himself on his backside, with snow down his shirt and pants, staring at the sky. He raised his head, and the pounding in his skull almost overpowered Braf's shouts. Braf grabbed his hook-tooth and attacked again. This time he hooked Sashi's ankle from behind.

She barely noticed, dragging Braf from his feet and ripping the weapon from his hands as she walked toward Jig.

"Don't you know you're on fire?" Jig asked. She acted like she'd happily let the meat cook from her bones as long as she got to slaughter a few goblins first.

Jig pushed himself to his knees. Where had his sword landed?

Sashi screamed. Oh, there was his sword, protruding from the flames that now engulfed her back and shoulders. Behind her, Grell hobbled back to retrieve her canes.

Sashi reached around, trying to grasp the sword, but her arms didn't bend enough to reach. She spun around in circles, like a tunnel cat chasing her tail. Finally she appeared to give up. She took several shaky steps toward Jig, then collapsed face-first on the ground.

"Is she dead?" Braf asked.

Jig crawled toward the still-burning body. He would have

walked, but he wasn't sure his trembling limbs could hold him yet. "I think so."

Braf used his hook-tooth to catch the handle of Jig's sword and tug it free. Snow and steam hissed where it landed. Jig decided he could wait a few minutes to retrieve his weapon.

A loud whoop startled him so badly he fell back into the snow. Braf was shaking his hook-tooth at the sky and laughing. "Three goblins against an ogre. Did you see when I hit her with my hook-tooth? And, Jig, the way you flung that muck was brilliant! That ought to teach her not to attack goblin warriors."

Grell rolled her eyes. With a pained groan, she hobbled closer and spread her hands, warming them over the still-burning ogre. "So does this mean we're finished?" she asked.

"No!" Jig said quickly. Once their quest was over, Grell and Braf were free to kill him. "I mean, we don't know Walland's dead, and he did ask us to help his people. We should at least find out what's been enchanting them. Whatever it is, they're not doing a great job." He stared at Sashi's body. "We should be dead."

"What?" Braf stopped dancing. "But you're Jig Dragonslayer."

Jig ignored him. Hot footsteps dotted his leg as Smudge returned. There was a distinct bulge in the fire-spider's fuzzy belly. Smudge headed straight for Jig's belt pouch, no doubt for a long nap.

"Jig's right," Grell said. "The only way so few goblins have ever overpowered an ogre is by sneaking up and killing him in his sleep."

Braf chuckled. "Yeah, I know that song." He raised his voice and began to sing.

"Their weapons drawn, the goblin party snuck through darkest night,
lusting for revenge after the morning's failed attack.
But tonight the goblins meant to wage a goblin's kind of fight.
With numbers great they stabbed the ogre squarely in the back."

"Do you remember the last verse?" Jig asked.

"The ogre yelled in red-hot rage, the goblins yelled in fright,
and as he died the ogre seized a goblin's neck and . . . crack!"

Jig clenched his hands together like an ogre killing his attacker. "Ogre Attack" was a children's song, with gestures to accompany each line.

"We shouldn't have survived," Jig said. Whatever was controlling the ogres, it slowed their reflexes, made them clumsier. That might also explain why Sashi hadn't seemed bothered by the flames. The enchanted ogres would be less effective fighters, but they wouldn't stop fighting until they were dead.

Jig stared through the trees at the gray sky beyond. He doubted very much that Shadowstar had sent him here to kill the ogre he was supposed to be saving, but so far, the god hadn't chastised him. Come to think of it, Jig had heard nothing at all since they descended into Straum's realm.

Shadowstar?

Silence. What a wonderful time for the god to abandon him.

Grell had retrieved one of her knives, and was helping herself to a bit of well-done ogre meat from the shoulder, where the flames had died down. "So tell me, Jig. With all that running around, do you have any idea how we get back to the ladder?"

Jig stared. Already the snow had begun to cover their tracks. The trees all looked alike to him. It was one of the things he hated about this place. No tunnels, no walls, nothing but open land spreading in all directions. How was anyone supposed to find their way around?

"I—"

Grell snorted. "That's what I figured."

And people wondered why Jig hated adventures.

CHAPTER 4

"The difference between a Hero and an ordinary man is that when the ordinary man comes upon a flaming death swamp full of venomous dragon snakes, he turns around and goes home. The Hero strips down and goes for a swim."

—Saint Catherine the Patient, mother of Glen the Daring
From *The Path of the Hero (Wizard's ed.)*

SNOW AND ICE CUSHIONED VEKA'S FALL, BUT the impact still knocked the wind out of her. She groaned and rolled over, spotting her staff a short distance away. She crawled over and used it to prop herself up.

From atop the ladder, Slash grinned down at her. "Where's all your fancy magic now, wizard? I'll bet you can't cast your spells on a target you can't see." He disappeared, no doubt heading back up to the lake tunnel.

He was laughing at her, just like the other goblins had always done. Between one tight breath and the next, Veka forgot all about Jig and ogres and heroic quests. She shook her staff and shouted, "And how exactly are you planning to get past the lizard-fish alone, you ugly mound of dragon droppings?"

Slash reappeared soon after, looking far less cocky than before. "About that—"

That was as far as he got. Veka drew back her arm and threw her staff like a spear. It caught Slash right in the stomach.

Slash grunted and doubled over, clutching his gut. Time seemed to slow as Veka watched him recognize his mistake. His spear fell, and his eyes widened. He reached out, flailing for the edge of the pit. His fingers scraped the stone as he tumbled forward. In a slow, graceful dive, Slash somersaulted down and landed flat on his back, almost in the exact same spot Veka had fallen.

She picked up her staff and Slash's spear while he gasped for breath. Large as she was, Slash was even bigger, and he had landed far harder than Veka. She nudged him with her toe. "Get up. Quickly, before we're discovered."

Slash touched his head, as though he were testing to see if the skull was intact. A fall from that height could easily result in broken bones, but hobgoblin skulls were notoriously thick. "Discovered by what?"

Veka pressed her toe to Slash's head, turning it to one side. "Those things, for a start."

Twin streaks of fire raced over the trees in the distance. Given the subdued coloration of everything from the sky to the rash on Slash's face, which looked like old rust, the brilliance of the two flames was even more startling. The nearer of the two was bright green. The other was a deep red. They swooped back and forth, their paths crossing again and again.

"They look like they're searching for something," Slash said as he got to his feet.

Jig and the others. She wondered if they were in trouble. The two flames appeared to be coming from the direction of Straum's cave. "What are they?" That they were magical in nature was beyond obvious, but they were too far away to make out any details.

"They're dangerous." Slash reached for his spear.

Veka yanked it back, out of reach. "You're lucky I don't kill you for pushing me through that pit. If I weren't in the midst of a quest, I—"

Slash leaped forward, seized the spear just behind the

head, and yanked. Veka stumbled, but she didn't let go. She tugged back, putting all of her considerable weight into it.

With a wicked grin, the hobgoblin released the spear.

For the second time, Veka landed in the snow. Slash pounced, grabbing the spear with both hands and twisting. He nearly snapped Veka's wrist as he wrenched it from her grasp. Before she could recover, he smashed the butt into her forehead. "Some wizard."

Right then Veka would have given everything for just one spell that would take away that smug, arrogant smirk. Maybe something that transformed his teeth into worms. That would be fun to watch.

Slash looked at the ladder. The closest rungs were little more than shadows. Even with his spear stretching as high as he could reach, the tip barely scraped against the lowest solid rung. "We should get out of this clearing," he said.

Blood heated her face. She had read Josca's book so many times she knew most of it by heart. Nowhere did it say anything about the Hero being shoved into pits or taking orders from her own sidekick. A true Hero would have wrestled the spear away from Slash and beaten him senseless.

"We need to find Jig Dragonslayer," Slash said.

Veka rubbed her head. "Why?"

"Unlike a certain oversize goblin braggart, Jig won't have been stupid enough to come down here without a plan for getting out. If nothing else, that ogre he had might be big enough to hoist us up to the ladder. Unless you want to try your magic?"

Slash didn't wait for an answer. Veka bit back a squawk as he grabbed her by the ear and yanked her toward the trees. He released her after a few steps, apparently trusting her to keep up.

Veka's mind filled with all the things she would do to him once she was a real wizard. Her books thumped against her stomach as she ran, painful reminders of how far she had to go to truly follow the Hero's Path.

They found Walland's body sprawled upside down against half a broken tree. Another of the flaming lights, a yellow one this time, had already discovered it. Veka and Slash crouched behind a cluster of pine trees. The brown needles were encased in so much ice and snow it was nearly impossible to see beyond them.

"So much for your idea," Veka whispered.

"Maybe if we dragged him back and used him like a stool?" Slash said.

Shadows twitched back and forth as the yellow light behind the body moved, almost as though it were pacing. Veka flattened herself to the ground. There were fewer branches down here, but now the snow began to chill her whole body. She gritted her teeth and remained, her ears wide as she listened to the high-pitched mumbling coming from the light.

"No life left in this one," the voice said. "Is it really so difficult to subdue an enemy without smashing them to a pulp?"

The light brightened abruptly, shooting sparks in all directions as it leaped up to land on Walland's shoulder. This was it: Veka's first real view of her enemy, her nemesis, the foe she would battle as she traveled the Path of the Hero.

"The ogres were beaten by a bunch of pixies?" Slash whispered. He sounded as if he was fighting not to laugh.

Standing atop the ogre was a small winged man. If he stood on the ground, the top of his head wouldn't even reach her knees. He had two sets of wings, like an insect, and the yellow sparks seemed to come mostly from the lower set. The wings had an oily shimmer around the edges. Otherwise they were clear as glass, save for faint yellow lines that spread through them like veins on a leaf.

Black cloth crossed around his chest, cinched into a knot at his waist. His black trousers were decorated with red beads that took on an orange shine when they caught the light from his wings.

The pixie gave Walland one swift kick, then flew into the air. "Where have your friends run off to, ogre?"

A low growl made Veka jump, but it wasn't Walland. The sound came from an enormous dog that sniffed the air as it approached the dead ogre. It walked with a limp, and one of its rear legs was matted, probably with old blood. Gaps in its fur showed older scars, mostly near the throat. Strings of drool swung from its flat, wrinkled face as it bared its teeth and snarled at the pixie.

The pixie barely hesitated, glancing back only long enough to swing one hand in a lazy gesture.

The dog took a few more steps, snapping at the sparks falling from the pixie's wings, before giving a sharp, pained yelp. As the pixie flew through the branches and disappeared, the dog sat and began to gnaw at its rear paws.

"What happened?" Veka whispered. Slash's jaw tightened, but he said nothing.

The dog snarled, attacking its own legs with even greater ferocity. The pixie didn't appear to be coming back, so Veka crawled out from behind the tree.

"That dog will rip you apart," Slash warned.

Veka was more curious than afraid. What had the pixie done?

She was almost at Walland's body when she saw. The roots of the nearby trees had coiled around the dog's paws, anchoring it to the ground. Smooth black bark crept up its legs. Blood and splinters sprayed from its panicked jaws, but the pixie's magic was too strong. No matter how the dog struggled, the bark continued to spread. It had reached its hips by the time Slash joined her. The dog's yelps grew higher in pitch, and foam dripped from its mouth as it panicked. Slash reached for the dog and nearly lost his fingers.

"That's no way to die," Slash said. "Can you stop this?"

Veka shook her head, too fascinated to lie.

He grabbed the end of his weapon and swung it like an oversize club against the dog's neck. There was a loud crack, and the dog dropped.

"Stupid pixies." Slash nudged Walland's body with his toe. "The dog was just looking for a meal."

"How did it get down here?" Veka asked. "I've never seen a dog like that before."

"Probably came with a group of adventurers." He pointed to a worn scrap of leather buckled around the dog's neck. A few rusted spikes protruded from the collar, though most had torn away over time. "They bring their animals along on their little quests, get themselves killed, and their pets either wind up in some other creature's belly, or they go feral like this poor thing. I remember one fellow who carried around a pair of trained ferrets who could disarm traps, chew through knots, all sorts of tricks."

"What happened to them?" Veka asked.

"We caught one of his companions and tied her up for the tunnel cats. Sure enough, he sent his ferrets to free her while he fought the cats." He grinned. "He should have taught them to be sure nobody had spread poison on the ropes they chewed."

Veka turned her attention back to the dog. By now the tree had nearly consumed the body. Only the wrinkled face and one ear still showed, and soon those too disappeared. Tiny branches began to sprout from the dog-shaped stump.

The pixie had done this with nothing more than a wave of his hand. No wonder the ogres were so desperate for help.

Slash gave the wooden head a sympathetic pat. "What now?"

Veka didn't hesitate. "Walland said they had taken over Straum's lair. We'll sneak into the lair and discover their secrets. That should give us the key to destroying them."

For a long time Slash simply stared at her. When he finally spoke, he sounded almost resigned. "There's something very wrong with you, even for a goblin."

Veka didn't answer. If she tried to explain, he'd only laugh at her. That, or he would go ahead and kill her.

But deep down, she knew. These pixies were her nemesis. Nemeses? It didn't matter. The magic she had seen proved they were the archenemy she must defeat to finish her journey along the Hero's Path. If she could overthrow these pixies, it would be a triumph unmatched in goblin history. Nobody would even remember Jig and his stupid song. When she returned, she would be Veka the Great. Veka the Mighty. Veka the Bold. She would have so many adjectives, the other goblins would take all morning just to greet her!

Better yet, Jig and the others might be in trouble. They had lost their ogre companion, after all. What a thrill it would be to rescue the great Jig Dragonslayer.

"Come on," she said, tugging Slash by the arm. He

wrenched free, staring at her as if she had suggested raw carrion-worms for dinner. He didn't understand. The longer they stayed here, the more time Jig would have to save himself, and that would ruin everything.

She started to walk in the general direction of Straum's cave. She wondered if the pixies would have spellbooks she could steal. She would have given anything for the kind of power she had just witnessed. Well, maybe not that spell in particular. The ability to make trees swallow your enemies wouldn't be much use back in the stone tunnels and caves of the goblin lair. But if the pixies could do that, they certainly had other spells she could use.

Crunching footsteps told her Slash had decided to follow. The scowl on his face made it plain he would have preferred to leave her broken body here with the dog, but given what they faced, it was smarter to stick together.

That was how a sidekick was supposed to behave.

Veka kept her ears twisted, tracking Slash's footsteps to make sure he didn't try to stab her in the back. Though he could just as easily throw his spear, if he really wanted her dead. But to do that, he would have to shift his weight, which she would also hear, thanks to the crunch of ice and snow. Hopefully that would give her enough warning to dive behind a tree.

Her enthusiasm began to wane the longer they walked. She found herself constantly stumbling over snow-covered roots or bumping into branches which dumped snow down her neck. The sky had begun to darken, making progress even more difficult. The last branch had nearly cost her an eye. "This whole place is out to get me," she muttered.

By the time they reached the edge of the woods, Veka was hungry, cold, and soaked. Her only consolation was that Slash had been equally abused.

"Straum's lair is there, the edge of the cavern," Slash said.

"You think I don't know that?" Veka tried to sound haughty and disdainful, but her stomach gurgled as she spoke, ruining the effect. She should have brought food, or at least grabbed a few bites of Walland.

A wide clearing separated them from the edge of the cavern. In Straum's time, the dragon had kept that stretch empty so nobody would be able to sneak into his lair without being seen. Over the past year, shrubs and saplings had begun to pop up, though none were tall enough to use as proper cover.

Veka leaned on her staff as she studied the entrance to Straum's lair. The horizontal crack was like a dark mouth in the cliff curving up before them. Vines hung over the entrance like unwashed hair. The ground closest to the cliff was overrun with dying wildflowers. Over the centuries, Straum had tried many things to relieve his boredom, including gardening. The sweet, rotten smell made her nose wrinkle.

A knotted rope hung down the cliff, courtesy of some early traveler. Even from here Veka could see it was frayed and useless.

She saw no sign of any guards. The pixies should be easy to spot. The one by Walland had lit up most brightly when he used his wings, but even when resting, he gave off as much light as a good lantern. If there was a pixie anywhere near that cave, Veka would see.

"Stay with me," Veka said, stepping into the clearing.

Slash's fingers snagged her cloak and yanked her back. She fell, banging her shoulder on a tree. "What are you doing?" she shouted, climbing to her feet and shaking her staff at him so hard one of the glass beads broke and fell into the snow.

"Keep your voice down, idiot! If you're so eager to get yourself killed, at least let me do it." He used his spear to knock her staff to one side. "Any hobgoblin child would know better than to go out there."

Veka stared back out at the clearing. "It's not even guarded."

"Exactly."

Veka's fingers traced the outline of *The Path of the Hero* beneath her cloak, wondering if Josca included any instances of the Hero killing her own sidekick.

Then she spotted it. The body of a small rabbit, half buried in the snow. In the dying light, she had mistaken it for a bit of wood or dirt. She couldn't see any blood, so it hadn't been killed by predators. From the amount of snow on the rabbit, it had been dead a while. Someone could have killed it with a rock, she supposed. A number of goblins were quite good with rocks. But why would they leave the corpse?

No, this had to be a trap of some sort. Judging from the angle of the body, the rabbit had been coming from her left. It had died a bit short of the cave. The trap must cover the area in front of Straum's lair. Using the rabbit as a marker to judge the distance, that meant it probably extended right up to the edge of the woods. A few steps and she would have triggered it.

That only made her angrier at Slash. A Hero shouldn't need her sidekick to save her. She knelt, determined to figure this out for herself. Slash leaned against a tree with his arms folded, amusement plain on his face.

The land looked no different. Ice encased the grass and shrubs poking up from the snow. The grass was a bit taller here, maybe. And there were holes in the snow where the ice protruded, almost as if the grass had melted the newfallen snow around it. But if that was the case, why hadn't the ice melted as well?

She pushed her staff forward, breaking bits of ice and snow. She glanced at Slash for some clue whether this was a good idea, but he only smirked. Her face burning, she jabbed the staff farther.

The ice didn't break. She tried again. A bit of snow fell away, but the ice was solid as rock. It seemed to pulse with a dim red light. Another jab confirmed it. "There's something inside the ice."

The taller shards of ice were literal spikes. She could see it now, how they came to a sharper tip than the rest of the grass. They had to be magical, probably strong enough to pierce the leather soles of her boots, as well as her feet.

She crawled forward, using her staff to test and break the ice until she reached the closest of the spikes. With one finger, she brushed the snow away.

The base was as thick as her thumb, and appeared to extend a little way into the dirt. The ice was perfectly smooth, so clear she could see something coiled at the base. She gave it a quick tap.

The ice flashed red as a thin tendril uncoiled, shooting up to the very tip of the spike.

"Looks like the rabbit managed to hit two of them," Slash said. "I'm guessing whatever's inside is poisonous. Their prey dies on top of their little trap, and they get enough food to last for weeks."

Veka's stomach rumbled again at the mention of food. "So how do we get past them?"

"If it were me, I'd toss a bunch of goblins out there. The spikes would hold them in place, and all I'd have to do is stroll along the goblin path."

What she needed was the ability to fly, like the pixies. If only she could make her levitation spell work. She pulled out her spellbook and opened it to the spell. The covers were cold on her hands where the copper was exposed through the peeling leather. The darkening sky made it almost impossible to read, even if she hadn't accidentally burned the page, but it didn't matter. She had long ago memorized every word on the page.

She knew the spell. Even though it had never worked before, it would work now. She had set foot on the Hero's path. This was the time when her powers would blossom, giving her the means to complete her journey. She glanced at Slash. Should she warn him, or simply pluck him from the ground and drag him along behind her as she flew? The latter, she decided, smiling as she imagined his frightened cries.

Her fingers twisted through the binding charm, and she closed her eyes as she finished the spell, wrapping tendrils of magic around herself and her companion and hoisting them both from the ground.

Nothing happened. She couldn't even complete the binding spell. Slash cleared his throat. "Go on, keep waving your hands like a madwoman. Maybe the little ice creatures will all get scared and run away."

Veka blinked back tears. Heroes didn't cry. Not even when their magic deserted them. She slammed the book shut.

The book . . . She stared at it for a long time. Perhaps the answer she needed was within her spellbook after all.

* * *

"You look like a fool," Slash said.

Veka didn't care. Planting the butt of her staff on the ground in front of her, she took another step. Already she was halfway across the clearing.

Strips of black cloth bound the copper covers of her spellbook to her feet. The ragged edge of her robe flapped behind her as she took another step. Red lights flashed beneath her feet. Elation at her success helped to ease the pain of ripping the covers from her spellbook. Most of the binding had torn in the process, and already the pages were separating. She had ripped an extra strip from her robe and used it to tie the pages together for now. She had hoped she would be able to repair the covers, but one look at the stiff, torn leather told her it was probably pointless.

"That doesn't matter," she whispered, taking another step. The pixies would have new books, better spells.

The ice gave way beneath her, and she clung to her staff to keep from falling. The end of the staff caught her in the chin, but she managed to keep her balance. She had reached the cliff, and the patch of ground here appeared to be natural. This was where the smell of dying flowers was strongest. Maybe the smell repelled the ice worms as well, or maybe Straum had done something to the soil to protect his garden. It didn't matter. She was safe.

She slipped the copper plates from her feet and sent them spinning through the air toward Slash, then turned back to the cliff. By stretching, she could just reach the old rope hanging down from the cave. A quick tug snapped it, and dirt sprinkled her face as the rope fell. She spat and tossed the rope aside. An ogre could probably reach the lower lip of the cave, but it was well beyond her. Or Slash, for that matter.

Slash hopped down from the field of spikes and walked over to test the vines dangling down over the cave. One tore loose in his hand, and he tossed it aside. "Kneel."

Veka raised her staff. "What?"

"Unless you have a better way to get up there?"

Oh. Veka looked up, then at Slash. "You should kneel. I'll climb up and—"

"Break my spine," Slash said flatly. He tossed the covers

of her spellbook on the ground. "I'm taller, stronger, and lighter. If you're serious about getting up there, this is the only way it's going to happen."

Had he laughed, had he even smiled, Veka would have punched him in the face. For once, he didn't appear to be mocking her.

He studied the cave entrance carefully. "You really think we'll find something in there to help us?"

"Do you have a better idea?" Veka shot back. She picked up her battered covers. The leather covering had torn completely loose on one, flapping from one corner and revealing dented, tarnished copper. The other wasn't in much better shape. She stuffed them both into her pocket with her spellbook and dropped to one knee.

Slash leaned his spear against the rock and put one foot on her outstretched thigh. Keeping his hands pressed to the rock, he placed his other foot on her shoulder and jumped. Veka fell flat into the snow and mud, but Slash had managed to grab the edge of the cave. He pulled himself up and whispered, "Pass me my spear."

Veka wiped mud from her face and grabbed his spear. "You did that on purpose," she hissed.

"Of course I did. Now give me my spear!"

Only the fact that she needed his help to get to the cave stopped her from throwing it. She handed the weapon to him, and he wrapped both hands around the end, beneath the spearhead.

Veka passed her staff up, then grabbed the other end of the spear. Her feet scraped against the rock as she searched for traction. She heard Slash grunt, and the spear slipped slightly. At least if he let go, the spearhead would probably take a good slice out of his hands.

The vines tickled her wrists as she struggled to climb, digging her boots into every crack and irregularity she could find. Dirt stung her eyes, and already her hands were beginning to cramp, but she said nothing. A Hero didn't complain about such things, even when her muscles were burning and she was hungry enough to eat hobgoblin cooking.

After what seemed like an eternity, her fingers found the

edge of the cave. Slash grabbed her other wrist, bracing her. She tried to swing one foot up to the ledge, but she couldn't stretch high enough. She tried again.

On her third attempt, Slash snorted with disgust and reached down to grab her ankle with his other hand. She half climbed, half rolled her body up into the cave and lay there gasping for breath.

"That was pitiful, even for a goblin," Slash commented.

Forget hobgoblin cooking. What Veka really wanted were some of Golaka's special spiced hobgoblin ribs, with lots of gravy.

Ignoring Slash's mocking grin, she grabbed her staff and set off down the tunnel. The dim light from outside soon faded to total blackness. Normally the dark didn't bother her. She had lived her life in the goblin tunnels and moved around comfortably by sound, smell, and touch alone. But as she listened to the breeze whistling past the cave mouth behind them, she found herself wishing they could risk lighting a lantern.

She kept to the left of the tunnel, one hand following the rough stone. Her staff she kept extended in front of her. As the sound of the wind faded, even her breathing began to sound loud.

Her heart pounded. The journey through darkness . . . could she have reached The Descent so soon? According to Josca, the Hero first endured The Trials, a series of tests through which she would prove her worth and gain the power she needed to triumph. The Descent was the fifth chapter, in which the Hero explored the darkness and prepared for the final confrontation.

Her toe hit something hard, and she fell, landing on what felt like a metal boulder. Her staff clattered to the ground next to her.

"What was that?" Slash asked. He sounded anxious.

Veka's hands explored smooth, cold metal until it gave way to dry flesh. "A body. An ogre, from the size of it." She frowned. The skin felt . . . crunchy, and was almost as cold as the armor. The ogre had been dead for some time. Long enough it wouldn't be safe to eat, she thought regretfully.

The armor had a few dents and dings, but it was still intact. She couldn't find any holes or wounds in the ogre's exposed flesh, either.

"How did it die?" Slash asked.

Veka hissed with pain as she sliced her fingers on the sword still clutched in the ogre's hand. She shoved her bleeding fingers into her mouth. "How should I know?" she said, her voice muffled. "Maybe he killed himself so he wouldn't have to listen to stupid questions."

She found a second sword in his other hand. Several knives were strapped to his belt and thigh. "He's got enough weapons to fight half the creatures in this mountain," she added.

"Probably looted them from Straum's lair."

Among the dragon's other eccentricities, Straum had been a bit of a collector, saving trophies from the various failed Heroes who tried to slay him over the years. Weapons of all conceivable design had lined his walls, along with the armor, lanterns, jewelry, even the chamber pots of the men and women he had slain.

Most of those valuables had disappeared soon after Straum's death. Centuries' worth of weapons were looted in mere days as ogres, goblins, and hobgoblins poured into the cavern. This new influx of weaponry caused a brief escalation of conflicts, decreasing the goblin population by about a quarter. Veka wasn't sure how many hobgoblins had died. Not enough, at any rate.

In many cases it was the looters themselves who died, learning too late that a sword that had done nothing but gather dust for centuries tended to break at the most inopportune times.

She could hear Slash crouching on the other side of the body. "Feels like he was burned."

Before Veka could begin to guess what might have killed the ogre, she realized she could just make out the shape of Slash moving around. In the distance, a dim green aura filled the tunnel. She tapped Slash with her staff to get his attention, then pointed to the light.

"We must be getting close," he said.

Veka watched a little longer before answering. "No. That's coming to us." Now she could hear the buzzing of wings, slightly lower in pitch than the pixie they had seen in the woods. "I only hear one. If we're fast enough, we should be able to kill it before it can use its magic." Or if not, hopefully the pixie would go after Slash first. She would have time to hit it from behind, and she might even get to see a new spell.

The light brightened as the pixie neared. The tunnel curved a bit up ahead. Soon the pixie would come into sight. "Get ready," she whispered.

"I'm . . ." Slash's voice trailed off, and he stared at her hand. Even in this dim light, she could see that his face had gone pale.

She glanced down. Blood from her cut fingers had run down her arm and begun to dry. She flexed her hand, grimacing at the sting of sliced skin.

"You're bleeding," Slash said. He swallowed and turned away. He appeared to be swaying.

"What is it?" Veka asked.

Ever so slowly, the hobgoblin fainted. His spear clattered against the rock.

Veka blinked. Hundreds of hobgoblin warriors, and she wound up with the one who was afraid of blood. She couldn't wait for him to wake up so she could taunt him.

But first . . . she raised her staff and strode toward the oncoming light. From the sound of it, the pixie had picked up speed. It had probably heard Slash drop his spear.

Time to show these oversize bugs what a Hero could do.

CHAPTER 5

"This is my quest. I shall be the one who leads us to victory."

—Prince Barius Wendelson, Adventurer (Deceased)

BY THE TIME JIG AND THE OTHERS MADE THEIR way back to the clearing, the sky was dark. The land, on the other hand, still gave off enough light to keep them from walking into the trees. The light appeared to be trapped within the ice and snow, which had grown steadily deeper in the time they had been searching. The snow came to their ankles now, and beneath it the ice was thick enough to support their weight. Braf had fallen three times already.

Jig stared across the clearing, refusing to accept what he saw. "This is the right place. The ladder should be here."

He glanced at his companions, hoping they might have a suggestion. Braf yanked his finger away from his nose and tried to look nonchalant. Grell passed gas, something she had done quite regularly since their fight with Sashi.

"Ogre meat disagrees with me," she snapped. "You have a problem with that?"

Jig pulled off his spectacles and cleaned the lenses on his shirt. Given the condition of his shirt, it didn't help much.

"If the ladder's gone, how do we get back?" asked Braf.

Jig didn't have the slightest idea. They were still looking to him for answers, as if he were supposed to conjure another ladder out of thin air. Or were they simply getting ready to kill him? With Walland dead, it could be argued that their little quest was at an end. Jig squinted at the sky, pretending to search for the ladder as he stepped away from the others.

"Maybe we could ask those ogres," Braf said.

Jig tensed, one hand going for his sword before he spotted the ogres in question. They were marching through the trees on the far side of the clearing. Jig counted six, maybe seven. He had trouble distinguishing the shapes, even with the lantern the lead ogre carried.

"Don't ogres usually use torches?" Grell asked. "I thought wood burned orange, not pink."

The pink light coming from the lantern popped and sparked as the ogres made their way through the woods.

"They might be using muck," Jig said. "Hobgoblins change the recipe a bit to get those blue flames." He had always believed they did it on purpose, purely so they could have flames the color of goblin blood. But why would anyone want pink fire?

"Where are they going?" Grell asked.

Jig clenched his fists. How was he supposed to know these things?

"We should ambush them," Braf said. "We can torture them until they show us the way out. There are three of us, and we have the element of surprise."

Grell smacked the back of his head.

"Thanks," muttered Jig.

Walland had acted nervous from the moment they arrived, glancing around and jumping at the slightest sound, like . . . well, like a goblin. These ogres could not have cared less who saw them, which meant they were probably controlled the same as Sashi had been. Hopefully, that meant they shared her lack of alertness as well. "We'll follow them," he said.

"Why?" asked Grell.

"Because I don't know what else to do!"

Grell grunted. Braf looked disappointed.

"We can cut around the clearing. That light carries pretty far in the dark, so we should be able to keep them in sight."

A noise in the woods made him jump. He turned, orienting his good ear toward the darkness as he peered into the trees. The branches had been creaking in the wind since he arrived, and occasionally the weight of the snow and ice would cause one to break. The first time it happened, Jig had yelped and drawn his sword. Braf had hidden behind a tree, proving himself smarter than Jig in at least this one thing. No doubt this was just another branch collapsing beneath the snow and ice.

Another crunching sound, like a footstep.

Braf was already looking for a place to hide, while Grell hobbled after him. The tightness in Jig's stomach grew as he realized he was probably the most capable warrior in the group.

He drew his sword and pressed his back to the nearest tree. Smudge was still safe in his pouch. If he could have, Jig would have crawled in after him.

There were at least two sets of footsteps. Had it been only one, Jig might have been able to kill whoever it was without alerting the ogres. Any real battle would no doubt be loud enough to bring them running.

"Jig?"

For a moment, Jig stood frozen. Then he recognized the voice. "Veka?"

Veka crept out of the darkness, her staff rattling, and her cloak dragging through the snow. A hobgoblin trailed along behind her.

"Well met, Jig Dragonslayer!" she said.

Jig stared. "Huh?"

"A good thing I changed my mind about helping you," Veka added, a huge grin on her face. "Beating those pixies is a job for a Hero."

Pixies. Jig had encountered only one in his adventures. The Necromancer had been one of the fairy folk, a little blue-haired man with a nasty sense of humor. It was cosmically unfair that anything so small could be so frightening. The tiny dark wizard had nearly turned Jig and his companions into animated corpses. Pure luck had kept Jig alive.

"How many pixies?" he whispered. Ogres couldn't hear as well as goblins, but he wanted to be safe.

"A lot," Veka said cheerfully. "They're holed up in Straum's lair. I killed one, then we fell back to plan our next attack."

Grell limped toward them. "These things enslaved the ogres, but you and your hobgoblin pet killed one and got away?"

The hobgoblin growled, pointing his spear toward her. Grell smacked his hand with her cane, and the spear dropped into the snow.

"We were sneaking through the tunnel toward the lair," Veka said. "Slash here was—"

The hobgoblin snarled again, loud enough to make Jig cringe.

"He was distracted," Veka said. "I picked up my staff and waited as the pixie came closer . . . closer . . ." She waved her staff, clearly enjoying the tale. "Suddenly he spotted me. His eyes widened with surprise. Surprise, and a little fear. He tried to cast a spell on us, but I was too fast. I leaped out and hit him with my staff, sending him flying into the far wall. He was stunned, but not out. He tried again, and the air tingled with the power of his evil magic. Another moment, and we would have been done for."

"Did you win?" Braf asked.

Veka rolled her eyes. "Just as his hands began to burn with magic, I reached him, crushing his skull with my staff." She showed them the end of the staff, then frowned. "I guess the snow washed the pixie blood away."

"So you beat this all-powerful pixie by hitting him with a stick?" Jig asked.

"That sounds like fun," Braf said. He hurried away, presumably to look for a pixie-hitting stick.

"How did you find us?" asked Grell.

"We didn't." Veka pointed to the ogres. "We were following that pink pixie."

"That's a pixie?" Jig asked.

"A lazy one," Veka said. "She was making the ogres carry her so she wouldn't have to fly."

She walked to the edge of the clearing, ignoring the others as if she had nothing to fear and making Jig wonder what had really happened. Normally, putting a goblin and a hobgoblin together was a sure way to rid yourself of the goblin, but here was Veka, turning her back on Slash and the spear that could punch a bloody hole through the middle of her back with one thrust.

Smudge was squirming out of his belt pouch. Jig loosened the ties enough for Smudge to scurry up to his leather shoulder pad. Flakes of snow hissed as they landed on him. The fire-spider turned this way and that, trying to keep an eye on Veka and the hobgoblin both. Jig didn't blame him. He had healed enough victims of hobgoblin traps to know how dangerous they could be, and as for Veka, what could be more dangerous than a goblin who wanted to be a Hero?

"Well?" Veka asked. She had already begun walking after the ogres. "Our way lies with those ogres, and I for one will not shirk away from the call of destiny."

Jig glanced at the hobgoblin, his fear unexpectedly giving way to sympathy. "Has she been talking like that the whole time?"

"Ever since she fought that pixie." Slash's nails dug into the shaft of his spear. "When she wasn't narrating her own little adventure, she was trying to compose a song about her triumph. I nearly ripped off my own ears."

"Wouldn't it make more sense to rip out her tongue?" Braf asked.

"Come on," Jig said. He didn't like the thoughtful look Slash was giving Veka. The pink light of the lantern—no, the pixie—was already fading with distance. They would have to hurry to keep up.

As he walked, he comforted himself with the thought that at least Slash didn't have orders to kill him when this was all over. On the other hand, when had a hobgoblin ever needed orders to kill a goblin?

Light had begun to return to the sky when the ogres finally reached their destination. Jig's legs felt like dead wood, and his socks and boots were soaked through. He would have blisters the size of his fist from all this walking.

The others seemed to be doing a little better. Jig didn't know who surprised him more, Veka or Grell. Despite her weight, Veka hadn't stopped once, nor had she shown any willingness to rest so the others could catch up. As for Grell, she hobbled along at a steady pace, never quite losing sight of the group. She didn't even appear to be breathing hard.

"I work in the nursery," she explained when she caught up. She waved one of her canes at Veka. "I spend every night chasing idiots. The only difference is, I don't have to clean her arse after she squats."

Jig hurried ahead to see what the ogres were doing, as much to drive that horrible image from his mind as anything else. They had come to the edge of the huge cavern. "Are we near Straum's lair?"

As soon as he asked, he realized the stone wall ahead of him wasn't the same as the one he had seen a year before. For one thing, the trees grew right up to the edge of the rock. The only exception was a small area of freshly cut stumps. The stone itself was covered in dying brown moss, and it sloped upward at a much gentler angle than he remembered.

He also realized something else. The snow and ice were thinner here by the edge of the cavern. The few flakes that blew onto the rock were white, not gray. The ogres' skins started to lose their metallic hue as they gathered around the cliffside. Their coloration still wasn't right, but it was closer to normal than anything Jig had seen since he arrived down here. Whatever was affecting the cavern, they seemed to be reaching the edge of its range.

One of the ogres dropped to his hands and knees to crawl into a dark hole in the cliff. Rock and dirt had been piled to either side of the hole, suggesting this was a new addition. Jig had always believed the hardened obsidian walls were indestructible, but he had believed the same thing about the ladder back at the clearing.

A high-pitched scream made Jig shrink back. The ogre's feet reappeared. He backed out, both hands clutching a rope as thick as Jig's wrist. The others crowded around, blocking Jig's view.

An answering scream came from one side of the cleared area, where an enormous brown bundle flapped and struggled against a rope. Powerful wings knocked into the branches, spilling snow and sticks. Even Veka seemed a bit taken aback by the size and ferocity of the trapped bat.

Farther on, Jig realized that what he had first assumed to be a pile of rubble was actually the bodies of several more giant bats.

"Ugly things, aren't they?" Braf asked.

Jig nodded. The ogres were dragging another trapped bat from the tunnel. The rope was looped around the bat's neck, and the wings were folded and pressed tight against its body. Tiny black eyes bulged from a flat, pale face. The bats' only redeeming feature was their oversize flopping ears, which reminded Jig a little of goblin ears.

Given how roughly the ogres grabbed and pulled, Jig wasn't at all surprised by the number of bat corpses in the pile. What he couldn't figure out was why they were collecting giant bats in the first place.

With a flash of pink, the pixie launched herself into the air. She waited until the struggling bat was clear, then darted into the tunnel. The ogres looped more rope around the bat, securing its wings to its body. Several ogres began to do the same to the other bat. The smell of guano grew stronger as the bat struggled, but it was no use. Soon the ogres had both bats tightly bound. A pair of ogres hoisted each bat onto their shoulders and set off into the woods.

Several more ogres were now crawling out of the tunnel. Brushing dirt and rocks from their bodies, they hurried to join their companions.

By the time the pixie returned, the ogres were already heading back the way they had come. Jig crouched behind a tree, holding his breath and praying Braf or Veka wouldn't do something stupid like challenge the ogres to single combat.

The pixie looped through the air toward one of the ogres. She landed on what appeared to be a small hammock tied to a wooden handle. The ogre held the handle perfectly flat as the pixie settled into place. Her shimmering wings twitched slightly, folded to either side of the hammock.

All of this was accomplished without the pixie or anyone else ever speaking a word. Jig was still staring, trying to understand it all, when Veka strode past.

"Come on," she said, stepping around a tree stump. "This is our chance."

"Our chance to do what?" Jig asked. "The only thing we know about that tunnel is that wherever it goes, there are giant bats on the other side."

"The Path will present itself to the True Hero," Veka said. She was quoting that book again. She always tilted her head back the same way when she did that, with her eyes half closed and one corner of her mouth curled up. "But the Hero must have the strength and courage to follow where the Path leads."

"What about the book's last owner?" Jig asked. "His path led him straight into Straum's stomach!"

Veka sniffed and turned away. "Then clearly he was no Hero, was he?" She reached into her cloak for her book, eliciting a pained groan from Slash. Ignoring him, Veka flipped through the pages and read, "Sa'il stared at the mountain of skulls leading to the temple of the black goddess, and his friends urged him to turn back.

"'Do you not see the bones of those who have tried to reach the goddess?' pleaded his faithful companion Tir.

"'Without those bones, there would be no path to climb,' replied Sa'il."

Jig glanced at the others. Slash was using his finger to test the tip of his spear. Grell looked ready to fall asleep. Braf, on the other hand, was wide-eyed as he listened.

"I don't understand," said Braf. "There aren't any bones here. And wouldn't all those skulls roll away when you tried to walk on them?"

Veka slammed the book shut. "It means you can't let the failure of others block you from the Path." She walked to the hole in the cliff and peered inside. "Hurry, before they return."

They looked at Jig, who shrugged. It wasn't as though he had a better suggestion.

Veka had already stepped into the tunnel. Where the ogres had crawled on hands and knees, Veka merely had to duck her head a little. Jig started to follow, when a surge of heat seared his neck.

"Veka, wait!" Jig shouted. He leaped back, poking Smudge with his fingers to drive the fire-spider away from his neck. Smudge's heat dissipated almost as quickly as it had begun. Jig searched for a source of light, a lantern, a bit of dry wood, anything that might burn. All the lanterns had either run out of muck or been broken during the fighting.

"If you're afraid, you can wait here while I explore the tunnels," Veka said.

It would serve her right to let her go on and get eaten or stabbed or killed by whatever Smudge had sensed. Jig ran to the dead bats and ripped tufts of fur from their brown bodies. They smelled faintly of mold. He rolled the fur between his palms, spinning it into a crude bit of rope. He held one end up to Smudge as he returned to the tunnel.

A smelly orange flame appeared on the end of the rope. Jig moved quickly to catch up with Veka. Already the rest of the fur was beginning to burn. He saw Veka's shadow just ahead and tossed the fur to the ground beside her.

"What are you doing?" she snapped.

Jig pointed. "What's that?"

Pairs of tiny yellow eyes hovered in the darkness. There were too many to count. Veka untied her robe and searched through her pockets, finally producing a small cloth packet. She unfolded the cloth and dropped a long, thick tube of brown fungus onto the fire. Jig recognized it as a firestarting stick. The fungus would burn slowly and steadily, and was far safer than flint and steel for lighting fires in the distillery. The flames brightened, taking on a greenish tinge.

"That is another trial I must face," Veka said.

"No, that is a multiheaded snake thing," Jig snapped, grabbing her arm and pulling her back.

Jig counted at least fourteen heads on the tangle of snakes, all of which were watching him and Veka. This must have been what the pink pixie was doing when she flew into the tunnel. Even the ogres would have had trouble getting past it. The creature completely blocked the way. Looking at any one segment of the snake, it would appear to be a normal rock serpent. Reddish brown scales perfectly matched the obsidian tunnels. A whiplike black tongue flicked the air, sensing prey.

The pixie had apparently taken a group of rock serpents and joined them into a single creature. Their bodies merged into an irregular ball of scaly flesh at the center of the tangle. There were no tails. Every sinuous length of snake had sharp venomous fangs at the end.

Jig could see why Smudge had been afraid.

"Out of my way," Veka said, pushing Jig back. Jig hopped out of the tunnel, Veka's staff rapping the ground at his heels. She strode to Slash and said, "I need your spear."

"The pixies left a snake creature to guard the tunnel," Jig explained. Though what Veka planned to do with the hobgoblin's spear was beyond him. He doubted it would be enough to kill one of the bodies. Killing a segment of a carrion-worm only made the rest of the worm angry. She would probably have to kill every piece before the thing would really die, and while she was going after one head, the rest would go after her. "Veka, if you try to fight that thing with a spear, you're going to get killed."

Slash's expression brightened. "Here you go," he said, handing over his weapon.

Veka set her staff against a tree and marched back into the tunnel.

"What are you doing?" Jig asked, hurrying after her. Her triumph over the pixie had obviously damaged her mind. What did that say of him, though? He was the one following her back into the tunnel.

"Chapter Four: The Trials." She handed her firestarting stick to Jig. Her hands gripped the shaft of the spear near the bottom. "All Heroes must overcome a series of harder and increasingly dangerous obstacles."

Jig stopped, momentarily puzzled. "Why do the obstacles always get harder? Why wouldn't the Hero face the most dangerous one first? The rest should be easy after that."

Veka ignored him. Raising the spear, she thrust the point at the center of the snakes.

Every head, except those few supporting the creature's weight, lashed out at Veka. Four sets of fangs sank into the wood of the spear, wrenching it from her hands. Smudge curled into a ball on his shoulder pad, and Jig smelled burning leather.

Splinters flew as the snakes ripped the spear apart. The thought of what those snakes would do to a goblin nearly made him throw up. They were clearly ravenous, some of them so desperate they were actually trying to swallow the broken bits of wood before spitting them to the ground.

Jig gathered up some of the splinters and used the fire-starting stick to light a small fire on the side of the tunnel, then studied the snakes more closely. If he wasn't mistaken, the pixie had made a mistake when she created this monstrosity.

"Stupid hobgoblins can't make a decent spear to save their lives," Veka muttered. Jig grabbed her sleeve and tugged her back outside.

"So did you kill it?" Slash asked, a wide grin on his scarred face.

"I need your help," Jig said, cutting Veka off. "Help me butcher one of those dead bats."

"I'm a hobgoblin warrior," Slash said. "I don't do that kind of work. And where's my spear?"

"I'll help," said Braf. "I was getting hungry again anyway."

Jig didn't bother to explain. He and Braf worked together, cutting chunks of meat from the body while Slash stormed off to search for a replacement weapon. Veka watched, her arms crossed.

"What do you plan to do, beat them to death with raw meat?" she asked. "That's the best plan the great Jig Dragonslayer can devise?"

"Come on," Jig said, scooping some of the meat into his arms. His shirt would be ruined, and it would take ages to get the smell of dead bat out of his nose. Even before he dropped the meat, he could see the snakes quivering eagerly. The pixie's magic seemed to bind them in place, but the heads stretched and strained toward the smell of food.

Jig was happy to oblige. He tossed every bit of bat meat at

the snakes, trying not to watch as the heads fought one another in their eagerness to gorge. Then Jig retreated back out of the tunnel to wait.

"What did you do?" asked Slash. He had returned empty handed, and the glare he aimed at Veka's back promised murder. "They're not dead. I can hear them from here."

"Give it time. It will die soon enough," Jig said.

"Poison?" Grell guessed.

Jig shook his head. "Most poisonous creatures have some immunity to toxins." He peered into the tunnel. The flames were dying again, but he could just make out the shape of the creature. Already several of the heads drooped to the ground. This was working even better than he had expected.

"What did you do?" Veka demanded.

"It's what the pixie did. She bound those snakes together, but she didn't think it through." They stared at him. "Look, that thing just ate most of a giant bat, right?"

Braf nodded.

"What happens next?" Jig asked.

"Dessert?" Braf guessed.

"What happens to the *food*?"

Grell snorted. "If you're me, it builds up in your gut until you need some of Golaka's special mushroom juice to get things moving, and then—" She broke off, hobbling past Jig to stare at the creature, following the lines of the snakes' smooth, unbroken bodies back to the juncture. "They can't—"

"The back part of those snakes got lost when the pixie put them all together," Jig said.

Grell pursed her lips. "Poor thing. That's a horrid way to die."

Jig was all too happy to let Veka be the first to climb over the dead snake creature. Even though Smudge was cool and calm, he still half expected one of those heads to lurch to life and sink its fangs into Veka's leg. Only when she was safely past did he stop worrying about the creature.

That simply meant he could resume worrying about other things, not the least of which was what he would say to Kralk when and if they found their way back to the goblin lair. "Let's see, our ogre escort was killed by his sister. We lost the ladder to the upper tunnels. And oh yes, the pixies have conquered the ogres and should be coming along shortly to do the same to the goblins."

Jig tried to console himself with the fact that he was unlikely to survive long enough to see that invasion. This tunnel seemed to slope downhill, carrying them deeper into the mountain and farther from home. Even if they evaded the pixies, the odds were good he would never make it back to face Kralk.

It was scant comfort.

It's not the pixies you should be worried about.

The voice of Tymalous Shadowstar, coming after such a long silence, made Jig jump so hard his head slammed into the top of the tunnel.

"What is it?" asked Braf, his face barely visible in the dull glow of Veka's firestarting stick.

"Nothing." Jig rubbed his head and glared upward. *Where have you been? I could have used some help down here. I had to fight an ogre and a snake thing and what do you mean it's not the pixies I should worry about? Do you remember the Necromancer? He was just one pixie. Now we have—* He didn't actually know how many pixies had taken up residence in Straum's lair. *—more than one,* he finished.

That pixie was not the original Necromancer, Shadowstar said. *Don't you remember?*

I try not to. But Shadowstar's prodding had brought the experience back to the surface: the smell of decaying flesh, the screech of the Necromancer's voice as he gloated about killing the original Necromancer and stealing his magic.

He wasn't from our world, Shadowstar said. *Whether he came willingly or was exiled, he left his world behind to enter ours. The pixies below haven't done that.*

But I saw them! I saw the snake creature that pixie created. And what about the ogres? They—

Shut up and listen, Jig.

Jig blinked. Rarely had Shadowstar sounded so abrupt.

The pixies haven't left their world behind because they're bringing it with them. That's why I couldn't reach you. Even gods have limits, and my power doesn't extend into other worlds.

The snow, the strange colors, that's—

It's an imbalanced juxtaposition of realities, said Shadowstar, escalating Jig's headache from "pained throbbing" to "Dwarven drinking party inside Jig's skull." *It's a bubble.*

That was better. Jig could understand bubbles. *So what's going to happen?*

I'm not sure. Shadowstar actually sounded embarrassed. *It may be a temporary thing, a transitional zone to help the pixies to acclimate to this world. Or it could become a permanent pocket of their world within yours. I suppose it could also pop, to further the metaphor. In that case, I imagine the magic of the pixie world would simply disperse.*

Jig's headache was getting worse. *What do you expect me to do about it?*

I don't know, snapped Shadowstar. *I was the god of the Autumn Star, remember? A god of evening, of peace and rest. Protector of the weary and the elderly. I didn't spend a lot of time repelling pixie invasions.*

Jig stopped so suddenly that Grell bumped into him. Up ahead, Veka turned back to ask, "What's the matter?"

Let me make sure I understand this, Jig said. *You, a god, can't set one metaphysical foot down there, and you have no idea how to fight them. Yet you expect me, a goblin, to take care of it? To beat an army of ogres, pixies, snake-monsters, and whatever else they fling at us, and also to push their little world-bubble back into their world?*

Bells jingled, Shadowstar's equivalent of a shrug.

Jig glanced at his companions. A hobgoblin, an old nursemaid, a warrior who was more likely to kill himself than the enemy, and a muckworker with delusions of wizardry. *Is there anything else you want to tell me before I go back to getting myself killed?*

Veka and her hobgoblin friend. They're cocooned in the magic of the pixie world. I'm guessing they've been enchanted. The pixies are probably watching every move you make.

Jig massaged his skull, trying to ease the pounding in his

head. His fingers warmed, swelling with a brief pulse of healing magic. The throbbing receded slightly. *Thanks.*

He glanced ahead to where Veka was impatiently tapping her staff on the ground. Slash was right behind her. At least Veka had destroyed the hobgoblin's weapon. Still, an unarmed hobgoblin could beat an armed goblin nine times out of ten, and the tenth time applied only when the hobgoblin was asleep.

So everyone here either had orders to kill Jig, or else they were controlled by pixies who would also kill him.

With an exaggerated sigh, Veka plopped herself down and drew out her spellbook. The spellbook was worse for wear, little more than a handful of ragged pages. She picked one and, after shooting an annoyed glare at Jig, began reading. Behind her, Grell sucked on a candied toadstool.

Is there any way we can break the enchantment? Jig asked.

Not that I know of. They may not even realize they're being controlled. Sorry.

I don't suppose there are any other gods I could talk to?

Tymalous Shadowstar didn't bother to answer.

CHAPTER 6

"True heroism requires the wisdom to find the proper path, the courage to face all obstacles, and the magic to blast those obstacles to rubble."

—Aurantifolia the Blackhearted
From *The Path of the Hero (Wizard's ed.)*

VEKA WALKED WITH HER FIRESTARTING STICK in one hand and the pages of her spellbook clenched in the other. Her staff was clamped beneath her arm as she muttered under her breath, reading through the tattered pages. She had already rapped Braf in the head twice and knocked one of Grell's canes from her hand, but she couldn't help it. She *had* to keep reading. For the first time, as she read through the mystical incantations and charms, things began to make sense. Her body tingled with magical energy just waiting to be released.

A bit of ash dropped onto the instructions for distilling pure bile from rat corpses. She wasn't sure what she was supposed to do with the rat bile once she had it, but with so many pages damaged or burned, she was picking up a lot of random tidbits. One page gave instructions for calling fire from river stones. Another listed step-by-step instructions for planting elvish corn, which apparently required the use of a platinum-gilded spade and water collected from the morning dew of an oak leaf, all of which was way too much trouble for a silly vegetable.

She grabbed another page. Most of the spell was illegible, but as far as she could tell, it was supposed to turn the caster invisible. In the margins, the previous owner had scrawled a note in blue ink:

Fire-breathing cat guarding Lynn's chambers can apparently pierce invisibility spells.

Veka crumpled that page back into her pocket and picked another. Before she could start reading, another chunk of ash fell onto her wrist. She jumped, blowing frantically to dislodge the burning ash. Her staff clattered to the floor, stirring dust into the air.

Jig whirled, his sword halfway out of its sheath. He and Slash had squeezed past her to lead the group, which would have irritated her if she hadn't been so absorbed in her spells.

She ignored him as she squatted to retrieve her staff. Chunks of rock and dirt covered the tunnel, a far dingier place than the smooth, polished stone of home. Ogres dug ugly tunnels. In several spots, rough wooden planks were wedged against the walls and ceiling to provide extra support.

Jig still hadn't relaxed his grip on his sword. He didn't trust her. Veka saw the way he had been watching her ever since she returned. He was jealous, threatened by her victory over the pixie. That was why he had shoved her aside to fight the snake creature. She would have defeated it eventually if he hadn't been in such a hurry to prove himself.

"Be more careful," Jig said at last. "I don't know when those ogres are going to come back, and we don't know what else might be hiding down here."

Slash laughed softly. "Don't worry, if the ogres show up, I'm sure she'll use her mighty magic to stop them."

Veka's ears grew warm. She brought the dying flame of her firestarting stick closer to the pages and kept reading, hiding in her book. The stick had burned down until it was as short as her thumb. Soon she wouldn't have enough light to read.

She sorted through the pages until she found the illumination spell. Old water damage smeared part of the middle, but most of the spell was still legible. She had tried this one before, in the privacy of the distillery. If she could find a way to create light without fire, it would make the muck work so much safer. In the past all she had managed was to burn herself.

But now her eyes devoured the page. "Nothing more than a basic transference and enhancement enchantment, really."

She blinked. She didn't even know what that meant, though the rhyme was catchy. Her mind was clearly leaping ahead, instinctively grasping more advanced concepts of magic. Her heart pounded as the arcane instructions became clear. She squinted at the damaged section. "Probably talks about providing an initial source of light, like the spark to start a fire. Pretty basic spell. Not so much generating magical light as stealing it from somewhere else."

Her fist tightened around the firestarting stick. First she needed to use the binding spell to tap into the surrounding magical energy. "That should be simple. There's enough magic trapped in this place to light up half the world."

"Hush," said Grell, poking her in the backside with one of her canes.

Veka ignored her. She spread her fingers, drawing a web of magic in the palm of her hand. The silver lines connecting her fingertips were far stronger than anything she had managed before. "That's only the first part of the binding. The magic needs to be linked to the light itself in order to manipulate it."

Veka smiled as she studied the binding. The silver lines weren't true light. Bringing her hand closer to the page didn't illuminate the words, nor did the light cast any shadows. The others didn't seem to notice it at all. Her hand felt warm . . . healthy. She began to mutter the second part of the binding, then changed her mind.

"Why bother? The words are useless, a crutch for the weak-minded." Her hands flexed of their own volition, and the silver web bowed outward. A tendril of light crept through the air until it touched the flame of the firestarting stick.

"Interesting," she muttered. "Magic is more sluggish here. Probably an ambient effect of the sterile nature of this world."

Veka stared at her hand, trying to understand the words coming from her own mouth. More sluggish than what? She tried to convince herself she was simply remembering passages from her reading. Josca liked to use big words, many of which Veka still didn't understand. What was the historical unification of mythological heroism anyway? So she blurted out a few strange phrases as she cast her spells. It was part of her growing awareness, nothing more.

Josca did say the Hero would tap into previously unknown reserves of strength and power as she traveled along the path. This crisis had simply helped her discover those reserves.

She giggled. She should have snuck away years ago instead of waiting around for Jig Dragonslayer to teach her his worthless flavor of magic.

"What's so funny?" Slash asked.

Without thinking, Veka pushed the flame with her mind. Orange light leaped from the end of the stick, splashing as it collided with Slash's nose. The firestarting stick went dark.

Slash's nose lit up like a muck lantern with an oversoaked wick. He leaped back, smacking his head against the wall, then falling as he tried to scramble away from his own nose. Dirt and dust swirled around his body. "What did you do to me?"

"Quiet," Veka said sweetly. "We wouldn't want the ogres to hear you."

Jig had turned around, his hand again going to his sword. The tunnels had widened a bit, back at the junction where the ogres' tunnel breached a larger one, but Jig still had to squeeze past Braf to reach her. "What happened?"

She tossed her firestarting stick aside. "The light was dying. I made a new one."

"Take it off, goblin," said Slash, "before I—"

Veka shook her staff, rattling the beads and trinkets at the end. Slash cringed and took a step back. A gleeful giggle tried to escape her lips at the sight of his fear, but she fought it down. Heroes didn't giggle. "Calm down, hobgoblin," she said. "Right now I've only channeled the light to you. Would you like the flames as well?"

Slash's eyes crossed as he stared at his nose. The orange light turned his face pale, almost white. Veins traced dark lines throughout his nose, especially around the nostrils. "Could you at least dim it down a little? You're giving me a headache."

"He looks like a pixie flew up his nose," Braf said, grinning. Slash stepped toward him, and that grin vanished.

Veka thought she was going to explode from sheer joy. She had cast a spell. She had mastered the magical energies around her and harnessed them to do her bidding. And she had shown that stupid hobgoblin a thing or two in the process. That would be the last quip he made about her magical abilities. He was lucky she hadn't done anything worse.

"The light *is* pretty powerful," Jig said. They had left the ogres' tunnel behind, crossing once again into familiar obsidian, and the orange light reflected from the rock for a fair distance in both directions.

"Say no more," Veka said, waving her hand in what she hoped was a gesture of generosity. She turned to Slash, reached out her hand, and tried to pull some of that light back into herself.

Nothing happened. She frowned and tried again. The spellbook said the caster would have total mastery of any effects they produced.

"I . . . I've changed my mind," she said. "Leave the hobgoblin to his discomfort. He can tie a rag over his face if he wants. At least that would spare us the ugliness of his features."

She saw the muscles of Slash's neck and shoulders tighten, but he didn't say anything. He was too afraid of her!

"Here," said Grell, handing him an old stained cloth.

Slash's hands shook with anger as he tied the cloth around his nose. The light shone right through the cloth, but it was significantly softer. "What is this?" he asked.

"Old diaper," Grell said. "Don't worry, I rinsed it out before I packed it."

"Veka. . . ." Jig's voice trailed off. He looked nervous. Was he starting to realize she would soon replace him in the eyes of the other goblins? Already Braf stared at her with new respect, and Grell . . . well, Grell looked annoyed. But she always looked annoyed.

Veka smiled. "Shall we proceed, Jig Dragonslayer?"

Beside her, Grell shrugged. "Might as well. I've got no interest in standing here staring at the hobgoblin and his amazing glowing nostrils." She turned away and started walking. With a shrug, Braf fell in behind her.

Veka gave Slash one last smile before she followed. Fortunately, Slash had no magic of his own. Otherwise the hatred on his face would have melted her to a puddle of goo right there.

Veka found herself walking beside Slash, to the annoyance of them both. Without her firestarting stick, the only way for her to read was by the light of his nose. Several of the glowing bugs she had seen in Jig's temple circled Slash's head, evading his angry swats.

"I'm going to kill you and feed your body to the tunnel cats, you know," Slash said.

Veka ignored him. His bluster reminded her of the goblin guards boasting about what they planned to do to the hobgoblins. They were too afraid to follow through. Those few who tried tended not to return.

"What are you planning to do when the ogres and the pixies find us?" he asked. "Making pixies glow isn't going to do much good."

"There are other spells," she said, giving him a sidelong glance. Though they would be far simpler to master if her spellbook weren't in such wretched condition. Here was a spell to fling fire at one's enemies, but most of that page was blackened beyond legibility, all except the warning at the top: *Do not cast near a privy.* Another page contained the first few steps in what seemed to be a very advanced spell, but the last part of the title was smudged.

"Shadow Beam of what?" she muttered. Shadow Beam of Darkness? Shadow Beam of Death? This could be Shadow Beam of Endless Belching for all she knew. If the rest of the spell had been present, she would have tried it on Slash anyway, but without the later instructions, the page was worthless.

A draft of warm air brushed her face. She glanced up and, for the first time since leaving the woods, really noticed their surroundings.

The dust ahead was heavily scuffed. She spotted large footprints ahead of Jig and the others. Ogre footprints.

She could hear a humming sound farther down the tunnel, like a giant playing the world's largest wind instrument. The air was drier than before, and it smelled of bat guano.

Ahead, Jig had stopped moving. He looked frightened.

"What is it?" Veka asked.

"I know where we are. Where we're going, at least. I hoped I was wrong." He leaned against one wall and wiped sweat from his face. "The Necromancer transformed his tunnels into a labyrinth full of traps and spells, and every tunnel led to the same place: a bottomless pit where he could dispose of those who weren't 'worthy' of joining his dead servants."

"I know the song," Veka said. Keeping her voice low, she sang,

"Deep in the mountain, to the blackness below,
that's where the Necromancer's victims all go.
Your screams start to fade as you plummet and fall,
so bring a good snack and don't bounce off the wall
of the Necromancer's Bottomless Pit.
The Necromancer's Bottomless Pit.
You can fall for a lifetime, if you come prepared.
Bring food and klak beer, there's no need to be scared
of the Necromancer's Bottomless Pit."

Slash grunted. "We hobgoblins sing something like that. The chorus is a little different, though.

"How many squirming goblins will fit
in the Necromancer's Bottomless Pit?
Keep tossing them in as they beg and they shout,
keep tossing them in if you want to find out
just how many terrified goblins will fit
in the Necromancer's Bottomless Pit."

"Will you please both shut up?" Jig asked. "Those giant bats, there was a whole nest of them living in the pit. That must be where the ogres are going to collect them. You can already feel the wind. This tunnel leads to the pit. We'll be trapped if we go there."

"So let's go back," Veka said. The others stared. "We passed at least one other tunnel, back where the ogres had broken through. All we have to do is—"

"The ogres have been following us for a while now," Jig said. "Can't you hear them?"

Veka's ears swiveled, trying to shut out the sound from ahead as she listened. She flushed. Jig was right. The sounds were faint, but the grunting and clomping of the ogres was unmistakable. How could she have missed it?

"They don't know we're here though, right?" she asked.

"I wouldn't bet on that," Jig mumbled.

Braf was looking back and forth between them. "So what do we do?"

"We go forward," Veka said. "Follow the path."

"And hope it branches off again between here and the pit," Jig added. He mumbled something about ogres being the least of his worries, but by then Veka was once again scouring the pages of her spellbook.

The wind picked up, ripping the page Veka had been studying from her hands. She barely managed to clamp down fast enough to keep the rest from following. She watched as the instructions for transforming urine to beer fluttered down the tunnel. The wind was making it impossible for her to study.

She grabbed Slash by the arm. "Come on. I need the light."

Slash growled deep in his throat as she led him back down the tunnel, chasing the flapping paper. After several failed attempts, Slash shoved her aside and stomped on the page. He picked it up, ripping the edge, and shoved it into her hands.

"Thank you," said Veka.

Grell shook her head. "Next time you go running off like that when we're trying to avoid an ugly, ogre-inflicted death, I plan to put a knife in your belly. I thought you'd like to know."

Veka bristled. Didn't Grell understand this was the magic that would save them from the ogres and the pixies, not to mention this bottomless pit? Well, maybe not the urine-to-beer spell, but magic in general.

The wind grew stronger, tugging wisps of hair from her braid and whipping it into her face. Grudgingly she conceded the older goblin might be right. If she kept trying to read, it would probably cost her any number of spells.

Her muscles tightened as she shoved the pages into the pocket of her cloak. It was as if her body were physically rebelling against the idea of giving up her studies, even for a short time. So many things had begun to make sense, so many possibilities were becoming clear, and she was supposed to simply set it all aside?

The noise was louder here. Despite Jig's hopes, the tunnel had taken them farther and farther down, following a relatively straight line through the rock. They were trapped between the ogres and the pit.

The pit itself was visible now, a black shadow at the end of the tunnel. Jig stood to one side, staring at the darkness as if he could somehow transform it into a bridge or a ladder.

For a goblin who had fought and triumphed over adventurers, the Necromancer, and even a dragon, Jig didn't act like a Hero. He acted . . . well, more like a goblin, really. He preferred to cower and hide, to run away from danger and avoid the glory of battle.

Jig was what Josca called a Reluctant Hero. Chapter ten discussed the various kinds of heroes. For herself, Veka had every intention of becoming a Hero of Legend, one whose triumphs would inspire her people for generations after she was gone.

But Jig was clearly a different breed. She rested one hand on the comforting weight of the book, reciting the passage to herself from memory. *The Reluctant Hero wants nothing more than to be left alone, but such is not the fate of the Hero. The Hero is destined for great things, and destiny is not easily fooled. Destiny uses a variety of prods to push the Hero into adventure, the destruction of his village being one of the most common. The murder of friends and/or family is also popular.*

If you feel you may be a Reluctant Hero, you are advised to go forth into the world as soon as you can. It may be your only chance to protect your loved ones from the cruel, crushing hand of destiny.

Yes, Jig was definitely a Reluctant Hero. Given what she had seen, Jig was a Dragged-Along-Kicking-and-Fighting-the-Whole-Time Hero.

How had he survived everything that happened to him in "The Song of Jig"? He wasn't strong. He looked more like a child than a full-grown goblin. His poor vision handicapped him further, even with those ridiculous lenses. His magic seemed to be limited to fixing wounds. Faced with an impending battle against the ogres, his whole heroic plan was to run away.

Veka moved past him, keeping her head and shoulders high to project an air of confidence. Whatever luck had saved Jig in the past, it didn't appear to be helping him now. He didn't know what to do.

She beckoned to Slash. "Come with me." His silent obedience was proof of how far she had come since leaving the goblin lair.

Crumbling, sloping rock marked the end of the tunnel. The ground tilted downward, and it would have been easy for her to lose her footing and fall. Bracing the end of her staff against the opposite wall, she pressed her other hand to the stone and crept forward until she could see out into the pit.

Orange light from Slash's nose barely reached the far side of the pit. The wind rushed downward, sending a low hum through her bones as it passed the tunnel entrance. Slash had stopped a few paces back. His tiny pupils never left the emptiness beyond.

Veka leaned forward and looked up, trying to see how high the pit went. The pit itself seemed to extend as far upward as it did down. She supposed it couldn't go up forever. The mountain itself only went so high. That started her wondering if the pit were truly bottomless. Not that it mattered much. If the bottom was deep enough, a regular pit was just as effective as a bottomless one. A bottomless pit just sounded more impressive.

A good thirty or so feet up, a dark shape arched over the center of the pit. That would be the bridge at the center of the Necromancer's maze. This last tunnel had sloped deeper down than she had realized. "Bring your nose closer."

Slash took a half step, then folded his arms, refusing to take another. Veka squinted, trying to make out the details of the bridge. She could see square gaps where the blocks or tiles or whatever they were had fallen loose, but the bridge itself still appeared to be stable. All they had to do was reach it.

"The ogres will be here soon," Grell commented. "If you're through sightseeing, maybe we ought to figure out how to fight them."

Veka was tempted to wait. Once the others were dead and dying, she would stride through to stand in the center of the tunnel. The ogres would pull back, momentarily confused by her confidence. There, with the wind rushing past her face, fluttering her cloak in a dramatic fashion, she would slam her staff against the ground and say in a booming voice, "Go home, you stupid ogres!"

No . . . that wasn't dramatic enough. Slamming the staff was good, but the dialog needed work. She would have to sit down with *The Path of the Hero* and reread Appendix C: Heroic Declarations and Witty Remarks.

The end of her staff slipped, and she fell back, kicking to keep from falling. On second thought, maybe fighting wasn't such a great idea. Not when a misstep could send even a Hero tumbling into the darkness.

She could hear Jig mumbling to the others, trying to come up with some sort of battle plan. She ignored him, setting her staff to one side as she yanked the pages of her spellbook from her pocket. The pages rustled and slapped her hands in the wind, fighting to escape, but she held tight until she found the burned page with her levitation charm. Still prone on the ground, she tucked that page beneath her arm and shoved the rest back into her pocket.

She had to sit up in order to read the charm. Slash had turned away to listen to Jig's plan, but he was still bright enough for her to skim the words that hadn't been seared away. A quick binding spell to tap into the magic. A second to anchor the spell to her staff. She ignored the margin notes and a doodle of an overly endowed elf girl as she read the true heart of the charm.

"Another straightforward bit of sympathetic magic, with the magical component providing the necessary leverage." Whatever that meant. She tucked the page back into her cloak pocket, grabbed her staff, and finished the charm, carefully enunciating each tongue-twisting syllable.

Slash yelped as his head bounced against the roof of the tunnel. He kept yelling as he floated and bobbed, so the damage couldn't have been too bad.

"Veka, if we're going to fight the ogres, we'll need that hobgoblin!" Jig shouted.

She could hear the ogres running, and the far end of the tunnel had begun to take on a pinkish tinge. "Not yet," she muttered. "I'm not ready."

A twitch of her staff shot Slash out of the tunnel and into the pit. His shrieks grew higher in pitch as his arms and legs whirled, as if he were trying to swim through the air itself. Veka slowly spun her staff, rotating him until he was facing the tunnel.

"What are you doing?" Braf asked.

"Saving our lives," said Veka. She gave him a fierce grin as she cast the charm again.

Nothing happened. She tried a second time, tracing the binding with her free hand, then connecting Braf to her staff. He should have floated out to join Slash in the pit. She had done the spell correctly. Why wasn't he flying?

"You're doing that?" Jig asked, pointing to Slash.

She nodded.

Jig glanced at the approaching light, then back at Slash. Sliding his sword into its sheath, he moved to the end of the tunnel, muttering, "I hate magic." When he reached the end he braced himself and leaped. His arms clamped around Slash's waist, his legs locked around the hobgoblin's knees.

"Get off of me, you stupid goblin!"

"Don't squirm," Jig yelled. "Do you want me to bite you to keep from falling?"

Slash stopped moving. A wise choice, given where Jig's face had ended up.

"Bring him closer to the tunnel," Jig yelled. "If we all pile onto Slash, can you float us up to the bridge?"

This was *her* plan! Why was Jig giving orders? She scowled, trying to come up with a reason it wouldn't work. But she was having no trouble levitating the additional weight, and the bridge wasn't too far away. It would probably work, darn it all.

She turned away. "Grell, you go next," she said quickly, before Jig could make the decision.

Grell tucked her canes through her belt and limped to the edge of the tunnel. Veka twitched her staff, bringing Slash and Jig closer . . . closer. . . . Slash stretched out his arms, trying to reach the rock. Veka spun him around again, rapping his head against the stone for good measure. "None of that, you."

She lowered him a bit, and Grell half stepped, half skidded off the edge. Her arms circled Slash's neck, and one of her feet kicked Jig in the ear.

A high-pitched scream echoed through the pit, and for a moment, she thought Jig had fallen. She froze, trying to sort out whether she should feel guilty or relieved. Perhaps a little of both? But as the scream repeated, she realized it was too loud and too high to have come from goblin lungs.

"Veka, we have a problem," Jig shouted.

A flick of her staff moved them to one side as she peered into the pit. Far below, a giant bat flew toward them, its huge wings flapping hard against the wind.

"You there, goblin!" Two ogres had come into view. One pointed a crude wooden spear at her and Braf. "We've come for Jig Dragonslayer."

Veka felt as though the ogre had walked up and slammed a fist into her stomach. "Jig?" she repeated. "You want *Jig*? I'm the one doing all the work!"

Beside her, Braf squeezed past to leap onto Slash. She was too stunned to even notice whether or not he made it. After everything she had done, the ogres wanted Jig. She was the Hero here, not him. She was the one wielding the magical energies. Didn't they see the floating, glowing hobgoblin?

"Veka," Jig shouted. "The bat!"

She ignored him. "Why do you want Jig?"

"That's not your concern, goblin." The two ogres began to move forward. The pixie still hadn't shown herself.

"Veka, stop playing around and do something about this bat," Grell shouted, her tone so sharp Veka started to obey without even realizing it.

The other ogre shoved past his companion. "Jig is there, in the pit. Kill the fat goblin and grab him before he escapes."

Kill the fat goblin. She was nothing but an obstacle to be tossed aside. Her fangs bit into her cheeks, and her hands shook with the grand injustice of it all. Nothing she did would ever be good enough to erase the mighty Jig Dragonslayer. Forget her victory over the pixies, forget her mastery of powers Jig couldn't even understand, none of it made one bit of difference. She was nothing. Nobody.

A squeal from the pit told her the bat was here, its wings adding to the wind as it hovered beside Slash and the others. Feet with claws as long as her hands stretched toward Braf. He dangled at the bottom of the group, clinging to his hooktooth, which was hooked through Slash's belt.

Braf kicked uselessly, nearly dislodging himself. "Jig, help!"

Veka screamed. She tilted her staff, flinging Slash and the goblins aside. At the same time, she reached out with her other hand, her fingers curled into claws. Magic swirled through her arm as she bound the bat to herself, forcing the binding spell into the bat's body, until her power pulsed through every vein, every bone, every drop of blood. Like a magical web, her will closed around the bat, controlling its every motion.

Veka closed her eyes and leaped from the tunnel. She could still see, using the bat's own senses. To the bat, Veka was a sharply defined shadow arching into the emptiness, and it was a simple matter to fly beneath and catch her.

The bristling fur stank, and the pounding wings nearly dislodged her, but she clung with one hand to the bony edge of the wing where it joined the body. Pulling herself up, she pressed her knees into the bat's side. For one horrifying moment, she thought the bat would be unable to carry her, but this was an animal built to snatch and carry prey even larger than Veka. Wings pounded, moving them away from the tunnel and wrenching Veka's arms as she clung. She opened her eyes, seeing the others both with her own vision and with the colorless shadow-senses of the bat. Never had she seen so sharply, and the bat's hearing made goblin ears seem feeble and weak as a human's. She heard every footstep the ogres took, every curse Slash whispered, everything.

Giddy excitement swelled through her. She fought to keep from laughing, afraid she wouldn't be able to stop. Even Jig was staring at her, fear and awe etched on his scrawny face. Let Jig Dragonslayer try to take credit for this rescue. Never again would she have to suffer the mockery of goblin guards or the disdain of a hobgoblin. She was Veka the Batrider. She . . . she . . .

She had no absolutely idea how she had cast that last spell. The bat tilted to one side, fighting to break free of her control. It didn't appear to be going after Slash and the others anymore. It simply wanted to get away. And it wanted to be rid of the goblin clinging to its back.

"No, fly up to the bridge, you stupid bat." She moved her staff, floating the others higher. Why wouldn't the bat obey? "Of course. It can't understand me. I have to control its actions."

The bat was a stupid animal. When Veka first sent it flying beneath her, it had assumed the idea was its own, and taken over. All she had to do was start it moving, and the bat would keep going until something changed its mind.

Something like bait. She made the bat raise its head, fixing its attention on Slash and the others. At the same time she increased the speed of its wings, forcing it higher. "You want to eat them, you ugly, filthy, smelly creature. Eat them!"

Slowly the bat seemed to get the idea. A spear flew past, barely missing Veka's arm as the bat flew upward. The ogres stood at the edge of the tunnel, staring.

Veka moved Slash higher, twitching him back and forth to keep the bat's interest. "That's right," she said. "You're hungry. You'd rather eat a good meal than worry about me."

"Hurry up, goblin," Slash shouted. "My legs and shoulders are killing me, and if that fool Braf keeps squirming, I'm going to lose my trousers!"

In a moment of inspiration, Veka moved them toward the wall of the pit, directly above the ogres. If the ogres leaned out to try to throw their spears, they would probably fall into the pit. As long as Veka kept them close to the wall, they should be safe. "Unless the pixie comes out after us."

They were about halfway to the bridge when a flicker of motion caught her eye. She closed her eyes, allowing the bat's senses to take over. It saw much more clearly than she ever could. She spotted another crack in the wall, a tunnel immediately ahead of Slash and the goblins. Standing at the edge of the tunnel, an ogre flung a thin line into the pit. A loop of rope settled around Slash and the others, drawing them toward the tunnel.

Before she could react, a second rope flew out, cinching her to the bat. She could feel the bat fighting to breathe as the rope tightened around its throat.

She tried briefly to goad the bat into flying back, dragging the ogre into the pit, but the bat was already tired from carrying Veka, and it was too panicked to obey. The harder it struggled to breathe, the faster it used what little air remained in its lungs. Soon Veka found herself swinging toward the rock, tied to an unconscious bat. The bat hit first, cushioning the impact. She twitched her staff, trying to use her levitation charm on Slash to drag the other ogre down, but they were too strong.

So be it. Fighting was more heroic than fleeing any day. She tightened her grip on her staff and prepared for battle.

CHAPTER 7

"Keep your enemies close, but your friends closer. That way your friends are between you and your enemies."

—Goblin Proverb

NORMALLY JIG WAS GOOD AT CONSIDERING HIS options and discovering the best way out of whatever situation he had been flung into. He was finding that much more difficult now, as the ogres' rope squished his face against Slash's hard leather vest. He didn't know what the hobgoblin carried on his belt, but a number of pouches and tools kept jabbing Jig in the chest and armpit. Adding to his discomfort was the cheeselike odor of Grell's right foot, currently resting on Slash's hip, so close Jig could have licked her sandal.

The only options he could come up with all centered on how they were going to die. The male ogre carried a large ax on his belt, which seemed a likely way to go. Though ogres were known to enjoy crushing their enemies bare-handed. They could also settle for simply tugging the rope tighter until it squeezed Jig and the others to death, though that probably wouldn't be as much fun for the ogres.

He glanced at Veka. Given what she had already done, she might be even more dangerous than the ogres and pixies. At the moment though, the ogres' second rope had her face pressed against the back of the strangling bat. Jig doubted she could cast a spell with a mouth full of bat fur.

That meant Braf was their best hope. Perhaps "hope" wasn't the right word. Dangling from his hook-tooth, Braf had been low enough that the rope only caught his wrists. He had been wiggling and squirming ever since the ogres pulled them into the tunnel. With a triumphant snarl, Braf yanked himself loose and dropped to the ground. Jig and the others floated slightly upward as Braf fell.

Unfortunately, Braf had left his weapon hooked through Slash's belt. That didn't seem to bother him. He spread his hands and snarled, "Set the others free, ogres, before I—"

The closer of the ogres, the female, tugged her rope. Jig yelped as he, Slash, and Grell were yanked forward, crashing into Braf from behind. Braf stumbled forward, directly into the path of the ogre's fist. He slammed into the wall and slid to the floor. The female ogre grinned and scooped him up, tucking him under one arm. She hadn't even bothered to release the rope.

The male ogre followed them into the darkness, dragging Veka and the bat along the ground behind him. Jig did his best to protect himself as he bounced off the walls and ceiling. He couldn't use his arms, but he kept his feet out to absorb the impact when he could. He heard Veka spitting and cursing.

Jig wrinkled his nose. Wherever this tunnel led, it stank worse than any part of the mountain Jig was familiar with. The smell of rotting garbage and burned meat overpowered even the fungal scent wafting from Grell's toes. Small brown-shelled insects scurried away, avoiding the light.

These ogres don't seem to be possessed like Sashi or the ones with that pixie who were chasing you through the tunnels, said Shadowstar.

That's good.

Don't get me wrong. They're just as likely to kill you.

Jig didn't answer. He closed his eyes, trying to orient himself. Every goblin learned to navigate the darkness, but as far as Jig knew, none of them had ever tried to do so after floating about in the darkness. If he had to guess, he'd put them thirty or forty feet below home. He wondered if they were out from below the Necromancer's maze yet.

Once they had gone far enough from the pit for the wind to die down some, the ogres stopped. The female pushed Grell with one finger, rotating the group. Jig was starting to feel motion sick. The light from Slash's nose illuminated moldy rock and ground so caked with mud and dust the stone beneath was invisible.

"Do something about that nose," the ogre said. She tugged them closer, so Jig could see the pine-colored freckles on her leathery face. An emerald-studded loop of gold hung from one ear. Jig could have worn it as a bracelet.

"Unless you want to lead the pixies to us," added the male. He was larger than his companion, a hulking brute whose hair hung in dirty braids past his shoulders. Spiked gauntlets covered his fists. A single blow from one of those gloves would leave the victim perforated in four places.

The female rolled her eyes. "I don't need your help, Arnor."

"Don't be like that, cousin. I was—"

"Just because you're older doesn't mean you can—"

The male, Arnor, tossed Veka and the bat to one side and stepped toward his companion. "Look, Ramma, I'm only trying to help."

Dumping Braf on the ground, Ramma used her free hand to draw an enormous blade from a curved leather sheath on her belt. There was no handle. Oversize finger holes pierced the base of the crescent blade. She slipped it on like a glove, so the edge covered her knuckles, and shoved the blade toward Slash's face. Glancing at Arnor, she said, "Like I told you, I don't need your help."

"Threaten her, not me," Slash said, frantically tilting his head toward Veka. "She's the one who did this to me."

Ramma handed the rope to her cousin. With one hand, she hauled both Veka and the bat into the air.

"Release us," Veka said haughtily, or as haughtily as was possible considering she was still spitting bat fur from her mouth. "Then I'll consider your request."

Veka didn't seem the least bit frightened. She stared defiantly at the ogre, silently daring her to proceed. If Jig had retained any doubts about Veka's sanity, those doubts would have been dispelled.

Ramma pressed the edge of the blade against the knot of the rope. Both Veka and the bat dropped to the ground. Moments later Jig and the others had been cut free as well.

Jig didn't know whether to feel grateful or worried. The ogres wouldn't have freed them if they felt the slightest bit threatened. Given that their goblin warrior was currently snoring on the ground while the hobgoblin squirmed and swore from the ceiling, pinned by Veka's spell, Jig really couldn't argue with the ogres' assessment.

Veka stood, brushing dirt and fur from her robes.

"End the spell," said Ramma, tugging Slash down by the ankle. "Or I'll slice the nose from his face."

Veka grinned. She was actually thinking about defying two ogres.

She's a goblin, said Shadowstar. *Brains have never been your strong suit.*

"Stop fooling around, girl," snapped Grell. "I'd bet my canes there are more ogres farther down this tunnel. All it will take is one with a crossbow to put an end to your wizarding nonsense." She jabbed a cane into Veka's belly. "If you're so eager to die, run back and throw yourself in the pit. Don't take the rest of us with you."

Veka glared, her mouth still open. Jig held his breath, fully expecting to see Grell floating into the air and flung back to the pit. Eventually, Veka nodded. How did Grell do that?

Grell walked to the side of the tunnel and eased herself down, groaning as her joints cracked and popped. "Goblin trying to be a wizard. Never heard of anything so ridiculous."

Veka's face turned a darker blue, but she didn't react. Had the comment come from Jig, he had no doubt Veka would even now be turning him into a carrion-worm, but something in Grell's tone kept Veka from reacting. Jig really had to learn that trick.

"Well?" Ramma asked, waving her blade. "The longer he shines, the greater our danger."

"I'm trying," Veka snapped. She picked up her staff and pointed it at Slash. "I . . . the spell . . . I'm having a little trouble, that's all." She reached into her cloak and grabbed the ragged pages of her spellbook. "It's not . . . the binding, it's stronger than . . . I'm trying. Let me find the right page."

Ramma shrugged and stepped forward. "No skin off my nose." She raised her blade, adding, "So to speak."

"No, wait!" Slash's voice squeaked, almost unrecognizable. "Move me toward the goblin. Let me talk to her."

The ogre gave him a shove, sending him floating toward Veka. She looked up, and her words dripped disdain. "What do you intend to do? You're no wiz—"

Slash's heel caught her square in the forehead, knocking her back into the wall. Her head smashed into the stone, and she slumped to the ground.

The light vanished. Slash squawked as his body came crashing down. A pained groan marked the hobgoblin's location.

Jig rubbed his forehead. "If you'll give us a little more time, we'd be happy to finish incapacitating ourselves, and then you can do with us whatever you'd like."

He heard the ogres picking up Slash and the two unconscious goblins. "Follow," said Ramma. "Try to escape, and I'll beat you to death with your own wizard."

That was good enough for Jig. "Where are we going?" he asked.

"We're taking you to meet my mother," said Arnor.

Jig kept his good ear up, listening to the footsteps of the ogres and the tapping of Grell's canes. The stench grew worse as they walked, despite the breeze. Jig shuddered to think how much worse it would be without the wind of the pit to circulate the air through the tunnels.

Despite the darkness, the ogres navigated the tunnel without a single misstep. They had been living here for a while then. The tunnel followed no pattern, veering left and right, upward and downward, all seemingly at random. Though the aches in Jig's thighs and hamstrings suggested they were walking mostly uphill.

Several times he felt shifts and eddies in the air that marked other passages. From one came the sound of dripping water, and the heavy, sickly sweet smell of mold. Another breathed warm, dry air onto Jig's skin, carrying a smell like charred bones. Smudge stirred as they passed that one, climbing halfway down Jig's arm. Jig could feel the fire-spider quivering, as if he were ready to leap away and flee. Jig stroked the spider's fuzzy back to reassure him.

"Hold," said Ramma. She chuckled softly. "We don't want our guests to die before they meet Aunt Trockle."

Jig listened as Ramma jogged ahead, wondering what she meant. That they wanted him and the others alive was the best news he had heard in days.

The only sounds came from Ramma's bare feet on the stone and the raspy breathing of the still-unconscious Braf. From the sound of it, his nose still wasn't properly healed.

Tell him to keep his finger out of it, and maybe it will improve, said Shadowstar.

A loud hiss and the dry scrape of scales on stone interrupted the ogre's footsteps. Jig heard a muffled thump, like a fist striking a mattress.

"You little—" Ramma grunted. "Got you."

The hissing grew louder and more frantic, then stopped abruptly with the sound of cracking bone.

"Are my ears failing me," asked Grell, "or did your friend just tangle with a rock serpent?"

"They like to hunt these tunnels," said Arnor. "They give one another space, but there's always a few between here and camp."

And ogres were immune to most poisons, which made the rock serpents ideal guardians . . . assuming you didn't mind a few fang wounds. Rock serpents would eat just about anything, even carrion-worms. More than once Jig had been rushed to the garbage pit to heal some unsuspecting kitchen goblin who had dumped the spoiled remains of a meal and found himself face to face with an enraged, if somewhat greasy, rock serpent.

Now that he thought about it, the smell here was similar to the garbage pit back home. Stronger and fouler, but the same basic filth.

The ogres knocked two more rock serpents out of the way before they reached the end of the tunnel. Jig could see the orange flames of torches, and a voice called out, "Who's there?"

Both ogres spoke their names at once, then glared at once another. They reminded him of young goblins competing for the chief's favor. "Fetch my mother," Arnor added.

They had stopped at a wide, arched opening before a cavern. For an instant Jig thought they had somehow returned to the goblin lair. But the smell alone was enough to dispel that idea. He turned to his left. Straum's caverns should be in that direction, somewhere beneath them.

A few small fires brightened the cave, but the putrid smoke was enough to make him gag. Most of it pooled at the top of the cavern before flowing through a crack to Jig's left.

Thick columns of obsidian were scattered throughout the cavern. The ogres had built crude shelters at several of the larger columns, stringing rag curtains for privacy. Jig guessed there couldn't be more than a dozen ogres living here. The few he spotted appeared weary, dirty, and *hungry*. Jig comforted himself with the fact that Slash was a much meatier meal than he was, and the hobgoblin was already conveniently knocked out and ready to roast.

Braf coughed and gagged. Arnor dropped him, and he landed hard on the ground. "What is that stench?" Braf mumbled.

Ramma pointed to an open doorway at the far side of the cavern. Bits of wooden framing and rusted hinges still clung to the stone. "The pit you goblins use to dispose of your waste passes close to this cavern. Some of it is worth burning."

"Even goblin dung burns, if it's dried first." The speaker was an older, hunchbacked ogre, presumably Arnor's mother. Her knuckles were swollen and callused. A small, hooded lantern hung from a thick metal chain around her neck. With her spine so badly bent, the lantern never touched her body. The flames probably helped keep her warm. One whiff of the sweet-smelling smoke told Jig she had added something extra to the lantern fuel, something with a bit of a kick to it.

"Aunt Trockle—" said Ramma. That was as far as she got.

"We found these goblins fleeing the pixies," said Arnor. "Ramma and I spotted them coming up the pit, and—"

"I said we should kill them," Ramma piped up. "But he—"

"You told us you wanted to know of anything strange at the pit," Arnor said, glaring at Ramma. "This—"

"Shut up, both of you." Trockle stepped forward, scowling at the goblins. Her fingertips brushed the floor as she walked.

"Sorry, Aunt Trockle," said Ramma. At the same time, Arnor said, "Sorry, Mother."

"I told you I wanted to know what was happening at the pit," Trockle went on, her voice growing more and more shrill. "I didn't say you should bring goblins into our homes."

"He's a hobgoblin," Braf said, pointing to Slash. Grell smacked his head before he could say more.

"They were coming up the pit," Arnor said. "I thought we could question them to learn what's happening back home."

"They were running away from the pixies," said Trockle, her voice stern. "So you thought you'd lead them straight to us?"

"I told you," Ramma said, elbowing Arnor in the side.

"And you went along with him," Trockle said sharply. Ramma flushed and glared at Jig.

In that instant, Jig knew exactly what was about to happen. He had been on the receiving end far too many times. Ogres were larger and stronger, and their family arrangements were bizarre, but the humiliation and anger on Ramma's and Arnor's faces was universal. Just like goblins being chewed out by the chief, they had been shamed in front of the others. Next they would need a victim, someone upon whom they could vent their rage, to help them regain their sense of power and strength.

How many times had Jig been punched, chased, tormented, and teased because a larger goblin got caught messing around on duty?

"Do you want me to—" Arnor began, stepping toward the goblins.

"No, I can—" Ramma interrupted.

Jig was already moving. He grabbed Braf by the arm and said, "Get behind me."

Braf stared. Jig pulled his sword, swiping the blade past Braf's face so he stumbled away. Jig spun around, waving his sword back and forth at the three ogres.

"Just kill them and be done with it," snapped Trockle. Her face scrunched with annoyance as she regarded Jig's sword. "Leave the bodies by the pit. Make it look like they turned on one another."

"That won't work," said Braf. "The pixies will never believe we just killed each other for no reason."

Jig answered without turning around. "Sure they will. We're goblins."

Arnor pulled out his ax. Next to the ogres and their weapons, Jig's sword looked little better than a kitchen knife.

"But they won't believe it when Braf runs screaming down the tunnel," Jig continued, praying Braf would understand. He would have preferred the hobgoblin. But Slash and Veka were unconscious, Grell was far too slow on her feet, and if Jig tried to run, he had no doubt the others would do the same. So Jig clutched his sword with both hands, tightening his jaw to keep it from trembling. "Go, Braf. Grell and I will slow down the ogres. You tell the pixies they missed some ogres. They'll probably retreat through one of those tunnels on the far side of the cavern. I'm sure the pixies will be fast enough to catch them."

He glared at Trockle, who hadn't moved. "That way we all die."

Arnor glanced at Trockle. "Mom?" Beside him Ramma had drawn her weapon and stepped sideways.

Grell limped forward, and her cane made a ringing sound against Ramma's blade. "You wait right there until your aunt tells you what to do, girl."

"The pixies will kill you anyway," said Trockle. "They plan to kill every last thing in this mountain. My boy here will make it quick. Put away that sword, and he and my niece will finish all three of you before you can feel it." She sounded completely calm and reasonable, as if letting the ogres kill them was the most sensible thing in the world.

Jig shook his head. Trockle might be right about the pixies, but the pixies weren't here yet. The ogres were.

And they were still going to kill him. For the moment they were at an impasse, but already Jig could see other ogres moving toward the tunnel. From the sound of it, Braf had taken a few steps back toward the pit, but even if he did manage to reach the pixies, it wouldn't do Jig much good. They couldn't stand here forever. Arnor was playing with his ax, and Ramma had drawn back her fist to strike.

"You take your ogres to safety," Jig said. "I'll take care of the pixies."

His heart pounded as Trockle stared at him. Slowly she began to chuckle. "You? You're going to fight the pixies?"

"You must have knocked this one on the head when you caught him, cousin," said Arnor.

"How exactly do you intend to do that?" asked Trockle. "We saw what they did to our people, and you're nothing but a goblin runt."

Jig straightened his spectacles. "No," he said, feeling like a fool. "I'm Jig Dragonslayer." Gods how he hated that name.

"Jig Dragonslayer?" repeated Ramma.

Jig's cheek twitched. "That's right."

Ramma glanced at the others. "He's the one who—"

"I know who he is," snapped Trockle. She studied Jig more closely now. "You're shorter than I imagined."

Jig couldn't think of a suitable response, so he said nothing.

"You're no ordinary goblin, that much is obvious," said Trockle. "Most of you would have either run away or charged in like idiots."

Both of which were time-honored goblin tactics, and both would have gotten them killed. Jig waited. His arm was beginning to hurt from holding his sword like this.

"Go on then," said Trockle. "Fight the pixies."

Jig lowered his sword, resting the tip on the ground. His hands were shaking, and if he tried to put it back in the sheath, he would probably cut off his own belt.

"We should wake up Veka and Slash," Braf said, stepping toward them. "Veka's magic would help against the pixies. Maybe she can fling the hobgoblin at them."

"Not with the pixies controlling them," Jig said wearily. "More likely she'd fling us all into the pit."

Absolute silence. Jig could feel Smudge growing warmer. Slowly Jig realized what he had just said.

"These two are pixie-charmed?" asked Trockle.

"Um." Jig glanced at the other goblins. Braf was still staring at him, as if he didn't quite understand. Grell looked annoyed. Ramma and Arnor had both raised their weapons again. Jig could feel his brief respite disappearing as quickly as gold from the dead.

"Kill them all," said Trockle.

"Wait," said Jig. "We can tie them up."

"The pixies can see through their eyes," said Arnor, reaching toward Jig.

Jig twisted away from that huge hand and nearly lost his balance. "We'll blindfold them," he said. "Even if they woke up, they wouldn't know where they were or how they got here."

"They'll know we exist," said Trockle. "That's enough."

"What if—" Jig bit his lip. Once again he could see what was about to happen. His stupid comment was about to get them all killed. And this time he couldn't see a way out.

"Oh, for Straum's sake," Grell said. "You know what you have to do, Jig."

Jig stared. She was looking at his sword. Did she expect him to fight the ogres? "I can't—"

"That's your problem." With an annoyed grunt, Grell pushed Jig to one side and grabbed the sword from his hand. "Sorry about this, hobgoblin," she muttered. "At least it'll be quick." With one cane hooked over her arm, she shoved the blade into Slash's chest.

Slash jerked once, then his head dropped to the ground. Grell lost her grip on the sword and stumbled back. She would have fallen if Braf hadn't caught her shoulders.

"A shame," Grell said. "He wasn't such a bad sort, for a hobgoblin."

Slash's breath turned to tight, wheezing gasps. Jig didn't move. Neither did the ogres.

"Otherwise they kill us all, chief," said Grell, stressing the last word. "Now, are you going to take care of Veka, or do I have to do that too?"

Before Jig could respond, the voice of Tymalous Shadowstar overpowered everything else.

Jig, heal the hobgoblin.

Grell was wiping blood from her hands. "Should have stayed on brat duty," she muttered.

JIG, HEAL THE HOBGOBLIN.

The force of Shadowstar's command made Jig clutch his head. *I didn't know Grell was going to kill him, but you can't blame her for—*

He's not dead yet, and the spell dissipated the instant your blade pierced his chest.

Jig stared at Slash's body. His sword stuck up from the hobgoblin's chest like a skewer in one of Golaka's barbecued rat kebabs. *So all we have to do to break the pixies' spell is stab the victims?*

Now, Jig.

Jig moved forward until he stood in the puddle of blood seeping from Slash's body. He knelt, cutting his fingers on his own sword as he probed the wound. In the corner of his vision, he could see the ogres reaching for him.

"Let me help him," he said. He ripped the sword free, and blood spurted like a miniature fountain onto hands and arms. He put both hands over the wound, feeling hot blood cover his fingers and seep onto the ground. He would have hobgoblin blood all over his favorite boots. "Bring that torch closer."

"What are you doing?" asked Ramma.

A new kind of heat flowed through Jig's limbs, past the blood and into Slash's body.

Grell missed the heart, but she nicked one of the arteries. This is going to require a bit of precision. Put your fingers inside the wound.

"Ick." Jig closed his eyes and pressed two fingers through the skin. Something scratched the back of his finger. Was that bone? And what was that pulsing thing pressing against his knuckle? Everyone talked about how Jig Dragonslayer could cure any wound, but nobody realized how truly gross the process could be.

Got it.

The flow of blood slowed. Jig slid his fingers free and

wiped them on Slash's pants. He reached down to retrieve his sword. It was warm to the touch, or maybe the intensity of Shadowstar's magic had left his body feeling cold.

"When Grell stabbed him, it broke the pixies' spell," Jig said to the confused onlookers.

He couldn't have gotten a stronger reaction if he had told them Straum himself had returned from the dead and would be dropping by later for deep-fried bat wings. Arnor and Ramma started talking again, each trying to drown out the other.

Trockle rolled her eyes and grabbed each one by the ear, her nails digging cruelly into the lobes. "Stop talking."

To Jig's great surprise, they obeyed. Arnor and Ramma were both younger and stronger than Trockle. If this scene had been played out by goblins, Trockle would have found herself beaten and tossed into the cavern. But the ogres merely glared at one another and rubbed their ears.

"After the invaders began killing us, we sent a group to Straum's cave to try to bargain with them," Trockle said. "We offered to share the cavern, or even to leave the mountain altogether. Those ogres returned the next day, enslaved. They killed dozens of us before we managed to stop them." Trockle stared at nothing. "I cracked my own cousin's skull with a club, and he remained a slave of the pixies until the last breath left his body. How can you be so certain this one is free?"

Jig hesitated. *Because my god told me so* wasn't the most convincing answer, but it was the only one he had.

"They want us dead, Jig Dragonslayer. Only when this mountain belongs entirely to the pixies will they feel safe."

"Aunt Trockle," whispered Ramma, "the hobgoblin is stirring."

"I see that," Trockle snapped. The ogres stepped closer, forming a partial circle around Slash, with Jig crouched near his feet.

Slash's tongue slipped out, moistening cracked lips. He groaned. "My chest feels like Veka sat on it. What—" His fingers touched his bloody vest. His eyes widened, and he sat upright. "Which one of you ugly, blue-skinned rat-eaters stabbed me?" He looked around, and his eyes fixed on Jig.

Jig glanced down. Hobgoblin blood covered his arms and sleeves. If that weren't incriminating enough, his sword was dripping with the stuff. Blood had dripped down the blade to form a sticky mess near the hilt. Really, Jig's entire outfit had been recolored in a kind of "slaughtered hobgoblin" theme.

"You did this!" Slash roared, pushing himself to his feet. The ogres glanced at Trockle, who shrugged, obviously waiting to see what would happen.

"Wait, I didn't—" Jig scrambled back. "Oh, dung."

Slash took two steps, and then the color faded from his cheeks. He stared at the blood on Jig's clothes. His breathing quickened, and he wobbled a bit. "I hate goblins," he muttered.

With that, he dropped to his knees and passed out.

"I think you might be right," said Trockle. "I've yet to see a pixie-charmed slave faint." She reached over to pluck the bloody sword from Jig's hand. "It doesn't seem to be an enchanted blade," she said, holding it close to her lantern. She wiped a bit of blood away from the blade by the hilt. "Magical steel wouldn't tarnish like this."

She handed the sword back to Jig, who nearly dropped it. He was still shaken by Slash's near-assault. "Do you mind if we tie him up before he wakes up and tries to kill me again?"

Trockle produced a thick coil of what appeared to be gray string and handed it to Arnor. He shoved Slash onto his stomach, then began binding his arms and legs.

"Are you sure that stuff is strong enough to hold a hobgoblin?" asked Braf.

Arnor gave it a sharp tug. "This is elven rope. Got it from Straum's lair. Thin as string but strong enough to hold four ogres. After a few of us escaped to these tunnels, we tried to use it to haul the rest of the family up after us."

"What happened?" asked Jig.

He spat. "Ever try to climb string? It's impossible to grip the stuff. It's so darned thin you slice your hand to the bone. Stupid elves."

Jig stared at his sword, wondering if he should stab Veka as well. If it worked for Slash, there was no reason it wouldn't work for Veka. Of course, there was no real reason it would work, either. Perhaps it would be better to simply tie her up until he figured out what had broken the spell.

He glanced around, and his stomach began to hurt again. "Um . . . does anyone know where Veka went?"

There was no sign of Veka. She must have fled while they were busy stabbing and saving Slash.

"I should have stabbed 'em both," Grell muttered.

Jig had a hard time disagreeing. He was a bit surprised Veka hadn't attacked them the moment she awakened. If she could fling Slash about and seize control of giant bats, surely she could do a fair amount of damage to a few goblins and ogres. He remembered the wild glee on her face while she was riding the giant bat. The only reason Jig could think of for her to retreat was so she could return with reinforcements.

Trockle seemed to be thinking along the same lines. She scowled at her son and niece. "You've brought the pixies down upon us."

"Sorry," said Ramma and Arnor in unison.

Trockle turned to Jig, and he raised the bloody sword. She shook her head. "Killing you wouldn't help us now. Go fight the pixies, if you can. You might buy us a brief head start. Or if you prefer a quick death, we can— "

"We'll fight the pixies," Jig said.

Trockle turned and punched Arnor in the arm. "As for you and your cousin, you're going to be on dung-drying duty for the next month!" Both ogres shot hateful glares at Jig as they left.

Grell and Braf looked at Jig.

Jig knelt, wiping his sword on Slash's pants. Why did they keep expecting him to tell them what to do? Any other goblin would have killed Slash and Veka the moment they learned of the pixie spell. Because of Jig, Veka had escaped to warn the pixies.

You goblins are so quick to deal out death. What happens when you err? Some deserve death, it's true, but can you restore life to those who don't?

Jig glanced at Slash's body. *Well, it was pretty gross, but—*

That's not what I meant, Shadowstar said, sounding cross.

I'm a goblin, remember? We don't care who deserves death and who doesn't. We care about not getting killed ourselves.

Will you just go fight the pixies? snapped Shadowstar.

Right. Jig stared at his sword. One old goblin, a runt, and an idiot against Veka and the pixies. Not to mention a fainting hobgoblin warrior.

"Braf, would you wake Slash up?" Maybe this time the hobgoblin would stay conscious long enough to help.

Not that he really expected it to make much of a difference.

CHAPTER 8

"A lot of fledgling heroes have asked me to teach them, but I tell them to take a hike. Mentor a newbie, and next thing you know you're getting slaughtered by some demon from the depths while your student escapes. Sure, the Hero eventually avenges the poor Mentor, but I'd rather be the avenger than the avengee any day."

—Nisu Graybottom, Gnomish Illusionist
From *The Path of the Hero (Wizard's ed.)*

THERE WAS NOTHING QUITE LIKE WATCHING someone run a sword through your traveling companion to help you shake off the last vestiges of unconsciousness.

Veka kept her free hand on the rock as she hurried through the tunnel. Blind panic had brought her this far, with no thought except to put as much distance between herself and Jig Dragonslayer as she possibly could.

She should have expected this. Jig had seen her true potential back there in the pit. He felt threatened. He preferred the old, pitiful Veka. Josca had warned of the jealousy a Hero could expect from those closest to her. She touched the comforting outline of the book through the outside of her cloak.

Veka was a victim of jealousy, just like Li'ila from chapter five: The Descent.

And when Li'ila had flung her attacker to the ground and bound him with the mystical energies of the earth, she drew her sacrificial moon blade and demanded of him, "Why do you accost me here, as I enter the domain of the foul one to complete my destiny?"

And the frightened mercenary responded, "Have mercy, Li'ila. I come on behalf of your husband, who wishes only to save you from these powers that have seduced you into dark witchery."

"This is how he proposes to save me?" the astonished Li'ila demanded. "Using a hired thug to accost me in the dark and drag me back to his cottage?"

Too cowed to lie, the mercenary hung his head and said, "Not precisely. He hired me to cut out your heart and bring it to the temple of Plinkarr, that he might purify your soul."

Like Li'ila's husband, Jig feared her and hoped to do away with her before she grew too powerful. That didn't explain why they had killed Slash, too. Then again, Slash was a hobgoblin. How much reason did they need?

Veka turned around. Maybe she should go back. Jig might try to hide and flee from battle, but she was Veka. She had the power to defeat ogres and goblins both. She grinned, remembering the giddiness of riding the giant bat through the pit, her cloak billowing, her hair blowing in the wind. All she lacked was her staff.

She scowled, trying to recall where she had lost it. She had been trying to release the spell on Slash. For some reason, she hadn't been able to undo the magic, and then . . .

"He kicked me!" Remembering that indignity was the final insult. She rubbed her scalp, feeling the blood clotted to her hair. Of all the ungrateful, cowardly, hobgoblinish things to do! It made her feel a little better about his ugly demise.

She wouldn't have been so upset if it were Slash who had been planning to kill her. She was a little surprised he hadn't tried already. But to hear Jig and Grell talking about who should be the one to stab her . . . "They wanted to kill me." The words sounded distant and unreal.

Her throat hurt, as though she had tried to swallow a rock, one with lots of corners. "I went to Jig for help!" How many times had she imagined the day he would see her potential and share the secrets of his magic, teaching her the things he had never shared with any other goblin.

He had seen her potential all right, and it had terrified him. Jig was no Hero. Nor was he a Mentor. What kind of Mentor plotted the murder of his own apprentice? Even if she had never officially been his apprentice.

But Jig had failed. He had made a mistake, killing the hobgoblin first. Veka was no longer the helpless fool everyone thought she was. She would go back there and show Jig Dragonslayer what real magic could do. She would—

She glanced at her legs, which refused to budge. She pinched her thigh and winced. Why couldn't she move?

She tried an experimental step backward, toward the bottomless pit. Her legs obeyed, but when she tried to go forward again, her muscles went rigid.

"What's wrong with me?" Maybe it was a curse of some sort. She wouldn't put it past Jig. She turned around and tried walking backward toward him, and again her body rebelled. She could flee, but she couldn't go back to confront him.

"Trying to fight Jig Dragonslayer will get you killed, either by Jig himself, or by the pixies searching for him," she whispered.

One hand reached up to touch her lips. That was her voice, but it certainly didn't sound like anything she would say. Though it was a reasonable point. Assuming the pixies were searching the pit, they would eventually find this tunnel.

"Jig means well, but he's going to get every last goblin killed."

It was her mouth. Her voice. Her teeth that nearly pierced her fingers when she grabbed them and tried to stop herself from talking. She waited to make sure the voice had finished before asking, "What's going on?"

"Currently, you're standing in a tunnel with your fingers in your mouth." The inflection was slightly off, emphasizing different syllables and blurring the sentence together so it sounded like one long word. The fact that her fingers were still probing her lips didn't help her enunciation much either.

"Who are you?" She folded her arms and braced herself. Her legs twitched, but she tightened the muscles. She might not be able to walk back to the others, but she could stop herself from leaving. "I'm not budging until I get some answers."

"Fine. My name is Snixle," Veka's own voice said, sounding exasperated. "I'm the guy who helped you cast that illumination charm on your hobgoblin friend. The one who guided you through the levitation spell. The one who helped you take control of that bat before he could eat you. I'm the guy trying to save your life, who can teach you far more powerful magic than anything you've done so far, but only if you get out of there. It's much more difficult to teach the dead."

Veka started to argue, but her lips refused to open. Her neck and jaw muscles began to cramp as she struggled against herself.

From the direction of the pit, a faint purple light began to fill the tunnels. "Pixies." She couldn't tell if she or Snixle had been the one to speak.

Veka frowned. "The pixie following us was pink, not purple."

"Which means there's probably a second pixie. Lights combine into new colors. Don't you goblins know anything? If they're sending another pixie out into your world, they must really want your friend Jig."

The rock in her throat grew sharper at the mention of Jig's name. "Why him?"

"Look, if I promise to answer your questions, will you please get out of the tunnel? We passed a crevasse near the floor a little way back. You can hide down there."

"Heroes don't hide," Veka said. "If these pixies are coming for Jig, they won't expect me. I'll have the element of surprise."

"I'm sure that will be a tremendous comfort when your bones begin to grow through your skin. Look, no matter how surprised they are, they'll either kill you on the spot, or they'll wrest control from me and make you fling yourself into the pit or slam your own head against the wall until your skull cracks. You can fight me, but you won't be able to resist them. Is that really how you want to meet your end?"

"I can—"

"No, you can't," Snixle said, cutting her off. He sounded absolutely certain. "Not yet, at least. You can't save your people if you're dead. Do you really think the pixies would send anyone but their strongest warriors to hunt in your world?"

Reluctantly, Veka allowed Snixle to take control of her legs, hurrying back a short distance. A smell like damp seaweed marked the place. She lay flat on the ground, feeling the outline of the opening, an irregular crack on the edge of the floor. She hadn't even noticed it before. Snixle must have been attuned to her senses for some time.

She should fit, though it would be tight. The ground beyond angled sharply downward. She heard water trickling from overhead. The crevasse extended up as well.

"Goblins have a rule about surviving strange tunnels," she muttered. She pulled her cloak tight around her body and slipped her feet into the hole. "A rule for figuring out which ones are dangerous."

"What rule is that?"

"They're all dangerous." She scooted deeper, grimacing as her hips and stomach scraped the rock. By now the approaching pixies were bright enough for her to distinguish the individual colors. The left side of the tunnel was more pink, while the right was bluer. If they found her here, wedged halfway into a hole, they wouldn't even need to attack. She would die of humiliation.

The soles of her boots touched the far side of the crevasse. She squeezed her fingers in next to her stomach and pulled. Her feet searched for traction, anything she could use to help drag herself through. This was worse than the time a group of older goblins had threatened to plug a privy with her.

No, on second thought, it wasn't quite that bad.

Her hand slipped, scraping skin from her knuckles. Gritting her teeth, she reached down and tried again, straining and tugging.

The edge of the crevasse scraped her stomach as she finally slid inside. She clung to the rock as her feet searched for traction. The crack fell away at an angle, passing underneath the tunnel. Water trickled along the bottom. Already it had begun to soak into her cloak.

"They're almost here," Snixle whispered. Without warning, her hands relaxed. Only Snixle's control of her jaw kept her from screaming as she slid into the darkness.

She stopped moving almost at once as her legs jammed into the rock. Cramped as it was, it would be nearly impossible to really fall. The hole dropped more sharply here. She lay on her stomach, staring up at a crack of light with one leg dangling into the drop-off. The other pressed against the rock, bracing her in place.

As the pixies passed, their lights briefly illuminated the crevasse. Water and brown sludge covered the rock. A quick glance showed that same sludge now covered her cloak and boots. She waited until the light disappeared, then pushed herself up.

"What are you doing?" Snixle whispered.

"The pixies are gone. I'm getting out of here."

"There will be others. Pixies and worse. They'll be even more vigilant now that the queen has awakened. All they care about is eliminating every possible threat to the queen's safety."

"The queen?"

"She came over before, asleep in a shell of magic to protect her from the shock. This place is so warm and dry. Even with all of the changes below, the transition will be quite a shock. But soon she should be ready to leave the dragon's cave. She might already be on her way. That's why they must capture Jig Dragonslayer."

Veka decided right then that the next one to mention Jig Dragonslayer's name would get a knife in his gut. "Why does everyone—?"

Her jaw clamped shut. Through pressed lips, she heard Snixle say, "This place isn't safe. We have to go deeper. Then we'll talk."

The water was cold enough to chill her hands and arms, and her sodden cloak was beginning to weigh her down. Gritting her teeth, she pressed her hands against the rough stone and lowered herself farther, searching for footholds in the algae-slick stone.

Her stomach rumbled as she climbed. How long had it been since her last meal? Heroes' stomachs weren't supposed to rumble. Of course, Heroes weren't supposed to have to squirm down dark, tight, wet holes, talking to themselves and hoping their friends didn't come along to stab them in the back either.

Her fingers slipped. She dropped hard, landing in a shallow puddle on a ledge. The rock fell away by her ankles. As the water soaked into her undergarments, she closed her eyes and fought for control. When she thought she could speak without screaming, she said, "We're deeper."

Snixle didn't argue. Maybe he heard something in her tone. "The tunnel slants back down toward the pixie cavern. If we're lucky, we can just follow the water all the way home."

Veka rested her head on the rock. "We're running away from two pixies so we can drop in on a whole army of pixies?"

"Most will be busy preparing to escort the young queen to her new home. This place still isn't safe for her. There are a few ogres roaming free, not to mention you goblins and hobgoblins. But no pixie queen likes to wait. Everyone will be concentrating on her, so depending on where this drainage crack leads, we should be able to get you out unnoticed."

"Why do they want Jig?" Veka asked.

She felt Snixle taking control of her hand, running through the familiar motions of the binding spell. She recognized the enchantment; he was trying to create light. "It's no good," she told him. "Without a source of light, the spell won't—"

Her fingers began to glow from the inside with a soft green light. The bones and veins in her hand appeared as dark shadows.

"*That* is why they wish to capture Jig Dragonslayer," Snixle said. Veka suspected it was supposed to sound dramatic, but mostly it just irritated her. "That is why they would want you as well, if they knew what you could do."

"They would?" Knowing the pixies would want to capture her made her feel a little better. She stared at her hand. "They want us to make light? I wouldn't think that was a problem for pixies."

"The magic of your world follows different rules. Your magic is richer, full of power, but also rigid. Learning to manipulate magic here is like learning to breathe stone. We can learn faster if we have a practitioner of your magic."

"You're one of them, aren't you?" she asked, turning her hand. Even her claws glowed.

"I used myself as the light source," Snixle said.

The dragon's cave. When she and Slash had gone to spy on the pixies. The pixie who found them in the tunnel had been this exact shade of green. But she remembered defeating him. She had told the others how she bested him. "You changed my memories from Straum's cave."

"No, you did that all by yourself," said Snixle. "You swung at me with your staff. That's when I cast my spell. By the time you got back to the others, you must have convinced yourself you'd killed me. We control the body, not the mind. We can't touch your thoughts or emotions. Well, the queen can, but not the rest of us."

Veka shook her head. "I remember hitting you, and then—"

"Your staff only brushed the tip of my wing. Then you turned around and dragged your friend out of the tunnel."

"He's not my friend." So why had she bothered to drag him out, unless that had been Snixle's doing? He must have enchanted them both. "That's why Grell stabbed Slash. They knew you were controlling us."

"They must have," Snixle agreed. "Jig's smarter than I realized."

Jig hadn't been threatened by her after all. He wasn't afraid of her. He was afraid of Snixle and the pixies. To him Veka was nothing. Just like she was to every other goblin.

"Why did you let us go?" she asked, her voice dull and flat. "Why not turn us over to your queen when you had the chance?"

"I . . ." Snixle's voice trailed off. Her shoulder blades flexed, and she stared at the ground. After a moment, she realized these were Snixle's movements. He must be flexing his wings. A nervous gesture? "I'm not strong enough," Snixle said. "If I tried to force you both, I was afraid you'd break free. I thought I'd let you and the hobgoblin go back so I could try to learn more about you, maybe find something that would help me earn the queen's respect. She was so depressed at the thought of leaving our home. I never imagined you held the key to this world's magic."

Her spellbook. "That's why you wanted me to hide from the other pixies," she said. "So you could keep me for yourself."

"If I bring you to the queen, she'll reward us both," Snixle said. "Veka, right now they mean to cleanse the mountain, to kill every last hobgoblin and goblin. Come with me, and maybe we can show her she doesn't have to kill you. She may let your people leave peacefully."

Veka shook her head. She didn't like the sound of that *may*.

"Look at what I've already shared with you," Snixle said. "Imagine what else we could accomplish. You can tap into the magic of your world. I can teach you to use that power to save your people. Jig Dragonslayer wants to fight us. The queen won't like that. She'll order you all killed. She'll send more pixies up into the tunnels to—"

"I thought you couldn't use magic here," Veka interrupted. "Our tunnels should be safe." She frowned. If that was true, the two pixies who had flown through above should have been powerless.

"*I* couldn't," Snixle said. "But the strongest warriors can wrap a bit of that magic around themselves when they leave the safety of our home. It's like a magical blanket. They have enough power to fight you goblins at least. Eventually our magic will fill this entire mountain. Then all your people will be destroyed, unless you help me."

"I know what you're doing," Veka said, shaking her head. "This is the Temptation of the Hero."

"The what?"

"Josca wrote all about it. This is part of The Descent, where the Hero is tempted away from the Path, drawn by promises of power and glory. You're trying to trick me into betraying my companions."

"The same companions who wanted to stab you in the back?"

That was a good point.

"We need you, Veka," Snixle said softly. "There's a limit to the power we can bring from our own world. We're exiles, every one, and we would be killed if we tried to go back. We must learn to live in your world. Help us, and you could be the savior of our people. Our people and yours as well."

Before Veka could answer, a loud snarl rose from the darkness below.

"What's that?" asked Snixle.

Veka's stomach tightened. "Tunnel cat." Naming the beast made her mouth go dry. She nearly lost control of her bladder. Which, given that the tunnel cat was creeping around beneath her, would have only made the situation worse.

This chimney of rock would be the perfect hunting ground for a tunnel cat. They had little fear of water, and their paws could find purchase on the smoothest stone. Prey would be hard-pressed to escape in such close, treacherous confines.

"Can you take control of the tunnel cat?" Veka asked. "Like you did with the bat?" Her heart pounded as she imagined herself returning to the goblin lair astride her own pet tunnel cat. She could almost hear the terrified screams of the goblins as they fled. Hobgoblins might be able to train the tunnel cats, but Veka would master them. She—

"No," said Snixle, shattering her fantasy with a single syllable. "The bat was stupid and frightened, both of which made it vulnerable to my magic. I doubt this beast shares those weaknesses."

"No." As far as Veka knew, tunnel cats didn't have any weaknesses.

"I might be able to help another way," Snixle said. "But you have to choose. Save us. Save our queen. In return, I can save you, and I can help you save your people. If not, you and the rest of the goblins will die."

Veka hesitated. Josca was quite clear on the fate of so-called Heroes who yielded to temptation. In the end, most broke away from their evil ways, but a high percentage died in the process. No, defying the temptation was almost always the right choice. Though in this case, defiance seemed to have a high chance of death too, and that couldn't be right.

"Wait, you said you were exiled?" Veka asked. She fumbled for her books.

"This is hardly the time to catch up on your reading," Snixle said.

Veka ignored him, flipping through *The Path of the Hero* until she came to the appendices. "Appendix A," she said, reading by the light of her hand. "One Hundred Heroic Deeds and Triumphs." She skimmed through the list. " 'Number forty-two: saving a village from invasion.' The goblin lair isn't exactly a village, but I think fighting off a pixie invasion would count."

"What are you doing?" Snixle asked. "I told you, if you try to fight us, you—"

"Shut up and listen to this," she said excitedly. " 'Aiding a banished prince or princess to regain his or her throne' is number thirty-seven!"

"Thirty-seven?"

"Do you know what this means?" Veka said, slamming the book closed. "Helping your exiled queen is even more Heroic than trying to save the goblins. Josca says so himself!"

"Does that mean you'll help us?"

She could save the pixies and the goblins both. Better still, she would save the goblins from the very doom Jig Dragonslayer would bring down on them. Jig still wanted to fight, but Veka would be the one who led them to safety.

"Can we fight the tunnel cat now?" Snixle asked.

She blinked. "Sure."

"Put your hand into the water."

Veka obeyed. Snixle gave her an extra push, thrusting her hand forward until her fingers smooshed into the wet, fibrous mass of algae. The slime and water shone green with the light emanating from her hand.

She twisted her head, trying to see into the darkness below. She couldn't see the tunnel cat, but she could hear it making its way toward her. The rough barbed skin of those paws let them climb almost as quickly as they walked. Those barbs would also strip the skin from their prey in a single swipe.

"Okay, I *think* we need to cast another binding. That's the key, you realize. Back home, we're constantly tied in to the magic, but here—"

Veka yanked her hand back. "You think? You don't know?"

"Do you have a better plan?"

Scowling, Veka relaxed and allowed Snixle to trace a quick binding. Lines of magic wove from her fingertips into the algae, knitting them together.

"Excellent. Now push, like so, joining your power to the very life of the algae."

Her hand flexed, and a bubble of magic pulsed outward from her palm. Veka grimaced. "It feels like I'm farting through my hand."

"You should have been a poet."

The tunnel cat's nose poked up through the darkness, surrounded by a halo of long white whiskers. A pale face stared up at her, the pink eyes never blinking.

A new sensation flowed through her hand and arm: a cool, calm feeling, as if the water were trickling over her own body, refreshing and reenergizing her flesh. She was feeling what the algae felt.

"You're bound to the plant," said Snixle. "Forget the clumsy second-rate sympathetic magic you were doing with that levitation spell. This is pure power. The magic is an extension of your body, and the algae is an extension of your magic. Now reach out and grab that tunnel cat before he rips your legs off."

The cat climbed closer. Muscles twitched along its back as it shifted its weight, searching for the next hold. Tunnel cats rarely rushed. They climbed easily and surely, waiting for prey to panic and fall.

"Grab it how?" Veka asked.

"Less thinking, more doing." Before Veka could react, Snixle took control of her feet and yanked them from the wall. She began to slip.

Veka grabbed the algae, and the algae grabbed her. Slime coated her fingers and wrists. Even as her legs kicked the air, drawing a hungry growl from the cat, the sludge tightened its grip. Hair-thin tendrils coiled around her fingers, stronger than any rope.

"Excellent! Now do the same thing to that beast below."

"Shut . . . up," Veka said. She could feel the cat now as it crept through the slime. Each time a paw pressed into the algae, she felt it on her own skin. The tail tickled as it lashed through the water.

The next time that tail splashed into the water, Veka grabbed it. A great mass of brown plant matter clumped onto the tail and held fast.

The tunnel cat yowled, a furious squeal that echoed through the tight crevasse.

"Don't let go!" Snixle yelled.

Stupid pixie. As if she couldn't figure that much out on her own. Veka fought to hold on. Slime crept farther up the cat's tail, tendrils weaving through fur and clamping around the bones and joints beneath. By now the tunnel cat was clinging to the rock with all four paws, pulling and twisting to escape. It twisted its head, bending its spine nearly double to bite at its own tail. Veka reached out, using another bit of algae to pluck several whiskers from its face.

That was too much for the poor tunnel cat. Fur ripped free as it dropped away, hissing and spitting. She could hear claws scraping against stone as it fled down into the darkness.

"Not bad. We'll have you commanding the elements and smiting your enemies in no time."

Veka laughed, no longer caring whether anyone heard. Forget Jig and his temple tricks. Had Jig ever ridden a giant bat or turned plants against a tunnel cat? Josca wrote that the Hero descended into darkness, where she would face her greatest trials and come into true power. Well, this crevasse was not only dark, it was smelly too. And if facing a hungry tunnel cat wasn't a trial, she didn't know what was.

"Do you think I should have a new name?" she asked. "Josca says a lot of powerful wizards have more than one name." Plus it might stop the other goblins from ever calling her Vast Veka again. "According to Josca, a truly heroic wizard name should be several syllables, often with some kind of animal worked in. Birds are best, but any powerful animal will do. What about Kestrel Shadowflame? Or maybe Olora Nightcrow?"

"Veka Bluefeather of the Flatulent Hand?" asked Snixle.

She rolled her eyes. Not even the pixie's mockery could pierce her excitement. She was going to be a wizard!

Veka rested with one leg propped against the top of the tunnel. By twisting the upper part of her body, she could press one cheek into the dripping water. After climbing for so long without food or drink, the sharp, silty water tasted like the finest wine. Wine mixed with plant slime and the occasional slug, but that simply added flavor.

She massaged her hand, trying to work out the worst of the cramps. Her magically glowing hand was fine. Somehow the enchantment kept the muscles loose and strong. If she could, she would have spread the spell over her entire body, but Snixle said that would only dilute the magic.

"Hurry up," said Snixle. Veka found herself glancing around, searching the darkness overhead as his nervousness translated into her body.

"Why are you in such a rush?"

"I have to get you to the queen. If she finds out I concealed your presence— " Veka's body shivered. "Queens are especially temperamental after drastic changes. That's one of the reasons for transforming your caves, to give her a familiar space. I remember how long it took my former queen to adjust after the death of her favorite mate. She ordered her guards to rip the wings from a worker's body simply because she didn't like the color of the shimmers he had brought to her quarters."

"Shimmers?"

"Wingless insects," said Snixle. "They weave intricate patterns of light wherever they crawl, which lures smaller bugs toward them. My former queen hung them for decoration. The bugs are nasty to feed, though. A bite will ooze blood for days."

"Why did this queen come here at all?" Veka asked. "Weren't there better places to invade? Places that would have been less of a change from your world?"

Snixle shook her head. "Opening a gateway is easy enough. The trick is to stabilize the other side. Magic calls to magic, even between worlds. The more magic you have on the other side, the stronger the link. Otherwise your gateway might flash off to some other world, and suddenly you're flying into a flaming mountain or the middle of an icy sea. This mountain was full of magic, especially the dragon's cave. That makes it safe."

Veka nodded. "Legend says the whole mountain was carved out by magic." She flicked a snail away from her hand and pushed herself away from the water, wincing at the tightness in her back and shoulders. She kept the algae twined around her hand and wrist as she lowered herself off the ledge. The crevasse was nearly vertical here.

"Best of all," Snixle added, "this place was unguarded. Aside from a few ogres and you goblins and such, of course."

"Jig will still try to fight you," she said. "He's like that."

Snixle was shaking Veka's head. "If he fights, he condemns you all to death."

"What if—"

"Less talking, more climbing," Snixle snapped. "The pixies have probably already captured him." Her shoulders twitched with his anxiety. "If they bring him to the queen before we get there—"

"I don't think so," Veka said. "Not Jig." Her mind leaped ahead. Jig would escape somehow. He always did.

Snixle didn't appear to be paying attention. "Do you see that? Down below?" Golden sparks floated upward, some nearly reaching her feet before disappearing.

This tunnel couldn't have been much longer than the one they had walked through before, on their way to the bottomless pit. But she felt as though she had been crawling and climbing through the tight confines for an eternity.

"We're almost home. I'm not sure where this comes out, so be careful."

Veka's heart started to pound. She knew what she had to do. She had to stop Jig Dragonslayer before he doomed them all.

She relaxed her legs, using the algae to slow her descent as she slipped toward the hole at the bottom of the rock. A thick haze filled the air below. Her feet emerged into open air, and only now did she stop to wonder how she would reach the ground. There was no ladder, and she—

Her shoulders spasmed, and her hand released the algae. With a loud squawk, Veka fell. Her arms and legs wheeled madly, and then the ground hit her like an angry ogre.

"Sorry," said Snixle. "I was excited. I forgot you don't have wings."

Veka spat snow and blood. One of her lips was split, and her face would be one enormous bruise. She rolled onto her side.

Slabs of ice covered the ground, high enough to completely hide the dead grass and bushes. Snow swirled through the air, reducing visibility to nearly nothing. That was good, she decided. Hopefully nobody had seen her graceless fall.

"So flat," Snixle muttered. "So overrun with plants and dirt. I miss the ice spires of the palace back home, watching the young pixies light up the mists from the nests as they flew their mating dances. . . ." He turned her in a slow circle and began to mumble. "Magic is flowing from your right. That should be the direction of the gateway. From the feel of it, you're on the far side of the cavern, well beyond the Necromancer's pit."

"Can you lead me to the Necromancer's lair?" Veka interrupted.

"What? No, we have to get you to the queen."

Veka shook her head. "What if there's a way for me to bring Jig Dragonslayer to your queen?"

She shivered. A drenched cloak didn't provide much warmth in the best of times, but down here it was little better than going naked.

"You can do that?" Snixle asked.

"Can you teach me to command creatures like that bat?" she countered.

"I think so. Like I said, I'm not the greatest warrior, but—"

"Teach me that spell, and I'll bring you Jig Dragonslayer." She cocked her head to one side. "If you're no warrior, exactly what *do* you do?"

She found herself walking as Snixle talked. Hopefully he was guiding her to the Necromancer's lair.

"Mostly I use magic to . . . well, to clean things."

Veka frowned. "What do you mean?"

"I'm a worker. I may not be a trusted bodyguard for the queen, but I'm wicked fast when it comes to getting stains out of clothing. Spills, infestations, anything like that. I was coming to dispose of that dead ogre when I found you and your friend."

That couldn't be right. Her Mentor simply could not be the pixie equivalent of a carrion-worm.

"There," said Snixle. He pointed.

Veka squinted, barely able to make out the dark rock overhead. The illusory sky Straum had maintained for as long as anyone could remember was gone. She searched the rock, trying to make out the spot he was pointing to. "That's the Necromancer's lair?"

Snixle was already casting a levitation spell. Moments later, the snow was gone, and Veka stood in the dusty emptiness of the Necromancer's throne room. She untied her belt and tossed her cloak on the floor, grimacing at the sloshing sound it made when it landed.

"Jig says the Necromancer was a pixie," she whispered. Something about being in this place alone made her uncomfortable, as if the dead still lurked beyond the doors, waiting for the slightest sound to resurrect them once again.

"Probably exiled here," said Snixle. "I wonder how long it took him to learn the laws of magic."

"Can all pixies command the dead?"

"Technically, yes," said Snixle. "The magic is the same kind of spell I'm using on you. We don't do it, though."

"Why not?" Forget commanding a giant bat. If he taught her this magic, Veka could lead an army of the dead!

"It's . . . icky. Necromancy is like wearing a corpse. You need a lot more power to keep the bodies from rotting, or else your host starts to drop bits and pieces everywhere they go. And you always have to be careful not to let your body get too connected to the host. That's bad enough when the host is alive, but you can imagine what happens if you get too attuned to a corpse."

Right. Forget Necromancy then.

"Are you serious about being able to beat Jig Dragonslayer?"

Veka retrieved her copy of *The Path of the Hero* and wiped water from the cover. The edges were damp. She opened the book and fanned the pages to dry them. "I can beat him," she said. "I have to. It's the only way to save my people and yours, right?"

"Assuming he hasn't already been captured," Snixle said nervously.

Veka didn't bother to respond. Clearly these pixies didn't know Jig Dragonslayer. But they would . . . just as Jig Dragonslayer would soon learn to know and respect the real Veka.

CHAPTER 9

"Sure he killed the Necromancer, but can you imagine a bunch of goblins trying to sing 'Hail Jig Necromancer-slayer'? And then you've got to come up with a rhyme for it."

—Goblin Songwriter

THE OGRES DIDN'T LEAVE JIG COMPLETELY EMPTY-handed. No, they did something worse: they gave him a torch.

Regular torches were annoying enough. Unless you dipped it in muck, the flames would flicker and start to die every time you moved. Nor was muck the answer, not unless you wanted the stuff dripping onto your hand and burning your fingers off.

This was worse. The ogres had no muck, so they had fallen back on what they did have.

"Flaming goblin dung on a stick," Slash muttered, waving one hand in front of his nose. He kept his eyes averted from Jig, whose shirt had begun to stiffen with drying blood.

"Would you rather leave it behind?" Grell asked. "You can go first. Let us know if you find any rock serpents."

"What does it matter?" Slash asked. "The pixies are going to kill us all anyway."

"They're not—" An unfortunate puff of wind sent smoke directly into Jig's face. He held the torch at arm's length, coughing and gagging. To make matters worse, the smell was drawing flies that constantly buzzed about Jig's head and landed on his ears. Smudge kept climbing onto Jig's head, trying to catch them.

"Here," said Grell, fishing a knotted bit of cloth from her shirt pocket.

"What is it?" Jig asked, his voice hoarse.

"Sugar-knot. Hardened honey candy." She grabbed his fang and pulled him down. With an easy, well-practiced motion, she tied it around his fang and tucked the knot inside his lower lip. "It calms the kids down. Ought to block the smell a bit."

Jig gave the sugar-knot a tentative suck. The cloth was rough and gritty, but the candy inside had a too sweet, fruity taste. Better than dung smoke, at any rate, though it left a bitter aftertaste. He frowned as he recognized it. "Is that klak beer?"

Grell shrugged. "Like I said, it calms the kids down."

His tongue and mouth tingled as he sucked the candy. He could still smell the smoke, but he no longer felt as if he were about to vomit.

"So what do we do?" asked Braf. He was swinging his hook-tooth through the air, probably attacking imaginary pixies.

"How should I know?" Jig had the overpowering urge to smash the flaming end of the torch right into Braf's face. Why did they keep asking him? "The only reason Kralk sent me on this little quest is so I'd get myself killed. I don't know how to fight pixies. I don't know how we're going to get back home. Stop asking me! I don't know."

Braf had stopped in midswing. Slash stood leaning against a wall, his arms folded.

"No more sugar-knots for you," Grell muttered.

His outburst finished, Jig's weariness returned. He stifled a yawn, knowing how foolish it would appear to the others.

"You told the ogres you'd take care of the pixies," Braf said.

"They were going to kill us!" Jig said. "This way—"

"This way the pixies do it instead." Slash snorted. "Nice of you to save the ogres the work."

They were right, and Jig knew it. But it was their own fault. They were the ones who kept calling him Jig Dragonslayer, expecting him to find a way out of any situation. Didn't they understand how many times he had nearly died on that stupid quest? He could barely keep himself alive, let alone two other goblins and a hobgoblin.

Smudge tickled the back of Jig's neck as he scooted to the other shoulder, trying to get away from the torch smoke.

Okay, so he had managed to protect Smudge so far, too. He stroked Smudge's head, wishing he could scurry away and hide in a crack somewhere until the pixies gave up. Really, wasn't that what the ogres had done? Hiding deeper in the tunnels and hoping the pixies wouldn't follow? Of course, if Jig tried to lead the others after the ogres, one of two things would happen. Either the pixies would find them and kill them, or the ogres would find them and kill them. The only thing left was to decide which would be the quicker death.

Even Tymalous Shadowstar didn't know how to fight an army of pixies. What was Jig supposed to do?

One step at a time, Jig. First you need to beat the pixies who are hunting you. Then you worry about the rest.

If Tymalous Shadowstar had been a physical being, Jig would have punched him in the face. *This is your fault! You're the one who told me to go with Walland. You—*

The pixies were here whether you went or not, Jig. Sure, you could have hidden in your temple like you always do, but in the long run you're better off facing them now.

How does that help me if I die in the very short run? Jig asked.

The god didn't answer. Jig sat down, sucking hard on his sugar-knot. Fine. So he was supposed to fight the pixies. No, wait. Shadowstar said he had to beat them. That didn't mean he had to fight them himself. He could order Slash or Braf to do it.

One look at them did away with that idea. Slash had no

weapon, and as for Braf, the pixies would fly circles around him until he killed himself with his own hook-tooth.

Smudge twitched, growing a bit warmer. The pixies were coming. What Jig needed was a giant fire-spider. With smaller prey, Smudge could be as vicious as any goblin, catching and cooking his food in a single jump.

Slowly, Jig climbed to his feet. On the way in, they had passed an opening that smelled of soot and ash. He hadn't recognized it then, being a bit distracted by his ogre captors, but the air had smelled a lot like one of Smudge's abandoned webs. Only stronger.

"What is it?" asked Braf.

"The pixies are coming," Jig said. He stepped away from the others, who made no move to follow. Good.

Grell coughed and spat. "You've got a plan, then?"

"I'm a goblin, remember?" Jig said, fighting a completely inappropriate giggle. Was giggling in death's face a sign of hysteria? "We don't make plans."

Jig hadn't gone far when he spotted the pixies approaching in the distance. Purple light slowly resolved into sparkling pink and blue orbs. The pink one flew ahead of the blue, wings humming. She folded her arms as she drew to a halt, hovering in front of Jig. He could feel the wind from her wings.

"You're Jig Dragonslayer." It wasn't a question.

Jig nodded. "Who are you?" To his surprise, he got the words out with barely a tremor.

"Pynne." She landed on her toes. Her wings continued to buzz, supporting most of her weight as she stared up at him. Her small face was overly round, almost swollen, with puffy cheeks and a wide forehead. White hair surrounded her head like a cloud. Yellow beads decorated her white wrap. Her nose wrinkled as she studied his torch, but she didn't say anything.

Jig had grown up a runt, always looking up at the other goblins. Dodging the larger goblins' fists, to be precise. Now he found himself staring down at his enemy. Pynne was so small. She looked like one good kick would break her against a wall.

"Try it," Pynne said softly.

Jig didn't move. Despite their difference in size, those two whispered words were enough to make him feel as though Pynne were the one looking down at him.

"*You're* the one who killed the dragon?" Pynne asked.

Annoyance momentarily overpowered his fear. Hadn't he been through this once before with Walland? "Yes, that was me."

"There were others with you when you escaped the bottomless pit," she said. "What happened to them?"

Jig hesitated. Where was Veka, and how much did the pixies already know? "The ogres killed them."

Pynne frowned. "What ogres?"

Whoops. Trockle wouldn't be happy. But how could they not know about the ogres? *Are you sure Veka was being controlled?*

I'm sure, said Shadowstar.

Pynne sighed, a whistling, chittering sound. "I told the others some ogres had escaped, but did they believe me?"

Behind her the blue pixie rolled his eyes. "Yeah, yeah. You're always right and everyone else is wrong. You want me to fly along to deal with them?"

"No, Farnax" said Pynne. Her light had brightened as Farnax spoke, and even Jig could hear the annoyance in her voice. "We've found Jig Dragonslayer. Our duty is to bring him to the queen."

Farnax drifted higher, and sparks exploded from his wings as he brushed the ceiling. He dropped to the ground, cursing and flexing his wings. "How do you creatures survive in these horrible, hot, filthy tombs? You've barely room to breathe without hitting stone."

"Enough," snapped Pynne. Farnax shrank back, then nodded. No question who was in charge here.

"Why does the queen want me?" asked Jig.

Pynne's wings stilled. "You are Jig Dragonslayer. When you killed the dragon, you opened the way for us. You served the queen once, and you will serve her again by helping us master the magic of your world."

"What about—?" Jig clamped his jaw before Veka's name

slipped out. Somehow Pynne didn't know about Veka. If she did, would she still see any reason to keep Jig alive?

Jig stared at her as the rest of her comment sank in. *He* had opened the way? The pixies had to be mistaken. Jig was certain he would have remembered opening a portal to another world.

"What about what?" asked the Farnax.

"The other goblins," Jig said. "The ones up above in the lair. What are you going to do to them?"

Pynne shrugged and hopped into the air. "The same as we would do to any pest who infested our home."

She turned, gesturing at a smaller rock serpent who had been creeping up the tunnel toward them. At first nothing appeared to happen. Then the snake hissed and began to bite at its own scales. The snake's struggles grew more frantic, dissolving into spasms and convulsions that flung it right off the ground. The snake made one last, frantic attack, sinking its fangs deep into its body, and then it was still.

Only when the rock serpent was dead did Jig see clearly enough to understand. Blood seeped from the edges of the scales. Pynne's magic had caused the scales to grow inward, digging through the skin until they killed the snake.

"Do we understand one another, goblin?" Pynne asked, smiling.

Jig thought he might throw up. It wasn't fair. Goblins worked so hard to be loud and ferocious and intimidating. Pynne had them all beat with a smile and a wave of her hand.

Jig stared at the snake. They intended to kill or enslave every last goblin in the mountain, and they thought Jig would help them do it, just to save his own life.

They knew goblins pretty well. Jig took a step back. "You said you wanted to control the magic of our world?"

"That's right," said Pynne, moving so close Jig could feel the warmth emanating from her wings. Smudge was still hotter, and growing more so the closer Pynne came, but the pixie generated a respectable warmth.

"When I ran away from the ogres, I was coming to get the power to fight them," Jig said. He was a horrible liar, but hopefully Pynne would have as much trouble reading his expressions as he did with the pixies. "After I fought Straum, I found a wand, one with more magic than I could ever hope to keep for myself. Enough to reshape this entire mountain."

The pixies glanced at one another. "Where is this wand, goblin?" asked the blue one.

Jig stared at the snake. He had never imagined he could feel sorry for a rock serpent. "I'll take you to it."

There were advantages to traveling with pixies. For one thing Jig could do away with that awful torch. Almost as good, the insects that had been harassing Jig now turned their attention to the pixies, drawn to their bright lights. Jig smothered a grin as he watched Pynne swing her hand at a particularly amorous moth.

Another advantage was that Jig no longer needed to worry about the rock serpents. Twice more the snakes slithered toward them. Pynne didn't bother with such dramatic magic this time. She simply used her power to make the snakes bite themselves to death.

"I thought you didn't know how to use our magic," Jig said as he watched the second snake die, fangs still sunk into its own back.

"We don't," said Pynne. "The strongest among us learn to store magic within ourselves, but if we're away from our world for too long, our power will fade. Even the enchantment we use to speak your language would dissipate."

Farnax scowled. "Don't misunderstand her, goblin. We're still strong enough to destroy you if you betray us."

"Oh, Jig wouldn't dream of such a thing," Pynne said, smiling. It was the same smile she had worn after murdering the first rock serpent. Her light turned a brighter pink as she circled Jig's head. "Tell us more of this wand."

Jig tugged his ear as he tried to remember the stories. "A wizard used it to create these tunnels and caves. It has the power to transform people, things, just about anything."

"A perfect tool," said Pynne.

"If you know about this wand," said Farnax, "why haven't you used it against us?"

"I didn't have it with me." Even if he had, he wasn't sure

the Rod of Creation would work inside the pixies' world-bubble. "I have a hard time just keeping the other goblins from taking my boots."

Jig held up one foot. All his climbing and running away had scuffed the blue leather, and the white-furred fringe at the top was tangled and matted. "Goblins have a different view of property and ownership than most races."

"A communal relationship?" asked Farnax. "Things are shared and passed along to those who need them?"

Jig shook his head. "No, things are taken by those who are bigger and stronger than the ones who had them."

"With the power you describe, you could destroy anyone who tried to take the wand from you," Pynne said.

"I'd have to kill the whole lair," Jig muttered. Not to mention he would never again be able to sleep. How many times had he woken up to find goblins tugging at his boots?

The wind had begun to increase as they moved toward the pit, and the air was drier. Both pixies were having a bit of trouble flying. Farnax in particular kept bumping into the rock and swearing.

Jig coughed, trying to clear his parched throat. His nose wrinkled. The pixies certainly smelled better than the ogres' torch, but in some ways, their scent was equally disturbing. They smelled of burning metal mixed with something sweet, like the flowers that used to grow by Straum's cave.

"Why did you leave your world?" Jig asked.

"We had no choice, once the queen was born," Pynne said.

"She ordered you to leave?" Jig didn't know much about kings and queens, but that made no sense.

"Her birth was an accident," Pynne explained. "The current queen almost never gives birth to a successor until she nears the end of her life, but occasionally it happens. Once the new queen was born, exile was the only option. Otherwise war would have devastated our people."

So it was a power struggle, and the pixies in this world had been the losers. Given what Jig had already seen them do, that wasn't as reassuring as it might have been. "Why didn't the other queen just kill the new one when she was born?"

Both pixies froze. Was it his imagination, or had their lights grown brighter?

"Nobody can kill a queen," whispered Pynne.

Alien though the pixies might be, Jig could still read them enough to know this was a good time to stop asking questions. All his instincts screamed at him to change the subject. Of course, if he had listened to his instincts, he never would have left the goblin lair to begin with.

"Even if she's too powerful, wouldn't another queen be equally powerful?" he asked, cringing in anticipation. "She has to sleep sometimes, doesn't she?"

Pynne actually shivered, a strange sight, since she was still hovering in the air. Her whole body vibrated, and it hurt Jig's eyes to look at her. "You couldn't understand. None can look upon a pixie queen without loving her. That's her power. That love is even stronger when the queen is young. When she is asleep or vulnerable. A newborn queen will even steal the loyalty of her mother's followers. She was raised in isolation until she was old enough to travel to your world. The most black-hearted villain would die to protect her, once he laid eyes upon her."

"As will you, goblin," added Farnax.

Jig struggled to comprehend that kind of loyalty. Goblin politics were swift, decisive, and deadly. Goblins followed their chief because they would be killed if they didn't. The trouble was, the chief couldn't be everywhere at once. In the midst of battle, the immediate threat of an enemy with a big sword took precedence over a chief who might or might not survive long enough to punish you. If Farnax and Pynne were telling the truth, the pixies would never flee from battle. They would never stop fighting, and they would use every bit of their strength to destroy their enemies. Enemies like Jig and the other goblins.

He was so absorbed in the ramifications, he nearly missed his destination. Only Smudge's sudden excitement made him stop and look around.

"There," he said. A flat opening near the top of the tunnel, to his right. That was the origin of the ashen odor he had smelled before. If he was wrong, the pixies would probably kill him. But if he was right . . .

Who was he fooling? The pixies would probably kill him either way.

"The wand is in there?" asked Farnax, flying closer to the entrance.

Jig jumped and grabbed the lower edge of the hole, then struggled to pull himself up. His boots scraped uselessly against the moss-slick rock. Finally, muttering under her breath, Pynne grabbed the bottom of one pantleg and flew up. Farnax did the same with the other leg. With the pixies' help, Jig managed to pull himself into the cramped tunnel.

There was barely room to crawl, and Jig tried not to imagine what would happen if the tunnel grew any narrower.

"This had better be worth it," Farnax said from behind Jig. "I can't stand much more of these tunnels. I feel like I've been buried alive." He had landed on the ground, and he glared distastefully at the rock with each step. There was no room for them to fly. They probably couldn't even see anything but Jig's backside. No wonder they were so grouchy.

Jig's sword hilt jabbed his side as he started to crawl. Smudge crouched on his shoulder. The fire-spider was warm, but this wasn't the intense heat of fear. Heat wafted from Smudge's body in waves, in time with the spider's rapid heartbeat. Smudge was making no attempt to hide. Rather he seemed eager to continue, racing down Jig's arm, then turning as if to ask what was taking so long.

Jig hoped that was a positive sign. He had heard other goblins talk of fire-spider nests, but he had never seen one. Usually fire-spider eggs were abandoned in pools or puddles of water, and the young spiders that survived scattered throughout the tunnels to find their own hunting grounds. But down here, with all the insects attracted to the filth and garbage, there would be no need to leave. At least, he hoped so.

Jig stopped to remove his spectacles, doing his best to wipe the lenses on his shirt. Sweat and steam still streaked his vision. Tiny insects kept landing on his neck and ears.

"This seems a strange place to hide your treasure," said Farnax. "A dismal cave you can't even reach? How would you have retrieved it if we hadn't been here to help lift you into the tunnel?"

Jig bit his lip. Most goblins wouldn't have caught that discrepancy. "I can reach it," he protested. "My arms were just tired from fighting ogres, that's all."

He wished there was enough room to look behind so he could try to guess whether the pixies believed him.

"More likely your legs were too tired from running away from the ogres," Farnax muttered. The pixie didn't seem to like him much.

Jig twisted sideways to pull himself up and through a narrower bit of tunnel. As he did, his body blocked the light of the pixies, and he noticed a faint red light coming from farther on. The air was warmer, and the smell of ash was even stronger. "Almost there," he whispered.

Smudge hopped off Jig's shoulder and skittered ahead. Jig grabbed for him, but he was too slow. The fire-spider disappeared. "Smudge, wait!"

No, this was probably for the best. If things went wrong, Smudge would be safer away from Jig. Still, as Jig pulled himself along, a hard lump filled his throat. Smudge had been his companion for so many years, and now the stupid fire-spider had abandoned him.

Jig crawled past a drop in the tunnel and looked up. His breath caught.

The cave was larger than he had imagined, and it was full of fire-spiders. Hundreds of webs stretched across the walls and ceiling, dotted with dried bugs of every size, from tiny gnats to a green moon moth as big as Jig's hand. There were so many spiders that their combined heat and magic actually generated the red light he had seen: just enough to attract more insects.

"How far must we travel?" asked Pynne. "I feel like these tunnels are shrinking around me."

Fire-spiders twitched and crawled in response to her voice, some crawling deeper into their webs, others moving toward the source of the sound. Jig searched for Smudge, wondering if he would even know his own spider from the rest.

"We're here," whispered Jig, trying to block the cave from their sight. He spotted a patch of mirrored ebony on the ground near the back of the cave. That would be the pool where the fire-spiders laid their eggs.

The pixies would kill him the moment they suspected betrayal. No, that wasn't true. Farnax already suspected him. Regardless, Jig would have to move swiftly.

He studied the webs. The majority hung near the entrance, which made sense. Few insects would survive to make it deeper into the cave. The only real gap was directly in front of the tunnel, which helped the air flow freely through the cave. That opening gave Jig his only chance. He tensed his legs, drawing them up as much as he could in the confines of the tunnel. His hands gripped the rock to either side.

"What is it?" asked Pynne.

Jig kicked her as hard as he could. He heard Farnax swear as Pynne crashed into him, and then Jig was launching himself into the cave. He stayed low to the ground, but his ear tore through one web, then he caught another with his arm.

The fire-spiders reacted instinctively, the way fire-spiders always reacted to threats. They retreated, igniting their webs as they fled. Jig crawled as fast as he could, flinging himself into the shallow pool even as his sleeve and hair went up in flames. Water hissed and steamed. Jig rolled over and squinted through streaked lenses as the pixies burst into the cave at full speed.

Farnax was first through, flying too fast to avoid the webs. His blue light nearly disappeared as he tore through the flames. His body crashed into the far side of the cave and dropped, completely engulfed.

Pynne fared slightly better. Farnax had torn enough of an opening that only her wings caught fire. She spun and flew back into the tunnel, tumbling to the ground.

Jig crawled back out, doing his best to avoid the furious fire-spiders and the remains of their webs. Up ahead Pynne was frantically trying to rip the flaming bits of web from her wings. Jig slid his sword free, holding it ahead of him.

Pynne's light brightened when she saw him. Ignoring her smoldering wings, she raised her hands to cast a spell. Jig didn't have room for a proper attack, but he managed to smack her arms with the flat of the blade.

Pynne screamed, clutching her arms. Jig crawled closer and pressed the tip of his blade to her chest.

"Stop!" Pynne shouted. She twisted back, breaking part of her burned wing in her desperation to avoid the sword. "Please, keep it away." Dark burn marks covered her arm and hand where Jig had struck her.

Her right wing was mostly intact, but the left was barely half its previous size. The ragged edge glowed orange, like an ember.

Jig risked a quick glance back, to make sure Farnax was dead. He needn't have bothered. Fire-spiders swarmed over the body, leaving only the faintest cracks of blue light visible.

He heard Pynne moving and lunged, but she twisted aside. She pointed at Jig, and his sword twisted in his hand. No, not the sword itself, but the leather wrapped around the hilt.

Pynne stumbled back. "Your blade might be death-metal, but the leather is nothing but dead flesh." Already the tightly wound cord slithered between Jig's fingers, loosening from the hilt and wrapping around his hand and wrist. He tried to drop the sword, but the leather dug cruelly into his skin, binding his hand in place.

"You betrayed us," Pynne said.

"I'm a goblin." Jig tried to grab the cord with his other hand, and nearly managed to get both hands bound to his sword. He yanked his free hand away so hard his elbow smashed into the tunnel wall.

"The queen would have honored you for your help," said Pynne. "Instead, the last thing you feel will be your own weapon choking the life from your body. You thought this ruse would defeat us? I promise you, goblin, we will destroy every last one of your ilk." Her face glowed with pink light as she lay back, gasping.

The cord was already coiling around his elbow. Jig shook his hand, trying to fling the sword away. The blade clanged against the rock, jarring his bones. "Wait. I thought you needed me to learn how to use magic in our world."

Pynne smiled and shook her head. "You would have simplified the process immensely. But we have adapted to other worlds before. And there are always others willing to share their knowledge in exchange for the rewards you've thrown away."

The end of the cord tickled Jig's chin. He twisted his head away, but how was he supposed to avoid his own arm? The leather brushed his neck, waving like one of Smudge's fore-legs, reaching . . . reaching. . . .

Jig looked down. Only a single loop of leather remained knotted around the bare wood of his sword hilt. The leather wasn't quite long enough to reach his throat.

Pynne realized it at the same time. She raised her hands, and Jig lunged. This time Jig was faster. His sword was nearly as long as Pynne herself. She died quickly and messily.

Jig pulled his hand back, hoping the spell would dissipate with Pynne's death, but the only change was that the end of the cord grew still, stiff as rock. It jabbed his chin when he turned his head.

The sword rang against the rock as Jig turned to search for Smudge. So many fire-spiders, all feasting on crispy pixie. He tried to smile. Crispy Pixie would make an excellent title for a song.

"Good-bye, Smudge." Jig backed away from the cave. Smudge was probably safer here anyway. There was plenty of food, and he was surrounded by other fire-spiders. Most importantly, he wouldn't be anywhere near Jig when the pixies came to wipe out the goblins.

A small, dark shape broke away from the mound of spiders, scurrying toward Jig. He could see it dragging something with its rear legs, something that glowed faintly blue.

Jig grinned so hard his cheeks hurt as he set his free hand down for Smudge. The fire-spider crawled up to his shoulder pad and began to feast.

"I'm sorry about that," said Jig. "It's been a while since I fed you, hasn't it?"

Come to think of it, he hadn't eaten in quite some time either. Jig turned back around to where Pynne had collapsed. . . .

* * *

Braf, Grell, and Slash were still waiting where Jig had left them. Jig heard their voices long before he got close enough to see the light of their small fire. They were arguing loudly enough Jig was surprised a tunnel cat hadn't eaten them all.

"I say we go after the ogres," Slash was shouting. "They're so busy running away with their tails between their legs they won't notice us tagging along."

"Ogres don't have tails," countered Braf. A moment later he grunted sharply, as if he had been struck with a cane.

"All it takes is for one of them to glance back, and they'll squash us like bugs," said Grell. "The way you smell, I'd notice you at a hundred paces."

"What choice do we have?" asked Slash. "Head back and ask the pixies to let us through? Beg them not to hurt us, the way you goblins do when you want to pass through hobgoblin territory?"

"Jig should have let you stay dead," Braf said. "When he gets back—"

"You think Jig's coming back?" Slash asked, laughing. "If he's smart, he ran like a frightened ogre. If he really tried to fight those pixies, he's probably—"

Jig's sword banged against the ground. He had been trying to hold it out in front of him, but the blade seemed to grow heavier with every step. "It's me," he called out. He could hear them shifting positions.

"What are you doing still alive?" Slash asked.

Jig could see them now, standing behind a small, foul-smelling fire. Braf had his hook-tooth out. Grell held one of her canes like a club. Slash had a rock. Jig couldn't tell whether they had been preparing for a pixie attack, or if he had arrived just in time for them to start killing one another.

"The pixies are dead," Jig said.

"All of them?" Braf asked.

With his sword pretty much permanently attached to his arm, it would have been so easy to run Braf through. "No," Jig snapped. "The two who were following us."

"Looks like you had a little trouble with your sword," Slash said. "Lost a bit of hair, too."

Jig reached up to touch the short, singed patch of hair. Hair wasn't supposed to feel so crunchy.

"How do we know they're really dead?" asked Grell. "You told us the pixies were controlling Veka and the scarred simpleton here. They—"

"Hey," said Slash. He stepped toward Grell, only to catch the butt of her cane in his throat. He turned away, gagging.

Jig pulled a bundle from inside his shirt and tossed it onto the ground between them. "Here's your proof."

"What's that?" Braf asked, poking it with his hook-tooth.

"Leftovers." Jig's sword dragged against the ground as he walked toward Grell. His whole arm tingled with every movement, and his fingers were swollen and cold.

Consider yourself lucky. If I hadn't strengthened the vessels and forced your blood to keep flowing through your arm, your fingers would have fallen off by now.

Jig grimaced. Given that the pixies were going to wipe them all out anyway, and the only way he could think of to get back home was more than a little unpleasant, he was having a hard time feeling lucky. "I need to borrow your knife," he said to Grell.

Braf had already opened the bundle and stuffed a bit of glowing meat into his mouth. As Grell slapped the handle into Jig's free hand, she said, "Going to carve up what's left for the rest of us?"

"No," said Jig, sitting down beside the fire. He tried to work the tip of the curved blade beneath the cords on his arm, but the leather wouldn't budge. All he managed to do was slice his skin. He changed tactics, trying to cut the leather where it looped around the hilt. The blade didn't even scratch it.

He knew the knife was good. The blood dripping down his arm proved that. Pynne's magic must have hardened the leather. "Stupid pixies." Jig was going to spend the rest of his short life with a sword stuck to his arm.

"So how do you propose we get out of here?" Slash asked.

Jig handed the knife back to Grell. "The ogres said that stench came from goblin garbage."

Grell was the first to figure it out. "I've dealt with some vile messes in my time, but I'm not climbing through that."

"Fine," said Jig. "Stay here and wait for the pixies." He stared at his sword, wondering if he would be able to climb the crack one-handed. Grell would certainly need help as well, assuming she changed her mind. "Braf? Slash?"

"You want us to climb through goblin filth?" asked Slash.

"I really don't care." Jig was too tired to argue. His sword dragged along the ground as he trudged toward the ogres' abandoned cavern. He heard the others fall in behind him, not without a bit of muttering on Slash's part.

A short time later, Jig realized he had given all three of them a clear shot at his back. As the smell of rotting garbage grew strong enough he could taste it in the back of his mouth, he was almost disappointed they hadn't taken advantage of his vulnerability.

CHAPTER 10

"The astute reader may notice gaps in the old tales, unexplained spans when the Hero disappears from the narrative. The Hero emerges later, more powerful and prepared for the final conflict. Some argue these omissions are due to the highly secretive nature of the Hero's transformation. Others say the storyteller simply wanted to skip to the good parts."

—From the introduction to Chapter 7 of
The Path of the Hero (Wizard's ed.)

DESPITE THE AWKWARDNESS OF THE BLADE AFfixed to his right arm, Jig still managed to climb a goodly distance. From his own informal calculations, he had now climbed approximately twelve times the height of the entire mountain. That was what it felt like, at any rate. In reality, it couldn't be more than thirty or forty feet from the ogres' cavern to the goblin lair.

Jig's sword arm hung leaden at his side. His thigh throbbed with every movement where he had sliced himself before thinking to tie the scabbard over the naked blade. He stank of rotten food, mold, and far worse things. And tiny burning stings covered his scalp and shoulders from brushing against . . . he still wasn't sure what the nasty things were.

At least they give off light, Shadowstar offered.

True, and Jig would take a few stings over the stench of the ogres' torches any day. He peered upward, where more strands of what appeared to be blue-white hair dangled from the filthy stone. The ends of the strands slowly changed from blue to green and back again. Jig braced himself, watching as a huge black fly approached one of the strands, drawn by the shifting light.

The instant the fly touched the end, the strand flashed, shocking the unfortunate insect. The rest of the strands shot out, coiling around its body and dragging it toward the oversize sluglike body stuck to the underside of the rock.

Shadowstar thought it must have come from the pixies' world. Jig didn't care where it had come from, as long as it was too busy with the fly to go after him. He had moved Smudge down into his belt pouch after the first attack. Smudge was a tough little fire-spider, but these creatures had a lot more filaments than Smudge had legs.

He reached up with his left hand and pressed his feet to either side of the rock, dragging himself a bit higher. The creature ignored him. A tiny carrion-worm scurried over Jig's fingers, clutching a broken bit of bone in its claws as it fled. The light of the tendrils turned the worm's white skin pale blue.

"Ouch," shouted Slash. "I'm going to rip that hairy glowing slug apart with my bare—Ouch!"

"Keep your hands to yourself before you kill us all," snapped Grell. They had rigged a crude rope harness to help her climb, using scraps of rope scavenged from the abandoned ogre camp. Braf and Slash both supported some of Grell's weight, leading to numerous complaints from all involved.

"Are you sure this will take us home?" asked Braf.

"Smells like goblin filth to me," muttered Slash.

"Quiet," said Jig, twisting his head so his good ear was aimed upward. Footsteps, and the creak of a door.

His sword clinked against the rock as he drew himself higher. He could see light from above: not the pale, sickly light of the slugs, but the cheerful green of a goblin muck lantern. They were here. They had made it to the goblin lair. He opened his mouth to tell the others.

Broken, dripping shards of pottery showered down on them. Jig yelped as one piece jabbed the top of his head. The shards smelled of spoiled beer.

Jig pushed himself up. He dug his toes into the rock and summoned one last burst of energy to drag himself out of the pit.

He found himself staring at a young goblin girl. Before Jig could say anything, she screamed, threw her lantern at Jig's head, and ran screaming.

Jig dropped back into the pit, barely dodging the lantern. One foot landed on Slash's shoulder. The hobgoblin grunted and strained to keep from falling, which was probably the only thing that stopped him from flinging Jig down with the rest of the garbage.

"Sorry," Jig muttered as he climbed back out. The muck lantern had shattered on the back wall, casting green light over the small, stuffy cave.

"At least that oversize, rat-eating wizard never made me swim through goblin trash," Slash muttered as he followed Jig out. He turned and hauled on his rope, pulling Grell and Braf out after him.

"Where is Veka, anyway?" asked Braf.

"I wish I knew," said Jig. He had been wondering the same thing. Pynne and Farnax hadn't said anything about her. Maybe she was dead. She could have run afoul of a tunnel cat or rock serpent, or maybe she had tried to jump onto another giant bat and missed. Given that she was still pixie-charmed when she escaped, Jig's life would be much simpler if she were dead. That, more than anything else, convinced him she was still alive.

A heavy door blocked the only way out of the cave. Jig gave it a quick shove, but the door was barred on the outside. The goblin lair had few real doors, since the rock was too hard to work, but there were a few areas deserving of special attention. In this case a full frame had been constructed around the cave opening, secured with a batch of Golaka's raknok paste. The sticky-sweet paste was great on fish, but more importantly, raknok was the favorite food of a kind of black mold that clung tightly to both wood and stone. After a week the frame would be secure enough to support a door. After a month an ogre could probably still rip down the door, but it would take at least four or five goblins working together to do so. Given how often goblins worked together, the door would likely stand for years.

Jig jabbed his sword tip into the crack at the edge of the frame, trying to reach the bar on the other side, but the blade was too thick.

He stared at the sword, remembering the fear on Pynne's face as he shoved his sword at her. She had called it death-metal. The blade had left burns on her skin. If all pixies shared her vulnerability, the goblins might have a chance.

No, the only reason he had gotten close enough to kill Pynne was because they wanted him alive. The pixies wouldn't make that mistake when they came to wipe out the goblins.

They might not attack right away, Shadowstar said. *The first two pixies to venture out from the protection of their world were killed by a single goblin. They'll be more cautious next time. You might have bought your people a little more time to prepare.*

A strong hand shoved Jig aside. Slash pounded on the door. "If you don't let us out of here now, I'll feed your private parts to the tunnel cats!" He stepped away, searching the debris-strewn cave. "There has to be something we can use to bash this thing down. If I have to spend another moment immersed in this stench—"

"You call this a stench?" asked Grell. "Try changing diapers when the whole nursery comes down with the green squirts." She shook her head. "Babies never get sick alone. Once one of 'em starts dripping and crying, you can bet the rest of them will come down with it in a day or so."

Jig grimaced and stepped toward the edge of the waste crack, away from the others. He had managed the entire climb without relieving himself, but if he didn't go now, his bladder was going to burst. He stared at the sword tied to his hand. This was going to be tricky.

He fumbled a bit, giving himself a nasty pinch involving the sheath and crossguard, but he managed. Then he got another shock. Apparently the pixies' glow followed them through death and beyond.

Jig's sword dragged along the ground as he returned to the door. He could hear several sets of footsteps outside, along with low voices. Slash and Grell were still arguing.

The door creaked open. Slash started to push past Jig, then noticed the armed goblins gathered around the cave. He moved aside. "Why don't you go first?"

As Jig stepped outside, he breathed deeply for the first time in what seemed like forever. The air smelled of muck smoke and the sweat of too many goblins, but compared to the waste pit, this was paradise . . . if paradise included one very angry goblin chief.

Kralk stepped forward, her morningstar hanging from one hand. To either side goblin guards stood with drawn swords. The rest of the lair had gathered at a safe distance, no doubt eager to see who would get a taste of that morningstar.

"You've returned," Kralk said. "Alive." That last was added with a long stare at Grell and Braf, who still waited in the shadows. "And you've swapped your ogre for a hobgoblin. Not a wise trade, I think."

A few goblins laughed at that. Slash growled.

Kralk hesitated, taking in Jig's bedraggled appearance. No doubt she had already gotten past her disappointment at seeing him alive and was now trying to figure out how best to turn this to her advantage. She began with mockery.

"So tell us, Jig Dragonslayer. What menace so terrified the ogres that they turned to you for help?" She smirked. "Perhaps we can make a new song for you. 'The Triumph of the Filth-Strewn Hero.' "

To Jig's great annoyance, his mind seized on the title and spliced a tune to it.

In comes the filth-strewn hero,
his sword nicked and rusted,
his bones bruised and busted,
his body still sticky with blood so blue.

Beware the filth-strewn hero.
His temper is strained,
a stink fills his brain,
and he'll triumph by running you through.

Jig allowed himself a quick, wistful sigh. "Pixies," he said.

Kralk cocked her head, momentarily taken aback. "Did you say pixies?"

"They've enslaved or killed most of the ogres," Jig said. "The rest have fled the lower cavern. The pixies are going to destroy us and the hobgoblins if we don't stop them. We—"

A harsh laugh cut him off. "Pixies conquering the lower cavern?" Kralk said, her face twisting into a sneer. "That's the best story you can invent? How could they have gotten to the ogres without first passing through our tunnels?"

She turned to glare at the other goblins, who started to jeer and laugh. The sound of their mockery triggered flashbacks from Jig's childhood. Most of his adulthood too, for that matter.

Jig hunched his shoulders, remembering what Pynne had said about him being the one to open the way for the pixies. He still didn't know what she meant by that, but why would she make up such a lie? "They opened a magical gateway into Straum's lair. A portal from their world."

To Jig's surprise, the laughter began to die. They actually believed him?

"Have you seen this portal?" Kralk snapped.

Jig hesitated. "Not exactly." He had thought his problem would be in convincing the goblins to fight the pixies, not in proving the pixies existed in the first place. Perhaps he should pee for her.

He pointed to the waste room, where Slash and the goblins still waited. "They were there. They've seen—"

"You expect us to take the word of a hobgoblin?" Kralk said quickly. "Or two goblins who failed to carry out their orders?"

"What orders?" Braf asked. Grell grabbed his ear, yanked his head to her mouth, and whispered. Braf's eyes widened.

"Oh, that's right. I forgot." He drew his hook-tooth. "Should I do it now?"

Grell dragged his head back down and smacked his forehead with her other hand.

The head of Kralk's morningstar swung back and forth as she twitched the handle. As Jig watched, it slowly dawned on him that she wasn't nervous about the pixies. She was worried about *him*.

She had sent him on this mission hoping to be rid of him. Instead he had returned alive, if a bit smelly, and bringing word of an invasion into the mountain. Kralk couldn't afford to believe him. If she did, she would make Jig a hero all over again. He would be the one who had discovered the threat and returned to tell of it. He would be the logical choice to lead the goblins against their new enemy. No matter what happened, Jig, not Kralk, would be the one the goblins remembered.

"You're lying," said Kralk. "And even if these pixies did exist, why should we worry? They'll have to fight through the hobgoblins first."

"You rat-eaters think we're going to do your dirty work?" Slash shouted, stepping forward. One of the goblin guards advanced to stop him. Slash shoved him, knocking him into the crowd. Several more goblins rushed forward with swords and spears.

"Wait!" Jig said. He grabbed Slash by the arm and tugged him back.

Kralk and the others were all watching him. Jig had always thought hobgoblins were the experts on traps, but the one Kralk had created when she sent Jig out with Walland Wallandson had ensnared them both. Kralk had to kill him. If he was lying to the chief, death was the only punishment. If he was telling the truth, she had to kill him to keep control of the other goblins.

On second thought, it seemed like Jig was the only one who had been snared in this little trap.

"You should probably talk to the warriors," Jig stammered, searching for a way to back down. "You can prepare the lair against the pixies. I wouldn't be much use. I barely escaped. They nearly killed me. Look what they did to my arm."

He stepped forward, flourishing his arm so everyone would see the way the leather bindings bit into his skin. As he did, the sheath slipped free, flying from the blade and striking Kralk's shoulder.

Jig's throat tightened so quickly his breath squeaked. He now stood with a bare blade pointed directly at the goblin chief.

Kralk's smile threatened to split her face. She flexed her arms, then switched to a two-handed grip on her weapon. The other goblins fell back like ants fleeing a muck spill. Kralk kicked the sheath away, out of Jig's reach, so he had no way to cover his weapon. "I wondered when you'd finally summon the courage to challenge me, runt," said Kralk.

Jig backed away. It appeared as though Pynne was going to succeed in getting him killed after all.

Kralk was stronger, larger, and faster than Jig. He didn't need the warmth coming from Smudge's pouch to tell him he was in trouble. *Help?*

Jig, she might be stronger, but you're smarter. You can defeat her.

Right. What was the smart thing to do? That would have been not going on this stupid mission in the first place!

Kralk stepped forward, swinging her morningstar in a wide arc. The spiked ball smashed Jig's sword, spinning him in a full circle. Shock and pain tore through his arm, shaking his very bones. He staggered back, barely dodging a second blow.

Like most goblins, Kralk attacked with brute force but very little technique. Unfortunately, she had a great deal of brute force.

Her morningstar whooshed through the air, driving Jig toward the garbage cave. Her attacks were predictable enough for Jig to avoid getting hit, but he couldn't attack without opening himself up at the same time.

If he timed it right, he might be able to dive through the door of the cave and crawl back down the waste crack before Kralk smashed his skull. He doubted that was what Shadowstar meant by "smarter," though.

Kralk switched her grip, swinging at an angle that knocked Jig's sword downward. Jig dropped to one knee. Kralk's morningstar blurred in a circle, smashing Jig's sword against the floor. A handsbreath of steel snapped off the end.

Jig stumbled into the doorway, staring at the broken end of his weapon. At least the blade was a little lighter now.

Kralk was still smiling. She was sweating a bit, but Jig was so tired he could barely keep his sword up. She didn't even have to hit him with her morningstar. Much more of this, and he would drop from exhaustion.

"Your precious god isn't going to save you this time, Jig," said Kralk.

Jig snorted. His precious god was the one who had gotten him into this mess to begin with. He pushed sideways, trying to get to the doorway. The morningstar gouged the door frame near his head.

"See how he scampers," Kralk shouted. "Jig Dragonslayer, cowering like a cornered rat."

Jig tried to stab her while she gloated. He barely avoided having his elbow shattered as a reward for his clumsy lunge.

Kralk's foot shot out, catching him in the shin. He rolled away as the morningstar rang against the floor next to his head. The next strike was even closer. He flattened his ears, trying to shut out the worst of the noise as he scrambled to his feet.

"They'll sing a new song before this day is done," Kralk yelled. "How Kralk the Chief triumphed over Jig the Coward." She glanced around as she was speaking, but it wasn't long enough for Jig to attack.

She was playing with him, stretching out the fight for the other goblins. She wanted to make a show of it, to prove beyond any doubt who was the strongest. To Kralk Jig was already dead. She fought now to defeat anyone else who might have considered trying to overthrow the chief.

If there was one thing Jig knew, it was fear. Kralk was afraid. Afraid of Jig, and afraid of the other goblins. She had seized control through treachery and deceit, which meant she had to live every day in fear that someone would do the same to her.

Fine. Treachery and deceit it would be. Jig raised his sword and shouted, "Now, Braf! Attack her now!"

Kralk never took her eyes from Jig. She smirked as she twirled her morningstar. "A poor choice for a bluff, Jig. Braf lacks the imagination for treachery."

She raised her morningstar, and a wooden hook caught her wrist. She staggered sideways. A powerful jerk of her arm yanked her attacker to the ground.

Jig thrust as hard as he could. His shoulder nearly wrenched out of its socket as the broken tip of his sword skidded off her breastplate. Jig fell forward. He twisted to keep from squishing Smudge. As a result he landed off-balance, hitting his chin on the floor hard enough to rattle his teeth.

Kralk's eyes were wide, her teeth bared. Jig didn't know why she was so upset. His attack hadn't even scratched her armor. She raised her morningstar to crush Jig's skull . . .

. . . and a yellow hand snaked out to catch her right fang. The other hand seized her by the hair. With a sharp twist, Slash broke Kralk's neck.

Jig stared at Kralk, who lay twitching on the ground. Then he stared at Grell, who was climbing back to her feet, Braf's hook-tooth in one hand. Then he stared at Slash. The hobgoblin was looking around at the stunned goblins with a wary expression that suggested he wasn't sure whether to gloat or run away.

"Why did you do that?" asked Jig.

Slash wiped his hands on his vest. "No blood this way."

That wasn't what Jig meant, but before he could clarify, one of the goblins whispered, "Does this mean the hobgoblin is our new chief?"

"What's that?" Slash looked like he had swallowed a rock serpent. "Me?"

"You did kill Kralk," Jig said. From the muttering of the crowd, they didn't like the idea any better than Slash did.

By now Braf had retrieved his hook-tooth, and was walking toward Jig. He nudged Kralk's body with his foot. "That was great. Everything worked exactly the way you planned it, Jig."

"The way I what?" Jig bit his lip. Throughout the cave goblins were whispering and pointing and generally wondering what was going on. Jig knew exactly how they felt.

"Yeah," said Braf. "Jig knew Kralk would try to kill him, so he made a plan to kill Kralk instead." He clapped Jig on the back, hard enough to stagger him. "Grell told me all about it when she borrowed my hook-tooth."

Jig turned to stare at Grell, who shrugged and said, "Good plan. I guess that means you're chief."

"Me?" His voice squeaked.

Kralk's body lay face-up, a grimace of rage frozen on her dead face. *I suppose it's too late to heal her so she can be chief again?*

Even if she wasn't already dead, how long do you think you'd keep breathing if she could get her hands on you?

How long do you think I'll keep breathing now? Everyone was watching him. No matter which way he turned, half the goblins would have a clear shot at his unprotected back. What was a new chief supposed to do in a situation like this anyway? Usually they bellowed something loud and triumphant and scary, but Jig's throat had constricted too tight for him to say anything at all.

Grell nudged Kralk's body with her cane. "Hey Jig, if you don't want to claim that malachite necklace, I'll take it."

She didn't wait for an answer. With a bit of groaning and creaking, Grell hunched down and began untying the necklace. Braf picked up the morningstar and handed it to Jig.

The weapon was heavier than he had guessed, especially one-handed. The handle was still warm. He dug his claws in to keep it from slipping out of his sweat-slick grip. Should he tuck it through his belt, the way Kralk had always worn it? The weight would probably drag his trousers down to his knees.

"Feast!" shouted one of the goblins, a cry that swiftly echoed through the crowd.

Feast? What . . . oh. The chief was dead. Goblins usually marked the occasion with a feast. The choosing of a new chief always provided plenty of fresh meat.

They hadn't feasted when Kralk became chief, but that was because the former chief's body had already been eaten by hobgoblins, and nobody had been certain whether her other opponents' bodies had been poisoned or not. "What about the pixies?" Jig asked weakly.

"You really want to deny this crowd their feast?" Grell asked, glancing up. The necklace hung nearly to her waist. Malachite clinked as she held the rough spikes to the light.

"What's going on out here?" The voice thundered through the cavern, cutting a path through the goblins as Golaka the chef stormed from her kitchen. Even larger than Braf, and strong enough to give Slash a good fight, Golaka waved her huge stirring spoon like a sword as she approached. She stopped when she saw Kralk. "Who did this?"

Every set of eyes turned toward Jig.

Golaka shook her spoon. "I've been marinating a pan full of moles all day, and now you're telling me I have to throw them out and cook her?" She tilted her head to one side, and her voice grew thoughtful. "Though the hobgoblin opens up some interesting possibilities. I could make skewers, alternate goblin meat with hobgoblin, add sliced mushrooms and rat livers, and garnish the whole thing with fried cockroaches for texture. Hobgoblin, do you drink a lot of alcohol?"

Slash stared. "Why do you want to know?"

"It affects the taste of the liver," said Golaka. "Doesn't matter, I can always baste you with—"

"No," Jig said. Blast it, he was squeaking again. "No," he repeated.

The lair fell silent, and Jig tried to remember if anyone had dared say no to Golaka before.

Golaka tilted her head. She was older than any goblin had a right to be, and her hearing was as poor as a human's. "What did you say?"

"Slash—the hobgoblin, I mean, we—"

"Slash the hobgoblin!" yelled one of the younger goblins, raising a sword.

"No!" They didn't understand. They hadn't seen the entire lower cavern transformed. They hadn't talked to the handful of ogres who had survived the invasion. They didn't care about pixies.

This was a hobgoblin, a threat they knew. How many of

them had endured the taunts of hobgoblin guards? How many bore scars from the hobgoblins' "playful" jabs? And now Jig's first act as chief would be to deny them their revenge?

Jig turned around, wondering if it was too late to retreat back into the garbage pit. Anywhere he could put a heavy door between himself and the rest of the goblins would do. But the only places that merited doors were the nursery, the distillery, the kitchen, the garbage pit, and Kralk's quarters.

No, *his* quarters now. "The hobgoblin comes with me," Jig said. He forced a smile, trying to appear as nasty as possible while he reached up to stroke Smudge's head. "I've got something special planned for him, and my pet hasn't eaten in far too long."

Jig started to walk toward the brass-hinged door on the far side of the cave, only to draw up short when Golaka refused to budge. Jig held his breath as he stared into those greasy, dark-veined eyes.

Eventually Golaka shrugged. "Bring me the leftovers, chief. We haven't had hobgoblin jerky in a long time."

The goblins cheered, shaking their weapons and causing several injuries in the process. Golaka stepped aside.

Glancing back at Slash, Jig whispered, "You can either follow me, or you can stay with them."

"Do you want us to help carve?" one of the goblins asked before Slash could respond.

Jig shook his head. "I think I can handle one hobgoblin by myself." Slash cocked his head at that, but the only sign of annoyance was a convulsive twitch in his hands, his fingers curling much the way they had when he broke Kralk's neck. Silently he followed Jig across the lair, glaring at any goblin who dared approach too closely.

The bottom of the door scraped the rock as Jig hauled it open. Inside, two muck pits sat to either side of the doorway. One was empty, the other nearly so. The lone flame flickered weakly, but it was enough. Gleaming metal lined the walls, like a miniature version of Straum's old hoard. Swords, spears, knives, as well as more exotic weapons, were all stacked against the walls, some piled atop one another. To one side, a longbow with a broken string sat half buried in a rickety stack of yellow-fletched arrows. A spear so long it barely fit within the cave was propped against the opposite wall.

The door slammed shut behind him. Jig spun, nearly cutting Slash's ankle with his sword. Slash stepped to one side, and his hand clapped Jig's shoulder. The nails dug through Jig's shirt. "I've killed one goblin chief today," he said. "Do I need to kill a second?"

Jig shook his head. Slash was too close for him to stab with the sword, even if his arm hadn't been useless after the fight with Kralk. "They would have killed you," Jig said.

Slash stared at him for a long time. "Pah. You rat-eaters are too cowardly to take on a hobgoblin warrior." But he made no further move against Jig. He picked up a peculiar-looking knife with two thin spikes angling out from the main blade. "They're going to eat you alive, you know. You're no chief."

"I know." Jig stepped away, rubbing his shoulder. Out in the lair, Jig could still hear the chant of "Feast, feast!" from the goblins, and then Golaka shouting, "If you don't shut up, there'll be more than one goblin on the cookfires!" The lair was much quieter after that.

Jig's new quarters were relatively small, and the abundance of weapons made the place feel even more cramped. A mattress made from the skin of a giant bat sat against the far wall. Jig could smell the dried moss stuffed within the skin. His eyelids drooped at the mere thought of such luxury. He stepped toward the mattress, but Slash grabbed his ear and yanked him back. Jig yelped, then covered his mouth and hoped nobody outside had heard.

Slash pointed to the floor, where a thin string stretched through a metal loop, up to a tripod of battle axes beside the door. The base of the nearest ax was secured to a wooden rod. From the look of it, the ax would swing down to split the skull of anyone who snuck in uninvited.

"A three-year-old hobgoblin could do better," Slash muttered, kneeling by the string. "The line's too high. Not only does it catch the light of the muck fires, but it leaves a clear shadow. If nothing else, you ought to blacken the line." He studied the ax briefly. Holding the handle in place, he broke the string with his other hand.

Jig examined the room with new respect, not to mention fear. What other surprises had Kralk left behind? Several vials and clay jars sat in a rack by the far wall, padded with dried leaves. Her collection of poisons? A wooden box with rusting hinges sat open on the other side of the room, revealing rumpled clothes in bright blues and reds and oranges. Near the head of the bed sat a jar of candied toadstools. Jig's mouth watered, but he stopped himself after a single step. Knowing Kralk they were probably poisoned.

Slash squeezed past him to examine the mattress. Strange that Jig felt safer in here, alone with a hobgoblin, than he would have with another goblin.

Slash poked the leather in a few spots, then grabbed the edge and lifted the mattress to reveal a thin metal spike affixed to a broad wooden base. Moss flaked out of the hole in the bottom of the mattress where the spike had been. Jig tried not to think what would happen to anyone who snuck in to catch a quick nap.

"Some of these are hobgoblin tricks," Slash said. "Poorly done, but I'm guessing your chief had help setting this place up. Another benefit of your precious truce." He sat by the door and dipped his fingers in the empty muck pit. Humming to himself, he began to smear the ashen film along the string. "The first thing we need to do is run the line from the top of the door, where nobody will see it," he muttered. "Those axes are too obvious. Though if I could mount one to the ceiling, it might work. That's the first rule of traps: nobody ever looks up."

Jig sat gingerly on the corner of the mattress, half expecting it to stab him in the backside or trigger an avalanche of sharp rocks. Smudge started to crawl down to explore, but Jig snatched him and shoved him into his pouch. Until he knew everything Kralk had done to this place, he wasn't about to let Smudge wander about. The fire-spider probably wasn't heavy enough to trigger most traps, but paranoia had kept Jig alive so far.

Now that he was chief, paranoia might not be enough. *Why did you do this to me?* he asked.

What are you talking about? I didn't do anything. Despite his vast powers, Tymalous Shadowstar was a piss-poor liar.

When my sword came unsheathed. You did that. I could feel the magic. Jig was too exhausted to be angry.

She was going to kill you one way or another.

Jig shook his head. *You've been pushing me ever since Walland showed up. Why?*

You would have preferred to go back to your little temple? To hide all alone while the world goes on without you?

That was unfair. *Better than another adventure. I hate this.*

I know. But I also know your people would never survive against the pixies. I'm trying to keep you all alive.

No, said Jig. *You didn't know about the pixies. You didn't know anything except that Walland 'felt wrong.' Oh, you also knew Kralk wanted me killed, and that she would probably use this as a way to get rid of me.*

But you're still alive, and Kralk is getting basted as we speak.

I'm chief, Jig said. *Do you know how long most goblin chiefs survive?*

Jig, it doesn't—

Less than one day. Usually we go through at least seven or eight goblins before one survives long enough to really seize control. Kralk had been an anomaly, killing her foes with a ruthless efficiency that had gone a long way toward cowing the other goblins into submission. Jig, on the other hand, had nearly died. He would have died, if not for the help of an old woman and a hobgoblin. No doubt half the lair was already plotting his death.

Jig stiffened as he realized what Shadowstar had done. "You set me up," he whispered.

"What?" asked Slash, glancing up from a half-assembled crossbow.

You didn't want me to save Walland. You wanted to pit me against Kralk. You wanted me to be chief.

I wanted both. I wanted to know what was happening, and I wanted to help you change things for the goblins. You can lead them, Jig. You can help them be something more. You've already begun to change the goblins who are closest to you.

Grell saved your life when Kralk was about to kill you. Doesn't that seem like an odd thing for a goblin to do? Why do you think she did that?

Jig hesitated.

Grell saw you go off to fight those pixies. She saw something few have ever seen: goblin courage.

Lots of goblins run into battles against more powerful enemies.

Goblin stupidity is as common as lice, but you're not stupid. Grell saw that. So did your hobgoblin friend. You saved his life. Look at him, sitting there and not killing you. When you defeated those pixies, you inspired them. You showed them they could be something more, something greater.

Jig's stomach was starting to hurt again. Hunger and anxiety worked together to twist his guts into a knot. He wondered if he would be able to keep anything down at his own chief's feast. He grabbed his numb arm by the wrist, setting the sword across his legs to examine the broken steel.

It's rude to ignore your deity, snapped Shadowstar. No goblin could sound half as petulant as a cranky god. *Forget the pixies, think about your people, living and dying in the dark, trapped in a cramped, smelly cave as they kill one another off. Would you rather live like you did before you faced Straum, scurrying about on muck duty and hoping the bigger goblins didn't try to unclog the privy with your head?*

Jig didn't answer. To tell the truth, he rarely thought ahead. Most of the time he was content simply to make it through the day without getting killed.

Horrible as that adventure a year ago had been, his life was better now. It had been free of privy-related incidents, at least. *We happen to like caves*, he said. As protests went, it was weak and he knew it.

What do you want, Jig? You're chief now. You're responsible for what happens to the goblins.

That was even more frightening than an imminent pixie invasion.

What do you want? Shadowstar's voice was louder, more insistent, prompting Jig to blurt the first thing that came to mind.

"Stuffed snakeskins and klak beer."

"What?" asked Slash. He held several crossbow quarrels between the fingers of his right hand, and a length of copper wire in his left. A steel tool like a tiny flat-tipped dagger protruded from his mouth.

"That's what I want," Jig said, ignoring a sigh of divine exasperation. He wanted one brief respite where he didn't have to worry about pixies or ogres or goblins trying to kill him. Or hobgoblin traps misfiring, he added as a crossbow quarrel shot into the ceiling and ricocheted into the mattress beside him. "And now that I'm chief, I should be able to get it."

He headed for the door. Golaka's stuffed snakeskins were legendary. She stuffed shredded meat, sautéed mushrooms, and boiled tubers into snakeskin, fried the whole thing, then sliced them into bite-size chunks. Best of all, snakeskins and klak beer would help wash away the sour aftertaste of pixie meat.

You can't run away from this, Jig. You have a responsibility to your people.

Can't you see I'm busy? Jig asked. *Besides, if I order them to do anything before they've had their feast, they'll throw me onto the fire alongside Kralk.*

As he thought about the pixies, wondering how he could possibly lead the goblins against them, he couldn't help wondering if maybe Kralk had been the lucky one.

CHAPTER 11

"You have to understand, this truce doesn't mean we can't kill goblins. It only means we can't get caught."
—One-eyed Tosk, Hobgoblin Weaponsmith

JIG STOOD IN THE MAIN CAVERN, BURPING UP snake and watching the satiated goblins. As a rule, goblins with full stomachs were slightly less dangerous than hungry goblins. He had no doubt they would still kill him if he dropped his guard, probably even if he didn't, but maybe now they wouldn't be quite so brutal about it.

He remembered how foolish Veka had looked with her cloak and staff, trying to be a wizard. Jig's pretense at being chief was even more absurd. One look and anyone would know Jig was no chief.

His sheath once again covered his sword, but with the blade broken, the end of the sheath flopped limply along the ground. He had already stepped on the end twice, nearly tripping himself as he walked.

His clothes had been so saturated with blood and filth there was nothing to do but burn them. Even his favorite boots were scuffed and scratched. The pixies would pay for that.

Unfortunately, most of Kralk's clothes were ridiculously large on Jig's scrawny frame. Given the choice of raiding Kralk's wardrobe or facing the lair naked, Jig had chosen the ridiculous.

His belt cinched garish yellow trousers that ballooned over his thighs. He had also picked out a red vest with silver tassels. On Kralk those tassels would have hung just below her waist. On Jig they tickled the tops of his knees when he walked.

"Well?"

Jig jumped. He hadn't noticed Grell sidling up to his right. Braf followed close behind her, groaning and rubbing his stomach.

Why now, when he was in more danger of being killed, was Jig having such a hard time staying focused?

"They're waiting for you to tell them what to do," Grell said. "They know things aren't right. They may not have seen the pixies, but they know the air is colder, and they see how restless the snakes and bugs have been. One of the guards says a rock serpent attacked his muck lantern, and Topam swears he saw a giant bat flapping around over the lake a few days ago. There have been more carrion-worms crawling around the tunnels, too."

Which you would have known, if you didn't spend all of your time in your temple, Shadowstar whispered.

"The tunnel cats have been pretty restless lately, come to think of it," said Slash as he stepped out of Kralk's—out of *Jig's* quarters. "By the way, don't push your door open more than forty-five degrees, and you should probably let someone else light that muck pit from now on."

Jig wondered if he would ever have the courage to set foot in that room again. This was probably for the best, really. If not for Slash's traps, Jig would be too tempted to retreat back to his quarters and lock the door behind him.

Shadowstar was right. They had to do something about the pixies. The longer they waited, the more time the pixies would have to adapt to this world. The next time Jig faced pixies, they would be far more dangerous than Pynne and Farnax.

He stepped away from the wall to address the goblins, and his throat went dry. It looked as though every single goblin in the whole mountain was here, joking and smirking and waiting for him to speak. So many goblins, all staring at him.

Wait . . . all the goblins? "Who's on guard duty?" Jig asked.

A pair of well-fed, belching goblins near the back raised their hands, and Jig groaned. "I told you the pixies were going to try to kill us. Don't you think someone should guard the lair?"

The guards nodded, but made no movement to return to their posts. "Someone should, yeah," said one. The other laughed.

"Don't ask them," Grell whispered. "Tell them. You're the chief!"

Jig cleared his throat. Both guards waited, silently daring him to utter an order. How was he supposed to make them obey? His sword arm was so numb he could barely move it, even if the sword hadn't been broken. Jig looked at those guards, and all he could see was himself as a child, fleeing the older, bigger goblins who wanted to put a carrion-worm down his pants.

"Fine," Jig said, anger helping his voice carry throughout the cavern. "Leave the lair unguarded." He glanced at Grell, hoping she had been right about the goblins' mood. "I'm sure the pixies will appreciate it, when they send their ogre slaves to slaughter us." He raised his voice and pointed at the guards. "When the ogres start tearing you apart, and the pixies are disemboweling you with their magic, remember it was those two goblins who let them stroll right into the lair."

Finally the attention of the goblins shifted away from Jig. Angry muttering spread through the crowd.

"We're going, we're going," said one of the guards, shooting a hateful look in Jig's direction.

They didn't make it out of the lair. A loud snarl announced the arrival of a group of armed hobgoblins. Two tunnel cats strained to break free of braided leather harnesses, nearly pulling their hobgoblin keeper off his feet. "Where is Jig Dragonslayer?" shouted the largest of the hobgoblins.

And that brought the attention right back to Jig. He didn't get the chance to speak before the hobgoblins were making their way toward him, tunnel cats snapping at anyone who failed to get out of the way.

"Our chief wants a word with you, goblin."

Another of the hobgoblins stared. "Hey, Charak. What are you doing with these rat-eaters?"

Charak? They were looking at Slash. From the look of things, he had been trying to disappear into the shadows.

"Chief's going to want to see you, too," said the hobgoblin holding the tunnel cats. "He's going to be real happy when he finds out you're still alive. Now where's Kralk? He told us to bring back the goblin chief, too."

Maybe I should have just stayed in the garbage pit. Jig raised his hand. "I'm the chief." The words sounded strange, like someone else had spoken.

A tunnel cat swatted a goblin who had gotten too close, sending her to the ground with four gouges bleeding down her arm. "Makes our job easier, I guess," said a hobgoblin. "Come with us, rat-eater."

"You can't come in here and give Jig orders," Braf shouted. "He's the chief. You're lucky he doesn't slay every last one of you hobgoblins."

"Braf?" Jig asked.

"What?"

"I'm chief now, right?"

Braf nodded.

"So you have to do what I say?"

Braf nodded again.

"Good. Shut up." Jig studied the hobgoblins. Two tunnel cats and five warriors to escort a few goblins. The hobgoblin chief was serious. Still, if the whole lair attacked together, they would overwhelm the hobgoblins. Judging from the nasty smiles beginning to spread through the crowd, the goblins had figured that out too.

What they hadn't figured out was what the rest of the hobgoblins would do in reprisal. The last thing Jig needed was to have hobgoblins screaming through the layer on a vengeance raid when he was trying to worry about pixies. He could only manage one war at a time.

Actually, he doubted he could manage even one.

"Braf and Grell, I want you to come with us to the hobgoblin lair," Jig said loudly. "The rest of you, keep the muck pits filled and burning, and could somebody please make sure we get a guard at the entrance?"

"Why us?" asked Grell.

Because Grell and Braf had both been under orders to kill him, and neither one had done so. Jig hoped that trend of not killing him would continue. "Because I'm chief and I said so."

Jig tried to look on the bright side as he followed his escort out of the lair. If the hobgoblins killed him, at least he wouldn't have to worry about the pixies.

The lead hobgoblin took one of the tunnel cats, who sniffed the air and the ground as they walked. Another cat followed behind, straining at its leash. That one actually drooled as it watched Jig, barely even blinking.

Hobgoblin lanterns painted the tunnel the color of goblin blood. Jig glanced at Slash, trying to guess whether he was a captor or a prisoner. The other hobgoblins hadn't given him a weapon, but they weren't jabbing him in the back of the legs with their spears either. Lucky hobgoblin.

Jig jumped and walked faster, trying to avoid another poke as he studied his escort. A large, ugly bruise covered one side of the lead hobgoblin's face. Recent, from the looks of it. They didn't say much, but they didn't have to. Three lanterns were overkill for such a small group. They kept peering into the shadows and letting the tunnel cat peek around bends and turns. They were afraid.

"Have the pixies attacked already?" Jig asked.

That earned him another jab, this one in the thigh. From then on, Jig kept his guesses to himself.

When they reached the hobgoblin lair, Jig saw that the number of guards had doubled. Four hobgoblins stood in a rough square at the junction of the tunnels. Lanterns hung from both ears of the glass statue. Several of the guards growled softly as they saw the goblins approaching.

Braf puffed his chest and opened his mouth. Jig smacked him with his sheathed sword. Whatever Braf had intended to say came out a startled, "Hey!"

"No weapons," said one of the hobgoblins, catching Jig's wrist. Jig's arm was so numb he could barely feel the fingers digging into his skin. The hobgoblin grabbed the crossguard and gave a quick yank that nearly dislocated Jig's shoulder.

"Try cutting it off," suggested the hobgoblin who had yanked Braf's hook-tooth away.

"I already did," said Jig. "The leather is enchanted. Cursed, really. It's too strong to cut."

The hobgoblin grinned. "I didn't mean the cord." He drew a short, flat-tipped sword from his belt. The blade was only sharp on one side, an obvious chopping weapon.

"Go on, cut it off," Grell said, leaning against the wall. "Course, then you'll have to explain why your guest bled to death before he could talk to your chief."

The hobgoblin's smile melted away. The thought crossed Jig's mind that nobody had actually specified whether they wanted Jig alive or dead. Though if they wanted him dead, they probably would have killed him by now.

The hobgoblin shoved Jig's arm away. "Draw steel, and you'll wish I'd killed you, goblin." He pushed Jig for good measure, knocking him to the ground next to the glass statue. Blue light reflected from the chipped glass. The hobgoblin warrior stood so tall his head nearly touched the top of the tunnel. Aside from a helmet, he wore only a loincloth, no doubt to emphasize the muscles covering his body.

Lying on the floor, Jig wondered if anyone else had ever bothered to examine the statue from this angle. He also wondered why the sculptor had made the hobgoblin anatomically correct.

"Get up." Strong hands hauled Jig to his feet, then dragged him through the open archway. They pushed Slash after him, saying, "Make sure he doesn't step in anything." Grell and Braf followed, probably assuming they were safer with Jig than out here with cranky hobgoblin guards.

One of the tunnel cats stayed behind. A guard tied the leash around the legs of the statue. The statue would keep the cat from running off, but all the guard had to do to loose the cat on an enemy was cut the leash. Whatever had happened, the hobgoblins were taking no chances.

A few paces into the tunnel, the hobgoblins pressed themselves to the walls as they walked.

"Pit trap," said Slash, shoving Jig against a wall hard enough to bang his head. Grell did the same to Braf who, despite Slash's warning, had almost walked right into the trap. "Fall in there, and the goblins will have to find someone else to play chief."

"What's down there?" Jig asked, keeping his body as close to the wall as he could.

"Used to be a pair of giant carrion-worms." Slash shook his head glumly. "A group of adventurers fell into the pit and slaughtered them. Do you have any idea how long it takes to breed and raise giant worms? The chief decided rusty spikes at the bottom would be faster and easier. Not as much fun though."

"Oh. I see." Jig fought to keep his face neutral, though he couldn't quite stop a shiver at the memory of those worms.

A few paces later, Slash pushed him again. "See that stain on the ground?"

Jig stared. The ground was dusty rock, the same as the rest of the tunnels. Squinting, he could just make out a faint discoloration in the dirt where Slash was pointing.

"We spread a mix of blood, rock serpent venom, and diluted honey there. The venom keeps the blood from clotting, and the honey makes it stick to whoever steps in it." Slash licked his lips. "Tunnel cats love the stuff. Step inside the lair wearing that scent, and they'll be on you before you can draw your sword." Indeed, even as Slash explained, the tunnel cat tugged its leash, trying to reach the dried stain. The hobgoblin kicked the cat in the side, earning a loud hiss, but the cat didn't attack. That was a well-trained animal. Jig wondered if the hobgoblins would be willing to train the goblin guards.

Before Jig could say anything, Slash hauled him to one

side. This time it was a scattering of tiny metal spikes resting on the ground.

"They're so small," Braf said.

"And they're coated in lizard-fish toxin," Slash said.

Oh. Jig stared at the hobgoblins with newfound respect. If he tried to set such traps to protect the goblin lair, half the goblins would be dead within a week.

"Watch your step," said Slash.

Jig stopped, fully expecting to be shot, poisoned, crushed, or maybe all three at the same time. "What is it now?"

Slash pointed to a pile of brown, slimy goo in the center of the tunnel. "Hairball."

Eventually the tunnel opened into a broad cavern, similar in size to the goblins' lair. But the hobgoblins had carved out a very different home for themselves. For one thing, instead of using muck pits in the floor, the hobgoblins hung wide metal muck bowls from large tripods, so the light came from overhead. Every time Jig took a step, three shadows followed him along the floor. As if he wasn't jumpy enough already!

Even stranger, there were hobgoblin *children* running about. Jig stared at a girl whose head barely came past his waist. She had a knife tucked through her belt, and was swinging a club at a larger, similarly armed hobgoblin boy. As Jig watched, the boy knocked her club away, then kicked her in the stomach. The girl crawled away to retrieve the club. To Jig's amazement, the boy stood there, waiting as she attacked again.

"What's she doing?" Jig asked.

Slash glanced over. "Practicing."

Jig could see other children working throughout the cavern. A few near the entrance scraped lichen from the walls by one of the lanterns, while a boy farther in helped butcher a pile of lizard-fish. Jig even saw a baby hobgoblin slung to the back of a female. He grimaced. The baby had wrinkly yellow skin, green toothless gums, and a misshapen skull.

"Hobgoblin babies are ugly," said Braf.

Grell snorted. "You weren't exactly pleasant to look at yourself."

The female with the baby noticed them staring and bared

her teeth in a scowl before ducking behind a large, painted screen mounted on a wooden frame.

Similar screens were set throughout the cavern, partitioning the space into smaller chambers. Crude paintings decorated most of the screens. They seemed to tell stories of hobgoblin triumphs, whether it was a single hobgoblin leading a troll into an ambush, or a group tossing goblins into a pit full of tunnel cats.

The guards led Jig and the others toward the rear of the cave. Several hobgoblins spat as Jig passed. He heard two others making a wager over how Jig would be killed. He held his sword close to his leg, trying to appear unthreatening. So many hobgoblins. Men and women, young and old, armed and . . . well, they were all armed. And they all looked angry.

"What happened?" Jig asked.

One of the guards shoved him forward. "That's for the chief to explain."

"No," said another. "That's for him to explain to the chief."

The chief was an older hobgoblin, sitting on a much-abused cushion near the back of the cavern. A half-eaten skewer of lizard-fish meat sat on the ground beside him. Screens to either side created a smaller artificial cave. Another frame stood in front, but the screen had been rolled up and tied overhead, opening the small chamber to the rest of the cavern.

The hobgoblin chief rose, ducking past the wooden frame to stand in front of Jig and the others. He slipped a bit of greasy lizard-fish to the tunnel cat, then wiped his hands on his quilted, brass-studded jacket. A long wavy sword hung on his hip. The cast bronze head of a hobgoblin warrior capped the hilt, and the crosspiece was a pair of long barbed spikes. Jig had seen the sword once before, when he and the chief had negotiated the truce between goblins and hobgoblins. According to hobgoblin law, whoever held that sword commanded all hobgoblins.

"Hello, Jig," said the chief. His thinning hair was bound into a dirty white braid. He glared at the other hobgoblins. "I said I wanted to speak to the goblin chief too."

"That's me," Jig said.

"I see." He studied Jig, his expression never changing. His cool appraisal was far more worrisome than the gruff threats of the other hobgoblins. At least with them, Jig knew what to expect. Not so with this hobgoblin. He might offer Jig a bit of lizard-fish or cut the head from his body with that huge sword, and he would do both with the same stone expression. Finally he grunted and said, "About time someone killed that overbearing coward Kralk."

He turned to Slash. "Ah, Charak. The others tell me you let a goblin outwit you. A fat female, one who claimed to be a wizard of some sort. They say she humiliated you and led you away, slinking like a cat who's been beaten once too often."

Jig took a small step away from Slash. Charak. Whoever.

"Doesn't matter anymore," Slash said. "The stupid rat-eater went and got herself enchanted by pixies."

"Pixies?" the chief asked. "What are you talking about?"

As fast as he could, Jig stepped forward to explain about the pixies and their conquest of the ogres. He told the chief how they had fled to the Necromancer's pit and how the steel of his blade seemed to have broken the spell on Slash. "Ask them," he added, pointing to Braf and Grell. "They've all seen the pixies and what they can do."

The chief was shaking his head. "So, Charak. Not only does a mere goblin get the best of you, but then you let yourself fall prey to a fairy spell? I should probably kill you now and save us all the trouble."

The threat was uttered in an easy, casual tone, but Jig saw several hobgoblins reach for their weapons.

"Falling in battle against an invading army I could forgive," the chief continued. "But letting a goblin get the better of you?"

Slash mumbled something incomprehensible.

"And now she returns," said the chief.

Jig's ears perked up. "You have Veka?"

"Not exactly." The chief took another bite of lizard-fish as he studied Jig. Pale strings of meat protruded from between his teeth. "Your goblin wizard killed nine of my men. She refuses to let anyone get to the lake. If we can't get down to hunt in the caverns below, we'll be reduced to scavenging for bugs and rats. Living like goblins, in other words."

He stepped closer, until Jig could smell the meat on his breath. "She tells me she'll let us through if we present her with Jig Dragonslayer."

For once, Jig wasn't afraid. He raised his chin and said, "You can't. She'll turn me over to the pixies, and they'll kill me."

The chief shrugged and spat a few bones onto the floor. Jig could hear the guards moving closer, and Smudge crouched down at the junction of Jig's neck and shoulder to hide.

"If I die," Jig went on, "the truce between goblins and hobgoblins ends today. The truce, and everything that came with it. The same goes if you kill my companions. Even him," he added, nodding toward Slash. He tried to fold his arms defiantly, but he had forgotten about the sword. The sheath whacked him in the leg, to the amusement of the hobgoblins.

The chief stared at Jig for a long time. His wrinkled face gave no clue what was running through his mind. He was a crafty one, even for a hobgoblin, and Jig began to wonder if he had miscalculated.

"Veka told us she wanted Jig Dragonslayer," the chief finally said. "She never specified how she wanted him delivered . . ."

The hobgoblins guarding the entrance to the lair appeared quite surprised to see Jig and the others alive.

"Give me that," Braf said, reclaiming his weapon.

One of the guards stared at Slash. "What happened?"

"We're going to kill Veka," Slash said, grinning.

"I don't suppose any of you mighty warriors know how we're going to accomplish that?" Grell asked.

Nobody answered. Personally, Jig had been giving serious thought to running away and hiding back in the goblin lair. If Veka had slaughtered nine hobgoblin warriors, Jig and his companions weren't going to last very long.

But retreating would only lead to other problems. Problems like angry hobgoblins butchering their way through the goblin lair, demanding Jig's head.

Slash grabbed one of the muck lanterns, but Jig shook his head. "No light. We don't want her to see us coming."

Jig studied his companions as they left the hobgoblin lair. Grell's canes made too much noise. They might be better off leaving her behind altogether, but she seemed to do a good job of keeping Braf in line. As for Braf, he was barely bright enough to know which end of a sword to grab, but Jig needed all the help he could get. Without the two goblins, his only backup would be a hobgoblin who fainted at the sight of blood.

"Wait," Jig said, struggling to draw his sword. After the incident with Kralk, he had used a bit of cord to knot the sheath in place. Those knots had tightened, and he had to bite through them to free the blade. His shoulder burned with newly awakened pain as he used the sword to cut off the tails of his vest. "Grell, give me one of your canes."

He wrapped the material around the end, then used a broken piece of twine to tie it into place. He did the same with the other cane. Hopefully that would muffle the noise a bit.

He shoved the sword back into the sheath and rested the whole thing over his shoulder. Smudge scurried to the top of Jig's head for safety.

As the light dimmed toward blackness, Slash stepped closer. "Why didn't he kill you?"

"Who?" Jig asked.

"The chief. You defied him, and he let you live."

"A good thing, too," said Braf. "You hobgoblins need to treat us with a bit more respect, or else—"

The thump of Grell smacking Braf was quieter than usual. The cloth Jig had tied around the ends of her canes appeared to be working.

"Because of the truce," Jig said. That earned a disbelieving snort. "No, it's true. He's afraid that if I die, he'll lose what he got out of the deal."

"I've always wondered about that," said Slash. "A lot of us have. What possible reason could you give us to leave you rat-eaters alone?"

Jig brushed the fingers of his free hand along the wall for guidance as blackness swallowed the last of the lantern light.

"He was sitting on his cushion when we arrived, right?" Jig asked. "Before the truce, when was the last time you saw him sit?"

"He didn't," Slash said. "He was always up and moving. Training the warriors, inspecting traps, overseeing the cats' handlers. He's chief. He doesn't have time to—"

"No, he *couldn't* sit. He had . . . an injury. I healed it." He grimaced at the memory. "Not an experience I'd choose to repeat."

"What?" From the sound of things, Braf was barely holding back his laughter. "You mean this whole truce was nothing but a reward for you healing a hobgoblin's ugly behind?"

Jig stopped. "What did you think, Braf? That I threatened them? That I stomped through the hobgoblin lair and told their chief I'd bring the full wrath of the goblins to bear if they didn't stop killing us?"

"Well . . . yeah."

Jig shook his head. How in the world had Braf survived to adulthood?

The smell of water told Jig they were close, as did the sudden flare of warmth from Smudge. Faint light shone from the beach ahead. Pixies? Jig hoped not. The hobgoblin chief hadn't known about the pixies, which suggested Veka was alone.

"Hello, Jig." Veka's voice was as cheerful and grating as ever. "I know you're there. You and your three companions. Why don't you come out and meet my new friends?"

So much for Veka being alone. How could she know they were coming? Jig wrapped his free hand around his sword handle. With the muscles of his sword arm bound and numb, this was the only way he'd be able to use it.

Veka *couldn't* know, not unless one of his group was possessed.

No, none of you have the taint of pixie magic.

Then how? They had been as quiet as tunnel cats stalking their prey. Veka couldn't have heard them. Jig backed away.

He had only gone a few steps when Smudge grew warmer.

Had Smudge only now recognized the danger? Jig was moving away from Veka. That should be safer!

Jig ripped a handful of frayed threads from the bottom of his vest. Putting the threads in his mouth, he reached up to move Smudge to his shoulder. Much hotter, and Smudge would burn the rest of Jig's hair . . . which would give him the light he wanted, but Jig preferred to keep what little hair remained. Once the fire-spider was crouched on his leather pad, Jig twisted the ends of the threads together and reached up to poke Smudge from behind.

The threads burst into flame. "Eight eyes, and I can still scare you," Jig whispered. In the faint, dimming light, he could see Grell, Braf, and Slash standing behind him, weapons drawn.

"No light," Slash said, mimicking Jig's voice. "We don't want her to see us coming."

"Here," said Grell, holding out a rag. She touched one corner to the dying flame, and the tunnel brightened.

"What is that?" Braf asked.

"Another diaper. Useful things, really." She knotted the burning diaper around the end of Jig's sword. "Don't worry, it should be clean."

Normally the odor would have bothered Jig, but the ogres' torches seemed to have overloaded his sense of smell. And the diaper burned quite well, he had to admit.

Mold covered the tunnel walls, thriving in the damp lake air. Jig saw nothing out of the ordinary, aside from himself and his companions. Maybe Smudge was getting jumpy in his old age. Considering everything they had been through together, Jig could certainly understand that. He took another step back.

"What's wrong, Jig?" Veka shouted. "Running away won't save you."

"It's always worked before," Jig muttered. She could see every move they made. "That's not fair," he whispered, turning toward the others.

As he did, a shadow overhead caught his attention. No, three shadows.

"Good fire-spider," Jig whispered. Clinging to minuscule

irregularities in the obsidian, three lizard-fish watched Jig from the ceiling. They were so still they could have been a part of the rock, save for a slight quiver in the closest lizard-fish's tail. "First rule of traps," Jig muttered, remembering what Slash had said before. "Nobody ever looks up."

He tried to watch them without moving his head or giving Veka any indication that he had discovered her spies. He stepped toward Slash, a move that brought him almost directly underneath the lizard-fish. The tails of the other two began to twitch now. Jig recognized that motion. They tensed their muscles like that right before they lashed out with those poisonous spines.

Why hadn't they struck when Jig and the others passed underneath the first time? Something must have held them back. The same power that had driven them from the comfort of their lake, pushing them beyond the damp sand and onto hated rock. Veka.

Jig locked eyes with Slash, hoping the hobgoblin would understand. Slowly and deliberately, Jig turned his eyes upward.

"Look out!" Braf shouted. "Lizard-fish!"

Even as Jig thrust his sword at the closest lizard-fish, a part of his mind hoped he would live long enough to hide a few lizard-fish in Braf's undergarments.

His sword clanged into the ceiling, still sheathed, but the flaming diaper drove the lizard-fish back. They circled around, their tiny legs scrambling in unison. How could they cling upside down like that? Then he remembered Veka's levitation spell, back at the bottomless pit. She must have been practicing.

A rock cracked off the ceiling, and one of the lizard-fish fell. It wasn't dead, but its body bent sharply in the middle, and the tail was still.

Jig leaped back as the other two lizard-fish dropped to the ground to attack. One landed on its back, while the other scurried after Slash. Jig saw Grell crushing the inverted lizard-fish with her cane.

Slash was still unarmed, and he leaped out of the way as the lizard-fish charged. He grabbed Braf by one arm. As Braf squawked in protest, Slash kicked the back of the goblin's knees and flung him to the ground. Braf landed on his back, directly on top of the attacking lizard-fish.

As Braf scrambled to his feet, cursing and spitting, Jig could see the squished lizard-fish still stuck to the wooden shield strapped to Braf's back.

A crunching sound told him Grell had finished off the first lizard-fish, the one with the broken back. "Who threw that rock?" Jig asked, as much to distract Braf from going after Slash as anything else.

"Oh, that was me," said Braf. "I've always been good with rocks."

"You've always . . ." Jig's voice trailed off. He stepped away, shaking his head in disbelief. He waved his light around the floor until he found the stone Braf had thrown. Tucking it into his shirt, he wandered farther down the tunnel, collecting a few more. He came back and dumped the rocks into Braf's hands. Without a word, he snatched the hook-tooth away and handed it to Slash.

This time, there were no taunts from Veka as Jig approached the lake. He could hear the others following behind.

Jig peeked around the edge of the tunnel and nearly wet himself.

Hundreds of lizard-fish waited on the beach. Veka must have emptied the entire lake to amass so many. They stood facing the tunnel, each one about arm's length from the next. Aside from the occasional flicking of a tongue, they were absolutely motionless.

Then they spotted Jig. Each and every head turned in unison.

Braf tugged Jig's arm. "I think I'm going to need more rocks."

Veka herself sat atop the tunnel that led into the lake. The edges of her cloak trailed along the surface of the water. Her eyes were closed, but she was smiling at Jig. "I knew those pixies wouldn't capture you." She patted a pocket in her cloak, doubtless one of those stupid books. "The end of the

Path brings the Hero to her final, fateful trial. I should have known destiny's decree would bring us together for this climactic confrontation. You've thwarted me at every pass, Jig Dragonslayer, mocking my efforts to master the mysteries of magic."

Jig rolled his eyes. Veka's "Heroic" dialog had grown even worse. Had she always used such clumsy alliteration?

He turned his attention back to the beach, particularly to the hobgoblin corpses scattered among the lizard-fish. He counted eight or nine, most of which had died within a few steps of leaving the tunnel. A few dead lizard-fish lay beside them.

"What we need is about a hundred more hobgoblins," Grell said.

"Don't worry, I can get her," said Braf. Before Jig could react, Braf stepped into the open and flung one of his rocks. It arced through the air, directly toward Veka's head. The rock slowed as it neared, coming to a halt just before it hit Veka's forehead. Without opening her eyes, Veka reached out to tap the rock with her finger. It reversed direction, picking up every bit of speed it had lost and more.

Jig ducked, and the rock slammed into Braf's stomach, knocking him onto his back.

"Nice try," Veka called out.

"We should run," said Jig, keeping his voice low. "Her magic is too strong."

"Don't you have magic of your own?" asked Slash.

Jig shook his head. "She's using wizard magic. I only have priest magic."

What are you talking about?

Jig jumped. *I can't do wizardly things like Veka. I can only—*

Magic is magic. The universe doesn't divide its mysteries into priest magic and wizard magic any more than you divide the air down there into goblin air and hobgoblin air.

Wait, does that mean I'm a wizard? Jig's eyes widened. *But I have a sword! And I don't have a staff or a beard or long robes or—*

You're as bad as Veka, you know that?

Jig stiffened. *So why can't I use magic to make those lizard-fish turn on Veka?*

That kind of magic takes years of study and discipline.

A gritty wind began to blow. Veka held her fingers fanned toward the tunnel, her magic shooting sand into their faces.

Years of study and discipline, or getting possessed by pixies, Shadowstar amended.

Can you help me fight her magic or not? Jig demanded.

You'll need time to learn and practice that style of magic. Ask Veka to meet you back here in about a year or so.

Jig grimaced and spat sand from his mouth. "I can't fight her magically." He stared at the beach, using his fingers to block the worst of the sand from his eyes. Why hadn't Veka simply sent the lizard-fish into the tunnel to kill them?

He studied the lizard-fish more closely. Even the twitching of their tails was synchronized, just like the three that had been spying in the tunnel. The only time that had changed was when the lizard-fish dropped from the ceiling and their instincts had taken over. If Jig and the others hadn't been in the way, would the lizard-fish have left them alone? Free of Veka's control, they might have fled for the comfort of the beach.

How much power did Veka need to control all those lizard-fish? "We have to go out there," he whispered.

"If you don't want to be chief, there are easier ways to quit," said Grell.

Jig shook his head. Already the sandstorm was beginning to die down. She couldn't have much power left. Enough to deflect a few rocks maybe. "All the hobgoblins charged straight through the middle," he said, pointing to the line of bodies. "We need to split her focus. I don't think she can send them against us all at the same time."

"So you're saying only some of us will get killed?" Braf asked.

Jig's shoulders slumped. That was precisely what he was saying. And they reacted precisely the way he would have expected goblins and hobgoblins to react. Grell chuckled.

Braf shook his head and backed away. Slash rapped the end of his hook-tooth against the wall, testing its weight.

"Surrender to me, Jig," Veka said. "Come with me, and your companions will survive. The pixies will spare you all, but only if Jig gives himself up."

"Sounds good to me," said Slash, stepping toward Jig.

"Wait!" Jig waved his sword at them. The flaming diaper dropped to the ground. He licked his sand-chapped lips, searching for sympathy and finding none.

If he tried to run, Slash and Braf would both be able to tackle him. Or Slash could loop the hook of his weapon around Jig's feet. Jig would never get past them both. "She's lying," said Jig. "Remember what Trockle said? The pixies want us all dead!"

"Trockle said they wanted all of the ogres dead," said Braf. "Who can blame them?"

"Braf, think about it," said Jig. "If she gives me to the pixies, who's going to help you the next time you get a fang rammed up your nose?"

He turned to Slash. "And you, hobgoblin. I guess this means you'll be heading back to your chief to tell him how one goblin female was too much for you to handle? Veka's been getting the better of you since she first laid eyes on you!"

He had saved Grell for last, mostly because he wasn't sure what he could say to convince her. She was too old to threaten, and too smart to fall for any bluff. He stared at the dwindling diaper fire on the ground, and then it came to him.

"Help me, and when we get back, I'll take you off nursery duty forever. You'll never wipe another goblin butt as long as you live."

Nobody spoke. Braf and Grell glanced at one another. Slash had a scowl on his face, but he always had a scowl on his face.

"You really think Veka and the pixies will just go away and leave you all in peace if you give me to her?" Jig asked.

"I've been patient with you until now," shouted Veka. "It's time to make your choice."

The others looked at one another. Slash was the one who broke the silence. "I'd never hear the end of it," he said.

"Do you really think this will work?" asked Grell.

"Of course," Jig said.

Grell poked him with a cane. "Liar." Groaning, she limped toward the beach. When nobody else moved, she turned around again. "Well, what are you all waiting for?"

CHAPTER 12

"Great power carries a great cost. But there's no rule that says you have to be the one to pay it."

—Grensley Shadowmaster
From *The Path of the Hero (Wizard's ed.)*

NOWHERE IN EITHER THE RAGGED REMNANTS of Veka's spellbook or in her copy of *The Path of the Hero* did there exist a single warning that the overuse of magic could leave the wizard with such a raging headache. She had never seen Jig suffer this kind of pain after one of his little healing spells. On the other hand, Jig had never tried to control well over a hundred individual minds.

She kept her eyes closed, seeing through the eyes of the lizard-fish and struggling to merge it all into a single coherent image. So long as she remained still, the feeling that a team of ogres were digging a hole through her skull wasn't quite as bad. Only a single ogre, and he wasn't using quite so heavy a pickax.

"How much longer?" Snixle whispered. By now, she had gotten used to the pixie speaking with her mouth. He had a tendency to curl her tongue into a tube, though, and that was annoying. She could do without the twitching of her phantom wings, too. No wonder Snixle had a hard time controlling other creatures: he insisted on treating them like pixies.

Veka knew better. Her lizard-fish weren't miniature goblins to command. The more she tried to control their every movement, the clumsier they became. One of the hobgoblins had crossed half of the beach before she realized she could let the lizard-fish's own instincts take over, keeping only enough control to aim them at the appropriate prey.

"Throw more sand at them," Snixle said, trying to raise her hands. The pounding in her head grew worse. Three ogres worth, at least.

"I'm not sure I can." She probably could, but if Braf threw another rock at her, she might not have the strength to stop it. "Be patient. Jig will be out soon, one way or another. The others have a choice between their lives and his. I have no doubt what they will choose."

She concentrated on the lizard-fish closest to the tunnel. Lizard-fish didn't see very well. Their vision was blurred, and she had a harder time distinguishing colors. Not to mention how odd it was to have to look *up* at everything. On the other hand, lizard-fish had excellent hearing. Not as sharp as the giant bat she had ridden, but good enough to hear the goblins whispering. She couldn't quite hear Jig's words, but she could make out the rising fear in his voice. If they hadn't killed her three lizard-fish in the tunnels, she could have listened in on the conversation easily.

"Once Jig realizes he's out of options, he'll be ours," she said. Excitement made her shiver, which sent new pangs through her skull. This was worth the pain. Her former days of sitting alone in the back of the distillery, painstakingly struggling through the faded instructions of an old spellbook, were behind her now. Veka had become a wizard. Or sorceress. Sorceress sounded more impressive. *Veka the Sorceress.*

"At least send a few more lizard-fish into the tunnel," Snixle whined.

"Jig will come to me," Veka said. Whether he came willingly or was thrown out by his companions was another question.

As if he had heard her thoughts, Jig stepped out of the

tunnel. Even through the blurry vision of the lizard-fish, Veka could see that he was breathing fast, like a rat about to be dropped into the stew pot. He had his sword drawn, but he didn't seem to be attacking the lizard-fish. The broken tip of his blade hung by his ankle. What was wrong with his arm? A sour taste hinted at pixie magic. The pixies had cursed his sword, from the look of things. Apparently Jig hadn't come through his last battle unscathed.

Behind him, Slash poked a weapon toward Jig's back, urging him onward. Veka's throat tightened. The hobgoblin was supposed to be dead! She had seen Grell shove a sword into his chest. Jig must have healed him, though she couldn't understand why he would waste that much magic on a hobgoblin.

Grell held a makeshift lantern of some sort that burned with a foul black smoke. Braf stood on Jig's other side, seemingly empty-handed.

"Go back," Veka shouted to them. "Tell your people not to resist, and the pixies may let you live."

"Right," Jig said, turning around to leave. "I'll pass that along."

"Not you," Veka snapped.

Jig stopped at the edge of the sand. His eyes fixed on the closest lizard-fish.

"Fear not, Jig Dragonslayer," she said. "They obey my will, and mine alone." To demonstrate, she commanded those lizard-fish nearest Jig to move aside, opening a path for him.

"Veka, do you really believe the pixies will let us live?" Jig shouted.

"They want this mountain," Veka called. "Whether we're dead or departed doesn't matter. The strongest will rule this place. Isn't that the way it's always been? Before it was Straum and the Necromancer who commanded the bulk of the mountain. The pixies are even more powerful, and they've chosen this place as their own."

She could see Jig shaking as he stepped forward, past the hungry lizard-fish. Veka gritted her teeth as she continued to clear his way. Would it kill him to walk a little faster?

"Drop your weapon," Snixle shouted, using her voice.

Jig struggled to raise his sword arm. Now Veka could see

how leather ties secured the sword to his hand and arm. The skin had turned purple where it bulged between the cords. "I wish I could."

When he was halfway across the beach, Veka raised her hand. "That's far enough, Jig Dragonslayer. From this point onward, you shall submit to my will." Let him try to fight. His healing magic was no match for her power. She stilled the lizard-fish and opened her eyes, focusing on Jig alone. Controlling lizard-fish was one thing. This would be her first attempt at controlling another intelligent being. She grinned. Not just any being, but Jig Dragonslayer.

"Look out!" Snixle yanked her to one side, nearly dumping her in the lake. A stone grazed her head, clattering off the top of the tunnel before splashing into the water. Veka recovered to see Jig running as fast as he could, his sword dragging through the sand. He wanted to test himself against her power? So be it. She drew herself to her feet.

Before she could do anything more, her vision erupted into rippling, blinding light. No, not her vision, but that of her lizard-fish. One segment of her sight now burned with orange fire, rippling through her composite view of the beach as the burning lizard-fish frantically tried to escape the flames. She severed the spell binding her to that lizard-fish, then turned to see what had happened.

Grell! She had flung a rag of some sort onto the lizard-fish. Even now another burning rag flew from her hand. Trapped by Veka's spell, the lizard-fish were unable to dodge, and another segment of her vision exploded into flame.

Veka cut that lizard-fish free, then commanded the others to surge forward. They had barely begun to move when yet another layer of her sight began to spin and whirl. Slash had crept out of the tunnel, and was using the hook end of his weapon to fling lizard-fish into the air.

Another lizard-fish died as a rock smashed its skull. Braf was throwing rocks again, aiming for the lizard-fish nearest Jig. She tried to intercept the next stone with magic, but Grell lit a third lizard-fish on fire, and Slash was still flinging them to and fro. Much more and Veka would lose the contents of her stomach.

Enough of this. She relaxed her control over those lizard-fish closest to their attackers. Some immediately scurried for the water, but others were too close to Slash and the goblins. Braf shouted a warning as the lizard-fish broke formation, and he began throwing at the lizard-fish racing toward Grell.

"Now we help them," Snixle said, bouncing with eagerness. Seizing control of her arms, he moved her through a quick binding, then cast a levitation spell. The spell ripped the hook-tooth from Slash's hands and sent it flying point-first toward Braf.

"Nice move," Veka said.

Slash kicked a lizard-fish and shouted, "Watch out!"

Braf yelped and ducked, and the point of the hook-tooth splintered against the wall.

"Drat," said Snixle.

"It doesn't matter," Veka assured him. Braf was almost out of rocks, and Slash was unarmed. She turned to Grell, casting another levitation spell to try to rip the rags from her hands.

Grell had a surprisingly strong grip for such an old goblin.

"Concentrate on Jig," Snixle said. Jig was the only one not fighting lizard-fish. He seemed solely intent on reaching Veka. He ran at top speed, several times practically stepping on lizard-fish in his haste.

Veka grinned in anticipation. Here was the battle she had dreamed about. Veka the Sorceress against Jig Dragonslayer. The new Hero stepping forth to vanquish the old. He had suppressed her for so long, but finally she was ready. She would have to make sure at least one of his companions survived to take the story back to the goblins and the hobgoblins. Grell would probably be the best choice. Slash was a hobgoblin, and Braf would mess everything up in the telling.

Veka strode toward the front edge of the tunnel, where it rose out of the lake. Here atop the arching stone, she had the advantage of height. Jig would have to scramble up to face her. Would it be better to wait for him, or should she strike him down as he climbed? The former would make a better story, but she might be wiser to kill Jig when he was most vulnerable. Strictly speaking, that might not be the most heroic decision, but it was certainly a goblin decision. She cast another levitation spell, lifting one of the lizard-fish and floating it spine-first toward Jig's back. She would plunge those spines into Jig's neck as he climbed, and—

The lizard-fish squealed in pain as a rock smashed it aside. Braf! She clenched her teeth, wishing she had tossed Braf into the middle of the lake, but there was no time. Jig was almost upon her. She braced herself, releasing the rest of the lizard-fish as she prepared to strike.

Jig disappeared.

Veka's mouth opened in disbelief. Jig had run straight into the tunnel. He hadn't even stopped to fight her. He was fleeing to the Necromancer's domain. What kind of Hero ran right past his enemy without even a token exchange of insults?

She stepped to the edge.

"What are you doing?" asked Snixle.

"The Necromancer's home was a maze of tunnels," she said. "Jig could disappear in there for days, and we'd never find him."

"You promised me Jig Dragonslayer," complained Snixle.

"Relax. We'll get him." Snixle was such a whiner. A wave of her hand cleared the lizard-fish from the tunnel mouth. Another spell gathered the flaming rags from the sand, summoning them to Veka. Jig might be fast, but he couldn't have reached the end of the tunnel yet.

Her magic compressed the rags into a single ball as she prepared to fire the flames into the tunnel. He would be badly burned, but he should survive. With the fire hovering over her hand, she jumped to the sand below.

Snixle screamed as Jig's broken sword took Veka in the chest.

Veka could hear lizard-fish splashing back into the lake. There was sand in her hair, and Jig's knees dug into her belly. Every time she inhaled, someone punched her in the chest. No, that was the sword. There was tremendous pressure, but less pain than she would have imagined.

Her body began to spasm as her lungs fought harder and harder for breath. "Snixle?" Her lips formed the word, but no sound came out.

Someone was shouting. Jig? He appeared to be in pain. With an effort, Veka managed to focus her eyes. Only one set of eyes . . . how odd.

Jig's arm was twisted at a painful angle, still lashed to the sword which had sunk into Veka's body. He must have wrenched his shoulder when Veka fell.

She would have laughed, had she been able to catch her breath. The only injury Jig had taken in his fight with Veka, and he had done it to himself.

Through watering eyes, she saw Grell come up beside Jig, carefully carrying a burning lizard-fish for light.

"Help me get her on her side," Jig said.

Grell was no use, but Veka felt a large boot slide beneath her shoulder, kicking her to one side. Jig flopped into the sand.

"Thanks, Slash," Jig said, spitting sand. He braced his feet on Veka's chest and yanked.

A true Hero would have made one final, defiant declaration as her blood spilled onto the sand, but all Veka could manage was a whimpered "Ouch." Then she passed out.

When she awoke, she found her face pressed against Slash's back. There was no light, but the smell of hobgoblin hair grease was unmistakable. Her arms were around his neck, and her feet dragged along the rock as he hauled her through the tunnel.

"Jig, she's drooling again," the hobgoblin complained. "It's gross."

"Could be worse," Braf said. "At least she's not bleeding on you."

Slash groaned, and Veka felt him swallow.

"You're alive?" Veka asked. It came out a dry croak. "All of you?"

Slash dropped her. Her fangs cut into her cheeks as her jaw hit the ground.

"The lizard-fish all fled back into the water when you dropped your spell," Jig said. "You kept them out of the lake for too long. Their skin was dry and cracked, and they were climbing over one another to get back."

So once again Jig had escaped unscathed. An entire army

of lizard-fish, and he had won. All her power, and she was the one who had taken a sword through the stomach.

Hesitantly, afraid of what she might feel, she reached down to where she had felt the horrible pinching sensation of Jig's sword. There was a ragged hole in her cloak. Both the cloak and the shirt beneath were still sticky with blood. But her skin was soft and whole. Jig had healed her.

"You were under a pixie spell," Jig said. "They've been controlling you since you left Straum's cave."

Veka kept silent. Let him believe the pixies were responsible.

"What happened after you ran away?" Jig continued. She could hear him sitting down beside her, his sword dragging on the rock.

"I descended," she whispered. Her hands automatically moved to check her pockets. Both books were still there. She pulled out *The Path of the Hero*, holding it with both hands. "I descended through darkness and sludge and tunnel cats, and emerged into the silver light of Straum's cavern."

Her eyes watered as she quoted chapter five. " 'The Hero's Path shall descend into darkness, but upon the Hero's return, her symbolic rebirth, she shall have the power to triumph.' That's what Josca said. And I descended!" Her hands shook so hard she could barely hold the book. "I descended and returned, and you stabbed me!"

"You were trying to kill us," Braf said.

"You don't understand," Veka said, tears tickling her face. "I was supposed to be strong. Jig wasn't supposed to beat me. All that magic, and he still beat me."

She flung the book away. Pages flapped, and the book thumped against the tunnel wall.

"Watch it," snapped Slash. "Stupid goblin. Jig should have left you for the lizard-fish. Gods know there's enough of you to go around."

Veka sniffed. She couldn't summon up the slightest bit of anger at Slash's jab. It was no different from the taunts goblins had flung at her all her life. Slash was right. Jig should have left her to die. Now there would be new songs of Jig Dragonslayer and his victory over Vast Veka at the lake.

"I did everything Josca said," she mumbled. She had followed the Path, descended into darkness, acquired an admittedly unusual mentor, and returned to face her greatest challenge. But Josca said the Hero was supposed to win.

"The pixies said the queen had come into our world," Jig was saying. "Do you know where she went? How many pixies are we up against? Where are all their ogres?"

"I don't know," Veka whispered. *The Hero was supposed to win.*

"She's useless," Slash said.

"Like a hobgoblin guard who's afraid of blood?" asked Braf.

"Shut up, both of you," snapped Jig. "The pixies will know Veka's no longer enchanted. Next they'll probably send their ogres up to wipe us out."

Jig had beaten her.

"So what?" asked Braf. "They'll have to go through the hobgoblins before they can get to us."

"You rat-eating coward!" shouted Slash.

"We've taken the brunt of every group of adventurers, explorers, and heroes who ever came to this mountain," Braf shouted back. "It's about time you hobgoblins took a turn."

"Or else the pixies could wait and let us kill each other," Grell said.

Veka coughed and spat. Evidently she had gotten a bit of blood in her throat after Jig stabbed her. It tasted awful. "Snixle said something about bringing the queen to her new home."

"Snixle?" asked Braf.

"The pixie who . . . who controlled me." She flushed, ashamed. Let them think it was Snixle who had lost the fight against Jig Dragonslayer, not Veka.

"Where was this home?" Jig asked. "In Straum's cavern, or somewhere else?"

She shook her head. "He didn't say."

"Why leave Straum's cave at all?" Slash asked. "That's the safest place in the whole mountain. In all those years, how many adventurers ever reached the dragon?"

"The cave is too cramped for pixies," Jig muttered. He was

sitting so close. She could reach into her cloak and pull out her knife. In the darkness he would never know it was coming.

No, his pet fire-spider would know. Smudge would warn Jig, and Jig would stab her again. No matter what she tried, Jig would beat her. Just as he had beaten the dragon and the Necromancer. Just as he had beaten the pixies who tried to capture him. Just as he had beaten her at the lake, destroying Snixle's spell.

"How did you overcome the pixie's control over me?" she asked.

"Steel," Jig said. He sounded distracted. "The pixies called it death-metal. Something about it disrupts their magic. That's how we freed Slash. When he got stabbed . . ." His voice grew faint, barely even a whisper. "Oh, no."

"What?" asked Grell.

"The pixies told me I opened the way for them when I killed Straum," he said softly. "They said it was my fault. Do you remember what Straum's lair was like, right after he died?"

"Full of clutter and junk," said Braf. "Books, pots, paintings, coins, armor, every bit of garbage that old lizard had collected in his lifetime."

"Including weapons and armor," said Jig. "Every sword, every knife, every shield and breastplate, all of it was mounted on the cave walls. He lined the whole cave with steel, and after he died—"

"We picked the place clean," said Braf. "Oh. Whoops."

Veka felt herself nodding. "Snixle said it took powerful magic to open a gateway. The greatest concentration of magic over here would have been Straum's cave, where the dragon's own power had seeped into the rock over thousands of years."

"We should get back to the lair," Jig said. "We'll send some of the goblins to help the hobgoblins, in case the ogres come up through the lake."

"Kralk will never agree to that," Veka said.

Slash began to chuckle. "I don't think Kralk's going to object too much, seeing how she's dead."

"Dead?" Veka asked. "Then who . . . ?" She didn't finish

the question. She knew. Who else could it be? While Veka had been descending and returning and wasting her time trying to master pixie magic, Jig had not only fought off ogres and pixies, he had taken control of the goblins as well.

"Come on," said Jig.

Veka trudged along behind them. Her foot brushed her copy of *The Path of the Hero* where it had fallen. She hesitated, then continued after the others.

Veka remained silent as Slash tried to convince the hobgoblin guards she was their prisoner and that Jig was taking her back to the goblin lair to make her pay for what she had done. The hobgoblins were reluctant at first. One kept twitching the leash to his tunnel cat and talking about how hungry the beast was.

Then Jig stepped forward. He looked filthy and exhausted. In that pitifully small, squeaky voice of his, he said, "We fought through an army of enchanted lizard-fish to get this goblin." He grabbed his sword in both hands and pointed the bloody tip at the closest guard. "Move aside."

The hobgoblins backed down. Jig was small, his weapon was laughable, and any one of the guards could have killed him bare-handed, but they backed down. How did he do it? He didn't boast, he didn't raise his voice, he didn't even try to threaten them. He simply . . . told them the truth.

Jig had defeated the lizard-fish, and Veka as well, and the hobgoblins knew it. They knew what Jig Dragonslayer could do. Jig didn't have to boast. He simply had to remind them who he was. Jig was a Hero.

Two goblins stood outside the goblin lair, and they actually appeared to be standing guard.

"Come with us," said Jig. The guards grinned. Why wouldn't they? Jig had just ordered them to stop working.

Veka could feel the tension the moment she stepped into the lair. The muck pits were all full and burning. Goblins cast wary looks at the entrance until they saw who it was. A pair of young goblins outside the kitchen were strangely quiet as they played Stake the Rat. From the look of it, the female had a three-rat lead.

"Now what?" asked Slash.

Jig raised his battered sword over his head and slammed it three times against the ground. Sparks flew from the steel, and a shard of metal broke away, but it got the goblins' attention.

Jig took a deep breath. "The pixies and the ogres have taken over the lower caverns. Soon they'll be coming after us. I'm betting they'll come through the lake to attack the hobgoblins."

Immediately the goblins began to whisper to one another, setting odds and making wagers. A few goblins gave a tentative cheer. Veka kept her attention on Jig. His face shone with sweat, and his clothes were torn and bloody. His sword arm hung limp at his side, and he kept playing with his right fang. Hardly the picture of a Hero.

Jig swallowed and said, "So we're going to help them."

Silence blanketed the lair, broken only by the occasional cough.

"Help the hobgoblins or the pixies?" someone asked.

"The hobgoblins," Jig said.

"Why?"

Veka could see Jig searching the crowd, trying to pick out the speaker. Not that it mattered. Every goblin was silently asking the same thing.

"Why not let the hobgoblins wear them down, then we can finish off whoever survives?" yelled another goblin. Veka thought it was one of the guards from outside, but she wasn't sure.

Nobody had ever questioned Kralk's orders. Then again, Kralk had never given such bizarre orders.

Veka waited to see what Jig would do. How would he prove himself, bringing the goblins into agreement and obedience?

But Jig simply stood there, looking more and more nervous. If he rubbed that fang anymore, he was going to twist it right out of his jaw. The goblins were starting to whisper among themselves again.

Veka couldn't believe it. Jig didn't know what to do.

Grell's canes rapped the floor as she stepped forward. Her

dry fingers dug into Jig's shoulder, pushing him aside. "You idiots couldn't stop one lone ogre from marching through this place before, and he wasn't even trying to kill you. What are you going to do against an army of 'em? Hobgoblins too, most likely. Every hobgoblin who falls could be enchanted, sent out to fight the goblins. If we help the hobgoblins fight, we might be able to do some damage, but only if you stop asking stupid questions and start listening to what the chief has to say!"

"There's an even better reason," said Braf, coming around on Jig's other side. "If we help the hobgoblins, then every time you see one of those yellow-skinned freaks, you can gloat about how we had to save their worthless hides from the ogres!"

That earned a rousing cheer. Several goblins pointed at Slash, snickering. Others were grinning and nodding to one another.

Slash, on the other hand, was staring at Braf and clenching his fists.

"You should do it because it's Jig's idea." The words slipped out before Veka even realized she had spoken. She almost thought Snixle had taken control of her again, but no . . . the words had come from her. She saw Jig's mouth open in disbelief.

She couldn't even look at him as she stepped forward to address the goblins. "Jig fought an ogre and won, down in Straum's cavern. He killed two pixies. He killed the Necromancer. He killed Straum himself. Not only did he win every one of those battles, he kept his companions alive as well." She sniffed and wiped her nose on the sleeve of her robe. "If Jig says we have to help the hobgoblins, you can bet it's the only way we're going to survive."

"Actually we're probably going to die," Jig whispered. He was still staring at Veka.

"I'm thinking you shouldn't mention that," Grell answered just as softly.

Many of the goblins were already swinging their weapons in anticipation. Veka saw one warrior nearly slice the ear from his neighbor with a crude hand ax. Others had begun to sing "The Song of Jig."

"The strongest warriors will go to the hobgoblins to help fight," Jig shouted. "The rest stay here. Some of you will barricade the lair, and a handful will come with me."

Only Veka was close enough to hear him mutter, "And you're not going to like where we're going."

CHAPTER 13

"No plan survives the first encounter with your enemy, so why bother to make one?"

—Farnok Daggerhand, Goblin Warleader

TWENTY-THREE GOBLINS WAITED OUTSIDE THE doorway as Jig and Slash searched through Kralk's armory, collecting every knife, sword, mace, morningstar, and ax they could find. Anything would do, so long as it was steel.

"Any reason you didn't share these toys with the goblins heading out to the hobgoblin lair?" Slash asked.

"I'm betting they won't be fighting pixies," Jig said. "Not many, at any rate. The pixies will stay in their own world as much as possible. That's where they're strongest. And if I'm right, we're going to need all the help we can get."

He picked up a quiver of steel-tipped arrows. He had also spotted an enormous bow, but he hadn't been able to find a bowstring. Not that he or any other goblin knew how to shoot a bow. And the only crossbow had been disassembled so Slash could use the string in one of his traps. But the arrows were long and heavy enough he might be able to use them as spears, which could be useful against an airborne enemy.

He had to make several attempts to get the leather strap

over his pixie-cursed arm, but once he managed, the quiver fit fairly well. Jig turned his head to search for more weapons, and the end of an arrow poked him in the ear.

Slash laughed as he stooped to pick up a nasty-looking barbed trident.

"Leave that," said Jig. "Leave everything longer than your arm."

"Why?" Slash asked. "You goblins not strong enough for real weapons?" He hefted a thick quarterstaff with iron bands around either end. "This could do some serious damage without drawing much blood, don't you think?"

Jig ignored him. Carrying weapons under his arm, he stepped through the doorway, being careful not to trigger Slash's traps. Several knives clanged onto the ground. Jig dumped the rest in a pile.

"Take whatever you can carry, but don't overload yourself," Jig said. He studied the goblins closely as they scrambled to arm themselves. He hadn't tried to pick and choose who would accompany him. Instead he had let the goblins choose for him when he ordered the strongest warriors to help the hobgoblins.

As a result, Jig had been left with the weakest goblins in the lair: the scrawny, thin-limbed goblins who slunk into the shadows and hid from danger. The ones who survived through thievery and betrayal rather than facing their enemies head-on. The ones who had to be twice as cunning as the rest of the lair just to survive. These were the goblins Jig wanted.

Braf and Slash towered over the others. Even Jig didn't feel like such a runt among this crowd. Most of the weapons had disappeared, and the goblins eyed one another warily as they waited for Jig to speak. However, the bulk of their suspicion was reserved for Jig himself.

Jig kept his back to the wall. They weren't going to like this. He thought about Farnax and Pynne, remembering their reactions to the cramped tunnels of the mountain. If the other pixies felt the same way, they wouldn't stay in Straum's cave. No, if Jig was right, there was only one place they would go.

"The pixie queen sent a handful of pixies into our world to prepare the way," he said. "They killed or enslaved most of the ogres, but instead of moving up into the Necromancer's tunnels, they burrowed through the rock until they reached the bottomless pit, where they've been hunting and destroying the giant bats."

To a goblin, a cave was the safest place to hide, with solid stone protecting you on all sides. For pixies, safety lay in the open. They would choose a place where they could fly, where they could ride the wind, and where any attacker would face an enormous disadvantage.

"They're building their lair in the bottomless pit," Jig said. "That's where they'll bring the queen. If we can get there before they do, we might be able to ambush them."

As he had expected, his own companions were first to understand the implications. Unless they wanted to make their way through the Necromancer's maze and a possible ogre attack, there was only one way to get back to the bottomless pit.

"I still smell like goblin filth," Slash shouted. "Now you expect me to climb back down through—"

"No, I don't," Jig said. He had counted on Slash being the first one to complain. "This is a goblin mission. I'll understand if you prefer to stay behind, where it's safer."

"I'll go!" Braf yelled. "The hobgoblin might be a coward, but I'm—"

"Who are you calling coward, rat-eater?" Slash demanded, shoving goblins aside as he advanced on Braf.

Jig's plan had worked. Now all he had to do was keep them from killing one another.

"I'll go too." Veka's flat voice momentarily drew the attention away from Slash and Braf.

"Why, so you can get yourself pixie-charmed again?" Slash asked.

"You were enchanted too," Braf pointed out.

Grell hit them both, one with each cane. Braf took it on the shoulder, and Slash received a sharp smack on the knee. Grell staggered forward a few steps before recovering her balance. Then, to Jig's surprise, she whacked him on the arm as well. It was his sword arm, and the flesh was so numb he barely felt it.

"Stop standing there with your mouth hanging open," Grell snapped. "You're chief, remember? Try to act like it."

Jig nodded. "We're going to climb down through the garbage, to a tunnel that will take us to the bottomless pit." He glanced at Braf and Slash. "You two stay in the back. Make sure nobody tries to sneak away. You too," he added, nodding at Grell.

Grell raised both eyebrows but said nothing as Jig turned to lead the goblins toward the waste pit. More than pixies or the bottomless pit, this was the part of his plan he had been dreading. But it had to be done.

He stroked Smudge, perched comfortably on his left shoulder. Climbing down the pit was too dangerous . . . too vulnerable. It wasn't a question of whether one of the goblins would try to kill him. It was simply a matter of when.

He strained to keep his sword from dragging along the ground. His good ear twisted back as he listened for every whisper, every footstep. What was taking them so long? They didn't actually believe everything Veka had said about Jig being so dangerous and heroic, did they?

There it was. A slight change in footfalls. One set drawing nearer, while the others pulled back, giving the chosen goblin room to make his or her move. Smudge crept closer to Jig's neck, warmer, but not yet hot enough to burn.

Jig kept walking. His timing would have to be perfect. What were they waiting for? Working up the nerve to attack? His back was turned. How hard could it be?

There, a quick indrawn breath. At the same time, Smudge's feet seared Jig's skin. Jig lunged forward, hunching his head and shoulders as he grabbed his sword arm with his free hand and spun, hoisting the blade into the path of his would-be killer.

His attacker slammed onto the broken sword, knocking them both down. Jig found himself staring into the face of Relka, one of Golaka's kitchen assistants. The knife in her hand clattered to the ground.

Jig kicked her off of his sword. His shoulder felt as though someone had ground metal shavings into the socket.

Relka wasn't dead. She clutched her bleeding stomach and scooted back, her huge eyes never leaving Jig's sword.

"Stay here," Jig said. "Have Golaka bandage you up. If you're still alive when we get back, I'll heal you then. Assuming we get back."

He turned his back on Relka, trying not to feel too bad as she crawled away. He hoped she would survive. She made the best snake egg omelettes. But her attack had done what Jig hoped. The other goblins looked terrified.

Jig shook his head. *It wasn't hard to guess one of them would try to kill me.*

Maybe, said Shadowstar. *But think about what they saw. You just took out a potential assassin without even looking. They won't try to stab you in the back again any time soon.*

No, Jig agreed glumly. He had never imagined he would feel sympathy for Kralk. *Next time, they'll try something sneakier.*

Climbing up through the waste pit had been bad enough. Climbing down, leading a group of twenty-plus goblins and one grumbling hobgoblin was far worse. Only the cramped confines of the pit, which kept them all moving one at a time, prevented bloodshed. Even so, goblins were constantly stepping on one another's hands, or dislodging dirt and worse onto the ones below.

Jig had ordered several goblins to carry muck lanterns. As an unexpected bonus, the light and heat seemed to frighten off the tendriled slugs that had stung Jig before. Unfortunately, the goblins kept accidentally igniting the waste that clung to the sides of the pit.

Even with several ropes anchored in the goblin lair, it was a miracle nobody had fallen.

Jig relaxed his grip and let himself drop a bit, away from the bulk of the group. His sword tip caught a rock, jamming his arm and nearly breaking his elbow before he managed to stop. To make things worse, his spectacles kept sliding down his nose. He tried to use his shoulder to scoot them into position, but they immediately slid back down his sweaty face.

"How many ogres and pixies do you think we'll get to kill?" Braf asked, nearly falling as he shoved past another goblin to catch up with Jig.

"None if you keep talking so loudly," Jig said. The noise shouldn't give them away, not this far from the pit, but better to silence Braf now. They should be about halfway down by now, roughly level with the Necromancer's maze.

Braf bit his lip and nodded.

Jig frowned as he studied the other goblin. "You didn't get a weapon?"

Braf tried to shrug, and ended up hoisting his body higher on the rope. "I stocked up on rocks instead. If we're going to fight pixies at the pit, I thought we'd want some kind of ranged weapon."

Jig hesitated. "You thought of that yourself?"

"No," Braf said quickly. A strange, frightened expression flashed across his face, then disappeared again. "Grell did. She told me I'd better stick to rocks, or else I'd hurt myself." He scrunched up his forehead. "Or did she say *she'd* hurt me?"

Jig climbed a bit lower, thinking hard. "Braf, back when I was trying to get the goblins to help the hobgoblins, you told them they should do it because we'd be able to gloat. What made you say that?"

"Because it's true!"

Maybe, but it had also been the perfect thing to say, the pebble that had started a rock slide, bringing the lair around to Jig's plan. Just as Braf had done later, outside Kralk's quarters, when he mocked Slash. Once again Braf had helped to persuade the goblins to do exactly what Jig wanted them to do.

Jig squinted up through sweat-smeared lenses, and in that instant, he saw it. Braf was studying Jig . . . trying to figure out whether Jig had guessed his secret? The expression vanished as soon as Jig noticed, but it was too late.

"You're not as dumb as you pretend to be, are you?" Jig whispered.

Braf's eyes narrowed. Suddenly Jig was very aware of exactly how big and strong Braf was. And Jig's sword was pointed down toward his feet, with no easy way to lift it here in the cramped confines of the pit.

"Maybe," Braf said, his voice as quiet as Jig's.

They were still at least a body's length ahead of the next closest goblin. Higher up Jig could hear Grell cursing and trying to rearrange her canes. Slash was swearing right back, threatening to cut the rope that held her harness. Others still stood around up top, waiting to follow.

Jig turned his attention back to Braf. "Then why—"

"You'd do the same thing if you were me."

Jig stared, not understanding.

"How does a goblin captain take command of his group?" Braf asked.

"The same way a goblin becomes chief. Kill the former captain, along with anyone else who opposes you."

"Look at me, Jig. Big, strong, and threatening. If you're . . . well, someone like you, you'll see me as a bully, and you'll try to kill me in my sleep. If you're a warrior, you'll see me as competition. If you're a captain, you see me as a threat. If you don't kill me outright, you'll send me out to fight tunnel cats or ogres or order me to march into a hobgoblin trap. You think it's coincidence there are no old goblin warriors?"

Slowly, Jig shook his head.

"So I play dumb. I drop my weapon. I let others play their stupid tricks." He grimaced and rubbed his nose. "I didn't expect to get a fang punched up my nose, but the point is, if I'm dumb, I'm not a threat. The teasing and the jokes are annoying but better than the alternative. Oh, and a carrion-worm is about to crawl onto your hand."

Jig yanked his hand away from the wall, which knocked his back and shoulder into the rough stone. The pale, segmented worm was almost as big as his arm. Jig waited until the worm squirmed away, dropping into the darkness with a bit of charred meat and bone clutched in its black pincers.

"So why do you let Grell hit you all the time?" Jig asked.

Braf laughed. "Grell knows what I'm doing. She helps me. I can pretend to be stupid, and she stops me before I do anything too dangerous." He gave Jig a sheepish smile. "It's kind of fun."

"Fun?"

"Sure. You're always so uptight, so afraid of messing everything up. With me, people expect it." His smile faded.

"Naturally, if you tell anyone, I'll strip the skin from your body and feed it to the worms."

"Naturally," said Jig.

Braf grinned. "Hey, when did it get so cold down here?"

Sweating and warm from climbing, Jig hadn't really noticed, but Braf was right. The stone was cool to the touch, and the air below . . . "Can someone lower one of those lanterns?"

A flare of heat from Smudge warned him just in time. Jig twisted, pressing himself to one side as a burning muck lantern tumbled past, splattering green flames as it went. Braf swore and flicked a bit of muck from his arm. Overhead, goblins yelled and cried out in pain as they tried to pat themselves out. Then the goblin who had dropped the lantern squealed as his fellows pummeled him for his mistake.

Still, it did what Jig needed. The droplets of burning muck illuminated a silver fog creeping slowly up the pit below.

"Where are we?" The words echoed through the abandoned cavern.

Jig wasn't sure who had asked the question. He could feel the heat of the goblins gathered behind him. He took a few steps to the side, trying to get his back to the wall. He probably didn't need to worry. These goblins hadn't seen the pixies' world yet, and they were too shaken to think about killing him . . . at least for the moment.

The rippling texture of the obsidian combined with the lead-colored frost created the illusion of being surrounded by molten metal. The light of their lanterns had taken on the same bronze tinge he remembered from his excursion into Straum's cavern.

Shadowstar? Can you hear me?

Silence. The pixies' world was expanding much faster than he had expected. That couldn't be good.

Jig looked around, and for one panicked moment he wasn't sure which tunnel led out to the pit. Everything was so different with the fog and the snow. They had come from the right, hadn't they? Rubbing his fang, he began following the cavern wall. His sword dragged lines through the frost beside him.

"This looks a bit like our lair," Braf commented.

Jig glanced around. Braf was right. The cavern was larger, but he could easily imagine goblins or hobgoblins making a home of this place. He hadn't seen much the last time he was here, being too eager to escape, but now he looked more closely. Bits of rotted rope still circled one of the obsidian pillars, far too old to have been left by the ogres. When they reached the tunnel, Jig spotted a rusted hinge hanging from a scrap of wood beside the opening. He tried to pry it free, and the wood crumbled in his hand.

Jig had never heard of goblins living this far down, but clearly someone used to inhabit this cavern. Their own lair might look like this one day, if they failed to stop the pixies.

"Keep your weapons ready," Jig said as he stepped into the tunnel. "The last time we were here, we faced ogres and pixies both."

"And rock serpents," Braf piped up. "Don't forget about them!"

The response from the other goblins was less than enthusiastic. Jig saw several glance longingly into the cavern, no doubt wondering if they would be better off climbing back through the garbage. Veka remained at the rear of the group. She hadn't spoken at all since they left the goblin lair. He still wasn't sure bringing her along was such a great idea, but so far she seemed safe enough, if a bit subdued.

"Come on," Jig said, hurrying into the tunnel.

They passed a mass of carrion-worms, a knee-high mound of the squirming creatures huddled together to one side of the tunnel. They seemed to be climbing over one another, all trying to get to the top of the pile.

"They're freezing to death," Grell said. "They pile together for warmth. We do something similar with the babies, tossing them all into a single crib when the air gets too chilly." She kept her arms close to her chest, and she kept stamping her feet. She was wearing an old pair of sandals, and her toes had already begun to turn a paler shade of blue.

The cold appeared to be even harder on the rock serpents. Jig saw several snakes coiled into tight spirals for warmth. They weren't dead—one snake still struck out when a goblin poked it with his sword—but the snake's reflexes were so slow the goblin actually survived the attack. For all practical purposes, the tunnel was unguarded.

"Smother the lanterns," Jig whispered. As the flames died, he began to make out the open space at the end of the tunnel. A long stiff shape lay on the ground near the edge: Veka's staff, right where it had fallen when Slash kicked her in the head. Jig glanced back. Veka had seen it too. She stepped past him, her eyes never leaving the staff. Several of the beads and cords broke free as she pried the staff up, leaving a perfect impression of the wood in the frost and ice. Jig wrapped his good hand around the handle of his sword, wondering if Veka was about to try something heroic again. But she seemed content to stand there staring at the staff.

Jig edged around her, wondering if the pixies had damaged her brain. Some of the other goblins were pointing and whispering. Jig heard muffled laughter. They hadn't seen what Veka could do, back at the lake. He held his breath, but Veka appeared deaf to their jokes.

Praying it stayed that way, Jig crept to the edge of the tunnel. Wind blew snow and dirt into his face. The buzzing of wings warned him, but even so, when he looked out into the pit and saw the swarm of pixies darting through the darkness, he found himself wondering if he should just throw himself over the edge. At least that way he might hit one on the way down.

They had changed the pit itself. Shimmering silver bubbles, each one larger than Jig himself, covered the walls. In most places, the bubbles pressed against each other, their sides flattening where they touched. In one spot the bubbles were two or three layers thick.

As Jig watched, a pair of green pixies flew out to hover near a bare patch of rock. These were smaller than the pixies Jig had seen before, and they had only two wings, not four. Their lights faded somewhat as they touched the stone. When they drew back their hands, a thin transparent bubble followed. Ripples of color spread across the bubble's surface as it grew. The pixies floated, motionless except for the blur of their wings, as the bubble grew. When it was as large as the others, they dropped away. The color continued to spread across the bubble's surface, rings bouncing back and forth before gradually fading to a more uniform silver.

One of the green pixies pressed her hand against the bubble. Her hand disappeared, and the pixie squeezed through the surface and disappeared inside the silver shell. Her companion floated back, allowing the wind to carry him up until he reached another patch of bare rock.

"What is it?" Braf asked.

Jig took a deep breath. "They're building a hive."

The other goblins had crept up behind Jig, straining to see into the pit. A younger goblin, Grop, was leaning so far out that his shadow was visible on the roof of the tunnel. Jig grabbed him by the hair and yanked him back.

"How are we supposed to fight that?" Grop asked, rubbing his head.

"Quiet," Jig snapped. He didn't think anyone could hear them over the wind, but he wasn't about to take any chances. He lay down in the frost and peered up, toward the old bridge connecting the Necromancer's tunnels. A handful of pixies buzzed around the bridge. Darker shapes resolved into ogre warriors as a pixie flew past. Wonderful.

"It gets worse," Veka said.

Jig didn't even blink. "Of course it does."

She pointed down to the thickest cluster of bubbles, down where the pixie tunnel emerged from Straum's cavern. "The queen is down there."

"Are you sure?"

Veka nodded. "It's hard to describe. I can feel their magic, like a wind."

"Do you think maybe, just maybe, that could be the wind?" Slash said.

Veka ignored him. "It's like she's sucking the magic into herself and drawing the rest of the pixies to her. Not physically, but their magic, their minds, everything about them revolves around the queen."

Jig adjusted his spectacles. He thought he saw a spot of pure white light below, but it was hard to be sure. What had Pynne said? *None can look upon a pixie queen without loving her*.

Either that light wasn't the queen, or Jig was too far away to be affected. The only thing he felt was sheer, gut-churning fear.

"We should go back," said Grop. "We can help the others barricade the lair and—"

"And what?" asked Jig. The pixies were moving too quickly. Look what they had accomplished in a single day. "Why didn't they leave guards in this tunnel?"

"This crack isn't easy to see from out there," said Veka. "The overhang makes it look like part of the rock. The pixies aren't telepathic. If you killed the only two who found the tunnel, they might not know about it yet. And Snixle . . . he didn't tell anyone about me and Slash."

"Lucky us," Slash muttered.

Jig peeked into the pit again, trying to see how high the pixie's world reached. Only the occasional spark marked the expanding border between their world and his own, but that border appeared to be well past the Necromancer's old bridge. "They needed weeks to take over Straum's cavern," Jig whispered. At this rate their world would overtake the goblin lair within a day at most.

"We need to cut off the source of their magic," said Veka.

"I know that," Jig snapped. "I thought we could destroy their gateway after we killed the queen and eradicated her army of pixies. And then I figured I'd resurrect Straum the dragon and use his breath to toast my breakfast rats."

He closed his eyes, trying to calm himself. Why worry about future battles when he probably wouldn't survive this one?

"Are you sure we shouldn't go back?" asked another of the goblins, Var.

Jig shook his head. They were spreading too quickly. If he and the others left, that hive would fill the pit by the time they returned. "The pixies are like insects," he said. Magical bugs with ogre slaves and enough magic to conquer the whole mountain, but bugs nonetheless. "What do you do when you find wasps building a nest in the lair?"

"Burn it," said Var.

"Knock it down and use a stick to hide it in Captain Kollock's chamber pot," muttered Grop.

Jig grinned despite his fear, wishing he had thought to try that. "Everything the pixies do, they do for their queen. We attack the nest, kill the queen, and their whole purpose for coming here is gone."

Grell scratched her ear. "You know, I've seen wasps get pretty riled up when someone pokes their nest. Even if we manage to kill the queen, we're still going to have an army of angry pixies after our hides."

"We'll have that anyway," Jig said. He was trying very hard not to count the number of bubbles. How long would it take them to produce a pixie for every chamber in that nest? If pixies reproduced as quickly as they did everything else . . .

"Jig's right." Veka stepped away from the others, her staff clutched tightly in both hands. "As long as the queen lives, every pixie you see will fight to the death. With her gone, they might be willing to negotiate." Her eyes widened, as if she were surprised at the words coming from her own mouth. "Like Jig did with the hobgoblins."

"Or they might kill us all for revenge," said Slash.

Veka shook her head. She closed her eyes, and said, "The climax of the Hero's journey is the battle through death. No reasonable person could hope to survive this final conflict, but the true Hero shall discover a way." Her smile was wistful, almost sad. "This is that battle, and Jig will get you through it."

Grell shrugged. "Only one way to find out."

Before Jig could think up something inspirational to say, Veka moved closer. Jig started to back away, but she reached out and tapped his sword arm with her staff.

"What are you— " Jig stopped in midprotest as the leather cords on his arm began to loosen. The ends slipped from his shoulder. "You mean you could have done that the whole time?"

"I'm sorry," Veka whispered. "I didn't . . . I couldn't bring myself to try any magic until now. I should have, but— " She swallowed. "The spell is straightforward, even easier than controlling the lizard-fish. Just a simple command to the residual life in the leather."

The sword dropped to the ground. Jig winced and glanced

out at the pit, but the pixies didn't appear to have noticed the sound. His fingers were still molded to the shape of the hilt, and deep wrinkles marked his arm. The flesh was so pale it was almost white, with dark lines and bruises where the skin had pinched and folded over itself. "So why didn't you—"

That was as far as he got, and then the blood began to flow through his veins again. Jig clamped his jaw, biting back a high-pitched squeal as he fell back. With every heartbeat, a thousand hammers smashed the bones of his arm and hand. Tunnel cats chewed the joints from the inside out, and the skin was molten lead.

Jig stared at the frosted rock overhead until tears blurred the patterns into a field of gray. If he could have reached his sword, he would have cut off his own arm at the shoulder to stop the pain. *Shadowstar?*

The god couldn't hear him, not down here. He felt fingers prying at his jaw, shoving something between his teeth: one of Grell's sugar-knots, laced with klak beer. He bit down on the sugar-knot so hard his teeth crushed the candy inside.

"Give him a little time." Grell's voice sounded as if it were coming from the far end of a tunnel.

Easy for her to say. His arm felt as if it had swollen to triple its normal size, but when he opened his eyes, he found he was mistaken. It was only double.

Gradually the pain began to ebb a bit, becoming a deep prickly feeling that began at the skin and penetrated all the way to the marrow. Jig grabbed his sword with his left hand and used it like one of Grell's canes to push himself to his feet.

"See, I told you he'd be fine," said Grell. "So tell us how you plan to get through this battle, oh heroic one?"

Jig scowled and sucked on the crushed remains of his sugar-knot. He had been wondering the exact same thing. He could tell the other goblins weren't happy about the situation. Goblins weren't subtle when it came to expressing displeasure. Weapons drawn, they were moving into a rough circle, trapping Jig between the edge of the pit and a lot of sharp steel.

Jig raised his sword. His right arm was still useless, but so was the sword, really. The blade had lost another chip from the end. Old blood stained part of the hilt blue. The hilt itself was bare wood, held in place only by the dinged, worn pommel. A long string of leather dangled down to the floor. The nicked, dented edges of the blade would have a hard time cutting even the skin of a child. Unfortunately, it was all he had.

The goblins stopped. "Well?" asked one.

"Well what?"

"When do we attack?"

They weren't preparing to kill him. They were preparing to kill pixies. They . . . they were getting ready to follow him into battle. To follow *him*!

He turned back to the pit, trying to flex his arm. His hand and wrist twitched a bit. He spotted Braf watching him. Now that Jig knew what to look for, he saw past the slack-jawed expression to the way Braf's eyes shifted from Jig to the other goblins to the pit and back, watching for threats from either side.

"Braf, what's the best way to stir up a big wasp hive?" he asked.

Braf grinned and fished a rock out of his trousers.

"How many rocks are you carrying down there?" Jig asked with a grimace.

"Don't ask. I'm fine as long as I don't sit down." He slipped past Jig and hefted the rock. "Who do you want me to hit first?"

Jig pointed to a bubble on the far side of the pit. "No, wait." Why bother throwing rocks when Veka could use her magic to shoot them across—

He glanced around, searching the shadows. Veka was gone. So was Slash.

"What is it?" asked Grell.

"Nothing." If he pointed out that two of their number had already slipped away, who knew how many would follow? "Wait for my signal to throw. The rest of you, back into the darkness. We don't want to reveal our numbers yet. Braf might be able to hit two or three pixies before they figure out where the rocks are coming from. They'll send a few up to investigate, and we'll draw them into the tunnel. They hate it in here, and they can't maneuver as well."

He turned back to Braf, wishing he could talk to Tymalous Shadowstar about this plan. Annoying and condescending the god might be, but he had helped Jig through a few messes in the past. Not to mention that Shadowstar would have been able to help him heal any injuries the goblins might sustain . . . starting with Jig's arm, which felt like one enormous blister.

On the other hand, at least this way Shadowstar wouldn't be around to make snide comments if they failed. Jig raised his sword and backed into the shadows. "Do it."

CHAPTER 14

"The gods mark their favorites. I was born with a birthmark in the shape of a flying dragon, and I became the mightiest beastlord in history. My sister wasn't so lucky. Her birthmark looked like a lopsided bowl of raisin pudding."

—Theodora of June, Beastmaster of the Elkonian Isles
From *The Path of the Hero (Wizard's ed.)*

VEKA HURRIED THROUGH THE DARKNESS, PULLing her cloak tight with one hand for warmth. She had ripped the remaining beads and bones from her staff to stop them from rattling, but she couldn't quite bring herself to leave the staff itself. The thick wood was her best weapon, and who knew what creatures she might encounter on the way to Straum's lair? She needed the staff for defense, that was all. It had nothing to do with her shattered dreams of wizardry. Nothing at all.

She slowed, searching for the crack where she had descended to the pixies' cavern. She poked her staff at the rock as she went. Several times she nearly slipped on the frost and ice. Stupid pixies. No wonder they flew everywhere. Who could walk on all this ice?

Her cloak helped against the cold, but it did nothing to block the sensation of alien magic that permeated the air like the stench of a dead hobgoblin. The pixies' magic was like a living wind, cutting right through her clothes to chill her skin. The pixies flew upon that magic just as much as they did the air, riding its currents and drawing power through themselves, replenishing their strength with every breath. Magic was as much a part of their diet as food and drink.

Veka could barely grasp that power long enough to channel it into a spell.

But she had done it before. Snixle had shown her the way. How many times had he taken control of her body, dictating her gestures as he struggled to master the magic of her world? Those gestures had made little sense in the beginning, but she had learned. Pixie magic was less a matter of control and more about suggestion. The slightest whisper was enough to shape that magic. Grasp too hard, and it crumbled in your fingers. But she could do it

If she could figure out how to use their magic, the pixies could do the same. That was the only explanation, the only way their world could have begun to grow so quickly. The pixies had found a way to tap into this world's magic to feed the expansion of their own.

The only one who could have helped them do that was Snixle, and the only one he could have learned from was Veka.

This was her fault.

Muttered curses interrupted her thoughts. The sound came from behind her. She raised her staff and sniffed the air. "Slash?"

She heard him hurrying toward her. "I hate that name, you know."

"What are you doing here?"

"I saw you slipping away from the others."

Her shoulders slumped. "So you came to stop me from running away like a coward?"

Slash snorted. "I came to join you. If you really thought Jig had any chance at all, you would have stayed. No, the only thing that crazy runt is going to do is get himself and the rest of his little band slaughtered."

Veka shook her head, forgetting he couldn't see her. Jig would survive. He might even keep a few of the others alive too. Her lip trembled. How did he do it? He had magic, but hers had been stronger when they fought. She was bigger, stronger, and younger, but Jig had beaten her.

Jig had been the Hero all along, not Veka. She was simply another of Jig's trials, an obstacle to be overcome and forgotten. She wondered if she would even rate a line in Jig's next song.

"I'm going to destroy the gateway from the pixies' world," Veka whispered.

"My mistake. For a moment there I forgot that *all* goblins were crazy."

"Most of the pixies will be with the queen. She's more important than anything." Though Veka doubted they would be foolish enough to leave the portal completely unguarded. She didn't know if she would find pixies at Straum's cave, but she would not enter unchallenged. Perhaps she would have to face something like the multiheaded snake creature the pink pixie created in the tunnels, only without that construct's intestinal design flaw.

She shivered as she thought about it. Before, she would have been eager to face such a challenge, but that was when she had believed herself the Hero. Now she was afraid, and she hated it.

She turned her attention back to the rock, searching for the opening. How far had she run when she fled from Jig and the ogres? She hadn't bothered to count her steps or memorize every twist and turn, and her struggle to control her own body had further confused her sense of distance. She stopped, fighting despair. Was she even on the right side of the tunnel?

With one hand, she tried to conjure up a light, but without a source she could do nothing. Pixie magic swirled around her fingers, taunting her with her own impotence.

"So you have a way to sneak down into Straum's lair?" Slash asked.

"There's a crevasse, where water runs down through the rock. Snixle brought me down, before I –" She bit her lip.

"Before you came back to murder some hobgoblins?"

Veka backed away.

"That's right, I was under the pixie's spell too, remember?" Slash asked. "But I didn't march into the goblin lair and start slaughtering rat-eaters. Nobody forced me to do anything. You *wanted* to kill those hobgoblins."

Veka tried to remember if Slash had taken any weapons from Kralk's old chambers. He had Braf's broken hook-tooth, if nothing else. And in the darkness blood wouldn't bother him one bit.

"I didn't care about the hobgoblins," she whispered. Let him kill her, if that was what he wanted. "I wanted to fight Jig."

"Why?"

She started to repeat the reasons she had given to Snixle, the reasons she had repeated to herself. Because Jig had treated her like a child when she came asking for help. Because Jig would get the goblins killed, and Veka could save them. Because it was the only way.

No. Part of being a Hero was making your own way, like Jig was doing.

"I wanted to prove I was better than he was." She tried again to create a light, but as before, nothing happened. "Better than all of them."

"Oh." Slash stepped past her. "Well come on, where is it?"

Veka wiped her nose on her sleeve. "Where is what?"

"This secret runoff of yours."

"I don't understand. You're not going to kill me?"

He snorted. "With enslaved ogres going after the hobgoblins up above, and Jig fighting the bulk of the pixies down here, I'm starting to think you've got the best idea. Straum's cavern might be the safest place in this whole cursed mountain." His voice changed, becoming quieter. "It's not like I'd be much use in battle anyway."

The very first casualty would leave him passed out on the ground. For the first time Veka wondered what it had been like for him, a hobgoblin warrior who couldn't bear the sight of blood.

"This way, I think," she said. She raised her ears, listening for the sound of water, but either they weren't close enough to hear it, or else the water had frozen in the cold. "Tap your weapon along the other side of the tunnel, near the bottom. Let me know if you find it."

Slash sighed as he began rapping his hook-tooth against the rock. "Just promise me we won't have to climb through any more garbage."

Veka found the crack eventually. The water had indeed frozen, turning the rocks even more treacherous. The algae and slime were dying, but enough life remained for her to use them to help control her descent. She moved faster than before, thinking about Jig and the other goblins.

Her staff she simply dropped. It clattered down a short distance before getting stuck. She kicked it again, knocking the end loose so it fell a bit more. Above her head Slash yelped as his feet slipped. Like Veka's staff, he fell only a short way before catching himself on the rock. She couldn't hear everything he said under his breath, but she caught her name, along with the phrase ". . . grind her into tunnel cat kibble."

Though she never would have admitted it, especially to Slash, she felt better with the hobgoblin along.

"There," she whispered. Below her feet, silver light outlined a jagged opening. Her staff had dropped through and now lay in the snow and ice below.

She squinted, waiting for her eyes to adjust. She could probably use pixie magic to levitate herself down. Her backside was still bruised from the last time.

Slash made the point moot, losing his grip and falling hard enough to knock her free. With frozen, dying algae still twined around her hand, she slipped into the open air and landed, once again, on her behind. This time Slash came with her. His legs slammed into her stomach, knocking the wind from her lungs.

"Graceful, as always," he said, resting his head in the snow.

The top of the cavern appeared to be much lower than before. If she held one end of her staff, she would be able to tap the rock overhead. She rolled onto her side, wincing as the movement revealed new bruises on her elbow and shoulder. "We're here."

Here was an enormous slab of silver ice. The top of the

cavern wasn't low at all. Instead the ice lifted them to the height of the trees. Veka could see withered treetops poking through various spots. The slab itself had cracked and broken in places, leaving the surface slightly tilted. Pushing herself to her knees, Veka could feel her body starting to slide to the right, away from the crack. She grabbed her staff and jabbed the end against the ice for balance.

The ice directly beneath the opening overhead was smooth, almost like a puddle. Water must have continued to drip down after the cavern froze. She wiped her hand on her robe, leaving a dark, damp algae stain.

"Which way?" asked Slash.

Fog and snow swirled through the air, and the ice made every direction the same. She closed her eyes, concentrating on the flow of the magic. Down here it was strong enough to make her feel like she was standing in the center of a river. A fast river, deep enough to cover her head and strong enough so she nearly fell.

Veka pointed toward the source of the flow. That should be the gateway, clear on the far side of the cavern. Tightening her cloak, she took one step, lost her footing, and began to slide down the ice. She tried to grab a tuft of pine tree in passing, but the brown branch snapped off in her hand, and then she was falling. Again.

This time snow cushioned her landing. She found herself in a canyon of ice, three times as tall as any ogre. The gap was barely wide enough for her to fit. The fog was thickest here, curling up from the snow and the icy walls.

She could hear Slash laughing as he made his way after her. She closed her eyes again, tapping into the magic to cast a quick levitation spell, just enough to nudge the hobgoblin behind the knees. Moments later Slash plunged into the snow beside her, cursing.

The ice had a copper, cloudy hue when viewed from down here. Veka imagined a huge slab covering the entire cavern, then fragmenting into uneven blocks like these. Was this what the pixie world was like, a world of ice and fog and cold? That would explain their glow at least. It would be the only way for them to find one another.

"This way," she said. The canyon didn't go in precisely the right direction, but she could always levitate them out and over the ice. For now though, staying down here kept them out of sight of any pixies who might have stayed behind.

Then again, trying to cross the ice above offered the possibility of sending Slash for another spill.

Reluctantly, she decided to stick with the canyon. The ice walls closed in on them before they had walked very far, but the slab on the right tilted upward enough for them to crawl beneath the edge. Veka sighed and tightened her robe, then dropped to her knees. A short distance away, she could see a triangle of light from the far side of the slab. It should be a simple matter to scoot beneath it and continue along the other side. Keeping her staff in one hand, she began to crawl past a thick tree trunk that rose right through the ice.

She had only gone a short distance when Slash seized her ankle. Veka yelped and twisted, and Slash slammed into the ice above them.

"Sorry," Veka said. A part of her was delighted at how easily she had used magic to defend herself, but her heart was still pounding too hard to truly enjoy it.

Slash's hands and knees dug long gouges through the flattened, muddy earth as he tried to break free, but his body remained pinned to the ice overhead. After a few more undignified attempts to pull himself down, he asked, "Would you mind?"

She dropped him.

"Stupid goblin witch," Slash muttered. Silver clouds floated from his mouth as he spoke. "I ought to let you keep going for that."

Veka hesitated. "What do you mean?"

"Look at the ground," Slash said. "Dead and dying grass, broken splinters that used to be saplings, a few stray vines, and muddy ice overhead. Except for that spot right in front of you."

Veka stared, trying to understand. "So there's a puddle. Do you think it might have something to do with all the ice?"

"Do you see any other puddles? It's a trap. Look at the ice."

Most of the ice was rough and muddy, full of stones and twigs and at least one buck-toothed squirrel still clutching a nut in his claws. He had probably frozen to death and been trapped in the swift-forming ice. If she hadn't been in such a hurry, she would have chipped him free to see if the meat was still good.

Directly in front of her, however, the ice was clear and clean. A few bronze-colored vines crept around the edges, defining a roughly circular patch. Clusters of swollen globules dangled from the vines by knifelike leaves. Within the clear patch, long needles of ice hung like the malachite formations back at the lizard-fish lake. She could see water dripping from the ends. They looked a bit like the ice spikes she had seen in front of Straum's lair, but these were thinner, and she saw no sign of the wormlike creatures she remembered. As she watched, a drop of water fell from one of the spikes. "What is it?"

Slash reached into one of the pouches on his belt and pulled out several metal objects no wider than his thumb. Each one had four barbed spikes protruding from the center.

"Goblin prickers," he explained, grinning. "You scatter them on the ground and wait for some dumb goblin to run past. If you're feeling really nasty, you do it near a tunnel cat lair. The goblin steps on the pricker. His scream wakes up the cats. The cats smell the blood, and we sit back and make wagers on how far the goblin will be able to limp before the cats get him."

He crawled past her and tossed one of the goblin prickers into the puddle. The instant it hit the water, the ice above exploded. A coiled snake of gold fire streaked to the ground and seized the goblin pricker in its mouth.

The snake was fairly small, about the size of the average carrion-worm. Veka could see several sets of rudimentary wings pressed flat against its burning scales. The snake wasn't truly on fire, she saw. Like the pixies, it gave off a great deal of heat, light, and sparks. Those sparks brightened, turning almost white as the snake realized what it had caught. Water splashed as the snake flailed its head, trying to rid itself of the goblin pricker. One of the barbs had stuck in its lower jaw. Smoke trailed from the snake's mouth.

"I guess they aren't too fond of steel either," Slash said.

Eventually the snake dislocated its own jaw, then used its fangs to rip the goblin pricker free. With its wings folded back like armor, it shot up into the ice and disappeared.

Slash scooted ahead to reclaim his goblin pricker. "I doubt the pixies did this. The labor-to-victim ratio is all wrong: too much work for too few victims. This is a natural trap, probably how that thing hunts for food. Lizard-fish do something similar. They'll hide in the sand beneath the water, waving their spines until some stupid cave fish swims over to take a nibble."

Veka rolled onto her back, trying to see where the snake had gone. How many more might there be? Snakes could be the least of the predators. She squinted, imagining she could see faint lines of light wiggling through the hazy silver ice.

Her back scraped the damp ice overhead as she turned around. "We need to get out of here. We'll go over the ice and hope they don't spot us. That will be faster anyway."

Slash was still muttering about goblin indecisiveness as he followed her out from beneath the ice. When they reached the canyon, Veka wiped damp, muddy hair from her face and stared at the sky.

"How many of those goblin pricks do you have?" she asked.

"Goblin *prickers*," Slash said. "Eight, though one is still a little slimy from that snake. Poor fellow."

Veka stared, but he appeared serious. He really felt sorry for the snake that would have killed them. Hobgoblins were weird. "Give them to me."

He handed her a small jingling pouch. She pulled out one of the goblin prickers and tried to levitate it. Almost immediately the metal grew so hot she had to fling it away. The pricker bounced off the ice and dropped to the ground, completely unaffected by her spell.

"Interesting strategy," said Slash. "How exactly is this going to get us to Straum's cave?"

"Shut up." While she waited for the first goblin pricker to cool, she pulled out another and examined it more closely. The whole thing was steel, rusted a bit toward the center, but gleaming brightly at the points. She drove one of the goblin pricker's barbs deep into the wood of her staff, then concentrated.

The staff began to float. She could feel heat coming from the metal, but as long as she focused her spell on the wood, she could control it. "Help me find more wood. Small pieces, but solid enough to hold a goblin pricker without splitting."

After a bit of scrounging, they gathered enough broken branches for all eight prickers. She embedded each one into a chunk of wood. The last goblin pricker ripped a long splinter from her staff when she pulled it free. She grimaced and rubbed the wood. She would have to sand that out with a rock later, assuming she survived. She tucked most of the goblin prickers back into her pouch, but kept a few in her hand just in case. "Ready?"

"Ready for what?" Slash asked.

Veka grinned and waved her staff. Ideally her robe should have fluttered around her feet as she floated into the air, but after her aborted crawl through the mud, all it did was drip a bit. A casual glance at Slash was all she needed to summon the hobgoblin up after her.

"You'd better know what you're doing this time," Slash snapped. "Otherwise I'll give you a lot worse than a kick in the head."

They flew over the cracked plain of ice, the wind ruffling her cloak. She spun Slash over and raised him higher, until his nose nearly scraped the top of the cavern, then brought him back down. "Keep an eye out for pixies. Most of them will probably be with the queen, but there may still be a few down here with us."

She flew between the protruding treetops, trying to stay as low as possible. Avoiding the brown, dying branches was easy enough. Keeping Slash from crashing through them was trickier. More than once she heard him plotting her death and spitting dead leaves from his mouth.

Veka grinned and increased their speed.

At most Veka had expected to face only a handful of pixie guards. She had been correct. Only five pixies perched on the rock around the entrance to Straum's lair, clinging to the icy stone like glowing flies. A sixth stood on the back of what might have been a cousin to the winged burning snake that had tried to ambush them beneath the ice. The only real difference was that this snake was as wide as Slash's thick head, and long enough to wrap its body around them both from head to toe without a bit of space between the coils.

"So much for sneaking in," said Slash.

Veka guided herself and Slash down behind the top of a nearby tree. Dry papery leaves offered some cover, assuming the pixies hadn't already spotted them. The snake reared up, wings fluttering as it looked around. It actually left the ground, flying low over the ice as it hunted. A tongue of green fire flicked from its mouth. She could feel tremors passing through the magic around her, like waves in a pool. The snake was *tasting* the magic, searching for them. For her. The instant she tried to cast a spell, the huge snake would find her.

"Amateurs," she muttered.

"What are you talking about?"

She pointed to the snake. "Making giant versions of normal creatures. It's a fairly basic bit of magic. Most apprentices learn to do it in their first year of studies. There were notes in my spellbook. Giant bats, giant rats, giant snakes, giant earwigs . . . most of the time they all die within a few days. The larger body isn't proportioned right. But occasionally someone gets lucky. That's why you get giant weasels rampaging through a village, or giant toads hopping around and crushing people, or giant dung beetles rampaging across the country in search of giant privies."

"Can you do it?" Slash asked. "Better yet, can you undo it?"

Veka flushed. "The notes in my book . . . they weren't complete."

Slash didn't say anything. She almost wished he would.

She opened her hands, staring at the goblin prickers she had carried. Her palms were dotted with blood from clutching them too hard. She hadn't even felt the spikes pierce her skin.

They were outnumbered. Any magic she used would give

them away. Not to mention that six pixies could bring a lot more magic to bear than a single goblin. And then there was the giant flaming snake.

"What next?" Slash asked.

Veka had no idea. She stared at him, then back at the pixies. *Jig would have found a way.*

The thought made her stomach hurt. Jig would have slain not only the pixies, but the giant snake as well.

No, he wouldn't. That was the sort of thing a Hero from her book would do, but Jig wasn't like that, whatever "The Song of Jig" said. He would have done something different. Something unexpected. Something goblinish . . .

"I think I have an idea," she whispered.

CHAPTER 15

"Hero or coward, they all taste the same with a bit of harkol sauce."

—Golaka, Goblin Chef

JIG'S HANDS SHOOK AS HE WATCHED BRAF throw his rock. It arced through the air toward the silver bubbles on the far wall. Would the pixies attack en masse, or would they see Braf standing alone and decide he wasn't worth a full assault? If they sent only a few pixies, the goblins might have a chance.

The rock hit one of the silver bubbles and stuck.

Nothing happened. Jig glanced at Braf, who shrugged. Eventually another of the two-winged pixies flew up to investigate the rock. This one was orange in color. He glanced up, then back at the bubble. With both hands he pried the rock free and dropped it into the pit. He whistled loudly, presumably to warn the pixies below to watch out for falling rock.

"Tough nest," Braf muttered.

"Yes, it is," said Jig.

The pixie was already descending toward a lower cluster of bubbles.

Movement up above drew Jig's attention. Apparently one

of the pixies up on the bridge had noticed something. He started to fly lower, in the general direction of Braf and the others.

"Can you hit him?" Jig asked.

Braf produced another rock and let fly. The pixie tried to spin out of the way, but he was too slow. Purple sparks exploded as the pixie spiraled downward, his light fading.

Two more pixies hopped off the bridge, searching for their attacker. These were the four-winged pixies, who seemed to be the warriors and guards. Jig could see the ogres peering down as well. "Them too?"

Another rock flew. This time the pixies managed to dodge, though the rock did hit an ogre on the shoulder. The ogre didn't appear to notice. One of the pixies pointed toward Braf. "Get him!"

The enslaved ogres leaped from the bridge and began to plummet into the pit.

Jig stared. Grell shrugged and said, "Nobody ever said ogres were bright."

That was when the first of the ogres spread her wings. On Jig's shoulder, Smudge grew so hot he began to glow. Jig could smell his hair burning as it curled away from the terrified spider. Jig patted out the hair with one hand, never looking away from the flying ogres.

"Unfair," he whispered. He counted four ogres, circling lower on enormous black wings. Bat wings. The pixies had been hunting giant bats, trying to capture them alive. Somehow they had grafted the wings onto the ogres, creating flying ogres. Similar to what Pynne had done to create the snake guardian with too many heads and no tail. Jig doubted he could defeat these ogres by feeding them though. "Weren't ogres scary enough already?"

He wondered briefly what had happened to the bats. Without their wings, they were essentially giant blind rats. Then the first ogre reached the tunnel, and Jig and Braf were leaping away to avoid a spear thrust.

Braf threw another rock, which bounced off the ogre's wing with no apparent effect. The ogre stabbed again. Braf fell, yelping with pain.

"Are you hurt?" Jig asked.

Braf shook his head. "She missed me. I landed on my rocks, that's all."

Beyond the tunnel, the ogre dropped out of sight. Another appeared from above, armed with a large club. He hovered for a moment, then flung his club at Jig.

Jig's sword dropped as he rolled out of the way. Arrows spilled from his quiver, and he nearly squashed Smudge. "Sorry," he whispered. He tried to scoop Smudge off his shoulder, but the little fire-spider was too terrified, not to mention too *hot*, for Jig to move. Sucking his blistered finger, Jig turned his attention back to the ogre. He peeled away from the cave, to be replaced by yet another.

"They can't get into the tunnel with those wings," Jig said, gathering his fallen arrows. Their wingspan was too great, and if they stopped flapping, they would fall. "Braf, get back. They can't come in after us."

The new ogre scowled. He couldn't reach Braf or Jig, but he did manage to use his spear to drag his companion's club back out of the tunnel. Jig cursed himself for not throwing it out of range. They could have disarmed at least one of the ogres.

"Well this is an amusing little standoff," Grell said from the darkness. "What next?"

The ogre with the club returned. This time a bright green pixie warrior rode her shoulder.

"Rock!" Jig shouted.

Braf fumbled for a stone, but the pixie was faster. He flew into the tunnel and pointed. Braf fell, fumbling at his boots and howling in pain.

The pixie turned to Jig. Jig grabbed his sword and prepared to charge, already knowing he couldn't get there fast enough. But before Jig had taken a single step, the pixie yelped and clawed at his shoulder. Smoke spiraled as the pixie fell to the ground, where he yanked a tiny dart from his shoulder and flung it away.

Jig ran up and kicked the pixie. He slammed into the wall and slid to the ground.

"That's mine," Grop said, hurrying to retrieve the dart. He

lowered his voice. "I use it back at the lair. The others blame it on wasps. If you tie a thin line to the dart, you can yank it away before they swat it, and nobody knows—"

Jig stepped away. Ogres hovered outside, and Jig could see other pixies streaking toward them from above and below. He turned to face the other goblins.

Braf was using Grell's knife to pry his boot from his foot. The pixie had tried the same trick Pynne had used on Jig, constricting the leather. Braf had managed to get one foot free before it tightened too badly. The other appeared immovable. His face was tight from pain.

"I heard bones snap," Grell said. "Can you fix him?"

Jig shook his head. "Even if I could, I can't break the pixie's spell on the boot." Veka could, but she had disappeared. "You and Braf stay here. Our attack should draw them away from the tunnel. If you see an opening, try to hit a few more pixies with rocks."

One of the goblins coughed. "Our attack?"

"I'm guessing their nest is strong enough to hold us," Jig said. "We can jump down and—"

"You're guessing?" repeated the goblin, Ekstal. He was another distillery worker, like Veka. Ekstal waved his sword at Jig. It was in far better shape than Jig's weapon. The slender, double-sided blade looked as though it had been forged solely to slide through goblin throats. "You're going to get us killed!"

"Probably," admitted Jig. He didn't have time to argue. He glanced at Braf, who nodded and pushed himself into a sitting position.

"I'm not going out there," shouted Ekstal. "If you try to—"

There was a sharp thud, and Ekstal's sword dropped to the ground, followed by Ekstal himself. A bit of blood trickled down his neck where Braf's rock had hit him.

Jig scooped up the sword and gave it an experimental swing. Much better than his own weapon. He pointed to two of the goblins. "Toss him onto the nest. Then we'll know whether it can hold a goblin."

The two goblins looked at one another, then at Ekstal. "Right!"

"What about the ogres?" one asked.

Jig scooped up the dead pixie. Hopefully the ogres wouldn't realize he was dead. He flung the body out of the tunnel.

All four ogres dove, trying to catch him.

"Go," said Jig.

Ekstal groaned. His eyes opened wide as the goblins pushed him over the edge. A high-pitched squeal echoed through the tunnel.

Jig peered down. Ekstal had nearly missed the nest. He lay at an angle, his feet pointed upward, looking as though the slightest movement would send him slipping into the abyss. Already the pixies were zooming toward the panicked goblin.

"Here!" Jig called. He started to throw Ekstal's sword down to him, reconsidered, and tossed his own old broken sword down instead.

Ekstal caught it by the blade, which would have been a problem if the weapon hadn't been so dull. He clawed his way back to the rock, where he stood and waved the sword with both hands.

That answered the last of Jig's questions. Sticky as the nest was, they could still move about. "Everyone get your weapons ready. Spread out. Try to cut your way into the nest. Make them come up close to fight so you have a chance to stab them before they use their magic."

A rock flew by his head, momentarily driving the pixies back. Below, Ekstal was frantically cutting a hole in the nest.

None of the goblins had moved. The two who had tossed Ekstal down were still standing at the edge, watching and cheering him on. Jig sighed, tucked his sword under his arm, and pushed them both down to join their frantic companion.

It took a bit of threatening, with both his sword and Braf's rocks, but eventually the other goblins followed. Jig caught the last three before they jumped.

"You're the smartest goblins I've got," Jig said.

"Why do you say that?" asked Grop.

"You haven't jumped yet." Already Jig could hear shouting and screaming from below. "So you're the ones I need with me."

"Doing what?"

Jig swallowed and tried to sound like he knew what he was doing. "We're going to kill the queen."

He unstrapped his quiver and handed a few arrows to each goblin. "The tips are steel. Throw them like spears to keep the pixies back, but save one or two for when we reach the queen. We'll have to fight our way through any guards."

Jig put two arrows back into the quiver, keeping a third ready in his hand. Ekstal's sword was too long and slender for his old sheath, but he forced it. A handspan of steel protruded from the bottom, but if he was careful, he should be able to avoid slicing off his own foot.

He stepped to the edge and froze. The others stood close behind, waiting for Jig's order. Wind buffeted his face. He tried to tell himself he was waiting for the right moment, giving the other goblins time to spread around the nest. Several had already fallen into the pit, and the rest were scrambling away and cutting into the silver bubbles as fast as they could.

He could imagine Tymalous Shadowstar's derisive laughter as he said, *Waiting for the right time? You're cowering while the others get themselves slaughtered.*

Jig shrugged. Cowering while others died was a perfectly acceptable goblin tactic. Unfortunately, once the pixies finished with the others, they would return to the tunnel.

The hive was right below, only a short jump. The others had landed safely. Well, aside from Jallark, who had leaped a bit too enthusiastically. Even Braf's rock had stuck. Jig wasn't going to fall. The nest would hold him.

"This is crazy," whispered one of the remaining goblins, Noroka.

Jig agreed completely, but he forced himself to shake his head, then gave them his best conspiratorial grin. "We're going to let the others fight pixies while we sneak down through the hive. Do you think I'd be doing this if it wasn't the safest part of the whole plan? If you want, you can stay behind, but look what happened to poor Braf."

With that, Jig sat down on the edge, put his arrow in his mouth, and before he could stop to think about what he was doing, pushed off. Fear locked his jaw as he fell, and he bit clean through the arrow. The short drop felt like an eternity, and he was certain he had somehow missed the nest. He would fall forever into the bottomless pit, unless one of the pixies was kind enough to kill him in passing.

His feet hit the nest. Jig spat splinters of wood from his mouth and tried to make himself start breathing again.

The silver bubble felt like warm clay, sinking beneath his weight and sticking to his boots. The smell reminded him of burned mushrooms. Some of the fog rose from the nest itself, the warm surface interacting with the cold, damp air. With one hand pressed to the icy wall of the pit, Jig made his way to the next bubble. He looked up. "Hurry!"

Nothing happened at first. Then he heard the distinctive sound of a cane smacking a goblin skull. Grop dropped down a moment later, rubbing his head.

Several pixies were already streaking toward them. Jig hurried to the next bubble. He could see where some of the goblins had cut their way into the hive. The punctured cells sagged and wiggled as the goblins moved about. Farther on the pixies had added a second layer of bubbles, thickening the hive. If Jig could reach that point, the extra layer might help to conceal him.

On the far side of the pit, a goblin poked his head out of a damaged bubble and threw his knife at an unsuspecting worker pixie. The pixie fell. The goblin's gleeful expression vanished as pixies and ogres swarmed toward him.

Jig drew one of his two remaining arrows and threw it at the closest pixie. The pixie veered away, and Jig hopped to the next bubble, landing beside the smashed body of one of his goblins. Peeling the goblin from the bubble, Jig flung him onto the head of an unsuspecting pixie below.

The goblins who had gone first all appeared to have followed Jig's instructions, spreading out and taking cover in the hive. They were doing quite well for goblins, which meant they weren't all dead yet. From what Jig could see, almost half were still alive and fighting.

One of the goblins crouched within a broken bubble, fighting a pixie. As Jig watched, the pixie flew away, and an ogre soared in to take its place. Instead of trying to escape, the goblin actually tried something heroic. He raised his sword and swung for the ogre's head.

The ogre took the blow on the shoulder without slowing. His body smashed the goblin against the rock. That was what happened to goblins who tried to be heroes.

So what am I doing here? The ogre dove away from the gruesome remains of the goblin, then swooped up again, apparently unaffected by the collision. He was coming directly at Jig. Jig drew his remaining arrow and waited. The ogre drew closer . . . closer. . . .

Jig feinted with the arrow, then leaped to the next bubble. The ogre hit the rock headfirst and fell back, clutching his scalp. The impact didn't seem to have stopped him, reinforcing Jig's private theory that ogre skulls were stone all the way through.

It did make the ogre an easy target, though. Grop threw one of his arrows. The point lodged in the ogre's wing, and he screamed and moved away, flapping his other wing harder to keep from falling.

Jig jumped one more time, and he was there. This part of the hive was firmer, supported by the second layer of bubbles. Praying this would work, he reversed his grip on the arrow and shoved the head into the silver surface.

Sour air rushed from the puncture. The walls were thicker than they looked. He could probably push his thumb into the hole, and his claw would just reach the other side. The wall sizzled and smoked where the arrowhead touched. Moving as fast and as carefully as he could, Jig carved an opening wide enough for him to squeeze inside.

This was too much for Smudge. The fire-spider raced down over Jig's chest, smoke rising with each step, and stopped near his pouch. He turned, all eight eyes pleading for Jig to open his hiding place. Jig loosened the laces with one finger to let Smudge scurry inside.

Sweat dripped down his face as Jig crouched within the bubble. These chambers might be quite cozy for a pixie, but Jig barely fit. He jabbed his arrow into the floor, punching through to the next one. The air was warm and damp, like the breath of a dragon with an infected tooth.

Purging that image from his mind, Jig prepared to cut through to the next cell. He bent down, and the end of his sword pierced the side of the bubble.

Jig grabbed his sheath, pulling the blade back, but the damage was done. A long, smoking gash opened into the next bubble, where a bleary-eyed yellow pixie was stirring. Apparently when pixies slept, they slept hard. The pixie blinked, horror replacing weariness as he spotted Jig. Jig drew back the arrow to throw, just as the pixie's light flared. The wooden shaft crumbled, and the feathers of the fletching twined together and tried to fly away.

Jig squeezed through the opening and punched the pixie in the face. The pixie bounced off of the far side of the chamber. Jig grabbed him by the wings and threw him against the flattened part of the bubble, the side that clung to the rock. As the pixie collapsed, Jig realized he was grinning. He liked being bigger than the enemy for once.

The nest muffled sound well enough he could barely hear the battle outside. No wonder this one hadn't woken up. He wondered how many more sleeping pixies they would encounter.

The bubble shook slightly as Grop dropped into the one behind him.

"Are the others still coming?" Jig asked.

"Var got pixie charmed and tried to stab me in the back, but Noroka tossed her into the pit." He scowled. "Or maybe she wasn't pixie charmed. Var never did like me that much."

Jig shook his head. If he was remembering right, they had a long way to go before they reached the thickest part of the nest, where he hoped to find the queen. He looked at his lone remaining arrow, then at his sword. The arrowhead was small enough to control, but the sword was faster.

He was a goblin. Caution was for those who actually expected to survive a battle. Jig returned the arrow to his quiver and climbed back into Grop's chamber. Squeezing past the other goblin, he drew his sword and slashed a hole in the far side. He lost his balance and fell. His sword opened a huge hole in the floor. The chamber below held another two-winged pixie, but Jig impaled him as he plunged downward.

Jig grinned. Sure he was down to three goblins against the pixie queen and all her guards, but in the meantime, this was how goblins should fight. Sneaking around, pouncing by surprise, and stopping only for a very quick snack.

One problem with cutting through the inside of a pixie nest was that you had no way to know when you reached the bottom.

No, that wasn't true. There was one way.

Jig rolled away from the gash in the floor, pressing his body against the rock and gasping so hard he nearly passed out. He rested his sword across his chest, making sure the steel came nowhere near the walls of the bubble. His shook so hard he could barely hold on. From below, the wind of the bottomless pit fluttered the edges of the gash.

He tried to tell himself he wouldn't have fallen through. The hole might be big enough for his leg, but not his whole body. "Don't come down!" he whispered to Grop and Noroka.

Grop poked his head down from the chamber overhead. Jig could see Noroka settling in above him. "Now what?"

Now he had to figure out where they were. He pulled out his remaining arrow and poked a tiny hole in the wall of the bubble, widening it just enough to see. He pressed his eye to the wall.

Only a handful of goblins still fought. Jig saw an orange pixie swoop in to cast a spell, then tumble to the side. Jig hadn't seen the rock that hit him, but he was relieved to know Braf had survived so far.

The queen was easy enough to find: a point of brilliant white light, orbited by pixies of every color. The white light perched in the center of a cluster of bubbles, a rounded area of smaller bubbles that bulged from the rest of the hive. Jig closed his eyes, hoping that one brief glimpse wouldn't be enough to enchant him. He didn't *feel* particularly loving.

"The pixies say all who look upon their queen will love her, so don't wait," Jig said, turning back to Grop and Noroka. "We're going to cut our way through the hive until we're close enough to attack. If we're lucky, we'll have one chance before she enchants us."

"And if we're not lucky?" asked Noroka.

One of the surviving goblins from the fighting above chose that moment to go tumbling past, screaming.

"Any other questions?" Jig stood up and began cutting a path to the next bubble. He used his arrow, unwilling to risk a mistake.

Noroka and Grop both had several arrows left. Grop had already proven his aim with that dart. A thrown arrow didn't have the force to penetrate deeply, but as they had seen with the flying ogre, even a weak hit was enough. As long as the steel lodged in the queen's flesh, they might actually succeed.

A few bubbles over, Jig poked another hole to gauge their progress. He tried not to look directly at the queen, judging her location from the shadows and the other pixies. It looked like the pixies had taken over a small cave to use as the queen's chamber. An ogre stood at the edge, two warrior pixies perched on her shoulders. Other pixies sat on the bubbles above the cave, like tiny, glowing gargoyles.

"How much closer do we need to get?" Grop asked.

"A few more chambers," Jig guessed without looking back. "We should try to attack from the side. Noroka, you distract the guards long enough for Grop and me to cut through."

This could work! What would Tymalous Shadowstar say if he could see Jig now?

That was when something punched him hard in the back. Jig twisted his head to see Grop's arrow sticking out from beneath his rib cage. There was no pain, just blue blood dripping down the shaft.

No, wait. *There* was the pain.

Jig dropped to his knees. Grop pulled out another arrow. "That was a good plan," he said to Noroka, who was staring from the next chamber. "The two of us will attack together. Help me toss Jig's body out for a distraction."

Goblins really are as stupid as they say. Less than a day as chief, and I already turned my back on another goblin. Are you happy now, Tymalous Shadowstar? You're the one who wanted me to lead my people. Is this what you meant when you talked about inspiring the other goblins? I inspired Grop so much he thought he'd try his hand at being chief!

He tried to reach around, but the effort made the arrowhead move inside him, and he squealed in pain. Maybe he would just hold still.

Shadowstar? Of course. The god couldn't hear him down here. Jig had no way to heal himself. He was alone.

At least Grop and Noroka might still reach the queen. Not that it would do Jig much good.

Then he saw Noroka contemplating her own arrow, looking from the tip to Grop's exposed back. Jig wanted to weep. They were so close! "Noroka, don't—"

Grop spun as Noroka leaped. She landed on top of Grop and stabbed her arrow into his hip. The arrow broke, leaving a splintered shaft in her hand. With a shrug she stabbed the broken end into Grop's side.

Grop screamed and elbowed her in the head. There was no room to fight, and both goblins kept stepping on Jig. Claws and fangs ripped flesh. Jig moaned and tried to curl his body into a ball, keeping his wounded back away from the fight.

The bottom of the bubble began to glow with golden flames. A hole opened in the floor beneath Noroka. Jig would have warned them, but he was too busy bleeding and cowering.

An ogre grabbed Noroka by the ankles and yanked her out. Grop followed, his fangs still locked in Noroka's arm. Another ogre caught Grop by the neck and squeezed until he let go. Jig grimaced. Goblin jaws were stronger than any other muscle in their bodies, and the ogre had plucked Grop off Noroka like he was a rat.

Jig yelled as another ogre pulled him down, bumping the end of the arrow against the nest. Hanging upside down by one leg, Jig closed his eyes and concentrated on not blacking out.

The beating of the ogres' wings was almost as loud as the pounding in Jig's head. As they flew toward the queen's chamber, he found himself feeling jealous of Veka. Wherever she had gone, at least she hadn't been stupid enough to rely on goblins to help her.

The ogres dumped them on rough stone. Jig raised his arms and tucked his head as he landed, trying to protect Smudge and keep from bumping the arrow in his back at the same time. He managed to avoid squishing Smudge at least.

Unlike the pit and the tunnel above, the air was warmer here, and there was no frost. Now that he was here, Jig realized this was the same tunnel that the ogres had dug from Straum's cavern. The back had been narrowed, with two-winged pixies constantly squeezing in and out, carrying small fruits or clearing bits of stone from the cave. Hardly a single speck of rubble littered the ground. Sparkling blue and green crystals covered the rock. They felt like sand, scraping Jig's skin when he moved.

He rolled onto his side, grimacing. The entire right side of his body hurt with every breath. His sword and arrow were both missing. The ogre must have taken them, or else they had fallen into the pit. Jig hadn't even noticed.

He touched Smudge's pouch and felt the fire-spider moving about inside. He loosened the ties. Hopefully Smudge would have a chance to escape.

Grop and Noroka lay bleeding beside him. Jig pushed himself up just enough to give Grop a quick kick in the stomach, a move that probably caused Jig more pain than it did Grop. Jig kicked him again anyway.

"I hate this place."

Jig still hadn't looked up, nor did he intend to. Faint shadows spun around his body as the pixies circled behind and overhead, but the white light shining from the queen overpowered them all.

"Everyone promised me we'd be safe. That you'd build me a nest even bigger than my mother's. You never said we'd be underground, in this hot, dark, horrible place. What if these goblins had gotten through? They could have killed me!"

Her voice jumped and dipped like music. Other pixies swarmed and buzzed overhead, drowning each other out with their hasty apologies.

Jig saw bare feet moving toward him and the other goblins. They were larger than he had expected. The queen must be almost as large as a goblin. Either that, or she was simply a normal pixie with grotesquely oversize feet.

Sweat dripped onto one of his lenses. Jig flinched and

closed his eyes. How much of the queen did he have to look upon to be enchanted? Were feet enough? He didn't feel overcome with love or worship yet. He raised his hand to block her from view as he glanced at the others.

Grop was doing the same thing, shielding one eye. The other was bruised and swollen shut. Noroka had gotten in some good blows.

Noroka looked equally battered, but she didn't seem to care about her wounds. She didn't seem to care about anything. The queen's light turned Noroka's skin to white gold. She lay on her back, her mouth open and her eyes wide as she stared up at the queen. Until now Jig had clung to the faint hope that goblins might somehow be immune to the queen's charms. So much for that.

Could they still attack? Jig twisted his head, quickly losing count of the pixies buzzing around their heads. He could hear several ogres hovering outside as well. Attacking now would be suicidally stupid.

Grop attacked. He had managed to palm his little dart, and he flung it at the queen. Four pixies swooped down to intercept the missile. Grop swore as one of the pixies squeaked and fell. He drew a knife from inside his shirt.

Noroka kicked him in the knees, knocking him to the ground. Moving faster than any goblin had a right to move, she pounced and sank her fangs into his neck. Grop stabbed his knife into her arm, but she didn't even notice.

The queen giggled. "Stupid goblins."

Noroka rose and backed away. Grop whimpered on the floor, blood dripping from his throat. He would be dead soon, from the look of it.

The queen stepped closer. Through squinted lids, Jig saw a slender, pale hand grab Grop's hair, wrenching his head back. Grop's eyes widened, and his face relaxed into a slack, peaceful smile.

"What's your name?"

"Grop." His wound bubbled.

"What an ugly name." She struggled to lift him up. Instantly four pixies flew down to help, hoisting Grop up until only his toes still brushed the ground. "Go away and leave me alone, Grop."

Still smiling, Grop turned and began to jog away. He ran right out of the chamber, dropping into the pit without a sound.

Jig began to tremble. Given the arrow still sticking out of his back, he wasn't terribly upset about Grop's death. But Grop had acted so cheerful about it. Jig hadn't seen the slightest trace of hesitation on that blissful face as he trotted to his death.

"Oh, yuck. This one's bleeding all over my cave."

Jig glanced down. His blood formed a small puddle on the floor. The pain had begun to recede a bit, but he was lightheaded, and every movement made him dizzy. Was he dying?

"That's Jig Dragonslayer," said Noroka. She moved in front of Jig, positioning herself between him and the queen. "He's the one who forced us to try to kill you."

Jig groaned. He scooted back, toward the edge of the pit. If he was going to die, wouldn't it be better to do so himself, while he was still his own goblin?

He stopped. Blood loss was starting to affect his mind. Death was death. Veka might opt to die heroically, but Jig planned to go out cowering and pleading for his life.

Smudge darted down Jig's leg and scampered up the wall. Nobody appeared to notice. Their attention was on Jig. He hoped Smudge would be able to climb back out of the pit. Did he still remember how to find the fire-spider nest?

"Make him look at me!"

Two pixies seized him by the ears, yanking his head up.

"Want me to cut off his eyelids?" Noroka asked.

Jig's eyes snapped open.

The queen stood before him. Her gown sparkled like platinum, though it was clearly too small for her. Several stitches had popped along the side, and the hem barely reached past her knees. Rows of black pearls highlighted the contours of her skinny body. A golden circlet was twined into her long black hair. Had she been a goblin, Jig would have guessed her to be no more than seven years of age.

Her ears were narrow and pointed, rising well past the top of her head. Her eyes were pure blackness, reminding him of the bottomless pit, save for the spot of white light at the center of each eye.

Her wings were small and shriveled. Jig wondered if that was a result of injury, or if queens simply didn't get real wings. He saw no scars, nor did the wings appear deformed. They were simply too small, too flimsy. She had four wings, like the warrior pixies, but hers gave off no light. The queen's light came from her skin, her eyes, even her nails.

"Stand up."

Sweat poured down Jig's face as he obeyed, despite the pain the movement caused. He stood hunched, one hand reaching around his back to hold the arrow still.

The queen was . . . beautiful. It was an alien beauty, but Jig couldn't look away. The angular features of her face, the curves of her body, the gracefulness of her movements that made her every step look like she was flying. . . . Every being Jig had ever encountered seemed crude and ugly in comparison. Admittedly, Jig had spent most of his life with other goblins.

"Jig Dragonslayer," the queen whispered. "I remember your name. They told me about you. You're the one who opened the way so we could come here. Everyone was so excited when they found this place. I would be safe. We could start our own kingdom, away from my mother. I could raise my own army of warriors as soon as I was old enough to breed. All thanks to you."

Jig shivered. What was he supposed to say? "You're welcome."

"I hate you!" the queen said. She stomped around Jig, her withered wings rustling with her despair. "Why couldn't *I* stay behind, and my mother come through?"

"You know your mother's followers were too great in number for—" one pixie said.

"Shut up! How many more of these horrible goblins are going to come crawling into my cave?" She wiped her nose on the sleeve of her gown. "I hate them," she said again.

She wrapped both hands around the arrow in Jig's side

and prodded him toward the edge. Tears streamed down his face, and he was gasping so hard he nearly passed out. Pixies and ogres flew back, clearing space for him to fall.

Jig turned around. Everyone was watching, waiting for that last order that would send him to his death. The queen wrenched the arrow from his back. Jig gasped, and tears filled his eyes.

"I wish you'd never opened that stupid cave for us," she whispered, too low for the others to hear. Even her tears glowed. "I wish you'd just left me there to die."

The poor queen was scared and miserable. Jig sympathized. He had felt the same way ever since that ogre first came to the goblin lair.

A small, dark shape dropped down to land on the queen's withered wing. She didn't appear to notice. Nor did she notice when smoke began to rise from that same wing. "Go on," she said. "Follow your friend into the pit."

Noroka acted first, leaping toward the queen and screaming, "Jig's fire-spider!"

That was too much for the young queen. She whirled around and flailed her arms in panic, knocking Smudge to the ground. "Somebody kill it!" she screamed.

Jig leaped. Agony tore his wound as he grabbed the arrow in the queen's hand and ripped it from her grasp. Before the queen could react, he plunged the arrow into the her back, directly between the wings.

She screamed. Jig flattened his ears against the terrible, high-pitched shriek. Pixies swarmed around the cave. Others fought their way through the opening at the back, bloodying one another in their desperation.

Before anyone could reach the queen, Jig yanked hard, pulling her toward the edge, then let go. The queen staggered, her arms waving madly. Jig saw her wings shiver once as she teetered on the edge, and then she was falling.

Every single pixie and ogre dove to follow, trying to save her. Jig scrambled out of the way and pressed himself to the floor.

When Noroka tried to follow the queen, Jig reached out with one hand and snagged her ankle. She flopped face first onto the rock and didn't move. Only then, with Noroka unconscious and the rest of the pixies and ogres gone, did Jig drag himself back to peer into the pit. A tiny spark of white was quickly fading into darkness, pursued by swirls of color.

Everything felt fuzzy. He thought something in his back had torn when the queen yanked the arrow free, and his blood was flowing faster than before. His head slumped to the ground, just past the edge. He watched a bit of his own drool fall into the pit. Why wasn't he dead? He had looked upon the queen, just like Grop and Noroka. Not that it mattered. He would be dead soon enough.

His ears and nose hurt. He pushed himself back and reached up to adjust his spectacles. The frames were so hot they burned his fingers.

The *steel* frames.

Jig started to giggle. Every time he had looked at the queen, he had seen her through circles of steel.

Shadowstar? There was no answer. He was alone.

Hot footprints made their way up his arm. Not alone after all. Jig smiled and rested his head on the stone. At least he would die with the one creature in this world he had always been able to trust.

CHAPTER 16

"You think Heroes have it rough? Try cleaning up after them."

—Chandra Widowmaker, Proprietress of
The Dancing Zombie Tavern
From *The Path of the Hero (Wizard's ed.)*

"SO WHAT'S THIS PLAN OF YOURS?" SLASH ASKED. He lay on his stomach, burning designs in the ice with one of his goblin prickers. Veka frowned and looked more closely. He had drawn a fat goblin cowering behind a tree. Now he sketched a pixie circling the tree, with bolts of lightning shooting from his hands. Slash appeared to be a fairly skilled artist. He held the pricker by the wood, pressing two points into the ice as he drew the parallel lines of the giant serpent's body.

By the cave, the flaming serpent undulated through the air, almost as if it were swimming.

Veka's fists clenched. "Can I borrow that?"

Slash sat up and handed her the goblin pricker. Veka jabbed one of the points into her forearm, then pinched the skin around the wound. Blood dripped down her forearm.

"What are you doing?" Slash asked.

She squeezed harder, and a tiny spray of blood misted Slash's drawing.

"Stop that." He turned away, his face pale.

Veka grabbed his shoulder. Blood dripped down her arm. The pain was annoying, but the discomfort on his face more than made up for it. "I need a distraction," she said. "The only way one of us is getting through is if the other gets the guards out of the way."

"I'm not going out there."

"If you say so." She squeezed again, spraying a bit of blood onto his chest.

That was too much for the poor hobgoblin. Slash groaned and fell face first onto the ice. Veka pressed the goblin pricker into his hand and closed his fingers.

Almost instantly Slash was up again, suspended by Veka's magic. She could see the giant serpent stiffen and turn, tasting her spell. She maneuvered the unconscious hobgoblin like a puppet, marching him toward the pixies. One of the pixies flew out to meet him, shouting a challenge. The pixie didn't appear worried. A lone hobgoblin shouldn't be much of a threat.

That was what he thought. Splitting her concentration, she cast a second spell that tore the goblin pricker from Slash's hand and propelled it upward. The point drove through the pixie's wing.

The pixie fell, screaming with pain and fury. Veka turned her full attention to Slash, levitating him over the pixie and dropping him several times. She didn't know if it would be enough to kill the pixie, but it should keep him from getting up any time soon. One pixie down. Five more to go, along with the flying fire snake.

"Sorry, Slash," she whispered. To her surprise, she realized she meant it.

Already the other guards were rushing to attack, the serpent in the lead. Veka sent Slash running as fast as she could, guiding him away from herself and the pixies. No hobgoblin could move so quickly, but the pixies probably didn't know that. Sure his movements were stiff and awkward, but so were most hobgoblins. And if his feet didn't quite touch the ground with each step . . . well, hopefully the pixies would be too intent on catching him to notice such details.

Veka edged out from behind the tree and began to run toward the cave. Slash's movements grew even clumsier. She couldn't watch where she was going and control him at the same time. Maybe she would have been better off trying to take over his mind, but that was a more complicated spell. Dominating lizard-fish was one thing, but Snixle had told her that intelligent creatures fought much harder. Grudgingly, she admitted that Slash would probably qualify as intelligent.

She glanced back in time to see Slash run right through the tip of a pine tree. He stumbled and slid along the ice. Veka tried to yank him back to his feet, but before she could, he simply dropped out of sight. He must have fallen into another crevasse.

Good enough. She was almost to the cave. The ice near the entrance was melted smooth and slick, probably from that oversize snake. She saw no sign of the tiny worms and their ice spike traps. In a way, the flaming serpent had done her a favor, driving off the smaller predators.

A few more splashing steps brought her to the darkness of the tunnel and relative safety. Thankfully the ice was high enough she didn't have to climb up to the entrance.

She was past the guards. Using her helpless companion as bait wasn't the most heroic tactic, but it had worked.

The tunnel had changed since her last visit. Orange insects filled the air, zipping this way and that, riding the currents of the magic. One tried to bite her arm, and she slapped it. She wiped glowing bug guts off her arm and hurried down the tunnel.

Glittering gray frost coated the rock. The dead ogre from before was gone. She looked back, wondering what the pixies would do to Slash. She hoped they wouldn't kill him.

The tunnel never became truly dark. The orange bugs continued to circle her. Their light reflected from the frost, illuminating the walls as she ran. As she neared Straum's lair, the light grew stronger. The warmth of the magic increased as well, making her sweat beneath her cloak. She pressed to one side of the tunnel and peered into the cave the dragon had once called home.

Crystalline ice lined the walls, the facets reflecting colored light in every direction. The ice itself seemed to glow, as if some of that light had been frozen within.

A bone-white mound sat in a depression on the far side of the cave. Golden sunlight spilled from a round, jagged hole in one side of the mound. She could feel the magic from here, enough to make the hair on her arms and neck stand at attention. If that wasn't the portal, she would eat her spellbook.

As far as she could tell, there were only two pixies in the cave. Two-winged worker pixies, not the warriors from outside. It would have been her luck to show up right as an army of pixie warrior-wizards were coming through, but for once, fate's dice had fallen in her favor.

A bright yellow pixie hovered on the far side of the cave. Her green companion crouched on the ground, struggling to maneuver a long pole-arm. Swarms of orange gnats circled angrily as he tugged. The point of the weapon slowly scraped along the rock, toward what appeared to be some kind of hive.

"You're mad," the yellow pixie said. Veka's heart pounded as the pixie flitted in Veka's direction, but then she turned back. "The queen ordered all death-metal buried beneath the ice."

"She also—" The green pixie grunted and strained as the pole-arm started to slip away. There was something wrong with his wings, but from this angle, Veka couldn't tell what. "She also ordered us to take care of the sparks. I for one don't intend to stand around swatting bugs all day."

The hive was a frosted, warty bulge in the ice about the size of a goblin's skull. The tip of the pole-arm brushed the hive, sending up a tiny geyser of steam. More gnats exploded from the hive, swarming toward the pixies.

"Don't drop it!" the yellow pixie shrieked.

The one on the ground grunted as he jabbed the tip deeper into the hive. He stepped back and fished a small bronze fruit from his vest. It looked like the globules she had seen growing beneath the ice. He popped it in his mouth, sucked for a moment, then spat out the wrinkled skin. "There's not enough metal in this stick to damage the portal."

"But if the queen comes back—"

"She won't." He pointed at the hive, and Veka felt the tremors of magic. It reminded her of the spell she had used on the lizard-fish, back at the lake.

Orange bugs streaked toward the head of the pole-arm. The pixie's magic drove them into the steel, where they died in tiny flashes of light. Bodies sprinkled down on the green pixie like rain. "Ha! What do you say now, Wholoo?" He laughed and danced a victory jig as the bugs continued to dive to their deaths.

Veka's jaw clenched as she realized who it was. She had never actually seen Snixle before, but she recognized the inflection of his voice, the way he moved. It was easier to recognize someone when they had inhabited your body for a time.

Why wouldn't Snixle be here? He was the muckworker of the pixie world, cleaning up their messes and doing the jobs nobody else wanted. While the others went off to defend the queen, he was stuck here fighting bugs.

With the worst of the bugs littering the ground, Snixle bent down to adjust the butt of the weapon. Where his wings should have been, two tattered fragments protruded from his shoulders. He gave off less light than the yellow pixie, Wholoo. A deep green fluid had oozed over the torn ends of his wings. This was a recent injury then.

That meant he wouldn't have adjusted to his loss yet. Veka had seen it before, watching the younger goblins torture rats. The maimed rats needed to learn how to move all over again. Snixle's reflexes would be wrong.

Veka grabbed the rest of her goblin prickers and launched them at the yellow pixie. The pixie saw them coming and tried to dodge, but it was too late. Two caught her in the back and leg. Wholoo fell like the bugs she had been working to kill. Snixle let go of the pole-arm, which tipped over backward.

Already Veka was up and running. She saw Snixle leap back, then fall, unable to complete his instinctive retreat to the air.

Veka smacked Wholoo with her staff, then pounced on Snixle, wrapping her fingers around his slender body.

Snixle squirmed briefly, then his head slumped. "Go ahead and eat me," he mumbled. "That's what you goblins do, isn't it?"

Veka hesitated. The maimed pixie was, in a word, pathetic. Skinny, too. There was hardly enough meat on those tiny bones to make him worth the effort. "What happened to you, Snixle?"

His head jerked back up, and his glow brightened slightly. "Veka?" A tentative smile spread across his bruised face. "Is that you? I thought Jig Dragonslayer killed you!"

Veka shook her head. "When he stabbed me, it broke your spell. Then he healed me."

"The disruptive effect of death-metal, yes," Snixle said, nodding. "That makes sense. But why did he save you?"

"Because he's Jig. That's what he does." She turned him around to examine his wings.

"The queen," Snixle whispered. "When she learned how I failed to capture Jig Dragonslayer, and that I had kept you a secret . . ." Tears filled his eyes. "I didn't mean to disappoint her. She should have killed me. You can't know the agony of disappointing her, Veka. I wish she had killed me, but she ordered me to remain, to clean the sparks out of our cave."

Glowing snot dripped from his nose. He was a pitiful sight. The queen's magic was strong indeed, to command this kind of loyalty. She wondered how Jig would overcome it. "Sparks?"

He tilted his head toward the insect hive. "Nasty things. They feed on the blood and magic of pixies and other magical creatures." He sniffled and bent his neck, wiping his face on Veka's thumb. "How did you get in? There were guards—"

"I snuck past," she said.

"You're going to try to close the gateway, aren't you?" He shook his head. "Twenty of the strongest pixies worked together to open that portal. You'll never be able to destroy it."

She stepped toward the white hill, feeling the magic wash over her body. Snixle was right. Even this close, the sheer power pouring from the gateway made her want to shield her face. Enough power to transform the entire mountain. She knelt, trying to peer through, to get a glimpse of the pixies' world, but the sunlight was too bright.

"It's not too late," Snixle said. "We could still go to the queen—"

Veka shook her head. "Jig's leading an attack against the queen."

"No!" He couldn't have looked more distraught if she had eaten his legs. He twisted and squirmed, pounding Veka's fingers with his tiny fists. "I have to help her. I have to fight—"

Veka gave him a shake. "You have to show me how this gateway works."

"I can't! I have to save the queen." He closed his eyes, and Veka felt a swelling of magic within her hand as Snixle fought to take control, to reestablish the spell he had used on her before.

Veka strode to the edge of the cave and rapped him against the ice on the wall. "Stop that."

Snixle's spell dissipated at once. He groaned and closed his eyes. Another rush of magic swept past her.

The buzzing of insects warned her what Snixle had done. Veka leaped aside as a swarm of sparks rushed after her. Her staff clattered to the ground. She spun and flung Snixle into the middle of the swarm.

He yelped and curled into a ball. Bugs flew in every direction. Snixle's torn wings fluttered uselessly, and then he hit the ground and skidded into the wall. Veka hurried to scoop him up, but she needn't have bothered. Snixle swayed as he tried to stand. Even with one hand on the wall, he could barely keep himself upright.

Veka picked him back up and flicked a spark off of his neck. "Next time, I'll just squeeze."

Snixle nodded. "But the queen. I can't abandon—"

"Hush." Her ears twitched. She could hear shouting from the tunnel. She bit her lip, recognizing Slash's voice. At least he was still alive.

Snixle used her distraction to try one more time to enchant her. Her skin tingled, and her muscles grew heavy. Veka couldn't help but admire the little pixie. Bruised and battered, he still tried to fight.

She bounced him against the wall again, then stuffed his unconscious body into her pocket as she searched for a place to hide. The only shelter was the hill itself, the white mound that housed the pixies' portal. She crouched behind it, pulling her cloak around her body. The dark material wouldn't do much to conceal her, not when everything from the ice to the bugs generated its own light, but it was the best she could do.

Flickering flames marked the arrival of the giant serpent. Several pixies flew into the cave ahead of the snake. "Hey, Snixle, Wholoo, we caught a hobgoblin prancing around outside. He says his friend was coming this way."

Veka's fangs pressed her cheeks. The stupid hobgoblin had probably started babbling the moment he woke up. Cowards, all of them.

Then again, she had sent him bouncing over the landscape as a distraction. She might not feel terribly loyal either, if he had done something like that to her.

"Down here," said another pixie. "Wholoo's dead."

"Where's Snixle?"

Their lights danced along the ice as they flew down to investigate the body of the pixie Veka had slain. She didn't have much time before they found her. She had to figure out how to destroy the gate.

"Stay back. Let Moltiki deal with her."

Veka peeked around the hill, trying to figure out which one was Moltiki. The other pixies retreated to the entrance. Surrounded by pixies, Slash pressed himself to the wall as the giant snake slid into the cave, sniffing the air. As Snixle had taught her, she tried to reach out, to touch the snake's body with her magic. She had commanded hundreds of lizard-fish. How hard could a single giant snake be?

She wove magic like a shell, a second skin she could use to surround Moltiki, to control the snake's movements. Slowly that shell shrank into place.

The instant the magic touched the snake's skin, her spell shattered. She bit back a scream of pain. Moltiki reared, tongue flickering madly. One of the pixies shouted, "She's by the hill!"

She wasn't strong enough to break their control over the snake. All she had done was reveal her position, giving herself a skull-splitting headache in the process.

She edged around the hill, toward the back of the cave. She thought about simply running through the gate, but what would she accomplish? Even if she survived, she would be alone and lost in another world. Better to end things quickly, but how?

She could sense the magic pouring through the portal, but she didn't have the slightest idea what to do with it. If she tried to block the flow, that magic would rip her apart.

Moltiki crept closer. Veka pressed her hands and face against the hill. The mound's rough surface scratched her skin. What was this thing made of? Unlike the ice and stone of the cave, this was dry and warm. Too hard and uniform for wood, and too rough for stone. More than anything else, it reminded her of bone.

Veka backed away, staring at the mound and imagining . . . That bulge around the base could be a tail coiled against the body. The other side of the hill narrowed like a neck, with the great skull resting between his feet.

The pixies needed a powerful concentration of magic to serve as an anchor for their portal, and what greater magic than the body of Straum himself? They had fused the bones into a single invulnerable shell. The skull housed the actual gate. To physically destroy the hill, she would need to shatter the skeleton of a dragon. Easier to rip apart the mountain itself. No wonder they hadn't left more guards. What could a single goblin do against this?

"I see her!" One of the pixies waved his hands, and Moltiki lunged for her. How could something so big be so fast? Veka's size had only ever slowed her down.

She dove away, stumbling into the icy wall. Strange that she didn't feel cold. Oh yes, that would be because Moltiki had set her cloak on fire. She stripped the cloak from her body and flung it at Moltiki's face. Wearing nothing but her old muckworking clothes, she backed away.

The giant snake slid around behind her, positioning his huge body between Veka and the exit.

"What did you think you were doing, goblin?" asked the lead pixie.

Moltiki's tail smashed her side. It was like being hit with a tree. A burning tree. With rough scales that shredded her apron and the skin beneath. Old muck stains on her clothes smoked in response to the flames. Veka cowered against the hill, her hands up in a futile gesture to ward off the next blow.

"This is what you want," Slash shouted from the entrance. He held up a small rectangular box that appeared to be made of wood. "This is what she planned to use to close the gate."

The pixies hesitated. Moltiki's burning eyes stared into Veka's. His mouth was open, and he could have swallowed Veka whole before she could draw breath to scream. For now, though, everyone's attention was on Slash.

Veka rubbed her head. What was that stupid hobgoblin talking about? Where had that box come from?

"I stole it from her," Slash said. His face was bruised and bloody, either from being dropped into the ice crevasse, or from the pixies' rough handling. "No hobgoblin would trust a rat-eating goblin with something this important."

One of the pixies flew toward Slash and plucked the box from his hand. "What is it?"

"There's no magic in that," said another. "If they think their little toys are powerful enough to scratch our gate, they're delusional."

Veka glanced at the pole-arm Snixle and Wholoo had been using against the sparks. Was that enough iron to scratch the gate? Probably not or they never would have used it here. She needed something bigger. A spell powerful enough to kill this stupid serpent and destroy the portal at the same time.

While she was at it, why not wish for the pixie queen's unconditional surrender to Veka the Sorceress?

"How do you open it?" asked the pixie, studying the box. "I see no hinges—No, I see it now. Clever workmanship." He pressed one end of the box. "The lid pops open like so, and—"

Even Veka's goblin ears could barely make out the sharp

twang from the box. The pixie screamed and flung the box away. A slender pin protruded from the center of his palm. Smoke rose from the wound.

"Kill him!" the pixie screamed. Moltiki rushed away, closing the distance to Slash before the poor hobgoblin had taken a single step. Moltiki's body blocked her view as he lunged, and then the giant snake drew back. Slash dangled from the snake's jaw. Moltiki's fangs had pierced the hobgoblin's leg. Slash flailed about, shouting in pain.

"No!" Before Veka even realized what she was doing, she had wrapped a spell around the pole-arm and launched it at the snake. The steel blade cut through the scales and lodged deep within the neck. Moltiki roared in pain. Slash dropped to the ground and didn't move.

"Get the goblin, get the goblin!" screamed another pixie.

The pole-arm was embedded too deeply in the snake for Veka's magic to remove it. She cast a second spell, grabbing her staff from where it had fallen and sending it spinning through the air. The whirling ends batted one pixie aside, then smashed a second. She shot the staff at a third pixie, but this one waved a hand, and the staff disintegrated. So she flung Wholoo's body at the pixie instead. She missed, but it bought her time to scramble around behind the hill.

Two pixies down, a third with a metal pin through his hand. That left two uninjured, along with one bleeding, very angry snake. She could try again to control it, but—

No. She stared at the hill, remembering Snixle's words. *Necromancy is like wearing a corpse.* But the magic was the same as she had used on the lizard-fish.

Straum had been dead for an entire year. His bones were warped and fused by pixie magic. She had never tried to control anything so big, or so dead.

And if she didn't try now, she would be snake food.

Blood dripped into her eye. When had she cut her head? Not that it mattered. As the pixies regrouped, she pressed her body against the hill and cast her spell.

Snixle had taught her that pixie magic was practically a living thing. So were Straum's remains. The dragon might be dead, but those bones were still warm with power. They welcomed Veka's magic, drawing her spell into themselves like a starving goblin stuffing himself in Golaka's storerooms.

Her vision blurred and darkened. Her joints felt like ice, stiff and cold. She slipped to her knees as the magic threatened to crush her. No, it wasn't the magic. It was Straum's remains. The weight of those massive bones pressed her to the ground, grinding her into the ice and stone. She couldn't hear. She couldn't see. Where were the pixies, the giant serpent? Moltiki could be rearing back to strike, and she wouldn't even know.

She fought to stand, but her body wouldn't obey. Straum's body. Magic and ice and decay had turned the skeleton into a solid mass of bone. She would have to break the bones to move them. This had been a mistake. How could she have been so foolish? She tried to release the spell, but even in death, Straum was too powerful. His body sucked Veka's power and refused to let her go. She was inside Straum's bones, but she couldn't move them. She would have laughed at the absurdity, but even that was beyond her.

Veka felt nothing. No cold, no pain, nothing but magic. The river of magic pouring from the portal in her mouth, the currents flowing through the room, the tiny spot of warmth on her side . . . no, that was Veka herself, felt through Straum's body. Her jaw throbbed, as if she had tried to swallow one of Slash's goblin prickers. Was that the portal causing her such pain?

There was Moltiki, crawling around the front of the hill toward Veka.

Would she even feel the strike, or would her existence simply end? Worse yet, would her mind remain trapped inside Straum's skeleton, blind and deaf and forever unable to move? Despair began to weigh her down as much as the bones themselves.

Time seemed slower, trapped inside the dragon. She could feel each ripple of Moltiki's muscular body as the great snake drew back to strike. The pixies darted about, sending currents through the magic like bugs on the lake.

As she waited for the serpent to finish her, a single thought wormed through her mind. *Jig would have found a way.*

Anger burned through despair. Jig *always* found a way. He

always won. Veka was the one who got captured by a pixie peon or eaten by a flaming serpent or stabbed through the gut by *Jig Dragonslayer*! Jig had slain Straum, and Veka wasn't even strong enough to overcome the power in the dragon's dead bones. It wasn't fair!

The portal pulsed in her jaw as waves of magic poured from the pixies' world. Veka tried to shut out everything except that portal. Forget the pixies. Forget Moltiki. Forget Slash. She didn't even know if the hobgoblin was still alive.

Jig would have succeeded. So would she.

Straining every bone in her neck and jaw until they felt ready to shatter, Veka wrenched Straum's head to one side and snapped the great jaws down on the serpent.

There was a moment of tremendous pressure. She thought about the younger goblins who, when harassed by mosquitoes and other bloodsuckers, would pull their skin taut to trap the bugs in place. Blood would continue to bloat the mosquitoes until they exploded. At that moment, Veka felt a great sympathy for those poor bugs.

The skull shattered, and Veka lost consciousness.

Rough hands shook Veka's arm. She opened her eyes and wished she hadn't. The light felt like knives going straight to her brain. "No goblin should have to wake up to that ugly face," she mumbled, shoving Slash away.

"About time you woke up." Slash sat against the wall of the cave. He had wrapped torn singed strips of her cloak around his leg. Water dripped down from the melting ice.

Veka looked around. Moltiki's body had been cut completely in half, either by Straum's jaws or by the explosion that followed. Huge shards of bone littered the cave floor. If the pent-up magic had done that to a dragon's bones, she wondered how bad the damage had been on the pixies' side of the portal.

She reached up to touch her face. Her fangs had driven right through her cheeks when she clamped Straum's jaws down around the serpent.

Blue blood. She stared at her hands. The metallic glow of the pixies' world was gone.

Slash was holding up one hand to block the sight of her blood. "Do you mind?"

She wiped her hands on her apron. "That box. What was it?"

"Needle trap. I pried it out of one of the Necromancer's doors a few months back. Dipped the needle in lizard-fish poison for good measure." He pointed to the pixie who lay dead near the tunnel entrance. "I had been planning to install it in a little chest and leave it in front of the goblin lair."

He gave a sheepish shrug. "The chief only told us not to kill goblins. Is it my fault if you hurt yourselves on one of my toys?"

Veka was too exhausted to do anything but shake her head. Even that was a mistake. The bones in her neck popped and cracked, shooting pain down her spine. All she wanted was to lie down and sleep for the next few days.

"How do you think Jig did?" Slash asked.

Veka snorted. "He's probably back at the goblin lair, sipping klak beer while the other goblins make up new verses for 'The Song of Jig.' "

Slash chuckled. "Forget 'The Song of Jig.' I want to know what they're going to sing about this." He waved an arm to encompass the snake, the bone debris, the dead pixies, and the multicolored slush dripping from the walls and ceiling. "I'll tell you this much, though. The first goblin to call me 'Slash' in a song gets a lizard-fish spine in her boot."

Veka stared at the scar running down his face. For the first time she thought to wonder how it had happened. "Who did that to you?"

He flushed. "I did it myself. An ax trap I was working on misfired." He shrugged. "Could be worse. You should see what my friend Marxa looked like after her fire trap went off prematurely."

Veka nodded absently. Reality was gradually beginning to seep through her shock. She was still alive. The portal was destroyed. The pixies had all died or fled.

She glanced at the tattered remains of her cloak, wondering what had happened to Snixle. She had forgotten all about him when she tossed away the burning cloak. If he had remained inside her pocket, she would have been able to smell his burned remains. She crawled over and poked the cloak. A bit of ash floated free, all that remained of her spellbook.

"Hey, Veka." Slash still wouldn't look at her. "That snake was going to kill me. One more bite. . . ." He grimaced and touched the bloody bandages on his leg. "I mean, if you hadn't stabbed him like that. He . . . you . . ." He shook his head. "Sorry, I can't say it. Not to a goblin. If the other hobgoblins found out a stupid, fat, ugly rat-eater like you had saved my life, they—"

"Shut up, Slash." Veka rolled her eyes. After everything else she had been through, the hobgoblin's insults were no more bothersome than gnats. The normal kind, not the orange pixie gnats. Besides, if he got too uppity, she could still bounce him off a few walls. "You're welcome."

She tried to stand up, and her head began to pound. "Forget that," she muttered. With the portal closed, she had to try several times to cast her levitation spell. The pixies' magic was still here, but it was dissipating fast, like smoke in the wind. Eventually she managed to tap into that fading power. Ever so gently, she lifted herself from the ground. A second spell scooped Slash after her. Together they floated out of Straum's lair and into the wider cavern, toward home.

CHAPTER 17

"Well, that didn't go quite the way we had planned."
—Poppink the Pixie

JIG HAD EXPERIENCED PLENTY OF UNPLEASANT awakenings in his life, from the time he woke up to find a group of goblins preparing to drop a baby rock serpent in his mouth to the time he discovered Smudge building a web in his loincloth. This one topped them all. Not only was Tymalous Shadowstar's voice booming loudly enough to crack his skull, but when he finally opened his eyes, Braf's face filled his vision.

Braf grinned so widely a bit of drool slipped from his lower lip. "It worked! You're alive!"

You weren't joking, were you? asked Shadowstar. *Less than a day, and already you've got goblins trying to kill you.*

Jig groaned and sat up. "Yes, I'm alive." He stopped. The pain in his back was gone. Drying blood covered his vest, but the wound itself had disappeared. *Why am I alive?*

Because Braf fixed that nasty hole in your back.

Jig stared, trying to absorb that piece of information. Braf had healed him. Braf, who was now standing next to Jig. Standing on two bare, perfectly healthy feet. Grell sat on the ground behind him, tending a small fire. She had taken the remains of Jig's muck pouch and set the whole thing aflame.

You . . . he healed me? But I thought you couldn't do anything down here. The pixies—

Look around, Jig.

The tunnels were the same red and black obsidian he was used to. The flames rising from his muck pouch were a healthy green. This was the chamber where he had fought the pixie queen. Without the sparkle of magic and the flurry of pixie lights, Jig barely recognized the place. The blood on the ground gave it away though. A sticky blue puddle showed where Jig had passed out.

Noroka still lay face first on the ground, snoring loudly. "You healed her too?"

Braf nodded. "Those pixies broke her nose pretty good, but she wasn't dead."

"Pixies. Right." Jig looked out at the bottomless pit. "How many others survived?"

"Counting us?" Grell asked. "Maybe five or six. I'm not counting you, because you should have been dead. Would have been, if Braf hadn't stuck his finger in your back and—"

"Thanks," Jig said, cringing.

"The others already started climbing back up to the lair," Grell went on. "I wanted to follow, but this clod kept insisting you were alive, talking about how he had to save you. When I asked how he planned to do that with the bones of his foot all crushed to gravel, he sat down and started fixing his own foot. After that I figured maybe he knew what he was talking about for once."

"How did you get here?" Jig asked.

Braf pointed to a rope hanging down the side of the pit. "One of the ogres tried to fly straight into the tunnel. Snapped his wings, but he nearly got me. Grell snuck up and jabbed a knife in his ear. We tied the rope around his body and climbed on down."

Jig stood up, testing his balance. He was filthy, hungry, and exhausted, but everything appeared to be working. He crouched by Noroka and shook her until she stirred. "Watch her," Jig warned. "Stop her if she tries to go over the edge."

Braf and Grell looked confused, but they didn't argue. Braf stepped toward the pit, arms spread.

"My head hurts," Noroka said. "I think the mountain punched me in the face." She gasped. "Grop. He—"

"Took a dive into the pit," Jig said. "Do you want to do the same?"

Noroka scowled. "Is that a threat?"

"No." Jig realized he was grinning. He didn't know how long he had lain there, but it was long enough for the pixie queen's magic to disperse. If the steel arrowhead hadn't killed her, the wind would eventually do the job, smashing her against the walls of the pit. Most of the pixies had probably suffered the same fate as they flew so recklessly after their queen, trying in vain to save her.

He stepped to the end of the tunnel and looked into the darkness. The muck fire gave enough light for Jig to see the nearest bubbles of the pixie nest. They sagged gray and broken from the walls. He saw pieces flaking away, spinning as they disappeared into the dark.

Of all the goblins who had come with him, only a handful still survived. He wondered how the goblins back at the lair had done against the ogres. If things had gone as poorly there, Jig might have single-handedly overseen the extermination of half the goblins in the mountain.

Is that why you spoke to Braf? he asked. *To replace me with a follower who doesn't get everyone around him killed?*

Don't be daft, snapped Shadowstar. *I spoke to him because it was the only way to keep you from bleeding to death. I actually asked Grell first, but she told me to go to hell. I wiped it from her mind, so she doesn't remember. But that left the idiot.*

Braf isn't—

I know he's not as dumb as he pretends to be, but he's still a goblin.

Thanks.

"What now, Jig?" Braf asked.

Jig stared for a long time before realizing what Braf meant. Jig was still chief. Braf and the others still expected him to tell them what to do. Jig groaned and rubbed his head. "We should go home," he said. "We have to find out if anyone survived up there."

"Braf and I will go first," Grell said. "He can haul me back up, and then you two follow. We shouldn't put too much weight on the rope. That ogre was a big fellow, but we don't want to push our luck."

Jig nodded.

"Watch out for that nest too," Grell added. "Those chunks are hard as wood when they fall, and they'll scratch you good. The big ones could knock you clean off the rope."

"I will," Jig said.

"Of course some of the pieces are pretty sharp. We'll be lucky if one doesn't cut the rope clean through as we're trying to—"

"Will you just go?" Jig snapped.

"Hmph." Grell grabbed a bit of rope and began tying herself to Braf. "See if I ever share my sugar-knots with you again."

Jig climbed slowly, despite his fears. He had hesitated at first, not sure whether he should go first and give Noroka a clear shot at his back. But if he followed, it would be just as easy for her to cut the rope, sending him into the pit. In the end he decided he was too tired to worry about it. If she killed him, at least he wouldn't have to be chief anymore.

His mind hurt as he tried to absorb it all. What had happened to the pixies' world? No matter how he thought about it, he kept coming to the same answer: Veka. She and Slash must have found a way to close the gateway. Jig spent a fair amount of time wondering how in the name of the Fifteen Forgotten Gods she had managed to pull that off.

Then there was Braf and Shadowstar. By all logic, Jig should have been happy. Let the goblins come to someone else for a while with their broken bones and their bloody wounds. Let Braf be the one the ogres sought out when pixies invaded. Braf could have Tymalous Shadowstar, and Jig could have some peace and quiet.

Yet every time he thought about it, the idea of Braf taking his place made his teeth clench tighter.

Why, Jig, I think you're jealous.

Jig rolled his eyes. *Can't you snoop around in his mind for a while?*

I did. It's boring. Besides, who says I can't snoop in two places at once? Now tell me, what's really bothering you?

You, said Jig. *You pushed me to go to the lower caverns with Walland. You pushed me to fight the pixies. You pushed me into that fight with Kralk. You've been trying to control me all along, just like the pixies controlled their ogres.*

Haven't we already been over this? Shadowstar asked, sounding a bit testy. *Jig, what do you think would have happened if you hadn't gone? The pixies would have swept through this mountain, and every last goblin would be dead or a slave.*

Jig wrapped his arms and legs around the rope and rested briefly. *Kralk could have led that fight.*

Jig, the goblins are dying.

Jig snorted. *That's what happens when goblins fight ogres.*

That's not what I mean. Think about that cavern where the ogre refugees were hiding. Who do you think used to live there, and what happened to them?

Jig didn't answer.

You goblins have always lived in the dark, dank holes of the mountain. Even before you sealed the way out a year ago, you isolated yourselves from the world. You hid, and you fought, and you died.

I sealed the entrance to protect us, Jig snapped. *And if this is your solution, I'm not impressed. All you did was speed up the process.*

No, the pixies did that. Jig, you can't go back to hiding in your temple, and the goblins can't keep hiding in their mountain. Straum's cavern is wiped out. The Necromancer's tunnels were already dead, if you'll forgive the pun. And there are other empty lairs, places where goblins and hobgoblins and other creatures used to live before they died out. If things don't change, empty lairs will be all that's left.

You want us to leave? Jig asked.

I want you to stop isolating yourselves. Jig, your race was brought here to help protect the treasures of the mountain. Those treasures are long gone. The goblins have no purpose. All you do is fight the hobgoblins and the other monsters, when you're not fighting yourselves.

Jig shook his head. *I can't—*

You have to lead, Jig. Kralk couldn't have done it. The hobgoblins won't. If the goblins are going to survive, you have to be the one to guide them.

It all sounded so reasonable. Jig rested his face against the rock. *Why didn't you tell me? Why not trust us to make our own decisions?*

Shadowstar didn't respond, and Jig didn't bother to repeat himself.

The goblin lair was empty. Braf and Grell had opened the door from the waste pit, and the cavern was as quiet as the Necromancer's throne room.

"Do you think the ogres won?" Braf asked.

Jig shook his head. The pixies' control over the ogres should have been broken, but that probably didn't matter. The ogres would have found themselves free, in the midst of a battle with goblins and hobgoblins. Being ogres, they probably reacted the same way the goblins would have: by finishing the battle. But if that was the case, why hadn't they overrun the lair? Where were the goblins who had remained behind? There were no bodies, no signs of battle, aside from day-to-day goblin messiness.

He hurried past the others, running toward the kitchen. Dying muck fires flickered to either side as he peered through the doorway.

The kitchen was empty. The cookfire was little more than embers.

"Golaka left her kitchen?" Braf whispered, sounding shaken.

Jig wanted to weep. He didn't have the strength for another battle. He reached up to pet Smudge. The fire-spider didn't seem worried. Maybe the events of the past few days had burned out his ability to feel fear.

By now Noroka had emerged from the waste pit. She cocked her head to one side and said, "Jig, listen."

He tilted his head and twitched his good ear. Screams coming from the hobgoblin lair. He started to reach for his sword, forgetting the pixies had thrown it away. Grimacing, he snatched a large kitchen knife and headed for the tunnels.

The closer they came to hobgoblin territory, the stranger the sounds became. He didn't hear the ring of steel or the high-pitched squeals of wounded goblins. The taunts and shouts weren't as loud or hateful as he would have expected either. Some of the voices actually sounded like they were singing.

A group of hobgoblins stood near their statue, guarding the entrance. One raised a copper mug. "Who goes there?"

"Filthy beasts, aren't they?" asked another of the guards.

Jig glanced down at himself. Perhaps he should have changed clothes after coming through the waste pit.

"Looks like a bunch of carrion-worms masquerading as goblins." That earned a laugh from the other hobgoblins.

"This is Jig Dragonslayer," snapped Grell. "The goblin who singlehandedly killed the pixie queen."

Jig flushed as the hobgoblins peered closer. A horrible thought entered his mind. Would they start calling him Jig Pixieslayer now?

"Jig Dragonslayer, eh?" The guard was clearly skeptical that the goblin chief would be wandering about in such a state. He glanced at his companions and shrugged.

"Put that thing away," said the largest of the guards, pointing at Jig's knife. Two others ducked into the hobgoblin lair. "They already carved the meat."

Already carved the meat? Jig stared at the knife in his hand. It wouldn't do much good against the hobgoblins anyway. The blade fit loosely into the empty sheath on his belt. "I don't understand. What—"

The other hobgoblins returned carrying large, wooden buckets. Before Jig could react, they tossed the contents over him and the other goblins. Jig barely had time to shield Smudge before the frigid water knocked him back.

"That's better," said the closest guard, swishing the half-empty bucket. "Folks are trying to eat and drink back there. If we don't rinse you down, you're going to ruin their appetites."

Jig was too confused to do anything but nod and turn around. They had a point, he supposed. He did smell pretty rank. Smudge was even worse, since fire-spiders cleansed themselves by burning whatever dirt clung to their bodies.

Still, there was no reason the water had to be so cold.

Eventually they were deemed suitable for hobgoblin society, whatever that meant, and led into the larger cavern. The dead goblin they passed along the way did nothing to calm Jig's fear. The hobgoblins stepped around the body. One of them muttered, "Makkar was supposed to clean up the traps. Looks like she missed one."

"This is weird," whispered Noroka.

Jig only nodded. Most of the partitions that had divided the hobgoblin lair were gone, torn down and piled to the sides. Hobgoblins and goblins crowded around an enormous bonfire, and as far as Jig could see, nobody was killing anyone else. He spotted a few fights, but they were weaponless spats. A hobgoblin bludgeoning a goblin here, a gang of four goblins piling on a hobgoblin there, nothing out of the ordinary. And those few fights were the exception to the overall sense of . . . of celebration.

Jig made his way toward the fire, where two hobgoblins were turning an enormous spit. Both hobgoblins cast nervous looks at Golaka, who rapped her ever-present wooden spoon against her palm as she supervised.

She supervised one hobgoblin on the back of the head, hard enough to knock him away from the spit. "Don't turn it so fast," she shouted. "Give the ogre time to cook. Give the sauce time to work through the meat. Otherwise you might as well eat him raw!"

Braf tapped Jig on the shoulder and pointed to the bonfire. "Isn't that Arnor?"

Jig squinted. Golaka's garnishes hid some of the features, but he thought Braf was right. Apparently some of the ogre refugees hadn't managed to escape from the pixies.

Grell sniffed the air. "Smells like Golaka broke out the elven wine sauce."

A loud, harsh voice cut through the noise. "Jig Dragon-slayer!" From the far side of the cavern, the hobgoblin chief waved his sword. "Someone drag that scrawny excuse for a leader to me."

Jig waded through the crowd, doing his best to avoid the larger goblins. Cheerful as things appeared, he was still the goblin chief, and there were a lot of ambitious goblins crammed in here. Nowhere near as many as there had been before, thanks to the fighting, but more than enough for Jig's comfort. Not to mention the hobgoblins, one of whom left claw marks in Jig's arm as he tried to hurry Jig along.

The chief sat on one of the rolled-up partitions, basically a log of heavy red cloth. One of his tunnel cats sat with its paws tucked beneath its chin as it worked the marrow from an ogre bone. Veka and Slash stood to one side, drinking klak beer. Veka had lost her robe and staff. Both she and the hobgoblin looked bruised and battered, and it was strange to see Veka in her ragged muckworking clothes. They made her look smaller somehow. Younger.

The hobgoblin chief pointed his sword at Jig. "A beer for the goblin chief!"

Veka rolled her eyes, then gestured. Across the room a cup jumped from a hobgoblin's hand and floated toward Jig. Veka bit her lip. From the looks of it, she was concentrating much harder than she had before. That thought cheered Jig immensely.

"You're using your magic to serve drinks now?" Jig asked. Veka scowled, and the cup wobbled just enough to spill beer onto Jig's arm. He grinned and snatched the cup. The smell of klak beer would help mask the odors still coming from poor Smudge.

"What a battle," the chief said. "They'll be singing songs about this one long after you and I are gone. Those blasted ogres drove us all the way through the tunnels to the entrance of our lair." He pointed. "That's where we hit them with our first ambush. I had your goblins come at them from the tunnel. Pathetic as you rat-eaters are in a real fight, it was enough to confuse the ogres. They're tough to kill, I'll tell you that much. No matter how many times we drove them back, they kept coming. Eventually they broke into the lair. We led them into the tunnel cat kennels near the back. Your little wizard here showed up around then, using her magic to fling weapons left and right. Not enough to kill an ogre, but she certainly kept them on their toes while our cats tore into them."

Veka's mouth wrinkled, as if she couldn't decide whether or not to take offense at the "little wizard" remark.

"A number of the ogres fled in the end. Your wizard thinks some pixies survived as well. I don't know where they'll get to, but I plan to be ready." He waved at Slash. "Charak here has been sharing some ideas for pixie traps, and I want them set up in your lair as well as ours."

Slash pulled a folded packet of parchment from his vest. Charcoal arrows and drawings covered the page. "I'm designing a pixie net using steel wire," he said, sounding more excited and animated than Jig had ever seen him. "I haven't figured out how to set a trigger for an airborne target yet, but I will. We can also stretch netting across any opening we don't want pixies coming through, like your waste pit or the privies. Can you imagine sitting down right when a pixie—"

"We'll need to do something about Straum's lair too," said Jig. "The dragon lined his cave with steel and iron to keep the pixies from coming through. Most of those weapons will have to be returned. Otherwise what's to stop the next group from recreating the portal?"

"The fact that I blew Straum's remains to pieces," Veka mumbled. She sounded dejected, which confused Jig. From the sound of things, she had done everything she ever dreamed of: fought pixies, destroyed the gate, and helped to save the goblins. Her magic was clearly stronger than before, and somehow she had survived the whole mess. What was wrong with her?

"You want us to give up our weapons?" The hobgoblin chief scowled, and Jig took a step back.

"Not all of them," Jig said. "But enough to line the walls of Straum's cave. Goblin and hobgoblin weapons both."

The chief's scowl faded. "Why not? If we need more swords, we can always come pound a few more goblin warriors and take yours, right?" He clapped Jig on the arm and stood up. "If we're going to do it, best to start now, before these fools sober up."

Despite his age, his shouts cut through the noise of the celebration like . . . well, like his sword. "Listen up! We're going to lock those pixies out of this mountain forever. To do that, I need you hobgoblins to gather every sword, knife, shield, and any other bit of steel or iron you can find. Once we see what we have to work with, we'll decide how much we need."

He glanced at Jig, clearly expecting him to make a similar announcement. Already hobgoblins were crowding around the chief, dropping weapons and armor at his feet. The sight of it confirmed something Jig had been thinking about ever since leaving the pixies' pit.

No matter how loudly he shouted, no matter how many songs the goblins sang about him, no matter how many pixie queens and dragons and Necromancers he killed, the goblins would never leap to obey him the way these hobgoblins did with their chief . . . the way the pixies obeyed their queen. Even the old ogre Trockle had been able to control her family.

Jig wasn't cut out to be a leader. Sure, they followed him into battle after a bit of prodding and bullying. Then he turned his back on Grop and nearly got himself killed.

His attempts to rally the goblins into battle with the hobgoblins had been humiliating, and his first official act as chief had been to flee to Kralk's quarters and hide.

Everyone stumbles in the beginning, Shadowstar said.

When a goblin stumbles, there's usually another goblin to make sure he doesn't get back up.

By now many of the hobgoblins were watching Jig, as were a number of goblins. He could see their suspicion building. Was this a trick to disarm the hobgoblins? The hobgoblins looked angry, and the goblins looked eager.

"Bring your weapons to the goblin chief," Jig said, wincing

at how hoarse his voice sounded. Drawing a deep breath and hoping it wouldn't be his last, he pointed to Grell. "Bring them to her."

Grell's cane jabbed him in the side before he could say anything more. "Did my withered ears deceive me, runt? If you think you can foist this job off on me, you—"

"Isn't it better than working in the nursery?"

"I'm looking after children either way. At least the babies don't poison you in your sleep. Not until they're two or three years old at least. If you want me dead, cut my throat and be done with it."

She was right, of course. Grell was one of the few goblins who would be even more vulnerable than Jig himself. He could already see the hunger in the eyes of the goblins, the calculating expressions. Jig had lasted several hours before his first assassination attempt. Grell would be lucky to last five minutes.

"Grell's smart enough to have survived this long," he said. "That's something we need from a chief."

Grell reached beneath her blankets and drew her knife, which she jabbed at Jig's throat. New odors wafted from Smudge as he grew hot from fright. "That's right. I survived by avoiding suicidal situations like this one. I'm not about to—"

"I'm not done!" Jig squeaked, backing away from that blade. He raised his voice. "I know you're already plotting to kill her, so I should warn you. Whoever kills Grell will die a slow, horrible death. I've cast a spell of protection on her. Every hurt I've healed over the past year, every broken bone, every gash, every split lip and chipped tooth, every gouged eye, hernia, and wart, all of them will be inflicted upon whoever dares lay a hand on her."

Oh, really? Shadowstar asked.

Shut up. As long as they *believe it, who cares?* The goblins looked nervous. They kept glancing from Jig to Grell and back again. He held his breath, hoping it would be enough. If not . . . if they didn't believe him . . .

"Yeah," Braf piped up. "And then I'll kill you." He was

unarmed, but he pounded his fist into his palm for emphasis. Whatever else he might be, Braf was a big goblin. The crowd began to mutter.

One of the hobgoblin swords floated from the pile of weapons and began to spin. Veka stepped forward to stand beside Braf. She didn't try to shout, but every other voice in the cavern went silent to listen. "But before he kills you, I'll seize control of your body. I'll make you smile as you eat your own limbs." The sword cut an arc through the air, driving the goblins back. "Cooked or raw, it's your choice."

The goblins backed down. A new pile of steel began to grow next to Grell. Jig knew most of the goblins were keeping knives or other weapons hidden, just as the hobgoblins were doing, but hopefully it would be enough. Given how sensitive the pixies had been to the touch of steel, they shouldn't need to line every bit of the cave. Just enough to disrupt their magic.

He turned to Grell. "Now will you be chief?"

Grell muttered and spat.

"I watched you," Jig said, lowering his voice. "You helped Braf. You helped me. You were the one who convinced the goblins to follow my orders. You know how to get them to do what you want. I don't."

He looked around. "You *care*. You won't let them die. You'll keep them safe and make them stronger." He swallowed, remembering what Shadowstar had told him. Angry as he was, he couldn't ignore the truth in Shadowstar's words. "We can't keep going on the way we have."

He held his breath. If he were in Grell's position, he would ram that knife right into Jig's belly. Sure, Jig and Braf and Veka had all sworn to avenge her death, but that didn't do anything to change the fact of her death, did it? Most goblins would be too afraid of Jig's bluff and the others' threats to do anything, but there were always a few clever enough to trick another goblin into doing their dirty work. Jig would have to keep an eye on those.

Grell poked him with her cane again. "If I'm going to be chief, I'm going to enjoy it. Grab me a pitcher of klak beer and a plate of Arnor."

Beside her the hobgoblin chief chuckled and turned his attention back to the growing pile of weapons and armor. Mostly weapons . . . neither hobgoblins nor goblins worried too much about armor. Jig reached around to rub the spot where Grop had stabbed him. Maybe he ought to snatch a scrap of armor for himself before all that steel went back to Straum's cave . . .

Two beers and a bit of heavily spiced ogre meat later, Jig was sneaking out of the hobgoblin lair toward home. Smudge sat on his shoulder, happily charring the scrap of meat Jig had saved for him.

"Jig, wait." Veka hurried after him, carrying a borrowed muck lantern. Blue light illuminated the tunnel, nearly washing out the few specks of orange that swirled around her head. "Pixie bugs," she muttered. "They were all over Straum's cave."

Jig didn't answer. She couldn't be planning to ask him about magic again. Whatever tricks Jig could do, Veka had clearly surpassed him. So what could she possibly want?

"Jig . . ." She grabbed his arm and dragged him to one side of the tunnel.

Jig tensed, suddenly very aware that he still hadn't replaced his sword.

But Veka only sighed and looked away. Her huge body seemed to deflate a bit.

"Jig, Braf told me what you did. How you led the goblins through the nest and killed the pixie queen."

Jig nodded, still unsure where this was going. For a moment, he nearly panicked, thinking Veka might somehow still be under pixie control, here to avenge his attack on the queen.

She swallowed, and her eyes shone. "How did you do it?" she asked softly. "I needed all of my magic just to survive, and even then . . . even then, Slash had to help me. I needed a hobgoblin's help to keep me alive long enough to kill the giant snake and destroy their gateway. I had all that power at my fingertips, and you had nothing. I know you couldn't talk to your god. You had no magic, nothing but a few goblins and some old weapons to fight an entire army of pixies and ogres, not to mention the queen herself, and you *won*. You killed her."

Jig touched his spectacles. "I was lucky."

Veka shook her head so vehemently her hair whipped Jig's face. "Nobody is that lucky." She patted her apron as though she was searching for something, and then her shoulders slumped even more. "In *The Path of the Hero* Josca wrote a list of one hundred heroic deeds. I read it so many times I could list the top ten in my sleep."

She closed her eyes. "For deed number one, Josca wrote, 'The mark of the true Hero, the one feat that scores above all others on the dimensions of courage, strength, cunning, and sheer nobility, is the slaying of an evil dragon.' "

With a weary sigh, she looked at him and said, "You're a Hero, Jig. A scrawny, half blind, weak runt with no real magic to speak of, but still a Hero."

"Thanks," said Jig.

She shook her head again. "You don't understand."

Should he tell her the only reason he had survived his encounter with the pixie queen was because of his spectacles? Or that if she examined every one of his so-called victories, what had kept him alive wasn't strength or nobility, but pure, unadulterated cowardice?

Veka swatted another bug. "I always thought you were weak. Hiding in your temple, letting Kralk bully you, flinching away from the larger goblins. I never wanted to be like you. But ever since you came back from your adventure, I wanted . . ." Her voice trailed off. Jig wasn't sure, but he thought she had said, "I wanted to *be* you."

"Veka, what—"

"I lost my spellbook. I lost Josca's book. I even lost that ridiculous cloak." She cocked her head to one side. "Which is probably for the best. That thing was too heavy for these caves. The material doesn't breathe at all, and I was always drenched in sweat. But, Jig, what am I supposed to do now?"

"I'm sure Grell wouldn't mind if you took one of Kralk's old outfits."

Veka rolled her eyes. "I thought . . . I wanted to go on adventures and save our people and discover ancient treasures and all that. But you're the Hero, not me. I'm not the one who killed the queen or slew the dragon. I—"

"Veka, I didn't kill the stupid dragon," Jig blurted.

She froze with her mouth half open. "What?"

Jig grimaced as he sang a bit of that blasted song, " 'While others fled, Jig grabbed a spear, and he threw.' The song doesn't say I actually killed Straum."

Veka blinked so rapidly Jig thought one of those orange bugs had flown into her eye. "I don't understand. Straum's dead."

"He's dead, but I didn't kill him."

"I *know* he's dead, Jig." She pointed to a long cut on her arm. "I got that when his bones exploded!"

Jig rubbed his head. Were goblins really this dense? "I threw the spear, just like the song says. I threw it right at Straum's eye, but the stupid dragon blinked. The spear lodged in his eyelid. Straum was going to have me for a snack when someone else grabbed the spear and finished the job."

"But you're Jig Dragonslayer."

He shook his head impatiently. "Not really."

Veka looked so stunned Jig thought she was going to fall down. Instead, she leaned against the wall and whispered, "You didn't kill the dragon."

"That's right."

Her quivering lips began to smile. "What about the Necromancer?"

Jig shrugged. "Well, yeah, I killed him."

"But . . . killing a Necromancer isn't even *in* the top hundred heroic deeds and triumphs. The closest thing would be defeating a dark lord who had returned as a spirit or body part. That was number eighty-three, I think. Though Josca wrote a footnote that you could score it a little higher if nobody else believed the dark lord had come back, and everybody teased you about your so-called obsession."

"Body part? Like a disembodied nose?" Jig cringed, trying not to think about a flock of glowing pixie noses chasing him through the tunnels.

"There was something about the black foot of Septor,"

Veka said. "Legend has it the foot appeared in the boot of the weather mage Desiron, and when he tried to pull on his boot, the black foot grew teeth and—"

"Veka, stop." It was too late. As if he needed more fodder for his nightmares. "If you want to go on adventures, go."

"But I'm not—"

"Not what? Not a Hero? Just because you didn't find 'Destroy a pixie portal in an abandoned dragon's lair' on Josca's list?" Jig couldn't believe he was saying this. "Would a real Hero let some dusty old book tell her what she could and couldn't do?"

"I guess not."

"And that giant snake you fought. Slash told me a bit about it. Flames and scales and wings and teeth . . . That sounds pretty dragonish to me."

Her face brightened. "That's true."

"Veka, we need goblins like you. Goblins who will delve into the abandoned tunnels and caverns of the mountain, or go out to explore the rest of the world."

"But you closed the entrance to the mountain," she said. Her eyes widened. "You're going to reopen the way?"

Jig gritted his teeth. Shadowstar hadn't spoken in some time, but he knew the god was listening. "I was wrong. We can't cut ourselves off from the rest of the world, Veka."

Veka stared at him for a long time, until Jig began to wonder if all this arguing had somehow broken her mind. When she finally spoke, her voice was quiet and tentative. "But what about you? Shouldn't you be the one to explore? To continue your adventures and add new verses to your song?"

Jig stepped back. "Nothing you, Grell, or even Tymalous Shadowstar say could make me set off on another adventure."

Ah, whispered Shadowstar. *That sounds like a challenge.*

No!

Veka had begun to smile. She looked like a nervous child, ready to bolt at the first sign of danger. "You really think I should be the one to go out there?"

"Better you than me." Jig pointed toward the goblin lair. "You'll want to gather some supplies. Clothes, food, weapons, that sort of thing."

"Thank you!" Veka grabbed his arms and squeezed. Then she was racing down the tunnel.

Jig watched the blue light of her lantern disappear into darkness. He was about to follow when he heard footsteps coming up behind him. Whoever it was, they were running. Only one person, from the sound of it. Jig backed against the wall, hiding in the darkness. Smudge remained cool, but Jig wasn't taking any chances.

His pursuer stopped almost within arm's reach and shouted, "Jig!"

Jig grabbed his ears and winced. "I'm right here, Braf!" He heard Braf jump away.

Hey, Jig said. *Couldn't you have warned him I was here before he deafened me?*

I could have, sure.

"What is it?" Jig asked. He sounded more brusque than he intended, but he didn't have time for another long conversation. Hobgoblins used big cups, and those two beers had gone straight to his bladder.

"It's about *him*," Braf whispered. "Tymalous Shadowstar. He never really told me what I was supposed to do. Except to heal you when you were dying, I mean."

Jig groaned. He wasn't even chief anymore. Why did everyone still expect him to tell them what to do? "Heal the other goblins. Hobgoblins too, if they need it. And he's not too keen on stabbing people in the back or killing them in their sleep."

"Weird," said Braf. "What else?"

Jig started walking. "Well, he might make you do stupid things like helping ogres or challenging the chief or battling pixies who can kill you with a wave of their hand." He glared skyward. "Not that he'd ever tell you what he's doing at the time."

"He's a god," said Braf. "They're supposed to be manipulative and incomprehensible to mere mortals, right?"

Jig scowled. "I guess."

"So that's it? Heal a few goblins, wake people up before you kill them, and fight a few creatures we would have had to fight anyway? That doesn't sound too bad."

"Wait until tomorrow, when you've got a mob of cranky goblins threatening to rip you apart unless you cure their hangovers."

Braf had stopped walking. "So what does he get out of it?"

"He gets to laugh at us as we're running around, trying to save our hides," Jig muttered. He waited for Shadowstar to chastise him, but his head remained mercifully silent.

"He did save your life," Braf pointed out.

Much as he hated to admit it, Braf was right. For all Shadowstar's meddling, he had saved Jig on several occasions.

"Um . . . Jig?"

"What?"

"You said Shadowstar's magic could cure hangovers?"

"I guess so," said Jig. "Why not?"

"Thanks!" Braf's footsteps retreated swiftly toward the hobgoblin lair.

There was a time when any priest of mine who drank himself into a stupor would have been stripped of his robes and driven out of town.

You want Braf to strip for you? Jig asked.

Gods forbid. No, these days one makes do with what one can. Goblins are a grubby, selfish, violent race, but they have their moments.

We're not children, Jig said.

What's that?

You're like Grell in the nursery, tricking and kicking the children to get them to do what she wants. Don't do it again.

Shadowstar's voice grew louder, and Jig imagined he heard thunder in the distance. *Are you trying to command a god, goblin?*

Jig didn't answer. He knew how far he could push Tymalous Shadowstar, and he had done nothing to truly enrage the god yet. He didn't think so, at least. There was one other thing he had learned about Shadowstar, something he hadn't shared with Braf: Tymalous Shadowstar was lonely. He had been one of the forgotten gods, alone for centuries until chance brought him and Jig together.

You're right, said Shadowstar. *I'm sorry.*

Jig was so surprised he nearly fell. He wondered how many people could claim to have gotten an apology from a god.

You know, back in the old days, worshipers wouldn't dare set terms to their gods.

Back in the old days, gods would rather disappear forever than take goblins as worshipers, Jig countered.

True enough.

Jig perked his ears. He could hear singing from the tunnels ahead, and faint green light flickered at the edge of goblin territory. He was almost home.

Go on. Eat, rest, and enjoy the peace while you can. You deserve it.

Jig stopped. *While I can? What do you know that I don't?*

Do you really want to spend the rest of your short life listening to that list?

The pixie queen is gone. The portal is closed. Veka and Grell and Braf can worry about helping the goblins to grow and explore. What's left?

Nothing. Nothing at all.

Jig grunted. "Good."

It's just that . . .

Jig closed his eyes. He hated gods. Almost as much as he hated himself for asking what he was about to ask. He knew he should let it go. Let Shadowstar taunt Braf with his foreboding hints and dire warnings. *What?*

Nothing really. You're right, you know. You beat the pixies, and you survived your little adventure, just as you survived that messiness with Straum.

So what aren't you telling me?

A faint tingling of bells filled the air: the sound of Tymalous Shadowstar's laughter. *Haven't you ever noticed? In all the songs and all the stories, adventures so often come in threes?*

Jig gritted his teeth. *I hate you.*

More bells, then silence. Shadowstar was gone.

Jig reached up to pet Smudge. He had no doubt Shadowstar was right. Shadowstar was always right about things like that.

With a shrug, Jig continued toward the goblin lair. Golaka should have plenty of leftovers, and with most of the other goblins still celebrating, Jig might actually be able to relax and rest for a little while.

Really, what more could any goblin ask for?

Goblin War

To Jamie.

Recitation of the Deeds of Jig Dragonslayer
(written by the goblin Relka, Founder of the Children of Shadowstar)

Relka: In the beginning, there was a muckworking runt called Jig.

Goblins: We stole his food and threw rats at him.

Relka: But destiny brought adventurers into our mountain haven. And lo, Jig set forth to combat these so-called heroes.

Goblins: Better him than us.

Relka: It was a battle of great chaos and bloodshed, and Jig did kicketh the human prince right in the rocks.

Goblins: Such should be the fate of all nonbelievers.

Relka: Though he was captured again, Jig was not afraid.

Goblins: Long may his loincloth remain unsoiled.

Relka: Jig led them into darkness, where he slew hobgoblins, the Necromancer, and even the dragon Straum with no more than a broken kitchen knife.

Goblins: Hail the miracle of the wobbly blade.

Relka: Jig returned triumphant, blessed by Tymalous Shadowstar with the gift to heal our wounds, though they be many and often self-inflicted. But lo, some were displeased with Jig's triumphs. The treacherous goblin chief Kralk sent Jig away, and none dared challenge her.

Goblins: For she was big and scary, and carried many weapons.

Relka: Guided by the light of Shadowstar, Jig descended into the mountain. There did he discover a great threat.

Goblins: Stupid pixies!

Relka: Jig and his companions returned to leadeth his fellow goblins in battle, but Kralk refused to believe. She fought, and she fell.

Goblins: Thus did Jig teach a great lesson: Never turn your back on a hobgoblin.

Relka: Jig set out to destroyeth the pixies, but still there were some who did not believe. A single kitchen drudge attempted to steal his glory for herself.

Goblins: And lo, Jig stabbethed you in the gut.

Relka: But Jig Dragonslayer was merciful. Upon his triumphant return from battle, and after drinking too much klak beer, he did heal my wounds, pouring the light and life of the Shadowstar into my very blood.

Goblins: Praise be unto Jig Dragonslayer, high priest of Tymalous Shadowstar. Long may he heal our wounds and fight our foes.

CHAPTER 1

STARLIGHT SPARKLED IN SILVER MORTAR AS TYmalous Autumnstar ran his fingers over the wall of his temple. The black stone was warm to the touch, constantly changing to record the prayers and gifts of his followers.

Every image and tribute ever created in his honor was here, preserved in the rock. To his right, the blood paintings of the Xantock Warrior Elves shone in the light, still wet after thousands of years. Overhead, the intricate carvings of the Undermountain Dwarf Clan spelled out their long-winded prayers.

The temple had gotten uncomfortably large over the years.

Tiny bells jingled on Autumnstar's sleeve as he touched a starburst a child had drawn in the mud. The ebony stone mimicked her painting so perfectly he could even discern the tiny whorls and loops where her fingertips had pressed the mud. Clumsy hieroglyphs below the picture read Tell gramma I miss her and please send me a puppy.

The painting was two centuries old, and the girl had long since followed her gramma. Autumnstar's forehead wrinkled. He had forgotten to take care of the puppy. That had been right around the start of the war, so he could probably be forgiven an oversight or two, but it still bothered him.

The temple shuddered, as if someone had taken the moon itself and smashed it against Autumnstar's roof.

Autumnstar's movements were slow, almost absent-minded as he raised a silver shield overhead. The second blow crumbled the ceiling to reveal the deeper darkness beyond. Mortar fell in glittering clouds as cracks spread through the walls. Stones shattered against Autumnstar's shield, centuries of worship and idolatry reduced to rubble.

Overhead, the Autumn Star burned red, casting a bloody glow over the remains of the temple. By the time the attack slowed and the dust began to clear, the remnants of the walls came no higher than Autumnstar's knees. He lowered his shield and used one foot to sweep some of the debris to one side. He preferred his home tidy.

The light of the Autumn Star vanished, blocked by the looming form of another god. Noc, a newly empowered death god, bent to touch a fallen shard of rock. The rock dissolved into smoke at his touch.

"Show-off," Autumnstar muttered.

Noc stepped over the broken wall and drew a sword of white light.

"You know," Autumnstar said slowly. "My temple had a door."

Goblin war drums wouldn't be so bad, Jig decided, if the drummers would only stick to a consistent beat.

He squeezed between a clump of pine trees. Snow spilled from the branches, most of it sliding down the back of his cloak. The rest landed in Jig's left ear.

Jig yelped and poked a claw into his ear, digging out the worst of the snow.

"We should stay quiet," Relka said behind him.

With great effort, Jig restrained himself from stabbing his fellow goblin. He wiped his nose on his sleeve and tried to ignore her.

Relka brushed snow from his back. "Don't you like the cloak I gave you? Why don't you use the hood?" She grabbed the hood before Jig could warn her. A moment later, she was cursing and shoving her singed fingers into the snow.

"Because that's where Smudge rides," Jig said, his annoyance vanishing as quickly as it had come. He grinned as he reached back to stroke his pet fire-spider. Smudge was still warm, but he settled down at Jig's touch.

"But you do like the cloak, don't you? I got it from an adventurer last month." Relka sucked nervously on her lower lip, tugging it between the curved fangs of her lower jaw. She did that a lot around Jig. Between that and the bitter cold, her lips were always cracked and bleeding.

Relka was one of the younger goblins, a kitchen drudge who worked with Golaka the chef. Her fangs were small for a goblin, and her face tended to be sweaty and streaked with soot from the cook fires. She had used an old tunnel cat bone to pin a blanket over her clothes for warmth.

Jig fingered the hole in the front of his cloak. Old blood had turned the frayed edges the color of rust where a goblin had gotten in a lucky blow with his spear. Still, even with the hole, at least the cloak was warm. Lavender wasn't exactly Jig's color, and he could have done without the embroidered flowers and vines running along the edges, but he wasn't about to complain. It was *warm*, and even better, the material was highly flame-resistant. Even if it did smell faintly of blood.

"You hate it, don't you?" Relka slumped. Even her wide, pointed ears sagged.

"It's not bad," Jig said grudgingly. "I like the pockets."

Relka beamed. Before she could speak, Jig quickly asked, "Shouldn't you be taking me to Grell instead of fussing about a cloak?"

Relka squeezed past him, close enough for her necklace to tangle in Jig's sleeve. She tried to tug it free, but only managed to jab Jig's arm.

"Sorry," she mumbled, her face turning a brighter shade of blue.

Her necklace was supposed to symbolize her devotion to Jig's god, Tymalous Shadowstar. Rat bones were lashed together to form a crude starburst. Pieces of a broken kitchen knife formed a lightning bolt, the lower tip of which was currently poking Jig's forearm.

Relka's obsession with Jig and Shadowstar had begun when she tried to stab Jig in the back. Instead, Jig had run her through, leaving her with a nasty belly wound while he led the other goblins off to fight pixies. Relka had crawled away to hide, terrified that Jig would return to finish her off.

Which he might have done, if Tymalous Shadowstar hadn't had this strange obsession with mercy and forgiveness. Also Relka made really good snake egg omelettes.

Jig clenched his jaw, driving his fangs into his cheeks as he waited for Relka to free her necklace. What was Grell doing outside in the first place, anyway? During a time of battle, a goblin leader traditionally stayed back where it was safe. Especially when it came to enemies like this.

The attack had begun this morning, and from what Jig had heard from the few goblins who limped back to the lair, this was no simple adventuring party.

"Grell?" He tried to speak loudly enough for the aging chief to hear, while at the same time keeping his voice low to avoid attracting any human attention. What emerged could best be described as "quavering."

"She said she was going to take care of the drummers," Relka said.

Oh. Jig felt a moment's sympathy for the goblin drummers. If they had caused Grell to miss her after-lunch nap, she would be even crankier than usual.

The area immediately around the goblin cave was flat, covered in small pine trees. If you walked directly away from the lair, you could go about fifteen paces before tumbling off a steep, rock-strewn drop-off.

The drummers would have taken the left path, which led along the cliffside and up toward the lake. The higher they climbed, the more people they could annoy with their drums.

The trees were denser as they approached the river. Their branches seemed determined to drop snow and needles down the back of his cloak. Trampled snow showed where goblin warriors had stormed through in search of humans to fight.

Pools of blue blood showed exactly where the humans had ambushed them. The bulk of the humans were still farther down the mountainside. They must have sent scouts ahead. It was a smart idea. The scouts could watch to see where the goblins were going, then report back to whoever was in charge. If they got the chance to surprise a few goblins, so much the better.

Jig didn't bother searching for the injured goblins. There were no bodies, which meant they had probably followed typical practice and fled like frightened rats. If Jig were smarter, he would be doing the same.

But where had the humans gone?

Relka hurried past before Jig could stop her. He crouched down, waiting for her to be shot or stabbed.

Nothing happened. She was already climbing up along the riverbank, using the shrubs and small trees to pull herself along the rocks. Jig held his breath and crept after her.

"It sounds like they're near the lake," Relka said. She drew a long, wickedly sharp knife. A cooking knife, from the look of it. Hopefully Golaka didn't know Relka had swiped it.

The drums grew louder as they followed the river back to the lake. Jig started to draw his sword, then thought better of it. Given the rocky, snow-covered terrain, he'd only end up tripping over a rock and impaling himself.

They scrambled on hands and knees to the top of a rise bordering the lake. As Jig pulled himself up, he heard the ripping sound of a dying drum, followed by the squealing sound of a dying goblin. He covered his eyes against the sun's glare. Only the edges of the lake were frozen, and the still water at the center created a second sun, reflecting the light into Jig's eyes and blinding him doubly. The amethyst lenses of his spectacles helped, but any relief they brought was balanced by splotches of melted snow. He wiped his sleeve over the lenses, but that only smeared his vision worse.

A short distance ahead, a human in leather and steel armor stood on the edge of the lake, surrounded by fallen goblins. He wore a green tabard with a picture of a giant four-legged boar standing in front of a tower. The animal appeared almost as large as the tower itself, and it held an enormous sword in one paw.

Humans wore strange clothes.

A dent in the human's helmet suggested the goblins had landed at least one good blow before they fell. Of the four goblin bodies scattered across the snow, only one was still moving.

"Oh, no," Jig whispered. The surviving goblin had fallen onto the ice at the lake's edge. She struggled to push herself up on twin canes of yellow-dyed wood. One cane punched through the ice. She fell back with a curse, losing her grip on the cane.

"Come on," said Relka. She started to rise, but Jig dragged her back.

"Humans have weird rules about killing unarmed old women," Jig said. "Some of them do, at least. Grell will be fine."

This human appeared to be one of the "honorable" ones. He kept his sword ready, but didn't try to stop Grell from crawling to the edge of the lake.

"At least you put a stop to that blasted drumming," Grell said. She took another step and her remaining cane slipped.

The human laughed.

"Oh, think this is funny, do you?" Grell rolled over and slammed her cane into the human's leg.

The cane broke. The human laughed even harder.

Jig shook his head. "It's not a good idea to laugh at Grell."

Grell stabbed the broken end of her cane into the human's thigh, right through the bottom corner of his tabard.

The human staggered back. He reached down with his free hand to rip Grell's cane from his leg.

"We've got to save her!" Relka grabbed Jig's hand and pulled him over the ridge.

They weren't going to make it. With only one cane to support her hunched body, Grell could barely even walk. The human was going to kill her, which would leave the goblins without a chief.

The last time that had happened was close to a year ago, when a hobgoblin named Slash killed the previous chief. The goblins had chosen Jig to take her place.

Jig still had nightmares about his short time as chief. Half of the lair had expected him to solve all of their problems. The other half had been busy plotting to kill him and take his place. Jig wasn't about to let that happen again.

He yanked his sword from its sheath. In the songs and stories, warriors sometimes threw their weapons as a last resort to kill distant enemies. As Relka ran ahead, Jig steadied himself, drew back, and flung his sword as hard as he could.

Either Jig was no warrior, or this wasn't the right kind of weapon for throwing. Probably both. The sword nearly cut off Relka's ear as it spun end over end. She dove into the snow.

The sword curved to the right and bounced harmlessly off a tree, halfway between Jig and the human. A bit of snow sprinkled down from the branches.

Everyone turned to look at Jig . . . who had now thrown away his only weapon.

Relka was busy digging through the snow. She must have dropped her knife when she tried to avoid Jig's sword. Wonderful. With a single throw, Jig had managed to disarm both himself and his companion.

Relka waved at him. "Don't worry! Shadowstar will guide you to victory!"

Jig stared at the limping human. Jig was unarmed, but the human carried enough weapons for three goblins. He switched his sword to his left hand and drew a knife with his right. He flipped the knife, catching it by the blade, and threw.

The knife spun past Jig's head, close enough for him to hear the whirring sound of its passage. With a loud thunk, the knife buried itself in a tree trunk.

Right. *Warriors* could throw their weapons. Goblins were better off running away.

Jig turned to run. He leaped over the ridge, skidding and flailing his arms for balance. He managed to run a whole three steps before tripping over a tree root. Rocks scraped his knees and hands, and the impact stole his breath. He pushed himself up. Snow smeared his spectacles, rendering them all but useless. He peered over the top of the frames at the blurry figure of the approaching human, who now carried swords in both hands.

That was simply unfair. Two swords against none? Jig squinted. Was that—? It was! The human was carrying Jig's own sword in his off hand.

"For Shadowstar!" Relka waved her knife as she charged to Jig's defense. It was a typical goblin tactic, with typical results. The human stepped to one side. Relka was running too fast to change direction, but she tried anyway, saving her life in the process. She stumbled, dropping her knife again as she fought to recover her balance. The human's follow-up attack missed, and then Relka was face-first in the snow.

"There's no place to run, goblin," the human said. He had faced four goblins, and he wasn't even breathing hard! "Turn around and die like a man."

Now there was a stupid suggestion if Jig had ever heard one. Jig pulled himself to his feet and searched his pockets for weapons. There were at least twenty pockets sewn into the cloak, enough for Jig to carry most of his belongings.

Unfortunately, that was far too many pockets to remember exactly where everything was. He found an old smoked bat wing, an extra pair of socks, some dead wasps he was saving for Smudge . . . hadn't he tucked a knife in here somewhere?

The human twirled both swords. The blades hissed through the air. His hands moved so fast Jig could barely follow, and his swords were all but invisible as they created a web of whirling steel. One limping step at a time the human advanced, bringing those blades closer and closer to Jig.

Jig reached into his hood and grabbed Smudge. For a moment Jig simply stood there, letting the fire-spider's warmth thaw his numb fingers. Then Jig threw him at the human.

Smudge landed on the human's chest and clung there, a blurry spot of black and red in the middle of the human's tabard. He had landed near the head of the beast embroidered on the tabard, like a tiny smoldering hat.

Unfortunately, the tabard gave no indication of bursting into flames. Either Smudge wasn't as frightened as Jig, or else the poor fire-spider was too cold to generate enough heat.

Well, on the bright side, Jig wouldn't have to worry about the other goblins trying to make him chief again.

The human's scream was so unexpected—and so terrifying—that Jig found himself screaming in response.

Both swords fell to the ground as the human grabbed the edges of his tabard and tugged it away from his body. He shook the tabard faster and faster, trying to shake Smudge free. Jig could have told him not to bother. Each of the fire-spider's legs had tiny hairs, like burrs, that let him cling to almost anything.

The human changed tactics. Still screaming, he dropped to his knees and tried to yank the tabard over his head. Unfortunately, he forgot to remove his helmet first.

Slowly Jig walked over to retrieve his sword. The human was still trying to rip the tabard off his helmet when Jig stabbed him.

He wiped his sword as he waited for Smudge to cool. Apparently all that flapping had been enough to wake Smudge up. The poor spider struggled to climb down off the human. The meandering path of smoldering spider footprints on the tabard was proof of Smudge's dizziness.

Jig stared at the dead human, trying to understand his reaction. You'd think he'd never seen a fire-spider before. Smudge wasn't even the biggest specimen Jig had encountered, being only a little larger than Jig's hand.

Humans were weird.

More shouts made Jig jump. He might have killed one human, but there were plenty more running about, and Jig didn't have enough fire-spiders to fight them all. He cocked his head and twitched his good ear. The other ear had been torn in a fight with another goblin, long ago. Still, a single goblin ear let him hear better than any two-eared human.

From the sound of it, the humans were getting closer.

Jig plucked Smudge from the human and stroked the spider's still-warm thorax before returning him to his hood.

"I knew Shadowstar would bring us victory," Relka said. Blood dripped down her cheek. Her fang had broken the skin when she fell.

"Right," said Jig. "Maybe next time Shadowstar can kill the human, and I'll stay in the lair where it's warm."

Grell appeared to be uninjured, judging by the volume of her cursing as she yanked her remaining cane from the ice. Jig grabbed the human's sword and gave it to her as a substitute. The tip sank deep into the earth, so Jig went back to retrieve the scabbard.

Grell took another step, resting her weight on the sheathed

sword. With a grunt of approval, she hobbled over to the human and whacked him with her remaining cane.

"Blasted humans," she said. "Don't they know the dragon's dead? Treasure's all gone."

"What were you doing so far from the lair?" Relka asked.

Jig was more interested in knowing how Grell had made it so far. Grell was the oldest goblin in the lair, with the possible exception of Golaka the chef. But where Golaka had gotten stronger and meaner with age, Grell got smaller and wrinklier, like fruit left out in the sun. Sometimes Jig thought the only thing keeping her going was sheer stubbornness.

Grell began walking toward the lair, wheezing and grunting with each step. "There are too many humans for them to be adventurers. Adventurers are like tunnel cats. A few of them might be able to live and hunt together, but if you add more, they all start biting and clawing and hissing at one another."

Relka cocked her head. "They're not exactly the same, though. When you eat tunnel cats you spend half the time picking fur out of your meal. You don't have that trouble with adventurers. Except dwarves."

Grell jabbed her cane at the human Jig had killed. "There could be a hundred of them. Far too many for us to fight. And a few of the warriors are saying they saw elves."

"That's why you wanted to stop the drumming." Goblins didn't have formalized signals for battle. So long as the drums kept beating, the goblins kept fighting. If the drummers died or ran away, that was the signal for everyone else to do the same.

Jig perked his ears. He only heard one drum now, off to the other side of the lair.

"I sent Trok out to shut that one up." Grell scowled. "Probably should have been more specific about *how* to shut him up."

Jig's skin twitched with every shout and scream. He reached for Grell's elbow to hurry her along, but a rheumy glare made him back down.

"Maybe they're hunting," Relka suggested. "For food, I mean. There hasn't been as much to eat since the snow came. Humans have to eat too."

"Humans don't eat goblins," Jig said. His stomach clenched at the thought of the things they did eat. Dried fruit and porridge and bread. What little meat they ate had all the flavor cooked out of it. Jig had been a prisoner of human adventurers for only a few days, but it had taken close to a month for his stomach to recover.

The last drum fell silent. After a lingering scream, so did the drummer. Shouts echoed up and down the mountain as the goblins began to retreat.

Jig squeezed through a clump of pine trees and waited, holding the branches out of Grell's way. He could see the lair from here. How bad would it be to let the branches slap Grell to the ground so he could scamper to safety? Smudge was already getting restless in his hood. The cloak was relatively fireproof, but the wisps of Jig's hair weren't.

A trio of limping goblins scurried into the lair up ahead. A fourth followed, hopping on one foot. His other leg bled from the thigh, leaving a bright blue path in the muddy snow.

The cave was partially hidden by a fallen pine. A heavy gate had once blocked the way, but that gate had disappeared a few months back. The hobgoblins had stolen it to build a bigger cage for their trained tunnel cats.

The pine tree didn't block anyone out, but it did hide the lair from casual view. The only drawbacks were the brown needles that tangled into your hair, and the sticky sap that covered your clothes, not to mention the overpowering pine smell. The smell had faded with time, but the tree seemed to have an endless supply of brittle needles with which to torment innocent goblins.

Two more warriors disappeared into the lair before Jig and his companions reached the tree. Jig played with one fang and tried not to let his impatience show as Grell hunched to step inside. Her joints popped, and she wheezed with every step.

Jig could hear the humans shouting as they closed in. Grell was right. There were an awful lot of humans out there.

Trok ran past, knocking Jig into the snow as he tried to get into the lair. He didn't make it. As he squeezed past Grell, she dropped her cane and twisted her claws into Trok's ear. With her other hand, she shook her borrowed sword until the scabbard fell free. "Relka, do you know any good recipes for goblin ear?"

"Four," Relka said. "Do you want something spicy?"

"Spicy food puts me in the privy all night." Grell gave up trying to draw the sword. She clubbed Trok's foot with the partly sheathed weapon. "Of course, I could put him on privy duty as part of his punishment."

Trok was a big goblin. He wore several layers of fur to make himself look even bigger, despite the fact that all of those furs made him sweat something awful. Trok's glistening face twisted into a sneer.

Grell pinched her claws deeper into his ear, drawing spots of blood. Trok yelped and backed down. He rubbed his ear as he waited for Grell to pass beneath the pine tree.

Neither Jig nor Relka received the same courtesy.

The obsidian walls of the tunnel muted the sounds of battle somewhat as Jig finally scurried into the darkness of the mountain. His eyes struggled to adjust. The warmer air had already painted a film of mist onto his spectacles. But no goblin who survived through childhood relied on vision alone. Jig could hear Grell grumbling and stomping her feet for warmth up ahead. A quick sniff assured him that Trok wasn't waiting nearby to take his annoyance out on Jig.

Grell's cane and sword tapped the rock as she moved on. From the sound of it, she was limping even worse than usual. The cold had been hard on her, and she had asked Jig and Braf for healing almost every night for the past month. Jig and Braf were the only two goblins "gifted" with Shadowstar's healing magic. That gift meant they both spent much of their time healing everything from cold-dead toes to rock serpent bites to that nasty case of ear-mold Trok had gotten a few months back.

The last glimmers of sunlight faded behind them, replaced by the comforting yellow-green glow of muck lanterns burning in the distance. Jig splashed through puddles of half-melted snow as he followed Relka and Grell through the main tunnel toward the rounded entryway into the temple of Tymalous Shadowstar.

Glass tiles on the ceiling portrayed the pale god looking down at the goblins. As always, Jig's gaze went to the eyes. Sparkling light burned in the center of those black sockets. No matter where you stood, those eyes always seemed to be watching you.

Once, Jig had painted a blindfold over Shadowstar's face. The god had not been pleased.

The temple was the first cave anyone saw after entering the mountainside. Looking back, Jig probably should have put it somewhere a bit more out of the way. Mud and slush covered the floor where goblin warriors had stomped their boots and brushed themselves off as they passed through. Other warriors stood dripping by the small altar in the corner, where poor Braf struggled to heal them as quickly as he could.

Relka touched her necklace. "Make way for Jig Dragonslayer!"

Grell coughed.

"And Grell," Relka added hastily.

The announcement of Jig's arrival didn't have the effect Relka was hoping for. Instead of spreading out to make room for Jig, the goblins split into two smaller swarms, one of which immediately surrounded Jig, the same as they had done with Braf.

"Why should Jig Dragonslayer provide the healing power of Shadowstar to nonbelievers?" Relka demanded. She wrapped both hands around her bone-and-knife pendant. "How many of you have donned the symbol of— Ouch." Shc stuck her finger in her mouth. Apparently the knife blades on her necklace were still sharp.

"Everyone back to the lair," Grell snapped. "You think those humans are going to stop once they reach the entrance? Go on."

Slowly the crowd dispersed through the three tunnels on the far side of the temple. All three merged a bit farther on. No doubt there would be further injuries to heal once the goblins reached that junction and fought to go first.

Grell grabbed one goblin as he turned to leave. A bloody gash crossed his scalp. "You don't have pine needles in your hair. How did you manage to get yourself injured without leaving the tunnels?"

"Bat."

"A bat did that to you?"

"No." He pointed to another goblin. "Ruk was trying to hit the bat with his sword, and—"

"I would have got him, too," interrupted Ruk. "But then he flew away."

Grell rubbed her forehead. "Ruk, go up the tunnel and wait by the entrance. Humans don't see well in the dark. They'll be disoriented. Stay there and kill anything that comes in. Anything that's not a goblin, that is."

She smacked him with a cane for good measure.

Ruk left, grinning and jabbing imaginary humans with his sword. Jig watched him go. "Do you really think he'll be able to slow down the humans?"

"Nope," said Grell. "But any idiot who'd slice his own partner is one I won't miss. When he screams, we'll know they've entered the mountain."

Despite the imminent attack from the humans, Jig found himself relaxing as he followed Grell deeper into the dark tunnels. The closer he got to home, the more the smell of muck smoke and Golaka's fried honey-mushrooms overpowered the scent of pine. His boots clopped against the hard stone. He ran one hand over the reddish brown wall, smiling at the familiar rippled feel of the obsidian. The warm air drifting from deep within the mountain helped drive the worst of the numbness from his fingers. Of course, that air also carried the faint smell of hobgoblin cooking, but at least it was warm.

A group of armed goblin warriors crowded near the entrance of the cavern, joking and boasting about what they would do to the humans. These were the same goblins who had shoved past Jig and Grell in their eagerness to flee back to the lair. But now that they were here, every last one shouted tales of triumph and victory, trying to top the rest.

Jig had seen it before. The worst part was that every goblin started to believe what the others were saying. Before long they would be charging back out of the mountain to prove themselves.

Grell solved the problem by jabbing the closest warriors with a cane. "You three go wait in the temple. Ambush anyone who comes in."

Relka shoved past Jig, clearing a path through the remaining warriors. She raised her voice, so her words echoed through the tunnels. "The high priest of Tymalous Shadowstar has returned!"

From the direction of the hobgoblin lair, a faint voice shouted back, "Shut up, you stupid rat eaters!"

"Stupid hobgoblins," Relka muttered. "Why aren't they out there fighting the humans too?"

"Because I sent Braf to ask them for help when the humans first arrived," Grell said.

Relka shook her head. "I don't understand."

"The fool went and told them the truth about how many humans and elves we were fighting. The hobgoblin chief told him. . . ." Grell shook her head. "Well, it doesn't matter. Braf's not flexible enough to do it, at any rate."

Jig hunched his shoulders and followed them into the deep cavern the goblins claimed as their home. Inside, goblins scampered about like rats with their tails on fire. A group off to thc right traded wagers as to how many goblins would die in the fighting. Others squabbled over the belongings of the dead and the almost-dead. Jig's attention went to a skinny goblin girl near the edge of the cavern. She kept her head bowed as she moved, carefully refilling the muck pits and lighting those that had gone out.

A few years ago, that had been Jig's job. The caustic muck could blister skin, the fumes made the whole cavern spin, and woe unto the careless goblin who let a spark land in his muck pot. Still, as smelly and humiliating as muck duty had been, at least it hadn't involved running out into the snow in the middle of a battle. Or fighting dragons and pixies and ogres. Or trying to avoid Relka and her band of fanatics.

Jig wondered if the muckworker would be willing to trade.

Several of Relka's friends were already crowding around Jig. Like Relka, they wore makeshift necklaces to show their devotion to Tymalous Shadowstar. Most were goblins who had been healed by Jig or Braf in the past. Given how the rest of the lair reacted to their endless praise of Jig and Shadowstar, they tended to need healing fairly often.

"Jig, come with me," Grell snapped. She hobbled through the crowd to one of the few doors in the cavern. Fixing wood to rock was tricky, but Golaka the chef made a paste that could be spread on the walls. The mold that grew on the paste clung equally well to stone and wood, enabling the goblins to erect a few crude doors. The chief's cave was the only one with a lock.

Grell grabbed the door with both hands. Goblins everywhere cringed as the wood screeched over the stone floor. Jig reached out to help, but a glare from Grell stopped him.

"I can open my own door, thank you." Eventually she managed to slide the door wide enough to slip inside.

A single muck pit cast a weak green glow over the cluttered space within. A handful of weapons sat beside a batskin mattress filled with dried grasses. Grell wheezed as she lowered herself onto the bed, a complicated process that involved much grunting and repositioning of her canes. Finally she sat back and pulled a blanket of tunnel cat fur over her body.

"Perhaps Jig Dragonslayer should lead the goblins while you rest?" Relka suggested as she dragged the door shut behind her.

Grell opened her eyes. "And perhaps you'd like me to find a new place to store my cane." She reached to the other side of her mattress and grabbed a clay pot. Jig's nose wrinkled at the smell of stale klak beer. "The dragon take this wind and snow. Every time there's a storm, my joints swell up like leeches on an ogre's backside. And I think I did something to my knee out there on the river."

Jig sat beside the bed. He shoved the blanket back and put one hand on her knee. He could feel the joint grinding as Grell straightened her leg, and her kneecap popped beneath his fingers.

No matter how often Jig healed Grell of one ailment or another, nothing seemed to last. Was Shadowstar's magic failing? The other goblins stayed healed. Well, except for Relka's friends. But when you interrupted a warrior's dinner to sing the praises of Tymalous Shadowstar, you had to expect a plate-size bruise on your face.

The warmth of Shadowstar's magic flowed through Jig's fingers, driving away the last of the snow's pain as Jig healed Grell's knee.

I can help you fix the damage she did on the ice, but it won't last. Tymalous Shadowstar, forgotten God of the Autumn Star, sounded strange. His voice was softer than usual.

Why not?

Because she's old, Jig.

But what's doing this to her? Jig glanced around, frowning as he spotted the klak beer. *Is someone poisoning her?*

No, she's just old.

I know. Everyone knew Grell was old. That's why her skin was all wrinkly, and she had to run to the privy four times a night. *But why is she—*

This is what happens when people get old. Their bodies begin to give out. Don't goblins ever die of old age?

Jig shook his head.

Oh. Right.

The tendons twitched beneath Jig's hand, and Grell gasped. She bent her leg, and this time the kneecap stayed where it was.

"That's a little better," Grell said with a sigh.

"Praise Shadowstar."

Jig glanced up at Relka, then bit back a groan. She had taken off her blanket. Her shirt was torn in the middle, revealing the scar where Jig had stabbed and healed her.

In the old days, you would have had hundreds of followers like Relka and her friends, Shadowstar said. *Well, not exactly like her. But it's only natural for them to look up to you and Braf.*

Can't they look up to us from a distance? Jig asked.

Shadowstar laughed, a sound that always reminded Jig of tiny bells. *Be thankful I'm not asking you and the others to perform the solstice dance.*

What's the solstice dance?

Another jingling laugh. *On the first night of autumn, when my star is highest in the sky, you and the others spread your yearly offerings on a great bonfire. The idea was that the smoke would carry your prayers to the stars. Then you dance from sundown to sunrise to celebrate another year of life.*

Jig wasn't much of a dancer, but that didn't sound too bad.

Did I mention that the high priest dances naked? added Shadowstar.

Goblin war cries erupted from the tunnels. Jig twisted around, his ears perked high. The door muffled the noise somewhat, but it sounded like the humans had reached the temple. He hoped Braf had made it away before the humans arrived.

"That idiot Ruk." Grell crawled off the mattress and rummaged through her pile of weapons. "He was supposed to scream before they killed him."

Smudge was squirming about in Jig's hood. Now that they were inside, the cold didn't suppress the fire-spider's heat. Jig grabbed Smudge and dropped him into a pocket in his cloak, one he had lined with leather. Then he stuck his fingers in his mouth. Smudge wasn't hot enough to blister skin, but he was close.

"Shadowstar will protect us," said Relka. "I am not afraid."

Another scream punctuated her words.

"Like he protected that poor fool?" Grell asked.

"If those goblins had truly believed, Shadowstar would have saved them."

"I miss Veka," Jig mumbled. Veka was a distillery worker with delusions of heroism. She had followed Jig around for a while, just like Relka. Veka had dreamed of learning the secrets of magic in order to become a sorceress and a hero.

Jig thought she was mad, but at least Veka had been useful in a fight. Unfortunately, she had left shortly after the battle with the pixies and the ogres, going out into the world to "pursue her destiny."

Jig had never worried about pursuing his destiny. Generally, destiny pursued him. Then it knocked him down and kicked him a few times for good measure.

This time it sounded like destiny planned to bully the entire lair. The humans had already reached the main cavern.

In the past, the goblins would have charged into the tunnels two or three at a time, to be killed at the humans' leisure. These days, they had learned to wait and allow intruders to charge into the lair, where they would be surrounded and outnumbered.

The twang of bowstrings and the shrieks of goblins told Jig how well that tactic was working.

"We should have covered the muck pits," Jig whispered. Humans didn't do well in the dark. Extinguishing the fires might have given the goblins more of an advantage.

"Come on." Relka grabbed Jig's arm and tugged him toward the door. She had her knife ready. "The goblins need their champion!"

"What am I supposed to do?" He pressed his ear to the door. The clank of armor and the clash of weapons had already spread. He heard shouts from the back of the cavern, where goblins were no doubt fighting one another in their eagerness to escape down the garbage crack that led to the lower tunnels.

"What do you think you're doing?" From the opposite side of the cavern, Golaka's outraged shriek was loud enough to make Jig flinch back from the door. A loud clank followed, as if an enormous stirring spoon had dented a soldier's helmet.

"Focus your efforts on that one!" A human's voice. Male, with a slightly nasal tone to it. "Form a line and drive the rest of these vermin back!"

"Clear room for the archers!" This voice was female. At least Jig thought it was. With humans, it could be hard to tell. They all sounded a lot alike, probably because of those tiny mouths and teeth.

An arrow punched through the door in front of Jig's nose. He leaped back so fast his head hit the wall.

"Jig, open the door."

"What?" Jig stared at Grell. How much klak beer had she drunk since they returned?

Grell pulled her blanket up to her chin and settled back. "We face them now and find out what they want, or else we wait until they've slaughtered every last goblin in the lair."

"I like waiting," Jig mumbled.

"Open the door, or else when we get out of this, I'll tell Golaka you've been stealing her fried rat tails."

"So you're the one!" Relka whispered.

"No!" Jig's toes curled in his boots at the thought of the last goblin Golaka had caught stealing her treats. Golaka had turned his ears into a spice pouch. "I mean, it was only a few. Smudge likes them, and—"

The loudest crash yet made the door shiver. Golaka must have flung one of her cauldrons at the attackers.

Grell bared her yellow teeth. "Enough of this. Relka, go tell Golaka—"

Jig shoved the door open a crack. Then another shout from the humans pushed any thought of Golaka from his mind.

"We have the spoon!"

"Oh no," Jig whispered. He peeked past the edge of the door.

The humans stood in a half circle in front of the main entrance. Another group battled Golaka and the other goblins near the kitchen. A ring of humans lay groaning at her feet. Skewers, forks, and other utensils protruded from their bodies.

One of the humans ran back toward the entrance, waving an oversize stirring spoon above his head. Several others shot arrows to stop the goblins from pursuing. One arrow rang as it ricocheted off the iron lid Golaka held in one hand. Another hit her in the arm. More arrows drove her back into the kitchen. Humans with spears pursued, keeping their weapons extended to break any counterattack.

"Where is your chief?" That was the female voice. She stood near the entrance. A tight ring of soldiers blocked her from sight.

The goblins backed away. Seeing Golaka driven to retreat had taken much of the fight out of them. Several pointed toward Jig.

"Him?" The human sounded skeptical.

"No!" Jig yelped. "Not me, her!" He shoved the door wider and pointed to Grell.

Whatever the woman tried to say was overpowered by screams from the kitchen. Spears clattered to the ground as the humans stumbled out, covered in steaming lizard-fish pudding.

"Forget the chef," the woman shouted. She and about twenty soldiers shoved their way toward Grell's cave.

Jig scurried out of the way as soldiers stepped into the room. One of them smirked as he studied the goblins. "Nothing to worry about, Highness. A runt, a girl, and an old woman."

The woman entered next. She was shorter than the others. Her tabard was black, as was the embroidered crest of that odd beast. Jig could barely see the shine of the thread. The hardened leather of her armor was black as well, reminding Jig of the shine of the lake deeper in the tunnels.

Her sword was thin and sharp, with a blackened guard like a metal basket that covered her entire hand. Even the gem that shone in its pommel was black. Her boots, her belt, her gloves, even her hair . . . it was as if someone had spilled nighttime all over her.

A round helmet—black, of course—left her pale face bare, and something about that sweaty expression seemed familiar.

She glanced at Jig and Relka, then turned to Grell. "I'm supposed to believe one of you leads these monsters?"

"That's right," said Grell. "And you're in charge of this mob?"

"My brother and I, yes. I am Genevieve, daughter of—"

"I don't care." Grell tossed her blanket to one side. In her hands she held a small, cocked crossbow. Before anyone could react, she pulled the trigger. The bolt flew into the woman's neck . . .

. . . and dropped to the ground. A small drop of blood welled up on Genevieve's neck where the point had—barely—penetrated the skin. The blood was surprisingly colorful against her pale skin.

Grell flung the crossbow to the ground. "Stupid, worthless piece of hobgoblin garbage."

One of the soldiers leaped to the bed and pressed a knife to Grell's throat. Another kicked Jig to the ground for good measure. Relka got the same treatment on the other side of the cave.

"Easy there," said Grell. "Cut my throat and you'll never find the antidote."

"Antidote?" Genevieve touched her neck and stared at the smear of blood on her glove.

"I keep that little toy by my bed to discourage younger goblins who think they should be chief," Grell said.

The soldiers stepped aside as Genevieve approached the bed. One slipped out of the cave and ran back toward the tunnels.

Genevieve leveled her blade at Grell's chest. "Give it to me, goblin."

"Tell your people to retreat and leave us alone," Grell said.

Jig glanced at the floor where Grell's crossbow bolt had fallen. With everyone's attention on Grell, he could snatch that bolt and plunge it into Genevieve's back.

And then what? Killing a goblin chief led to chaos. Half of the goblins turned on one another, eager to take the chief's place, while the rest fled to avoid getting drawn into the brawl. But humans weren't like that. They had things like discipline and loyalty, not to mention enough weapons to kill every goblin still in the lair. Killing their leader wouldn't stop them; it would only make them angrier.

"The antidote," Genevieve said. "Or I'll cut off your ears."

"Don't give it to her!" shouted Relka, earning another kick.

Grell sighed and pointed to a small box.

Genevieve grabbed it and wiped crumbs from the top. Inside was a wooden tube, plugged with wax.

Jig had never seen Grell give up that easily. Actually, he had never seen Grell give up at all. He stared at Grell, but her face was pure, wrinkly innocence.

Genevieve uncapped the tube and poured the cloudy liquid down her throat. She coughed and wiped her lips on her wrist. "What a foul concoction."

"So I've been told," Grell said. "I thought about mixing blackberry juice to mask the taste of the poison, but—"

"The taste of the what?" Genevieve stared at the empty tube.

"Poison. That's a mix of rock serpent venom and lizard-fish blood."

Relka snickered.

"You said that was an antidote to the poisoned bolt," Genevieve said.

"Poisoned bolt." Grell rolled her eyes. "You think I'd risk poisoned weapons with this lot?" She lay back and adjusted her blanket. "Call off your army."

"I'll not bargain with goblins."

Grell shrugged. "What about a wager? I'm betting the rock serpent venom will paralyze you before the lizard-fish blood starts to burn holes in your stomach."

"I'll bet a week's worth of dessert that the lizard-fish blood hits first," Relka said brightly.

"Fetch my brother," Genevieve said. "Tell him I've been poisoned, and—"

"Not to worry." The other human leader was already pushing his way into the cave, followed by a pair of elf archers.

Unlike Genevieve, this human wore elven armor: thin scales of magically hardened wood, each one polished until it gleamed like metal. "What's the trouble, Genevieve? Did the goblins turn out to be too much for you? You're not trained for such things, Sister. It's as I was telling Father."

Genevieve sounded bored. "If you'll recall, goblin treachery got the best of Barius, too. And he used to thrash you with ease. Tell me, Theodore, how many times did you run to Mother, crying because Barius had made you clean out the stables with your bare hands, or—"

"Enough," snapped Theodore. His face was bright red, and he looked like he had completely forgotten about the goblins.

Jig was barely listening. He should have learned by now. No matter how dark and dire the situation, things could always get worse. And they usually did.

No wonder they had known about Golaka's spoon. Prince Barius Wendelson had been one of the adventurers who came to the mountain two years ago in search of the Rod of

Creation. He and his fellows had killed the rest of Jig's patrol and dragged Jig deep into the mountain as an unwilling guide.

"Aye, enough indeed." A hefty, black-haired dwarf stepped into the cave. "Let's be getting that garbage out of your sister's blood before I have to go back and tell her folks how a goblin finished off their only daughter."

Jig pressed himself back against the cave wall. *I don't suppose your magic can make me invisible?* he prayed.

The dwarf glanced at the goblins as he moved toward Genevieve. He whirled back around, his mouth round with shock. "Jig?"

I'm afraid not, said Shadowstar.

Jig's shoulders slumped. "Hello, Darnak."

CHAPTER 2

HOW MANY OF AUTUMNSTAR'S COMPANIONS still fought? Blind Ama had been the first to fall after Noc's betrayal. Whose idea had it been to let a blind god charge into battle, anyway? The old fool had raced straight into Noc's lightning.

And now Noc had come for Autumnstar.

"You've gotten stronger," Autumnstar commented.

Noc's tactics were simple but effective. Lightning struck Tymalous Autumnstar's shield over and over until it glowed from the heat.

The bells on Tymalous Autumnstar's sleeves began to melt. Molten silver dripped over his free hand to splash upon the floor. He winced and raised his hand to his mouth, sucking the singed flesh.

"The two have pronounced sentence upon you and your fellows," Noc said. His voice had gotten deeper, too.

"The two gods of the beginning couldn't even pronounce my name," Autumnstar answered. "They're mindless, so caught up in their own struggles they never even noticed us." The lightning made it difficult to see, but Autumnstar thought he saw Noc shrug.

"The upper gods have pronounced sentence in their stead," Noc admitted. "Now stop interrupting. Entire civilizations

once looked to you for guidance and comfort, and you betrayed them. In punishment—"

"We tried to protect them!" Autumnstar dropped to his knees.

The lightning grew brighter. The edges of Autumnstar's shield began to smoke, the god-forged metal boiling away under Noc's assault. Vision was useless in such an onslaught. Closing his eyes, Autumnstar felt the floor for anything he could use to protect himself. His weapon had been lost in the last battle, but surely there was something. . . .

His fingers brushed one of the fallen stones. He traced the familiar impression of the child's starburst.

"As punishment, you and all who turned against our forefathers shall be erased from history. Civilizations shall fall, and civilizations shall rise, but none shall remember your existence. None shall ever again speak their praise to the Autumn Star. None shall whisper your name, begging for comfort in their final hours. You are forgotten, Tymalous Autumnstar."

"And you talk too much." Autumnstar threw the stone as hard as he could. It caught Noc in the chest, knocking him right out of the temple.

In that moment, Tymalous Autumnstar turned and fled like a frightened mortal.

So this was how a rat felt right before Golaka skewered it for lunch.

Everyone was staring at Jig. For the most part, they appeared confused. Except for the elves, who looked bored, and Darnak, who had begun to gnaw his knuckles.

"Sorry," Darnak said, yanking his hand from his mouth. "Bird habit."

Jig hadn't seen Darnak since he had used the Rod of Creation to transform the dwarf into an oversized, ugly bird. As a bird, Darnak had still been able to talk.

Darnak had known the rod was disguised as Golaka's stirring spoon, unknown to anyone in the lair except Jig. He must have instructed Theodore in its use.

Darnak appeared no worse for his time as a bird. His dark hair and beard were a tangled mess, coming well past his thighs. He kept one hand on the wall for balance. Unfortunately, Darnak had already started to chew his other hand again, which meant he had no way to close the oversized blanket which was his only item of clothing.

Apparently Darnak had forgotten to instruct Theodore to create clothes.

"Do you mind?" asked Genevieve.

"Right. Sorry about that." Darnak yanked the blanket tight, so that only the tips of his toes peeked out.

Darnak studied Jig just as closely, taking in the cloak, the spectacles, even Smudge, who had crawled out from Jig's pocket to perch upon his shoulder. "I see you found yourself another spider."

"Not exactly," Jig said. "Smudge was—"

"You know this creature, Darnak?" asked Theodore. He held Golaka's stirring spoon with both hands.

Jig looked longingly at the door, wondering who would kill him first if he tried to flee. Probably one of the elves. Or maybe Grell.

"Jig led us down through the tunnels two years ago. He even saved our lives once or twice." Darnak forced a grin. "Those oversized white worms were a bit of fun, eh?"

Dwarves clearly had a different concept of fun than goblins.

"This was your guide?" Theodore whispered.

Memory was a funny thing. In that moment, Jig remembered Barius and Ryslind so clearly they could have been standing before him. If Grell's room hadn't been so crowded, at any rate.

It was almost funny how Theodore got exactly the same cold, angry expression on his face when he was getting ready to kill you.

Jig braced himself, wondering if he had time to swipe some of Grell's klak beer first.

"Jig ran away when we got to the dragon's cave," Darnak continued. "Never thought to see him again."

"Typical goblin cowardice." Theodore's attention wandered back to Grell. He tried to give the rod a quick twirl, and accidentally thumped one of his guards with the spoon.

The guard scrambled back, tripping in his eagerness to get away.

Jig stared at Darnak, who blinked and turned his head. Darnak knew Jig had killed the princes. Why was he—

"That's a lie," Relka said.

Jig's chest went cold. Relka was too far away for him to stab, so he searched for something to throw at her.

"Jig is no coward," Relka continued. "He killed Straum himself, and then—"

"A goblin killed the dragon?" Theodore looked genuinely amused. "And how exactly did he accomplish such a feat?"

Relka folded her arms, a pose familiar to most goblins who had endured one of her lectures. "According to 'The Song of Jig,' he—"

Jig finally found something to throw. Grell's "poisoned" crossbow bolt bounced off Relka's forehead. She blinked and turned to Jig, her mouth compressed into a pout.

Genevieve coughed and rubbed her neck. "Much as I'd love to spend the afternoon listening to goblin songs, do you think we could cleanse the poison from my body first? If nobody has anything better to do, I mean."

"Right. Poison." Darnak rubbed his hands together, which had the unfortunate effect of loosening his blanket again. He stepped toward Genevieve, moving in a clumsy waddle. No doubt he was still adjusting to being a dwarf again.

"What were you thinking, coming in here before the area was secured? Are you really so eager to make your brother an only child?" Darnak squeezed between the goblins and soldiers until he was close enough to touch Genevieve's hand.

"There were only three goblins." Genevieve's cheeks were red. "Hardly a threat."

"That's the kind of thinking that got your brothers killed," Darnak said. He dug through his beard to retrieve a silver amulet. Either Theodore had restored the tiny silver hammer, or else it had somehow survived Darnak's transformation. "Don't you worry, lass. Poison can be nasty stuff, but it's no match for Earthmaker's magic."

"So can we execute this one now?" Theodore asked, pointing the spoon at Grell.

Genevieve waited for Darnak to finish, then turned to her brother. "Idiot." She took a deep breath. "She's the leader of the goblins. Kill her, and who's going to surrender to us?"

Theodore slammed the spoon onto the edge of Grell's mattress, raising a small puff of dirt. "As leader of these goblins, you will surrender yourselves to us. If you continue to resist, we will kill every last goblin in these awful caves. Your blood will seep into the earth, and your bodies will be left to rot. Not one goblin will be left to— "

"She gets the point," said Genevieve.

"I still say we should kill them all," Theodore muttered. "Father never meant for you to— "

"Father's not here. He charged me with Avery's defense, not you, remember?"

From the fury on Theodore's face, he most certainly did. "Father only allowed you to take command of that ill-gotten town because no self-respecting army would bother to attack it, even if— "

Grell groaned and lay back in her bed. "Would you mind going outside while you argue? I could use a nap. You're welcome to fight your way back in when you're finished."

Genevieve and Theodore glared at one another a while longer. Eventually Theodore huffed and stormed out of the cave, followed by the elves.

"Your strongest goblins will come with us," Genevieve said, turning back to Grell. "The rest will remain here, sealed within the mountain by the power of the rod."

"Why?" Jig asked before he could stop himself. He wasn't sure whether to laugh or cry. He had sealed the mountain himself, back when he first found the rod. Then, on Shadowstar's advice, he had opened the cave again to keep the goblins from stagnating and dying in their isolation. Had he known what would happen, he could have left the cave sealed off and saved everyone a great deal of trouble.

"Part of their orders from the king was to make sure the goblins wouldn't be a threat," Darnak said. "Only two ways to make that happen, and only one way that lets you keep breathing."

Relka cocked her head. "So you came onto our mountain,

slaughtered our warriors, broke into our lair, attacked our chef, and stomped into the chief's cave because *we* were a threat to *you*?"

Darnak shrugged.

"Gather your strongest goblins," Genevieve said. "Except for that chef. I get the sense she wouldn't be quite as easy to control."

That was quite the understatement. When nobody responded, Genevieve shrugged. "If you prefer, I can let my brother give the order to kill you all."

"Can't you take the hobgoblins instead?" Jig asked.

"No time," said Darnak. "Besides, hobgoblins are a nasty lot. We were thinking you goblins would be easier to manage."

"A difficult choice, we know," said Genevieve. "For a leader to willingly surrender those under her protection, or to—"

"Make sure you take Trok. That sorry excuse for a warrior keeps trying to poison my beer. Better yet, shove his arse over a cliff." Grell cocked her head. "Will you be passing any cliffs, do you think?"

They took Jig too, even though he was no more a warrior than he was an ogre. As Genevieve and the others were tying up the biggest and the strongest goblins, Theodore seized Jig's arm and tugged him along as well. "We should bring this one. He killed a dragon, after all. Surely he's the mightiest of goblins."

"You are such a child," Genevieve said, even though to Jig's eye she was significantly younger than her brother.

One of the elves looped a thin rope around Jig's neck and twisted a tight knot, adding him to a line of almost forty bound goblins. Jig found himself at the end of the line, directly behind Trok. He tried not to breathe through his nose, but it didn't help. The stench of Trok's sweat-soaked garments was so potent Jig could taste it.

Maybe if he told Genevieve and Theodore the truth about their brothers' deaths, they would kill him quickly and get it over with.

Near the front, Braf leaned out and waved at Jig. Whatever he started to say turned into a loud squawk as a passing elf tugged the rope, yanking him back into line.

"Wait!" Relka hurried out of the cave. She clutched her pendant with one hand. "Where Jig Dragonslayer goes, I go."

The elf glanced at Theodore, who shrugged. Soon Relka was bound behind Jig, close enough for him to smell her breath. Relka had been dipping into Golaka's honey wine again . . . which might explain why she had insisted on following Jig.

The elf took her knife, then grabbed the pendant.

"No!" Relka clawed the elf's wrists, to no avail. A sharp tug to the side choked off Relka's protests, and a quick flick of the knife severed the leather thong.

"You're an idiot," Jig whispered.

"Be not afraid," Relka said. She raised her voice. "Fellow goblins, this is but a trial of our strength. Believe in Shadowstar, and he shall set us free!"

Trok snarled and tugged the rope with both hands, pulling Jig off-balance. Jig lurched into Trok's furs, and then Relka crashed into Jig. Trok reached over Jig's head to punch Relka in the middle of her forehead. "Last I checked, both of Shadowstar's mighty priests were right here tied up with the rest of us."

Jig squirmed out from between them and spat in the snow. Trok's furs were shedding.

"They're going to eat us," Trok muttered. "That's why they wanted the meatiest goblins."

Jig shook his head. "Humans don't eat goblins."

Whatever they were going to do, Jig hoped it happened soon. Anything had to be better than Trok's smell and Relka's babbling.

As if to prove him wrong, Relka began to sing.

"My Shadowstar is a glorious star.
He shines upon us day and night.
We are but worms before him.
He guides his goblins from afar,
Forgiving us our every slight.
We are but dung beneath him."

With a snarl, Trok shoved past Jig, looped the rope around Relka's throat, and hauled her off the ground. Relka kicked and squirmed, then slammed her head back into Trok's chin.

There was little slack in the rope between goblins to begin with, which meant Jig found himself pulled tight against Relka and Trok as they struggled. Relka's heel kept hitting Jig's gut, and every time Trok shifted his weight, his elbow smashed Jig's spectacles against his face.

Where were the guards? Several of the humans were watching, hands on their weapons, but they made no move to intervene. The elves were looking up and down the line, bows ready. As for the other goblins, they mostly appeared relieved. Not that Jig could blame them. Relka's hymns were, in a word, awful. Jig had heard this one several times, and it only got worse, comparing goblins to rotting meat, vomit, and in the penultimate verse, hobgoblins.

Still, she was one of Shadowstar's worshipers, and the god had funny ideas about protecting Jig's fellow goblins. "Trok, put her down."

"You think just because these idiots worship you, that means you can run around giving me orders?" Watery blue blood trickled down Trok's chin when he spoke.

"No." Jig swallowed and pulled back as far as his bonds would allow. He managed to twist far enough that Trok's elbow hit him in the ear instead of the eye. "You think they're going to cut her body free after you kill her? They think this is a trick, a distraction so the others can escape. Look at the way they're watching the rest of the goblins. Most likely, they'll leave Relka tied up, and we'll have to drag her body along to wherever it is we're going. You might not mind hauling her weight, but I doubt the other goblins will appreciate it."

Low mutters spread through the line, but Trok didn't let go. Relka had turned a deep shade of blue, almost purple, and her kicks were weaker.

"Besides, what do you think Golaka will do when we get back and she finds out you murdered one of her kitchen drudges?" Jig added.

That did it. Trok dropped Relka as if she had sprouted lizard-fish spines.

"Shadowstar's wrath—" Relka coughed and clutched her throat, then tried again. "His wrath will smite you like—"

"Shut up, Relka," said Jig. The wind picked up, spitting snow at the goblins, and Jig shivered. He could feel Smudge burrowing in his pocket.

What did the humans want? Darnak had said they were supposed to make sure the goblins weren't a threat. But if that was all they wanted, why drag the strongest warriors—and Jig—away before sealing the lair?

Whatever it was, Jig was certain he wouldn't like it.

They marched throughout the day, until the sun was little more than a scattering of red-orange light through the trees. At first they had made their way through the trees, crossing back and forth down the rocky, uneven ground of the mountain until the muscles in Jig's legs felt as though they were on fire.

The most tortuous spot so far was a steep slide of loose stone, conveniently hidden by a blanket of snow. Braf had been the first to stumble, but his weight pulled the next goblin off-balance, and soon the entire line was tumbling down the hillside.

Hobgoblins could learn a few things about traps from this place.

Jig had taken some satisfaction in knocking the legs from beneath a few humans as he fell. Unfortunately, they hadn't stopped long enough for him to heal his scrapes. The blood seeping from his elbow kept sticking to his sleeve.

The goblins stayed close to one another as they walked, in part to keep from choking, but also for warmth and reassurance. Jig had never explored more than an hour beyond the lair, and that had been years ago, when he was fleeing from a bully named Porak. Most goblins spent as little time as possible on the surface.

"I hate the outdoors," Jig muttered, shoving his hands into his sleeves for warmth. The sound of the branches humming in the wind conjured images of dragons and worse. The trees here were skeletal, their dead leaves covering the ground to turn it even more treacherous. The clouds drifting overhead made him feel as though the ground were shifting beneath his feet.

The world was simply too *big*. Back home in the lair, there were only so many caves and tunnels to explore. Out here, they could be going anywhere.

Eventually they left the tree-covered stone of the mountainside for a road of frozen mud. Even more armed humans waited here. Most were tending to their horses.

Jig stared at the closest horse. He had never actually seen one before. Oh, adventurers would occasionally have an image of a horse painted on their shield or armor, and once the hunters had brought back most of a horse for dinner. But living, breathing horses were very different.

For one thing, they were a lot bigger. And scarier. The closest had gray fur with white spots. Its eyes were huge, and it bared a row of enormous flat teeth as the goblins limped forth from the trees. It pawed the road, and Jig realized it wore a heavy piece of curved iron on its feet. No doubt to help it crush goblin skulls.

Most of the humans were already climbing onto the horses. Theodore jabbed his heels into his horse's sides, and the horse trotted to the front of the line. The elves followed. They remained on foot, but seemed to have no problem keeping up with the horse.

The goblins were dragged into the middle of the road. Soldiers rode on either side, tugging the reins to keep their horses under control. Those horses were even bigger than tunnel cats! A single one could probably kill and eat half the goblins here.

Now, instead of tripping over tree roots and icy rock, Jig found himself tripping over ruts in the road and frozen horse tracks. The horses also left other less savory signs of their passage. Some of those piles must have been from the journey here, as they were frozen hard as rocks.

Trok had already thrown one at Relka's head.

Jig twitched his ears, trying to restore feeling to the tips. He could hear Theodore joking with one of the elves up ahead, though the wind kept him from making out their words. Genevieve rode behind, along with another group of humans.

A low hooting sound made Jig jump.

"They're going to feed us to the monsters," said one of the goblins.

"I'm doubting the owl would be interested in making a meal of you." Darnak chuckled as he jogged to catch up with the goblins. Thankfully, he had managed to find clothes. His trousers bagged out of the tops of his boots, and his shirttails hung down to his knees. He had twisted his beard into a rope and tied a knot in the end to keep it out of the way. Staring at Jig, he said, "Keep your mouth shut and do what you're told, and you'll be all right."

Jig nodded. "But why did you tell them—"

"Mouth shut I said." Darnak shook his head and stopped walking, allowing the goblins to draw away. "Ears the size of saucers, and they still don't listen."

The sky was dark by the time Prince Theodore ordered a halt. A yank on the rope punctuated his cry. "We're here!"

By now Jig had lost any sense of distance or direction. Even if he were to escape, he would never be able to find his way back to the lair. Jig pulled to one side, trying to see past the other goblins, but it was no use.

Genevieve rode to join her brother. Her horse was black, naturally, all except a spot of white above its front foot. Its tail flicked like a whip as she passed.

Jig cringed away from that tail, then turned around, trying to get a sense of their surroundings.

Black shadows rose in the distance to either side. The road appeared to run through a wide valley. Jig sniffed, hoping the smell of the air would tell him more. All it told him was that Trok had worked up a good, sour sweat over the course of the day.

The land immediately to either side of the road was flat and clear of trees. Jig squinted at a bulky shape to the left. Could that be a building of some sort? Tall, bulky animals stood in a tight group to one side of the building, letting out an occasional moaning cry.

"Get those goblins out of here," someone yelled. "They're scaring the cows!"

"Welcome to Avery," Darnak said as the line of goblins began to move again. He had made the entire journey on foot, and he kept muttering about how it would have been so much faster with wings.

Up ahead, flickering torches illuminated a wooden wall that rose four times as high as a goblin. There had to be some sort of platform near the top, supporting the soldiers who stood with spears and crossbows. The light of the torches turned them into flickering, ghostly figures. The platform was low enough that only the soldiers' upper torsos could be seen. It was a bit disconcerting, watching all those half-soldiers moving around to point their weapons down at the goblins.

Guards on the ground dragged open a door that was nearly as tall as the entire wall. Theodore and Genevieve were the first through. From where Jig stood, it looked as though they were steering their horses into one another, each one trying to shove the other aside so they could be first into the city.

"What's going to happen to us, Darnak?" Jig asked, wiping his eyes. His vision kept blurring, and his nose wouldn't stop running. The cold had been making his face leak all day, but the problem was even worse here.

"Genevieve means to put you to work," Darnak said. "You'll be helping fortify the town. Be careful. Folks around these parts aren't too fond of goblins."

"Nobody's fond of goblins," Jig said.

"True enough." Darnak's arms twitched as he walked, and he kept shaking his backside. Was he sick? It was only when he shook his head, fluffing out his black hair, that Jig recognized the movements. He had seen birds do the same thing, twitching their wings and shaking their tailfeathers when they were nervous. Darnak had spent far too long as a bird.

But why would he be nervous? Darnak wasn't afraid of anything!

"What about food?" Relka asked.

Farther up the line, Braf twisted around to add, "And a privy?"

"Some blankets would be nice," said another goblin.

"What about a nice hot cup of lichen tea?"

"And maybe some wood for a fire?"

"I'll need a new pair of trousers if you don't give us that privy soon!"

"That's enough," bellowed one of the humans. He pointed his crossbow at the line, and the goblins fell silent.

Jig blinked, trying to focus on the wall. Rather than the logs or planks Jig had expected, the wall appeared to be made of individual trees, growing so closely together that there was hardly a finger-width of light between them. The branches had been cut away, except for the very top, where they grew together into the bushy platform where the guards watched. And the bark appeared to be *moving*, rustling like a swarm of rats.

Jig sneezed, spraying the back of Trok's furs in the process. Not that anyone would notice.

As they walked closer, Jig realized it wasn't the tree bark that was moving. The trees were covered in drooping yellow flowers. Even the smallest was as large as Jig's hand. He sneezed again as the sickly sweet scent of the flowers overpowered even Trok.

"What is this place?" Relka whispered.

"Used to be an elf town," said Darnak. "There was a bit of a disagreement between the elves and the humans about sixteen or so years back. They eventually hammered out a treaty that gave this valley to King Wendel. It's not all that comfortable for humans, but the land is great for farming. Unnatural, the way elves and plants get along. One of them pisses on a rock, and the next day you've got a sapling. Avery produces twice as many crops as any other town its size. Of course, if you wander into the poison ivy on the south side, you'll pray for a quick death. Vines as thick as your finger. I suspect the elves planted it deliberately, as a going-away present.

"For the most part, the elves stay on their side of the border. But every once in a while, they try to 'recruit' a human to their way of thinking." Darnak scowled at Theodore as he spoke. "Humans are suckers for all that grace and so-called wisdom. Not to mention the hair. As if one of those pointy-eared tree-lovers could grow a proper beard."

Darnak stepped aside as the goblins passed through the

opening. The ground was softer here, covered in rotting flower petals. The walls were two trees deep. Thick branches grew together overhead, and a nest of birds squawked angrily from behind the flowers.

Inside, a wide path of snow-crusted wood chips led through more living buildings. Everywhere Jig looked, he saw vines and leaves and flowers of all colors and shapes. He wiped his nose again and blinked to clear his vision.

Genevieve dismounted from her horse. "Take them to the stables for now. Bring food and water. Blankets as well. I didn't drag these filthy creatures down here only to have them freeze."

"What about that privy?" Braf stood with his legs tightly crossed, and his voice was higher than usual.

Genevieve turned away. "Bring a bucket."

Jig had a hard time falling asleep that night. Maybe it was the fact that nobody had bothered to untie them, so every time Trok or Relka shifted in their sleep, Jig choked. Or maybe it was the human food they had been forced to eat.

The humans had brought two barrels. The first contained hard, green, smelly things called *pickles*. He had tried to feed some to Smudge, and the fire-spider grew so hot he nearly burned Jig's hand. The slimy, hard vegetables smelled a bit like Trok. Hardly an appetizing aroma.

The other barrel contained grungy brown bulbs with white shoots sprouting from them like tentacles. The humans called them *potatoes*, and they were cold, hard, and tasteless.

Still, after trying a pickle, "tasteless" was a significant improvement.

One of the horses snorted and shifted position. That was the real reason Jig hadn't slept. The goblins shared the stables with at least thirty horses. Sure, the horses were penned in their stalls, but Jig doubted those flimsy gates would stop them.

The dry air coated Jig's mouth and nose, though at least there were no flowers in here. He and the rest of the goblins huddled together at the far end of the narrow wooden building.

Do you know why we're here? Jig asked.

Shadowstar's answer was anything but helpful. *Probably because it's the only place in town big enough to hold forty goblins.*

"Jig?" Relka's whisper interrupted Jig's retort.

"What is it?"

"Do you think they're going to kill us?"

Jig closed his eyes. "Probably."

"Do you think I'll get to meet Tymalous Shadowstar when I die?"

He didn't answer. If he said no, Relka would spend the rest of the night praying and singing, trying to prove herself worthy. And if Jig said yes, he had no doubt that Relka would immediately provoke Trok into killing her, just to hurry things along.

Eventually exhaustion overpowered fear. Jig didn't sleep comfortably, not with Trok's elbow wedged into his gut and Relka's knees in his back, but he slept.

The clang of bells ripped him from a dream in which elves leaped from the walls to shoot pickle-tipped arrows at Jig and his fellow goblins. Trok leaped to his feet, nearly breaking Jig's neck in the process.

"Everyone out!" The stable door swung open to reveal the shapes of Genevieve and several of her soldiers. Thc bright sunlight made it impossible to discern anything more.

The horses in their pens bared their huge teeth as the goblins passed. Those round eyes seemed to bore right through Jig's skin. Maybe that was the real reason Genevieve had brought goblins to Avery. They had run out of horse food, and the horses were too smart to settle for pickles or potatoes.

"How are we going to fight them?" Trok whispered.

Jig looked around, trying to see who Trok was talking to. A tug of the rope yanked his attention back to Trok. "Me?"

"You're the dragonslayer, right? You're the one who fought all those pixies." Trok glanced at Genevieve. "So how are you going to kill this lot?"

Technically, Jig hadn't really killed the dragon. And while he had fought pixies, most of the goblins who had accompanied him in that battle hadn't come back.

"No talking," Genevieve said, saving him from having to come up with a response. She walked along the line, studying each goblin. Behind her, several men handed out more potatoes. Another dipped water from a barrel, offering each goblin a drink. These were no soldiers. They were unarmed, and their wide eyes barely blinked as they watched the goblins.

Other humans watched from windows and doorways. Those who passed walked faster, either staring at the goblins or averting their eyes.

The roads all seemed to stretch out from the center of town, with smaller paths between them. They reminded Jig a bit of branches growing from a tree. Buildings and trees crowded together between the roads. For the most part, the buildings appeared far younger than the trees. Many were wood and stone, though a few seemed to be built into the base of the trees themselves. Those looked like miniature versions of the wall surrounding the town.

A pair of children whispered and pointed from high up in one of the trees. An older man stood in his doorway holding an ax. They were afraid. Were goblins so terrifying? The rope around Jig's neck was clearly visible to anyone.

A rough-shaven man slapped a potato into Jig's hand, and his stomach clenched. He forced himself to take a bite. He picked one of the bitter sprouts from between his teeth. The white sprouts were the only part of the potato with any flavor, but Darnak had mentioned that they were also toxic. It figured.

Genevieve kicked her horse, yanking the reins to lead it back toward the gate. The goblins gagged down the rest of their food as armed guards escorted them out of the city after Genevieve.

There she slid down and drew a knife. Before she could speak, the horse butted its head into her shoulder, knocking her into the wall. Then it stepped past her and began to chew one of the flowers.

"Stop that." Genevieve reached up to tug the reins, then swore as the horse nipped her arm.

Theodore laughed as he rode his own horse alongside hers. Most of the elves rode behind him. Like the elves, Theodore rode bareback, though he still used reins. "If Windstorm is too much to handle, I'm sure we could find you a more suitable mount. I believe I saw an old mule in one of the farmhouses."

"I believe I see one riding horseback with the elves," Genevieve shot back.

Even their insults brought back memories of Barius and Ryslind.

Genevieve handed the reins to Darnak and stepped to the wall.

"This is steelthorn. It's an elf tree." She wrapped her fingers around the base of a flower, pulling the petals out to expose the brown stem. She placed her knife at the tip of the stem. The flowers must have been tougher than they appeared, because it took several hard tugs to cut through.

She dropped the petals and wiped her hand on her trousers. "Each of you will be given a knife." She tossed hers to the nearest goblin, who immediately tried to cut himself free. When the rope wouldn't budge, he shrugged and lunged at the princess.

An arrow pinned his rear foot to the ground. He screamed as he fell, and the knife dropped into the snow.

Genevieve picked it up. "Use your knife on anything but these flowers, and one of my brother's pet elves will put an arrow through your throat." She pointed to the top of the wall, where a slender figure waved his bow in salute.

"So you captured goblin warriors to fight flowers?" Trok asked.

Genevieve shrugged. "If you prefer, I can find other uses for you. Your bodies could fertilize the fields."

Jig studied the stem where Genevieve had cut away the flower. Thin, reddish-brown leaves had already begun to curl tightly around the stem. Smaller thorns covered the outside of the leaves.

"Every flower must be cut," said Genevieve.

Jig stared at the wall. The flowers in front of him were too many to count, and the wall stretched on to surround an entire town. Not to mention how high they grew.

"A waste of time," Theodore shouted as he rode his horse

to the gate. He pulled the Rod of Creation from his belt and held it overhead. He still hadn't bothered to take the metal bowl off the end of the spoon. "I take my leave of you, dear Sister. While you play with your pet goblins, Father and I shall protect our kingdom once and for all."

"And while you play with your rod, dear Brother, I shall restore this city."

Several of the goblins snickered. Theodore pointed the rod at the nearest, but that only caused the goblin to laugh louder.

"That's enough you two." Darnak walked right past the prince's horse, completely unafraid of those enormous hooves. "Teddy, you need to be getting yourself to Skysdale. Your father's expecting you. Genevieve, stop posturing for the goblins and put them to work already."

"You overstep your bounds, dwarf," Theodore said, wrenching at the reins with one hand. Jig watched him closely. If he dropped the rod, Jig could try to grab it, and . . . his shoulders slumped. The rod could only affect one person at a time. He could transform the prince into a worm, and then Genevieve and the humans and elves would all take turns slicing Jig into worm food.

Darnak pulled a slightly wrinkled red fruit from his pocket and held it up for Genevieve's horse. "My oath is to your father, boy." He waved the fruit in the air, and the horse calmed enough to pluck it from Darnak's hand. Darnak chuckled and grabbed a silver flask from another pocket. He took a deep swallow. "Get on with you. Elf steeds or no, you've a long ride ahead of you."

"The dwarf speaks the truth," Theodore shouted. He turned his horse around so he faced the small crowd. "I shall return, good people, with tidings of victory. Sa'illienth é traseth!"

Darnak choked on his drink. "Begging Your Highness' pardon, but are you sure you don't mean sa'illienth é trathess? 'Victory and honor' is the traditional elvish battle cry. Not that there's anything wrong with 'Victory and bacon,' mind you."

"Come my friends," Theodore said, his face red. "Alléia!"

Jig doubted human ears would have picked up Genevieve's muttered, "*Illéia*, you twit."

By the time the sun reached the top of the sky, Jig was ready to collapse. He and the other goblins had spent the entire morning cutting flowers from the wall. As he had guessed, the flowers were tough as leather near the base. His hands were cramped and blistered, and sweat kept dripping onto his spectacles. His nose was too stuffed up to breathe, and he sneezed every time he cut another steelthorn flower.

Their only break from harvesting flowers had come when humans passed out rakes, ordering them to drag the flowers off toward one of the farmhouses. There, some of the petals had been fed to fat, lumbering beasts the men called cows.

Jig paused to wipe his nose and study the wall. They had begun to the left of the gate, and had cleared an area roughly thirty paces wide and one goblin high. Where flowers had grown, shiny thorned spikes now covered the trees. Jig reached out to test one. It was surprisingly hard, considering how the leaves had curled so easily around the stems.

"Have you figured out how to escape yet?" Trok asked.

Jig shook his head. "This used to be an elf town." He touched another of the spikes. "These are the same color as the armor they wear. I'm betting they'll be hard as metal by tomorrow. And as deadly."

"Let's find out." Before Jig could respond, Trok grabbed the goblin to his right and shoved him into the wall.

The goblin, a warrior named Rakell, screamed and stumbled back. Only a few of the spikes were hard enough to pierce his skin. Puncture wounds in his chest and leg dripped blue. Several more of the spikes had broken away from the tree, leaving oozing wounds in the bark. Jig touched the sap, which was slick as oil. Anyone who tried to climb the wall would either impale themselves, or else the thorns would break away. The sap would cause them to slip and fall.

"What's all this ruckus?" Darnak asked. He and some of the humans were rolling a now-familiar barrel through the snow.

Trok snarled at the sight. "If they try to give me one more pickle, I'm going to beat them all to death with it."

Jig turned back to the wall. A small beetle crawled out of the bark. Jig smashed it with his thumb, then dropped the bug into his pocket for Smudge. At least one of them would eat a decent meal today.

Rakell finally recovered enough to punch Trok in the face. Trok snarled and grabbed Rakell by the throat. Goblins to either side stumbled, their ropes pulling them into the fight. Jig found himself pressed against Trok's furs, close enough to realize that what looked like a death-bite on Rakell's throat was actually Trok whispering to the other goblin.

With a shout, Trok shoved Rakell away, toward Darnak. Rakell raised his knife.

The human who had been helping Darnak with the barrel leaped away. Darnak simply waited.

An arrow buzzed from the top of the wall and punched through Rakell's throat. Darnak plucked the knife from Rakell's hand as he fell. A second goblin flung himself at Darnak, who caught him by the arm. A quick punch sent the goblin staggering back with one fang missing.

The goblins stopped moving. Darnak tucked Rakell's knife into his belt. "Anyone eager to join this poor wretch?" He nudged Rakell with his foot.

Nobody moved.

"Right," said Darnak. He turned his attention back to the barrel. "Then it's pickles and cheese for lunch."

"What about Rakell?" Relka asked.

"I don't imagine he'll be having much of an appetite," said Darnak. "Or did you mean the ropes? You'll have to wait for the elf to untie him. It takes a special touch to unknot an elven rope."

"No," said Relka. "What are you going to do with the meat?"

Darnak shook his head and muttered, "Goblins."

He and the human passed out the food. The morning's hard work had given Jig enough of an appetite that pickles sounded almost palatable. Almost. Jig accepted a pickle and a rock-hard lump of white cheese.

"Darnak, what is everyone afraid of?" he asked.

The dwarf shook his head. "Earthmaker willing, nothing at all."

Trok crunched into his pickle. "Your princess wouldn't be worried about preparing this wall unless she expected to need it. She's planning for an attack."

Jig turned to stare at the bigger goblin. That was more insightful than he expected, coming from Trok.

Darnak took a steel flask from inside his cloak. "His majesty the king sent Genevieve here at her own request. Restoring Avery is one of her pet projects. There's not a lot for a princess to do around the palace, you understand."

The dwarf's breath alone was enough to make Jig feel tipsy. He didn't remember Darnak drinking so much before. This didn't smell like dwarven ale, though. More like . . . old leaves.

"Theodore talked about tidings of victory," said Jig. "Victory against who?"

"Orcs," said Relka. Everyone turned to stare. "When you dragged us from the lair, I heard Theodore boasting about how many he'd kill."

"Idiot boy," Darnak muttered, too low for human ears.

Jig and Trok stared at one another. How had Jig not heard about the orcs? Oh, wait, that would have been when Jig had been clutching his ears, wondering if the pain of ripping them off would be better than the pain of Relka's hymns.

"Aye," said Darnak at last. "Not only orcs. Billa the Bloody has got goblins, too. Goblins and orcs and worse. Thousands of monsters, all marching this way. All of them after killing everyone in their path."

"Is Genevieve going to make *us* fight Billa's army?" Jig asked.

"Avery's a poor target." Darnak took another drink, then waved his flask at the distant rise. "We're right on the border of the king's lands, and there's no real strategic advantage to taking the town. The early snowfall would only make things messier for an attacking army. Wendel's men would sweep down from the valley to crush her. Billa's too smart to lead her forces into such a slaughter." He stared at the ground. "In part, Wendel sent his daughter here because it's likely safer than the palace itself. Not that the palace is in any true danger, mind you."

He had barely looked at Jig at all. How odd. Goblins never took their eyes off each other. The instant you stopped paying attention, that was when you'd take a knife to the gut.

"Darnak, what's going to happen to us when we finish the wall?" Jig asked, his voice soft.

"Don't you worry about that." Darnak took another drink, then stood to go.

Jig grabbed his arm. It was like grabbing rock. Two years as a bird hadn't softened Darnak at all. "Tell me."

Darnak sighed and tugged the end of his beard. He glanced back at the town, then nodded. "Aye, you've earned as much." He dug into his shirt and pulled out his tiny silver hammer. He twisted free of Jig's grip, and his own fingers clamped around Jig's arm. Before Jig could break free, Darnak rapped the hammer on his forehead.

Jig yelped. It was as if his skull were a bell that wouldn't stop clanging. He pressed his ears, but the sound came from within.

"Earthmaker's Hammer," Darnak said. He tucked the necklace away, then nodded toward the other goblins. Every last one of them was scowling at Jig, ears flattened against their heads. "It's a minor spell, but useful when you prefer a bit of privacy. They'll hear nothing but the blows of his mighty hammer."

Relka's mouth moved, but Jig couldn't make out the words. Trok said something as well. He started to reach for Darnak, and then Relka pointed back toward the town. Probably reminding Trok of the elf and his bow.

"You have to understand, Jig. King Wendel lost two sons to you goblins." Darnak pulled a tin cup from a pouch at his waist and poured a drink for Jig. "He would have marched his whole army into your tunnels two years ago, but we couldn't find the entrance."

Jig felt a moment's smugness as he sipped his drink. He had been right to seal the entrance after all.

And then he felt nothing but a burning sensation on his

tongue. He doubled over, dropping the cup as he coughed and scooped snow into his mouth.

"Elf beer," said Darnak. "Potent stuff, but it tastes like the trees' own piss."

Jig shuddered. His tongue felt as if it had grown a layer of mold. "What's going to happen to us?"

"Wendel decreed that any goblins found anywhere in the kingdom were to be executed on the spot. Genevieve managed to get around that law because she needed the extra muscle, but once the work is finished . . ."

Earthmaker's hammer pounded away as Jig stood there, staring. He wasn't surprised, exactly. Rather, he was more surprised the humans hadn't killed him and the other goblins already. "So if we come into their kingdom, they have permission to hunt and kill us like we're nothing but animals?"

"Well, no." Darnak took another drink. "The king has laws limiting the hunting of animals to certain places and times, and protecting—"

"But we didn't *want* to come into your stupid kingdom! You tied us up and dragged us. You can't kill us for being somewhere we never wanted to be. That's—"

"Easy, Jig." Darnak glanced at the other goblins. By now they had figured out that Darnak and Jig were the source of that awful noise. If it continued much longer, a few arrows wouldn't be enough to stop them from ripping the dwarf apart. "It wouldn't have mattered anyway, lad. That mountain you call home is a part of Wendel's kingdom too."

"Our mountain?" Jig stared.

"Wendel's, according to the treaty he signed with the elves." Darnak pointed to the other side of the valley. "He rules everything up to the top of those hills."

That was too much. "No matter where we go, they'll kill us."

"That's about the size of it. The story of Barius and Ryslind has spread. Everyone knows they were killed by goblins, and they're none to happy about having you on their lands." Darnak pressed the flask into Jig's hand. It was surprisingly heavy. "Forged that flask myself, with Earthmaker's help. You need it more than I do."

Jig nodded.

"You killed Barius and Ryslind, but you also saved our lives. You spared me, and I've not forgotten that. I've done my best to convince Genevieve to be merciful. The real trick is persuading her father. The royal children have skulls of granite, it's true, but they come by that honestly."

"Can't you let us go?"

Darnak shook his head. "I'm sworn to obey. Besides, there's no place to go. Theodore used the rod to seal your lair."

Jig could have wept. Without the rod, he could never go home again. And Theodore had taken the rod deep into the human kingdom, where everyone would kill Jig as soon as look at him. Though that really wasn't anything new. He was a goblin, after all.

"Grant me time to work on Genevieve," Darnak said. "She's a bit odd, that one, but she's got more control over her passions than her father. A bit too much control, really. Takes after her mother that way. If I can convince her it's in her best interest to keep you goblins alive—"

"Why would it be in her best interest?" Jig asked.

Darnak snorted. "If I knew, I'd be halfway there." He clapped his hands, and the ringing of Earthmaker's Hammer faded, to be replaced by the cursing of angry goblins.

"—with his own beard," Trok was saying.

"What about Jig?" asked another.

"Jig doesn't have a beard," said Braf. Trok and the other goblin both shook their heads.

Darnak raised his voice. "May the gods watch over you, Jig."

"They do," Jig whispered. "But it never seems to help."

I resent that, said Shadowstar.

Jig didn't answer. He turned around, studying the scattered farms, and the woods beyond.

So you plan to run away, do you?

Running away is a proud goblin tradition, Jig said.

So is getting shot by elves.

Jig glanced at Rakell's body, then looked back at the wall. Only one elf, but there were other humans there. Not to mention the soldiers and their spears and swords. The knife he had been given to cut flowers was better than the old kitchen knife he used to carry, but it still wouldn't do much against trained warriors.

"What did the dwarf say?" asked Relka. Trok and the other goblins crowded around him, curiosity overpowering their annoyance.

Jig took a drink from Darnak's flask and forced himself to swallow. "He said we're all going to die."

CHAPTER 3

FLEEING TO THE REALM OF THE MORTALS WAS A desperate move, but it almost worked.

Almost.

Tymalous Autumnstar had made it halfway across the world before Noc's attack struck him from behind, driving him to the ground. How long ago had it been? The black streaks of lightning that racked his body made it difficult to track the passage of time.

Surely when even the victim had grown bored of the torture, it was time to move on.

The desert sands where Autumnstar lay helpless had been transformed into irregular spikes and blobs of hot glass. Noc could have followed him and finished the job long ago, but to manifest in the real world would make him vulnerable, just as it had with Autumnstar. Noc was being cautious, mindful of another trick. Autumnstar approved, even though he was far too weak for tricks. Every time another streak of blackness shot down upon him, he grew weaker.

Noc was a boring killer. There was no banter, no gloating, nothing but lightning. Was it so much to ask that he at least vary his attacks? Pillars of fire would be a nice change, or maybe the sand could whirl in a blinding storm, each grain ripping at his skin. For a god of death, Noc showed very little imagination.

Between blasts, something tickled Autumnstar's awareness. A sand lizard, one of the tiny ancestors of the dragons, stood at the edge of the glass crater. The lizard's crest and wings were raised aggressively. He was probably hoping for a precooked meal.

Autumnstar and his fellow gods had often contemplated whether they were truly immortal, but not once had they stopped to consider whether or not they were edible.

Pressure built in the air as Noc readied another assault. Autumnstar closed his eyes and dropped his defenses, gathering what little power he had.

Jagged blackness cracked the sky, and then all that remained was the burned, lifeless body that had been Tymalous Autumnstar . . . and a lone sand lizard that scurried away as quickly as its squat little legs would take him.

Another goblin died by the time Jig finished his pickle. This one had managed to loop the rope around a human's throat.

The human leaned against the pickle barrel, shaking and touching his ear, as if to assure himself it was still there. Jig almost felt sorry for him. First a goblin had nearly killed him, and then an elf had shot an arrow past his face into that goblin's throat.

On the other hand, this was the human who had helped Darnak inflict another round of pickles on the goblins, which did away with Jig's sympathy.

Jig hooked a finger through the rope, tugging it away from his windpipe. The rope was thin and light, but not even Trok was strong enough to break it. Their knives did nothing. Trying to loosen the knot only resulted in broken claws. The elves could work the rope as if it were nothing but string. But Jig would have to cut off his own head to escape the bonds.

He had kept that last thought to himself, not wanting to give the others ideas.

"What's your fire-spider doing?" Relka asked.

Jig stared. Smudge despised the snow, but he had crept out of Jig's pocket and crawled down to the ground, climbing onto the edge of the cup Jig had dropped, the one with the elf beer. Apparently the dwarf had forgotten about it.

Six of Smudge's legs clung to the rim and handle. Smudge's head and forelegs disappeared into the cup. "Maybe he's thirsty?"

Back at the lair, fire-spiders would sometimes drink the muck the goblins used to fuel their lanterns and fire pits. The only problem was if an unwary goblin happened to startle one of the spiders in midfeast. On the other hand, Golaka never complained about precooked meat.

Smudge was still drinking. Compared to muck, elf beer might be almost palatable. Better than pickles, at any rate.

"Back to work," shouted one of the humans. He waved his spear at the goblins, then grabbed the end of the rope from the snow. Several of the goblins snarled, but nobody tried to fight.

Jig grabbed the cup and reached in to brush the bristly hair on Smudge's back.

A puff of blue flame shot from the cup, singeing Jig's fingers. Smudge tried to turn around to see who had touched him, and ended up falling headfirst into the cup. Jig squatted long enough to stick his burned hand into the snow.

Smudge looked as sheepish as it was possible for a spider to look. He climbed slowly out of the cup and onto Jig's wrist. There, all eight eyes stared up at Jig. Smudge continued to stare, even as he toppled slowly into the snow. Jig hastily scooped him up with the cup. "How much of that elf beer did you drink?"

Smudge curled his legs to his body. Steam rose from his back.

The humans swapped their knives for rakes, and Jig joined the other goblins in dragging another pile of flowers away from the wall. He carefully returned Smudge to one of the larger pockets in his cloak, tossing the empty cup away.

Jig worked with the other goblins, falling into an easy rhythm. Rake, then sneeze. Another sweep of the rake, then wipe his nose on his shoulder. If he stayed much longer, these flowers would be the end of him.

The humans directed them to a different farmhouse on the opposite side of the road. From here, Jig could see other humans working on the wall beyond the gate.

Jig slowed his efforts as they neared the farm, raking with one hand.

"No slacking, runt," Trok snarled. To his other side, Relka gave him a curious glance, but said nothing.

With his other hand, Jig reached in to retrieve Darnak's flask. Before he could do anything, Trok snatched it away and unscrewed the top. "You've been holding out on us!"

Jig started to protest, then changed his mind.

"Paugh!" Trok spat. "Tastes like something that came from the wrong end of a carrion-worm!"

Jig fought a grin as he took the flask from Trok, then poured a bit of elf beer onto the rope. He did the same on his other side, then put the flask away and grabbed Smudge.

"Hey, what are you doing?" Trok grabbed Jig's arm. His claws poked right through Jig's sleeve, until it felt as if they were gouging the bone beneath. "If you're going to escape, you're taking me with you."

"I can't," Jig said. Freeing himself would also free Relka, since she was tied to the rope behind him. But that couldn't be helped. And the longer he stayed, the more likely someone would notice. Already the human farmer was walking out with his pitchfork, either to help move the flowers or to protect himself from the goblins, Jig wasn't sure.

"You won't get far with a broken arm, either," said Trok.

Jig tried to tug free, but it was no use. "Fine," he said. "Give me your rope."

There was a choked squawk from the next goblin as Trok pulled his own rope into Jig's reach. Jig poured a bit more beer over the rope, then grabbed Smudge. He wasn't even certain this would work.

He placed Smudge on the rope.

Smudge listed to one side, faster and faster, until he swung down to dangle upside down from the rope. One pair after another, his legs gave way, and he dropped into the snow.

Jig picked him up again. Smudge promptly scrambled up Jig's sleeve and set it on fire.

"Stop that," Jig hissed. He patted himself out, and Smudge fell again. "No more elf beer for you," Jig muttered.

By now, the other goblins had slowed in their efforts so

they could watch Jig. They didn't realize what Jig was trying to do, but a drunken fire-spider was more entertaining than anything else they had seen since leaving the lair.

"Make him fall off the rope again," said Braf, grinning.

Jig wrapped his hand in the edge of his cloak and grabbed Smudge from the snow. He took the beer-soaked rope and yanked it down, choking Trok in the process. When he lifted the rope again, it burned with a merry blue flame.

"Smells like burned hair," Trok complained.

Jig said nothing. Next to Trok's own stench, the burning rope was almost pleasant.

Trok grabbed the rope on either side and pulled. The rope snapped. With a triumphant snarl, he flung his rake into the snow.

"Wait," Jig shouted. "We're still tied together!"

Trok began to run, dragging Jig and Relka behind him. Jig barely managed to get Smudge back into his hood. He hoped Smudge didn't set it on fire.

If any of the humans had missed Jig's attempted escape, the cheering of the other goblins took care of that.

"Get past the farmhouse," Jig shouted.

Trok veered away from the farmer and his pitchfork. The farmer did the same, fleeing in the opposite direction. Jig grinned as he struggled to keep up with Trok and Relka.

He craned his head to look behind. Several humans were running after them. The lead human tripped as a rake flew into his legs. Braf turned to Jig and waved.

The farmer was running back toward the town, shouting. Shouting to the elf on the wall. Jig squinted, trying to see through the smeared lenses of his spectacles.

The elf only needed to shoot one of them. Dragging the dead weight of a dead goblin would slow the other two enough for the humans to catch them. Jig watched as the elf drew an arrow from his quiver.

Jig grabbed the rope on either side of his neck, then lifted both legs from the ground. He fell, and his full weight yanked the rope, choking Relka and Trok. They collapsed on top of him.

Trok swore. "What are you—?"

An arrow thumped into the snow just ahead of them.

"Praise be unto Shadowstar," Relka whispered.

"I don't see Shadowstar down here, dodging elf arrows," Jig muttered. He crawled toward the farmhouse, craning his head to watch the distant figure on the wall. The elf would be mad now. They didn't like to miss. Jig waited, trying to hear over the shouting and his own gasping breath. There it was, the sharp *twang* of another shot.

Jig pulled out Darnak's flask and turned it over, gripping it in front of his throat with both hands.

The impact flung him back into the snow, but by now they were almost to the farmhouse. Trok and Relka hauled him the rest of the way, ducking behind the corner of the building as another arrow buzzed past.

"How did you do that?" Relka asked. She plucked the dented flask from Jig's hands. "It's like you knew exactly where the arrow was going to hit. Did Shadowstar bless your vision so you could see the future?"

Jig shook his head. He was still gagging from being dragged through the snow. "No self-respecting elf is going to shoot someone in the chest, not if they can make a harder shot to the neck." He glanced at the dented flask and shivered. Darnak made a good flask. This thing was thicker than armor.

"At least I grabbed the arrow," Trok said, grinning. The tip was bent from the impact.

"Good," said Jig. He tugged Trok around. "You can use it to fight the humans with their swords and axes."

Trok's grin disappeared. Goblins weren't the smartest warriors, but even he knew better than to take on armed humans with nothing but a sharp stick. He handed the arrow to Jig.

As soon as Jig recovered enough to stand, they were off again. They made for the trees, keeping the farmhouse between themselves and the elf.

It didn't stop the elf. Arrows continued to arch over the roof, landing disturbingly close. "Unfair," Jig complained as another arrow hissed past his ear.

And then they were shoving past branches and stumbling

over roots and low-growing plants. A branch snapped into Jig's face, making him yelp.

Trok grinned. Deliberately, he reached out to bend another branch. Jig ducked, and this one hit Relka instead. Then Trok ran face-first into a tree.

"Concentrate on running away," Jig said. Trok grunted his agreement as he rubbed his jaw.

One of their pursuers shouted, "Their tracks go this way!"

"Tracks?" Relka asked.

Jig looked back. The snow was thinner here, little more than a white crust sprinkled with fallen leaves and pine needles. But even Jig could see where he and his companions had gouged the snow with every step. He kicked the snow, trying to fill in a footprint, but only made things worse.

"Go deeper into the woods," Jig said. "There are more trees, so there's less snow."

According to what Darnak had told him, this was the human side of the valley, which meant he didn't have to worry about crossing some invisible boundary into elf lands. For once, luck was with him.

On the other hand, fleeing through elf-infested woods would at least have resulted in a quick death.

Jig tugged the rope, leading Trok and Relka to a long cluster of thorn plants. He tore his cloak and scraped his hands on the way through, but hopefully the thorns would slow the humans, too.

"Don't let them escape!" That was Genevieve. Jig cocked his head, aiming his good ear at the sound. He heard hoofbeats, but he guessed she was still at the edge of the woods. He still had trouble judging distances and sounds out here in the open, though.

"She never should have brought those monsters into our town to begin with."

Jig swore under his breath. *That* voice was far closer than Genevieve's. Jig was still thinking like he was back in the lair, assuming the humans would have to follow the same route the goblins had taken. But there were no tunnel walls here, and the humans had spread out. They could send an entire line sweeping through the woods to make sure they didn't miss the runaway goblins. They had probably even avoided those stupid thorns.

He didn't know how many of the humans were soldiers, but it was a good bet they all had better weapons than Jig's lone arrow.

He could hear two sets of footsteps closing in from the left. "Under here," Jig whispered, hurrying toward a small stream. The water was frozen save for a thin trickle in the center. There were fewer trees here, but one was a fat pine with branches sagging to the ground. Jig crawled beneath the branches, then waited while Trok and Relka crowded in behind him. Jig reached out with one hand to smooth the pine needles the best he could.

"Where'd you go, Samuel?" shouted one of the humans.

"Stopped for a rest."

Jig gripped the arrow with both hands. He could see the second human, Samuel. His legs, at least. Samuel had stopped less than a stone's throw from their hiding spot. He rested his weight on a large, double-headed ax.

Trok pressed something cold and scaly into Jig's hand.

"What's that?" Jig whispered, once he regained control of his breathing.

"Pinecone. I thought you could pour more of that elf piss on it and set it on fire, then maybe throw it at the humans."

"You want me to use flaming pinecones against humans and their axes?" Jig barely stopped himself from shoving the pinecone in Trok's ear. Only the knowledge that Trok would probably eat Jig's arm in return stopped him.

"I got the idea from a story. Apparently there was this great wizard, and—"

"And the best he could do was set pinecones on fire?" Jig bit his lip as the humans moved closer.

"Think they took to the stream to hide their tracks?" asked one.

Jig grinned. That was a clever idea. Though knowing his luck, he'd slip on the ice and break his knee.

"Who cares?" said the other, Samuel. "If you ask me, we

should cut them all loose. Better yet, take the axes to them. My little girl had nightmares all through the night after seeing those monsters."

"I hear they eat their young." The first human tromped closer.

"Only if they can't get ours," Samuel answered. "And you'd better mind your wife, Virgil. You know how goblins lust after human women."

Jig glanced at Trok, who grimaced. How could any self-respecting goblin be attracted to a human female and her tiny ears? Not to mention their flat teeth and pasty skin.

"Genevieve's mad, bringing them here. Who knows what kind of disease they're carrying? My cousin Frederik knew a man whose sister's husband got his arm scratched by a goblin. The wound spread, and they had to take his arm at the shoulder."

Diseases? Well, there was that toenail fungus Jig had been fighting. Shadowstar's magic helped, but the yellow gunk kept coming back. He didn't think the humans could catch that, though.

"I hear if they bite you, you turn into one of them."

Samuel smacked his companion on the arm. "That's wolf-men, you idiot."

"Doesn't matter. I'm not losing my arm to some stinking goblin."

Jig hoped that was merely a figure of speech. If the humans could smell Trok from there, the goblins were as good as dead.

"Forget this." Samuel cupped his hands to his mouth and shouted, "No sign of the goblins. We're heading back."

Jig couldn't believe it. Even as the humans turned and hurried back through the woods, he kept peeking around, waiting for an elf to pop out of a tree and shoot them.

"Why are they leaving?" Relka whispered.

Jig thought back to what Darnak had said. "They're afraid of us." These weren't heroes or adventurers. They were ordinary humans, and they had probably never seen a goblin in their lives before Genevieve dragged them all to Avery.

It was like the stories the goblins used to tell about the

Necromancer. Even though no goblin before Jig had seen the Necromancer and survived, they still told tales frightening enough to make children cry.

In the Necromancer's case, most of those tales had turned out to be true, but that was beside the point. The humans were afraid of them!

"What do we do now?" Relka asked. "Go back to the lair and rescue Grell and the others?"

"We can't," Jig said. "Theodore used the rod to seal the lair." Not to mention he wasn't sure how to find his way back. The woods and mountains were all so big. *Could you lead us to the lair?*

Probably, said Tymalous Shadowstar. *Where you'll be killed by whatever guards Theodore left behind. Or if he left the lair unguarded, you can sit around and starve to death.*

"What's wrong with him?" Trok poked Jig in the neck.

"Stop that," said Relka. "He's talking to Tymalous Shadowstar. You can tell, because his eyes cross a little, and sometimes he drools."

You'll need help to save your people, Jig Dragonslayer.

Jig wiped his mouth. *You mean Billa and her army of orcs and goblins. They could help us fight the humans.*

Shadowstar hesitated. *This goes beyond the humans, Jig. Not once in my memory have orcs and goblins come together like this. An army of monsters . . . something is wrong. Do you remember when I warned you about the pixies?*

I remember that you nearly got me killed!

This is worse.

Maybe this was why gods stayed on another plane of existence. If they stayed here in the mortal world, their followers would be too tempted to punch them in the face. *Of course it is. I don't suppose you'd be willing to tell me exactly what you're worried about?*

I would if I knew, said Shadowstar.

I hate you, you know.

Shadowstar didn't answer.

Jig waited to make sure he could no longer hear the humans' voices, then crawled out from beneath the tree. "Come on," he muttered. "We can follow the stream, and— "

Jig stopped. Far downstream, Genevieve sat on her horse, staring at them. She looked as startled as he felt. Even as Jig watched, she kicked her horse into motion. So much for humans being scared of goblins.

He handed the arrow back to Trok, then pulled out Darnak's half-empty flask. With shaking hands, he poured the remaining beer over the pinecone.

"I thought you said that was a stupid idea," Trok said.

"It is." Jig dropped the flask, twisted around, and snatched Smudge from his hood. He poked Smudge with the tip of the pinecone.

Nothing happened. Smudge had fallen asleep.

Genevieve had her sword pointed toward them as she charged. Toward Jig in particular.

"Wake up, you stupid spider!" Jig blew in Smudge's face. The fire-spider stirred. He took several tentative steps, then fell off the edge of Jig's hand. He dropped slowly, suspended by a silken line that ran from his backside to Jig's palm.

Jig thrust the pinecone into Smudge's face. The pinecone burst into flames. So did the line of web. Smudge plopped into the snow, and Jig threw the pinecone as hard as he could.

He was aiming for Genevieve's cloak, but he had thrown too low. The pinecone was going to hit the horse instead.

The horse reared back on his hind legs, and Genevieve tumbled to the ground.

Jig sucked on his hand. Smudge's web had burned swiftly, like any fire-spider web. Jig could already see a nasty blister where the line had stuck to his skin.

Genevieve tried to stand, then yelled and clutched her knee. She toppled onto her side, one hand holding her knee, the other reaching for her sword.

Trok was already dragging Jig and Relka toward the princess. He extended his arrow like a lance. Jig wondered if he had learned the tactic from watching Genevieve's people kill goblins the same way.

Genevieve reached her sword. A single swipe of her blade snapped the arrow in half, and then Jig was wondering whether Trok's body was bulky enough to stop the backswing from hitting Jig, too.

Trok leaped back. Genevieve stretched far enough to slice his arm, but the effort overbalanced her. She yelled again, and tumbled slowly into the snow. This time she didn't get back up.

Trok studied the broken arrow. Genevieve's sword had cut cleanly through the wood, leaving a nasty point. With a shrug, Trok raised it overhead like a knife.

Jig grabbed the rope and pulled him back.

"What are you doing?" Trok said, gasping for air. He turned the broken arrow toward Jig.

"She's faking to lure you close enough to kill." Jig pointed to her hand. "See? She's still holding her sword. And she fell with her good leg bent, so she could push off and run you through."

"How did you know?" asked Relka.

Genevieve turned her head. "Yes, how *did* you know?"

"I fall down a lot," said Jig. "I've never landed as softly or comfortably as you did."

Trok grinned. "Great. Jig, help me throw Relka at her."

"What?" Relka yelped.

"Genevieve will stab her, but by the time she gets her sword free of Relka's body, I can kill her with my fangs and arrow."

To his shock, Relka merely nodded. "If it helps to protect Shadowstar's chosen." She closed her eyes. "May Shadowstar guide your fangs."

"Who?" Genevieve sat back, shaking her head. "Never mind. Kill me, and every goblin at Avery will be executed."

Trok grinned, showing off his fangs. "But we won't be at Avery." He started to shove Relka at Genevieve.

"Wait." Jig braced himself, yanking her back by the rope. "Princess, we can either kill each other, or else you can let us go and limp back to town. Darnak can fix your leg."

"If my brother were here, he would sooner die than bargain with a goblin."

"Your brother is an idiot," Jig snapped.

Genevieve tilted her head. "True enough."

"And what would your parents say if they lost another child to the goblins?"

"My mother would weep. Father would probably say something along the lines of 'I told you so.' And then he'd spend the next month in mourning, wearing nothing but black and talking more about his dead daughter than he did in all the time she was alive." Still, Genevieve nodded, conceding the point. Goblins paid no attention to parentage, but such things were important to humans and other surface dwellers. "He hates black."

"*You* wear black," Relka pointed out.

Genevieve almost smiled. "It annoys my father."

"Give us your dagger," said Jig. He glanced at Relka and Trok, then added, "And tell us where to find Billa's army."

Genevieve switched her sword to her left hand, pulling her knife with her right. A flick of her wrist sent the knife into the ground at Jig's feet.

Jig clenched his teeth, hoping nobody had heard his frightened squeak. He grabbed the knife and sliced back and forth on the rope.

"Did you really guide my brothers through the mountain?"

The knife slipped. Genevieve kept a sharp blade. Not sharp enough to cut elf rope, but more than enough to slice deep into goblin flesh. Jig could barely feel the cut on his hand, despite the blood. "They didn't give me much of a choice."

"No, they wouldn't." Genevieve shook her head. "To get so close . . . to actually find the Rod of Creation, only to fall to goblins."

"Well, there were a lot of goblins." Jig glared at Relka, silently begging her to keep her mouth shut.

"Did they fight well?"

"Sure. Dead goblins everywhere. It took months to clean up the mess." Jig cut himself again, in almost exactly the same spot. A few more tries, and he should be able to completely sever his own thumb.

"Elf ropes," Genevieve said. "The knife will never get through them."

"It doesn't matter. Smudge can do it once he's sober." Jig pointed to the sheath on Genevieve's belt. "Could I have that, too? It's awfully hard to carry a knife otherwise."

Genevieve shook her head as she tossed him the sheath. "Billa is on her way to Pottersville. Follow the road to the west for five days, keeping to the base of the mountains." She studied the goblins. "Make that a week."

"We're taking your horse, too," said Trok.

"What?" Jig didn't know who said it first, him or Genevieve. He stared at the horse, which had wandered a short distance away to munch a sad, half-frozen fern. Was it his imagination, or was the horse watching him? The horse's tail twitched like a whip. "We'd be safer on foot."

"Horses are faster," Trok argued. "It's big enough to carry us all. We could ride in comfort, like the humans." He stared off into the distance. "An ax in one hand, a spear in the other, cutting down anyone who dared stand in my way. Anyone I missed, my warhorse would trample into the earth."

"Warhorse?" Genevieve glanced at the horse. "Windstorm?" Her face tightened. It almost looked like she was trying not to laugh. "Only if you swear to take proper care of him."

"We don't need a horse," Jig said. "We can—"

Trok grabbed the rope around Jig's neck, choking Jig and Relka with one tug. "Come on. You two go around and distract him. I'll sneak up and grab the reins."

Genevieve grinned and moved out of the way. "Windstorm can be a little stubborn. If he won't run, all you have to do is dig those claws into his ear and twist."

Trok was right about at least one thing. Windstorm did speed their progress. Not in the way Trok had imagined, perhaps. . . .

"He's running back to the road," Relka called. Jig groaned. His stomach had already begun to cramp from all of the running.

"Don't let him turn back toward the town." Trok threw a rock at Windstorm's head. He missed, but the horse snorted and veered away. They were actually making better time than Jig had hoped, running after the horse.

Windstorm had crossed into a farmer's abandoned field, which was overgrown with dry, withered vines. Dead, half-frozen orange gourds the size of Trok's head were scattered about like hobgoblin traps. No matter how closely Jig watched, he kept tripping over the rotting things. The toe of his boot was stained orange from the last one he had kicked. Why would the humans work so hard to grow these things, only to abandon them?

Cold flakes tickled his face, spotting his vision. He glanced at the sky, remembering what he had heard back at Avery. Snow had come early this year. Maybe they hadn't meant to leave their plants to die.

"Try to get in front of him!" Trok crossed Jig's path, trying to get behind the horse. "Keep him distracted while I sneak up and grab the reins."

Windstorm stopped to munch the plants at the edge of the field. Either that or he was playing with them, giving them the chance to catch up before darting off again. Just as he had waited for Jig to finish burning through their ropes before running away. Jig was starting to think horses were even smarter than he had realized. This one clearly intended to defeat his goblin foes by running until they passed out, at which point Windstorm could consume their unconscious bodies at his leisure.

Relka stepped into the road and raised her hands. "In the name of Jig Dragonslayer and his glorious god Tymalous Shadowstar, I command you to halt!"

Windstorm flicked his tail and began to relieve himself.

Trok crept up behind the horse. As Windstorm finished, Trok lunged. His fingers closed around the reins. "I caught him!"

Jig winced, waiting for Windstorm to bite Trok's nose off or smash his skull with one of those huge, iron-shod hooves. But Windstorm only snorted.

"Help me into the seat," Trok said.

Slowly Jig moved closer to the horse. Maybe Windstorm was waiting until all three goblins were close enough to kill.

"I think the humans called it a saddle," Relka said.

Humans climbed into the saddles by putting one foot in the metal loop on the side and swinging their bodies up onto the horses' backs. But humans had longer legs than goblins.

Trok solved the problem by punching Relka in the gut

with his free hand. She dropped to her hands and knees, and Trok put one foot on her back. Pushing himself up, he managed to swing his other foot into the metal loop.

Windstorm trotted a few more steps to eat another bit of snow-covered plant. Trok tried valiantly to hold on, but there was only so far his legs could stretch. He squealed and fell onto the ground, still clutching the reins with both hands.

Relka's fury slowly eased, giving way to amusement as they watched Trok dragged through the snow, flopping about like a broken toy.

Trok tried to pull himself up and punch Windstorm in the head. But he had to release the reins to swing. In the time it took to recover his balance, Windstorm trotted easily out of reach.

"Stupid horse," Trok shouted.

Relka glanced at Jig. "I'm starting to see why the princess let us take him."

This time, Trok threw himself onto the saddle before Windstorm could move away. Trok scrambled to hold on, kicking his leg around and gripping the saddle with both hands. He straightened, and his triumphant grin faded. In his haste, he had managed to seat himself backward.

"Aw, pixie farts," Trok said.

Before he could straighten himself out, Windstorm reared back on his hind legs. Trok tumbled into the snow and dirt.

Windstorm's whinny sounded a lot like laughter.

Goblins like Trok lived by making sure everyone else was afraid of them. When that fear faded, he did whatever it took to restore it. Apparently that went for horses too. Trok snarled and grabbed the front of Windstorm's saddle. With his other hand, he stretched up to grab the horse's ear.

"Wait," said Jig. "I don't know if you should—"

Windstorm squealed.

"Ha! Think you can best a goblin warrior, do you?"

The horse slammed his head into Trok's chest. Given the size of Windstorm's head, Trok flew back as if he had been punched by an ogre. Windstorm snorted, then reached down to nip Trok's ear.

"Make him let go!" Trok screamed, but Windstorm had

already released him. Jig didn't blame him. If Trok tasted as foul as he smelled, Jig would have rather eaten plants too.

Trok grabbed his bloody ear with one hand. His other clenched into a fist.

"Trok, wait."

"What is it, runt?" Trok pulled out his broken arrow. "You think you get to give the orders, just because you got lucky with those pixies?"

"And the dragon," Relka said. "And the Necromancer. Don't forget the old chief, Kralk. And the hobgoblins. Also, he's the one who saved you from taking Genevieve's sword through the belly. Personally, if Jig Dragonslayer told me to wait, I'd listen."

Jig stepped back. From the look on Trok's face, the only thing stopping Trok from killing them all was that he couldn't make up his mind who to kill first.

"There are probably still some humans out looking for us," Jig said. He was tempted to let Trok and Windstorm work things out. But Trok would be more useful as an angry goblin warrior than as a blue smear of slush in some farmer's field. "We'll need your help if we're going to make it to Billa's army."

"Why?" asked Relka.

"Because there are a lot more humans out there." Jig took a deep breath, never taking his eyes off of Trok's weapon. "Look, even if you do manage to ride him, we—"

Trok snarled.

"I mean *when*! When you ride him. Well, it's still going to take a few days to get to Billa's army, right?"

"I suppose," said Trok. "What does that have to do with anything?"

"Well, none of us brought any food."

Slowly both Trok and Relka turned toward Windstorm. . . .

CHAPTER 4

AUTUMNSTAR STRETCHED HIS WINGS ON THE broad stone, basking in the sun's warmth. It had taken a few years to adjust to his new body, but all in all, being a sand lizard wasn't too bad. Though he doubted he'd ever get used to eating bugs.

After seven days of smoked horse meat, Relka and Trok were beginning to look tasty. Jig was certain they were having similar thoughts about him.

He was almost sure Relka wouldn't murder him in his sleep, and Trok seemed more annoyed by Relka than Jig, so he would probably kill her first. That would give Jig time to flee. And Relka was the only one who knew how to cook, which was likely the reason Trok hadn't already strangled her. If Trok's frustration ever outweighed his need for a good meal, Relka was in trouble.

For the past few nights, Jig had taken to sleeping with Smudge in his hand. Hopefully his burning fingers would wake him up if the humans found them, or if either of the other goblins tried anything. He debated again whether he would be better off running away. He couldn't decide whether the protection of having two additional goblins around was worth the threat of having two additional goblins around.

"I still say we should have killed the human," Trok said as they crossed another bridge. The first time Jig saw a human bridge, he had been convinced it was magical. How else could an arch of stone hold together with nothing beneath it?

Now he merely groaned. Another bridge meant another treacherous crossing over icy wooden planks stretched between those unnatural arches. There was no railing or wall, only a row of taller stones to either side. The stones were gray and white, with dying grass and moss growing in the cracks. Beneath them, mud turned the thread of flowing water a strange reddish-brown color.

"She attacked our lair, and you just let her go. Besides, the human lied to us," Trok continued. "We've crossed half the world, and I've seen no sign of Pottersville or any army."

"We'll find it," Relka said. She coughed and spat to clear her throat, then sang:

"I walk through darkness and through cold.
Tym gives me strength. He walks beside me.
When I was hungry and alone.
Tym gave us food. Windstorm was yummy!
Trok wiped himself with toxic leaves.
Jig's magic caused the itch to flee."

Jig had been trying so hard to forget the leaves incident, too.

A hard-packed ball of snow and ice hit Relka in the face. "Next time it'll be a rock," Trok said. From the expression on Trok's face, he would definitely be killing Relka first.

"If we had killed Genevieve, the rest of the humans would still be chasing us," Jig said. Though he understood Trok's feelings, not to mention his hunger. How many times did they have to fight humans and pixies and everything else until they all just left the goblins alone?

He glanced down at the icy river as he crossed the bridge. Glinting yellow eyes stared up at him.

"Who are you?"

The voice sounded more female than male, if you could get past the growling and the snapping of her jaws. Jig had never seen such a creature. She was slightly shorter than a goblin, with a long face that reminded him of a wolf or dog.

Her armor was . . . unique. She appeared to have taken a heavy blanket and cut holes for her head and arms. Scraps of metal were fastened to every part of the blanket. Rusty metal rings decorated the hem, jingling when she moved. Bits of twine secured enormous iron hinges to her shoulders. A rusted key, a bit of old chain, and several of those crescent-shaped bars Windstorm had worn on his hooves all clanked together on her chest.

Bristly brown fur covered her exposed skin. She carried a short spear, which she jabbed in Jig's direction. The gesture was less intimidating than it might have been, thanks to the fish still flopping on the end of the spear.

Trok was the first to react. He grabbed Jig by the arm and flung him off the bridge at the creature.

Jig twisted, trying to avoid the spear. The creature did the same, presumably to protect her fish.

His shoulder hit first, slamming into her chest and stamping a key-shaped bruise into his shoulder. They crashed to the ground together, and then the creature's feet shoved Jig back into the stream. Jig ducked as the creature swung her spear back and forth. She scrambled back to the riverbank, where she threw back her head and yipped.

Trok jumped down and tried to grab the spear. She dodged and smashed the shaft against his knuckles. As Trok howled, she swung the other end, smacking him in the face with her fish.

"Take that, smelly goblin!" She did a triumphant dance, never taking her eyes from the goblins. In the distance, Jig could hear other yips and howls. Whatever this thing was, she wasn't alone.

"Wait," Jig said. "Darnak said Billa had put together an army of monsters. Goblins and orcs and worse. This thing is probably from that army."

Trok scowled. "This thing is supposed to be worse than a goblin?"

At the same time, the creature growled and bared an impressive number of sharp teeth. "Kobold! Stupid goblins."

"Can you take us to Billa?" Jig asked.

The dog-woman—the *kobold*—tilted her head to one side. "First you pay me. Then I let you go find Billa's army."

"What?" Trok yelled. "Why should we pay a mangy dog like you?"

Relka tapped his arm and pointed. Jig counted eight more kobolds—with eight more spears—running toward the bridge.

"What kind of payment?" Jig asked.

"Metal." As her companions arrived, she straightened and said, "Metal for everyone."

The rest of the kobolds jangled to a halt, pointing their weapons at the goblins. One wore a helmet made from an old pot. Another had armor made entirely of tarnished copper coins with square holes in the centers. A third wore a suit of arrowheads, with the metal points sticking out like animal spines. His fellow kobolds gave him a wide berth.

"What's going on, Hessafa?" asked the spiny one.

Hessafa pointed her spear and said, "Smelly goblins won't pay."

Jig could feel Smudge stirring in his hood. The fire-spider wasn't giving off the searing heat of imminent death, but that could be because of the cold.

Nine armed kobolds against three goblins. Jig still had the knife he had taken from Genevieve, and Trok had his stick. But the kobolds were all armed and wearing armor . . . such as it was.

Jig made his way to the edge of the ice. "That's not true!"

"So the smelly goblins *will* pay?" Hessafa asked.

"We did pay." Jig stepped to the side, out of reach of her spear. "We paid her lots of metal. Coins and nails and a dwarf shield. She didn't want to share!" He pointed back at the road. "She buried it in the snow so she could keep it all for herself!"

"Lies!" Hessafa shouted. But the other kobolds had begun to mutter to one another.

"Lots of shiny metal," Jig said. "Iron and copper and steel and brass."

"Where?" demanded a fat male. The butt of his spear was studded with rusty metal fishhooks.

"Back on the other side of the bridge. She made us close our eyes, so I don't know exactly where she buried it."

"*Hessafa* knows," said a kobold who wore a shovel blade for a breastplate.

"That's right," said Jig, trying to look surprised. "Hessafa does know. She could show you."

"No!" Hessafa shouted. "Smelly goblins lie!"

But it was too late. Hessafa yipped and snarled as the other kobolds dragged her across the stream.

"Come on," Jig said. The kobolds had to have been nearby to respond so quickly. He glanced over his shoulder, wondering what they would do to Hessafa. Would they believe her when she couldn't lead them to her stolen metal, or would they try to pound the truth out of her?

And then he crested a low hill, and all thought of Hessafa vanished. They had reached Pottersville.

Pottersville was built on the intersection of several roads, as well as that annoying river. One road led off toward the mountains to the north. Another bridged the stream and disappeared up into what Darnak had said were elf lands.

As with the town of Avery, Pottersville was surrounded by a low wall. From the look of things, it hadn't done much to protect the town.

Whole sections were ripped down, with figures moving in and out like bugs. Big bugs, with swords and axes and spears. To the right of the smashed gate where the road passed through the wall, goblins swarmed over abandoned farmhouses. There had to be hundreds of goblins down there. Some worked to load barrels and other bundles onto wagons. Others chased after a group of fluffy gray animals who had apparently escaped from inside a battered wooden fence.

The kobolds had taken over the other side of the road. Small groups of kobolds crept along the edge of the woods. Hunting for food? Or perhaps they were guarding against human survivors who might come back for revenge.

"What are those?" Relka pointed to where huge, long-limbed creatures with rubbery green skin chopped a fallen section of wall into individual logs.

"Trolls," said Jig. He hadn't seen one since his involuntary quest a few years ago. There had been a few trolls living down in the lower caverns with Straum the dragon back then. As far as Jig could tell, they had been eaten by the ogres.

Being uneaten, these trolls were better off than the ones back home, but not by much. As far as Jig could tell, they were prisoners. They were chained together by metal collars, a bit like the goblins had been back at Avery.

"And those monsters guarding them must be orcs," Relka said.

The orcs wore dingy metal breastplates and shields, all painted a dull black. Or maybe they were just dirty. Either way, Genevieve would have appreciated their sense of style.

"Look at them," Trok whispered, his tone very similar to Relka's when she talked about Tymalous Shadowstar. "They're so tough, the cold doesn't even bother them!"

Most of the orcs kept their muscular arms bare. Though when Jig squinted through his spectacles, he could see a few shivering as they marched through the broken gate. And they did march quite close together, presumably for warmth. It was still an impressive sight.

Jig wondered if the grayish tinge of their skin was their natural coloring or an effect of the cold.

His breath caught as he glimpsed more orcs within the town walls. Between the kobolds and the goblins and the orcs, there had to be thousands of monsters gathered here. Strong monsters. Warriors and fighters who would have no problem defeating Genevieve's little band of soldiers. All Jig had to do was persuade them to help.

As he watched, one of the goblins snuck away from the others to relieve himself on a rather out-of-place tree with thick, bare branches. The tree shivered, sprinkling snow. Then, before the goblin could react, the tree stomped him into the earth.

"First rule," Jig said, his throat dry. "Don't pee on the trees."

"Right." For once, Trok spoke without his usual bluster.

Jig watched as the tree wiped its . . . foot in the mud, then wrapped several branches around the remains of the goblin. It lifted the goblin, bent back until the body nearly touched the ground behind it, and then snapped straight. From the trajectory, the goblin landed somewhere near the back wall of the town.

Maybe this hadn't been such a great idea. For goblins, safety lay in numbers. Billa's army had sounded like the safest place to hide.

Back at the lair, Jig had always been able to disappear into the background. Well, up until everyone found out about that healing trick. But nobody here knew he could do that.

He glanced at Relka and sighed. Even if he asked Trok to cut out Relka's tongue right now, he would never blend in here. He was scrawnier than any goblin in sight. A part of him wanted nothing more than to flee and hide.

One of the goblins broke away from the others and jogged up the road. Toward them. Waving a sword in the air. "What are you worms doing away from your regiment? If Oakbottom catches you, he'll toss you all! He's still convinced he can clear the far wall if he finds a light enough goblin."

"Who are you calling worms?" Trok still carried his sharpened stick, and he jabbed it at the approaching goblin.

Jig and Relka glanced at each other and took a quiet step back, leaving Trok to his fate.

"Threatening a superior officer is grounds for summary execution." The approaching goblin was smaller than Trok, but his sword made up for any difference in size. His left ear was gone, sliced off at the scalp, and he was missing two fingers on his left hand. He wore a simple helmet of hammered metal, shaped like a bowl with large crescents cut on either side for the ears. Given this goblin's handicap, his helmet listed a bit to one side.

He pulled out a flattened stack of stained, rat-chewed pages and waved them under Trok's nose. "Regulations also give the condemned soldier a choice. Would you rather I force feed you your own weapon or toss you to the trolls?"

"We're not soldiers," Jig squeaked. "The humans attacked our lair, but we escaped, and—"

"You mean you're here to enlist?" The goblin's entire demeanor changed in an instant, as if the word "enlist" were a magical spell. "A wonderful choice. You won't regret it, I can promise you that. I'm Gratz. Corporal in the army of Billa the Bloody."

He sheathed his sword and hurried over to clap Trok's shoulder. The move was so unexpected that Trok didn't even stab Gratz. "Joining Billa was the best choice I ever made. Changed my life. Come on, I'll take you to Silverfang."

"Silverfang?" asked Relka.

"One of Billa's lieutenants," said Gratz. "He's in charge of the whole goblin regiment. He'll be the one to decide whether you're fit to join us."

"What if he decides we're not?" asked Jig. He doubted Trok had much to worry about, and even Relka was bigger and stronger than Jig. But the more Jig saw of this army, the more out of place he felt.

Gratz studied Jig closely, and his forehead wrinkled. "Don't you worry," he said, though his cheerful confidence had disappeared. "Silverfang will find a use for you, one way or another."

Somehow Jig wasn't reassured. He glanced behind, wondering if it was too late to flee.

The angry yaps of the returning kobolds answered that question.

"Right," said Jig. "The sooner we get to Silverfang, the better!"

Growing up, Jig had learned to avoid the warriors whenever possible. The warriors were the goblins most eager to prove themselves. For some reason, proving themselves always seemed to involve tormenting Jig. Whether it was dropping rats in his muck pail or locking him in the garbage pit, they all took their frustrations out on Jig.

So he had learned to watch for the signs. If a band of adventurers slaughtered some goblins in passing, Jig would hide in the nursery or the distillery for a few days. If Golaka blackened a warrior's eye for trying to steal a toad dumpling from her kitchen, Jig would do his best to stay on the opposite side of the lair, along with the rest of the weaker goblins.

Here in Billa's army, there were no weaker goblins. Only Jig. He tried not to make eye contact, but he could feel them staring as he followed Gratz toward the walls of Pottersville. Slitted eyes peered out from crude tents. Mud-covered goblins working down by the river paused to look. Farther on, a line of goblins stopped stabbing stacks of hay to watch Jig. Why they were attacking hay was beyond Jig's comprehension, but better hay than him.

Beside him, Trok was grinning and pointing and babbling like a child. "When can I get an ax like that?" he asked. "And that shield with the big spikes on the edge. I want one of those, too. And that helmet with the animal horns on the sides."

"One thing at a time," said Gratz. "Recruits start off with standard arms and armor. Regulations give you the right to claim better equipment from the enemy. Or from the bodies of your fellow goblins. Just make sure they're dead first." He pointed toward the wall, where several wide planks of wood had been lashed together and propped up to create a makeshift cave. "First you talk to Silverfang."

They passed a small cook fire, where two goblins were roasting one of the fluffy gray animals.

Relka stopped. "That's not right."

"What do you mean?" asked Gratz.

"They're not even saving the blood. How are they supposed to make the gravy?"

Gratz laughed. "Gravy? With this lot, you're lucky to know where the meat ends and the bones begin."

As if to prove his point, the spit holding the animal broke and fell into the fire. Both goblins immediately began to shout at one another. Neither bothered to try to get the meat out of the fire. The smell of burned fur made Jig's eyes water.

"That's enough!" Both of the would-be chefs jumped. Neither one made a sound as the biggest, meanest-looking goblin Jig had ever seen ducked out of the wooden cave.

"Lieutenant Silverfang, sir," Gratz snapped, his body stiffening.

A scar on the left side of Silverfang's face twisted his mouth into a grimace. His left fang had been replaced with a round steel spike, apparently held in place by the three small pins protruding from his jaw. He wore black plates of metal for armor, like the orcs Jig had seen in the town, and on his back he carried a curved sword that was almost as long as Jig was tall.

Silverfang's heavy boots crunched through frozen mud. His sword slid free, and both chefs closed their eyes. Silverfang thrust his sword into the burning animal. With a grunt, he hauled it into the air and flung it to one side, nearly hitting another goblin. He turned to jab a thick finger at the nearer of the two chefs. "Fetch another goat. Ruin this one and I'll make you eat the coals."

He beckoned the other chef closer, then grabbed him by the shirt. A whimper slipped from the goblin's lips.

Turning that huge sword with one hand, Silverfang wiped the blade on the goblin's collar. When he let go, the poor goblin fell on his backside in his eagerness to scramble away.

Silverfang turned to Gratz. "Fresh meat?"

"They want to enlist," said Gratz.

Silverfang came closer. His left eye was cloudy and oozed blue-black crud from the corner. He fixed the right on Trok. He grunted, then turned to study Relka. This time, his grunt sounded amused. He poked Relka's shoulder hard enough to knock her back a step.

Finally he turned to Jig.

"*You* want to join Billa's army?" He chuckled. "You're not even worth feeding to the kobolds."

Relka had done nothing when Silverfang poked her. But now she stepped in front of Jig, standing so close she could have bitten Silverfang's nose.

"That's Jig Dragonslayer. He's smarter and stronger than any warrior in your—"

Silverfang punched her in the jaw. She landed on the ground, spitting blood.

"Stronger than me?" Silverfang asked.

Jig thought about the knife tucked through his belt. Should he kill himself and get it over with, or would it be better to stab Relka first?

Silverfang stabbed his sword into the ground. With one claw, he traced the scar on his face. "A dwarf's ax did that. Took my tooth and my eye with one swing, and still I bested him. He forged this tooth before I tossed him to the wolves." He raised his voice. "Gather round, men. Let the little dragonslayer show off *his* battle scars."

"My what?" Jig tried to back away. He bumped into another goblin who had come up behind him. Jig turned to find himself ringed by goblin warriors, most of whom shared Silverfang's disdainful smirk.

"Your scars," said Gratz. "To prove your experience and worth as a warrior. It's how we measure the experience of new recruits. Regulations even allow you to enlist at a higher rank, if your scars meet certain criteria."

Silverfang rolled his eyes.

"Jig *is* a warrior." Relka still sat on the ground where she had fallen.

"But wouldn't the best warrior be the one who didn't get stabbed?" Jig asked.

Utter silence told him exactly how big a mistake those words had been. He cringed as he turned back to Silverfang, who was rubbing the huge scar on his face. "I didn't mean *you're* not a good warrior. I only—"

"Show us your scars, or I'll give you some," said Silverfang.

Scars. Right. Jig's hand shook as he pushed back his sleeve. "That's a sword cut from a few years ago," he said, pointing to a nasty gash on his forearm. He didn't think anyone needed to know it was self-inflicted.

He pulled off his cloak. The cold wind made him shiver even harder. Tugging down the shoulder of his shirt, he pointed to a small hard circle of pale skin. "That's from a wizard's arrow." He turned around to show them the matching spot on his back, beside the shoulder blade.

By now the goblins had stopped laughing.

Jig tugged his shirt up. "I can't reach it, but there's another stab wound in my back, below the ribs." He reached to touch the wrinkled scar on his ear. "I tore that in a fight with another goblin, years ago."

He wondered if he should include the various burns Smudge had inflicted over the years.

"How did a runt like you survive all that?" Gratz asked. Silverfang scowled, and Gratz's face went pale. "Sorry, sir.

Didn't mean to speak out of turn. Won't happen again. My apologies. I'll make sure—"

"Gratz talks too much," Silverfang said. "But he has a point." He grabbed Jig by the shoulder and spun him around, poking the arrow scar. "Most of this lot would have curled up and died from a wound like this."

"That's nothing!" Trok shouted. "A tunnel cat clawed half my leg off once." He yanked his trousers down to his knees, revealing a row of scars crossing his thigh. "I still killed that beast with my bare hands."

Relka snickered. "I was in the kitchen when you brought that 'beast' in for Golaka. It was so old there was barely any meat. It was missing most of its teeth, not to mention a leg." She sat up on the ground and pulled up her shirt, revealing the scar in the middle of her belly. "My wound was given to me by Jig Dragonslayer himself, for daring to challenge him. Not by some crippled old beast who gummed my leg a few times."

"You shut up!" Trok drew back his leg to kick her.

Silverfang was faster. He punched Trok in the side of the head, knocking him to the ground beside Relka. Silverfang flexed his fingers. "Next one of you who acts up gets the sword. Got it?" He turned back to Jig. "If the best warrior is the one who doesn't get stabbed, I guess you're one lousy warrior."

"Definitely," Jig said.

"And I suppose you expect me to believe her nonsense about you slaying a dragon?" Silverfang asked.

For once, Jig managed to keep his mouth shut. He doubted there was anything he could say that wouldn't infuriate Silverfang even further.

"So does he qualify for enlistment at a higher rank?" Gratz asked.

Silverfang closed his eyes. His fingers tightened around the hilt of his sword, and every goblin backed away.

"First they ought to prove themselves, don't you think?" Silverfang turned to Gratz. "Take them to the wolf pens."

* * *

The sound of goblins wagering on their survival did nothing to calm Jig as he followed Gratz through the camp. Nor did Trok's babbling about Silverfang and the army.

"Can you imagine if we had a chief like him?" Trok was saying. "We'd chase those hobgoblins right out of our mountain! The humans and elves wouldn't dare set foot in our territory." He paused to spit. His blood was bright blue against the snow. "Did you see how fast he hit me?"

"Do you think we could get him to do it again?" Relka muttered.

Gratz grinned. "I was the same way when Billa came to our lair. All those goblins and orcs, and even the kobolds. We had been living near a dwarven copper mine. They mostly left us alone unless we ventured near their tunnels. Those tunnels used to be ours, but the dwarves ran us off." He punched the air with both hands. "The dwarves didn't stand a chance against Billa the Bloody. They'll never set foot in our territory again!"

Relka grinned at Jig. "Ask him about our lair."

"Me? Why can't you— Oh, never mind." Jig turned to Gratz. "The humans attacked our lair. They used magic to seal the entrance. Do you think Billa could beat them?"

"Nothing can stop Billa the Bloody," Gratz said. He sounded as earnest as Relka when she talked about Shadowstar. "Armies, magic, even the gods."

Cocky little goblin, isn't he? Shadowstar asked.

"Unfortunately," Gratz went on, "regulations prohibit me from sharing our marching orders until Silverfang accepts you into his regiment."

"What regulations?" Trok asked. "What are you talking about?"

Gratz beamed and pulled out the folded pages he had shown them before. "I've written down everything Billa and her lieutenants have ordered since I joined up with her. Rules, punishments, every order from how to use your shield in combat to the best way to clean your fangs. These pages right here are what turn us into the most dangerous army in the world."

"Where are we going?" asked Relka.

"You get to clean up after the wolves." Gratz pointed. Up ahead, the walking tree they had seen before was lifting logs into place to reinforce what appeared to be a long, roofless building outside the wall. Oakbottom, Gratz had called him. The tree's branches creaked loudly as he worked. He had no joints, but the branches appeared to bend more where they forked into smaller branches. Jig saw no sign of eyes or a mouth, but the tree could clearly see what he was doing.

"That's enough, Oakbottom," Gratz shouted. "Silverfang wants these three to feed the wolves today." He turned to Trok. "Normally Oakbottom cleans the pens. He's strong enough to take care of himself, and the wolves don't like the taste of wood. Oakbottom tends to the wolves, and in exchange, Billa lets him toss as many humans as he likes when we go to war. Goblins and kobolds too, if anyone falls out of formation. It's the one thing he actually seems to enjoy."

The tree tromped off, his roots digging deep, muddy grooves in the earth.

Gratz gathered up shovels and buckets from the base of the wall. "Say, did you really face a dragon?"

"Sort of," Jig said. "I faced him, and then he smashed me into a wall. How big are these wolves?"

"Compared to a dragon, they're not so bad," Gratz said. "I've been riding for close to a year now, you know. A goblin warrior on one of these wolves can take out a human on horseback."

Jig glanced at Trok, who was practically drooling at the idea. Actually, he *was* drooling, but that was mostly due to his swollen lip.

"And Silverfang wants us to clean up after them?" Relka asked.

Jig could hear snarls and the snapping of jaws coming from behind the walls. The nearest wall shook as something huge slammed into it. Snow and dirt sprinkled from the top of the wall.

"Does Silverfang make everyone do this before they can join?" Jig asked.

"Only the ones he doesn't like." Gratz frowned as he led

them around to an iron-clad door. It looked like the door and wall had been ripped out of another building, then carried here. Probably by that walking tree. Ropes and planks secured the mismatched sections of wall. "He made me do it, actually."

The walls shook again, making Jig jump. Smudge was already uncomfortably warm in his pocket. "How did you survive?"

"Don't know that I should say." Gratz scratched his ear, then shrugged. "But there's nothing in the regulations against it. There were three of us, just like you lot. I stabbed the others in the back, pushed them in, and then shoveled out the pens while the wolves were eating."

A typical goblin solution. Jig could see Trok nodding his approval. Both Jig and Relka moved away from him.

Gratz pressed his face to the crack at the edge of the door. "They're beautiful animals. Take a look."

Trok practically shoved him to the ground in his haste to see. "They're enormous! Those things could toss a tunnel cat about like a toy! Do we get to choose which one we ride? When can we take them into battle?"

Jig moved to another corner of the pen. The walls were tightly secured with loops of thick rope, but a bit of light still shone through. He pressed one eye to the gap.

He had to grab the ropes to keep from falling. His legs had simply gone numb. Which was the only thing preventing him from running away as fast as he could.

The beasts inside the pen were the size of small ponies. Jig counted fourteen in all. To these creatures, a goblin would be little more than a rat to a tunnel cat. Their teeth were the size of his thumbs, and they had an awful lot of them. Bristly brown fur covered their bodies. The fur stood straight up on their necks and backs, except where it was covered by heavy leather harnesses.

One turned to snarl at Jig. Long tufts of fur dangled from the tips of the wolf's ears, an effect that might have been comical on another creature. Like one that wasn't currently gnawing on an arm.

Any snow or plants here had long since been trampled

into the mud. Red-brown earth was caked onto their legs and fur. Looking at the slick mess of mud and worse, Jig doubted he would be able to take two steps without slipping.

"The big one is named Bastard," Gratz shouted. "He's the pack leader."

Jig had no trouble picking Bastard out of the pack. He would be the one who had wandered over to casually lock his jaws around the throat of the one with the arm. The arm dropped to the mud, and Bastard snatched it up.

Wolf discipline had a lot in common with the goblin kind.

"The one rolling around in the back is Smelly," Gratz continued. "Nobody rides him unless all the other wolves are taken. The one with the patchy fur is Fungus. Ugly is the girl whose food Bastard just swiped. The one with the scarred muzzle and missing eye. She tried to steal Bastard's food once. Not smart."

Jig barely listened as Gratz named the other wolves. *You're one of the forgotten gods, right?* he asked silently.

That's right. We were cursed after—

And now Braf and I are your only real followers? Jig continued.

What can I say? Anyone's standards will slip a bit after a few thousand years of solitude.

It wasn't easy to shout inside your own mind, but Jig managed. *So if we goblins are all you have, why aren't you working harder to keep us from being eaten by wolves?*

I'm a little busy here, Jig. Fight your own wolves.

The abruptness of Shadowstar's response left Jig too stunned to reply, and then Gratz was dumping shovels and buckets in front of the gate. "Make sure they don't get out of the pen. Silverfang gets really mad when the wolves escape. They gorge themselves on whoever's closest, and then they're too stuffed to fight for at least three days."

Relka was the first to move, picking up a battered shovel and walking toward the gate. "I'm not afraid. Shadowstar watches over me."

And laughs, Jig added.

Only sometimes.

"They do their business near the back," Gratz said. "That spot where Smelly keeps rolling." He handed shovels to Jig and Trok.

Jig took the shovel with both hands and slammed it into the back of Gratz's head, knocking him face-first into the door. He bounced back and collapsed in the snow, groaning and holding his nose.

"Ha!" said Trok. "Good thinking, Jig!" He grabbed the bar holding the door shut. "Come here, wolves. Snack time!"

"Tymalous Shadowstar frowns upon the murder of our fellow goblins." Relka tried to push Trok aside, but he barely noticed.

"I'm not the one killing him," Trok said. "Shadowstar can talk it out with the wolves."

"Maybe we could feed them one of those goats instead." Relka turned to Jig. "Does Shadowstar say anything about killing goats?"

"I don't think so." Jig grabbed Gratz's sword and glanced around. A few other goblins were watching them, but nobody tried to interfere.

"Hey, that's right! He told us we were allowed to loot the dead," said Trok, seizing Gratz's helmet. "What else does he have worth taking?"

"I don't think he's dead yet, but. . . ." Relka shrugged and started tugging at Gratz's boots.

"Wait," said Jig. Relka backed away. "Trok, stop."

"Why, did you want the belt?" Trok glanced at Jig. "I don't think it will fit you."

Jig shook his head. If Silverfang were like other goblin leaders, this wouldn't be the last time he tried to feed Jig to the wolves. Next time Jig might not have the chance to whack his captor with a shovel.

There had to be a better way to control the wolves. The goblins couldn't feed someone to the wolves every time they mounted up for battle. Well, they could, but it would be awfully messy, and it probably wasn't a good idea to keep feeding them goblins. Not if you didn't want them to start seeing goblins as meals instead of riders.

Jig knelt beside Gratz and poked him a few times until he groaned. "You're one of their riders. How do you keep them from eating you?"

Gratz reached up to touch his fang, which was loose from his collision with the gate. "According to the manual, as a prisoner I'm required to give you only my name and rank. You already know all that, so I don't have to tell you anything."

"Fine." Jig stood. "I'll open the door. Trok, you throw him through."

"Of course, the manual also says that as victors, you're entitled to any spoils," Gratz said hastily. "Like that blue sack dangling from my belt."

Trok held the belt while Jig slid the sack free. The smell of old meat and blood made his eyes water. He reached in and pulled out what felt like a rock wrapped in leather. Something sharp jabbed his palm. He turned the object over to see a thick, yellow-green toenail.

"Troll toes," Gratz said, struggling to sit up. "The wolves love them. And trolls heal quick. You can get ten toes a week from the healthy ones."

There had to be thirty or forty toes in there. Jig stepped toward the pen and tossed one over the wall.

Snarling broke out even before the toe hit the ground. Jig peeked through the crack in the doorframe as the wolves lunged for the toe. Bastard bit another wolf on the rump, and suddenly he was alone. He dropped to the ground and began to gnaw the toe.

"Order them to sit," Gratz said. "Now that they know you've got toes, they should obey. Make sure to reward them all when you're done. They'll remember if you don't."

Before Jig could move, Trok shoved him out of the way and yanked open the door. Bastard leaped to his feet and snarled.

"Sit!" Trok shouted. The wolves obeyed, and Trok laughed. "It works!"

Gratz sat up and rubbed his head. "Go on, then. The sooner you start shoveling, the sooner you'll be done."

Relka was already following Trok into the pen. Jig stared

at his shovel. How did he know the wolves weren't just waiting until all three goblins were within reach?

"I told you Shadowstar would protect his followers," Relka said. "And Trok, too." She didn't sound as happy about that part.

Jig tucked Gratz's sword through his belt, gritted his teeth, and stepped through the doorway. Shadowstar wasn't the one walking past hungry wolves to clean up six varieties of filth. No, he was busy with more important matters.

Maybe I just trusted you to take care of this one on your own, Jig.

Jig reached the back and stabbed his shovel into the nearest pile. A crunching sound startled him, and his feet slipped. He landed on his side, looking back at the wolves. Bastard had gone back to playing with his troll toe, cracking the tiny bones in his jaw.

Relka began to sing as she shoveled.

"The wolves of war are drawing near.
They want only to eat him.
He shovels their filth with no fear.
He trusts his god to guard him.
Their furious howls he will not hear.
He trusts his god to save him.
He falls and gets scat in his ear.
He trusts his god to wash him."

Jig threw the contents of his shovel at her. He missed, but it was enough to shut her up. He heard divine chuckling in his mind.

I like her, Shadowstar said.

Eventually they shoveled the entire mess into buckets, to be dragged into the woods and dumped. It still wasn't as bad as privy duty back at the lair on those nights when Golaka made extra-spicy bat skewers.

Jig made sure to feed troll toes to all of the wolves. He dropped a few into his pocket, thinking they might make a good snack for Smudge. He shut and barred the door behind him just as Silverfang arrived.

Silverfang stared. "What are all three of you doing still alive? Haven't you cleaned those pens yet?"

Trok pointed to the buckets.

Silverfang went so far as to sniff the contents. He turned back to Jig. "You just cost me one of my good knives, runt. I had a bet with Gratz that there'd be nothing left of you but a few bones and scraps of that elf-ugly cloak." He bent to pull a knife from his boot, then slapped it into Gratz's hand.

"So now are we part of your army?" Jig asked.

Silverfang's face twisted as if he had choked on a troll toe, but he nodded. "Gratz, take them to get weapons and armor. And take your sword back from the runt. The orcs want us to send out a few more hunting parties to find those blasted elves that have been harassing our flanks."

"Elves?" Gratz looked surprised. "What are they doing in human lands, sir?"

"Who cares? They've been snooping and killing Billa's officers for the last day or so with their damned bows. She wants them dealt with."

They were going to hunt elves? Jig wondered if Silverfang would let him stay here with the wolves instead.

"What about our lair?" Relka asked. "Our warriors are imprisoned at Avery, and—"

Silverfang grabbed the front of her apron with one hand. He twisted the material so tight she could barely breathe, then lifted her off the ground. "You're a part of Billa's army now. I said to get weapons and armor. The next time you run your mouth instead of obeying, I'll eat your face." He opened his mouth, and the tip of his steel fang dented the skin beneath her jaw. All he had to do was let go, and Relka would be impaled.

He tossed Relka to the ground and walked away. Jig prayed she wouldn't say anything stupid, but for once she kept her mouth shut.

Gratz had pulled out his parchment and an ink-stained quill. "Running your mouth instead of obeying," he mumbled. "Punishable by having your face eaten." He tucked the regulations back into his shirt. "Come on, let's get your equipment. And don't worry too much about Silverfang. He's much more likely to just turn you over to Oakbottom. I think he's lost his taste for goblin, to tell you the truth."

Jig wasn't worried about Silverfang. He and the others were being sent to hunt *elves*. Jig suspected he would be dead long before either Silverfang or Oakbottom had the chance to kill him.

CHAPTER 5

AUTUMNSTAR WATCHED FROM BEHIND A CLAY pot of pickled rattlesnake eggs as a wrinkled woman with spider silk hair set a trap for him.

"Blasted sand lizards," she muttered, scooping a pile of dumplings into a clay bowl. "I was cooking that rabbit for my daughter's birthday feast." She set the bowl on a mat of woven leaves. Furniture was a luxury in the desert, where trees were scarce. Benches, shelves, and even beds were carved from the sandstone of the great cliff city . . . which probably explained the woman's leathery skin.

Autumnstar belched softly, wrinkling his snout at the aftertaste of overcooked rabbit. He crept closer to the edge of the shelf, watching as the woman slipped a string noose in among the dumplings. Her name was Anisah, and her traps had kept Autumnstar's life interesting for many years now. His followers had long forgotten him, and Anisah was the closest thing he had to a companion . . . even if she was always trying to lure him into a basin of sticky resin or brain him with a rock.

He felt no guilt about the rabbit. He had seen Anisah's daughter, and she could afford to miss a few meals.

Autumnstar crossed his front legs and settled his chin on his feet, staring out the open window. Even his enemies had for-

gotten him. He had sensed nothing from Noc since their battle in the desert, and Noc was not a patient god. If Noc thought Autumnstar had survived, he would have hunted him down years ago.

Wet coughs drew Autumnstar's attention back to Anisah. She was on her knees, doubled over as she hacked and struggled for breath. Flecks of blood and saliva sprayed the dumplings. A single look told him she wouldn't survive. Anisah's time was nearly over. She would be frightened and hurting.

Autumnstar climbed over the edge of the shelf, his claws finding easy purchase in the sandstone. Clinging to the edge, he spread his wings for balance and prepared to jump.

Noc may have taken away his followers, but he was still the God of the Autumn Star. For thousands of years he had brought comfort to the elderly and the infirm as their lives faded into darkness. Noc would have to send him back to the void before Autumnstar would give that up.

Anisah's coughs were growing weaker. Her hands pressed the floor, and her arms trembled.

Autumnstar glided to the ground, then scurried past spilled dumplings until he reached her side. He hadn't dared use his powers since fleeing Noc, for fear of being noticed. But he couldn't turn his back on suffering. He might not be powerful enough to stop death, but he could ease its sting. He spread his wings and reached out to touch her arm with his claws.

Nothing happened.

Rather, something did happen, but it wasn't what he had intended. Withered fingers clamped around Autumnstar's long neck.

"Got you at last," Anisah wheezed. For a dying old woman, she had a very strong grip. "This must be the gods' reward for a pious life."

Her last act before dying was to smash Tymalous Autumnstar's small body into the floor.

The town walls—what was left of them—rattled in the wind as Gratz led the goblins through a jagged gap. Jig wasn't sure what he had expected. Smoldering ruins, perhaps. A mob of orcs scrounging through the remains.

Instead, for the most part, the buildings inside were undamaged. Most were various shades of red, brown, and orange. As they passed, Jig saw that mud had been layered onto the wooden structures to give them their coloration. He half-expected to see humans peeking out the doors, as they had done back in Avery.

Gratz noticed him staring, and grinned. "Most of the humans had already fled by the time we arrived. They're scared of us, Jig. We haven't fought a true battle in over a month. Though Billa says we'll see real combat soon enough."

Jig and his companions were the only goblins in sight. Only orcs lived inside the walls. Everywhere Jig looked, he saw orcs hurrying between the thatch-roofed buildings or working to repair a broken wagon or hauling bundles of chopped wood.

This was Jig's first time seeing orcs up close. Their gray skin was bumpy, with a greenish tinge. Their flattened noses reminded Jig a little of boar snouts. Many of the orcs had scarred faces, though the scars were too precise to be battle wounds. The one carrying pots out of a home had three short lines running up the cheeks. Another who was hauling a wagon full of blankets had a broken line over her eyebrow. They all seemed to have a single scar beneath their noses as well.

"Tribal scars," Gratz said. "Each tribe of orcs has its own pattern. But they'll all have that scar on the nose. That's Billa's scar. All the orcs wear it to mark their loyalty."

"They let Billa cut their faces?" Jig asked.

Gratz shook his head. "They're orcs. They do it themselves." He gestured to another orc who was carrying a bundle of spears. Most of the orc's nose was missing. "Sometimes they get a little carried away."

"We don't have to do that, do we?" Jig asked, trying not to stare.

"No scars until you become an officer. Even then, only the orcs of Billa's tribe receive extra facial scars to mark their ranks. The rest of us get different marks, on our arms." Gratz actually sounded disappointed. He pointed to a pair of orcs standing guard in front of a building with swirls of darker mud blended onto the walls. Pot shards hung from one corner of the roof, clinking in the wind.

The orcs watched them approach. Neither said a word. Jig wondered how close the goblins could come before being cut down by those huge, double-headed axes.

"I need weapons and armor for these three," Gratz said. "Lieutenant Silverfang's orders."

One of the orcs grunted and disappeared into the building. Jig stared in wonder. Back home the guards would have been playing a game of Roaches or drinking stolen klak beer. Here they were actually *guarding*. The remaining orc was like a statue, barely blinking as she stared at the goblins. Though a statue wouldn't have had pimpled skin on her arms from the cold.

"How many of them freeze to death?" Jig whispered, staring at the muscles on those bare arms.

"A handful each week," said Gratz. He didn't bother to lower his voice. "They believe an orc who isn't strong enough to survive doesn't deserve to survive."

Jig could only imagine what they thought of him. Of all the goblins and kobolds, actually. How did they feel, traveling with so many "weaker" monsters?

The first orc returned carrying an armload of leather and steel, which he dumped into the snow.

"What's this?" Trok said, picking up one of the swords. If it could even be called a sword. The blade was a simple length of rusty steel, sharpened on one side. There was no crossguard. Twine held a bit of padding around the end for a handle. "Why can't I get an ax like yours?"

Relka grabbed a suit of armor. Heavy pads of leather were sewn together to form a crude breastplate. She stared at the various straps which connected it to smaller pads. "Could I get a suit without an arrow hole? One that doesn't smell like blood?"

The orcs ignored her.

Jig picked up a helmet, a simple bowl of metal like Gratz wore. He placed it on his head, then yanked it off. "They're freezing!"

"Put it on," Gratz snapped. "That helmet is your best friend. Not only can it save your life, but it also serves as a stool, a pillow, and a bowl for your meals. I know one fellow who uses it as a backup chamber pot, but I wouldn't recommend that."

Judging from the smell, this one had been used to serve a stew of mold and fetid meat. The edge of the helmet pressed down on the earpieces of Jig's spectacles.

Jig grabbed another suit of armor. Relka was having little luck with hers. Jig turned the armor about, then glanced at Gratz, trying to guess how everything fit together. If he put his head through the straps at the top, then those heavy pads would fall across his shoulders. . . .

The shoulder pads came nearly to his elbows, and the bottom of the breastplate brushed his thighs when he tried to walk. He pulled out the hood of his cloak, transferring Smudge there so the armor wouldn't squish the poor spider. No matter how tightly he tied the armor's straps, he still felt like a dried seed rattling around in a pod.

"A little large, but it should do," said Gratz.

"Why do they bother guarding this garbage?" Trok asked.

Gratz drew his own sword, which was far nicer than Trok's. Without a word, he swung the edge of the blade into Jig's stomach.

Jig staggered back. Why hadn't he taken a sword, too? He tried to grab his knife, but he had donned the armor over his cloak and belt, so this involved sticking his hand inside the breastplate.

"That's why," Gratz said. "You wear your armor at all times, follow orders, and you might actually survive your first battle."

Before Jig could respond, a second blow slammed into his back. This one knocked him face-first into the snow by the orcs' feet. He rolled over to see Trok grinning down at him.

"Hey, this is fun!" Trok raised his sword again, and then Relka slammed her own sword into his side.

"Watch it," Trok snapped. "You almost hit my arm." He thrust the blunt tip of his weapon into Relka's gut, and she doubled over.

"That's enough," Gratz shouted. "One of the first rules states that if you strike a fellow soldier, Billa gets her choice of your ear, your eye, or your hand." He reached up to rub his own missing ear. "It's how she keeps discipline. And believe me, you don't want to be drawing her attention."

"Does that mean Silverfang can't really kill me?" Jig asked hopefully.

"Oh, it's different when it's an officer doing the killing," Gratz said. "Silverfang could kill every last one of us, if he felt the urge. But then who would clean the wolf pens?" He laughed loud and hard at his little joke as he grabbed Jig's wrist and hauled him from the ground. "Now come on. We've got elves to hunt."

Jig picked up the remaining sword. The weapon was horribly balanced, like someone had strapped heavy rocks to the end of a stick. Testing the edge on his cloak, he decided rocks on a stick might actually be a better weapon.

Once they were away from the orcs, Gratz glanced around and said, "Billa brought along some orc smiths who make those swords. I think they deliberately blunt the edge. It's harder for new recruits to rebel when they're spending all their free time trying to hone their weapons."

That made sense. Unfortunately, it also meant Jig would be hunting elves with nothing more than a metal stick for a weapon.

Relka stopped so abruptly Jig bumped into her. "What's that?"

The building she pointed to was covered in large tiles. The doors had been ripped away, revealing an enormous brick oven at the rear of the building. The mouth glowed orange, and Jig could feel the heat from here. He moved closer, raising his hands to the warmth.

"Humans call it a kiln," Gratz said. "They use it to make pots and such. I'm told this town's famous for it. I think the orc smiths tried using it as a forge, but they couldn't get it hot enough." He kicked a broken shard near the doorway. "The walls broke almost as easily as the pottery. I don't understand why Billa chose this place as a target. No real fighting, and no tactical value that I can see. But that's why I'm only a corporal, eh?"

Relka didn't appear to have heard a word of it. "I could bake two bodies at a time. Three if they were dwarves. Golaka's oven is full of cracks, but this one . . . do you realize how much faster I could cook? We have to get one for the lair, Jig!"

"Maybe we should figure out how to get into our lair first," Jig pointed out.

Trok stomped another bit of pottery. "It doesn't sound like Silverfang's interested in helping us."

"You're welcome to complain," Gratz said. "You wouldn't be the first. Back when Billa first brought the orc tribes together, they didn't get along at all. They were stabbing each other every time you turned around. So Billa ordered that anyone who couldn't resolve their own problems should come to see her."

"And that worked?" Jig asked.

"They say that first day there had to be thirty orcs lined up at her tent. Billa marched out, took one look, and ordered them all butchered for breakfast. Things have been a lot calmer ever since. Still, if you catch her in a good mood, she might listen." Gratz continued toward the walls, leaving the goblins little choice but to follow. Jig didn't want to know what the punishment would be for fresh recruits found wandering through the town.

Gratz waved to a small group gathered by the gate. "Oh, good, they're ready for us."

The shabby weapons and armor were similar to Jig's own, but it was the kobold who caught his attention.

"Hessafa?"

"Kobolds aren't worth much in a fight," Gratz said. "But they're fast little things, and the best trackers in this goblin's army. They're not too fond of goblins, though. Being assigned to help us is punishment among the kobolds. I wonder what this one did to get herself into trouble."

Hessafa's lips pulled back, showing off her teeth. Her yellow eyes never blinked. Jig wasn't sure how to read kobold expressions, but he suspected it was a very good thing that Billa's law prohibited her soldiers from killing each other.

* * *

"Kobold, make sure you stay at least ten paces ahead of us, as spelled out in procedures," Gratz shouted. He turned to check the other goblins. "The rest of you spread out far enough that your weapons can't touch if you start swinging. Keep your ears up and your eyes wide. Elves are tricky bastards, but we'll find them."

"Only one elf," said Hessafa. "This way."

Jig kept his arms spread for balance. Hessafa had insisted on taking them over the frozen swamp. Dead trees and brown weeds jutted through the ice all around them, like an enormous version of the spiked pits the hobgoblins built back home.

Jig's boots were soaked from breaking through the thin ice, and most of the goblins had slipped and fallen at least once. Hessafa seemed determined to lead them through every pool of mud, filth, and foul-smelling slime she could find, while somehow avoiding them all herself.

"You can really track the elf through the swamps?" Jig asked.

"Hard to track elf over smelly goblin, but elf stink is here. Always trust scent, goblin." She sniffed the air and bared her teeth. "Scent goes this way."

"Up those icy, bramble-covered rocks?" asked Trok.

Hessafa's yips sounded suspiciously like laughter. "Goblin skin is so fragile. Try not to bleed too much. Spoils the scent."

The sun was low, nearly touching the horizon. Jig's stomach gurgled. They had already missed dinner. How much longer did Gratz plan to hunt this elf? "Why would an elf be sneaking around here anyway?"

"Hard to say." Gratz scratched the scarred nub of his ear. "Normally, elves stick to themselves. They look at humans like short-lived savages. Kind of how humans see us, actually."

"No, I mean why here?" Jig asked. "What good can a few elves do against an entire army?"

"They're scouts," Gratz said. "They shot a few arrows, killed an officer or two here and there, but mostly they're spying. It takes time to move an army. They want to know what we're doing and when we do it. If you can anticipate your enemy's actions, you can crush them."

"What *are* we doing?" Trok asked.

"We're changing things." Gratz's voice was soft, but his eyes were afire. "You said those humans attacked your lair. Well, Billa the Bloody is going to make sure no surface-dweller ever threatens us again!"

He drew his sword and shook it overhead. "It started a few years back, when Billa led her tribe against the trolls. She drove those trolls right out of their mountains. The trolls had nowhere else to go, so they started lurking about human villages, raiding their farms for food.

"Naturally, the humans didn't take kindly to this. Trolls, orcs, goblins, it's all the same to them. They began hiring adventurers to come into the mountains. They paid gold for every orc ear or troll head. So Billa summoned the other orc tribes, slew those who wouldn't follow her, and led the rest into battle."

He picked up a handful of snow. "They say the gods themselves were on her side that day. Snow blinded their soldiers. The wind fouled their arrows. Billa the Bloody sent those surface-dwellers fleeing for their lives. Everywhere she goes, she draws new monsters into her army. She plans to conquer every last inch of this land."

He crunched the snow into a ball and ate it. "At least, that was the plan. Turns out this land is a bit bigger than anyone realized."

Jig studied the other goblins. Trok was in heaven, beaming as he jabbed his sword at imaginary humans. Relka was fingering her necklace—when had she found time to make a new one?—and smiling to herself. Even Jig had to admit Billa's plan was appealing. Drive the surface dwellers back once and for all. No more adventurers sneaking in to the mountain to kill goblins and hunt treasure. No more humans and elves dragging goblins off as slaves. After all these years, they would be *safe*.

Was that why Shadowstar had sent him here? So Billa could protect them once and for all?

Not exactly, Shadowstar said. *The danger isn't from the humans and elves.*

Billa and her orcs? Jig guessed.

No. Something else.

Jig tugged his ears, using the pain to distract him from his frustration. *Is it too late for me to start worshiping a different god? One who isn't so vague with his warnings? Maybe one who will tell me to stay in the lair where it's safe, and eat hot rat stew and drink warm klak beer all day?*

You want Rionisus Yelloweyes, God of Revelry. But I don't think he'd be interested in goblin worshipers. Shadowstar paused. *Jig, you and the other goblins are my window to your world. In my prime, with worshipers throughout the world, I probably would have been strong enough to sense exactly what threat you faced. But now . . . I'm sorry.*

"How much farther?" Trok asked. "I want to kill an elf!"

"Quiet, smelly goblin." Hessafa dropped to all fours, pressing her nose to the rock. They had finally left the swamps, climbing into a rocky, lightly wooded area. Now if they could only leave the stench of the swamp as well. Unfortunately, Jig and every other goblin was caked in the stuff.

"It is elves?" Trok asked.

"Quiet means no talking." She crept forward, sniffing hard. A clump of snow balanced atop her nose when she next looked up. She sneezed and spat. "Elf scent. Smells like fruit and flowers. Better than goblin stink, though."

"So what do your regulations say about stabbing our tracker in the back?" Relka asked.

"They're vague," Gratz said.

Hessafa continued to mutter to herself as she scrambled up the rocky earth. "First goblins lie to kobolds, saying Hessafa stole metal. Then kobolds punish me by making me track for stupid goblins! Elf this way."

"Where?" asked one of the other goblins. An instant later he lurched back, slamming into the goblin behind him. An elven arrow pinned the two goblins together.

"There!" Hessafa dove to the ground. "Hessafa tracked elf. Goblins go kill it now!"

Jig could see the elf standing halfway up a snow-covered tree. He balanced easily on a branch, not even disturbing the snow as he nocked another arrow.

"Down!" Gratz shouted. He needn't have bothered. The

other goblins were already scrambling for cover, hiding behind trees and rocks and each other. There wasn't much cover on the rough hillside. The trees were sparse and thin.

The elf's second shot pinned a goblin's exposed ear to the earth.

Gratz was actually smiling as he glanced at the other goblins. His voice was loud enough to carry over the frightened screams. "Regulations say the best attack formation for a small group like ours is the Grab-and-Squeeze. Spread out like a giant hand, then everyone closes in at once. As commander, I'm the middle finger, so I'll charge up the center."

He jabbed his sword at the other goblins. "You three are the thumb and pointer. To my left. Jig, you and the kobold are the little finger. You head to the right. Now go!"

The goblins spread apart, obeying without thinking. Had they been thinking, Jig was sure they would have run the other way. But even he had jolted into motion at Gratz's sharp tone.

Hessafa threw her short spear as she ran. The elf twisted easily out of the way, but at least he couldn't shoot anyone and dodge at the same time. Trok stooped to grab a rock, then threw it without breaking stride.

The elf caught it. With a crooked smile, he threw it back.

Trok ducked his head. The rock that would have crushed his face instead rang off of his helmet. Trok staggered and toppled into the snow. Even from here Jig could see the dent in the top of his helmet.

By now the remaining goblins had almost reached the elf. Still smiling, the elf stepped back from his branch, dropping lightly into the snow. He used his bow to parry the nearest goblin's attack, then whirled, putting himself behind the goblin. A kick to the backside launched the goblin straight into the tree. The sound of skull hitting wood reminded Jig of the war drums back home.

Gratz and Relka reached the elf next, and both attacked at once. The elf tossed his bow into the air, where it hooked neatly over one of the branches. He caught Relka's wrist and twisted her arm so her sword pressed her neck. Had the blade been sharper, it would have cut her throat. The elf pressed harder, then grimaced in disgust. He slammed his elbow into Relka's temple, knocking her to the ground, and then Gratz swung his sword down onto the elf's bare wrist.

Nothing happened. Gratz tried again, and this time the elf caught the blade and yanked it from his hand.

Jig stopped running. He looked at Hessafa, who had started to follow him up the hill. Both took a tentative step back.

Another goblin screamed as he charged the elf, sword swinging. Jig wasn't sure if he was screaming to try to intimidate the elf, or because he still had an arrow dangling from his ear. Either way, the elf barely blinked as he parried the attack with his arm, then used Gratz's sword to run the goblin through. The body tumbled down the hill toward Jig's feet.

Dull or not, that blow should have shattered the elf's arm. And Gratz's weapon was certainly better than anything the others carried. Yet the elf hadn't even flinched as he grabbed Gratz's blade.

"Elf magic?" Hessafa whispered.

"No, this magic is worse." He recognized this elf now. This was one of Theodore's companions. Theodore must have used the Rod of Creation to strengthen the elf's skin, turning it tough as armor. The elf flexed his arms, stretching as though he had just awakened from a pleasant nap, then retrieved his bow from the branches.

"Run?" Hessafa asked.

Jig didn't move. They couldn't run fast enough to escape an elven archer. *Is this the part where we all die?*

No, said Shadowstar. *Well, it's not the danger I've been sensing, at any rate. That danger is magical and widespread. This one should be quick and efficient.*

Jig lay flat, hiding behind a tree and the dead goblin with the arrow in his ear. The upper edge of his armor pressed into his throat, cutting off his breath, but it didn't matter. He was too scared to breathe anyway.

Hessafa crouched beside him. He could see the elf approaching.

Why didn't goblins ever get the magical armor and the enchanted weapons and the— Wait. Jig reached out to yank the elf's arrow from the dead goblin's ear. If Theodore had used the rod to strengthen the elves, would he have done the same to their weapons? Jig brushed a finger over the arrowhead, grinning as a dot of blood appeared. The tip was so sharp he hadn't even felt the cut.

I don't suppose you could distract him for me? Jig asked.

There's one thing I could try, said Shadowstar. *I haven't done it in several thousand years, and it probably wouldn't work, but—*

Jig would have laughed if his throat hadn't been so tight. *A magic elf is about to snap me in half. Try it!*

Stand up.

Jig cradled the arrow in both hands. *What?*

Warmth rushed through Jig's body. The sensation was similar to what he experienced when he used his healing magic. But where the healing magic was concentrated in his hands, this bubbled up from his chest and spread outward. And while healing magic usually warmed his hands, this felt as though he had swallowed a fire-spider.

Rise, Jig Dragonslayer. Rise, and tell your kobold friend to close her eyes.

Why?

Shadowstar sighed. *Because if you don't, the elf is going to kill you.*

"Cover your eyes, Hessafa," Jig said. Hessafa buried her face in the snow. Jig wasn't sure if she was obeying his instructions, or if she just didn't want to see the elf kill her. Not that it mattered.

Smudge scurried out of Jig's hood and leaped off of his shoulder, a single line of silk slowing his fall. Snow melted beneath the spider's body, and he disappeared as he scrambled toward the shelter of the tree. Smart spider.

Jig stood. The elf was almost within reach. Would he shoot Jig with his bow and arrow? Break Jig's neck with one hand? Use Jig as a club to beat Hessafa to death? There were so many possibilities.

The elf hesitated. His skin and armor had a reddish tinge. So did the snow. Jig glanced behind, but the sky had only begun to take on the orange hue of the sunset.

The red light grew brighter and brighter. Blinking didn't

help. In fact, it made the glare worse. The light was coming from Jig's own skin, including the inside of his eyelids.

The light didn't bother Jig too much, but the elf was squinting. Jig raised his arrow. If he could attack while the elf was distracted—

Wait.

Jig stared at his hands. Red fire danced over his fingers. Curls of flame danced out from his skin, spitting wisps of fire into the air. *You're turning me into a fire-spider?*

A fire-spider? This is the Light of the Autumn Star! The divine mark of my champions! Well, a mild version of it, anyway. Still, the universe hasn't seen this aura of power in thousands of years!

The light brightened faster now, painting everything the color of human blood.

Hessafa whimpered. The elf moved quick as thought. An arrow buried itself in the tree in front of the kobold.

The elf had *missed*. The light must have blinded him. Already the elf had begun to retreat.

Jig stepped closer.

An arrow tore through Jig's armor. And through Jig. He could see the hole where it had entered the armor. He could feel a matching hole in the back, though this one was wet with blood.

It cut your side and grazed a rib. You'll live. Shadowstar hesitated. *Unless he shoots you again, I mean.*

Jig clamped his jaw, trying not to whimper. Even blind, elves were dangerous archers. There were no fancy throat shots here. The elf was shooting for Jig's chest. A handspan to the left, and he would have taken Jig in the heart.

Stupid snow. Jig couldn't move without his boot crunching loud enough for even a human to hear. Tears streamed down his cheek from the pain. He held his breath. The elf had to realize Jig hadn't fallen. He should have fallen down and pretended to die. Then when the elf came closer, Jig could have stabbed him.

Either that, or the elf would have put a few more arrows into him to be safe. *I don't suppose you can do anything about his hearing?*

Sorry. I wasn't even sure I could still do the Light of the Autumn Star anymore. What did you think? Pretty impressive, isn't it?

The creak of wood drew Jig's attention back to the elf and his bow. He held the string steady at the side of his face, listening. Jig's chest hurt from holding his breath, but he didn't dare exhale. He could throw the arrow to distract the elf, but throwing away his only decent weapon wasn't much of a plan.

Behind him Hessafa craned her head and howled. Jig flinched and flattened his ears against the sound. Another arrow buried itself in the tree, but Jig could barely hear the impact over the echo of Hessafa's cry.

He stared at the arrow. If *he* couldn't hear . . . Jig leaped forward and stabbed his own stolen arrow into the elf's chest.

The elf dropped his bow. Both hands touched the arrow. He squinted at Jig, and his expression was one of mild puzzlement. Slowly he toppled back into the snow.

Jig's whole body sagged with relief. Terror must have helped block the pain, but now that his terror was fading, the hole in his side felt as though it were on fire. Jig reacted by screaming and clutching the wound with both hands.

Hessafa scurried out from behind her tree. She retrieved her spear and prodded the elf. "Killed by noisy goblin. How?" Her fur bristled as she turned to point her spear at Jig. "More magic?"

"No, it—" Jig clenched his jaw. His breath hissed past his fangs. *Would you mind helping me?*

What? Oh, sorry.

Jig gasped with relief as the skin along his side began to heal. Eventually he managed to stand. He grabbed the hem of his cloak from beneath his armor and tried to wipe the snow from his spectacles, but between the snow, swamp muck, and various colors of blood, his cloak was a complete disaster. Albeit a colorful one. He ended up cleaning the lenses on the sleeve of the elf's shirt instead.

He checked Relka next. She would have a nasty bruise on her head, but she should live. Trok was snoring, so Jig figured he was okay. So was Gratz. His arm was broken from when the elf had tossed him aside, but that could wait until Jig checked the others. Of the two goblins who had been pinned by the same arrow, the one in back still lived. Barely. Jig managed to keep him alive as he pulled the arrow free, then did his best to heal the wounds.

By the time he finished, Jig was exhausted and covered in goblin blood. But only two of his companions had died.

"First you catch on fire, then you kill the magic elf. Now you heal stupid goblins." Hessafa was still staring, her fur making her head appear comically large. Her teeth were bared, and her eyes wide. "What are you, goblin?"

Don't tell her, Shadowstar said.

I don't want to. Can you imagine what it would sound like if she and Relka started singing together? But how am I supposed to explain catching on fire in the middle of a battle, not to mention—

Jig, you're not going to like this.

Jig closed his eyes. If Shadowstar was bothering to warn him, the news had to be truly unpleasant.

When I placed the mantle of my star upon you, something noticed.

The mantle of your star? Oh, you mean the light. Jig stiffened as the rest of that sank in. *What noticed? Are there other elves out here?*

They didn't notice you, Jig. They noticed me.

From Shadowstar's tone, this was a bad thing. Yet Jig couldn't help feeling relieved. For once, the unimaginably scary monster wasn't after him!

That's true, but anything searching for me is going to find you as well. Don't tell her anything, Jig. Don't tell anyone until I learn more.

So much for relief.

"What are you?" Hessafa asked again.

Jig glanced at the other goblins. Gratz was groaning, and Relka had begun to stir. "Hessafa, I didn't kill the elf."

"Kobolds not stupid. I saw!"

Jig shook his head. "You killed her."

"Elf attacked stupid goblins. Hessafa hid. Then you—"

"Think what the stupid goblins will say when you explain how you saved them," Jig said. "How you snuck up and stabbed that elf with his own arrow. The kobolds sent you with us because they're mad at you. Imagine how they'll react when you tell them you killed the elf."

Hessafa hesitated, glancing at the elf, then back at Jig. She straightened. "*Hessafa* killed elf!"

"Did I hear that mutt right? A kobold killed an elf scout?" Gratz's voice was hoarse but firm. He sat up and rotated his arm. "Huh. I could have sworn I heard bone crack."

Jig glanced around, searching the hillside and the trees. Shadows had begun to stretch as the sun sank lower.

Trok was the next to recover. He groaned and climbed to his feet, brushing snow from his furs. His ears perked when he saw the body. "Hey, fresh elf!"

"No eating." Gratz rubbed his arm again. "The last thing we need is for an entire squadron to come down with the runs from raw elf."

"Who said anything about eating him raw?" Trok asked. He jabbed a finger at Relka. "She's a cook!"

Their brief argument ended when Trok realized his knife wouldn't pierce the elf's skin. They might be able to cook the elf, but they had no way to eat him.

Even though Jig's stomach gurgled at the thought of roast elf, he was just as happy to move on. Cooking the elf meant more time alone in the woods, with wild animals and magically armored elves and whatever was hunting Tymalous Shadowstar.

What could possibly hunt a god?

Generally, nothing but another god, said Shadowstar.

As Jig followed Gratz and the others back toward Billa's army, he tried very hard not to think about that. He failed.

Do you remember what Darnak said, back when he first told you about me? Shadowstar asked as they crossed through the swamp.

Jig could feel Smudge rustling in his hood. Was he sensing Jig's nervousness, or was Shadowstar's hunter already closing in on them?

They had been deep in the tunnels of the mountain. Jig had seen Darnak's own healing powers and had asked about the gods. Darnak had been delighted to have an audience, and he had talked until Jig's ears were literally numb. *He mentioned you were one of the fifteen Forgotten Gods, and said something about a war.*

The War of Shadows. Bells rang sharply, which Jig had come to recognize as a sound of annoyance. *Stupid name, I know. I'd bet anything Noc was the one who thought it up. It suits his sense of melodrama. Still, it's simpler than "The Folly of Fifteen Gods Who Thought They Could Challenge the Two."*

That would be difficult to work into a song, Jig agreed.

The realm of the gods is a convoluted place, Jig. At the end of the war, vast stretches of that realm were cast into shadow and darkness. The fifteen rebellious gods were destroyed, their homes eradicated.

All fifteen? Jig repeated. Including Tymalous Shadowstar. *They thought you were dead.*

I nearly was. I've kept quiet since then. None of the magic I've used should have drawn the attention of another god. Not unless they were already searching for me.

Jig shivered. The evening had grown colder, and his breath clouded in the air. *I thought gods were supposed to be immortal.*

Some of us are more immortal than others.

Jig glanced at Relka. What would she say if she knew? For most of a year, she had praised Tymalous Shadowstar to anyone who would listen, and many who wouldn't. She sang about his strength and wisdom. But what Shadowstar had revealed made him sound less like an all-powerful god and more like . . . well, like a goblin. A goblin among gods, hiding and afraid.

I resent that. I'm far better looking than any goblin.

Jig ignored that. *Do you know which god is hunting you?* And, more importantly, would that god bother with Shadowstar's goblin followers?

I have my suspicions. Noc ascended to the role of death god during the war. He earned the name Godslayer. I trust you can figure out why?

"Weapons ready, men," Gratz barked, drawing Jig's attention back to this world. "Jig, Hessafa, spread out to either side. Stay out of sight. Flanking formation."

"What does that mean?" Jig asked.

"It means you get your scrawny arse out of sight and wait for orders. If this is another elf trick, you and Hessafa attack from either side."

Jig hurried away, crouching down in the swamp and barely noticing the stench. A part of him wanted to keep on running. Nobody would bother to follow a lone goblin runt.

But where would he run? Even if he managed to avoid elf scouts and Billa's warriors, he didn't know how to hide from a vindictive death god. Though he would probably freeze to death long before that became a problem. He squatted in the snow and tried to keep his teeth from chattering too loudly.

"Gratz, is that you?" The voice was Silverfang's. What was he doing out here? Jig peeked through the trees.

Silverfang sat astride Bastard, clutching the wolf's ropes in both hands. Bastard snarled and tugged his head. Silverfang leaned down and punched him in the head, after which Bastard settled down. Two other wolf-riders waited to either side.

"We were on our way back," Gratz said. "We found and killed an elf scout."

"I see you lost the runt." Silverfang looked pleased.

"No, sir. Jig, Hessafa, get back here!"

Jig stomped his feet as he walked. His toes were starting to go numb. That couldn't be good.

"Stupid goblins," Hessafa muttered. "First go hide. Then come back. Can't make up their minds."

"Corporal Gratz, report," Silverfang said, his voice strange. He wasn't yelling, exactly. He sounded like he wasn't sure whether or not to be angry. "Exactly what happened when you fought this elf?"

"He had some kind of magical protection," Gratz said. He hesitated, then grudgingly added, "The kobold finished him off."

"That's right!" Hessafa raised her spear. "Hessafa killed him. Goblins just fell down a lot."

"Is that so?" Silverfang scowled at Gratz. *There* was the anger. "You let a useless kobold fight your battle?"

"We used the Grab-and-Squeeze formation," Gratz said.

"Just like regulations say. We goblins did the bulk of the fighting, wearing the elf down so the kobold could—"

"Save it." Silverfang smiled. "You can explain it to the orcs. It seems Billa herself would like to ask you a few questions about your little battle."

CHAPTER 6

TYMALOUS AUTUMNSTAR DUG HIS FRONT CLAWS into the sandstone and slid his broken body across the floor. His rear legs and tail were limp and lifeless. From the feel—rather, the lack of feeling past his wings—Anisah had snapped his spine. Fortunately, it was difficult to truly kill a god.

Not so difficult to smash one senseless, as it turned out.

Finally he reached the wall, where various pots and sacks provided shadows and shelter. He squeezed behind a stack of fleshy cactus leaves. Hopefully nobody would need the pungent, needle-covered leaves for tonight's meal. Anyone who found Autumnstar here would either toss him into the pot for dinner or break his neck to put him out of his misery.

His tongue flicked out, smelling the cool night air. He rested his head against the barrel and looked out at Anisah's body.

Well, at least she had died smiling. Even if Autumnstar hadn't planned to comfort her in quite that fashion.

What had gone wrong? Healing a mortal body needed only the tiniest pinch of magic. He should have had no trouble easing Anisah's pain. Or fixing his own crushed spine, for that matter.

He closed his eyes, fighting off fear as he peered beyond the stone walls of the city. Surely the gods weren't still hunting him after all this time. A quick peek into the realm of the divine shouldn't draw any notice. Priests did it all the time, using purely mortal magic. And sometimes a particular type of mushroom.

He braced himself as his surroundings appeared to fade, but nothing more happened. Autumnstar rested his head on a cactus leaf and tried to relax.

It was strange to see the stars from down here. The constellations were recognizable, but altered. Tarvha the Trapper was much skinnier from this angle. The Three-Headed Dragon appeared to have his leftmost head wedged in a very improbable location. Then again, dragons were quite flexible.

He turned, trying to orient himself. A half-moon hovered over the eastern horizon, which meant The Guardian should be to his right. The Guardian looked like a potbellied dwarf from here. Autumnstar followed the tip of The Guardian's nose, toward—

"It's gone," he whispered. He searched again, making sure the oddly distorted constellations hadn't tricked him, but there was no mistake. Before, a lone star had burned red in the sky between The Guardian and Elsa the Drunk. Now there was nothing.

No, not nothing. He squinted, trying to make out a spot of darkness that was somehow blacker than the surrounding space. A point in the sky that seemed to absorb the light of nearby stars.

He should have guessed. Noc was nothing if not dramatic. No doubt the death of the Autumn Star had been a great spectacle, seen by gods and mortals throughout the universe.

"I hope you burned your eyebrows off," Autumnstar muttered.

A circle of orcs waited at the edge of the swamps. Jig counted at least eight, though there could have been more in back.

They stood with swords and axes ready. How much time did they spend polishing their blades, to get them to shine like that? And had they deliberately positioned themselves so their weapons would best reflect the moonlight?

Intentional or not, it worked. Jig didn't even realize he had slowed down until one of the other goblins bumped into him.

"Say nothing unless Billa talks to you," Gratz whispered. "Don't make any sudden moves, either. If one of those orcs decides you're a threat, you'll be dead before you can spit."

Jig pulled his cloak tight, tucking his hands into his armpits. His fingers felt numb, as if the blood had frozen. Even the inside of his nostrils felt like they were coated in a thin layer of ice. He stared longingly at Trok's furs, then gave a tentative sniff. Cold as it was, the icy breeze couldn't completely kill Trok's stench.

Silverfang pulled Bastard to a halt a few paces away from the lead orcs. The wolf snarled, but the orcs didn't so much as blink.

Billa was awfully confident, to come with so few guards. Sure, any one of those orcs could probably kill every goblin here, but with enough goblins and wolves, there was always the chance one would get lucky. Most of the goblins were new recruits. How did Billa know there wouldn't be trouble?

"General," Silverfang said, bowing his head.

The frontmost orcs stepped to either side, revealing Billa the Bloody.

Jig's first thought was that Billa looked awfully skinny for an orc. Her skin was paler, too. Her hair was a dirty white, pulled into a thick, snarled rope at the top of her head. Despite the white hair, she appeared quite young. Her face was unwrinkled, marred only by the tribal scar on her nose and a sprinkling of pimples on her forehead.

She wore a cape of white horsehair over her armor. Like the rest of the orcs, her arms were bare, but she didn't appear to notice the cold. Her skin wasn't pimpled like the others, nor did her face have the same flushed appearance.

She chewed her thumbnail as she contemplated the goblins. The rest of her nails were bitten raw.

Jig would have sworn the air got colder when she turned to look at him. Even the wolves backed away as her gaze swept them. She spat a bit of nail into the snow. One hand brushed the hilt of her sword.

"What happened tonight?" Her voice was softer than Jig expected.

Gratz cleared his throat. "We found and killed one elf, sir."

"Good. Who killed it?"

Gratz made a face like he had bitten into a fried rat, only to have it bite him back. "Her," he said, pointing to Hessafa. One of the orcs snickered.

Billa chewed her lower lip as she studied the kobold. "You killed an elf scout?"

Hessafa glanced at Jig, then grinned. "Goblins fight stupid. Hessafa killed elf."

"Nothing stupid about the Grab-and-Squeeze formation," Gratz muttered.

Billa drew her sword. Gratz squeaked once and was silent.

No wonder Billa hadn't worried about a few goblins and their wolves. With a sword like that, she could kill—

A god, said Shadowstar.

Most of the blade was a cloudy gray, rippled like sand on the shore of the underground lake back home. The edges were clear as glass. Fog rose from the surface, and frost soon covered the blade from hilt to tip. Cold spread from the sword like stink from Trok, so powerful Jig might as well have been standing naked in the snow.

So it isn't Noc after all, Shadowstar said absently. *This could be bad.*

Jig snorted, then tensed, hoping nobody had noticed. *What's worse than a god of death hunting us?*

"So I'm to believe a kobold summoned the power of Tymalous Autumnstar to help her overcome this elf?" Billa asked, her voice still mild.

For an instant, Jig felt hope. *You're Tymalous* Shadowstar. *Maybe she's confused you with some other god?*

Isa, Shadowstar whispered. *I thought she was dead.*

"Tymalous who?" Hessafa glanced at Jig again before asking, "Is that another stupid goblin?"

So who is Isa? Jig demanded.

Another goddess. She created that sword during the war. For Billa to carry it means Isa has taken her as her champion.

Billa stepped toward Jig. "Tell me what you know of Tymalous Autumnstar, little goblin. Lie to me, and I'll cut out your tongue."

Relka stepped forward. "Jig is—"

Silverfang punched her in the head. "No speaking out of turn!"

Jig gave silent thanks for Silverfang and his temper. Relka would get them all killed if she didn't keep her mouth shut. "I've never heard that name before," Jig said.

Too late he wondered if Billa could read his thoughts. No . . . if she could, Jig would already be dead. He tried to imagine how an innocent goblin would act. Terrified, most likely. Jig could do that.

"She probably means Tymalous Shadowstar," Trok said.

Silverfang drew back a fist, but Billa held up her hand, and he hesitated.

"Tymalous Shadowstar?" Billa stepped toward him, leaving Jig to shiver uncontrollably from cold and fear. "Tell me where you heard that name."

Trok folded his arms. "If I do, will you make me a wolf-rider?"

Gratz started to say something about regulations and orders, but Silverfang was faster. He reached for Trok, bellowing, "I'm going to rip off your arm and—"

"Yes," said Billa. "Tell me what I want to know, and Silverfang will make you one of his wolf-riders."

Silverfang's scowl wrinkled his face so badly his metal tooth pricked the skin beneath his eye. A drop of blue blood trailed down his cheek like a tear. But he said only, "Yes, sir."

Even if Jig could have stopped shaking, there was nowhere to run. The wolves would be on him in a single leap, assuming Billa didn't simply run him through with that sword. He stared at Trok, waiting for him to condemn Jig to death.

"You want her," Trok said. He nudged Relka with his foot, then reached down to grab the new pendant she had made.

Relka groaned and tried to take it back.

"She won't shut up about Tymalous Shadowstar," said Trok. "You should hear the hymns."

His feral grin made his motivation obvious. He might not

know why Billa was asking about Shadowstar, but anything that rid him of Relka's presence was a good thing. As a bonus, he would get to be a wolf-rider and keep Jig around to heal whatever injuries he might suffer . . . up until Relka opened her mouth and told Billa the truth.

"She's not— " Jig swallowed and tried again. "Relka's not the one you want."

"Is that so?" asked Billa, turning that frigid glare on him once more. Trok looked angry too, but he was a minor worry compared to Billa.

"You want Shadowstar's priest." He blurted it out quickly, before his sense of self-preservation could render him mute. "A goblin named Braf. Relka might have prayed to Shadowstar while we were fighting the elf, but Braf is his one and only true priest."

Come to think of it, Relka probably had prayed to Shadowstar during the fighting. Jig wouldn't be surprised if she prayed for Shadowstar's blessing every time she washed a pot or cooked an omelette.

She does. Why do you think they taste so good?

"Go on," Billa said.

"Braf cast spells for his followers. He put them on those necklaces. But he's not very good with magic." That last part was true, if nothing else. Braf had trouble concentrating on what he was doing. Jig still remembered the time Braf tried to heal one of the kitchen workers Golaka had stabbed for swiping fire-spider eggs. Braf had pressed two fingers into the wound, guiding Shadowstar's magic deep into the goblin's body. Jig found him there hours later, having healed the wound with his fingers still inside.

With a grimace, Jig said, "Relka must have used that magic to try to help her during the fight." He shrugged. "I didn't notice anything. Shadowstar never struck me as being a very helpful god."

Billa took the necklace from Trok and studied it closely. "What happened to Braf?"

"He died," Jig said quickly. "When Princess Genevieve attacked our lair."

"Champions of a god aren't so easy to kill." Billa waved at

Relka. "Take her." Two of her orcs hauled Relka upright. "Prepare your goblins, Silverfang. We march tonight."

"Tonight?" Silverfang cleared his throat. "Begging your pardon, but I've got two squads out with boot rot, and we haven't finished—"

"Leave them." Billa glanced at another of the orcs. "Spread the word. We march through the night."

Relka's feet dragged through the mud and snow as the orcs hauled her away. She watched Jig the whole time, hardly even blinking.

Billa sheathed her sword. "And give this goblin a wolf," she added, waving a hand at Trok.

Now what? asked Shadowstar.

Jig's shoulders slumped. *I was hoping you would tell me.*

Goblin drums beat out a steady rhythm as Billa's army marched up the road. At first Jig had been delighted to hear drums actually pounding in unison. Such a nice change from the cacophony of battle back at the lair. Row after row of goblins, all marching in step. Not one knew where they were going, but that didn't seem to matter. What mattered was staying in line and not drawing Oakbottom's attention.

The walking tree wandered through the ranks, his bare branches lashing out like whips at anyone who faltered. As far as Jig could tell, he never actually stepped on anyone. The base of his trunk split into four "legs," each one ending in a long mess of gnarled roots. He walked slowly, but with his size, he could take one step for every five of Jig's and still keep up. And his branches were long enough to strike seven lines ahead or behind, as the goblin next to Jig had learned earlier. The poor fellow was still limping.

As one of the newest, and presumably one of the most expendable recruits, Jig found himself near the front line. A group of orcs on horseback led the way, followed closely by the goblin wolf-riders. Trok rode Smelly, which seemed a perfect match. To either side of the main column, small groups of kobolds jogged along, presumably searching the woods for ambushes.

He glanced behind, still amazed at the sheer size of Billa's army. They filled the road and much of the land to either side. Billa and most of her orcs were toward the rear, followed by troll-drawn wagons. Presumably Relka was back there as well, assuming Billa hadn't killed her.

She's alive, said Shadowstar. *Frightened and exhausted, but alive.*

She hadn't told Billa about Jig, either, judging from the fact that Jig was also still alive. *What does Isa want with you? Who is she? What happened to Noc?*

Isa was Goddess of the Winter Winds.

That would explain the cold. If Jig had to face another god, couldn't it have been a god of warm, comfy breezes?

She was also my wife.

Jig stopped walking. Goblins behind him cursed and swore as they collided with one another. Jig hunched his shoulders against a punch to the back that sent him staggering. He hurried to catch up with the rest of his line, hoping Oakbottom hadn't noticed.

Your wife? he repeated. Goblins didn't mate for life, but he knew surface-dwellers had different habits. Habits apparently shared by the gods. *I don't understand. Shouldn't you be happy to see her then?*

I'm glad she's alive, Shadowstar said, though he sounded less than certain. *I'll be happier when I know why she's hunting me.*

Another goblin crashed into Jig as a small brawl erupted behind him. He tried to hurry away, but the formation was too tight. He had no place to go.

That didn't stop Oakbottom. He kicked goblins aside like pebbles in a tunnel. Branches shot out, hauling goblins into the air. Jig counted eight goblins, all squirming and kicking and helpless as bugs in a spiderweb.

"Most of you are new to Billa's army," Oakbottom said. He had no mouth or face that Jig could see, though the thick branches concealed much of his trunk. Many of his words were punctuated by a sound like boards clapping together. "So most of you probably don't know the punishment for brawling on duty."

More branches wrapped around one of the goblins, and

the great tree spun in a quick circle. The goblin flew in a long arc over the rest of the formation and into the darkness beyond. His scream faded with distance, then cut off abruptly.

"Now you know," Oakbottom shouted. He tossed the rest of the goblins to the ground, where they scrambled back into line.

A short distance ahead, Gratz chuckled. "That ought to keep things quiet for a few days." He glanced back at Jig and lowered his voice. "Oakbottom's a very angry tree. Doesn't like anyone, but he's especially mad at humans. Makes him a great asset during battle, and he's good for discipline."

"Why would a tree hate humans?" Jig asked.

Gratz winced. "Not so loud."

It was too late. Oakbottom was already stepping toward Jig. Despite the lack of visible ears, Oakbottom could hear as well as any goblin.

"You think you blood-sacks are the only ones to be abused by the humans?" Oakbottom asked.

"Here he goes again," one of the other goblins whispered.

"When I was little more than a sapling, there was a little boy who used to visit me," Oakbottom said. "Every day he came. He would swing from my branches. He slept in the shade against my trunk. Sometimes he shot stones at squirrels and birds with his little sling. I loved that little boy. We were happy."

"What happened?" Jig asked.

"Time passed, and the boy grew older. He stopped visiting as often. But one day he returned. He had fallen in love, and he wanted to make his girl a gift. So I told him, 'Take my leaves and branches and weave a beautiful headband.' And so he did.

"He came back a year later. He and this girl were to marry, and he wished to build a great bonfire to celebrate. So I said, 'Cut more of my branches and dry them for your bonfire.' And so he did. Soon I saw smoke in the distance as they celebrated and danced.

"Seasons passed, and I thought the boy had forgotten me. Then one day he returned, carrying an ax. He said to me, 'Old friend, my wife is pregnant, and there is no space in my father's home for a baby. Give me your wood so I can build a house.' "

Oakbottom shuddered as he walked. "He slammed that ax into my trunk. You can still see the scar. And so I did what any self-respecting tree would have done. I ripped the ax out of his hands and gave him a taste of his own blade."

"He's been killing humans ever since," Gratz said. "Naturally Billa made him an officer. He doesn't like to be called sir, though."

"Trees don't concern themselves with ranks and titles," Oakbottom said. "Give me the sun on my leaves, damp earth beneath my roots, and humans to throw, and I will be happy."

"Hear, hear!" Gratz shouted. The other goblins joined in.

Lovely company you're keeping these days, Shadowstar commented.

Jig didn't answer. He would have gladly listened to a hundred such stories. Marching was dull, mindless activity, which meant he had far too much time to worry.

Where was Billa taking them? What would happen if Relka told the truth about Jig? Were the goblins back at Avery still alive? When would they stop to pee?

The wind blew harder, freezing the tips of Jig's ears. He pulled up his hood and transferred Smudge into a small pouch at his waist. *If Isa is a goddess of winter and snow and cold, does that mean it's not likely to warm up any time soon?*

No, said Shadowstar. *And the stronger she gets, the colder you'll be.*

It figured.

Three days later, Jig barely even heard the beating of the drums. The quick double-beat that signaled a halt hardly registered. He bumped into another goblin, then mumbled an apology.

Every part of him slumped. For the past three days, he had trudged along, staring at the boots of the goblin in front of him. He knew every blemish of the wet leather, every loose stitch, even the frayed threads hanging from the bottom of the goblin's trousers.

He rubbed the front of his thighs and hissed from the pain.

His legs had banged the hard lower edge of his armor so many times he felt like his thighs would be permanently dented.

"Sleep with your weapons ready," Gratz shouted. "We're getting close."

Other goblins had already begun to drop, curling up in the middle of the road and shoving one another for space. Gratz and Oakbottom walked through the ranks, kicking them awake.

"You know the drill, you lazy bastards," Gratz said. "Sleep in your armor and you'll be too stiff to move, come dawn. Any goblin who's too sore to keep up gets tossed."

Jig dropped his helmet onto the road, flexed his fingers, and fumbled with the straps of his armor. His hands were little more than blocks of ice. The buckles refused to move, and the straps slipped through his fingers. After four tries, he was ready to draw his knife and cut away the armor. He would have done it, but he suspected that would violate one of Gratz's precious regulations.

Finally he lay down on his stomach and pointed his arms overhead. Feeling like a fool, he wriggled backward.

He lost a bit of skin from his ears and nose, but he managed to squeeze out of the oversize armor. Pressing his back against the armor, he drew his knees to his chest and rested his head on the road. He kept one hand on his sword and closed his eyes.

He heard voices in the distance. Silverfang was shouting at the wolf-riders to take care of their mounts. Poor Trok. How long would he be awake, caring for Smelly?

Elsewhere, Oakbottom lashed a group of kobolds awake, sending them out to keep watch.

The rest of Gratz's squadron fell asleep fast, all of them exhausted. Jig soon found himself squeezed into a mass of snoring, squirming, farting goblins. It reminded him a bit of home. And at least he was warm.

Jig giggled quietly, a sure sign of exhaustion or terror. Maybe both. But the more he thought about it, the funnier his situation became. If it weren't for a forgotten goddess who was hunting for him, this would have been the safest Jig had ever been. Surrounded by goblin warriors, he was well-protected from adventurers and armies and anything else . . . short of the gods, of course. And Billa's rules protected him from those same goblin warriors.

No wonder Billa had amassed such a following. Her army provided security. Security and hope.

Shadowstar didn't even know why Isa was hunting him. Maybe she just missed her husband.

And maybe Braf will stop picking his nose with his fangs, but I wouldn't put money on it.

Jig rolled onto his back. Smudge scurried out from beneath his neck, climbing onto his chest. Jig absently rubbed the spider with one finger as he stared up at the night sky. The sight of the clouds drifting past the stars gave him vertigo, and he clenched his eyes shut. *How do you know? Not about Braf, but that Isa is dangerous?*

It would be easier to show you, said Shadowstar.

That's all right, Jig said hastily. *I don't need to see—*

The ground beneath him seemed to give way, as if Jig had plunged into an endless pit. He squealed and flailed about.

Open your eyes, Jig.

Brilliant sunlight made him squint. Moments later he was leaping out of the way as a sea of dwarves charged past, waving axes and hammers and shouting in a language he didn't recognize. Though the dwarves didn't appear to notice him, he somehow managed to avoid being trampled into the grass. When the footfalls had faded into the distance, he opened his eyes and squinted to block the worst of the sun.

"We have *not* lost!"

He turned around to see . . . Jig wasn't sure how to describe her. She reminded him of a dwarf, only taller. A giant dwarf? Clearly his mind was still delusional from fatigue.

She was taller than most humans, but her broad shoulders and stocky build reminded him of Darnak without the beard. Her armor and helmet shone like glass, and in one hand she held a sword of ice. The same sword Jig had seen in Billa's hand that evening.

"Isa?" Jig guessed.

"Have you lost your wits as well as your courage?" Isa

spat in disgust. Even though it felt like late summer or early autumn, the spittle froze before it touched the ground.

The jingle of tiny bells warned him Shadowstar was near. He turned, but saw no sign of the forgotten god. Silver hair drifted in front of his eyes, and—

Jig stopped moving. He had never had hair this long, even before Smudge came along. Jig reached to touch his scalp, and the bells jingled again. He wore a loose shirt of cool black material, striped with silver bells. Tymalous Shadowstar's shirt. And Shadowstar's hair on his head. He reached for his ears, and tried to bite back his dismay at the puny, misshapen things he found there.

"It's you who've lost your mind, Isa," Jig said. His chest tightened with fear. Had he just insulted a goddess? "Wait, I didn't mean to say that!"

Relax. This happened thousands of years before you were born. Nothing you say or do can change the outcome.

Ah. This was a stupid god trick. *Couldn't you just* tell *me how it happened?*

This is more effective. It's also more fun to watch. Now relax and enjoy being me.

Isa pointed. Across a field, the dwarves were attacking men mounted on giant serpents. "Old Sethina sided with the two over us. Perhaps she'll reconsider when her precious snake lovers have been wiped out."

The snake lovers were putting up quite a fight. The serpents' scales were strong enough to turn most blows, and like the rock serpents Jig knew from back home, they struck too fast to dodge. Unlike those serpents, these were large enough to take an entire dwarf in their jaws.

Jig wondered briefly how the men remained in their saddles. Or how they stopped the saddles from sliding down the snakes' scaly bodies, for that matter. Magic, he guessed. Probably the same magic that kept the riders from throwing up as the snakes slithered and struck.

Twenty dwarves fell for every snake that died, but there were enough dwarves to defeat twice this number. The dwarves fought without fear, driven by Isa's magic.

And how did Jig know that?

"Ama is dead," Jig said. He had no clue who Ama might be, but the words continued to pour forth. "Noc has betrayed us. Even now, Ipsep flees to his temple in the black lake, and Talla the Merciful weeps over the loss of her sister. We've lost, Isa."

"Then we will make them pay for their victory." Isa pointed her sword over the field, to where the last of the snakes were falling. "Beginning with Noc. My dwarves will march into the very halls of death, and there they will—"

"Die." Jig interrupted. His terror had begun to fade. He still wasn't completely sure what was happening, but Isa hadn't killed him yet, and that was a good sign. But now he felt himself growing angry. Not the loud, frightened anger of a goblin, but the deep fury of a god. Anger powerful enough to wipe out every dwarf on that field, if he chose to unleash it. Instead, he—or Shadowstar—turned to face Isa. "You're serious. You're going to send mortals to face a god in his home. Every last one of your followers will die, Isa."

Isa shrugged. "They'll take some of Noc's protectors with them. Death is inevitable, dear Autumnstar. You of all beings should know that."

Jig felt himself grinning. "And you of all gods should know better than to push me." His vision flashed. Isa shielded her face from the red light pouring from Jig's eyes. Across the field, those dwarves who survived began to age. From this distance, the dwarves appeared no larger than his thumbnail, but Jig could see them all clearly as his magic took effect. Tough, sunbeaten skin wrinkled. Gray spread through hair and beards. Joints grew stiff, and old injuries began to ache.

"Stop!"

Isa's scream made Jig want to disappear, but instead he shook his head.

"You would kill them yourself?" Isa shouted

"They're not dead, just old," Jig said. "Too old to fight. They'd make it three steps into Noc's temple before half of them lost bladder control. But they're dwarves. They should live at least another century. Longer than they would if they continued to follow you."

Isa drew back her sword. Jig whimpered, even as he raised his left arm. A silver disk appeared on his forearm, absorbing

Isa's attack with ease. Isa struck twice more, ringing the bells on Jig's sleeve but doing no real harm.

"Where can I get a shield like this?" Jig whispered.

Noc melted it a few years after this battle, when he came to kill me. Sorry.

Isa backed away. "You're a coward," she whispered. "You're afraid to face Noc." Her next blow came so suddenly that Jig barely raised his shield in time to deflect it. The force knocked him to the ground, but Isa didn't bother to follow up her advantage.

Moments later, Jig was alone, grimacing as he rubbed his arm.

Now do you understand why she makes me nervous?

His chest burned. Was this another of Isa's attacks? Fire seemed out of character for her. Jig opened his eyes just as Smudge raced over his face, jumping down into his hood.

There was an orc staring down at him. Scars split the orc's eyebrows, and his breath smelled like kobold. The orc grabbed Jig's fang.

With a squawk, Jig was yanked to his feet. The orc kicked his way through the groaning, snoring goblins, dragging Jig to the edge of the group. Jig was almost positive he recognized this orc as one of the guards who had been with Billa.

"Billa wants to know exactly what we'll be facing when we reach your lair," said the orc. "What's the size and makeup of this force that attacked you?"

"Well, Darnak's a dwarf, so he's pretty small," Jig said, rubbing his eyes. "Genevieve is average height for a human, but she's skinny." He stared. "Wait, did you say we were going to our lair?"

"What numbers will we face when we arrive at your lair?" The orc spoke slowly, like Jig was an addlebrained child.

"I don't know." Jig rubbed his eyes and adjusted his spectacles. "The humans sealed the entrance. The only way in is to get the Rod of Creation back from—"

"Never question the power of Billa the Bloody or Isa of the Winter Winds." A halfhearted punch to the chest drove the orc's point home and knocked Jig onto his back. "How many goblins did they leave in the lair?"

“A few hundred,” Jig guessed. He started to sit up, then thought better of it. If he stayed on the ground, the orc couldn’t reach to hit him. “All but the strongest warriors were sealed inside. The rest were taken away to Avery.”

“So what are you doing here?” The orc snorted and shook his head. “What else lives in this mountain of yours?”

“Hobgoblins, mostly,” Jig said. “There used to be ogres and a dragon, but we killed the dragon and then the pixies came and wiped out the ogres. We killed the pixies too, and—”

The orc leaned down. “Pixies? Goblins killing a dragon? Didn’t your commander tell you there was no drinking in Billa’s army?”

Jig said nothing. The orc hauled him upright and shoved him back toward the other goblins. Jig picked his way back, trying not to step on his fellow soldiers. The orc headed to the front, presumably to interrogate Trok.

Jig settled back down on the cold earth, but this time, he was unable to sleep. In the moonlight, he could just make out the shape of the mountains. Billa was bringing him home.

Why?

Billa’s army believed she would lead them to victory, protecting them from the surface-dwellers once and for all. Jig remembered how Isa had been ready to send her dwarves to their death, all so she would have the chance to slay her enemy.

Now Isa had a new army.

Jig just hoped he and Shadowstar weren’t her new enemy.

CHAPTER 7

THE WORST PART ABOUT LOSING THE POWER TO heal was that he couldn't heal himself either. Fortunately, Anisah's daughter Hana found his broken body. After cooing over Autumnstar for close to an hour, she had decided he was the reincarnation of her mother's spirit.

Hana had never struck Autumnstar as being overly bright.

Without his star, Tymalous Autumnstar's power was almost as limited as a mortal's. Even more than his temple, the Autumn Star had been both the symbol and the source of his power. But he was still a god. His willpower alone was enough to keep the sand lizard alive, and over time, this body would heal.

For more than a year, Hana carried him around in a woven sling, feeding him beetles and ants and whatever other insects she could catch. His bones knit, the torn membrane of his wings sealed itself, and he regained the use of his tail and rear legs . . . though Hana still insisted on wrapping tiny diapers around his backside.

There was something profoundly wrong about a god being forced to wear a diaper. Had Autumnstar been a vengeful sort, he would have conserved his power for some serious smiting.

Instead he found himself slipping into lethargy. It would be so easy to let go, to allow his awareness to dissipate into this body and truly become a sand lizard. His star was gone, and he would be killed if he ever tried to retake his place among the gods. Here he was warm and comfortable and safe.

But one day Hana would grow sick or old. He might have enough strength to help her, but then what? Wait another ten years until he was powerful enough to help another person? Turn his back on the rest of the sick and the dying, the old and the weak, and all those who needed his protection?

He tested his legs, digging his tiny claws into his sling and stretching. His back arched, and his wings fluttered. He jumped free, spreading his wings as he glided toward the floor. He fell faster than expected. Hana's incessant feeding had left him a bit heavier than before.

Before he could recover his balance, Hana snatched him by the neck. Autumnstar coughed and squirmed as she dropped him back into his sling. She held him in place as she hurried back to her room, where she looped a length of goat wool around his neck.

"I have to take care of you, Mother," Hana said. She started to tie the leash to the strap of her sling. "Don't you remember what happened last time? If I let you go, you'll get yourself crushed or eaten or lost, and you'll never find your way back to me."

Autumnstar bit her thumb.

He scurried out the door and raced up the wall, hiding atop the overhang of the roof. Hana followed, her shouts muffled as she sucked her bleeding thumb.

Autumstar snorted. Served her right for trying to leash a god.

They marched for two more days. Sheer exhaustion numbed Jig's fear. By this time, he would have happily cut Trok's throat for the chance to ride a wolf. Terrifying as the wolves were, Jig was almost willing to risk being eaten if it meant he wouldn't have to walk anymore. His feet were so blistered he was amazed his boots hadn't burst at the seams. His legs were numb, and his ill-fitting armor had rubbed bloody streaks along his neck and shoulders.

Then on the morning of the fifth day, as Jig was scarfing down a breakfast of goat meat and warm milk, he spotted Trok hobbling into the woods to water the trees. He walked bow-legged, and even from here Jig could hear him yelp when he adjusted his trousers. On second thought, maybe marching on foot wasn't so bad. Painful as Jig's blisters and sores were, others had injuries that were far worse. All Jig knew was that he wasn't about to heal *those* wounds.

"Hurry it up," Silverfang shouted. He still rode Bastard, and he held Trok's wolf by the ropes. Trok ran back, his face tight with pain. Silverfang tossed Trok the ropes and turned to face the goblins. "We march double time today!"

Jig gulped down the last of his meat, dropping a bit into his hood for Smudge. He turned to Gratz. "What's double time?"

Gratz grinned. "You'll see."

The drums began to pound a quick, sharp rhythm. Apparently "double time" meant hurrying along at an awkward pace that was too quick to be a proper walk, but not quite fast enough to be a jog.

It was certainly a more efficient pace. Normally it took Jig most of the morning before his stomach began to cramp and the muscles in his thighs knotted. Marching at double time, he reached that same level of pain before they were even out of sight of last night's camp. By the time the sun was overhead, he was about ready to cut out his stomach with his sword. He probably would have done it too, if his stupid armor hadn't been in the way.

The ground was steeper today. Roots and saplings fought to reclaim the edges of the road. Those soldiers unfortunate enough to be at the edges of the formation were constantly stumbling and cursing as they fought to keep up.

Three thunderous drumbeats signaled a halt. Jig turned around, standing on his toes to see past the other goblins. A group of orcs rode through the trees, toward the front of the lines. He recognized Billa by her white cape. Relka rode with her. Her eyes were squeezed shut, and her hands were tied. She looked like a child, squeezed onto the front of the saddle with Billa.

"The temple is nearby," Billa shouted. "Silverfang, bring your goblins."

Jig blinked. He had thought they were going back to the lair. What temple—?

Mine, said Shadowstar. *She must have sensed it.*

What would happen when she realized she couldn't get into the mountain to reach the temple? Jig stared longingly up the mountainside, wondering how the remaining goblins had fared since he left. They had survived for over a year the first time Jig sealed the entrance. They should be fine. Why, even now Golaka was probably preparing stuffed snakeskins and lizard-fish pudding.

Jig's mouth watered, and a bit of drool slipped past one of his fangs.

Silverfang turned Bastard in a tight circle. "Gratz, your squadron's with me. The rest of you take a break, but anyone who falls asleep had better pray I feed you to the wolves. At least they'll be quick!"

Jig and the rest of Gratz's squadron groaned. Behind them, goblins collapsed to the ground, leaning against one another for support.

Silverfang tugged Bastard's ropes and shouted, "March!" Bastard trotted after the orcs, and the rest of the wolf-riders fell in behind him.

Trok cursed as Smelly lunged away from the pack, teeth bared as he charged the closest of the horses. Trok yanked the ropes, fighting to get his wolf under control, but Smelly ignored him.

Silverfang threw a rock. No, not a rock. One of those troll toes. It flew past Smelly, who skidded to a halt. His front paws shoveled snow as he dug after the toe. "Next time you lose control of your mount, it's your toes I'll be feeding him," Silverfang said as he rode past.

Jig adjusted his helmet as he and the other goblins jogged up the mountainside after the wolves. His armor bounced with every step, deepening already-painful bruises.

They kept up that pace for what seemed like years, until Jig began to worry that his feet and legs would simply snap away from his body like twigs. Finally the horses and wolves slowed near a half-frozen stream.

"Gratz, take your men up the mountainside and scout around." Silverfang grinned. "If you find anything, scream really loud before they kill you."

Jig glanced behind, surprised at how far they had climbed. When he turned back, he realized he knew this place. Farther upstream was where he and Relka had come to rescue Grell from a human soldier a few weeks back. He was home!

"Spread out," said Gratz. "Weapons ready."

Jig tugged his sword free. The leather wrapping on the hilt did little to protect him from the cold metal, and he switched the sword from one hand to the other as he walked. His other hand he shoved into his cloak pocket, petting Smudge for warmth.

The snow had hidden most evidence of battle, but here and there Jig still saw signs of the humans' attack. A spear stood point-first in the snow. At first, Jig mistook it for a sapling. Farther along, a bluebird perched on an arrow embedded in a tree. The bird chirped and fluffed its chest, apparently trying to mate with the bright-colored fletching.

What Jig didn't see was any hint of humans or elves. Genevieve had taken her goblin slaves down to Avery, while Theodore and his elves ran off to join the king and await Billa's army. How long would it take them to discover Billa had chosen an alternate path? An army of monsters was hardly subtle.

"Jig!" Gratz's sharp whisper made Jig jump. "You're on point. Take us to this lair of yours."

Jig's chest tightened as he crept past the others toward the small clearing up ahead.

"Everyone else hold back," Gratz said. "Regulations say the best way to spring traps and ambushes is with a single scout. Be ready."

That made sense. One goblin would spring the trap, and then the rest could rush in. It was a great strategy for everyone except the poor scout. But Smudge was still relatively cool, and Jig heard nothing but the eager whispers of his fellow goblins. He crept forward, ears held high, until he reached the entrance. What remained of the entrance, at any rate.

Before, a fallen pine had sheltered the entrance, blocking the wind and hiding the cave from casual view.

Theodore must have used the Rod of Creation on the tree. The flat, brown needles now stretched in all directions, even into the rock of the cave. They were as wide as Jig's claws, and the edges appeared sharper than Jig's own sword. Smudge might be able to creep through the cracks between those tight-woven needles, but no goblin would fit. Not without first being chopped into spider-size pieces.

He decided to keep that last thought to himself, lest Gratz or Silverfang start to get ideas.

He would have given anything to be able to crawl through the tree and retreat to his lair. He wanted to be home, not stuck in the cold, waiting for Billa and her goddess to discover who he was.

This is your fault, he muttered. Shadowstar didn't argue.

"Is the lair secure?" Gratz called.

"Yes." It was more than secure. He rapped his sword against one of the needles. The needles bent slightly, like good steel, but when he tried to push them further, they sprang back.

Gratz shouted down the mountainside, then waved for the other goblins to join Jig. The orcs and wolf-riders had left their mounts a short distance below. Jig stepped as far to the side as he could to make way for Billa and her orcs. And Relka. Relka's bound hands clutched her pendant tight.

Billa scowled at the tree. "Cut it away," she said.

Orcs raced to obey. Goblins raced to get out of the way of the orcs. Swords and axes crashed against the tree, to no avail. Like the elf scout Jig had fought, the tree was hardened by the Rod of Creation. Indestructible, save for magic.

Billa shoved Relka into the snow and drew her sword. "I know you're here, Autumnstar. You can't hide from me forever."

Billa chopped her sword onto the branches. The magically strengthened branches snapped as though they were dead and rotted. A few more swings, and Billa had cleared away enough of the tree for her to slip inside. She grabbed Relka by the arm.

"Nobody comes into this cave, friend or foe," said Billa. Her orcs grunted and took up positions to either side of the cave.

Relka had time for one frightened look at Jig, and then Billa dragged her into the darkness.

"This is boring," Trok muttered, not for the first time. Silverfang had taken several of the goblins down to tend the wolves. The rest were supposed to help the orcs guard the cave, a duty made more difficult by the orcs' determination to kill anyone who came too close.

Trok was sitting beneath a tree, rubbing a stone over the flat tip of his sword to sharpen it. He raised the sword high, holding it by the blade so the tip pointed down at his boots. He let go, and the sword buried itself in the snow and dirt, a finger's width from his right foot. "It's not right, leaving us out here to freeze. This is *our* lair. Why should Billa get it all to herself?"

Jig didn't answer. Billa had opened the lair! All he had to do was wait until everyone left, and he could return home. He stared at the orcs guarding the cave. Would anyone notice if Jig slipped away to hide?

An angry scream echoed from inside the tunnels.

"On second thought," Trok said, "Billa seems to know what she's doing."

"That was Relka," Jig said.

"*Was* being the important word." Trok yanked his sword from the ground and began sliding the stone along the edge. "With the warriors gone, who do you think will end up eating the rest of the goblins? Tunnel cats or the hobgoblins? My bet's on the hobgoblins. The yellow-skinned sneaks are probably raiding the kitchens even now."

"I doubt it," Jig said. "They'd have to get past Golaka to do that."

Jig, you have to go in there.

What? Jig glanced at the cave. *Didn't you hear that scream? And what about all of those orcs guarding the cave?*

Billa is in the temple, Shadowstar said. *She's going to kill Relka unless I manifest before her.*

So manifest!

There was a long silence. *Billa carries Isa's sword. That weapon could kill even me, Jig.*

Then I'm pretty sure it would kill me, too!

Trok punched him in the shoulder. "You're doing that thing where you stare and mumble to yourself again. It's creepy."

Jig bit his lip to keep from mumbling. *She's your wife, not mine.*

Jig, now that Billa has entered my temple, I can hear Isa whispering to her. She means to kill me if I don't help her. I'm not strong enough to fight another god.

So help her! Jig sat in the snow as he realized what Shadowstar was saying. *You're afraid.*

So are you, said Shadowstar.

Well, yes. I'm a goblin.

Relka screamed again. She sounded more angry than afraid.

Wait, I thought Isa wanted to kill you. Now she wants your help? Jig asked.

She wants me to help her kill Noc.

Jig's head was starting to ache. *Didn't you say Noc was the one who betrayed you? If she has a way to kill him, why wouldn't you help?*

It's more complicated than that.

Jig wasn't surprised in the least. Gods were supremely talented when it came to complicating things. Most of the non-goblin races were, come to think of it.

He's my son.

But why can't you help Isa kill him?

Shadowstar's sigh rang through Jig's skull. *Why did it have to be goblins?* Without waiting for an answer, he said, *Imagine if Billa told you she would destroy you unless you helped her to kill Smudge.*

Jig scooped Smudge out of his pocket and shielded him in both hands. *Why would Billa want to hurt my fire-spider?*

Don't make me smite you. Another divine sigh, and then, *I don't expect you to understand, Jig. But I can't let Isa kill my son.*

Wouldn't he be Isa's son too? Jig asked.

Shadowstar paused. *No. That's another reason Isa isn't too happy with me. Jig, whether you understand or not, I need you to do this. I can't help her kill Noc, and I can't let her sacrifice one of my followers in my own temple.*

Save Relka. From an orc and a god. Tymalous Shadowstar was afraid to go into that cave, but he expected Jig to go in?

You swore an oath to me, Jig Dragonslayer. There was no room for argument in his tone. This was Shadowstar at his most serious. *Relka believes in me. She believes in you. You can do this.*

Jig stared at the orcs standing around the cave. He closed his eyes as another shout tore out of the darkness. *No.*

The answering silence spooked him more than anything Shadowstar could have said.

If I go in there, Billa will kill two of your followers instead of only one. How is that better?

Still Shadowstar said nothing.

Noc is a death god, Jig said. *Why does he need our help against Isa, anyway?*

Noc doesn't know we survived. Even a goblin can kill a larger foe if that foe doesn't realize the goblin is there.

Jig shook his head. *Isa and Billa know I'm here. So do those orcs guarding the cave.*

Be not afraid, Shadowstar whispered.

And like that, Jig wasn't. The knot in his gut relaxed. The tension in his shoulders loosened. He stopped cringing every time Relka shouted. *What did you do?*

"You're still mumbling, runt," Trok said. He grabbed Jig's arm. "It's weird."

Jig punched Trok in the jaw.

Trok stumbled back, eyes wide. The bigger goblin looked more stunned than anything. That wouldn't last, though. As soon as Trok recovered, he would snap Jig like a stick.

Jig knew what Trok would do to him, and he didn't care. He didn't *want* to die, but he wasn't afraid, either. He stared at Trok and said, "I don't like being called runt."

Trok didn't move. "What happened to you?"

"Shadowstar." Jig rubbed his hand. Next time he would

have to remember to punch something softer. Jaws were too solid. *You took my fear away.*

It's one of my gifts.

Had Tymalous Shadowstar been present, Jig would have punched him, too. Fear was what kept goblins alive! It didn't always stop them from running into stupid situations, but it helped. Which was presumably why Shadowstar had done this. To make Jig charge in like an idiot to rescue Relka.

What if I don't? Jig asked.

Then I'll hit you with the Light of the Autumn Star again. How long do you think it will take for Isa to sense that and send Billa out to get you. At least if you sneak in, you get the element of surprise.

True enough. Jig turned to Trok, who was still staring at him. Jig knew he should be afraid, but even knowing Trok was angry enough to kill him did nothing. It didn't help matters that Trok looked so goofy when he got mad. His eyes were all squinty, and his nostrils flapped with every breath. Jig fought the urge to reach up and pinch his nose.

"If a god ever decides to talk to you, the best thing you can do is pretend you don't hear him." Jig grabbed Trok's arm and tugged him toward the orcs. "We have to save Relka."

Trok's anger disappeared, replaced by laughter. "Why would we do that?"

"Because if you don't, I'll pull out my sword and cut your throat." Jig reconsidered the state of his weapon. "Or I'll bludgeon you to death with it."

Trok laughed even harder, until he started to cough. "Try it, runt."

Jig didn't bother to draw his weapon. He simply spun, smashing the sheathed blade into Trok's knee. Trok yelped and fell. A few other goblins glanced their way, then went back to whatever they were doing.

"I told you not to call me that," Jig said. "Now one of two things is going to happen. Either I kill you, in which case you're dead. Or else I'll try and fail, and you'll kill me."

"Let's find out," Trok snarled.

Jig pointed to where Gratz and Silverfang were yelling at another goblin who had been so careless as to get himself bitten by one of the wolves. "Kill another soldier in Billa's army, and they'll feed you to the wolves. Either way, you die."

Of course, the same was true for Jig. But Trok hadn't had his fear sucked out of his ears by a cowardly god.

Trok nodded slowly. "I'll help you."

Jig turned around. He suspected he would be dead very soon, but in the meantime, living without fear was kind of fun. He took a single step, only to have Trok yank him back by his cloak.

"*If* you support me as goblin chief once this is over," Trok finished.

Jig stared. "Grell is chief. She'd have us both for dinner if I tried to make you chief in her place."

"Grell won't live forever." Trok spun his sword in a lazy circle. "The goblins look up to you. They listen to you. If you tell them I should be the next chief, they'll believe you."

There had been a time, years ago, when Jig would have thought Trok was the perfect choice to be chief. The job had always gone to the biggest, meanest goblin, the one who could kill all challengers. And then Jig had helped kill the previous chief, and suddenly a nearsighted runt was in charge of the entire lair. Jig wasn't crazy, so he had surrendered power as soon as he possibly could, turning the job over to Grell . . . who had turned out to be the best chief Jig could remember.

She wasn't strong. She wasn't loud. She rarely bothered to kill anyone. People obeyed her not because she threatened them, but because she was *Grell*. She kept her enemies busy killing one another instead of trying to kill her. It was a trick Jig really wanted to learn someday.

Trok wasn't stupid, but he was a warrior. What kind of chief would he be? More importantly, what would he do to Jig once he took power? If Jig helped make Trok chief, it followed that Jig could take that away as well. The smart thing would be for Trok to immediately slit Jig's throat.

On the other hand, since both of them would probably die trying to save Relka, none of it made any difference anyway. "Fine. You'll be chief. Now go distract those orcs."

"How am I supposed to do that?"

Jig tugged Trok's sword from his hand. To his amazement, Trok didn't try to fight him. How had Jig ever been scared of him? Jig marched over to the orcs, stopping just out of reach of their weapons. "Do any of you know how to play Toe Stub?"

The orcs stared. Jig could see their eagerness. Just a few more steps, and they would have an excuse to kill a goblin.

Jig turned back to Trok. "See? I told you they'd be too afraid to play."

That got one orc's attention. "Afraid of a goblin game?"

Jig slapped the sword back into Trok's hand. "Trok here was the best Toe Stub player in our whole lair." That wasn't saying much, considering Jig had just made up the game. "But I made a bet that he couldn't beat a real orc warrior."

By now several other goblins had approached. They whispered and pointed, and Jig heard at least one wager being made.

Trok leaned down to Jig and said, "Toe Stub?"

"Watch," said Jig. "Trok holds the sword by the blade and drops it. The winner is whoever gets the blade the closest to their foot without cutting off a toe. If you get scared and yank your foot away, you lose."

"Give me that," said the orc. He grabbed Trok's sword.

Trok started to smile. "You have to hold it so the tip is at least as high as your face."

The orc dropped the sword. It plunged into the dirt, a good distance from his foot. He cursed and clutched his hand.

"A typical beginner's mistake," Trok said, chuckling as he eased into the deception. He picked up his sword and said, "You have to yank your hand back quickly, or else you'll slice your fingers."

Jig grinned and backed away. His luck appeared to be changing. Neither the orcs nor the goblins paid him any attention.

Of course, since his apparent good fortune was giving him the means to slip into the tunnels to confront an orc and her god-forged sword, perhaps his luck hadn't changed after all.

Jig crept through the darkness with one hand on the tunnel wall. Frost coated the obsidian, numbing his fingers. Up ahead, he heard a sound like smashing glass, followed by another angry shout.

"I'll kill you!" Relka's voice was hoarse. "I'll puree your ears for the toddlers. I'll use your bones to make soup! I'll—"

"Will you please shut up?" Billa snapped. "How does your god put up with all of this babbling?"

Orange light told Jig he was close, as did the steadily increasing warmth coming from Smudge. Jig reached back to rub Smudge's thorax. Smudge clung to Jig's finger with his forelegs until Jig tugged free. Jig might not be able to feel fear, but his fire-spider certainly could.

He stepped to the end of the tunnel and peered into the temple. What was left of it. The little stone altar had been shattered. Of the glass mosaic on the ceiling, only a few tiles still clung to the rock. The rest lay scattered on the floor.

Relka sat amid the remains of the altar, her knees hugged to her chest. Billa stood beside her, a lit torch in her left hand. In her right she clutched Isa's sword.

Was it Jig's imagination, or did the torch's flames actually bend away from the sword? Even fire feared the touch of that blade.

"Shadowstar will crush you for this." Relka spat at Billa's feet. "He'll destroy you. You think he fears your little army?"

From Jig's angle, he could see Billa roll her eyes. "*Please* can I kill her?" Jig didn't hear an answer, but he saw Billa's shoulders slump. "What if I just cut out her tongue?"

Relka laughed. "Go ahead and kill me. I would be honored to die a martyr for Tymalous Shadowstar."

Go now, Jig.

Jig didn't move. He wasn't afraid, but he saw no need to charge out and die on that sword, either. I *don't want to be a martyr.*

Isa will sense your presence soon anyway.

Jig gritted his teeth and stepped into the temple. He didn't bother to draw his sword. What good would it do? He cleared his throat and said, "Shadowstar says if you kill her—or me!—he'll collapse the entire temple and crush us all." Actually that wasn't a bad plan.

"What are you doing here, goblin?" Billa snapped.

Relka's grin shone with triumph. "That's Jig Dragonslayer, high priest of Tymalous Shadowstar. He's here to kill you, orc."

"You? You're the priest?" Billa stared. "Seriously?"

"We can't all have magic swords and armies." Jig glanced around. Three other tunnels led away from the far side of the temple. A pair of goblins lay dead in the rightmost tunnel. They appeared to be two of Golaka's kitchen workers. They must have been sent to investigate all the shouting and destruction. Each one had been stabbed through the torso, but there was hardly any blood.

Jig crept closer, keeping Billa in his sight as he knelt to study the bodies. Blue ice crusted the wounds on the two goblins. Billa's blade had frozen their blood. It made for a much cleaner corpse than Jig was used to. Most nights he had to wipe up the blood of the wounded before heading back to the lair. If all goblins would do him the courtesy of getting stabbed with magically cold weapons, he could cut his cleaning time in half.

"Does your god speak to you?" Billa asked.

Jig groaned. "Usually at the worst times."

"Isa was so excited when she first realized Autumnstar—I mean, Shadowstar—was still alive." Billa sat down and jabbed her sword at Relka. "She was as bad as this one. Gave me a headache like you wouldn't believe. Whenever she's riled, it's like my whole skull freezes."

Jig nodded in sympathy. "Shadowstar wears tiny bells all over his clothes. Sometimes it takes days for my ears to stop ringing."

Billa chuckled. "After we first conquered the trolls, the orcs held a feast to celebrate. I overindulged on the wine, and had to retreat into the snow. There I am, in the middle of spewing an entire bottle back to the earth, and Isa pipes up to talk about tactics for the next battle."

"Shadowstar once made me heal a hobgoblin's backside," Jig said, his voice mild.

Billa shuddered. "You win."

"Do the other orcs sing hymns about you?" Jig asked, glancing at Relka. He knew he was supposed to be saving

Relka, and maybe killing Billa too, but this was the first time he had ever found someone who understood what it was like having a god in your head. There was Braf, of course, but Braf wasn't much of a conversationalist.

"They used to," said Billa. "Growing up, I had horribly dry skin, and my nose was always bleeding. That's where they came up with the name Billa the Bloody." She glanced around, then sang,

"Billa the bloody-nosed orc,
armed with Isa's magic blade,
led her people to battle.
Soon the trolls were sore afraid.

Billa the bloody-nosed orc
triumphed over every foe.
None may stand against her.
Forever shall her nostrils flow!"

Billa coughed to clear her throat. She actually appeared to be blushing. "I cut out the tongue of the first orc to sing that song within earshot. They don't sing it anymore." She rubbed a finger beneath her nose. "This cold weather makes it even worse."

"My hymns are better," Relka muttered.

Billa straightened. "So has Tymalous Shadowstar agreed to help us? Imagine their power—*our* power—once they're free of Noc's curse. With Shadowstar and Isa working together, we can summon Noc and destroy him." She jabbed her sword into the air, then cocked her head. "I wonder what god tastes like."

"Noc's a god of death. He's probably poisonous." Jig stepped away from the bodies. They were beyond his help anyway. "How will you summon him?"

"Death," Billa said simply. "The gods aren't like us, Jig." Strange to hear Billa the Bloody addressing him as an equal. "They can't act against their natures. Isa summons the winds because she must. Just like Noc must attend when the death is widespread enough to warrant his attention."

Jig glanced at the entrance. "I don't see why you need me or Shadowstar."

"Even gods can grow lonely," Billa said. "I think Isa misses him. And Autumnstar—sorry. *Shadowstar* has the power to calm and comfort. He can lull Noc's suspicions, dulling his reflexes and giving me the chance to strike. He can do the same with the rest of the gods, easing their wrath. It's one of his gifts, to calm people's passions."

Or their fear. "He wants you to free Relka first."

Billa turned around. A touch of her blade severed Relka's bonds.

"Let me have your torch," Jig said. "Shadowstar's magic should be able to heal your nose so it doesn't bleed anymore."

The orc's eyes widened. "You can do that?"

"It wouldn't be the first nose I've healed." Jig took the torch and circled Billa, studying her nose and positioning himself closer to Relka. He smelled burning cloth—right, that would be Smudge searing the hood of Jig's cloak. If Shadowstar hadn't worked his magic on Jig, he would probably be just as terrified as the spider.

With his free hand, Jig reached up to touch Billa's nose. Her skin was cool to the touch, especially the rough, pale scar. Old blood crusted the edges of her nostrils.

I'm willing to help you heal her, Shadowstar said. *But I won't join Isa. I can't.*

Shut up. Shadowstar had taken Jig's fear, but that only left more room for anger. Showdowstar wouldn't allow them to kill Noc, but he was perfectly willing to let Jig risk his own life. After all, Jig was only a goblin.

That's not—

I said shut up. Jig shoved the flaming torch into Billa's face.

Billa screamed and staggered back. She swung wildly with her sword, but Jig had already leaped away. As hard as he could, he hurled the torch down the right-hand tunnel.

The temple went dark.

Jig dropped to his hands and knees and grabbed Relka's leg. He dragged her away from the altar, toward the central tunnel. "Come on," Jig said, loud enough for Billa to hear. He tried to make himself sound afraid. All his life, he had fought to keep his voice from squeaking. Now thanks to Shadowstar, he had to force it. "If we can make it to the lake, we'll be safe."

He took a few steps into the tunnel, then shoved Relka against the wall and pressed a hand over her mouth. One of her fangs dug into the fleshy part of his palm, but he barely felt it.

He twisted his good ear back toward the temple and Billa's pained whimpering. Her footsteps crunched on stone and glass. Would she run after the torch? Or would she try to follow Jig and Relka into the darkness? If so, she had a one-in-three chance of bumping right into them.

The smart thing for her to do was to retreat. She could bring her kobolds to track Jig, and orcs to finish them off. But Billa was angry and hurting, and if Jig wasn't mistaken, hitting her in the face had caused her nose to start bleeding. She wouldn't be thinking clearly.

"Run away, little goblin," Billa whispered. She grunted as she tripped over the two dead goblins. She was going after the torch. "I'll feed your eyes to the wolves when I find you."

Jig waited until her footsteps faded, then hurried back through the temple, pulling Relka along behind him. He hoped Billa did find her way to the lake. Maybe the poisonous lizard-fish would take care of things for him.

"I knew you'd save me," Relka whispered.

"I didn't have much of a choice." Jig dragged her toward the entrance. He hoped Trok was still there. If the orcs had gone back to watching the cave, Jig was dead.

He squinted as they neared the light of the outside world. The crack of steel on stone made him jump. One of the orcs howled.

"Ha!" Trok shouted. "A half-sever. I win again!"

Jig peeked out to see orcs and goblins gathered in a circle. Trok picked up his sword. "I can beat that with my off-hand. Double or nothing." His sword scraped the edge of his boot when it landed.

"It's not fair," complained the orc who was sitting in the snow, clutching his bloody foot. "Goblins are closer to the ground than we are."

"No welshing," Trok shouted. "Play or forfeit." The other goblins joined in, taunting and jeering.

"Come on," Jig whispered. He took Relka's hand and led her out of the cave. One of the orcs glanced up and spotted them, but he didn't say anything. He probably thought they were just another pair of goblin soldiers come to watch the game.

Jig and Relka had just reached the cover of the trees when another orc screamed. Jig glanced back to see him tugging his sword from his foot while the goblins laughed.

"I win again," Trok cried. "Pay up, orc."

"I am *not* running naked to the river and back," the wounded orc protested.

"We went double or nothing," Trok said. "You're going twice!"

"Hurry," Jig said. Before he had to add the sight of a naked orc to his list of nightmares.

"I'm not afraid," said Relka. "Shadowstar watches over us."

Jig's jaw tightened, but he said nothing.

CHAPTER 8

AUTUMNSTAR TRAVELED WITH NO REAL DESTINATION. With his star gone and his temple destroyed, he was forced to hoard his power like a mortal wizard.

Everywhere he went, he felt people calling. The pain, the fear of death, they whispered to him, begging for comfort and solace. He couldn't do much to help them, but neither could he ignore them. He wandered from a battlefield to the collapsed tunnels of a gnomish silver mine, from a village buried by early winter storms to a flooded town on the other side of the world. Always he watched for signs of Noc or the other gods. It would be safer to do nothing, but Autumnstar could no more turn his back on suffering than he could steal back his star.

One day he found himself drawn to an old man curled in a ball near a small pond, a day's march from the nearest village. He had been cast forth to die. This time Autumnstar needed no magic. The man was not afraid, nor did he appear to be in excessive pain. The village had too little food, and this man had accepted death in order to ease his family's burden.

Autumnstar folded his wings and rested his head on the man's thigh. The rough scales startled the man at first, but slowly he relaxed. His fingers scratched Autumnstar's neck, tentatively at first.

"I hope you mean to wait until after I die to eat me," he said, his voice hoarse. His smile revealed a few yellow teeth. "Sorry there's not much meat on these old bones."

A black scavenger bird circled low, landing in the grass nearby. Autumnstar raised his head and spread his wings. With a screech, the bird flew away.

"Thanks."

Autumnstar's tail quivered. He hopped away from the old man and sniffed the air. He smelled pond scum and goose crap, a dead fish rotting in the mud . . . and another god.

Autumnstar hissed and turned to flee, but then his reason caught up with his instincts. If Noc had found him, he would already be dead.

He crept toward the water. Was this what had drawn him here? The power was familiar, though it had been ages since Autumnstar had encountered another god. Weak and frightened, the presence reminded Autumnstar a little of himself.

His wings fluttered with excitement. Could one of his companions have survived? Noc was powerful, but he was also arrogant and more than a little lazy. Autumnstar had escaped. Why not others?

Water lapped his toes. He stretched his neck, squinting to see past the reflected sunlight on the surface.

Black-shelled fingers clamped around his neck and dragged him down.

And that's what he got for trusting reason over instinct.

Gut-twisting nausea combined with the damp sweat breaking out over Jig's body told him Shadowstar's magic had worn off.

"Where are we going?" Relka asked once they were out of sight of the orcs.

"I don't know." He hadn't really planned that far ahead. Running was good, so he did that. He hadn't figured out how to get past the rest of the goblins. Nor had he thought about how to avoid the rest of Billa's army, waiting farther down the mountain.

But he had thought about what Billa would do if she caught up with him. Given the choice, Jig would rather face the army.

The sound of Billa's voice helped him run even faster. "I ordered you to stand guard," Billa yelled. "Not to play games with goblins."

A strangled scream made Jig whimper. He kind of hoped Trok wasn't the one Billa had chosen to make an example of.

"Did anyone else come out of this cave?" Billa yelled. Jig tensed, but whatever answer she received only added to her frustration. "Tell Silverfang to send these useless goblins out to form a perimeter around the lair. Don't let anyone past. You, fetch a team of kobolds and send them in after me."

Kobolds tracked by scent. They would quickly realize Jig and Relka hadn't gone down any of the tunnels.

Jig shoved through another pine tree and emerged onto a wide ledge of stone. This spot was a common meeting point for hunters. From here, he could see much of the land sloping out below. An animal trail led higher into the mountain, toward a pond which was probably frozen over by now.

He turned back as another thought struck. Widespread death . . . what if Billa simply slaughtered the rest of the goblins in the lair to summon Noc?

Not likely, said Shadowstar. *The goblins know their lair. Most would escape into the lower tunnels. To summon Noc, she'll need something much bigger.*

Something like another army. King Wendel's army. She didn't want to defeat Wendel. She wanted to cause as much death to both sides as she possibly could.

"Avery," Jig whispered. "Darnak said Billa was too smart to lead her forces into such a slaughter."

Well, that settled that. Jig turned to climb higher into the mountain, as far from Avery as he could possibly get.

You have to warn them, Jig.

Jig's fists tightened. *You mean I have to protect your son. Even if it kills me.*

If you're afraid, I could—

"No!" Jig flushed.

"What's wrong?" Relka asked.

"Shadowstar wants us to go back to Avery and stop Billa."

Relka touched her necklace. "I warned her that Shadowstar's wrath would be terrible." She grabbed Jig's hand and tugged him toward the edge of the ledge. Her fingers were rough and callused from working in the kitchens. "We'll get there faster if we go this way."

Jig peered at the slope of fallen stone, made all the more treacherous by the snow. "We'll die faster, too."

"You said Shadowstar wanted us to go to Avery." Relka released Jig's hand and stepped off of the ledge.

Jig watched her struggle to control her fall. For the most part, she kept herself in a sitting position, sliding down the rocks. "I'm not healing those scrapes," he muttered.

"Come on!" Relka said.

Jig shook his head. She didn't even question why they had to go to Avery. Jig could have said Shadowstar wanted her to march back to the lair and kick Billa in the backside, and she would have done it.

Hm . . . it *would* slow Billa down.

"Hey!"

Jig spun to see a pair of goblins running up the trail, weapons drawn. Right. Jig sat on the edge, moved Smudge into one of the front cloak pockets, and hopped down after Relka.

He slid on his back, legs flailing in the air. His armor absorbed the worst of the damage, but his helmet clattered away after the second bounce.

His leg hit a pine sapling, spinning him around. He glimpsed the goblins standing at the ledge, laughing and pointing. Then Relka caught him by the wrist, presumably to slow him down.

Instead she overbalanced and fell across his legs. The goblins above laughed harder as Jig and Relka slid a short distance farther before thudding into a boulder. Then their laughter stopped. Presumably they had remembered they were supposed to chase after Jig and Relka.

Jig grinned and hauled Relka to her feet. "Come on."

"What are we doing?" Relka asked.

"Trust me."

The guards shouted a challenge, and then Jig heard curses and the clatter of stone. Jig kept fleeing, letting the downhill slope of the mountainside add speed to his steps, until he felt like he wasn't running so much as falling.

His cloak snagged on a tree branch. The branch snapped, but the tug threw him off-balance. He twisted as he fell, hitting the snow hard with one shoulder and sliding a good distance. Relka skidded to a halt and grabbed his arm. She pulled him up and started to run.

"Don't bother," Jig said. The delay had cost them their lead. The goblin guards waved their swords in the air as they charged.

Jig folded his arms and tried to catch his breath. This would never work if he was panting too hard to speak. He thought about Silverfang, remembering the loud, angry bark of his voice, like he was just dying for an excuse to eat you. Which was probably true.

The guards spread to either side. What had Gratz called it? Flanking. It was a good maneuver, making sure Jig couldn't focus on one of the guards without exposing his back to the other.

"Off for a romp in the snow?" asked the guard on the right.

"This runt's a bit small, girl," said his partner. "How about I show you what a real goblin—"

"A real goblin?" Jig snapped. "You?" He straightened his back and brushed snow from his cloak, trying to remember what it had been like to feel no fear. "You're a disgrace. What's wrong with you two?"

The goblins glanced at one another, clearly confused. Jig hadn't drawn his sword, and he wasn't trying to run away. "Us? What's wrong with you?"

"What were your orders?" Jig raised his voice. "Your orders, goblins."

"To guard the perimeter of the lair."

Jig pointed up the mountainside. "That lair? That perimeter? The one missing two of its guards, so that any elf who felt like assassinating Billa the Bloody could slip right through the gap you left when you came charging after us? Is *that* the perimeter you're supposed to be guarding?"

The goblins glanced at each other. "Well—"

"Well, *sir!*" Jig snapped. "What if I was a decoy for an ambush?" He stepped toward the closer of the two goblins, shoving the guard's sword to one side with his bare hand. His gritted his teeth and clenched his hand. Just his luck, to run into one of the goblins who kept his blade sharp. "What if the humans had paid me to lead you here so that their archers could kill you?" He pointed to a random tree, and both goblins leaped back in alarm.

"But you were running away, and—"

"And you followed," said Jig. He lowered his voice. "Save your excuses for Silverfang. I'm sure he'll be very interested to hear how you were busy propositioning this girl instead of obeying his orders."

He tugged the guard's sword out of his hand, then rapped the flat of the blade against the second guard's skull. "If you're lucky, he'll feed only one of you to the wolves. Knowing Silverfang, he'll choose whoever is slowest to get back."

The goblins fled. Jig waited until they were gone from sight, then turned to Relka. He meant to pass her the extra sword, but he was shaking so hard he dropped it in the snow.

"That was incredible," Relka whispered.

"Thanks," said Jig. Then he threw up on her boots.

Jig finished shoving his armor beneath a bush, then stretched his arms overhead. Without the weight of all that leather, he felt as if he could leap as high as the treetops. Better still, he could walk without the armor rubbing his limbs to the bones.

He tightened his belt and repositioned the sword back over his hip. He had given Relka his own sword, keeping the one he had taken from the goblin guard for himself. It was still junk, but at least it was sharp junk.

"Why didn't you stay to fight Billa?" Relka asked as they resumed walking.

"Because *my* god didn't give me a magic sword," Jig said. "The only weapon I had is that sword in your hand, and it's not sharp enough to cut wind."

"She was in your temple," Relka said. She jogged alongside him, staying just out of sight of the road below. "You're the high priest of Tymalous Shadowstar. You're stronger than she is."

She made it sound like such a simple fact, like she was telling him snow was cold or dragons were dangerous or hobgoblin cooking tasted like rat droppings.

The howl of wolves interrupted them before Jig could tell her exactly what he thought of Tymalous Shadowstar. Jig slowed, wondering if he should go back for his armor. Not that the leather would do much against angry wolves.

"Have faith." Relka turned around and raised her sword. "We are servants of a great god."

"So let him fight the wolves," Jig muttered as he searched for shelter. A cave, a cliff they could climb, anyplace the wolves might not be able to follow. But this far down from the lair, the ground was disgustingly gentle. He glanced at a tree. He doubted wolves could climb, but they could surround the tree and wait for him to come down. More likely, the goblins would pelt him with rocks, or maybe just cut down the tree with Jig and Relka in it.

Jig pulled out his sword just as the first of the wolves came into view. Silverfang yanked the ropes, pulling Bastard to a halt as the rest of the wolf-riders joined him. It looked like Billa had sent all fourteen of Silverfang's wolf-riders after Jig, including Trok, who struggled to keep Smelly under control.

"I knew you were trouble," Silverfang shouted.

His sword was much larger than Jig's. When he charged, the wolf's speed would probably give him the strength to cut clean through Jig and Relka both. At least it would be a quick death.

"The runt is mine." Silverfang grinned and kicked Bastard in the sides. The wolf began to trot toward Jig.

Jig backed away. He fumbled with his cloak. Which pocket had Smudge crawled into? Bad enough Jig was about to be wolf food. Smudge didn't need to die too. He didn't know how long Smudge would survive outside in the cold, but it had to be longer than he would with Jig. Where was the stupid spider hiding?

He plunged his hand into another pocket, and his breath caught.

"What is it?" Relka asked.

Jig handed his sword to her.

He couldn't tell who howled first, Silverfang or Bastard.

The two of them harmonized quite well together, actually. The wolf's huge paws flung dirt and snow into the air behind him. They ran like a single creature, half wolf, half angry goblin, and the only question was whether the wolf's teeth or the goblin's sword would kill Jig first.

Relka leaped in front of Jig, waving both swords in the air. It might have been an impressive sight, if she hadn't managed to clank the blades together, knocking one of the swords from her hand. Undeterred, she gripped the other with both hands and shouted, "Prepare to face the wrath of Tymalous Shadowstar!"

Jig kicked her in the back of the knees, knocking her down. Bastard and Silverfang were almost on top of him. He pulled the large troll toe from his pocket and waved it overhead. He saw Silverfang's eyes widen as he realized what Jig held.

"Bastard," Jig shouted. "Sit!" He threw the toe at Bastard's face.

The giant wolf tried to obey. He reared and twisted, snapping at the toe even as he tried to settle his hindquarters. He might have managed, if not for Silverfang roped to his back. Jig had seen tunnel cats manage similar midair twists to snatch a bat or bird from the air. But with an armed, armored goblin tied to his back, Bastard had no chance.

Jig pulled Relka out of the way as Silverfang's weight dragged Bastard off-balance. The wolf twisted sideways in the air, his legs flailing and kicking. His jaws closed around the toe, and then Silverfang's shoulder struck the ground. Bastard slammed down on his side, bounced, and barely missed sliding into a tree. The giant wolf staggered to his feet and shook, spraying snow and mud and goblin blood in all directions. He took a single step, then spun and tried to bite Silverfang's leg.

"Behold the fate of all who challenge Jig Dragonslayer," Relka shouted.

The other goblins appeared unimpressed. They spread out in a formation Jig didn't recognize. He decided to call it the "Make sure every wolf gets a bite of Jig" formation.

Slowly it dawned on Jig that Silverfang wasn't moving. At

least not under his own power. Bastard continued to snarl and snap at Silverfang's left arm. Silverfang slumped more and more to the side. His right hand was tangled in the reins, and his weight caused them to dig cruelly into Bastard's jaws, driving him in tighter and tighter circles.

One of the goblins laughed. Jig was fairly certain it was Trok.

Bastard appeared to have forgotten all about the troll toe. His eyes were wide, and foam sprayed from his jaws. Jig could see where the rope harness cut into his mouth and throat. His teeth clacked together, but he couldn't quite reach Silverfang.

One of the goblins threw a chunk of ice at Bastard's nose, spurring him into even faster circles.

"None of that!" Gratz pointed his sword at the other goblin. "A named wolf is as much a soldier in Billa's army as you. We came out here to do a job. Let's kill these two and be done with it."

"Wait!" Jig squeaked. "Silverfang ordered you to let *him* kill me!"

"Silverfang's dead."

"Are you sure?" Jig glanced behind. Bastard had planted his front paws together, swiveling the rest of his body around in circles. Silverfang's arm dragged through the snow, his battered body showing no sign of life. "What if he's just unconscious? If you kill me, you're disobeying an order. What's the penalty for that?"

Pain seared Jig's belly. Oh, *there* was Smudge. Jig tried to grab Smudge from his pocket, but he was too late. The terrified fire-spider burned completely through the fabric and dropped into the snow. He tunneled beneath the surface, leaving a line of melted snow to mark his progress toward a cluster of tree roots.

"Fair enough," Gratz said. He pointed his sword at Jig. "Close in. Drive him toward Bastard and Silverfang. They'll finish him off one way or another."

The goblins spurred their wolves forward. Turning around, Jig shouted, "Bastard, sit!"

Bastard ignored him, spraying snow and dirt in Jig's face as he spun. The other goblins moved closer. Jig could see them fighting to keep their wolves under control. Several were actually drooling at the prospect of sinking their teeth into Jig. So were the wolves, for that matter.

Bastard's tail flicked Jig's leg in passing. Stupid wolf. Bastard's tongue flopped from the side of his mouth, and his mouth sprayed spit and blood.

Relka waved her sword at the nearest goblins, who laughed. One wolf lunged at her. She backed away, bumping into Jig and knocking him off-balance, directly into Bastard's path.

Jig plunged his hands into his pockets, searching for more troll toes, and then the full weight of Bastard's rump collided with Jig's hip. It wasn't as bad as being hit by a dragon's tail, but it was close. Huge paws trampled Jig's side. Why had he thrown away his armor? He covered his head as Silverfang's body bounced past.

Jig grabbed Silverfang's arm with both hands and clung with all his strength. His added weight barely even slowed Bastard down.

The world spun past. If Jig hadn't already thrown up once today, the whirling would have cost him the contents of his stomach for certain. He tried to pull himself up onto Bastard's back, but it was all he could do to hang on. The goblins were laughing even louder, and Relka . . . was she *singing* again?

Jig slid one hand onto Silverfang's belt, trying to get to the front of the wolf. Silverfang tilted even further, spurring Bastard to increase his speed. Jig braced his foot beneath Silverfang's chin and tried to push himself up onto Bastard's back. Something tugged him back. Turning his head, Jig saw his cloak caught on Silverfang's steel tooth.

He pulled harder, and the cloth tore. Jig swung his other foot over Bastard's back. His fingers twisted into the sweat-matted fur.

Help me heal Bastard's mouth, Jig said. *If I can calm him down, maybe he won't eat me.*

That might not be a good idea, Shadowstar said. *We don't know whether Isa can sense that kind of magic.*

If Bastard eats me, you'll have to rely on Braf to stop Billa the Bloody.

Jig's fingers warmed. He reached out, his fingers brushing the edge of Bastard's jaws. Snapping teeth nearly took Jig's fingers. He tried again, directing Shadowstar's magic into Bastard's torn skin.

Gradually the wolf slowed. His tongue lolled, and he stopped trying to eat Jig's hand. Those huge ribs bellowed beneath Jig as Bastard gasped for breath. Jig reached down to draw his knife. He stretched forward, using the knife left-handed to saw Silverfang free of the harness. Both Jig and Silverfang slid to the ground.

Bastard moaned, a sound that reminded Jig of the wind back home as it passed over the entrance to the lair. He tried to walk, but his head kept twitching, and he staggered like a drunken goblin. He managed one sideways step before toppling over onto Jig and Silverfang.

Silverfang's body protected Jig from the worst of Bastard's weight. He continued to heal Bastard's mouth and neck. The sooner Bastard recovered, the sooner he might get off of Jig. Bloody bristles of fur tickled his palm. Bastard panted, dripping warm drool over Jig's wrist.

Eventually Bastard climbed to his feet, took a few tentative steps, then sneezed three times. Relka hurried over to grab Jig's arm.

"Good . . . wolf," Jig gasped.

Relka hauled him upright, then turned to glare at the other goblins. "Who will be next to challenge the champion of Tymalous Shadowstar?"

The so-called champion of Tymalous Shadowstar promptly fell down again, where he clutched his head with both hands and waited for the woods to stop spinning.

"I told you he'd survive," Trok said to another of the wolf-riders. "Come on, pay up." Jig looked over to see Trok trading his old weapon for a gleaming two-handed broadsword.

"He'll be dead by sundown," the other goblin muttered with a glare at Jig.

"Want to wager on that, too?" Trok asked. "Those are some nice boots you're wearing."

Bastard walked back to Jig. He still wobbled a bit, but he seemed to have recovered from the dizziness faster than Jig.

Or maybe this was just an advantage to having four feet. Not that it made any difference. Even if Jig could have stood, he wasn't fast enough to outrun a wolf.

Bastard shoved his head into Jig's side and licked his hand.

Gratz cleared his throat. "With Silverfang dead, I hereby assume command of this unit. Seize the prisoners."

Several goblins hopped down from their wolves and advanced, weapons ready.

Gratz jabbed a finger at one goblin after another. "Trok, you and Dimak tie Silverfang's body onto Bastard's back. We'll— "

Bastard's snarl cut off the rest of Gratz's orders. The goblins who had moved toward Jig leaped away.

"Even the wolves recognize the greatness of Jig Dragonslayer and Tymalous Shadowstar," Relka said.

Gratz dug into a pouch and pulled out a wrinkled troll toe. He tossed it into the air.

Bastard bounded up to catch it, knocking Jig back into the snow.

"Good wolf," Gratz said. He pointed at Jig. "Kill!"

Bastard lay down and crunched his toe. Gratz squirmed on his wolf. Trok chuckled.

"Look out!" Relka pointed to Dimak, who was struggling to cock a small crossbow.

Jig put his hands on Bastard's damp fur. Slowly he swung one leg over the wolf's back. He lay down, flattening his body against Bastard's, then looked over at Dimak. "Be careful. If you shoot Bastard by mistake, you might make him angry."

"Shoot him," Gratz shouted. "That's an order!"

Dimak stared at Bastard, then tossed his crossbow to Gratz. "You shoot him."

Gratz's face turned a darker shade of blue. "This is mutiny! Billa the Bloody will crush your skull with her bare hands for this. It's right here in the regulations."

Jig had no doubt that was true. But Billa the Bloody wasn't here right now. Bastard was. And Bastard was bigger than any other wolf in the pack. Jig cleared his throat. "Billa the Bloody can only punish you for crimes she knows about."

Slowly, Dimak and the other goblins turned toward Gratz.

Gratz backed his wolf away. He pointed the crossbow at one goblin, then another. "Stay back. I'm a corporal in the army of Billa the Bloody, and acting commander of this unit!"

"And that's a big, angry wolf," Trok said, pointing at Bastard.

Gratz pulled the trigger. The bolt slammed into the side of the nearest goblin. Instead of intimidating the rest of the goblins, the attack only seemed to solidify their rebellion. In part, no doubt, because Gratz didn't have another crossbow bolt. He tossed the crossbow down and pulled out his sword.

"Wait," Jig said. To his surprise, they obeyed.

"What are you doing?" Relka whispered.

"I have no idea." Jig started to speak, then dug his fingers into Bastard's fur as the wolf stood. Jig had never realized how tall the wolves were. Relka's head was now level with his waist. He swallowed and said, "Corporal Gratz, what do regulations say about surrendering to an enemy?"

Gratz frowned. "I don't think that particular situation has ever come up."

"Then there's nothing in the regulations to stop you from surrendering to me before Bastard eats you?" Jig asked.

Shaking his head, Gratz said, "Any soldier who quits fighting is to be executed on the spot by his commanding officer."

"You mean that commanding officer?" Jig pointed to Silverfang's body. "It's your choice, Gratz. Surrender, or I order Bastard to eat you."

Gratz's lips moved as he turned around. He appeared to be counting the other goblins. "Right. I hereby surrender command of this squadron to Jig," Gratz said. He lowered his voice. "According to regulations, this means you receive a field promotion to the rank of lieutenant, with all the inherent responsibilities and—"

"Fine," Jig said. "Now put your sword away before Bastard decides you're a threat."

Gratz flung his sword into the snow. His hand barely trembled as he snapped a quick salute. "Orders, sir?"

Jig glanced around. Trok was laughing at him. The other goblins appeared skeptical at best. Aside from Relka, naturally. She was beaming and mumbling to herself, no doubt composing another hymn. Jig dreaded to think what she would rhyme with "lieutenant."

Gratz cleared his throat. "Sir?"

Jig was tempted to order them all to return to Billa's army. But with Jig gone, Gratz would probably resume command and come after him again.

Stalling for time, he turned to Relka. "This is my second-in-command." Since Relka was probably the only one here who wouldn't happily murder Jig to take his place, she was the safest choice.

Relka grinned. "So they have to obey me now, right?"

"That's right, sir," said Gratz.

Relka's claw stabbed at Trok like a spear. "Sing."

"What?"

Relka's smile was pure evil. "I like to listen to music. Sing 'The Song of Jig' for me, soldier."

Trok started to draw his sword.

"Are you disobeying an order, goblin?" Gratz shouted. He hopped down from his wolf and grabbed his own weapon. "Shall I cut out his tongue, sir?"

Jig shook his head in disbelief. Gratz was serious. Moments before he had been determined to kill Jig himself. Now he was ready to kill anyone who disobeyed him. Or Relka. If Jig had ordered him to eat his own leg, Gratz would even now be marching over to Relka to borrow a fork.

Jig tucked that idea away for later. For now . . . "Tie up the wolves. Relka, they'll probably be hungry, so why don't you feed Silverfang to them? Gratz, help them make a new harness for Bastard."

The goblins scurried to obey. Jig rubbed his fang nervously as he watched them work. How long could he keep up this charade? He was no leader. Sooner or later the discipline Billa and Silverfang had pounded into them would wear off, and they would go back to being goblins. He wondered if that would happen before or after Billa sent her orcs to find out what had happened to Silverfang.

Jig's good ear twitched, following Relka's footsteps as she approached. He had done the same thing a year ago, back in the lair. He remembered the sound of her footsteps, the cold of his own sweat dripping down his sides as he waited for Relka to try to kill him.

If Jig had known where he would end up, he probably would have let Relka go ahead and stab him in the back.

"The wolves are fed," Relka said. She sounded almost perky. Jig wanted to punch her. "We had leftover Silverfang, but I wasn't sure whether you'd want to take the time to prepare the meat properly."

Jig shook his head. Back home, the tunnels and caves restricted the flow of smoke. Out here in the open, it would be a clear signal to anyone searching for him. And since pretty much everyone wanted him dead, a fire was a very bad idea. So was eating Silverfang raw, of course, but Jig would rather risk knotted bowels than whatever death Billa had planned for him.

"Billa was supposed to drive the surface dwellers away forever." Jig's throat tightened. No more adventurers slaughtering their way through the lair. No more princes and princesses dragging goblins away to build their stupid walls. No more quests and fighting and fleeing for his life.

Instead, Billa was just using them. At least when Princess Genevieve used the goblins, she was honest about it. She didn't pretend she was trying to help anyone. She simply tied them up and dragged them to Avery. Nor did she pretend she wouldn't kill every last goblin if they gave her a reason.

"I believed in her." He stared at Relka's pendant. Jig had been every bit as much of an idiot as Relka. "Shadowstar is afraid of Isa," he said. He wasn't sure why he had blurted it out.

Relka stiffened. "What do you mean?"

"He could have manifested in his temple to protect you, but he knows Billa could kill him. So he sent me instead. He'd rather let me die than risk himself. He used me. Just like everyone else." Jig waited, watching to see how she would react.

Suddenly Relka's face broke into a smile. "This is a test, isn't it? You want to know how strong my faith is, so you know whether or not you can rely on me for the trials ahead."

Jig wondered if Shadowstar's magic could heal whatever

was wrong with Relka's brain. "Trials? Shadowstar wants me to go to Avery and stop Billa the Bloody!"

"The life of a champion is not an easy one," Relka said.

"Not easy? I just shoved a torch into Billa's face. She's going to send her entire army after me, and when they catch me, they're going to—"

"You've got an army too," Relka said, pointing back at the wolf-riders.

Jig's mouth stayed open, but he had run out of words. Nothing he could say would shake Relka's faith. She fully expected him to save Avery, defeat Billa and her goddess, and save all goblinkind.

Jig stood and brushed snow from his legs and backside. *Why couldn't you have chosen Relka? She would love to be a priest of Shadowstar, running around fighting pixies and orcs and doing all of your dirty work.*

If I remember correctly, you sought me out, said Shadowstar.

Jig didn't have an answer to that, either.

If it's what you truly want, I'll leave you alone, Jig. Do this thing for me, and I'll never disturb you again.

Wait, Jig said quickly. Lose the ability to heal himself and the other goblins? Jig shuddered, remembering the long list of war scars he had displayed for Silverfang. Without Shadowstar, most of those injuries would have killed him. *That's not what I meant.*

Of course. Shadowstar sounded amused.

Right. Billa was probably starting to wonder about her wolf-riders. Soon she would send more troops out to find them. Jig turned around . . . which way was Avery, from here?

Follow the road to the east.

To Avery, then.

"We need to warn Princess Genevieve what she's facing," Jig said. "The humans think they're fighting a regular army of monsters, an army that wants to win. Billa doesn't care about beating humans. She wants her army to die, and she wants to take as many humans with them as they can."

"I'll tell the others to get the wolves ready." With that, Relka turned to go.

"Thanks," said Jig.

Relka hesitated. "Do you think the humans will listen to you?"

The king had ordered all goblins killed on sight. Jig's last encounter with Genevieve wouldn't have encouraged her to change that order. "Not really, no."

CHAPTER 9

TYMALOUS AUTUMSTAR SQUIRMED TO BREAK free as the black-shelled arm dragged him deeper into the water. He twisted his long neck about until he saw his attacker.

"Ipsep? Is that you?"

The former sea god looked awful. Pale cracks lined his shell, most of which was covered in algae and mussels. His thick green hair had fallen out or wilted; what remained was little more than brown tufts of seaweed stuck to his scalp.

"You betrayed us, Autumnstar," said Ipsep. "You abandoned us."

"Noc *betrayed us." He bit down on Ipsep's finger. Autumnstar's teeth were useless against the armor of Ipsep's shell. All he got for his trouble was a mouthful of seaweed and one angry snail.*

"You were the first to give up when Noc turned against us. You're a coward." Ipsep tightened both hands around Autumnstar's neck and shoved him deeper into the water. "You left us to be killed, or worse, to be forgotten."

Autumnstar didn't argue. Even if he hadn't been drowning, there was nothing he could say. Ipsep was right. He had turned his back on the war.

Ipsep stumbled, and his grip loosened. Instantly, Autumn-

star twisted free. His wings thrust him to the surface, where he gasped for breath.

The old man Autumnstar had comforted stood knee-deep in the pond. As Autumnstar watched, he threw another stone at Ipsep.

The first attack had startled the god. This time Ipsep hardly appeared to notice as the rock bounced off his shell.

Autumnstar threw himself on Ipsep's back, digging his claws into the cracks of his shell, but it wasn't enough. Ipsep's fingers clacked together. The old man shouted in fear as he was drawn deeper into the pond.

Ipsep turned his attention back to Autumnstar. Clawed fingers reached around to sever the tip of Autumnstar's tail. Ipsep's other hand caught him by the wing. Autumnstar's claws broke as he was pulled away from Ipsep's back.

Autumnstar stopped fighting. He had never been much of a warrior anyway. Even during the war, in the midst of battle, he had barely been able to stop himself from throwing down his weapons and comforting the wounded and the dying.

Ipsep was both, and he didn't even know it. Only rage kept his despair at bay, and even in a god, rage couldn't last forever. Especially once Tymalous Autumnstar began to soothe that rage.

"They've forgotten us, Autumnstar," said Ipsep. Already his voice was softer. "The mortals don't even remember our names."

"Rest, old friend," Autumnstar whispered. "Be at peace."

"Peace." Ipsep waded deeper into the water, pulling Autumnstar with him. "An eternity of cowering in the shadows, waiting for them to find us. What kind of peace is that?"

Autumnstar clung tighter, pouring what little power he had into the other god. Most gods would barely have noticed his feeble efforts, but Ipsep was as weak as Autumnstar.

Soon Ipsep sank beneath the surface and disappeared. Slumbering or dead, Autumnstar couldn't say.

He struggled to swim to his would-be rescuer. How long had the old man been submerged? Autumnstar's left wing was crushed and useless. His blood flowed into the pond with every desperate stroke.

By the time he touched the body, he knew it was too late. Autumnstar had spent most of his hoarded power in his fight with Ipsep. Even had he been strong enough to heal the body, the soul had already fled.

"Thank you," he whispered.

Moments later, Tymalous Autumnstar climbed out of the pond, took a single step, and fell flat on his face. He rolled over, examining his new body and wondering how long it would take to get used to having only two legs again.

Jig should have known better. Gratz was a goblin, and goblins didn't take kindly to losing their commands. Especially not to an upstart runt like Jig. But Jig had been so busy being afraid of humans and gods and everything else that he had forgotten to be afraid of his fellow goblins.

The knife in Gratz's hand was short and straight. Barely long enough to pierce Jig's heart, though if Gratz was smart, he'd go for the throat instead.

Gratz had intercepted him after Relka went back to ready the wolves. The other goblins were too far away to help. Nor would Jig have expected them to. This was his own fault. He should have killed Gratz. Failing that, he should have made sure Gratz was disarmed and bound. Gratz had snuck up on him as though he were a deaf human.

Jig backed away, one hand reaching for his sword. Could he draw it before Gratz pounced? Probably not. "Don't regulations say anything about drawing a knife on a superior officer?"

Gratz blinked. "What, this? Oh, no, sir. I was only going to offer to cut your officer's scar."

"Officer's scar?" Jig stared, trying to understand.

"Now that you're a lieutenant and all that, you'll be wanting the scar of rank to show everyone. Six cuts to the right forearm." He frowned as he studied Jig more closely. "You're skinny, so I'll have to cut small. . . ."

"No."

"But you're an officer now." Gratz smiled wistfully as he looked at the knife. "I remember the day old Silverfang gave me my first scar of rank. Couldn't use that arm for a month."

"No!"

Gratz looked hurt. "It's not that bad, sir. The actual designs are sort of pretty." He yanked down part of his shirt to reveal a patch of dark blue scars below the shoulder. A single zigzag, with two diagonal lines cut through the center. Tiny angular cuts dotted the right side of the mark. "General's scars are even better. There's a double circle around the whole thing."

Jig! Shadowstar sounded shaken. *You can't let him carve that mark on you.*

I'm not the smartest goblin in the world, but I had figured that much out on my own.

You don't understand, said Shadowstar. *Those scars are how Billa plans to kill everyone.*

Jig waited a long time before following Gratz back to the group. He sat for so long that Smudge crawled out and nipped him on the ear, just to make sure he was still alive. Jig winced and tugged the fire-spider from his ear.

"They're spells," Jig whispered to Smudge. Every officer in Billa's army carried a spell upon his or her shoulder. Shadowstar wasn't sure exactly what the spell would do, but he thought it powerful enough to kill everyone within ten paces. If Billa waited until her army was locked in battle with the humans and elves, she could destroy them all with a single command.

You have to go back, Shadowstar said.

With a numbness only partly due to the cold, Jig pushed himself up and trudged toward the rest of his "army." As he returned to the group, they stared at him with the same expression the wolves wore when they saw fresh meat. They all had to know it was only a matter of time before Billa caught up with him. Jig was a walking corpse.

What they didn't realize was that the same was true for them all. And if Jig told them what Billa truly planned, one of two things would happen. Either they wouldn't believe him, and Gratz would quote some regulation against letting madmen command the troops.

Or else they would believe him. Jig suspected that would

be even worse. Whatever self-control and discipline Billa had trained into them would shatter, turning them back into an unruly mob. A very angry mob.

Jig had never done well with mobs.

"We have a choice to make," Jig said. His voice cracked, and several goblins smirked. He cleared his throat. "We can return to Billa's army and rejoin the others. Go back to being soldiers in Billa's war." He began to pace, more to keep his feet warm than for dramatic effect. "*Billa's* army. *Billa's* war. Do you think anyone will remember the goblins, once this war is over?"

The smirks faded slightly.

"Billa sent you to capture me," Jig said. "But where's the glory in dragging a half-blind goblin runt back to be killed? You think anyone will sing songs about that? How fourteen wolf-riders triumphed over a pair of runaways?"

He saw Trok nodding. Hopefully the other goblins were of similar minds.

"You know what's going to happen to me," Jig said. "Billa wants me dead, right?"

The goblins shifted uncomfortably. Honesty was an unfamiliar tactic to most of them.

"Well, that's fine," Jig said, raising his voice. "But first I say we show her what goblins can do. We'll show Billa and her orcs. We'll show the humans. We'll show them all—"

The goblins cheered. What was the matter with them? Jig hadn't finished yet. Were they so eager to prove themselves? They didn't even know what they were cheering for!

He pointed down toward the road. "There's a human town up that road. They've taken—"

A whisper from Shadowstar broke his rhythm. He sighed and pointed in the other direction. "They've taken the warriors from our lair. I say we free them all and capture another town for Billa the Bloody! By the time we're through, everyone will be singing about our triumph at the Battle of Avery!"

More cheers. Were all goblins mad?

From what I've seen— Shadowstar began.

Shut up.

Gratz stepped forward. It was all Jig could do to stop himself from flinching away. If Billa suspected Jig was here, all she had to do was trigger that spell on Gratz's arm.

"Begging your pardon, sir," said Gratz. "But it's against regulations for us to engage an enemy force without orders, unless that force attacks first or—"

"Trok," Jig yelled. "The next time Gratz contradicts my orders, you have permission to feed him to the wolves."

Trok grinned. "Yes, sir!"

Jig pointed to a few random goblins. "Clean up this mess. The rest of you, finish getting the wolves ready."

He watched in amazement as they obeyed. Couldn't they see how desperate Jig was? That he was making this up as he went, and that every last one of them would likely die if they actually attacked Avery?

They're goblins, said Shadowstar. *I've grown rather fond of you as a race, but you're not so good at thinking things through.*

You're right, said Jig. *Otherwise I would have known better than to get involved with gods.*

"I've changed my mind," Jig said, staring at Bastard. They had rigged a new harness, mostly by tying extra knots in the old one. "The rest of you go ahead and capture Avery. I'll catch up."

"Don't be afraid." Trok yanked Smelly's ropes, and the wolf padded over to stand beside Jig and Bastard. "These beasts are magnificent!"

Bastard lowered his head and butted Jig onto the ground.

"See?" Trok said. "He likes you."

"He still has a bit of Silverfang stuck in his teeth," Jig mumbled. Bad enough the wolf could snap him in half with one chomp, but now every time he looked at Bastard, he saw Silverfang. A single stumble, and Jig would end up the same way. Silverfang's remains hadn't been pretty. "Well tenderized" was the phrase Relka had used.

Whose stupid idea had it been to put goblins on wolfback, anyway? The hobgoblins trained their tunnel cats, but no hobgoblin was mad enough to try to ride one.

"He's definitely fixated on you," Gratz said. "You'd best mount him soon, to show him who's boss. Otherwise, you're small enough he might decide to carry you like a pup instead."

"What does that mean?" Jig asked.

"Whenever the pups wander too far away, the adult goes and picks them up by the scruff of the neck." Gratz grabbed his own neck to demonstrate. "The pups have loose, thick skin at the neck to protect them. You and me, well. . . ."

Jig reached out to touch the leather-and-rope harness circling Bastard's chest and neck. Holding the harness with both hands, he slipped one foot into the small noose on the side.

"Not that way," Trok said. "Not unless you want to ride to Avery with your face in Bastard's—"

"Thanks." Jig switched feet. The wolf was so tall that simply sliding his foot into the rope stretched Jig's thighs uncomfortably far. He bounced on his toes, trying to get enough of a jump to throw his other leg over the wolf's back. Finally he managed to haul himself up.

"Well, I guess you'll learn," Gratz said. "Right. Your turn." He gestured to Relka.

"What?" Jig asked.

"The commander's mate rides with him."

"The commander's what?" Jig yelled.

Trok was laughing so hard he sprayed spit over Smelly's back.

Gratz's face, by contrast, was expressionless. "I thought, with the way she looks up to you and talks about you. . . ."

Jig started to argue, but it wasn't like he had much choice. Relka had to ride with someone, and Bastard was the biggest wolf.

Jig clenched his jaw and waited as Relka scrambled up behind him. Gratz tied extra ropes around her legs and waist, cinching her tight against Jig's back.

Smudge scrambled out of Jig's hood barely in time to avoid being squished. He settled down in Bastard's neck fur.

Relka's arms tightened around Jig's chest. "I'm ready."

Jig glared at Gratz. If the other goblin so much as smirked, Jig was going to order Bastard to eat him. But Gratz only grunted and returned to his own wolf. He climbed up, tightened his harness, and waited.

Oh, right. They were waiting for Jig. Bastard was the pack leader, and Jig was in command. Jig leaned down. "Come on, Bastard."

Trok chuckled again.

"Kick him in the sides to start him moving," Gratz said. "Tug the ropes to one side or the other and squeeze with your knees to turn. Pull back to slow him down or stop. If you want him angry, you can reach out and pluck his whiskers. Riles him into a frenzy."

"Kick him," Jig repeated. Gratz was crazy. Jig had survived this long precisely because he *didn't* run around kicking huge wolves that could eat his head in one bite.

Trok kicked Smelly, then tugged his ropes to guide the wolf in a tight circle. "Nothing to it."

Jig grabbed the ropes with both hands and gave them a light pull. Bastard pulled back, ripping the ropes from his fingers. Jig tried again, his face hot.

"Don't forget to kick," Relka said. Before Jig could answer, she slammed her heels into Bastard's ribs.

Bastard went from a standstill to a sprint so fast Jig's head snapped backward into Relka's jaw. The other wolves raced after them. Jig glanced back to see Trok waving one hand in the air and laughing like an idiot. Trok's hand hit a low branch, dropping snow onto the next wolf-rider.

"To Avery!" Relka shouted.

To Avery. Now all Jig had to do was figure out what to do once they arrived . . .

By the time Jig spotted the outlying farms of Avery, he was starting to wish he had let Billa kill him.

The insides of his legs were damp with sweat. Bastard's sweat or his own, he wasn't sure. But sweaty trousers were the least of his problems. These oversize wolves also had oversize backbones, and their gait was more than a little bumpy. He wouldn't be able to sit down again for days.

His back, and presumably Relka's front, were also soaked with sweat. Her necklace jabbed him between the shoulder blades, and she kept trying to rest her chin on his shoulder, which meant her hair tickled his ear.

The only one who seemed to be enjoying the ride was Smudge. He had climbed up onto Bastard's head, where he stood as tall as he could, the wind brushing his bristly fur.

"We're almost there," Relka said.

"I know." Jig tugged the ropes and tried to squeeze with his legs. Bastard turned. "Wrong knee," Jig muttered, pressing hard with the other leg. Slowly he steered Bastard toward the trees and tried to remember how to stop. He glanced at Trok, who was tugging Smelly's reins. That's right. Jig pulled hard, and Bastard came to a grudging halt.

Falling snow had streaked Jig's spectacles, but when he looked through the trees, he could still make out the wall surrounding Avery.

Jig fumbled with the harness, trying to escape. Relka freed herself first, sliding easily over Bastard's rump. Jig stared at the mess of ropes and knots. Which ones held him in place, and which were part of the hasty repairs to the harness?

Eventually Jig gave up and drew his knife. He freed himself in short order, though he ended up with a loop of rope still tied around one leg. Ignoring it for now, he turned to study his . . . his troops.

The wolves weren't even breathing very hard. For the most part, the goblins appeared eager to charge the town. Their weapons were ready, and they were joking and bantering the way goblins always did before they ran into battle and got killed.

Gratz was the exception. He had already dismounted and now sat on the ground, tugging off his boots.

"What are you doing?" Jig asked, his other problems momentarily forgotten.

"Reg . . . regulations, sir." Gratz shivered hard as the first boot slid free. "After any sustained ride, soldiers are advised to dry off. Prevents fungus and other . . . nasty things."

To Jig's horror, once Gratz was barefoot, he then began to unbuckle his belt.

"No time," Jig said quickly. "We'll dry ourselves in Avery, in front of a warm fire."

That earned a few quiet cheers. Jig turned back to the town. The gate was closed. The elf atop the wall would pick off half his goblins before they even reached the gate. "What do regulations say about attacking a town like this?"

"With a large force, you can cut them off from supplies and reinforcements and wait for them to surrender," Gratz said.

Jig glanced at his goblins. "What about smaller forces?"

"Try to gain the walls, or break down the gate," Gratz said as he rubbed his toes. "Either way, for an attack against a walled town, you're looking at about a ten-to-one casualty ratio. That means for every one of them we kill, they'll probably kill ten of us."

"Wait, what was that?" Jig turned back to Gratz. "We have fifteen goblins. You're saying we'd kill one or two humans before they wipe us all out?"

Gratz beamed. "You catch on quick! Of course that elf on the wall bumps the numbers closer to fifteen-to-one."

The other goblins had grown quiet.

"And our attacking force is made up of goblins," Gratz added. "That makes it more like twenty-to-one."

"But we have Jig Dragonslayer," Relka said. "Champion of Tymalous Shadowstar. Slayer of Straum the dragon and the Necromancer. Vanquisher of the pixie queen. Rider of Bastard. Companion of Smudge. Your regulations know nothing of Jig."

"Unless he's also the Deflector of Arrows and the Breaker of Gates, we're still going to die before we kill a single human," Trok said.

"No back talk," snapped Gratz. "I'm sure our commander has a plan."

Trok smirked as he turned to Jig. "Well, sir? What's your plan?"

Right. A plan. Jig covered his eyes against the sun, studying the goblins working near the gate. They had cleared the flowers from the lower section of the wall, and now they worked on ladders to reach the higher flowers. A single elf watched from above, bow in one hand. It looked like the same elf who had shot at them before. A few armed humans stood by the gate. They mostly appeared to be watching the goblins.

"Princess Genevieve is the key to taking Avery," Jig said. "We need to capture her alive." If she was anything like the rest of her family, she would die before she surrendered to goblins, but they didn't know that. Jig only needed a few minutes to talk to her, to force her to listen.

Though if she was anything like the rest of her family, she probably wasn't very big on listening, either.

"We need more troops," Jig decided. "Genevieve dragged at least forty goblin warriors away to Avery. It looks like at least twenty of them are still alive."

"How do we free them without getting killed?" another goblin asked.

Jig closed his eyes. *Tell Braf we're here.*

He waited while Shadowstar relayed the message. Moments later, one of the goblins on the ladders turned around and cupped his hands over his eyes. Jig squinted through his spectacles, trying to be certain that was Braf. Then the goblin waved and nearly fell off his ladder.

"How did you do that?" whispered Gratz.

Jig sighed. *Shadowstar, would you please smite Braf before he alerts the elf and everyone else that we're here?*

Braf jumped like he had been stabbed, then quickly turned back to the wall.

Thank you. Jig stepped closer to the edge of the woods. *Braf, we need to capture Princess Genevieve. We need her help to stop Billa the Bloody.*

Why do we want to stop Billa? Shadowstar did a decent job of conveying the slow, deceptively stupid tone of Braf's voice. Jig wondered what Braf heard. Was Shadowstar mimicking Jig's voice as well?

Because she plans to kill everyone, said Jig. *Goblins, humans, it doesn't matter. She wants us all dead. Also because Shadowstar said so.* Jig studied the goblin prisoners. They would still be tied together, which limited what they could do. They had their knives, but the human weapons were far better. Not to mention that elf on the wall. *How often does Genevieve leave the city?*

A few times each day, Braf said. *She's always there when they drag us in and out of town. Mornings are the worst. It's still dark and cold, and nobody wants to come out and work. Nights are bad too. Also midmorning, when you've been working a while and have to use the privy, but you know it's a long time until lunch. Afternoons are pretty lousy. There aren't any good times, really.*

Genevieve? Jig prodded.

Oh. Right. She and Darnak go for walks in the evenings sometimes, too.

"You're planning to use bound prisoners to help us fight?" Trok asked.

As if the unbound goblins Jig had brought were much of a threat. "They're going to be our distraction." He raised his voice. "We wait until evening. Genevieve will be outside the walls. The prisoners will draw the attention of the guards. When that happens, we attack. No matter what else happens, we have to capture Genevieve."

"Brilliant," said Relka.

No, brilliant would have been running deeper into the tunnels when Genevieve first attacked their lair, and staying there until this whole thing was over. Or minding his own business when Billa dragged Relka into the temple. Really, could anyone but a goblin have managed to pick a fight with *both sides* in a war?

Jig?

What is it? Jig couldn't quite tell whether it was Braf or Shadowstar talking.

Hold on . . . I just got a thorn in my ear.

Braf, then. Jig peered out of the woods, trying to pick Braf out of the group. There he was, clawing at his left ear. How had he managed to . . . on second thought, Jig didn't want to know.

Jig, it would be a lot easier to distract the guards if we weren't tied up.

I'm sure it would. Jig stared at the walls. *It would also be easier if Genevieve ordered her warriors to cook themselves for dinner. But I don't know how to make that happen, do you?*

Well, we're about ready to haul another load of flowers out to the farms, Braf said. *The guards are watching for goblins who try to escape. But they probably wouldn't notice someone who joined us. Then you could use Smudge to burn through some of our ropes while we worked.*

Jig forgot sometimes that Braf only pretended to be stupid. Probably because he did such an amazing job of pretending.

Slowly Jig started to smile. The best part of Braf's plan was that it would save him from having to ride Bastard again. He turned to the other goblins. "Relka, I'm leaving you in charge. You'll know when to attack. Try to be as quiet as you can. The closer you can get before they notice you, the less time they'll have to react. Remember, we have to capture Genevieve alive."

"I won't fail you." Relka saluted with every bit as much sincerity and stiffness as Gratz.

Jig tried not to laugh. She was worried about failing him? He was the one sending goblins into battle against humans.

The loop of rope from Bastard's harness finally slipped down from Jig's ankle. He kicked it to Trok. "Someone needs to fix Bastard's harness again," he said.

"What will you be doing?" Trok asked, his voice gruff with suspicion.

Jig stared at the mounds of flowers. "Trying not to sneeze."

Brown stalks tickled Jig's face as he crept through the field. He squinted, wiping his face as he watched the goblins climbing down from their ladders. Behind him, sunlight turned the snow-covered hills and mountains a fiery orange. He saw no sign of his wolf-riders, which was good. Hopefully, the elf couldn't see them either.

He jogged the rest of the way to the edge of the field, then stopped. Not only could he see the flower petals piled up beside the farmhouse, he could smell them. His vision blurred, and his nose began to drip. He covered the lower part of his face with his cloak. Smudge crept around Jig's neck and perched on his shoulder.

Holding his breath, Jig ran to the pile and lay down behind it, out of sight of the wall. If anyone had seen him, he was dead. Though at least then he wouldn't have to keep inhaling flower perfume. He pulled his hood over his head and tried to breathe as little as possible.

A tiny spider crept out from beneath the flowers, drawn by the warmth of Jig's body.

Smudge pounced. A quick burst of heat cooked the tiny spider, and then Smudge was retreating back to the warmth of Jig's hood, carrying his meal in his forelegs. Jig felt strangely sympathetic for the smaller spider.

His ear twitched as the goblins left the wall, trudging toward the farmhouse. Jig rubbed his eyes and peered around the side of the pile. That elf was watching the goblins closely now. This was the best opportunity for them to run off, so he would have an arrow ready to discourage them. After Jig's escape, he doubted the elf's pride would allow anyone else to take a single suspicious step.

As if the goblins would have cooperated long enough to escape. They had no way to cut the rope around their necks, which meant they would have to run together. Goblins rarely did anything together.

No, that wasn't true. *Billa's* goblins worked together. They marched as one, fought as one, and if Billa and Isa had their way, they would die as one.

The scritch of rakes signaled the arrival of the prisoners. Jig waited until they had all reached the pile, then darted into line behind Braf.

"Jig!" Braf grinned. So did the other goblins, to Jig's surprise.

"Braf told us he was talking to you," said one. He shrugged. "I figured all that human food had rotted his brain."

"So, how are you going to get us out of here?" asked another.

"Wait, before you free us, can you do something about these blisters on my hands?"

"And my feet are killing me!"

"Quiet," Jig snapped. He glanced at the wall. The elf was still watching them. Had he noticed anything? Probably not, since Jig was still arrow-free. He concentrated on looking like another miserable prisoner. Keeping his voice low, he said, "Once I cut everyone free, you're going to distract the guards."

"Us?" The goblins' grins began to fade. "We're supposed to fight armed humans?"

"And an elf," Braf said, ever helpful.

"Only until my . . . my army attacks." Jig braced himself, but the other goblins didn't even smirk. To his shock, they actually sounded reassured.

Jig sniffled and sneezed and did his best to help with the flowers. By the time they started back, he was about ready to cut off his own nose to stop it from dripping.

Jig bit the rope as they walked, clutching it in his fangs so that, from a distance, he might appear to be tied up with the rest. When they reached the wall, he climbed up the ladder after Braf. The goblin tied behind him crowded uncomfortably close, but hopefully he wouldn't have to stay here for long.

The goblin below climbed up another rung. His breath heated Jig's neck. Jig tried not to think about the fact that every one of these goblins carried a knife.

They wouldn't stab him in the back now. Not while they still needed him to cut them free.

After that, well, anyone who turned his back on another goblin deserved what he got.

Jig set Smudge on the rope. This time, unaffected by elf beer, Smudge clung easily to the thin rope. He turned around and stared up at Jig.

"Go on," Jig said. He poked a finger at Smudge's face, driving him back a few steps.

"What's wrong?" asked Braf.

"He's not scared enough."

Jig cringed as soon as the words escaped his mouth. But before he could take them back, Braf shrugged and tried to stab Smudge with his knife.

He missed, but the knife jabbed Jig's cloak in passing. Smudge scurried back toward Jig, the rope smoldering where he walked. But then he jumped onto Jig's throat.

"Well, he's hot enough to burn," Jig said through gritted

teeth. He tried to catch Smudge, but the fire-spider had already darted toward one of his pockets.

Holding the ladder with one hand, he reached into his cloak, trying to figure out which pocket— "Oh, no."

"What's wrong?" asked the goblin below him.

Jig tried to stop the explosive sneeze building in his skull. He failed. The sneeze shook the ladder. He gasped for breath, which only earned him another mouthful of flower smell. He sneezed again, and his hand slipped from the rung.

The next thing he knew, he was on the ground, sandwiched between Braf and the other goblins. From the pained shouts, a few of those goblins had fallen on their knives.

"Hey, what's going on down there?" Atop the wall, the elf gestured with his longbow.

Jig tried to burrow deeper into the pile of goblins, but they were already sorting themselves out.

Where was the rope? He had lost it when he fell. One of his fangs was loose. No doubt the rope had tugged it before snapping out of his mouth. Could the elf see that he wasn't tied up?

"You in the lavender cloak. What are you doing?"

"Purple, not lavender," Jig muttered. One of the humans near the gate was hurrying away, presumably to fetch more guards.

Jig didn't move. He didn't have to. The other goblins had already backed as far from Jig as their ropes would allow.

"Where did you come from?" the elf asked. "How did—"

A rock hit the elf in the middle of the forehead. He grunted, staggered forward, then slowly toppled over the edge of the wall. Apparently Prince Theodore hadn't remembered to strengthen this elf before he and the others left.

Jig turned around. "Thanks, Braf."

Braf picked up another rock. "I've wanted to do that for days!" His vicious grin was a reminder that Braf had been a warrior long before he was a priest.

Jig ran toward the elf. He kicked the bow as far away as he could. The elf wasn't moving, but Jig didn't mean to take any chances. He knelt and grabbed the knife from the elf's belt.

Forged from a single curved piece of gray metal, the knife

was light as air. The unstained wooden handle was warm to the touch. He tested the edge on the elf, then grinned. "Braf, come here!"

Braf hurried toward Jig, dragging goblins behind him. A single swipe with the elf's knife cut Braf free.

Jig managed to free four more goblins before the first of the guards arrived.

"Use your rakes," Jig shouted. "Knives are no good against swords and spears."

A crossbow bolt buried itself in the ground beside Jig. Atop the wall, several more humans leaned over the edge, searching for targets.

Jig started to flee, then changed his mind and ran to the base of the wall. He couldn't get too close without impaling himself on the spikes growing from the trees, but the humans would have to lean out awfully far to shoot him. They were shouting for reinforcement, and he could hear horses thundering out through the gate. "Stay close to the wall," he yelled. "Make them chase us!"

The farther the goblins fled, the longer the gates would stay open. If the wolf-riders were fast enough, they might still manage to get into the city and capture Genevieve.

Jig tried to follow the other goblins, but tripped over the elf. The goblins, being goblins, kept right on going, leaving him to be killed. He started to rise, but there was no way he could catch up with the others.

Jig snagged a broken crossbow bolt from the ground and clenched it in his armpit. Hopefully, anyone who passed would assume he was dead. If they didn't, he would be soon enough.

He turned his head slightly as movement from the woods caught his eye. He had never realized how quickly those wolves could move. Already the lead goblins were halfway to Avery. As far as he could tell, the humans hadn't yet noticed.

Several horses pounded past, the thudding of their hooves a startling contrast to the silence of the wolves. Jig held his breath, but nobody paid him any attention. Humans on foot followed. Some appeared to be guards, while others were ordinary men with axes and spears. No doubt everyone who had resented the intrusion of goblins into their town was taking this opportunity to express their unhappiness.

"It's an ambush!" The voice was familiar, and far closer than Jig preferred. Genevieve stood with her sword drawn, pointing toward the wolves. Jig held his breath and hoped she wouldn't notice him.

An arrow or crossbow bolt arched from the wall, hitting one of the wolves. Wolf and goblin tumbled into the snow, and neither one got up again.

"Everyone back inside," Genevieve shouted. "Forget the prisoners! Archers, concentrate on those wolves!"

Jig clenched his jaw. Genevieve had spotted them too soon. They wouldn't reach her before she got her people back inside the gate. Humans rushed past, their rage turned to panic at the sight of the wolves.

"That goes for you too, Ginny!" Darnak's voice, closer to the gate. "We can pick them off from atop the walls."

So much for Jig and his army. His first attempt at tactics and strategy had fallen apart before his goblins even had the chance to draw their weapons. Genevieve would reach safety, and then they would kill every one of the goblins at their leisure.

Unless someone stopped her.

"I hate this," Jig said as he got up and ran after Genevieve. She moved at a relatively slow pace, all of her attention on the wolves.

Standing at the gate, Darnak was the first to notice Jig. "Princess, 'ware the goblin!"

He was too late and too far away. Genevieve started to turn, and then Jig pounced. He landed on Genevieve's back and clung with one hand. With his other, he pressed his stolen knife to Genevieve's neck.

"Tell your people to stop fighting, Princess!" He had done it! He had captured—

Genevieve grabbed his wrist and twisted the knife away from her neck. Her elbow thudded into Jig's side. The knife fell. Genevieve's free hand snaked up to grab Jig's ear, and then he was flying over her shoulder to slam into the ground.

Genevieve's own knife appeared in her hand. "I know you.

You're the runt who helped steal my horse!" She knelt and placed the tip of her knife on Jig's chest. "Jig, wasn't it?"

Oh, dung.

Darnak ran toward them, his heavy boots clomping through the snow. "Princess, forget the goblin and get inside!"

Jig held his breath, waiting for Genevieve to kill him.

A snarling wall of fur shot over Jig, and Genevieve disappeared.

"Ginny!" Darnak raised his war club overhead and charged.

Ignoring the pounding in his head, Jig rolled onto his side. Genevieve lay pinned beneath Bastard's front paws, her knife lost. Bastard looked from Darnak to the princess and back, as if he couldn't decide whether to eat her before he killed Darnak or after.

"Bastard, down!" Jig yelled. Bastard turned, his head cocked in confusion.

Jig lay back down, fumbling through his pockets. He had only a single troll toe left. He threw it to the wolf. "Sit!"

Bastard obeyed. Genevieve had time for one panicked squeal before disappearing beneath Bastard's backside. Only her legs still protruded, kicking furiously.

"Let her go, Jig." Darnak stopped between Jig and Bastard. "I've no mind to fight you."

Bastard growled again. The other wolf-riders spread around Jig and Darnak, forming a ring of teeth and claws and swords. Darnak didn't seem to notice.

Jig glanced at the wall. Several humans stood with crossbows ready. They were watching Darnak, waiting for his order.

"I can't let you kill her," Darnak said. "Not Ginny."

"I don't want to kill her," said Jig.

"So what is it you're wanting, then?" Darnak lowered his club. "If you've come to free your goblins, so be it. Take them and be gone."

Jig waved the other goblins back. They obeyed, though Trok had to tug Smelly's reins several times to get the wolf to turn away.

He couldn't tell Darnak the truth. Not here. No matter how softly Jig spoke, goblin ears would hear. "If she surrenders, we won't kill anyone else."

Darnak turned in a slow circle. Most of the guards had retreated through the gates, following Genevieve's orders. Darnak was alone, surrounded by goblins. Normally, Jig still would have given Darnak the advantage, but even Darnak couldn't fight all of those wolves.

"You planned this, did you?" Darnak asked.

"Well, this isn't exactly what I planned."

Darnak actually laughed. "Every field commander knows that feeling."

Jig kept his eye on that club. Darnak might not be able to fight everyone, but he could certainly kill Jig before the wolves got him.

"Let Genevieve go." Darnak tossed his war club to the ground in front of Jig. He turned and waved both hands at the men on the wall. "Lower your weapons, men."

Goblins would have shot anyway, out of spite. But the humans obeyed.

"Bastard—" Jig hesitated. Was there a command to make a wolf get up off of a human?

Gratz cleared his throat. "Perhaps a 'Ready' command, sir?"

"Bastard, ready!"

Bastard stood and bared his fangs, head low. Genevieve coughed and crawled out from beneath him. Her normally bored expression was twisted into one of utter horror. When she spotted Jig, her hands clenched into fists. She spat fur and searched the ground for a weapon.

"Easy, lass," Darnak said.

"That wolf," Genevieve gasped. "He *sat on me!*"

Darnak chuckled, then coughed to cover the sound. "It's over."

If only Darnak were right. Jig looked around, confused. "What happened to Relka?"

Trok pointed toward the woods. Jig spotted Relka limping through the snow, her sword dragging from one hand.

"What happened to her?"

"She insisted on riding Bastard in your place. When Bastard saw you were in trouble, he took off like a tunnel cat with his tail on fire. Relka tumbled right off." Trok gave an innocent shrug. "Seems like *someone* missed a few ropes when he mended Bastard's harness."

CHAPTER 10

TYMALOUS AUTUMNSTAR UPENDED THE CLAY mug, finishing off the last few swallows of . . . he wasn't sure, actually. From the taste, it could have been anything from gnomish beer to fermented leopard urine. He belched and ordered another.

"Haven't you had enough, Grandfather?" The middle-aged man behind the bar sounded simultaneously impressed and annoyed. Amber earrings dangled from his ears, marking him as an acolyte of Rionisus Yelloweyes. For the right price, he could arrange all manner of mortal pleasures. So long as he contributed a good portion of his profits to the temple, the emperor's men couldn't touch him.

"Have I had enough?" Autumnstar repeated, adding the empty mug to the collection in front of him. "My followers are long gone. My star has disappeared from the night sky. Most of my companions are dead. Any who survive seem determined to kill me. And not one of you remembers my name. Do you *think I've had enough?"*

"More than enough. I think it's time— "

"My name is Tymalous Autumnstar." He leaned back, settling into one of the enormous pillows that littered the floor like giant colored animal droppings. There were no chairs in Yelloweyes' taverns. The bar was formed from overlapping

slabs of green shale, running along the walls at knee height. "Repeat it back to me, and I'll pay you ten times the value of these drinks. If not, you pour me another and leave the bottle."

The bartender sat down and clapped Autumnstar's back, not unkindly. "Can you hear yourself? Followers and stolen stars? Go home and sleep it off."

Autumnstar smiled. "My name." Though he hadn't raised his voice, the few patrons in the tavern fell silent. "Repeat it."

"Sure thing, grandfather," the bartender said, humoring him. And then he frowned. "Could you say that name again?"

"Tymalous Autumnstar." He waited while the bartender stammered a second time. In the edge of his vision, he saw one person raise his hand in the sign of the alligator, warding off evil magic.

Eventually the bartender turned and reached for a bottle.

As it turned out, conquering a town was the easy part. Controlling it was another matter altogether. Thirty-five goblins and fourteen wolves couldn't hope to hold a town of this size for long. Both Genevieve and Jig knew it. Which would explain that small smile on Genevieve's face as she stared at him.

Or maybe she was simply imagining all of the ways she could kill Jig once she escaped. Even though he had her weapons and she was tied up, Jig still felt as though he were standing before a dragon, waiting to be eaten.

"We need to talk," Jig said.

Genevieve kept on smiling.

"Aye," said Darnak. "Preferably somewhere other than the middle of the street."

Jig agreed completely, but so far, he hadn't managed to go more than three steps without someone accosting him for orders. Speaking of which. . . .

"The wolves are hungry, sir," Gratz said as he ran up to Jig. A few of the wolf-riders came with him. "They made short work of that dead elf, but they're still growling. Are you sure we can't feed them a prisoner? There are so many humans, they won't notice just one. I'll make sure it's a wounded one, and—"

"No," said Jig. "Talk to Braf. The humans must have food stored somewhere. Wait . . . where did you put the wolves, anyway?"

"That big building down the road. The one with the trees with red leaves."

"Blood oaks," said Genevieve. She snickered. "You put those beasts in the mayor's house."

"It was the sturdiest place I could find," said Gratz. "Last I saw, the wolves were ripping up the tapestries for bedding."

"Poor Detwiler," said Genevieve, a nasty edge to her tone. "Serves him right for fleeing like a coward when he heard about Billa's army."

"Well, if he comes back, he'll want to wash out his closet before he uses it again. I'd throw out the bedcovers, too." Gratz glanced at Jig and added, "Smelly's been rolling again."

Trok and a handful of warriors jogged down the road. "We've finished locking up the soldiers," Trok said, shoving past Gratz. He grinned and added, "We put them in the stables. The doors are barred, and we've got goblins watching the windows."

"What about the townspeople?" Jig asked.

"So far they've kept to themselves. Most of them retreated into that big church and locked the doors." Trok glanced at Gratz. "They're afraid we're going to feed them to the wolves."

Good enough. Jig started to turn back to Genevieve and Darnak.

"So when do we burn the stable?" Trok asked. "Relka says if we throw the right kind of wood into the fire, the smoke will flavor the meat, and—"

Jig groaned. "Nobody is allowed to kill anyone!" he shouted. "Any goblin who disobeys will be executed."

Gratz's forehead wrinkled. "Wouldn't whoever carried out the execution be disobeying your order to not kill anyone, then?"

"If we let them live, they're only going to escape," Trok said. "You know how humans are."

"I'll deal with that later," Jig snapped.

"To think that *he* defeated us," Genevieve whispered.

Darnak chuckled. "Your mother would say it's the gods' way of teaching us humility."

"What do we do now, sir?" Gratz asked. "Now that we've taken the town, I mean. This should be enough to earn Billa's forgiveness. Would you like me to send a messenger back—"

"No!" Jig swallowed and tried again. "No." That was better. He sounded more like a goblin again, and less like a panicked bird. "First . . . first I have to interrogate the prisoners."

"Billa would at least let us eat the dwarf," someone said. Jig searched the crowd, but he couldn't identify the speaker.

"We don't have to kill anyone," Trok added. "We could take an arm here, a leg there. Humans can survive that, can't they?"

"We're not eating the prisoners!" Jig said. Not if he wanted to convince Genevieve to listen. He started to say more, then broke off as Relka ran up and whispered in his ear. Jig sighed. "We're not eating any *more* prisoners."

From the looks on their faces, this was not how a goblin leader kept control of his men. They had fought and won, and now Jig was denying them the chance to celebrate. How long could he keep it up before he went from leader to lunch?

"All of the goblin prisoners are hereby recruited into our army!" he announced. That earned even more muttering, which he had expected. None of the former prisoners would know what this meant, and his wolf-riders looked annoyed that these strangers were now a part of their army. But Jig wasn't finished yet.

"Everyone who rode with me today is hereby promoted to—" His mind went blank. What was a good rank? Gratz was a corporal, and he had said Jig was a lieutenant. "To . . . to captain?"

That earned cheers and shouts, so Jig assumed it was a good rank. But Gratz was shaking his head. "You can't promote everyone. That's too many captains. You have to work your way up through the ranks, and—"

"Are you saying you don't want your promotion, Captain Gratz?"

Gratz licked his lips. "Actually, regulations say that a commander away from Billa's army does have the right to issue field promotions."

"Good." Jig grinned. "Captain Trok, you're responsible for keeping the new recruits in line. Nobody eats the prisoners."

Trok scowled. He knew what Jig had done, but he wasn't protesting. Good enough.

Jig wiped his nose and eyes on his sleeve. His head felt like one of Golaka's stuffed rats. Stupid elves and their flowers and trees. So many roads and buildings and alleyways . . . how did humans find their way around this place? He turned to Genevieve and asked, "Where can we go to talk? I mean, so I can interrogate you."

She pointed to a thick grove of ivy-covered trees to the left of the gate. The dark, knifelike leaves of the vines turned the trees purple. "How about there? It's as peaceful a spot as any."

Jig hesitated. "What is it?"

Genevieve's face was hard to read. "A graveyard." She stepped off of the road, into the snow. "I thought you might like to see where I'll be leaving you when this is over."

Gratz drew his sword. "Threatening an officer of Billa's army is grounds for—"

"Shut up and come with me, Gratz. Relka, go fetch Braf and bring him to the grove." Braf and Relka were the only two goblins in Avery who might be able to hear the truth without immediately killing him. Jig walked toward the trees. "Well? Are you coming or not?"

As soon as Jig stepped past the first trees, the air grew warmer. Not warm enough to thaw his nose and fingers, but the snow underfoot changed to mud and earth, and the air was still.

"Every one of these trees was planted in the body of a fallen elf," Genevieve commented, grabbing a branch and swinging back and forth. "Some of them are centuries old."

"The elves feed their dead to the trees?" Relka asked, staring up at the branches.

"Oakbottom would love it," said Gratz.

"Who?" Braf stared, confused.

Jig sat down in the dirt, trying to find a spot where his legs didn't touch the roots of the elf trees.

"Would you like to be buried there?" Genevieve asked. "I'll do it myself, once my father arrives."

"Wait," Jig said. "Your father's army is coming here?"

Genevieve rolled her eyes, triggering flashbacks to Jig's time with her brother. "We know Billa's army is headed this way. If not for this cursed weather, my father would have intercepted her already. But the passes are blocked. He won't arrive for several days. But we will retake Avery, and when we do—"

Jig lowered his voice. "Billa doesn't *want* this town."

Whatever Genevieve had been expecting, that wasn't it. She looked almost offended. "Why wouldn't she want Avery?"

That list could have kept Jig talking for the rest of the night. Instead Jig turned to Darnak. "If you don't help me, everyone is going to die. Humans and goblins both."

"What are you saying, lad?" Darnak asked.

Jig scooted to the left, trying to watch everyone at once. The goblins appeared puzzled. Genevieve looked annoyed.

"So you captured Avery so that we could help you?" she asked.

Darnak shook his head. "Easy, Princess. Jig's no fool. He saved our lives, mine and your brothers', when we fell into a hobgoblin trap."

"No doubt to save his own worthless skin," Genevieve said.

"No doubt," Darnak agreed. "But that doesn't make the saving any less real." He glanced at the other goblins, then back at Jig. Clearly he had noticed Jig's own wariness. "It's not like we'll be any worse off for listening to what he has to say."

"Unless he plans to torture us for information," Genevieve muttered.

Gratz brightened, and he reached into his cloak to grab his regulations. "I wrote down lots of different techniques. Um . . . we don't have a catapult, so that one won't work. We'd need Oakbottom's help for this one." He blinked and looked around. "Does anyone have a horseshoe?"

Jig took a deep breath. He didn't have time for this. "Captain Gratz, give me your sword."

"Yes, sir." Gratz grinned as he handed the weapon to Jig. Genevieve and Darnak tensed, like they were preparing to leap up and wrest the weapon away. Which was what usually happened when goblins took prisoners. Taking prisoners was the easy part. Keeping them was much trickier. Far better to toss them in the cookpot and be done with it. No prisoner had ever escaped after being eaten.

"Your knife too." Jig waited while Gratz obeyed. He took the knife and handed it off to Braf. "Now take off your shirt."

"Huh?" Gratz blinked. "I mean, huh, sir?"

"Your shirt." Jig glanced at the princess. She still reminded him of a tunnel cat about to pounce, but her curiosity had been piqued.

Gratz stripped off his armor, then pulled off his shirt. He shivered in the cold.

Genevieve made a face like she had eaten something sour. "So this is your plan? To overwhelm us with the horror of goblin nudity?" She touched her fingers to her forehead. "I salute you. A devious plan, and one which has certainly sapped my morale."

"Darnak, look at the scar on Gratz's arm," Jig said.

Darnak glanced at Gratz. "If you're asking me to heal him, those cuts are far too old to—"

"I could heal him," Jig snapped. "Just look at the marks. They're magic."

"What do you mean, you could heal him?" Darnak asked.

"Darnak, please." Jig pointed to Gratz's arm.

"I don't understand, sir." Gratz turned around. "Silverfang marked me himself, when he promoted me." He rubbed his arm.

With a shrug, Darnak grabbed Gratz. Caterpillar brows scrunched together. "These almost look like runes." He yanked Gratz closer, nearly dislocating the goblin's shoulder. "Come over here by the light so I can see better."

Jig followed, as did Genevieve.

"The penmanship is pretty sloppy," Darnak muttered. "Could be a coincidence, I suppose. People are always claiming to see mystic runes and holy images in everything from clouds to sticky buns. Now that I think on it, Princess, wasn't it one of your brothers who came running out of the privy, screaming how Tallis Van's visage had appeared in—"

"Is it magic or not?" Genevieve snapped.

"Could be, though how a goblin wound up with magic runes on his arm is beyond me," Darnak said. He pinched the outer edge of the scar, and Gratz yelped. "The skin is cold to the touch."

"He's half-naked in the middle of winter," Genevieve pointed out. "What is this magic supposed to do, anyway?"

"I'm not sure," Jig admitted. "Something bad. Something powerful enough to kill everyone in this grove, including Gratz."

"Some sort of suicide spell?" Darnak asked. "To prevent a captured soldier from giving away vital information? There's an assassin's cult that does something similar, but I wouldn't have thought goblins would have the courage to use such magic."

Gratz was looking more and more confused. He yanked free of Darnak's grip and turned to Jig. "Why are you telling them this, sir? Silverfang was no wizard. This is my scar of rank. All the officers have them."

"How many?" Jig asked.

Gratz tilted his head. "Well, you need at least two officers for every squadron. So at least fifty on the goblin side. Probably even more among the kobolds and orcs."

Jig turned his attention to Genevieve. "Imagine what will happen when your father's army arrives. Billa's forces will already be here, positioned in the valley. His men will drive through our lines, fighting deeper and deeper toward the heart of Billa's army."

"Hey now," Gratz said. "Don't underestimate Billa's forces, sir. We can—"

"Shut up, Gratz," Jig said. "Whatever magic Billa carved into her soldiers, I'm betting she can trigger it all at once. Hundreds of spells, killing men and monsters both."

"Ridiculous," said Darnak. "Such a strategy would still kill more of her own troops than her enemies. She might be victorious, but she'd find herself standing in a field of death."

"That's what she wants." Jig glanced at the other goblins.

Relka was rapt, drinking in Jig's every word. Not that Relka's attention meant much. Jig could have been discussing various colors of toe fungus, and she would have listened just as hard.

Braf was nodding to himself. Shadowstar was probably filling him in. Gratz looked angry. Jig took a cautious step away from him, then said, "That's the only way Billa can summon Noc."

Silence. Eventually Darnak coughed and said, "The death god?"

Jig nodded so hard his spectacles slipped down his nose. "Everything she's done has been part of a plan to summon and kill Noc. The only reason she gathered her army is so she could sacrifice them to—"

"That's a lie!" Gratz shouted. A flare of heat from Smudge gave Jig a moment's warning as Gratz attacked.

He made it a single step before Darnak grabbed him by the back of the trousers, halting him in place. Gratz spun and struck Darnak in the chin.

Darnak frowned. Gratz clutched his fist. And then Darnak tossed Gratz headfirst into one of the trees, hard enough that snow drifted from the branches.

He rubbed his jaw. "Not bad, for a goblin. So what were you saying about Noc, then?"

"When Billa kills everyone, the death will summon Noc to the valley. She's going to use Isa's sword to—"

"Isa?" Genevieve interrupted.

"Goddess of the Winter Winds," Jig said.

"Winter winds, eh?" Darnak twirled a finger through his beard. "That might account for the nasty weather we've had lately. And what would this goddess' name be?"

Jig stared. "Isa. She was one of the Forgotten Gods of the War of Shadows. Like Tymalous Shadowstar."

"Like who?" Darnak asked.

Jig didn't answer. Darnak was the one who had first told him about Shadowstar. What was wrong with him?

"I'm more interested in this so-called goddess Billa means to free," Genevieve said. "What's her name?"

"Isa!" Jig said.

The princess nodded. Darnak cocked his head. "I'm sorry,

but I'm having a bit of trouble here. Could you say that name one more time?"

Braf snickered. "I think you broke them."

You could stay here all day, and they'll never remember, Shadowstar said. *Our names slip from their minds the instant they're spoken. You could carve my name into his skin and he'd still forget.*

Jig shook his head. *Darnak was the one who told me about you, back in the tunnels. How could he—*

I nudged his mind a bit. Shadowstar gave Jig no time to process that revelation and its implications. *It's the curse Noc laid upon us.*

So that nobody could ever remember your names?

Shadowstar chuckled. *Nobody civilized.*

Oh. Civilized. Like humans and dwarves and elves. What a peculiar curse.

Noc was trying to sound haughty and profound, Shadowstar said. *I didn't discover the loophole in his phrasing for centuries. Apparently Isa found it sooner, since she's had time to build up an entire army.*

Jig turned his attention back to his captives. "Call her Winter."

"Winter, eh?" Darnak frowned. "I thought you said her name was. . . . Well, smell my socks. It's right on the tip of my tongue."

"The gods have many names," Jig said loftily. "As you of all people should know."

"True enough," said Darnak. "Why, Earthmaker alone has well over twenty names. To the dwarves up north, he's known as Old Ironballs, from the time when he was bathing in— "

"There will be time for tales of Earthmaker later," Genevieve said quickly. "Darnak, is the goblin telling the truth?"

Darnak touched the silver hammer pendant hanging from his neck. "Truth magic is tricky stuff, but Jig believes what he's saying."

"Could it work?" she asked. "If Billa slaughtered her own army as well as ours, could she summon a death god?"

"Possibly." Darnak clenched a fist around his hammer. "Noc is a cold, distant god, but the gods are bound by laws, just like us. More than us, really. Laws of men can be broken, but the laws of the universe. . . . If Billa the Bloody does this right, Noc will have no choice but to appear. I wouldn't want to be standing nearby, but if Billa has some way to kill a god. . . ."

Braf stopped in the middle of picking his nose. "If Noc is a death god, why doesn't he stop Billa before she can summon him?"

Relka reached over and gently plucked Braf's hand away from his face.

Shadowstar's laughter rang softly in Jig's mind. *It turns out that Noc and his fellow gods consider themselves civilized.*

Jig snorted as he realized what that meant. *Noc cursed himself into forgetting you?*

Really poor phrasing on his part. Of course, it's not like I could run into Ux's fiery domain and kick him in one of his asses. They can *remember us, but it's a distant memory. For mortals, it would be like your very first memories: broken and vague.*

Jig's first memory was of one of the other toddlers sinking sharp baby fangs into his leg. There was nothing vague about that one. "Billa is . . . hidden," he said. He wasn't about to try to explain the curse of the Forgotten Gods to people who wouldn't remember half of what he said.

"Hidden," Genevieve repeated. "From the gods."

"That's right."

"So how exactly do you plan to stop her, goblin?"

"I hadn't really planned that far ahead." Jig plucked Smudge out of his hood and ran a fingertip over the spider's fuzzy back. "Maybe your brother could use the Rod of Creation to transform her into a rock or something."

"Or a fish," Relka suggested.

Genevieve's face had gone still. "Even if I believed you, my father would sooner die than accept the help of a goblin."

"Aye, but your father's not the one charged with protecting this town and these people," Darnak said.

"That's true," said Genevieve. "Which is why he'll send Theodore, just as the goblin suggests. And then he'll disown me."

Darnak chuckled. "Lass, if he didn't disown you for setting his throne on fire, he'll not disown you for this."

Angry shouts from outside the grove made the other goblins jump. Not Jig, though. To be honest, he was a bit surprised it had taken so long.

"What's going on?" Relka asked.

"That would be the humans," Jig said. "The soldiers are breaking out of their prison and wrestling weapons away from the goblin guards. The rest of the humans have probably joined them. They'll be running about with their shovels and axes and pitchforks to overthrow their goblin oppressors."

"We've only been oppressing them for an hour," Braf protested.

Jig ignored him. Every monster knew better than to try to imprison surface-dwellers. They always escaped. That was simply the way these things worked. No sooner had you thrown them in a cave than they were bursting free, carrying dead goblins as shields and slaying everyone in their path with stolen weapons.

"Send word to your father," Jig said. "You don't have to tell him the idea came from a goblin. Isn't saving everyone's lives more important than your father's pride?" He bit his lip. King Wendel was the father of Barius and Ryslind, which made that a very stupid question.

Genevieve didn't answer. The shouts outside were drawing closer.

Braf glanced around. "Should we do something?"

"Probably." Jig leaned against a tree, still holding Smudge. He stiffened and moved away an instant later, remembering what those trees were.

"Darnak said you were their guide," Genevieve said, her voice oddly soft. She looked at Jig in a way that made him want to squirm into the dirt and hide. "You escaped. Just like you escaped from me before. Tell me, did you humiliate my brothers the way you've humiliated me?"

Jig dug his claws into his palms to keep himself from shouting. "I'm trying to save you! And us. Mostly us, really."

"Take it easy, lass," said Darnak. "This is hardly the time for—"

"My father gave Avery to me because it was worthless," said Genevieve. "Too close to the elves. Poor strategic location. An incompetent coward of a mayor. Now, thanks to this goblin, he'll take it away and give it to my equally incompetent brother."

"Theodore and his elves are nothing to laugh at," Darnak said. "I've never understood his fixation with the tree-lovers, but they've turned him into quite the warrior."

"Barius was a warrior," Genevieve said. "As was Ryslind, in his way. Yet they fell to the goblins, just as I did. And both times, this goblin was there." She stared up at the trees. "Tell me, Jig. Did you lead that ambush as well, or did you simply lure my brothers into the trap?"

Distracted by shouting from the streets, Jig didn't realize what she was saying until it was too late. He was too far away to stop Braf from blurting out—

"What trap?" asked Braf, turning to Jig. "I thought you killed them with the rod."

Darnak closed his eyes. Relka walked over and punched Braf in the gut.

"Thanks, Relka," Jig whispered.

"You did, didn't you?" Genevieve shook her head. "I didn't really believe it. How did those idiots let you get your hands on the rod?"

Jig's fingers crept to his sword, but so far, Genevieve wasn't making any hostile moves. She actually looked more amused than anything else. Amused and tired.

"You lied to me, Darnak." Genevieve shook. Her face was wet, and she made no sound, but it almost looked like she was laughing.

Relka glanced over her shoulder. "You definitely broke her."

"No, he didn't." Genevieve hugged her knees to her chest. Darnak moved toward her, but she waved him away. "Everyone talks about how my brothers were killed by goblin warriors," she said, wiping her face. "But *him*? He defeated Barius and Ryslind both? He's the one who turned Darnak into that hideous bird?"

She stared at Jig. "You had the rod, and you gave it back to your chef. Why?"

Jig shrugged. "If I kept it, the other goblins would just kill me and take it. I have a hard enough time holding on to my boots." Slowly Jig released his grip on his sword. He set Smudge on his shoulder. The fire-spider was warm, but not hot enough to burn.

"Why didn't you tell us the truth, Darnak?" Genevieve asked.

Darnak shrugged. "Knowing you lot, you'd have all killed yourselves from shame, and then I'd be out of a job."

Hearing that made Jig wish Darnak *had* told them. It would have saved Jig a great deal of trouble.

Darnak clapped a hand on Genevieve's shoulder. "Your brothers died because they were cruel, shortsighted, petty men. I'd not say as much to your father, but it's the truth. I loved them like my own sons, but had they been mine, I'd have boxed some sense into their skulls."

Braf tapped Jig's shoulder. "Is she going to try to kill you or not?"

"I don't know," said Jig.

"If Barius or Ryslind were here, they'd stab this goblin, slaughter the rest, and charge into battle against Billa," Darnak said. "And if Jig's right, they'd get themselves and everyone else killed in the process."

"My father would—"

"Your father's the one who raised his sons to be jackasses," Darnak interrupted. "What would your mother do, were she here?"

Genevieve's mouth quirked. "You mean before or after she lit your beard on fire for lying to us?"

"I just got this beard back," Darnak said, grabbing his beard in both hands. "Anyone comes near it, and they'll be tasting Earthmaker's wrath."

"She would work to save lives," Genevieve said.

Darnak nodded. "The king left your upbringing to your mother, which means you actually had a chance to learn a little common sense. Whether or not you choose to use it is another matter. But I swore an oath to Earthmaker himself that I'd serve your family, and that means not letting you wipe yourselves out through your own bloody stubbornness." Darnak hesitated, then added, "With all due respect, Your Highness."

"Of course," Genevieve said dryly. She stood and looked at Jig for a long time. "He's so small."

"Begging Your Highness' pardon," Darnak said. "But some of us view our small stature as an asset. There's an advantage to presenting less of a target."

"Darnak, order our people to stand down," Genevieve said. "Tell the soldiers to fall back and wait for orders. Everyone else . . . should leave Avery tonight. They can take the northwest road toward Jasper Valley. If the goblin is right, Billa shouldn't bother to pursue them."

Jig was too stunned that she hadn't killed him yet to really understand what was happening. "Does that mean we can leave too?"

"Oh no, little goblin." Genevieve's grin was enough to make Smudge sear black spots onto the shoulder of Jig's cloak. "You conquered Avery. As ruler of this town, it's your duty to stay and defend it. To the death, if necessary."

CHAPTER 11

THE SLOPED PAVING STONES AROUND THE TEMple were designed to draw people toward the entrance, where a woman in dark red robes stood waiting. The outline of her silver-trimmed mask suggested a skull.

The domed temple was taller than the surrounding buildings. The arched entryway made those who passed through look like children. Bits of metal had been mixed into the mortar between the stones, causing them to sparkle in the sunlight. "He stole that from me," Autumnstar muttered.

A marble path inside descended to a blazing fire in the middle of the building. Black smoke rose from the top of the temple, the deathpath of whoever's funeral they celebrated today. The smoke was said to guide the soul to the star of Noc.

"My *star," Autumnstar muttered. He had stood outside since before the ceremony, watching, trying to decide what to do. Finally, he turned to the priestess. "The masks are a bit much, don't you think?"*

"My mask?" She touched one bony cheek.

"Robes the color of blood. Skull masks." Upon closer inspection, the masks appeared to be painted clay. Heavy, hot, and uncomfortable.

"Our garments are a sign of respect. The masks are a re-

minder that death walks among us." Her voice held the certainty of youth.

The fire turned those within the temple to shadows. Autumnstar could see several acolytes tossing damp straw onto the fire, sending up new plumes of black smoke. Those nearest the fire did their best to smother their coughs. "Do you think Noc would mind if you wore trousers? A loose shawl, maybe? With a nice hat to protect you from the sun."

She drew a deep breath, visibly trying to compose herself, then extended a hand in a well-practiced gesture of welcome. "Most people come to worship in the twilight of their years. Perhaps you've felt the breath of Noc, heard his whispered call? Many choose to donate to the temple, in the hope of turning Noc's eye from their—"

Autumnstar dug a square coin from his purse and pressed it into her palm. "I hate to break it to you, but the breath of Noc always smelled of fish. He spent too much time eating seafood with Ipsep."

Even through the mask, Autumnstar could see the priestess struggling with his words. He grinned and stepped closer to the entrance. Being careful not to cross the threshold, he pointed to a series of carvings on the inside of the arch. "Tell me, who is this poor creature here? The one writhing in agony beneath Noc's lightning."

"Ah, the challenges." The priestess straightened her robes, clearly relieved to be discussing something familiar. "During the War of Shadows, Noc faced fifteen challenges before conquering death itself. Here he throws down one of the demons sent to—"

"War of Shadows?" Autumnstar shook his head in disbelief. "Is that what they're calling it?"

"Named after the demons who attacked from the darkness."

"Demons, eh?" Autumnstar ran his fingers over the carving. "Awfully handsome, for a demon. The nose is a bit off, though. Does anyone know the poor creature's name?"

"When Noc slew the demons, he erased their names from the scrolls of—"

"He slew them all, did he?" Autumnstar grimaced. "Whoever carved this got Noc wrong. His ears stick out like paddles from a boat. You'll see when you look upon him."

Autumnstar stared at the fire. A part of him wanted nothing more than to pass through that archway, to take the single step that would place him within Noc's domain. Revealing himself to Noc would put an end to centuries of weariness and solitude. Not to mention giving the priests and worshipers quite the show. But now that he was here, he couldn't bring himself to take that final step.

Other acolytes lurked around the edge of the temple, rushing to and fro without a sound. Autumnstar leaned in to watch as one collected a donation from a little girl and her mother, then disappeared into the shadows by the wall.

"Be not afraid." In what was clearly meant to be a helpful gesture, one intended to aid an old man in conquering his fear, the priestess took Autumnstar's arm and pulled him toward the arch.

Autumnstar twisted, but his aged body wasn't fast enough. He was already off-balance, and the priestess was strong and determined.

Autumnstar stumbled into Noc's temple.

They found the goblins trapped behind what Jig guessed was a bakery, judging from the foul smell of bread. Jig couldn't see his goblins through the humans, but he could hear their cries, both frightened and defiant.

The closest humans were armed with shovels, pitchforks, axes, and other makeshift weapons. They followed a young man in a leather apron, holding an enormous hammer in each hand.

"It's always the blacksmiths," Genevieve said, shaking her head. "Something about working at the forge all day melts their brains, makes them dream about being heroes."

Darnak stood in the middle of the crowd, bellowing, "Stand down, all of you!"

The blacksmith was the first to respond. "Let us finish them!"

"You want to prove yourself, you're welcome to try that hammer against me." Darnak folded his arms and waited. The others backed away to give him space. "Otherwise, you'd best be obeying the orders of your princess."

The smith lowered his hammer. One of the goblins promptly attacked, and the smith smashed his arm.

"Lower your weapons," Jig yelled, his voice pitifully weak compared to Darnak's. Now that the humans had spread out, he could see a line of soldiers on the other side of the goblins. The blacksmith must have sent someone to free them from the stables.

"Those of you who wish to stay can do so," Genevieve said. The humans fell silent when they realized who was speaking. "You can join me on the walls of Avery, to defend this town against Billa the Bloody and her army. Given the thousands of monsters Billa commands, I will need every last man willing to bear arms to help protect our fair town. You there, you hold your shovel like a warrior. Clearly you would be an asset to—"

The man in question dropped his shovel. "Sorry, Highness. I've got the gout." He limped a few steps and shrugged.

A goblin warrior grinned and started to lunge at him, only to fall squealing when Trok stabbed him in the leg. Trok stepped on the other goblin's ear, pinning him to the ground for good measure. "Your commander said to lower your weapons."

"I don't understand," said the goblin, struggling in vain to pull his ear out from beneath Trok's boot. This was Dimak, one of the wolf-riders. "I thought we were taking this town for Billa! Now we're working with the humans?"

Tell Braf to bring Gratz out. Jig turned to Genevieve and whispered, "If they don't believe me, order your people to kill them."

"You would kill your own warriors?" Genevieve asked.

"Better than letting them kill me."

Gratz shivered and squirmed as Braf and Relka dragged him up the road. He was still bare-chested. His face was bruised and bloody from being thrown into a tree.

Jig took a deep breath. He was fairly sure the goblins from his lair would listen to him, even if they didn't believe what he said. The wolf-riders from Billa's army could be harder to convince. But this was the best chance he was likely to get. "Billa the Bloody plans to betray us."

"Don't listen to that traitorous runt," Gratz yelled. "Follow him, and you'll be every bit as guilty of mutiny as he is! Billa will have your heads on spears. She'll eat your livers, every last one of you!"

"That's a lot of liver," Braf said. He tugged Gratz around.

"And don't call Jig a runt," Relka added, smacking Gratz's head.

Jig pointed to the scar on Gratz's arm. "Those are runes. They're part of a larger spell. Billa means to use magic to kill the goblins. The kobolds too, probably."

"Why would Billa kill her own soldiers?" To Jig's surprise, the question came from one of the humans, not a goblin.

"Because she's an orc, and we're only goblins." Jig's words sounded harsh and bitter, even to his own ears. "Do you really believe Billa cares what happens to us?"

Low, angry muttering spread through the goblins. Angry at Billa, or at Jig? He couldn't tell.

"Billa has led us to one victory after another," Gratz said.

"Her victories," shouted Relka. "And who does she send to take the brunt of those battles?"

"Goblins!"

Jig thought about the marching formation on the road. Any attack would have decimated the front lines—the goblins—leaving most of the orcs well-protected. "I'm tired of being used," Jig said. He hoped Shadowstar was listening too. "Anyone who wants to keep fighting for Billa the Bloody, pick up your weapons and have at it. The rest of you, put away your swords."

Nobody made any move to attack the humans. More importantly, nobody tried to attack Jig.

"They believed you," Genevieve said, her voice quiet. "What did you do to earn such trust from goblins?"

Jig shook his head. "Trust had nothing to do with it. They're outnumbered and surrounded. Goblins will believe just about anything if it keeps them alive."

Jig hunched his shoulders and tried not to look at anyone as he followed Genevieve and Darnak deeper into Avery. Humans glared at him from the windows. Other humans were already hurrying through town, their belongings bundled on their backs or dragging behind on crude sleds.

They came to an intersection of roads and paths, coming together like threads in the middle of a spider's web. Triangular gardens filled the spaces between the roads. A single tree grew in each garden, the branches twining together overhead to provide a bit of shelter from the snow. Even with most of the leaves fallen from the branches, the trees were large enough to provide a makeshift roof.

Unfortunately, the trees were also full of birds. Instead of being crusted with snow, the ground was now layered in fallen leaves and bird droppings.

"Elfhawks," Darnak said. "Back when Avery belonged to the elves, they raised their messenger birds here. When the elves left, the birds remained. They're none too fond of humans, for the most part. A lot like elves, really. Over the years, they've gotten a bit out of control."

The hawks were as blue as the sky. Black markings along the chest and face made them look as though they were wearing tiny masks, or maybe spectacles. As Jig watched, two hawks hopped from the branches and swooped toward a family dragging their sled along the road. They snatched a carelessly bound rabbit from the sled. By the time the family reacted, the hawks had already carried their prize back to the tree.

"They're brilliant hunters," Genevieve said. "But they're even better thieves. They're also the fastest things in the sky, short of a dragon. Smart, too, which means they're the perfect messenger."

Darnak sat down in the middle of the road and pulled out a sheet of parchment. He dug through his pack until he found a pot of ink and a quill. He uncapped the quill and penned a quick message, then handed quill and parchment to Genevieve, who signed it.

Genevieve rolled the message into a tube. She glanced at Jig. "I need a strip of your cloak."

"What?" Jig stepped back.

"The birds are trained by color. Different ribbons signify different destinations. My father's color is purple. Normally we use silk ribbons, but the birds got in through a window and stole them all last week." She pointed toward the top of one tree, where the most colorful nest Jig had ever seen sat amid the branches.

Darnak was already slicing a strip from the bottom of Jig's cloak. He gave it to Genevieve, who tied a tight loop around the parchment, then knotted a larger loop in the rest of the material.

"How do the hawks carry—" Jig began.

Genevieve held out the message so the loop hung down. Instantly, four of the closest hawks dove into the air. Three veered away, and the fourth shot past. His head fit neatly through the loop, ripping the message from Genevieve's grasp.

Jig could feel Smudge burrowing deeper into his pocket

The hawk was already shrinking in the distance, the message hanging from its makeshift necklace.

"He won't stop until he reaches my father," Genevieve said.

"Good," said Jig. Relief made him dizzy. Prince Theodore would bring the rod and stop Billa, Noc would be safe, and Jig would finally be able to go home again.

Genevieve turned to Darnak. "Close the east and west gates. Post double guards on the north and south. I want men on the walls as well."

"What?" Jig stepped back. "I thought Theodore was going to come stop her."

"Billa is too close, lad," said Darnak. He unstrapped his pack and pulled out a long leather tube. "It will be easier to show you with some maps."

With that, he unhooked his cloak and laid it on the road. He then began spreading out sheet after sheet of parchment, weighing the corners with fallen sticks, the ink pot, a dagger, and anything else he could find.

Each map was a work of art. Darnak's own art, judging from the way he puffed up as he unrolled each one. It was a miracle he didn't burst his shirt.

"Hey, that looks like a goblin," Jig said, pointing to a tiny blue figure painted among the mountains. Jig squinted through his spectacles, trying to comprehend the mess of colors and lines and tiny notes, all written in Darnak's painstakingly perfect handwriting.

"Your lair," Genevieve said.

Once the map was secure, Darnak pulled a wooden box from his pack. He opened it to reveal a collection of tiny metal figures. He plucked out a blue-painted goblin, which he set down by a star marked AVERY. He set two armored soldiers beside the blue goblin. The three figures completely blocked out Avery. "Call it about a hundred or so fighters, all told."

"Is this really the best time to be playing with toys?" Jig asked.

Genevieve smirked. Darnak looked indignant. "They're not toys. They're tools. Markers. Very valuable for visualizing tactics and strategy."

Jig picked up the goblin figurine. "Why did you paint blood on his fangs?"

"Give me that." Darnak snatched the goblin back and slammed it into place. "Now the rest of Billa's army followed you up to the lair, right?" He pulled out several thin stone blocks, each with the number 1,000 carved into the top. The sides were painted with various monsters. Darnak stacked four of them by the lair.

"King Wendel and Theodore will be coming from the capital." More blocks went down on the other side of the mountains, along with two more tiny metal figures. One wore a gold-painted crown, the other a silver crown. "He should be about here when he receives our message."

To Jig's eye, the armies looked equally matched, and equally distant from the tiny force at Avery.

"Even in good weather, it would take an extra day for Theodore's men to get through the pass," Darnak said, pointing to the mountains.

"Assuming he believes me." Genevieve stared at the map. "Knowing my father, he'll toss my warning aside as the frightened nonsense of a naive child."

"We'll mine that vein when we come to it," said Darnak. "Jig, do you have any guess when Billa would have left the lair?"

Jig shook his head. "She might not even know I escaped yet."

She knows, said Shadowstar. *Isa knows. They're hunting us even now, Jig. I've done my best to protect you, but she's stronger than I am.*

Jig swallowed and said, "But she's probably on her way."

Darnak tugged his beard. "She'll have an easy march up the road." He moved Billa's blocks toward Avery. His jostling knocked the goblin figurine onto its back. Jig hoped that wasn't an omen. "Billa could be here as soon as tonight."

Darnak moved the silver-crowned figure through the mountains, muttering to himself. "Teddy's fast, no question. And his elves can run over the snow like it's good, solid earth, even if they look like fancy-prance twits when they do it."

"We can hold Avery," Genevieve whispered. "Billa has no heavy siege equipment, from our last reports. Avery's walls are strong. The gates are reinforced with elf magic. We only need to stop her for a day, maybe two."

"You couldn't even stop me." Jig glanced at Genevieve's face, then scooted out of reach of her sword. "What about the southern side of the valley? Won't the elves—"

Genevieve shook her head. "The elves will do nothing unless Billa violates their borders. My mother negotiated a treaty with them years ago. No elf can set foot in human lands without permission."

Jig stared at the map. "So give them permission!"

"First you'd have to convince my father," said Genevieve. "He already thinks they're trying to steal his son."

She set the two human figurines in front of Avery. "We'll post our men on the walls." She reached for the goblin. "Your goblins will need to work on the walls, cutting the last of the steelthorn. We should be able to finish— What is it now?"

"I don't understand." Jig studied the map more closely. "What goblins?"

"Your goblins," Darnak said. "They're not much, but they've done a nice job preparing the wall. We won't be tying them up this time, of course."

"Wait, you think they're still here?" Darnak and Genevieve had been standing right there when Jig told the goblins about Billa's betrayal. They heard him tell everyone what was coming, but they still expected the goblins to be here? "They're probably in the woods by now, running away as fast as they can."

Genevieve frowned at Jig. "*You're* still here."

Jig said nothing. Where could he go to hide from a goddess?

"What about that one?" Darnak asked, pointing up the road. "She didn't flee either."

Jig didn't even bother to look. He knew who it had to be. The one goblin he would prefer had abandoned him.

"I brought this for you," Relka said, handing him a hard, brown roll with bits of burned leaves on top. "They say it's an elf biscuit. I'd have made you a real elf biscuit, but they wouldn't let me near their stoves. Also, we don't have any fresh elf."

Jig took a quick bite of the biscuit, which tasted about how he would have expected. If this was what elves ate, no wonder they were so skinny.

Darnak sighed. "Without the rest of those blue-skinned nuisances, we'll need to spread our men even thinner to watch the walls."

"Where are the goblins going to go?" asked Relka, staring at the map.

Jig, Darnak, and Genevieve all turned to stare.

"They haven't run away yet?" Jig asked.

"Most of them are resting in the stables." Relka shrugged. "I guess they got used to it. The straw is warmer than the caves back home, and—"

"They're *resting*?"

"Well, you didn't order them to do anything else," Relka pointed out.

Jig searched for something to say, but the words wouldn't come. The wolf-riders had spent enough time in Billa's army that they might have lost their sense of self-preservation, but why would the goblins from the lair still be here? Unless their minds had been dulled by eating too many pickles.

"Come on," said Darnak, rolling up his maps. "We'd best

be getting back. Leaving your soldiers with nothing to do is a recipe for bloodshed, as any commander should know."

As if goblins ever needed an excuse for more bloodshed.

Genevieve was the first to spot the smoke. She broke into a run, leaving the others struggling to catch up.

They arrived to find the goblins gathered around a small fire in the middle of the road. Several humans stood nearby, looking . . . nauseated.

Trok turned around when he heard them approaching. "General Jig!"

The other goblins cheered. The humans tensed and reached for their weapons. In the distance, the wolves broke into howls.

"Dimak," Trok snapped. "I thought I ordered you to feed those beasts."

Dimak hunched his shoulders. "Sorry, sir." He grabbed something from the fire, then turned and fled toward the source of the howling.

"What's he going to feed them?" Jig asked. He glanced at the uneaten elf biscuit in his hand, but trying to feed such a thing to wolves would only enrage them further.

"Grappok and I had a bit of trouble deciding who should be in charge, with you and Relka both gone." Trok flexed his arm, and Jig saw two bloody fang marks at the shoulder. "I won."

"I don't understand," Jig said. Despite his nervousness, he found himself edging closer to the cook fire. The air had grown colder, until his fingers seemed to burn from the wind. "Wait, why did you call me general? And what are you still doing here? I thought you'd have left the city by now."

"It seemed only right to promote you," said Trok. "Seeing how this is officially your army, not Billa's."

"We're going to teach Billa the Bloody a lesson about goblins," somebody said. The others cheered.

"But she has thousands of monsters," Jig said. "She'll slaughter every one of you."

"See?" said the same goblin. "General Jig, he tells it like it is! No lies from this one."

They cheered yet again, idiots to the last.

Jig grabbed Trok's arm and dragged him away from the others. "This is madness." Jig kept his voice low, pitched so nobody else would overhear. "You've seen Billa's army. I can understand humans making a suicidal stand. They're stupid that way. But we're goblins. We survive by running away when we're outnumbered. Or when we're evenly matched. Or anytime we don't have a twenty-to-one advantage, really."

"You stayed," Trok said.

"I'm stupid too. And I can't run away, because Isa would—"

"You're not stupid," Trok said, shaking his head. "You're a whiny, puny, irritating little runt. But you're not stupid."

"Oh, no?" Jig pointed in the general direction of the gate. "Weren't you there when I led everyone against Genevieve's soldiers? A handful of wolf-riders against an entire city?"

"Shut up, sir." Trok glanced at the other goblins. "You think we haven't been talking about you? How any one of us could break you with our bare hands? How Porak used to dangle you over the garbage crack by your legs, or slip bat guano into your drink when you weren't looking?"

"Wait. Porak did what?" And here Jig hadn't thought anything could ruin his appetite more than that elf biscuit.

"I was there the day you came back from slaying Straum," said Trok. "I remember how those adventurers followed you. You led them away from the lair and beat them all by yourself. I remember how you helped everyone fight off those pixies and their ogre slaves, too. I was one of the goblins you sent to help the hobgoblins fight the ogres. I figured we were all dead, and I'd rather die quickly, smashed by an ogre's club, than face the nastiness those pixies were dealing out. Blasted bugs and their magic. But you, you went down there and killed every last one of them."

He grabbed the biscuit from Jig's hand and tossed it into the snow. "You're the one who helped me and Relka escape from this lot," he said, pointing toward Genevieve. "You got us away and found Billa. Then, when she turned out to be a conniving, backstabbing orc, you escaped again. You killed Silverfang, and then you came back here and took an entire town away from the humans."

"They took it back," Jig said.

"Doesn't matter." Trok spat. "I'm not as smart as you, and I know it. But I like to fight. We all do. We're warriors, Jig. It's what we do. And we like to win. That doesn't happen too often when you're a goblin."

That was true enough.

"You're a pathetic excuse for a warrior, hardly worth killing, even for the food. But you're clever. If you're staying, so are we. Even if we lose, it should be a great fight." Trok grinned. "Besides, if you stay here all alone and get yourself killed, who's going to make me chief when Grell dies?"

He dug his claws into Jig's arm and dragged him back toward the fire. "Now hurry up and get your share of Grappok."

Jig shivered in the darkness of the stables. He pulled his blanket tighter over his head, tucking his ears in for warmth. Even if he hadn't been too scared to sleep, the snoring of the other goblins would have kept him awake. How many hours had he lain here staring into the darkness and trying not to think about what was to come? He was almost grateful when Darnak opened the door and whispered, "Jig? Genevieve's wanting to see you."

Jig's teeth chattered. "It's about Billa, isn't it? She's coming."

Darnak was little more than a silhouette, but Jig could see him tilting his head to one side like a bird. "Now, how would you be knowing that?"

"The cold. It's getting worse."

"Aye. Something unnatural in that wind." Darnak waited while Jig gathered his blanket and retrieved Smudge from the tiny web he had woven at the base of the wall.

Outside, lanterns flickered by the gate. Even as Jig watched, one of the lanterns died, extinguished by the wind. "Where are we going?"

Darnak pointed.

"Oh, no." Whereas the outer wall was covered in thorns and a few scattered flowers, the interior was formed of a different kind of tree, covered in smooth, slippery bark. But the tree Darnak indicated was wider than the rest, with some sort of lichen growing on it. The brown disks were spaced evenly to the ground, each one large enough for a man's foot.

"Don't worry about it," Darnak said. He planted a boot on the lowest shelf of lichen, grabbed a higher one, and pulled himself up. "Took me weeks to get used to this place." He shook his head. "Sticking a dwarf up a tree is a violation of nature, like expecting fish to fly and build nests."

Fear dried Jig's mouth and throat. Though that was better than his nose, which was frozen on the inside from the cold. If the lichen could support Darnak's weight, with all his armor and everything he carried in that pack, surely it would hold Jig.

Unless Darnak's weight weakened it. Jig looked back at the stables. "Are you sure Genevieve doesn't want to come down here instead?"

"Don't make me carry you," said Darnak.

Gritting his teeth, Jig grabbed the lowest lichen and hauled himself after the dwarf.

The wind was even stronger atop the wall than it was below. Jig would have been blown clear off if Darnak hadn't seized his wrist.

Genevieve stood nearby, blankets and furs protecting her from the cold. There were no lights.

"Did you enjoy your rest, goblin?" Genevieve asked.

"No." Jig clung to Darnak's hand as he took his first step. The platform was nothing but sticks and leaves, woven tightly together. There were enough gaps to allow the snow to slip through, but the branches were still wet and slippery. They creaked and moved under his weight. "I miss my lair."

Darnak chuckled.

The top of the wall was wide enough for two people to stand side by side, though it required both people to stand closer to the edges than Jig liked. Waist-high railings ran along either side of the platform. Jig crouched against the inner railing. The branches and leaves were woven tightly enough to block the worst of the wind. A thick vine ran horizontally along the top, a railing of sorts. Jig gripped it with both hands and tried not to move.

His ears perked. He could just make out the sound of drums in the distance.

"Are the gates sealed?" Genevieve asked.

Darnak nodded. "We didn't have time to finish preparing the steelthorn, but the lower portion is clear. Nobody's going to be after climbing these walls. The trees might not be as strong as dwarf stone, but they'll do."

Genevieve glanced back at Jig. "Billa's army is coming."

"He knows," said Darnak.

Jig took a deep breath, then lurched across the platform to the outer railing. Staring out at Billa's army, he wondered if it would be better to simply fling himself off the wall and be done with it.

Torches and lanterns burned like tiny fireflies, stretching back along the road as far as Jig could see. Was it his imagination, or had Billa's army grown since Jig fled? Maybe it just seemed larger compared to the paltry numbers here inside the town walls. His ears twitched with each beat of the war drums.

Genevieve pressed a wooden tube to her eye. "Goblins march in the front of the column. She has kobolds scouting ahead and to either side."

"What is that?" Jig asked, pointing to the tube.

"The lenses provide a closer view of our foe," said Genevieve. She barely even blinked as she stared out at the approaching army. "Goblin, how will your men react in the face of this threat? Do you trust them to obey orders and do their duty?"

Jig stared at her. "They're goblins, remember?"

Genevieve sighed. "Billa seems to have no problem controlling her troops. Perhaps the goblins need a stronger leader."

Jig agreed completely, but the disdain in her voice made his hands clench. "Do you know how Billa raised such a large army, Princess?" Jig asked. "She told them . . . she told *us* that if we joined her, we'd never have to worry about people like you or your brothers again."

Genevieve started to say something, then bit her lip and

turned back toward the approaching monsters. "We'll have to hold them for at least a day. Darnak, get every available archer to the walls. Nobody attacks until I give the order. Our arrows and quarrels are too limited. Goblin, rouse your men. Position them along the wall in pairs."

Jig didn't move. "And what will you do with us when this is over?"

"I'll figure it out then. Assuming any of us survive." She raised the scope to her eye again. "None of the reports said anything about winged creatures in Billa's army."

Jig rubbed his spectacles on his cloak. Given the condition of his cloak, that wasn't much of an improvement. But by the time he hooked the frames back over his ears, he could make out dark shapes against the moonlit clouds.

"Dragons?" Darnak guessed. Jig edged closer to the ladder.

"The wings are the wrong shape," Genevieve said. "And the tails are more birdlike than serpentine."

"They're coming from the north," Darnak said. "If Billa sent a force through the mountains, our scouts would have known."

"Those are elfhawks," Genevieve said softly. The hand holding the scope dropped to her side. "They carry men upon their backs."

"Theodore."

Genevieve's lips twisted into a sour expression. "He must have used the rod on those birds."

As bad as it had been riding Bastard, the mere idea of riding a giant elfhawk made Jig dizzy. He grabbed the railing for balance as he watched the birds approach. He could see the shapes of the riders, each one bent low against bird's neck.

The first rider drew a sword that burned with orange fire. Why didn't goblins ever get the magical weapons? The rider raised his weapon in salute as he circled toward the wall. Prince Theodore, Jig guessed. He couldn't discern the rider's features, but he doubted the prince's pride would allow anyone else to lead.

" 'Ware the goblin!" Theodore shouted. His hawk swooped toward the wall.

No, not toward the wall. Toward Jig. Talons the size of Jig's foot reached out.

Jig screamed and leaped away, barely avoiding the prince's magical sword.

Unfortunately, Jig's desperate leap took him to the gap in the railing. He tried to twist around, to catch the lichen ladder and stop his fall.

He missed.

CHAPTER 12

THE PRIEST IN THE MIDDLE OF THE TEMPLE missed a beat as Tymalous Autumnstar fell. He lay sprawled on the worn tile floor, waiting for Noc's response. Would it be the lightning again, or had Noc developed new skills since their last battle? Autumnstar was betting on the lightning. Noc had never been the most creative of the gods. Hopefully Noc wouldn't incinerate too many of his followers in the process.

"Are you hurt?" The young priestess knelt beside him and touched his arm. She had stripped off her mask, and her brown face revealed both her youth and her terror. No doubt there were rules against assaulting the elderly. "Forgive me. I only wanted to help you face your fear."

Autumnstar peeked around the temple as the chanting resumed. Noc was *present, as much as any god ever was in a temple. But Autumnstar couldn't sense any change in the death god's attention.*

"Isn't that why you came?" the priestess asked. "To prepare yourself for death?"

Autumnstar pushed himself to his feet. "I came because . . . because I'm tired." Tired of being alone. Tired of living as a mortal. Tired of being afraid.

Giddiness knotted his chest. For him to step into this temple was like walking up to Noc and punching him in the nose. Yet Autumnstar sensed nothing. "Noc doesn't see me."

"All come to Noc's domain," the priestess said, her voice stern. "Your time is written on the scrolls."

"Noc erased my name from the scrolls," Autumnstar whispered, remembering what the priestess had said before. He started to laugh. "He cursed us, sentenced us to be forgotten . . . and now he doesn't remember me."

People turned to stare. The priest in the center of the temple stopped again. The priestess tried to take Autumnstar's arm and pull him back outside, but he tugged free.

"I'm right here, Noc!" Centuries of hiding, all for nothing. He was invisible. Tears and laughter mixed, until he was gasping for breath.

The shadows shifted as the acolytes ran toward him. Autumnstar hadn't even noticed them lurking in the dark corners. He raced down the aisle, past rows of stunned worshipers, until he reached the center of the temple. He dodged the high priest and climbed onto the edge of the fire pit. "Tymalous Autumnstar lives!"

The fire flared higher, even as the air chilled.

"Whoops." Autumnstar bit his lip. Perhaps that last defiant shout had been a little too much. He gingerly lowered himself from the pit and allowed the acolytes to grab his arms.

Halfway out of the temple, he turned to the priestess. "This body has served me for more than a hundred years. Take care of it. The coins in my pouch should make up for any disturbance I've caused."

The acolytes caught his body as it fell, but Tymalous Autumnstar was already gone. He would have to remember not to flaunt his survival. Noc's curse hadn't blinded him completely. Like Noc's own acolytes, Tymalous Autumnstar would have to keep to the shadows.

The sound of bells was muted as he stepped through the broken doorway of his ruined temple. Tymalous Autumnstar—Tymalous Shadowstar*—was home!*

Jig's lcft nostril was on firc.

The first thing he saw when he opened his eyes was

Smudge's fuzzy backside. Four of the spider's legs clung to the edges of Jig's spectacles. Smudge reached out again, searing Jig's nose with one of his forelegs.

"Stop that," Jig mumbled. Smudge backed away. Had he been trying to rouse Jig, or simply checking to see if he was safe to eat?

"Jig!"

He tilted his head to see Darnak and Genevieve climbing down the wall. Prince Theodore was already on the ground.

Why was it that every time Jig faced a prince, he ended up flat on his back? He started to sit up, then gasped. His knee felt like someone had smashed it with a rock.

"Easy, lad," Darnak said. "You're lucky you didn't land on your head! A fall like that can be fatal."

"Goblins have thick skulls," Jig said. He reached down to touch his knee. All he learned was that his shoulder was in equally bad shape. He lay back, grabbing his shoulder with his other hand and drawing on Shadowstar's healing magic. His jaw clenched. The pain of rebuilding a joint was bad enough, but couldn't Shadowstar do something about the popping sounds coming from his shoulder?

"Stand aside, Darnak," Theodore demanded, waving that burning sword in the air. He strode toward Jig, and his eyes widened. "By the First Oak, there are more!"

Jig's ear swiveled, tracking the footsteps of approaching goblins. "What did you do to Jig?" Relka yelled.

"Everyone calm down," Darnak shouted. His voice made Jig think of a mountain cracking. Darnak hurried to put himself between Jig and the prince. "They're not your enemy, Theodore."

"They're goblins," Theodore said.

"They're deserters from Billa's army." Genevieve moved to stand beside Darnak. "Jig risked his life to bring warning of Billa's plans. Plans that your scouts failed to uncover."

"And you believed them?"

Genevieve hesitated only briefly. "Darnak's magic showed him to be telling the truth. And Billa *is* coming to Avery. Really, Theodore. Haven't you more important things to do than wag your elven blade at our allies?"

Jig tested his arm, wondering when he had been promoted to *ally*.

"But they're goblins," Theodore said again, as if Genevieve had somehow overlooked the blue skin and big ears and fangs.

"Forgive the interruption, Prince, but you're looking a bit changed from the last time we spoke," said Darnak.

Jig blinked. He hadn't noticed before. Atop the wall, he had been more concerned with avoiding the bird's claws and the prince's sword. He squinted through his snow-flecked spectacles.

"The Rod of Creation is a gift," Theodore said. He pointed to the top of the wall, where huge elfhawks perched. "How else could I have reached Avery in time to save you all from Billa's wrath?"

"And the ears?" Darnak asked.

Theodore tossed his hair—which was far longer and lighter than before—back over his shoulder. He ran his fingertips over the sharp lines of his pointed ears and smiled. "The rod has helped me to become my true self."

"Eighteen years I helped raise the whelp," Darnak muttered. "Changed his diapers, forged his first sword, even called upon the power of Earthmaker to clear up those pimples. *Four years* of pimples. And he turns himself into an *elf*."

The prince ignored him and patted his belt. The tip of a wooden stick protruded from a purple scabbard. He sheathed his sword on his opposite hip. "I strengthened our armor, our weapons, even the skin of our bodies."

Theodore combed his fingers through his flowing hair. "Even elven hair is superior to our own. I've flown nonstop since we received your message, and look! Nary a tangle!" He grimaced and said, "Though it does tend to flick in one's eyes. I'll have to braid it before we attack. So tell me, dear Sister, would you like me to do something about that nose of yours?"

"I have a better idea," Genevieve said, perfectly calm. "Why don't you take that rod and—"

"All that power, and you couldn't even give yourself a decent beard," Darnak snapped.

Before Theodore could respond, Genevieve asked, "What

did the king say about all this? Our father isn't terribly fond of magic these days. Or of elves, for that matter."

Theodore flushed. "I haven't exactly told him. But, Sister, look at me! I'm stronger than before. Faster." He drew the Rod of Creation and raised it overhead. Jig tried to scoot away, but the effort made his knee feel like tiny dwarves were pounding it with great big hammers. "The goblins had all this within their grasp. They too could have transformed themselves into something great, had they only known what it was they had."

"But then we wouldn't have been goblins," Jig said.

Theodore turned and stared. Jig got the impression he had completely forgotten about the goblin's presence. "Such shortsightedness will be the downfall of your race, goblin."

He whistled, and two of the giant elfhawks swooped down to land beside him. The rest of Theodore's elves simply jumped from the wall. They landed easily in the snow, showing no sign of strain or worry about a drop that had nearly killed Jig. Stupid elves.

The two elfhawks were heavily laden with weapons and armor. One of the elves began distributing wooden shields and helmets to the rest.

"Billa is a bloody fool." Theodore grinned at his own wit. "My elves and I shall soar down and destroy her. When our father's army arrives, they will find Billa's forces in chaos."

"There's a mite bit more to this battle than meets the eye, lad," said Darnak. "Billa has magic of her own, and—"

"Billa is an orc," Theodore said. "Barely better than a goblin."

"She's an orc who has raised an army," Genevieve said. "An orc who has marched freely through our land, terrorizing our people and—"

"You worry too much, Sister." Theodore grinned. "You did well to summon me, but now your worries are over. Run along and prepare a suitable meal for me and my friends. A victory breakfast, to celebrate our triumph. Something hot." He slapped his stomach.

Genevieve's fingers twitched over her sword, but she stopped herself. "Father charged me with the protection of Avery. I should—"

"And a marvelous job you've done," Theodore said. "Your people are fled, and your town is infested with goblins. Father will be thrilled."

Genevieve's face turned a deeper shade of red. Darnak placed a hand on her forearm.

"Have your men gather food for our hawks as well," Theodore said, turning away. "Perhaps you could feed the goblins to them and solve two problems at once."

Genevieve waited until they were out of earshot, then turned to Relka. "Someone said you were some sort of chef."

Relka nodded.

"And what meal would you recommend for a prince, goblin?"

Relka rubbed her chin. "My favorite is charred rat with klak sauce, garnished in black-edge mushrooms. The tails are especially good."

Genevieve's lips tightened into a smile. "What are you waiting for? Prince Theodore has requested a meal. I imagine you'll find plenty of rats raiding the granary."

Jig and the other goblins stood by the edge of the road, watching Theodore and his elves mount their hawks. Many of the hawks had perched on the rooftops, forcing their elves to scale the buildings. Not that this slowed the elves down at all.

"If they fail, I've got dibs on the dark meat," Trok said softly.

Jig ignored him. Theodore had the Rod of Creation. All he had to do was reach Billa and transform her into something harmless. Billa was the only one who could set off the spells carved into her goblin and kobold officers. With her dead. . . .

His shoulders slumped. With Billa dead, the humans would have an easy time of it. Wendel's army would arrive in a day or so to drive the monsters back into the caves and tunnels. For those who survived, everything would return to the way it had been.

Billa had the support of a goddess, but she was no goddess herself. Jig had seen the power of that rod. Prince Theodore wouldn't have to come within range of Billa's magical sword. He could swoop down, transforming Billa and her friends at will, or at least until he got tired. The rod could take a lot out of whoever wielded it.

As far as Jig knew, Billa had no flying monsters. Arrows and stones would do little against Theodore's magically hardened armor. Jig still remembered the way ordinary weapons had bounced away from that elf scout in the woods.

So why was Jig still here when he should be getting as far from Avery as he could?

He couldn't concentrate. He flattened his ears against the sound of the wolves. Ever since the hawks had swooped in, the blasted things hadn't stopped yowling. And then there was Billa's army. Thousands of monsters, all shouting and jeering and beating their armor as they approached Avery.

It's part of their strategy. They're trying to unnerve you, Shadowstar said.

"It's working!" Jig pulled up the hood of his cloak. The wind promptly blew it from his head. Yanking it back, Jig turned to scowl at the hawks. Theodore had climbed onto his hawk, tucking his legs beneath the wings and waving to the human soldiers. He made an impressive figure, illuminated by the rising sun.

"Circle a few times to gain some height," Darnak was saying. "The higher you fly, the faster your dive. Don't spend a lot of time hovering before you attack. Hovering takes too much energy, and you don't want to tire the hawks. And—"

The hawk spread its wings and shrieked loudly enough to overpower even the wolves. It took a few quick steps, then slammed its wings, launching itself into the air. The other hawks followed, hopping from the rooftops and causing goblins to scream and dive out of the way.

Darnak hurried after them, still shouting bird advice as he climbed the wall.

Jig continued to pace as he watched the hawks fly away. Something squished beneath his foot. His boot slid out from beneath him, and he waved his arms to keep from falling. His knee twinged with pain. Apparently he hadn't done a perfect job of healing the joint.

He glanced down to see another of the "gifts" Theodore's elfhawks had deposited throughout Avery. Giant birds meant giant droppings. Jig groaned and hobbled over to scrape the boot on a nearby house.

"It could be worse," said Relka as she hurried toward him. She pointed to one of the goblins who had thrown himself to the ground.

Jig grimaced. "Somebody get him a rag. And weren't you supposed to be preparing a meal for Prince Theodore?"

"I was," Relka said. "That's why I came." She held out a blackened rat. "I thought you might like a taste."

Jig snatched the rat from her hand. The meat was still warm, and he gobbled it down, surprised at how hungry he was. When had he last eaten? He forced himself to slow down, ripping off a bit of tail for Smudge.

Smudge flattened himself to Jig's cloak, clinging with six legs while he reached for the meat with his forelegs. Jig turned his back to the wind, blocking the worst of it. Even with all those extra legs, the wind could still rip Smudge from his shoulder and fling the poor fire-spider—

"Oh, no." Jig's stomach knotted. He shoved both Smudge and the rat into a pocket and spun toward the wall. The elf-hawks were already gone. Humans cheered them on from atop the wall.

"What's wrong?" Relka asked.

Jig ran toward the wall. "Darnak! Genevieve! You have to stop the prince!" The wind swept his words away.

Cursing, Jig scrambled up the lichen shelves of the wall as fast as he could. The walkway was crowded with humans, all staring out at Billa's army. Jig shoved past them until he spotted Darnak. The dwarf stood atop his backpack, still watching the hawks. Genevieve was with him, her face stone. She held one of those elven scopes to her eye, watching Theodore's progress.

"Darnak, you have to call them back!" Jig shouted.

Genevieve snorted. "Even if he were close enough to hear, my brothers have never been fond of others telling them what to do. And I certainly can't imagine Theodore would take orders from a goblin."

Jig squeezed his way between them and stood up on his toes. The front edge of Billa's army had reached the distant fields. Goblins and kobolds spread to either side. Some loosed arrows and threw spears, but their attacks had no effect on Theodore's hawks. A few of the humans cheered as those same missiles fell back down upon the monsters' heads.

Several of the elves drew swords that glowed like Theodore's. Jig had half expected them to start firing arrows back at the monsters, but apparently not even an elf could aim a longbow and steer a giant hawk at the same time.

"Billa's going to kill your brother if he doesn't turn back," said Jig.

Suddenly Jig had everyone's attention.

"What did you say?" asked Genevieve.

"It's Isa," Jig said.

Darnak frowned. "Who?"

Jig wanted to punch him. "The goddess Billa worships. *Goddess of the Winter Winds.*"

Darnak was the first to understand. He spun, nearly falling off his backpack. "Every last man into the field *now*! We have to—"

"Too late," Genevieve said.

Jig clung to the railing with both hands as a burst of frigid air fought to throw him down. In the valley, the elfhawks were flung to the ground as if they had been struck by a giant. They landed near the front of the orc lines. Some of the elves leaped down to fight. Others tried to urge their hawks into the air.

Beside Jig, Darnak leaned into the wind, his arms quivering as though he too were fighting to fly. Jig squatted to retrieve Genevieve's scope.

"It doesn't work," he complained.

Darnak reached over, swapped ends, and pressed the scope back into Jig's hand, all without looking away from the hawks.

This time when Jig looked through the scope, it was as if he stood on one of the farmhouse roofs, close enough to reach over and touch Theodore and his battered elves. That they had survived the crash at all was amazing, but none looked ready for battle.

The orcs cleared a circle as Billa strode toward them. The

closest elves drew their glowing swords. The hammering of the wind robbed the elves of their usual grace. Billa, on the other hand, seemed untouched by the wind, which was completely unfair. And her sword had no trouble cutting through the elves' magical armor.

"Use the rod, you daft boy," Darnak shouted. "Use the bloody rod, damn you!"

As if he could hear Darnak's voice, Theodore pulled the Rod of Creation from its sheath and pointed it at Billa.

Billa swung her sword.

"Earthmaker preserve us," Darnak whispered.

The Rod of Creation was the most powerful magical artifact Jig had ever seen. Which admittedly wasn't saying a lot. But Jig had seen what the rod could do. Created by Ellnorein, one of the greatest wizards in history, the rod had the power to create dragons and destroy mountains. For thousands of years, songs had praised its godlike magic.

Billa's sword sheared it in two as if it were nothing more than a rotted stick. A second blow, and Theodore fell. Billa stepped back, allowing her orcs to swarm over Theodore and his elves. Blue feathers as tall as a man swirled in the wind. A few of the elfhawks fought their way free, wings pounding hard enough to knock their attackers back.

"Theodore," Genevieve whispered.

Billa turned toward the wall, seeming to look right at Jig.

Jig yelped and flung the scope away. He started to shove his way back to the ladder, but a gust of wind drove him to his knees.

He pressed his back to the railing for protection. Those nearest Jig crouched low, battered by the wind. Most of them were still pressed against the other railing, watching the prince's failed attack. So Jig was the first to notice as the snow swirled together, flakes clinging to one another until the shape before him began to resemble a tall, fluffy woman.

Get out of there, Jig.

How? Jig asked. *It's between me and the ladder!*

That's not an it, said Shadowstar. *That's Isa.*

Jig had already recognized her from the vision Shadowstar had shared. The snow packed tighter and tighter, forming ever-finer details. Isa's exposed skin turned clear as any stream. Icy fingers flexed and stretched. She appeared to wear a tight gown of snow, far too low-cut for this weather. The snow clung to her bulky form like silk.

"Hello, Jig." She glanced at Darnak, then turned her head to take in the rest of the humans gathered on the wall. Flakes of snow fell from her hair, reminding him a little of Braf. Braf had developed a nasty scalp condition lately, and even Shadowstar's magic was having trouble curing him.

Jig scooted to the side and tugged Darnak's jacket.

"Not now," Darnak said softly. The wind whipped his beard as he stared out at the field. His face was wet with tears.

Jig grabbed his beard and tugged hard.

"Eh? What's—" Darnak spun. "What in the name of Earthmaker's singed beard is that?"

Isa spread her arms, and the temperature dropped still further, until Jig had to close his mouth to keep his spit from freezing. He flattened his ears, then reached into his cloak to check on Smudge. The fire-spider was curled into a tight, fuzzy ball, and he wasn't moving. Jig cupped him in both hands and held him close to his chest.

"I am Isa of the Winter Winds. I am the Frost Maiden. It was I who first summoned the snows of the north, and it was I who banished them again at the end of winter."

"What did she say her name was?" Genevieve asked.

Isa sighed, sending a puff of frost from her mouth. "Never mind."

She's crazy, Shadowstar whispered. *Even a limited manifestation like this uses a great deal of magic. She could draw Noc's attention before she's ready.*

"I wanted to give you and your god one more chance to join me." Isa smiled at Jig, though the effect of those gleaming icy teeth was less than reassuring. She crouched beside Jig. "Billa would prefer I freeze the blood in your veins and bring you to her as a frozen dessert, naturally."

Darnak thrust Jig to the floor and gripped his war club with both hands. "For Theodore!" he shouted, and swung his club at Isa's head.

The metal-studded wood shattered. Isa reached up to brush a bit of snow and wood from her shoulder.

An arrow ricocheted from Isa's neck. She waved her hand, and the wind flung three of Genevieve's archers from the wall.

Between the fallen humans and Darnak's broken club, only an idiot would continue to attack. Jig turned expectantly to Genevieve. But the princess was smarter than her brothers. Though she had her sword drawn, she didn't try to use it. With her other hand, she gripped the inner railing. "I am Genevieve Wendelson, Princess of Adenkar. I presume you're the goddess who murdered my brother."

"Billa murdered your brother," Isa said. "I just gave her the weapon to do it."

Isa turned her back on the princess and bent toward Jig. Her breath frosted the lenses of his spectacles. "Wouldn't you like to be on the winning side this time, Tymalous? You could be a true god once again. Your name would be sung throughout the world."

Until the rest of the gods showed up to destroy us, Shadowstar muttered. He sounded wistful.

"Whatever our differences, we belong together, Tymalous. Don't tell me you haven't thought about me." She reached up to stroke Jig's ear.

Jig didn't know whether Isa was going to kill him or kiss him. Nor did he know which frightened him more. Kissing a goddess of ice . . . he remembered what had happened after the first snowfall, a month or so back. One of the goblins had dared Braf to lick a steel shield that had been left out in the cold. Even after Shadowstar healed his tongue, Braf had talked with a lisp for several days. Jig had no desire to freeze his lips to a goddess.

Actually it's kind of fun, said Shadowstar. *The trick is to—*

I don't want to know!

Jig cracked his fingers to check on Smudge. The fire-spider cringed at the cold, tightening his mandibles. Faint flares sparked from his bristles as he struggled to warm himself. The poor spider couldn't take much more of this. Neither could Jig, for that matter.

Genevieve's cloak dropped over Isa's head. "Darnak, now!"

Darnak leaped to help the princess. They yanked Genevieve's cloak, trying to drag Isa over the edge of the wall.

It was a good plan. Being formed of ice and snow, Isa should have slid easily across the platform. Maybe her feet had frozen to the branches beneath. Or maybe she was just heavy. Either way, she didn't budge. One hand ripped the cloak away and tossed it to the wind. The other shot out, grasping Genevieve by the throat.

Even as she choked Genevieve, she continued to talk to Jig in that gentle, terrifying voice. "You could be God of the Autumn Star once again, bringing comfort and peace to your worshipers. It's what you are." She stood, hauling Genevieve into the air. Darnak picked up Genevieve's dropped sword and slammed it into Isa's arm, with no effect.

Tymalous Shadowstar sighed. *She doesn't miss me. She* needs *me. Once Noc is dead and his curse ended, the other gods will remember her. She can't hope to fight them all. Her only chance is to plead for peace. My power could influence things in her favor.*

To Jig, he almost sounded disappointed.

"Well?" Isa asked.

Tell her . . . Shadowstar paused. *Tell her that what I am requires me to protect my son. Just as what she is requires her to be a heartless, frigid—*

"He says he'll think about it," Jig said.

Fog snorted from her nostrils. "Indeed." Faster than Jig could follow, she grabbed him by the throat. Smudge grew hot enough to singe Jig's palms. "Perhaps I can encourage him to make up his mind."

Darnak slammed his shoulder into Isa's side. She scowled, but fortunately for Darnak, she was out of arms. Otherwise she probably would have tossed him off the wall.

"Sorry about this, Smudge," Jig whispered. While Isa's attention was on Darnak, Jig closed his hand around Smudge and reached out until the fire-spider was directly over Isa's head.

In that instant, as Smudge figured out what Jig was about

to do, the fire-spider burned hotter than Jig had ever known. With a hiss of pain, Jig dropped Smudge into Isa's hair.

Steam shot from the top of Isa's head. Her eyes widened. She tossed Jig and Genevieve aside. She reached up to swat her hair, but Smudge had already melted down into her head. Isa's eyes crossed as Smudge sank behind her face. Jig could see Smudge scrambling to climb out, but all he accomplished was to widen the icy pit in Isa's head.

"Cursed goblins," Isa said. Water dripped from the corners of her mouth. "Billa will—"

At that point, Smudge reached the neck, and Isa collapsed. The wind died down, and the biting chill began to ease a bit.

Is she dead? Jig asked.

It takes a lot more than a frightened fire-spider to kill a god.

Isa toppled over, nearly smashing Darnak's toes. Darnak was helping Genevieve to her feet. Jig crouched over Isa's body, watching as Smudge dug his way out of the back of her neck. Still steaming, he scurried up Jig's leg, where he sank his mandibles right through Jig's trousers, biting his thigh.

Jig clenched his teeth and tried not to scream.

With that, Smudge crawled back into his pocket on the inside of Jig's cloak.

When Jig climbed down from the wall, he found a group of goblins waiting for him. Trok, Relka, and Braf stood near the front.

" 'Ware the ice!" Darnak shouted from the wall.

Jig leaped away as Darnak and one of the humans tossed the remains of Isa's manifestation onto the street. She shattered like glass, scattering shards of ice in all directions.

"What was that?" Trok asked.

"Nothing," Jig said. The last thing he wanted to do was admit that Billa the Bloody really had a goddess on her side.

Sure, but so do you, Shadowstar said.

Can you control the weather and manifest in Billa's army and start throwing her people around like toys?

Braf shifted his spear to his left hand. With his right, he picked up a glistening ice finger and sucked on the end. "Is it all over? What did the prince turn Billa into?"

A broken shriek made Jig jump. One of the elfhawks flew overhead, blood trailing from its chest. Another perched atop the wall, where an elf was climbing down from its back. Falling from its back, really.

The first hawk flew straight for the huge trees in the center of town. Jig could hear squawks of protest from the smaller birds.

"He didn't turn her into anything, did he?" Relka asked.

"Billa killed the prince," Genevieve said as she descended the ladder. She rubbed her throat, then turned to stare at Jig. "How does an orc come to command such power?"

"She's the champion of a god," Jig said. "A mean, scary god." He watched as a stray dog darted from the side of the road to snatch a chunk of ice. The dog trotted away, crunching merrily on a bare foot.

"You fought Billa before." Genevieve tilted her head as she studied Jig. Red marks circled her neck where Isa had squeezed. "And now you've stopped . . . what was her name again? No matter. You saved my life."

"I saved *my* life," Jig said. "Smudge did the hard part."

Genevieve actually smiled at that. "Perhaps I should send your spider out to fight Billa."

From the wall, Darnak leaned out to yell, "Princess! We've got a hawk from your father and a kobold from Billa."

Genevieve waved him back. "Goblin, you—"

"Jig," Relka said. "His name is Jig Dragonslayer."

Genevieve's jaw tightened, but she nodded. "Jig. I didn't believe your companion when he said you killed my brothers. Now I do."

Jig stepped back, one hand moving toward his dagger. Genevieve's smile was a dangerous one. Her expression reminded him of Grell. Grell always smiled like that right before she gave Jig a particularly nasty duty.

"My father has decreed that all goblins be killed on sight," Genevieve said. "For murdering Prince Barius and Prince Ryslind, you are to be drawn and quartered."

"Drawn and quartered?" Jig glanced at the other goblins, who looked as confused as he felt. A few had drawn weapons, sensing the threat even if they didn't understand it. Shadowstar whispered briefly in Jig's mind, explaining the phrase in graphic detail. Jig's legs went soft, and he sat down in the snow. "Oh."

"I will spare your life," Genevieve continued. "If you slay Billa the Bloody for me."

Relka laughed. "You think Jig Dragonslayer fears your threats, human?"

Jig said nothing. Genevieve wasn't as frightening as Billa or Isa, but Genevieve was much closer. He was fairly certain his goblins could overpower her. But what would that accomplish, other than to turn the rest of the humans against him? Billa and Isa were still out there, and Isa was probably quite annoyed at Jig for melting her head.

"Why me?" Jig asked.

"Billa and her goddess want you." Genevieve nudged a bit of Isa with her foot. "You could get close to her."

"Sure I could," Jig agreed. "Billa has to get close to me so she can feed my eyes to the wolves!"

Tell her to spare all of the goblins, Shadowstar said.

What?

Tell her you'll face Billa, but only if she convinces her father to let your people live in peace.

What about letting me live? Jig asked. *In peace or otherwise?*

I'll be with you.

Why does that not make me feel any better?

Still, Jig wasn't exactly in a position to argue. "If I fight Billa, you humans have to leave us alone. Forever."

"That choice is my father's, not mine," Genevieve said. "But I'll do what I can."

Jig blinked. Where was the angry pride, the humiliation at having to deal with a lowly goblin? She had agreed far too easily. "And I want a new sword," Jig said.

"Done."

"And maybe something to eat that isn't pickled?"

Genevieve's lip quirked. "Anything else, gob—?" She glanced at Relka. "Jig."

"I'll think about it and let you know."

"Very well." Genevieve turned toward the wall. "I'll return shortly. I look forward to hearing your plan." With that, she hurried back to the ladder and climbed up to talk to Darnak.

Jig stood and tested his legs. The knees still felt a bit wobbly, and his thigh throbbed where Smudge had bitten him, but he didn't collapse.

"So now what?" asked Braf.

Jig rubbed his thigh. "That's a good question." All he wanted was to run away, but there was no place to run. The gates were likely to be guarded, and if he climbed over the walls, he would have to deal with that blasted steelthorn on the way down. Not to mention that Billa would never stop hunting him. Between Isa sniffing after Shadowstar and the kobolds following Jig's trail, there was no place he could go where he would be safe.

That's not quite true, Shadowstar said.

What do you mean?

It's time for you to become a champion of Tymalous Shadowstar.

Wait, you mean you were serious? Jig sat back down. *You really want me to fight Billa?*

You fought her before, and you won.

I ran away before she could kill me, Jig said. *It's not the same thing. And I don't think she's going to let me shove another torch in her face.*

I'll help you.

How? By making me stupid again? Jig shook his head. *No, thanks. I can get myself killed without your help.*

I didn't make you stupid, Shadowstar said. *I made you unafraid.*

Same thing, Jig muttered.

Very well, Jig. I hoped it wouldn't come to this.

Come to what?

Shadowstar's silence was far more unnerving than anything the god might have said.

"He's mumbling to himself again," Trok said.

The only response came from Braf, who asked, "Are you sure?"

"Yes, I'm sure," Trok said. "Can't you see his lips moving?"

"Oh. Well, if you say so." Braf blinked, and it slowly occurred to Jig that he hadn't actually been talking to Trok. His bleary eyes focused on Jig. "I'm sorry about this, Jig."

"Sorry about what?"

A burst of heat from Smudge was Jig's only warning. And then Braf slammed the butt of his spear into Jig's head.

CHAPTER 13

EVEN TO A GOD, THE UNIVERSE WAS A PLACE OF mystery. The realm of the gods was an extension of the gods themselves, a universe built on grudging consensus, constantly evolving with the whims of its inhabitants.

Tymalous Shadowstar stared up at Noc's star, burning black in the sky. The dark flames swallowed the light . . . even light from within. Certainly Noc would never think to search inside his own star. Even if he did, the odds of discovering the second, smaller star burning inside his own were slim at best.

Shadowstar's temple was equally well-hidden, built within the black realm of Xapthlux, the Sleeping God. Shadowstar would have to leave before Xapthlux awakened, but since that wasn't ordained to happen for another fifty thousand years, he didn't let it worry him too much.

He didn't worry about anything, really. Over the centuries, his power began to return. From time to time he reached out, spreading what little comfort he could without drawing the attention of the gods. Beyond that, he mostly slept. And cleaned. Xapthlux's domain was a dusty place.

He wasn't sure what had awakened him this time. Looking around, he sighed and plucked a rag from the nothingness.

A distant voice tore through his chest like a sword. The bells of his garments betrayed his nerves as he tried to calm himself.

The call had been so weak. A stammering, lisping excuse for a prayer, but after so many years of silence. . . .

"I think it says Tymalous Autumnstar." The speaker was a spindly blue creature with crooked fangs—a goblin, from the look of him. He sat in a hot cave, squinting at a yellowed tome. "It's hard to read. That human bled all over the cover."

"That book was supposed to go to the chief." A much larger goblin waddled over, brandishing a huge stirring spoon. Her other hand clutched her swollen belly. "Though why he can't use lichen when he visits the privy is beyond me."

The first goblin peered out of the cave. "He'll need half the book, the way he's gobbling down that adventurer." He laughed. "Golaka, look at how—"

"Get up!" Golaka knocked the book from his hand. "Bad enough you did this to me," she said, touching her belly. "If you're going to stay here, you're going to help! Otherwise you can go back to the distillery and play in your muck."

"I carved that adventurer and served him to the warriors, didn't I? Besides, I want to know how they made it all the way to Straum's lair and survived. Can you imagine if we had magic like that? This one would have escaped too if he hadn't succumbed to those lizard-fish stings in his leg. Imagine it, Golaka. If we could get their weapons and their magic, we could drive the hobgoblins back. We could fight off the adventurers. We could—"

Golaka dropped her spoon. "Did you say lizard-fish stings?" She grabbed the smaller goblin by the arms and hauled him upright.

"It looked like lizard-fish stings. A row of bloody holes that wouldn't scab over. But I'm not sure. I don't see too well, remember?"

"You mean you fed poisoned meat to the chief and his warriors!" Golaka shouted.

The smaller goblin paled. Outside, someone shouted, "Where is that miserable runt Jarik? His food's making the chief sick!"

Eyes wide, Jarik twisted free of Golaka's grip. He spun, reaching for a bread knife that lay next to a jug. Then he changed his mind and grabbed the jug instead.

"Klak beer for everyone!" he shouted. As the first angry goblin burst into the cave, Jarik shoved the jug into his hands. "Golaka's finest beer for our finest warriors!"

It was a good attempt, and it almost worked. By the time the lizard-fish poison killed the chief, most of the warriors were too drunk to care.

Unfortunately, drunken goblins were violent goblins, and when poor Jarik ran out of klak beer, the results weren't pretty.

Shadowstar sighed as he watched Golaka carry the blood-stained book to the privy. "Tymalous Autumnstar, huh?" she muttered. "Stupid name."

Shadowstar sat down on the edge of his temple, his legs dangling in nothingness.

They remembered him!

These weak, violent, uncivilized *goblins could remember his name. Not that most of them seemed the type to care about the gods. Who could blame them? Autumnstar couldn't think of a single god who would lower himself to take goblins as followers.*

And the one goblin who might have cared, who might have actually made a connection with Tymalous Shadowstar, was now roasting over Golaka's kitchen fires.

But perhaps his child. . . .

"Nice to see you again, Jig Dragonslayer."

Stars filled the sky. The air was dry and dusty, though at least Jig had escaped the eye-watering smell of all thosc leaves and flowers. He sat up and touched his face. His spectacles were gone, but he could see perfectly well. The only time that had ever happened was in the temple of Tymalous Shadowstar. His *real* temple, not the little cave back at the goblin lair.

Jig turned toward the voice.

The god stood leaning against a broken wall, his arms folded over his chest. He was unchanged from the last time Jig had seen him. Still short. Still skinny. The wispy silver hair was still thin on the top. He could have passed for human, aside from those freakish eyes. Where eyeballs should have been, Shadowstar's face held two spots of perfect blackness, each one broken by the twinkling of a miniature star.

Jig backed away. "You told Braf to kill me!"

Shadowstar gave a sheepish shrug. "I told him to knock you unconscious. That's not as easy as it sounds, you know. And . . . well, he's Braf. Don't worry, Darnak is doing his best to fix your skull. If it's any consolation, Braf broke his spear in the process."

Oddly, that did make Jig feel a little better. "Does it give you a headache?" he asked. "Having stars for eyes, I mean."

Shadowstar shrugged. "I can see in the dark, which is fun." He wore the same loose-fitting clothes of black silk, with tiny silver bells down the sleeves and trousers. Those bells jingled as he rubbed his eyes. "Though my vision is still a bit fuzzy from seeing the Rod of Creation explode. I may have to borrow your spectacles."

Jig frowned. "It didn't explode."

"That much pent-up magical energy, released with no spells to contain it? It was like watching a tiny universe form and implode in a single heartbeat. Just be grateful you don't have a god's sight," Shadowstar said, chuckling.

"What did it look like?"

"Mostly purple." Shadowstar rubbed his eyes. "Jig, there are things you have to understand. Starting with the reason the Forgotten Gods went to war all those years ago. Haven't you ever asked yourself why I fought alongside Isa and the others?"

Jig shook his head.

"The nameless twins, the two gods of the beginning, they're all but mindless. Vastly powerful, but dumb as gob— Well, they're dumb."

"So you went to war because they're stupid?" If Jig followed that sort of thinking, he'd have to declare war on half the lair.

"Some did," Shadowstar said. "They thought such power should be given to those wise enough to use it."

"Themselves, you mean?"

"Of course." Shadowstar picked up a fist-size chunk of stone and turned it over in his hands. "Isa was one such goddess."

"Why did you help her?" Jig asked, honestly curious. Also,

the longer he kept Shadowstar talking, the longer he could stay here. Broken and depressing as Shadowstar's temple was, it was the one place Jig felt safe. Plus he kind of liked being able to see without his spectacles.

"To understand that, you need to understand how the universe works." He ran one hand over his head, flipping silver hair back from his face. "The universe . . . it has layers."

"Like ogres?" Jig asked.

Shadowstar stopped with his mouth half open. "Excuse me?"

"After we fought the ogres last year, we had lots and lots of leftovers. Golaka made up a dessert that has a layer of ogre meat, mushroom gravy, rat liver, and another layer of ogre. You sprinkle blue fungus flakes on the top, to give it that sweet aftertaste." His mouth watered at the memory.

"The universe is *not* like ogres," Shadowstar said, his voice stern. He set the stone on the floor between them and brushed his fingers over the rough surface. "You mortals see only the upper layer. It's rare that any of you notice the depth between you. Rarer still for one to reach down and touch those depths."

"So you're saying we're like the blue fungus on the top of Golaka's dessert?" Jig asked.

Starburst pupils rolled skyward. "Sure, why not. And we gods can be the mushrooms. The important thing is to realize that you fungus flakes—" He grinned. "I think I like this metaphor."

"Do you have anything to eat here?" Jig asked, glancing around.

"Nothing that would be safe for you. Sorry."

Jig checked his cloak, but the pockets were empty. Smudge hadn't accompanied him, not that Jig had expected him to. But the leftover rat he had saved was gone too.

"The point is, you fungus flakes live in a universe supported by mushrooms. I mean, by gods. You may not see what happens in the realm of the gods, but what we do affects your world."

"Like if the pan is lopsided and all of the mushrooms slide to one side?" Jig licked his lips. "Then the top layer of meat sinks, and somebody gets stuck eating all mushrooms and no meat."

"If you don't stop obsessing about food, I'm going to throw you into the void," Shadowstar said, his voice light.

Jig swallowed, then nodded.

"The two gods of the beginning have fought one another since the universe began. Imagine living things struggling at the base of your dessert. Think of what that would eventually do to the surface."

Jig nodded. "Sometimes Golaka adds—"

"I don't want to know!" Shadowstar said quickly. "The point is, their battle will one day consume the universe. Your world, ours, all of it will be destroyed." The light in his eyes faded slightly. "I thought . . . I believed we could stop them. That we could save the universe from destruction."

Jig glanced at the sky. "How long do you think it will be before—"

"Nobody knows. The universe is vast and deep. It could survive for millions of years. Billions, even."

"Good." Jig still kept one eye on the stars, though.

"What I learned is that I'm really bad at being a warrior." Shadowstar gave a sheepish shrug. "I'm the God of the Autumn Star. I help maintain the progress of time, the changing of seasons. I ease the terror of death, and I create the opportunity for new life. I'm a minor god, Jig, but I'm no fighter." He stood and folded his arms. "That's why I need you to be my champion."

Jig gestured at himself. "Have you forgotten I'm a goblin?"

"But you're mortal. I'm a god. What I was is what I am. What I am is what I will forever be."

"Huh?"

Shadowstar sighed. "Mortals can change. Gods can't. I can help you move beyond your fear, Jig. You have the opportunity to become more than just a goblin."

Jig shook his head. "I don't want to be more than a goblin."

"Your people need you," Shadowstar said. "You have the chance to protect them, both from Billa and from the humans.

Stop Billa and you save them all. The goblins, my son, everyone."

Jig shook his head. The Rod of Creation was destroyed. If Theodore hadn't been able to stop Billa, how was Jig supposed to?

Shadowstar grabbed Jig by the arms and lifted him into the air. For one terrifying moment, Jig thought he was about to be flung out into the darkness beyond Shadowstar's temple. But the god set Jig down ever so gently by the archway. "Isa is stronger than me, but I have strength of my own, Jig Dragonslayer. For thousands of years I rested, gathering my strength. Rebuilding myself. Rebuilding this place."

Jig glanced at the edge of the floor, where the stone seemed on the verge of crumbling into nothingness.

"I never claimed to be a very good builder," Shadowstar admitted. "But what strength I have is yours. I can't fight Billa for you, but I can protect you."

Jig's ears perked up. He liked the sound of that. But Shadowstar had already said Isa was stronger. "What if I say no?"

"You're mortal," Shadowstar said. "Your fate is yours to choose."

"Good. I choose—"

"Though I'm not sure you'd appreciate the consequences." Shadowstar patted Jig's shoulder and stepped away, dragging his fingers over the broken walls and humming "The Song of Jig."

"What consequences?" Jig asked. He knew he shouldn't ask, but he couldn't help it.

"Reject me, and you reject all I've given you." Shadowstar still didn't look at him. "It would be as though you had never felt my power. Including all of that nice healing magic."

Slowly, Jig realized what Shadowstar was saying. Without that magic, any number of his wounds would have killed him. The worst was when another goblin stabbed him in the back last year, during their battle with the fairies. And that didn't begin to count all of the scrapes and cuts and burns—

"You're lying," Jig said. "You just told me you're a god of comfort and protection. You can't kill your own follower!"

Shadowstar shrugged, ringing the bells on his sleeves. "You wouldn't be my follower anymore, would you?"

Jig shook his head. "But you still can't—"

"Maybe not." Shadowstar turned around, and Jig could see him struggling to keep from laughing. His lower lip twitched, and his eyes literally sparkled. "But that's one of the wonderful things about you goblins. You're cowards. I don't mean that as an insult. Cowardice is a far better survival trait than heroism. But it means even if you're almost certain I'm bluffing, you're still not going to risk it."

Jig stared at him for a long time. "Please don't do this to me." Strange, to be so afraid of losing his fear. But fear kept goblins alive.

"I'm sorry, Jig." Shadowstar's amusement had vanished. He actually sounded like he meant it. He reached out to press one hand over Jig's chest. "Your people need you. I need you."

Jig tried to sit up and immediately regretted it. Shadowstar might have taken away his fear, but Jig would have preferred to lose his nausea. His head throbbed like a drum, and when he touched his scalp, his hand came away bloody.

"He's alive!" That was Trok, his voice sending new cracks through Jig's skull. Other goblins formed a loose circle in the road.

"Of course he's alive. Earthmaker's not failed me yet." Darnak's meaty hand pushed Jig flat. "This was a stubborn wound, but I'll have him up and about in no time."

"Good." That was Princess Genevieve, standing beside Trok and looking annoyed.

Jig squinted at the sky. Hadn't the sun been on the other side of town? And why was Darnak the one healing him? "Where's Braf?"

"I'll be healing him next, so we can ask him a few questions," Darnak said.

Healing Braf? Jig tried a second time to push himself up, but Darnak held him in place. Jig might as well have tried to move a mountain. He settled for twisting his head and squinting. His spectacles were covered in snow and blood, but he could still make out Braf sprawled in the snow a short distance away. "What happened?"

Trok started to snicker. "Relka nearly killed him. Big, bad Braf, knocked senseless by a little kitchen drudge."

"You should have let me kill that coward!" Relka shouted. Several other goblins held her by the arms as she kicked and struggled. Her face was wet. Had she fallen in the snow while she was fighting with Braf? And why had she attacked Braf in the first place?

You goblins are truly dense, you know that?

Fortunately, Jig had long ago learned to ignore his god's snider comments.

"There we go," Darnak said. The pounding in Jig's head eased. Darnak hauled him upright. "Any idea what led him to try to split your skull like that? I'm thinking he's one of Billa's men, myself."

"You mean a spy? Braf?" Jig grinned despite his pain. "He was just confused, that's all. It happens a lot. Relka, you don't have to kill him."

"But he—" She squirmed and wiped her nose. She was calmer now, but the other goblins still kept firm hold of her upper arms. Twisting to face Darnak, she said, "He's really going to be all right?"

"Good as new," Darnak said. He patted Jig's head hard enough to knock him down again. "So tell me, Jig, when have you been finding the time to get yourself a new cloak?"

"A new what?" Jig tugged his cloak out so he could see. The material was still torn and stained, with the same ugly vines along the edges. Only there was a new design over the chest, right where Shadowstar had touched him. A starburst and lightning bolt were embroidered in black and silver thread.

"Looks a bit like her pendant," Darnak said, cocking a thumb at Relka.

"It does, doesn't it?" Jig ran his fingers over the design.

I like her work, Shadowstar said.

Jig turned to Genevieve. "Why are you here? I thought you were busy reading that message from your father."

"That was six hours ago," she said.

Darnak tugged his beard. "Fixing your skull was easy enough, but waking you was a bit of a trick."

Six hours. That would explain the sun's movement. Jig shivered. The air always felt colder in the evening.

Genevieve rubbed her forehead and said, "There's been a lot of snowfall in the mountains. My father's army won't arrive until late tomorrow. When he does . . . he means to attack."

"What?" The revelation didn't frighten him one bit, thanks to Shadowstar's power. But the loss of Jig's fear meant there was plenty of room for other emotions. Dismay, anger, even a bit of despair. "Didn't you tell him about Billa's plan? That's what she wants!"

"He didn't believe me," Genevieve said. "He's ordered me to secure Avery and do nothing until he arrives. I've sent a second hawk to my mother, hoping she'll be able to talk some sense into him. But even if she could reach him in time, I doubt he'd listen."

"Wendel's a stubborn one, even for a king. He'll hear nothing of any plan that allows Billa's army to live." Darnak shook his head. "I'm sorry, Jig. I never should have told him of Theodore's death. He might have listened had I not—"

"My father? Listen?" Genevieve laughed. "You've been a bird too long, Darnak. He's never listened to me, and your counsel has been less than welcome since you returned bearing news of Ryslind and Barius."

"What about Billa?" Jig asked. "You said one of her kobolds had come with a message. Why would she do that?"

"She offered to let me and my soldiers go free," Genevieve said. She took a deep breath. "All I have to do is turn you over to her."

That made sense. Why waste her own soldiers coming after Jig when she could get the humans to do it for her? Jig checked to see if he was armed. He still had the knife he had taken from that elf, but Shadowstar hadn't given him any divine weapons.

I'm not that good at weapons, Shadowstar said.

Naturally. Embroidery he could do. Weapons, no. Resting one hand on his knife, Jig asked, "What did you tell her?"

Genevieve raised an eyebrow and touched her own sword, as if daring him to attack her. "That you were a sneaky, conniving little coward who had managed to escape. I asked that she give us until tomorrow night to capture you, at which time I would hand you over."

"And Billa agreed to this?"

"Aye." Darnak had wound his hands into his beard, presumably for warmth. It made him look like he was wearing snarly black mittens. "From what you said, Billa doesn't care about Avery. She'd rather preserve her forces for King Wendel. She'll want as much death as possible. Taking the town would cost her a few hundred soldiers, and every monster she loses is one less death to attract Noc's attention."

Before Jig could ask anything more, Relka shouted, "Watch out!"

Jig spun. A single goblin leaped from behind one of the houses and ran toward him. Jig squinted and lowered his head, trying to find a clear spot on his lenses. Through the smeared blood and snow, he thought he recognized Gratz.

"Traitor!" Gratz shouted. He pointed a crossbow at Jig as he ran. "Regulations require me to arrest you for treason. You are ordered to—" Gratz slipped on a patch of ice, and the crossbow discharged.

The impact as the bolt thudded into Jig's shoulder wasn't as bad as, say, being struck by a dragon. But it was enough to knock Jig backward several steps. He waved his arms to keep from falling.

Gratz was already drawing a sword from his belt. Where had he gotten all of these weapons? He was supposed to be locked up, not—

"Why am I still standing?" Jig whispered. He looked down. The crossbow bolt lay in the snow a few steps away. His cloak was unmarked, though Jig could feel a bruise forming on his chest . . . right below the symbol Shadowstar had created on his cloak.

I do make good armor, though, Shadowstar said smugly.

That won't do me much good if he stabs me in the face. Jig drew his knife and started toward Gratz. Maybe Gratz would stumble again and impale himself, but Jig doubted it. Gratz was a trained soldier. As trained as goblins got, at any rate.

Jig glanced around. The other goblins were already making wagers and grinning with anticipation, as goblins did. But these were supposed to be soldiers too. *Jig's* soldiers.

He sheathed his knife and stopped walking. "Why are you all standing about, you lazy bastards?"

He did his best to mimic Silverfang's disgusted anger. From the shocked expressions on the goblins' faces, it worked. Before they could respond, Jig pointed at Gratz and yelled, "Get him!"

The goblins roared as they charged. Soldier or not, Gratz was still a goblin at heart. He threw down his sword and fled.

Jig smiled. He kind of liked being a general.

The dining hall in the barracks had the largest tables, which made them the ideal choice for spreading out all Darnak's maps. Unfortunately, the barracks was also one of the original elf buildings, and the table was in dire need of a trimming. Budding twigs sprouted from the edges, tickling Jig's wrists as he leaned in to study the maps. He wiped his eyes and tried not to sneeze.

Candles burned in holders formed of living vines. The too-sweet smell of perfumed beeswax did nothing to help Jig's nose.

Darnak had placed the bulk of his figurines on one side of Avery to represent Billa's army. Others were scattered through the woods to either side. "Billa's sent scouts through the woods, probably to make sure you don't try to flee."

He set another group of blocks at the top of the valley. "Once Wendel arrives, he'll send his cavalry down, hoping to ride right over Billa's monsters."

A third line marked the elves on the opposite side of the valley. "If we could somehow drive Billa's forces across the border, the elves would help—"

"Billa's monsters won't retreat," Jig said. "It's probably against regulations."

"It doesn't matter," said Genevieve. "We have to stop Billa before my father arrives."

"Wendel ordered you to sit tight," Darnak said.

"I know." She picked up several of the figurines from within Avery, setting them in a line outside the walls.

Jig studied the map. Darnak didn't appear to have a figurine for Billa, so he had used a large gray pebble instead. That pebble was currently guarded by several thousand monsters, most represented by larger metal blocks.

Jig frowned and looked closer. The figurines Genevieve had moved outside the wall were all goblins, though there was something odd about the frontmost one. He picked it up and peered more closely. Darnak had painted amethyst spectacles onto the goblin's face.

"You promised to kill Billa for me, remember?" asked Genevieve.

"Your goblins will pretend you're a prisoner." Darnak split a path through Billa's forces, then moved the goblins through. "Once you're within range, you charge. It's a desperate plan, but you'll have the advantage of surprise. Theodore's mistake was to attack in plain sight. Might as well have sent a note telling Billa exactly when he'd be dropping by."

"*One* of his mistakes, anyway," Genevieve said.

"He was overconfident, and it killed him." Darnak's voice was tight.

Jig studied the map. Overconfidence wouldn't be a problem for goblins. He moved the figurines into the center of the army, near the pebble that was Billa. "Say we somehow manage to catch Billa by surprise and kill her. What happens then?"

Darnak fiddled with his quill. Genevieve stared at the map.

Jig reached out and pushed the blocks of Billa's army until they surrounded the goblins. "We're all going to die."

"I told you this one was clever," Darnak said quietly.

This was the point where any reasonable goblin would have fled for his miserable life. Yet Jig didn't move.

"The orcs will be closest," he said. "They'll probably be the ones to kill us. And then they'll turn toward Avery."

"Not necessarily," said Genevieve. "For those who do, the walls will hold until my father arrives."

"We're hoping there will be some squabbling," Darnak added. "The death of their leader will be an enormous blow to morale. Not to mention they'll have to sort out who's in charge, with Billa gone."

Jig tried to imagine the chaos. Whenever a goblin chief died, the smarter goblins made themselves scarce for the next few days, emerging to see who had survived long enough to seize control. Given the size of Billa's army, Jig wouldn't want to be anywhere near that power struggle. Though that likely wouldn't be a problem, since he would be dead before it began.

Genevieve plucked the blocks from Darnak's map. "With luck, they'll give up and go home. Can you imagine my father's face? Him and his army arriving to an empty field." Her expression was wistful. She frowned as she studied the map. "What if Jig's goblins betray him? If he's smart enough to realize what could happen, maybe they will, too. They'll rejoin Billa to save themselves."

"Not Relka," Darnak said. "I get the sense that one would walk into a dragon's maw for him. A few of the others, too. As for the rest, well, Jig's already told them what Billa has in mind."

"We should do this soon." Jig turned the tiny, spectacled goblin over in his hand. He wondered if Darnak could sculpt a little spider to go with it. "Before they have time to think about it."

"Sunrise would be best," Genevieve said. "The sun rises almost directly behind Avery. It will work in your favor."

Jig nodded. There were a few things he needed to take care of, if he was to lead the goblins into battle. He stood to go.

"Jig, wait." Genevieve hesitated, then reached down to grab a long, cloth-wrapped bundle from the floor. "I promised you a sword."

Jig took the bundle. It was lighter than he had expected.

"This was my brother's short sword," she said. "Companion to the blade he carried when he fell. The elves gave them to him as a gift, the first time he snuck into their woods."

"You really think he'd want you giving that to a goblin?" Darnak asked.

Genevieve grinned. "No." She reached out to grab Jig's arm. "My father passed the law ordering us to kill goblins on sight. The worst thing you could do to him is to succeed where his son failed."

Jig's answering smile made his jaw ache. He had been clenching it so long it hurt to do anything else. Whatever flaws Genevieve might possess, she certainly knew how to motivate a goblin.

CHAPTER 14

THE SON WAS BORN A TWISTED BLUE RUNT WITH comically oversized ears.

"Are you sure that thing came from Golaka?" One of the nursery workers hobbled over. She was a hunched, wrinkled thing, leaning heavily on a yellow cane. "I've seen rats with more meat."

The goblin holding the baby jabbed her claw into his belly. He batted weakly at her finger. "He's a pasty little mouse. He hasn't even cried."

"Nothing wrong with a bit of quiet." The older goblin tucked a bit of hard candy into her cheek. "Maybe he can teach you how to keep your mouth shut."

"Careful, Grell." The younger worker balanced the baby in one hand and drew a short sword with her other. She jabbed the sword in Grell's direction. The baby turned his head, eyes wide as he followed the tarnished steel. He was an observant thing, and if that goblin wasn't careful, she was going to drop him on his head. If that happened, Shadowstar intended to give her a smiting like the world had never seen.

"Put that away," Grell said, rapping the sword with her cane. "Kill me, and you're on your own come diaper-changing time." She grinned. "Remember those dried fruits I swiped from that last group of adventurers? Well, a few of the brats

found them. It's going to make diaper duty pretty exciting for the next few days. But by all means, run me through with your little sword and wipe their arses all by yourself."

The other goblin stared at her sword. She looked as though she was half tempted to fall on it. With a sigh, she rammed it back into her sheath. "Why don't you check diapers, and I'll take the runt outside for the wolves."

Tymalous Shadowstar shook his head. That runt had potential, for a goblin. Besides, it was kind of cute the way those ears kept flopping down into his eyes. Shadowstar couldn't simply let him die.

He concentrated on Grell, but she mentally swatted him away like a bug. So he turned to the younger goblin. Aggressive and angry, she was a true goblin, willing to do anything to get her way.

"Wait," she said. "I have a better idea."

"You have an idea?" Grell snorted. "And here I thought I'd seen everything."

Shadowstar whispered, and the goblin said, "I'll bet you a week's worth of diaper-changing duty that you can't keep the runt alive long enough to see his first full moon."

Grell's cane clicked against the obsidian floor as she limped over to take the baby. "A month," she said.

"A month it is." The other goblin touched the hilt of her sword.

"Try it, and I'll make you eat those diapers."

Shadowstar grinned. He was starting to like these goblins.

Jig scowled at his new sword. The blade was light as air, and stronger than any human steel. Had any goblin ever possessed so fine a weapon?

If they had, Jig suspected they would have soon thrown it away. For Jig had learned the true nature of the elves' magical weapons. In addition to being so strong and sharp and light, the sword glowed orange in the presence of orcs and ogres . . . and goblins. Every time Jig looked at his own sword, it burned an image of itself onto his eyelids.

"Stupid elves," Jig muttered. He turned to Darnak. "Can't you turn it off?"

Darnak chuckled. "The steel remembers the light of the forge. Be thankful it doesn't recall the heat as well." He closed the box of figurines and crammed it into his pack.

Actually, a heated sword would have been nice. At least he would have been able to feel his fingers.

Genevieve had already gone off to prepare her soldiers, leaving Jig and Darnak alone in the barracks. Jig bent to pick up the goblin figurine, which had fallen onto the floor beneath the table.

"Keep it," Darnak said. "As for the sword, the magic will wear off in time. Most elven blades lose their power after a thousand years or so. Two thousand at the most."

The sword cast about as much light as a muck lantern or torch. Still, it was a far cry better than the old kitchen knife he used to carry. Not that he expected it to make much difference. Sure, Jig's sword could help him avoid stubbing his toe in the darkness. Billa's could kill a god.

A tugging on his cloak drew Jig's attention. Smudge crept slowly up the hem, toward Jig's neck. He took slow, careful steps, as he did when he was hunting. Just beneath Jig's chin, the fire-spider stopped. One leg at a time, he turned to face the sword.

"Odd pets you goblins keep," Darnak said.

Smudge pounced. The move was so sudden Jig nearly dropped the sword. Smudge landed on the blade, slipped, and fell into the snow.

Instantly, Smudge was scrambling for Jig's leg. He climbed up again and crouched, waiting.

Jig started to smile. Smudge probably thought he had discovered the world's largest glow-fly. He waited until Smudge pounced, then flicked the blade out of the way.

Next time, Smudge was smarter. He simply ran down Jig's arm and onto the blade. He steadied himself on the crossguard and tried to take a bite out of the edge. After a few such attempts, he turned around, all eight eyes glaring up at Jig.

"Don't get mad at me. I never said you could eat it." Jig ran a finger over the bristly fur on Smudge's back. "Darnak, I have to ask you for something."

"Genevieve's in charge," Darnak said. "Not me."

Jig shook his head. "No, it's nothing like that. Will you take care of Smudge for me?"

Darnak cocked his head. "That's Smudge? I thought that little guy got himself squished back when you and Barius fought."

"He . . . he survived." Had he ever thanked Shadowstar for that miracle?

No.

Jig sheathed his sword and held Smudge out to Darnak. "He doesn't deserve to die out there."

Slowly Darnak opened his hand. Jig poked Smudge, gently at first, then harder. Smudge lowered his body, his feet heating Jig's palm. Finally Jig grabbed him with his other hand and pulled him free. "Don't let him get near your beard unless you want to lose it. And try to keep him out of the cold, if you can. When this is all over you can take him back to our lair. There's a fire-spider nest in the tunnels below our cavern. If you put him into the garbage crevasse, he should remember how to find it."

Darnak held the fire-spider at arm's length. "Wouldn't it be making more sense to give this beastie to another goblin?"

Jig shook his head. "Most goblins don't like them very much. Fire-spiders sneak into the distillery and the muck pits. They like to eat the muck. When I was young, a distillery worker startled a fire-spider that was hiding in one of the pans. The explosion killed four goblins and deafened nine more."

From the look on Darnak's face, Jig might as well have given him a pile of wolf scat. With his free hand, Darnak twisted his beard into a rope and tucked it down the front of his shirt. "You sure it's me you're wanting to look after him?"

"If you say you'll protect him, you will. You're like that." Jig glanced at the map. "And he's safer with you than with me."

Slowly Darnak nodded. "True enough. I'll do my best to care for the beast—for Smudge—and to get him back home where he belongs. My word on it."

Jig searched his pockets for something to give to Smudge.

He found one tiny troll toe, covered in purple lint, but Smudge wasn't interested.

Jig's throat felt as though *he* had tried to swallow a toe. A big one. He blinked and turned toward the door.

"Jig!" Trok burst inside and stomped snow from his boots. "We caught Gratz. He's outside. Nobody knew where you had gotten to."

"Oh." That was good. Maybe he could give pieces of Gratz to Smudge as a final present.

"Well?" Trok said. "Aren't you going to come kill him?"

Jig blinked. "He's still alive?"

"He said that as an officer, regulations required us to turn him over to our superior for questioning."

"Trok, those are *Billa's* regulations." Jig heard Darnak chuckling behind him. With a sigh, Jig pulled up his hood and adjusted his sheath. This sword was wider than his last, and the end kept catching on his cloak. "Forget it. I'll deal with Gratz. There's something else I need you to take care of."

"What's that?" Trok sounded wary.

"I'm down to a single troll toe, and I doubt the other goblins have enough to control the wolves when we attack." Jig pointed to Trok's sword. "Why don't you take some of the goblins and introduce them to Toe Stub?"

Slowly Trok grinned. "Yes, sir!"

"What's Toe Stub?" Darnak asked after he left.

"You probably don't want to know." Jig pushed open the door and stepped into the cold.

About half the goblins followed Trok to learn about Toe Stub. The rest surrounded Gratz, who was bloody and bruised, but still alive. That he had convinced them not to kill him was quite the trick, particularly given the way Relka kept playing with her torch. Jig got the feeling she would happily cook him right here in the street if Jig gave the word.

Braf stood on the opposite side of the mob, keeping a wary eye on Gratz. Or maybe he was watching Relka. His clothes were still torn and bloody from the beating Relka had given him.

The goblins quieted as Jig approached. Gratz straightened. "As a prisoner of war, regulations require me to—"

Relka cleared her throat. Gratz glanced at her, and his mouth snapped shut.

"How did you escape?" Jig asked.

"The humans don't have a proper dungeon," Gratz said. "So they tied me up in the bakery, surrounded by stale bread."

Jig grimaced at the thought.

"I tried to bite through the ropes. These weren't those blasted elf ropes you told me about, but they were still too tough to chew. I thought I was done for. And then I remembered Billa's regulations."

Jig groaned. He wasn't the only one.

"Regulations say you're supposed to dislocate your own thumbs to escape the bonds of the enemy."

Jig studied him with a bit more respect. "You did that?"

Gratz shook his head. "I tried. Screamed and passed out from the pain. When I came to, one of the humans was staring down at me, so I kicked him in the giblets and took his weapons. That's in the regs too, you know."

Jig really needed to read those regulations. He gestured at the other goblins. "And then you attacked me in front of everyone. What do your regulations say about that?"

"It's a bit unclear," Gratz admitted. "Audacity is one of the keys to victory. But it also tends to get you killed."

Audacity. So be it. Jig stepped back and raised his voice so all the goblins would hear. "We're going to attack Billa in the morning." Several of the goblins cheered. The smarter ones looked worried. Jig tried to ignore them all. "And you're going to lead that attack," he said to Gratz.

That took care of the cheering.

"Are you sure Darnak finished healing your head?" Braf asked. "I hit you pretty hard."

Jig turned and walked toward the wall. "Bring Gratz. The rest of you get some sleep." He swiveled his ear, tracking their footsteps in the snow and waiting for one of them to try to kill him. It's what he would have done, had someone told him he had to attack Billa's army. But apparently the goblins were too stunned to act.

Jig climbed to the top of the wall, stepping onto the walkway without any hesitation. He found Genevieve and Darnak standing there, watching Billa's army.

"Bring Gratz," Jig shouted.

Relka sank her claws into Gratz's arm and dragged him to the ladder. Jig waited until they reached the top. There were no lanterns or torches, probably so that Billa's monsters would have a harder time targeting anyone.

"What are you doing?" Genevieve asked, lowering her elf scope.

"Planning tomorrow's attack."

Gratz clung to the railing as he stepped onto the wall. Jig didn't bother. He had no fear of falling. He had no fear of anything. That was the only reason he could walk up to Gratz and grab him by his lone ear.

He tugged Gratz to the opposite railing, yanking his head around so he was looking out at Billa's army.

"You mean to attack *that*?" Gratz shook his head. "You should have let me kill you. It would have been faster."

"What do Billa's regulations say about attacking a town?" Jig asked. Scattered campfires burned as far back as Jig could see. They had taken over the farmhouses too. At least one was on fire, though Jig wasn't sure that had been deliberate. Goblins swarmed around the burning building in a panic. "Billa has thousands of monsters. We have—"

"Eighty-seven soldiers and twenty-nine goblins," Genevieve said.

"And one dwarf," added Darnak.

"Given the weather, Billa's best choice would be to strike hard and fast," Gratz said. "Audacity, like I said. Surround the town and hit it from all sides at once. Use ladders and siege towers to—"

"What ladders?" Jig pointed. "Do you see any ladders? Or siege towers?" Not that he knew what a siege tower was.

"We left the siege equipment back in Pottersville," Gratz said. "It got pretty beat up in the attack, and—"

"So why aren't they building more?" Jig asked. "All those trees, but they're just sitting there. Waiting. Billa gave Genevieve until tomorrow to surrender."

Gratz shook his head. "That doesn't make sense. Giving humans time is always a mistake. They'll find a secret way out of the city, or some unassuming farm boy will sneak away to summon help, then before you know it a wizard shows up out of nowhere with reinforcements, and everything goes straight into the privy."

Jig shrugged and leaned against the railing, his back to Billa's army. "So this must be some sort of trick," he said. "Billa's secretly moving her forces into an attack formation."

Gratz shook his head. "That's no formation I've ever seen. Most of them seem to be sleeping!"

"You said the casualty ratio against a walled town was ten-to-one," Jig said.

"Billa has goblins and kobolds out in front," Gratz mumbled. "Make it fifteen-to-one."

"She has plenty of monsters," Jig said. "She could take Avery by noon tomorrow if she wanted. Then her forces would be safe behind the walls. Doesn't that make sense?"

Slowly Gratz nodded. "I don't understand it. No siege equipment. No sappers."

"That wouldn't work anyway," said Genevieve. "Steelthorn roots spread wide and deep."

Jig frowned, trying to understand what sap had to do with anything. He knew sap came from trees, and the walls were made of steelthorn trees, but why—? It didn't matter. He could see Gratz's confusion. Now it was only a matter of pushing.

"Her formation does make sense," Jig said. "Her lines are spread to face the north. She's waiting for Wendel's army to arrive."

"Why would she do that?" Gratz's fingers dug into the railing.

"Because I was telling you the truth before. She doesn't want to beat the humans. She wants to kill them. Them and us, all at once."

"No!"

Relka started forward, but Jig waved her away.

Gratz turned to Jig. His tone was pleading "That's not possible. Billa the Bloody is a liberator." He rubbed his arm, the one with the scar of rank.

That gave Jig an idea. "If you're still not convinced, I could try to trigger the spell she carved onto your arm."

Gratz stared at his arm.

"We should probably lower you down outside the wall, first," Jig said. "Genevieve, do you have ropes? I don't know exactly how much damage this is going to do."

"No!" Gratz blinked, and cocked his head, as if he wasn't sure who had shouted. In a softer voice, he said, "No."

Genevieve was staring at Jig just as intently as the goblins. "You could do that? Trigger the spell? That could destroy Billa's army!"

It wouldn't work, Shadowstar said. *Every spell includes a rune binding the magic to Isa. You'd have to rip each one away from her, and neither of us are strong enough to wrest control from Isa. I doubt you could even trigger Gratz's spell.*

I don't have to. Out loud, he said, "No, I can't," Jig said. "Billa created those spells. She's the only one who can use them."

Gratz's face turned a darker shade of blue. He grabbed the front of Jig's cloak. "But you said—"

Jig kicked him in the shin. "And you believed me! Deep down, you know that scar isn't just a sign of rank." He bit Gratz's arm until he let go of Jig's cloak. And then Relka slammed into Gratz from the side, knocking him down hard enough to make the branches tremble beneath them.

Jig knelt and grabbed the sheaf of paper sticking out from Gratz's shirt. The corners were wrinkled and filthy, speckled with dirt and Gratz's blood. He waved them in Gratz's face. "Doesn't Billa's plan to kill everyone qualify as treason?"

"Technically, since it's her army, she can't commit treason," Gratz said.

Jig fought the urge to try out his brand new elf sword. "At sunrise the other goblins are going to pretend to take me prisoner. We're going to get as close as we possibly can, and then I'm going to kill Billa." At least that was the plan. So far, his plans had been falling apart with annoying regularity. "It would be much more believable if you were the one leading that group. Billa knows you. Everyone knows you. Even the kobolds said you were a stuck-up, rule-bound arse-kisser."

"That's true," Gratz muttered. Then, to Jig's confusion, he began to laugh. He hugged himself, shaking so hard Jig worried he would fall down. Tears dripped from his cheeks.

"Goblins have the strangest sense of humor," Genevieve said.

"She could have done it," Gratz said, gasping for breath. He wiped his face on his sleeve. "Billa raised an army. She could have beaten the humans. She could have won, Jig."

Somewhere toward the middle of town, a goblin screamed. Genevieve had her sword drawn in an instant, her eyes wide. Her men raised crossbows, searching for a target.

"That's probably just Trok," Jig said. He turned his head, perking his ears. As the screaming quieted, he could hear other goblins jeering. Hopefully he would have time to heal the losers before it was time to leave. He reached out to grab Gratz's arm. "The princess gave me her word. If I stop Billa, she'll make sure the humans leave us alone."

Gratz grabbed the railing with one hand and pulled himself up. "Billa played us all for fools, Jig." His hand shook as he pulled out his battered regulations. "Always wash between your toes," he whispered.

"What?" Jig asked.

"First regulation I ever learned." Gratz stared out at Billa's army. "If you don't keep clean, you get fungus and rot and all sorts of nastiness."

"Good advice," Darnak agreed. "And it's not just toes, either. My cousin Dinla spent too much time in the mines one summer and got herself the worst case of armpit mold you'll ever see."

Behind him, Genevieve looked faintly nauseated.

"You'll want to hide that sword," Gratz said. "Regulations require all prisoners to be disarmed. If anyone sees it, they'll know something's wrong." He stretched his arms, then laced his fingers together to crack the joints in his hands. "I never liked those stinking orcs anyway. Always strutting about like they're better than us."

"So you'll help us?" Jig asked.

Gratz nodded.

To Darnak, Jig asked, "Is he telling the truth?"

"What's that?"

"When I first told you about Billa, Genevieve had you cast a spell to figure out if I was lying." Jig pointed at Gratz. "Is he telling the truth? If he means to turn me over to Billa, we should throw him off the wall and I'll have Trok lead us instead."

"Betraying your commanding officer gives your superiors the right to . . . hold on." Gratz flipped through his pages. "Ah. The right to use your skin as a blanket." He shoved the manual back into his shirt. "You're my commanding officer, General Jig. I have no interest in becoming a blanket."

"He means it," Darnak said, shaking his head. He looked both surprised and sad.

Jig wasn't surprised. Gratz was as bad as Relka. Without Billa to believe in, Gratz had latched on to Jig instead. Relka would have him wearing his very own starburst if he wasn't careful. Goblins were fools.

Their faith gives them courage, said Shadowstar. *Neither of them needed divine intervention to help them overcome their fear. They'll stand beside you and die with you.*

Jig nodded. *Exactly.*

Jig didn't sleep much that night. Maybe being a champion of Tymalous Shadowstar meant he didn't need as much sleep. Or maybe the idea of leading an attack against Billa the Bloody was enough to keep him awake, even without his fear. He kept thinking about all the things that could go wrong, and wondering which would be the one to kill him. Falling off of his wolf and breaking his neck would be embarrassing, but at least it would be quick. Slipping in the snow right as he reached Billa would be worse.

When he could lie there no longer, he got up and tiptoed out of the stables, past a heap of snoring goblins. Wrapping an extra blanket tight around his body, he hurried to the wall.

To his surprise, Genevieve was still there, staring out at the campfires of Billa's army.

Jig announced his arrival with a wet sneeze. At least tomorrow would see him free of all these plants.

Several of her guards moved toward him, but Genevieve waved them back. She started to speak, then wrinkled her nose. "What is that smell?"

"What smell? Oh, wait." Jig tugged a pouch from one of his cloak pockets and handed it to her. Genevieve's face went pale as she opened the bag.

"We were almost out of troll toes," Jig said. "Trok says the hardest part was convincing everyone to take off their shoes. I guess that makes it easier to score a full sever. I healed them the best I could. The wolf-riders will still be able to ride, and the rest . . . well, they can limp along behind us."

"Goblins." She tossed the sack at Jig's feet. One toe rolled free and disappeared into the cracks of the woven walkway. "For years, my brothers fought to earn our father's attention and respect. All they accomplished was to get themselves killed." She sighed and rested her arms on the railing. "I never blamed the goblins for killing Barius and Ryslind. I blamed him."

"Your father didn't kill them. I'm the one who turned them into trout." And that was why goblins needed their fear. Fear would have stopped him from saying something so incredibly stupid. He braced himself for Genevieve's response. At the very least, he expected a quick punch to the face. If he was unlucky, Genevieve would just run him through.

She did neither. "My mother says I'm too harsh. He's fought for this kingdom his whole life. I remember watching him teach my brothers how to fight. He was *laughing*." She shook her head. "He never laughs when he wears that stupid crown."

"Maybe he should give it to someone else," Jig said.

"My mother has said the same thing, in private. She even used to joke about changing the law so that the youngest daughter could inherit the crown. Then she and my father could retire to Silver Lake and spend their time fishing and watching the griffins on the cliffs. When I told her I'd use that crown to bludgeon the first person who tried to put it on my head, she smiled and said that only proved I was smarter than my brothers."

"That's not saying much." There he went again. But Genevieve only smiled.

"This coming from the goblin who tried to attack an entire city."

"We won!" Jig said, trying not to sound defensive.

"Only because I wasn't smart enough to come inside the walls when Darnak told me to." She yawned again, then fumbled through her cloak until she found a long wooden pipe. She walked to the closest lantern and lit a taper, which she used to start the tobacco burning. "Dwarven tobacco. It helps my nerves, and it's nice to be able to breathe without feeling like my lungs are about to freeze. Please don't tell my father, though. He'd kill me."

Jig managed to keep from rolling his eyes. "I'll try to keep it to myself."

She blew a puff of smoke, which quickly disappeared into the cold wind. "You deserve better than this, you know."

"Tell that to Tymalous Shadowstar."

"Who?"

Jig sighed. "Never mind." He tried to count the campfires, but quickly gave up.

"I can't imagine what my father would say if he saw me up here talking to a goblin." Her grin appeared strained. She tugged a leaf from the railing and pulled it apart. "I don't blame you for hating us, you know."

Jig shook his head. "We don't hate you. At least not any more than we hate the lizard-fish and the tunnel cats and the hobgoblins and everything else that kills us."

"Oh."

Jig had a hard time reading her expression.

"You should try to sleep," Genevieve said. "Nobody dies faster than a tired soldier."

"What about a goblin?" Jig asked.

That earned a soft chuckle. She blew another stream of smoke into the wind and stared up at the moon. Jig turned to go, then hesitated. "Aren't you going to get some sleep too?"

"Eventually." She sucked another breath through the pipe. "Darnak used to tell us stories about the great dwarf commanders, and how they would walk among their men the night before the battle." She ducked her head and added, "Besides, I get nightmares."

Jig started down the ladder. He had just lowered himself down so his hands clutched the top disk of lichen when Genevieve said, "For what it's worth, I'm sorry, Jig."

She sounded almost drunk, but her breath didn't have the stink of alcohol. Humans were weird.

It's time, Jig.

Shadowstar's voice yanked Jig from a dream in which Billa and her orcs had been pelting him with potatoes. He blinked and rubbed his eyes, then hooked his spectacles over his ears. The sight of all those snoring, drooling goblins was anything but pretty.

The stable door slid open, and Gratz peeked inside.

"You're awake." Gratz sounded surprised.

"What are you doing?" The idea of Gratz out and moving around on his own made Jig nervous.

"Checking on the wolves, sir. I thought it best to make sure they were fed before we attack. Not too much, of course. Hunger gives a wolf his edge, right?"

"Sure." Jig staggered toward the door. He stopped long enough to nudge Trok awake. "Get the wolf-riders ready," Jig said, fighting a yawn.

"Get them yourself, you scrawny little—" Trok rubbed his eyes. "Er. Sorry." He leaned over and punched the closest goblin in the gut. "Get everyone awake, and be quick about it."

That wasn't exactly what Jig had intended, but it worked. Soon his entire command was gathered outside the stables, shivering in the wind. The sky overhead was a dark blue color. Most of the stars had faded, and the moon was gone from sight. Over the far wall, Jig could see a faint trace of red.

"Beautiful morning, eh?" Darnak shouted as he jogged toward them, followed by Genevieve and several other humans. "Nothing like the chill of the predawn air to get the blood pumping."

Darnak was the closest thing Jig had to a friend here, but if the dwarf kept grinning like that, Jig was going to stab him.

Dark smudges beneath Genevieve's eyes made her look a bit like a raccoon. Her expression was one of complete understanding. "It could be worse," she muttered. "When he woke me up, he was *singing*."

Jig grinned and checked his sword. Orange light spilled from the end of the scabbard. Jig hurried back into the stable and grabbed a blanket. He pulled it over himself, wrapping one corner around the sword to hide it. "Gratz, Trok, take some of the goblins and go get the wolves."

"What about food?" Relka asked.

"Billa's troops will be breaking their fast soon," Darnak said. "Attack now, and we catch them in the middle of their meal. They'll be reluctant to abandon their food, and that gives you the advantage."

"Here," said Relka. She handed Jig a strip of meat so dry it crunched. "I swiped it from the humans last night."

"What is it?" Jig asked warily.

"They called it bacon." Relka glared at Darnak. "It's quick, and we can eat it while we prepare. No goblin should die hungry."

Jig took a bite, and the smoky, spicy taste caused his mouth to fill with drool. He stuffed the rest into his mouth and grinned. "You're sure this is human food? It's *good*!"

Relka handed him another greasy strip of bacon, then turned to the other goblins. Soon all of Jig's troops were wiping greasy fingers on their clothes, their hair, and each other.

Snarls and growls signaled the arrival of the wolves. Gratz, Trok, and a few other goblins strained at the ropes. The wolves tugged and fought, but Gratz and Trok had tied them well. The ropes circling the wolves' necks were knotted in front of the throat. The more the wolves pulled, the deeper that knot pressed into their windpipes.

Of course, if you were Bastard, you could simply double back and bite the arm of the goblin holding your leash. With blue blood dripping from his jaws, Bastard bounded down the road toward Jig, his rope bouncing along the road behind him.

Darnak drew his club and stepped in front of Genevieve, shoving her out of Bastard's path. Several of the humans fumbled with their weapons. The goblins, being smarter, fought to get out of the way. Jig grabbed the sack Trok had given him. By the time his cold fingers closed around a toe, Bastard was almost on top of him.

"Bastard, down!" Jig squealed, throwing the toe.

Bastard twisted, snapped the toe out of the air, and crashed into Jig. Still chewing, Bastard bent down to sniff Jig's face.

"Argh," Jig gasped. "Toe breath!"

Relka grabbed Bastard's leash and tugged. Bastard barely noticed, but then Darnak added his weight to Relka's, dragging the wolf back enough for Jig to wiggle free.

Thirteen wolves in total, including Bastard. Fourteen if you counted Fungus, who was still limping from an arrow wound. Jig had already tried to get close enough to heal Fungus' wound. The attempt had almost cost him a hand.

He stood and brushed wolf fur from his cloak. Amazing how much these animals could shed.

"Do you have riders picked out?" Genevieve asked.

Jig nodded. Keeping his voice low, he said, "A mix of our goblins and the ones from Billa's army. Mostly goblins who are too dumb to realize what's going to happen to them. Gratz and I will be on Bastard."

It was a good thing Shadowstar was still muffling Jig's fear. Bad enough he would be riding with the goblin who had tried to kill him yesterday. Without Shadowstar's help, the idea of riding Bastard again would have sent Jig running from town.

Jig handed out the toes Trok had collected and watched as his goblins climbed onto the wolves. Seeing them knot themselves into place made him think about the way Silverfang had died. "Everyone make sure you have a knife as well as a sword. If something happens, you'll want to cut yourselves free before your wolf falls on you."

Darnak cleared his throat. "Not that I'm one to tell goblins how to ride a wolf, but I'm thinking you might want to use a slipknot for those harnesses."

"A what?" Gratz asked.

Darnak walked up to one of the wolves, apparently unworried by the huge, growling jaws. Maybe his god took away his fear, too. Or maybe dwarves just didn't know how to be afraid. He twisted and tugged the rope, forming a small loop. A few more twists gave him a second, larger loop.

"This will hold you tight as a babe," Darnak said, tugging the loop. He switched his grip and grabbed one of the ends. "Something goes wrong, pull here." A swift jerk, and the loop fell apart.

Jig waited while the other goblins climbed onto their wolves. Trok was riding Smelly again, and looked as happy as Jig had ever seen him. Relka was on Ugly, and Braf was feeding Fungus a few extra toes, distracting the wolf long enough to heal his leg.

"Sir?" Gratz said. "I . . . I don't think Bastard will let me ride him without you."

Jig nodded and stepped past Gratz. Bastard licked his face, nearly knocking him into the snow. Jig shoved the wolf's muzzle aside and climbed onto his back. His legs and groin were already aching from the memory of his last ride.

He raised his hands while Darnak tied him into place. A second slipknot secured Jig's wrists. Anyone looking would assume he was a helpless prisoner. He pulled his cloak and blanket so they covered his sword.

Gratz climbed up behind him and reached around to grab Bastard's reins.

"Wait!" Jig shouted suddenly. He yanked the release ropes and hopped down.

"What is it, sir?" Gratz asked. "What's wrong?"

Relka leaped from her own wolf. "Is it an omen from Shadowstar?"

"Not exactly." Jig's face was burning. "I just . . . if I'm going to ride Bastard, I really need to use the privy first."

CHAPTER 15

JIG WAS MARVELOUS! SELFISH AND COWARDLY and completely untrustworthy, but also clever and resourceful and desperate to be something more than he was. Unfortunately, he was also so busy staying alive that he rarely thought about things beyond his little world in the caves . . . until now.

Did the adventurers who had captured him realize how Jig was studying them, how he drank in every word, every action, trying to learn how he too could be such a hero?

And did Jig realize what he had already accomplished? He had survived the ambush of his patrol and single-handedly helped the adventurers survive a hobgoblin trap. He had even played a part in overcoming the various surprises the Necromancer had scattered through his tunnels. They were currently resting, having explored much of those tunnels to no avail.

This was Shadowstar's chance. He had seen how keenly Jig watched the dwarf, fascinated by Darnak's healing abilities. Shadowstar reached out, subtly nudging Jig until the goblin's curiosity overpowered his fear.

"Tell me of the gods," Jig said.

Shadowstar gathered his power. With no worshipers, he had to forge and maintain his own connection to the mortal realm. He would have to wait for the perfect moment.

Darnak started talking. And talking. The other adventurers retreated to the far side of the room. Jig's eyes began to glaze. Still the dwarf talked.

Was he even stopping long enough to breathe? Jig hadn't asked for a lecture on the romantic preferences of Olin Birch, one of the woodland gods, let alone the resulting diseases that had followed him through succeeding centuries.

Shadowstar grinned at the memories. Old Olin Knottytwig, they had called him.

On and on the dwarf talked. Despite himself, Shadowstar was impressed. Darnak knew the gods' histories better than most gods.

Finally, Darnak paused for a drink. Shadowstar reached out, channeling his power into a single seed of thought and praying it would take root in the dwarf's mind.

He chuckled when he realized Darnak's earlier tale had gotten him thinking in tree metaphors.

Darnak belched. "Then you had the Forgotten Gods." He frowned, apparently confused, and took another sip of wine.

Jig stared, hardly hearing a word of it. A bit of drool trickled from one side of his mouth. He was exhausted and bored out of his mind. Shadowstar gathered himself and poked Jig as hard as he could.

"What was that?" Jig asked.

Shadowstar turned his power back onto Darnak, who blinked. "Eh? Oh, the Fifteen Forgotten Gods of the War of Shadows?"

"Who were they?"

Shadowstar could already feel his connection to the dwarf fading. "Remember," he begged. The curse had been laid by a god, so a god should be strong enough to break it, even if only for a brief time. "Remember, blast you!"

"Take the Shadowstar," Darnak said. "They stripped his mind, flayed his body with blades of lightning, and cast him loose in the desert."

Shadowstar's grip on the dwarf slipped. Had it been enough?

Darnak babbled a few moments longer, and then his voice trailed off. He glanced about in confusion. "What was I saying just then?"

It didn't matter. Shadowstar could already feel Jig reaching out, searching.

For the first time in thousands of years, Tymalous Shadowstar had a follower.

Jig kept one hand on his rope, ready to loosen his bonds at the first hint of trouble. The fingers of his other hand twisted into his cloak, holding it shut to hide his sword. He grimaced and hunched his head. He wished he could have put up his hood, but they needed his face to be visible so everyone would see he was a prisoner. But that meant Gratz's breath kept tickling his neck as they rode.

The gates of Avery swung shut behind them. Given the size of the gates, he expected a loud clang, or at least a heavy thud. Anything to mark the drama of the moment as the small goblin force set out to get themselves killed. The only sound the elf-grown doors made was an annoying squeak.

Jig wouldn't have thought it possible, but Billa's army appeared even bigger from the ground. Goblins and kobolds huddled around feebly burning campfires. The monsters had camped on the road as well as in the fields, so there was no clear path to Billa.

Gratz guided Bastard toward the goblin ranks, avoiding the kobolds. Hopefully the goblins would be less suspicious of their own kind. Even so, goblins everywhere stopped what they were doing to stare.

Gratz tugged the reins as they passed the first few goblins, trying to keep the wolf from investigating the rabbit turning over a fire, or the particularly smelly goblin who scampered past.

Familiar odors surrounded them. Smoke from the damp wood of the campfires. Burning meat. Filthy soldiers. Sheep droppings. Jig hadn't realized how accustomed he had grown to the smells in his short time with Billa. Then the wind shifted, and the stench of Smelly the wolf overpowered it all.

An armored goblin approached, a spear clutched in his hands. "Gratz, is that you? What happened to Silverfang?"

Jig held his breath. It wasn't that he was afraid of Gratz's response. Fear had nothing to do with it. The simple fact was that Gratz was a goblin, and this was the best chance he would have to betray Jig.

"The runt killed him." Gratz slapped the back of Jig's head. "Billa has plans for this one." He leaned his head down and whispered, "Sorry, sir. I know regulations say I'm not allowed to hit a superior officer, but if I act like you're my superior officer, nobody's going to believe—"

"Shut up," Jig said.

The guard grinned at Jig. "Try not to scream too loudly when she kills you. Some of the troops are still sleeping."

Jig did his best to look afraid. Strange, to have to force his features into an expression of terror. He hoped it wasn't too fake.

Goblins whispered and pointed as they rode, but none moved to stop them. Word spread quickly in the army. Jig could hear Gratz muttering, sounding more and more annoyed with every step.

"Regulations require them to challenge everyone who passes. They should have stopped us before we ever reached the perimeter." He glared back at the goblin with the spear. "He doesn't even have his spear in a proper grip. With thirteen wolves, he should have brought reinforcements. He should have insisted on searching the prisoner, to make sure you're not smuggling anything in."

"I am," Jig said. "I'm smuggling a sword, remember?"

"I know. That doesn't make it any less shameful. Silverfang would have—"

The creaking of branches interrupted whatever Gratz was saying. Snow shivered from Oakbottom's branches as he waded through the goblin camp, moving to intercept the wolf-riders. Several of the drowsy goblins were too slow to move out of his way. Their screams made Jig wince.

"What's this?" Oakbottom asked, stopping directly in front of Jig.

"That's more like it," Gratz said. "Though by rights, he never should have allowed us this deep into—"

Jig jabbed an elbow into his ribs.

Gratz coughed, then said, "The humans decided to surrender Jig to Billa the Bloody, and to let us go free!"

As planned, the other wolf-riders cheered and waved their weapons in the air. Jig studied Oakbottom, waiting to see whether he believed their story. How was Jig supposed to read the facial expressions of a tree?

How did Oakbottom even see? He had no eyes, as far as Jig could tell. It had to be even worse during the summer, when all his leaves grew in. Did he have someone trim his branches?

"Billa will be interested in hearing what took you so long," Oakbottom said.

"I'll give her my full report when I turn over the prisoner," Gratz answered, snapping off a quick salute.

"Bring your wolves to the pen." Oakbottom pointed his branches toward a small farmhouse. "Billa said I was to take the prisoner, if they turned him over. Apparently this one's tricky, for a goblin."

Jig waited, but Gratz didn't answer. Oakbottom stood unmoving, like . . . well, like a tree.

"Gratz?" Jig whispered. Hopefully Oakbottom's hearing wasn't as acute as a goblin's.

"Yes, sir?" Gratz's voice was equally low.

"Answer the tree!"

"What do I say?"

Jig groaned. Of course Gratz didn't know what to do. Regulations didn't say how to handle it when your plan fell apart and your superior officer couldn't bark out new orders because he was pretending to be a prisoner.

Jig glanced around. They were roughly halfway through the goblins. Too far to turn back, but not close enough to have any hope of reaching Billa.

Jig was used to his plans not working. All goblins were. But he had hoped to make a bit more progress before everything fell apart.

"Is there a problem, goblin?"

Was it Jig's imagination, or did Oakbottom sound hopeful? Maybe he hadn't been able to toss a goblin in a few days.

Before Jig or Gratz could respond, another wolf bounded past. Relka pointed her sword at Oakbottom and shouted, "For Jig and Shadowstar!"

Why had Jig insisted on bringing the stupid goblins along? He tugged the release rope, freeing his hands and giving himself a nasty rope burn on his wrists. "Split into two lines," he shouted. "Run past him and make for Billa!"

Gratz was already tugging Bastard's reins, leading him to the right. The other wolves began to charge, like a river flowing around a rock. Or around a big, angry tree who liked to throw goblins. Nobody wanted to come within reach of those branches.

Nobody except Relka. She and Ugly rode straight for Oakbottom. He reached out, and she slammed her sword into his branch.

The blade stuck. Oakbottom raised the branch. Relka tugged her rope, slipping free of the wolf as she rose into the air. Oakbottom plucked her free with another branch and grabbed her wolf with a third. He spun in a circle and threw both Relka and Ugly at Jig.

"Faster!" Jig yelled, kicking Bastard in the sides. He ducked as Relka passed overhead. With Ugly, Oakbottom actually did them a favor. The yelping wolf crashed into the charging goblins, knocking them back and clearing a bit of space for Bastard.

Jig drew his sword and waved it overhead. With this many goblins around, the elven blade shone like a beacon. Hopefully it would help the other wolf-riders to follow him through the chaos.

The goblins in front of them leaped away. Bastard's snapping jaws probably had more to do with their fear than Jig's sword, but he liked to think the glowing blade helped.

"For Jig and Shadowstar!" Gratz shouted, all but deafening him.

Jig's face burned as the other goblins picked up the cry.

"The orcs are fearless," Gratz warned him. "They won't budge." Up ahead, the orcs were already racing into formation, raising shields and spears to break Jig's charge.

Yes, they will, said Shadowstar.

A wash of heat was Jig's only warning before red light flashed from his body. When he fought the elf scout days before, he had lit up like a little goblin bonfire. Now it was as if the

Autumn Star rode Bastard into battle. Though the sun wasn't fully risen, the land around him was bright as daylight. Red-tinged daylight, sure. But daylight nonetheless. The orcs staggered back, raising their hands and shields to protect their eyes.

Jig twisted to look at his riders. They seemed unaffected by the light, but Billa's army fell away as though they were blind.

One of the perks of being a champion of Tymalous Shadowstar. There's a chance Noc or another god will notice, but it's a bit late for worrying about that, eh? Shadowstar sounded ridiculously cheerful, not to mention smug.

Jig grinned and clung to Bastard's fur as the wolf leaped past the first line of orcs. Jig kept his ears flat. The tips were ice cold from the wind. *I don't suppose you could provide the heat of the Autumn Star as well as the light?*

Only if you want to be burned to ashes before your wolf takes another step, said Shadowstar.

Where was Billa? Tents and wagons marked the orc camp. Billa had to be here, probably near the center, but which tent was hers?

Gratz waved his sword in the air. "Spearpoint formation!"

Most of the wolves closed into a single line with Bastard at the head. Two of the goblins—Braf and another warrior from Jig's lair—looked at one another in confusion then went back to laying about with their weapons. They had no idea what a spearpoint formation was, but the chaos and confusion they caused helped protect the main line.

With Billa's troops blind and confused, it was easy for the wolf-riders to hit goblins, kobolds, and anyone else who got in the way. But that led to a new danger, as Jig's goblins grew intoxicated by their momentary advantage. The formation wavered as individual riders laid about with their weapons. One goblin even swerved to attack a goat that had wandered too close. The blow killed the goat and dislocated the goblin's shoulder when he tried to hold on to his weapon, which had lodged in the goat's back.

Jig groaned as he counted his wolves. He was down to eight, counting Bastard.

"There!" Trok pulled alongside, grinning as he pointed his sword at one of the tents.

Billa stood barefoot in a heavy nightgown, her sword strapped over her shoulder. She looked as if she had just climbed out of bed. Did she sleep with that sword?

"Everyone, follow me!" Gratz shouted. "Sorry. I mean, follow Jig!"

Jig and Gratz both tugged Bastard's harness, guiding him toward Billa. Billa and the crowd of heavily armed and armored orcs who stood before her.

Why aren't they blind like the rest of her troops? Jig asked.

Isa is protecting them, just as I'm protecting your goblins and your wolves.

Trok kicked his wolf into the lead. "Left flank, help me hit the ugly one there!"

"Which one is the ugly one?" Braf yelled.

And then they were crashing through orcs. Jig saw one goblin go down, but the weight of the charging wolf still knocked the orc to the ground. Trok ducked and hamstrung a second.

Bastard trampled a third, which slowed them down enough for more orcs to close in. Jig gripped his sword with both hands, holding it at arm's length to block a much bigger sword that would have taken his head clean off and probably killed Gratz as well. The impact knocked Jig's sword back and numbed his arms.

"Parry at an angle," Gratz yelled. "You don't have to stop the weapon. Just knock it out of the way."

Blood trickled down Jig's face. Apparently he had cut his scalp with the back edge of his own sword. He hadn't even felt it.

A glancing blow bruised his ribs but failed to penetrate his cloak. He would definitely have to remember to thank Shadowstar for that.

Jig gave up trying to follow everything that was happening. The noise was worse than the lair back home on the nights Golaka brewed up a fresh batch of klak beer. The bloodshed was about the same, though.

Up ahead, Billa was waving her sword and shouting orders. Only a few orcs still stood between her and the goblins.

They were winning! The realization nearly made Jig drop his sword. Gratz had been right. Audacity was the key to victory.

"Get the leader," Billa shouted.

One of the orcs hesitated. "Which one is that?"

Jig stabbed that orc in the leg as he rode past. His sword cut through the orc's heavy furs and armor as if they were cobwebs.

Maybe elf swords weren't so bad after all.

Billa shook her head. "The one who's glowing, you idiot!"

There was only one more orc between Jig and Billa. Jig reached into his cloak and pulled out one of his last goblin toes. He threw it to the orc, who automatically reached to catch it with his free hand.

Bastard snapped up both the toe and the hand in one bite.

Billa sprang forward and swung her sword with both hands. Bastard yelped and staggered to the side, one leg cleanly severed.

Jig barely managed to yank the release line as Bastard fell. The world tilted, and Jig found himself sitting in the snow with a sore rump.

Gratz wasn't so lucky. He covered his head with both hands, trying to protect himself from Bastard's flailing. The poor wolf was completely panicked. He wasn't bleeding, thanks to the cold of Billa's sword. Not yet, anyway. But he was biting and snarling at everything that moved, including Gratz.

The remaining goblins and wolves circled around Billa, who took a cautious step back. Her face was still blistered and scabbed from Jig's torch, back in the lair.

With Bastard down, Jig had five wolves, one of which was carrying a dead goblin. Braf was holding a bloody gash in his side, and Jig could sense the pulsing warmth of Shadowstar's magic as he healed himself. Convenient, that magic. Trok's sword was broken and his leg was soaked in blood, but he was grinning like a madman.

Most of the orcs lay dead or wounded in the snow. For goblins, they had done exceptionally well.

"Orders, general?" Trok asked.

Jig pointed at Billa. There was probably an appropriate formation for something like this, but Jig had no idea what it might be. "Get her!"

Jig managed two steps before the wind slammed him to his knees. His cloak flapped behind him, tugging him onto his back. That would be just his luck, to choke to death on his own cloak. He fumbled at the clasp, but his numb fingers were all but useless.

At least Jig's spectacles provided some small protection. He could see the other goblins covering their faces as they huddled in the snow.

Several wolves toppled over, trapping their riders. The surviving orcs bent into the wind, but they were as helpless as Jig. Only Billa the Bloody appeared untouched by the frigid wind. Her gown fluttered about her legs, and her hair danced in all directions. Her expression reminded him of a tunnel cat toying with its prey.

Help? Jig asked.

I'm trying. Isa is stronger than I am.

Jig lifted his sword into a guard position. The wind caught the flat of his blade, and he nearly cut off his own arm before he managed to turn the sword so the edge pointed into the wind. He tried to climb to his feet, but the instant he stood, the wind tossed him onto his back. He actually slid a short distance.

"For Shadowstar!" The wind nearly swallowed Relka's defiant cry as she limped into the wind, using her sword as a walking stick to pull herself along. Apparently the wind lost strength the farther you were from Billa. Which meant the smart thing was to get as far from Billa as possible.

Relka stepped closer. One of the orcs near Jig turned around and took a cautious step toward her. With his second step, the wind pushed him into an uncontrolled run. He raised his ax and bellowed, his great leaps quickly closing the distance between him and Relka.

Relka raised her weapon, lost her balance, and fell over. She would never get up in time to protect herself. Even if she did. . . .

Jig switched his sword to his left hand, nearly losing it to the wind. More carefully, he pulled out his dagger to throw, then hesitated.

Warriors could throw their weapons. The last few times Jig had tried, the results had been laughable. He could imagine himself stretching his arm back to throw, only to have the wind rip the knife from his hand. Knowing his luck, the blade would jab him in his own backside.

Instead, Jig gently tossed the knife into the air.

Billa's wind caught the knife, flinging it with far greater force than he could ever have managed. It flipped through the air, buzzing like an angry insect. The hilt smashed into the orc's skull. He tripped over Relka and skidded face-first in the snow. Jig grinned and turned back around to face Billa.

Well done, said Shadowstar.

You told me once that when I die, I'll come before you, Jig said, watching as Billa advanced. *Is that true?*

It is.

Good. Because any minute now, I plan to walk right up to you and bite you in the—

Have faith, Jig Dragonslayer. Shadowstar's voice was firm. *Hold your strike until I give the word.*

What strike? Did Shadowstar actually think Jig would get the chance to attack before Billa ran him through?

I can't blind the orcs and protect you from the wind at the same time. Be ready.

"Isa spent centuries preparing for this," Billa shouted. "Do you believe she'd allow a goblin to interfere?"

"Not really," Jig said.

Now.

The blinding red faded, returning the world to its dreary palate of snow and mud. At the same time, the wind seemed to vanish. Jig could still hear it roaring past, but he couldn't feel a thing. It was like when he had turned his sword sideways, so the blade cut through the wind instead of fighting it.

Less introspection and more attacking!

What's introspection? Oh—right. Jig leaped forward, thrusting the tip of his sword at Billa's stomach.

Billa's sword was in the wrong position to parry, but she

managed to twist out of the way. Jig's sword grazed a line on her nightgown, but nothing more. Off balance, Jig had to jump aside as Billa spun around and tried to decapitate him.

Jig tumbled into the snow. He glanced down to see a long section of cloak hanging down around his feet. Any closer, and she would have taken his leg as well.

Billa stepped back. She scowled as she studied Jig. "Isa wants you dead, goblin. I've never heard her so angry. What did you do?"

"I melted her head with my fire-spider," Jig said.

Billa snorted. For a heartbeat, genuine mirth peeked through Billa's anger. She wiped her nose on the sleeve of her nightgown, then raised her sword so the blade angled up across her body.

Jig stepped sideways, searching for an opening. Billa's sword was longer than his. So were her arms, for that matter. By the time he got close enough to strike, Billa could run him through.

He would have to be quick. A feint to distract her, causing her to overextend in one direction, and then he could dash around and stab her in the belly. Once he was close, Billa's larger weapon could be a disadvantage. She wouldn't have room for a great, sweeping blow. Though with that sword, even a tiny cut might be enough to kill.

Jig cocked his head. "Your nose is bleeding again."

Billa reached up to touch her nostrils. As she did, her sword dipped lower. Jig screamed, doing his best to mimic the panicked fury of a goblin war cry, and stabbed at her foot.

Even as Billa lurched to parry, Jig pushed off hard, bringing his sword up to her stomach and—

Billa jumped back, sucking in her gut. Once again Jig scored a small cut, and then Billa's fist caught him in the side of the head.

His sword flew away. Jig hit the ground, then rolled away from Billa's huge feet as she tried to stomp on his face. He spat snow and blood. *You should have given me a helmet too.*

Sorry.

The light from his sword made it easy to spot. Unfortunately, Billa spotted it too. She kicked it out of Jig's reach.

Jig glanced around. The surviving goblins and wolves were ringed by orcs. And Oakbottom. The orcs appeared to be waiting for Billa to finish him off. Letting her prove how tough and scary she was, no doubt.

Jig started to grab his dagger, then remembered he had thrown it away to protect Relka. Relka, who had once again begun to sing.

"I looked upon the glory of the glowing blade of Jig.
He fought the ugly orc who had a nose just like a fig.
And though his light has faded and the orcs are
drawing near,
With him I have no fear."

Billa shook her head. "Is she always like this?"

"Pretty much," said Jig as he struggled to stand. "Sorry." He knew it couldn't be fear making his legs tremble. Therefore it must be an aftereffect of Billa's punch.

I'm sorry, he said silently. *Did you really believe I could beat Billa?*

Would he feel the blow that killed him? Billa was fast, and her sword was magically sharp. Any pain would be over in the blink of an eye. Unless she deliberately tried to prolong his suffering.

Billa thrust the point of her sword straight at Jig's throat.

The impact was lower than he expected, like a punch to the chest. He flew back, hitting the ground hard enough to make his ears ring.

The wind died. Nobody spoke. Unnerved by the silence, Jig reached down to touch his stomach.

The shirt was whole. But Shadowstar's cloak wasn't strong enough to block Isa's weapon. And why could he still hear ringing?

Jig jumped to his feet and stared.

Tymalous Shadowstar stood facing him, his hands still extended. He must have pushed Jig out of the way. The bells on Shadowstar's sleeves shivered as he reached down to touch the icy blade protruding from his stomach.

"Doesn't that hurt?" Jig asked.

Shadowstar nodded. "Very much, yes." He tightened his fingers around the blade and grunted as Billa tried to pull it free.

"You saved me."

"It's what I am." He winced. "I kind of hoped it wouldn't come to this, though."

There was no blood. Did gods even have blood? But as Jig watched, water began to drip from between Shadowstar's fingers where he held the sword.

"No!" Billa shouted. She grabbed the hilt with both hands, but it wouldn't budge. Rivulets of water dripped down to the tip to splash into the snow.

"Would you mind?" Shadowstar asked. He turned his head, and the starbursts in his eyes flitted toward Billa.

Jig moved toward his sword. Two orcs stepped in front of him, brandishing a club and an ax. Before Jig could react, they raised their own weapons . . . and then toppled over, asleep.

Jig glanced back at Shadowstar, who winked. "I am a god of protection, of peace and rest," he said. His voice was tight with pain. "They looked like they could use a nap."

"Stop him!" Billa shrieked. With a grunt, she stumbled back, nearly falling. She still held Isa's sword, but the blade was broken a short distance from the hilt. Shadowstar's grip had melted right through it. The broken blade continued to shrink away, dripping water over her hands. She flung it away and ran toward Jig's sword.

Jig didn't bother. He bent down, picked up a club one of the orcs had dropped, and slammed it into Billa's leg. She dropped and clutched her knee.

As Jig struggled to get the oversize weapon into position for a second blow, another goblin shoved him aside.

Gratz's clothes were a bloody mess. Shallow wolf bites covered his forearms. He clutched his sword with both hands. The blade trembled as he pointed it at Billa.

He and Billa stared at one another for several breaths, and then Gratz said, "The penalty for treason is death." He rammed his sword into her chest, and added, "Sir."

Nobody spoke as Billa toppled backward, Gratz's sword

still protruding from her chest. Only the heavy snores of two sleeping orcs disturbed the silence.

"Is Isa's sword destroyed?" Shadowstar asked.

Jig picked up the hilt. It was cold to the touch, but not unbearably so. The blade was completely gone. He brought it over to Shadowstar, who turned it over in his hands. A few drops of water fell to the ground.

Shadowstar smiled and sat down in the snow, one hand holding the hilt, the other clutching his stomach. There was no visible wound, but Shadowstar was clearly in pain. Without thinking, Jig reached out and put his hand over Shadowstar's, trying to heal the damage, but nothing happened.

"You're drawing—" Shadowstar coughed. *You're drawing on my power to heal me. It doesn't work that way.*

The monsters crowded around had begun to whisper. Very soon now the shock would pass, and then things would get messy indeed. Already the goblins were backing away from the orcs. The orcs were eyeing the goblins. The few kobolds who had come were still jumping up and down to try to see what was going on.

The only one who didn't appear to notice the tension was Relka. She seemed to see nothing but Shadowstar as she limped closer.

"Who is that?" she whispered. Her voice shook. She clutched her amulet so tightly her hands bled.

"He's the one who got me into this mess," Jig said.

Shadowstar chuckled. "It's one of my gifts."

Relka stopped just beyond arm's reach. For the first time that Jig could remember, she appeared unsure. She glanced at Jig, then back at Shadowstar, like a rat trying to decide which way to flee. "You're him, aren't you? Tymalous Shadowstar."

Shadowstar bowed his head.

"Billa was going to kill me," Jig said. "You pushed me out of the way. Why?"

Because you didn't think to duck. And because it was the only way to get my hands on Isa's sword long enough to destroy it. His bells rang as he coughed again, an odd combination of sounds. *I did say I'd try to protect you.*

"The runt killed Billa!" shouted one of the orcs.

Good job, said Jig. He drew a deep breath, pointed at Gratz, and said, "He did the actual killing."

Braf frowned. "Does that mean he's in charge of Billa's army now?"

Before Jig could answer, another orc snarled and raised an ax. "I'm not taking orders from some scrawny goblin."

The goblins began readying their own weapons. "Better than following another stinking orc!" someone shouted.

One of the kobolds chimed in, saying, "Orcs and goblins both stink."

Jig guessed it would be the orcs who killed him. They were closest, and they had the best weapons and armor. But instead of sheer, skin-chilling terror, Jig mostly felt sad. All of Billa's work was melting away with her death. The monsters would turn on one another, decimating their own ranks. The survivors would scatter, to be hunted by humans and other adventurers.

I never thought I'd say this to you, but I think you're being optimistic.

Jig turned to look at Shadowstar, who pointed to the northern side of the valley.

Maybe Shadowstar's wounds had sapped too much of his strength for him to continue stealing Jig's fear. Or maybe there was only so much terror a god could take away.

Regardless, the cloud of arrows arching from the upper edge of the valley was enough to shatter Jig's divine courage.

"Oh, dung." His voice was little more than a whisper.

"What is it?" Relka asked.

"Wendel's army."

CHAPTER 16

THE MANIFESTATION OF TYMALOUS SHADOWstar, currently resting in the snow as Jig panicked, showed no wound from Billa's attack. Unfortunately, things in his temple were quite different.

All that blood, dripping onto his temple floor. How messy.

"You've looked better." Isa stood in the doorway. Snow swirled around her white gown, and her breath turned to frost. "Really, Tymalous. Sacrificing yourself for a goblin?"

He coughed and said, "I like that goblin."

"He's going to die anyway. If my orcs don't kill him, the humans will." Isa ran one hand through her windswept hair, almost as if she were checking for spiders. "This isn't what I wanted, you know."

Shadowstar pushed himself higher, propping his back against the wall. "I know."

She stomped across the temple. "What were you thinking, throwing yourself between Billa and that goblin? Aren't you taking this whole protection thing a bit too far?"

"It's what I am." Shadowstar smiled. Her eyes were the color of the northern glaciers, and they shone when she was angry.

"I would have spared your pet goblin," she said. "If you'd—"

"If I'd helped you kill my son?"

Isa spun away, and Shadowstar chuckled. For thousands of years, mortal poets had associated passion and rage with the element of fire. That might have changed, if Noc's curse hadn't robbed their memories of Isa and her temper.

"Shortsighted as always, Tymalous." She kept her back turned, but Shadowstar could hear the pain in her voice. "Who will stop me next time? I'll raise a new army, recreate my sword—"

"That sword took years to make."

Isa laughed. "That's the beauty of Noc's curse, love. They've forgotten us. I have all the time in the universe."

Shadowstar closed his eyes, remembering the last time Isa had spoken to him of the inevitability of victory. That war had almost destroyed them, but Isa had learned nothing. She couldn't. She was the winter wind, returning each year without fail. Unstoppable and inevitable.

"Isa, what do you think will happen when this wound kills me?"

Isa turned to face him. "I'm sorry, Tymalous. I would save you if I could, but healing has never been my strength."

"That's not what I meant." He coughed, then grimaced as more blood seeped through his fingers. "Who comes to oversee the death of the gods?"

Isa went still. "There are several gods of death," she whispered. "It might not be—"

"He's my son, Isa. He will come for me, and he will remember."

"You planned this." She stepped toward him, hands balled into fists, then caught herself. Throttling him would only speed Noc's arrival. "I'm not ready! Without my sword—"

"You should leave now," Shadowstar said. "Get a head start. If you elude him long enough, he might even forget you again. But I'm told it's very difficult to escape death once he adds your name to his list."

"You let Billa kill you, all so you could destroy my sword and send your traitor son after me."

"I was hoping to avoid the part where Billa killed me, but otherwise, yes." Shadowstar shrugged and spread his hands. "He's my son."

Snow blinded him, and then Isa was gone. Frost covered the stones.

"I'm sorry about your orc!" Shadowstar called out. He chuckled to himself. "Maybe you should have gotten yourself a goblin instead."

The arrows fell like rain, landing mostly among the kobolds—either deliberately or because that was the limit of their range. The attack sent the kobolds into a panic. The injured howled and yipped. The healthy trampled the injured.

"I thought the humans weren't supposed to arrive for another day or so," Trok said.

"Brilliant tactical move on their part," said Gratz. "Using Jig to take out Billa the Bloody, throwing our forces into chaos."

Except that if Jig had failed, Wendel's strategy would have gotten his entire army killed when Billa triggered her spell.

"The goblins betrayed us to the humans," shouted an enormous, bare-chested orc with muscles like a mountain range. A scar on his arm showed him to be one of Billa's high-ranking orcs. Either that, or a wolf had gnawed on his shoulder for a while.

"No, the humans betrayed us to the other humans," Braf argued.

The orcs didn't listen. "Kill them all," said another, a cry which quickly spread through the ranks. The bare-chested orc snarled and stomped toward Trok and the goblins, waving an enormous ax overhead. Halfway there, a ball of snow and mud exploded against the side of his head.

Everyone turned to look at Jig. Jig wiped his hand on his cloak to dry it. He wasn't sure what surprised him more, that he had thrown the muddy snow at the orc, or that he had actually hit what he was aiming at. *Did you take away my fear again?*

Not this time, said Shadowstar. *You did that all by yourself.*

Right. Jig wouldn't be shaking so hard if Shadowstar was still stealing his fear.

The orc pointed his ax. "Pound that one into the mud."

"Pound me yourself," Jig yelled. He hugged himself to

hide his trembling. *You said you'd have to wrest control from Billa and Isa in order to use the spells in those scars. Are you strong enough—*

Shadowstar smiled and leaned back, closing his eyes. *Billa is dead, and Isa is . . . busy. I can guide you, but you'll have to trigger the spell.*

The orc was laughing as he readied himself, but at least the others had drawn back to see what happened. He swung his ax through the air, stretching the muscles in his arms. He managed to kill a goblin on the backswing. He blinked in surprise, then shrugged and wiped the edge of his ax on his trousers.

"Wait," Jig squeaked. "Let me get my sword." He scrambled away from the orc. Ten paces ought to be enough distance.

Make it twenty.

Jig kept backing away. Behind the orc, Jig saw Braf tugging the other goblins and dragging them back. Shadowstar must have warned him what Jig was about to do.

"Hey, you forgot your sword!" Another orc grabbed Jig's weapon and tossed it.

Jig dove out of the way, barely avoiding being impaled by his own weapon.

Focus on the scar, said Shadowstar.

Jig began to shiver. His skin pimpled from cold that seemed to come from within, as if the blood had frozen in his veins. His fangs were the worst. This cold had come on so quickly that they actually froze to his lips.

Concentrate, Shadowstar snapped.

Jig nodded and turned toward the orc. Even at this distance, he could feel the scar on the orc's shoulder, the bitter cold that threatened to freeze Jig's eyeballs in his skull. Those spots of cold were everywhere, scattered throughout Billa's army, but Jig concentrated on the orc.

Imagine yourself melting the ice within that scar to release the spell.

Jig closed his eyes. He could still see the scar, a blur of blue cold jostling about in the darkness. All he had to do was—

Limping footsteps crunched through the snow. Jig stepped

back, his eyes snapping open. Relka stood between Jig and the orc, holding a bloody sword in both hands. "I'll kill you all before I let you hurt Jig Dragonslayer."

"Fair enough," said the orc.

Now, Jig. Melt the ice.

Jig held his breath and imagined a fire-spider in his hand. He could almost feel Smudge's terror burning his palm. Praying Shadowstar knew what he was doing, Jig visualized himself throwing the spider.

His imagination was a bit too true to life. In his mind, Smudge flew wide and landed in the snow, where he turned to glare back at Jig.

The spider is in your mind, Jig! Shadowstar shouted. *How could you possibly miss?*

Jig concentrated, imagining a nest of whiteworms on the orc's arm. Plump, delicious whiteworms, one of Smudge's favorites.

His vision blurred. Was the cold freezing his eyeballs? He hoped Shadowstar would be able to heal them. He closed his eyes and concentrated on Smudge.

In his mind, Smudge raced up the orc's body and settled directly onto the scar to feast.

Hurry, Jig.

Jig could hear the orc approaching. Clenching his fists, he imagined Golaka the chef coming up to Smudge with a pot and spoon. Jig wasn't terribly fond of fire-spider soup, but many of the goblins loved it. The risk of biting down on a flame gland and burning through your lip was part of the fun.

The imaginary Smudge looked up from his whiteworms and reacted with the same terror anyone would feel when faced with a hungry Golaka. Heat seared the scar on the orc's arm, and Jig cried out as a wind colder than any Jig had known passed *through* his body.

The wind passed in an instant. Jig didn't know how much was in his mind, but the cold had been real enough to freeze Jig's fangs to his cheeks. He wrenched his lower jaw, tearing his fangs free as he looked around.

The lenses of his spectacles had fogged over, so he lowered his head and peered over the top of the frames.

A group of orcs lay unmoving in the snow. Jig's would-be executioner stood in the center, his ax still raised overhead.

A kobold ran up to kick the closest orc. The orc's hand snapped off.

With a triumphant howl, the kobold snatched up the hand and raced back to his fellows.

In the distance, arrows continued to pour into the far edge of Billa's army, but the screams seemed far away, like echoes from a distant tunnel. Jig sheathed his sword and hugged himself to try to control his shivering.

"Who did that?" asked an orc.

Trok was the first to respond. "Jig Dragonslayer." He pointed to Jig. "The new commander of Billa's army."

"Unless anyone else wants to end up like this lot?" Relka added. She folded her arms and contemplated the frozen orcs. "I wonder how long the meat will keep, frozen like that."

"Orders, sir?" asked Gratz. Billa's blood still covered his sword. The orcs kept staring at Jig and muttering to themselves.

How long before they decided to try again? Between Shadowstar's weakness and the horrible chill of the magic, Jig doubted he could freeze another orc if he tried. He needed to take control before they all killed one another and saved the humans the trouble.

"Tell the kobolds to pull back out of range," he said.

"Why?" One of the orcs laughed. "So they kill a few dogs. Why should we care?"

"Stupid orc!" A kobold darted past two of the orcs and plunged a knife into the taunter's leg.

"No!" How had Billa done it? All the monsters wanted to do was kill one another, even with an entire army ready to ride down and destroy them.

Relka tugged his arm and pointed. Slowly Jig started to smile.

"What's the penalty for brawling on duty?" he shouted. He wasn't loud enough for the orc or the kobold to hear him over their angry cries. If they had, they might have heard Oakbottom's approach.

The orc grabbed the kobold, and then Oakbottom grabbed

them both. Moments later both the orc and the kobold were soaring over the fields.

"Oakbottom, you have permission to toss anyone else who disobeys," Jig said.

"Hey, you're not—" That was as far as the orc got before Oakbottom launched her after the others.

Oakbottom didn't care about rank or loyalty, so long as he had the chance to throw people. Jig wouldn't be able to keep control for long, but he doubted anyone would survive long enough for that to matter.

"They're going to charge right over us." Jig stood on his toes, trying to see. The orcs blocked his view of Billa's army, but he could see movement atop the far side of the valley as the human archers advanced through the trees.

Gratz shook his head. "The valley's too steep and snowy for a true charge. Horses can't handle it, and the men will have to march slow and careful. But they'll be thorough. The king will probably send hunting parties out with dogs once he's broken our forces."

And the king wouldn't stop with the valley. They knew where the goblin lair was, and they knew it was once again open to the world. Wendel had lost yet another son. He wouldn't rest until every last goblin was dead.

"Billa the Bloody would have marched this army to victory."

Even Jig's ears couldn't pick out the speaker. "Billa's dead." He turned to Gratz. "How many wolves do we have?"

"Only a few of ours survived that attack," Gratz said. "The other goblin regiments have a few more squads of wolf-riders, though. We've probably got about eighty or so all total."

Good. "Trok, go get everyone mounted up and ready to retreat."

"Typical goblin," muttered one of the orcs. "Running away like a coward."

Jig nodded to himself. That described goblins pretty well. He thought about the tunnels and caves back home, the smell of the muck lanterns, the firm feel of obsidian beneath his feet, the taste of Golaka's cooking. . . .

Angry roars shook Jig free of his stupor.

"The trolls have gotten loose," Relka commented. Jig couldn't see the former slaves, but he could hear them rampaging through the ranks. From the screams, it sounded as though they were more interested in escape than revenge.

If he was going to do anything, it had to be now, before things got any more out of control. He turned to the orcs. "You're going to take Avery for us."

"How?" asked Gratz. "We have no siege equipment, remember?"

"Sure we do," Jig said, grinning. He pointed toward Oakbottom. "We've got him. Oakbottom, how would you like to toss an entire army of orcs?"

Oakbottom's branches quivered. Presumably that was a good thing, a sign of anticipation. Or maybe it was the wind.

"Do you think you're good enough to land them on top of the wall?" Jig asked.

"Let's find out." Oakbottom reached for the nearest orc.

"Not from here!" Jig shouted.

The orcs backed away. "I'm not about to let some walking tree throw me about," said one.

Jig folded his arms. "I understand if you're afraid. I jumped from the top of that wall and survived, but it was a little frightening. If you don't think you're tough enough—"

You jumped? Shadowstar asked.

Jumped. Fell. What's the difference?

The difference is that you had Darnak there to fix you.

The orcs were already charging toward Avery. Oakbottom scooped up a few orcs for practice, flinging them toward the walls as he followed. Jig tried to imagine what it would be like to be a human atop the wall, to see orc after orc hurtling through the air, screaming and waving their weapons. Even if most of the orcs died from the impact, Oakbottom would still be able to knock the humans off the wall. And it only took a few survivors to open the gates from inside.

He turned to the goblins and kobolds. The kobolds had already drawn back past the road, safely out of range for now. They really were quick.

"When Wendel's forces see what we're doing, they'll speed up the attack, sending more men to defend Avery." Jig wished he had thought to swipe a few of Darnak's maps. This would be much easier to plan if he could see everything.

"Is that when we attack?" asked Gratz.

Jig shook his head. "We're goblins. That's when we run away."

Goblin drums were bad enough. Combined with the braying of orcish horns and the shrill yowls the kobolds used to relay commands, the noise was enough to set Jig's teeth grinding. He flattened his ears and tugged the cloak off a fallen orc. The material was bloody, but tough. He wrapped it around two spears, tying the sleeves in a tight knot. He did the same with the bottom corners. "Help me."

Braf and Relka gently lifted Tymalous Shadowstar onto Jig's cloak. Each grabbed the spears and started to lift. Then Braf cursed and dropped his end.

Jig tried not to weep. "Maybe you should grab the spears *behind* the points."

"Sorry." Braf tried a second time. "Shouldn't gods be heavier?"

Loud howls made Jig jump, even though he had been expecting it. He turned to see Trok leading the wolf-riders past Avery. The kobolds fled in the opposite direction, scampering at top speed in the general direction of Pottersville. Just let Wendel's army try to catch them all.

Promise me something, Jig.

"What?"

Shadowstar managed a smile. *Don't let them eat me.*

Jig stared at Tymalous Shadowstar. There was no blood, but he looked like . . . well, like someone who had been run through with a big sword. His face was even paler than usual, and his eyes had dimmed.

Despite everything he had seen, Jig still couldn't accept the idea of a god dying. Gods didn't do that. Humans and orcs and kobolds and goblins, sure. Especially goblins. But not gods. Part of being a god was that you didn't die.

You could run away faster if you weren't carrying me, Shadowstar pointed out.

That's why I had Braf and Relka carry you instead of doing it myself, Jig answered. "We need to get to the edge of the woods. Make sure nobody crosses the boundary into elf lands."

"How will we know?" asked Braf.

"If everyone starts getting shot with arrows, we've gone too far."

The sharp scream of an elfhawk nearly made them drop Shadowstar. Everyone turned to stare at the two enormous birds flying from Avery. Jig squinted through his spectacles, trying to discern whether the hawks carried riders.

As the birds reached the edge of the army, a few goblins and kobolds hurled spears. Most missed, and those that hit didn't appear to do any damage. Prince Theodore must have hardened his hawks' skins against attack, the same as he had done to his men.

One of the goblins leaped and swung his sword. The hawk swerved, and its talons dug into the goblin's arm. Powerful wings pounded the air. The goblin screamed and kicked as the hawk hauled him higher, then dropped him.

To a bird that size, Jig was nothing more than a rat. A scrawny rat. So hopefully the hawks would go after plumper prey.

As usual, luck was not on Jig's side. The lead hawk banked sharply, then dove.

"They look like they're coming right at us," said Braf.

Jig dropped to the ground and crawled beneath Shadowstar. Braf and Relka promptly dropped the god on top of Jig and pulled out their weapons.

None of it made any difference. The hawk drew up sharply, and one of the enormous wings knocked Braf backward. The other batted Relka to the ground. Huge talons curled around Jig's neck and chest.

"Jig!" Relka pushed to her feet and leaped. Wrapping one arm around the hawk's other leg, she tried to drive her knife into the chest. And then they were airborne.

"Easy down there." Windswept black hair all but obscured Darnak's face as he peered down from atop the hawk. "Aha! No wonder she's having trouble climbing. If your friend was so eager to come along, she should have grabbed Genevieve's bird."

Jig tried to answer, but whatever faint squeak he might have managed was lost in the beating of wings. They were already far above the treetops. He could see Braf still standing there, a confused look on his tiny face. Behind them, Genevieve clung tightly to her hawk. Her black cloak flapped behind her.

"Let us go!" Relka shouted. She clung with her arm and both legs as she tried to stab the bird in the foot.

"Hey there, none of that. What are you planning to do if you actually hurt the beast, eh? Last I knew, you goblins couldn't exactly sprout wings." Darnak had abandoned his bulky pack, as well as his armor. He carried nothing more than his war club, no doubt to minimize the burden on his mount.

"What do you want?" Jig shouted.

Genevieve guided her hawk alongside. "My father sent orders to my men to confine me for 'collaborating with the enemy.' He lied about when he would arrive, because he didn't want to spur me into doing anything rash."

"Like breaking out and escaping on your brother's elf-hawks?" Darnak asked, chuckling.

"Why are you here?" Jig asked. "I mean, why am *I* here?"

"I gave my word I'd try to protect you," said Genevieve. "There's nothing we can do to help your army, but we can at least get you back to your lair. I'm sorry, Jig. It's the best I can do for you."

Darnak leaned out to rub the hawk's neck, ruffling the wide blue feathers. This close, Jig could see the leather harness and stirrups Darnak used to ride the hawk. If he leaned any farther, he would tumble right off.

"Be careful!" Jig yelled.

"Nothing to worry about, lad," said Darnak. "You know, if you'd told me two years ago that I'd miss this, I'd have called you mad. Flying through the air, not a care in the world. There's nothing like it."

Jig craned his head, trying to pick out Braf and Shadowstar, but he was too high. The goblins were little more than panicked blue dots on the ground.

He hoped the wind wouldn't knock off his spectacles. The frames hooked pretty securely around his ears, but still. . . .

There was Wendel's army, moving out of the trees. Lines of foot soldiers marched in unison, their shields and spearheads gleaming in the sun. Behind them, archers continued to loose their arrows. There were horses as well, but as Gratz had predicted, they weren't galloping after the monsters.

Wendel's army had broken into two distinct groups. One attacked the orcs, who were busy assaulting Avery. The other spread out to pursue the retreating goblins and kobolds.

From up here, it reminded him of a tunnel-sweep, where goblins would line up and march through the caverns and tunnels to drive out the rats and other pests. Usually a second row of goblins waited in front to catch the rats for Golaka's stewpot. In this case, the elves at the top of the valley would provide the second line, killing anyone who retreated a step too far.

Trying to move as little as possible, Jig turned to look up at Darnak. "I'm not very good at directions, but isn't our lair that way?"

"Er." Darnak scowled. The hawk was flying them to the opposite side of the valley, directly toward King Wendel's army. "Like any intelligent beast, they sometimes get ideas into their heads."

Without warning, Darnak threw his weight to the right. The hawk tilted.

Jig closed his eyes, but that only made things worse. He could feel his bacon from this morning fighting to escape. Thankfully, the hawk soon leveled back out. Once again it flew straight toward the humans.

"Your cloak!" Genevieve swore. "Jig, get rid of your cloak!"

"Oh, no." The hawks were trained by color. Genevieve had used a strip of his cloak to send one of the smaller hawks to her father. Jig tried to squirm free, but the hawk's claws circling his body made it impossible.

"Does this mean we're going to your father's palace?" Relka asked.

"They're not trained to deliver messages to the palace," said Darnak. "They're trained to fly to the king. Elfhawks have senses that go beyond ours. They know exactly where

Wendel is, and once they've accepted a message, nothing short of death will divert them."

Killing the hawk was hardly an option, even if Jig had a weapon that would penetrate the bird's skin.

"I'm not afraid," Relka said. "Shadowstar will—"

"Shadowstar is dying, Relka." It came out far angrier than Jig had intended. For all he knew, Shadowstar might already be dead. The thought made his stomach hurt.

I'm not dead yet, said Shadowstar. *This isn't how I'd choose to spend my last moments in this realm, though. Bouncing through the snow, staring up at Braf's backside. You'd think he could at least pull me headfirst.*

"Father's going to kill me," Genevieve said.

"He's going to kill *you*?" Jig yelled. As they reached the top of the valley, Jig saw bright green circles scattered throughout the woods. Tents, he realized. From the look of things, most of the camp's inhabitants were off chasing orcs and goblins and kobolds.

The hawk circled lower, giving Jig a better view. The humans had made their camp along a frozen stream. The tents appeared to be arranged in rings with the largest, fanciest tents near the center.

Jig spotted any number of horses, as well as other animals. Squat gray things, like miniature horses. Larger, dark-furred animals with curved horns, tied next to oversize carts. They reminded him of goats, only fluffier. Heavy tarps hid the contents of the carts, though Jig could see men unloading barrels from one. Closer to the middle of the camp, men and women melted pots of snow over the fires.

Darnak's hawk appeared to be flying toward one of the largest tents, near the center of camp. Genevieve followed, even though she probably could have flown elsewhere. Her hawk wasn't carrying a "message," after all.

A green and white banner hung limply from the center pole of the tent. The horses and other animals spooked and pulled away as the hawks swooped down. Jig did his best to keep from throwing up.

With a loud flapping, the hawk hovered lightly in the air, so Jig was roughly level with the top of the tents. The claws relaxed, and Jig dropped into the snow. Relka landed beside him.

By the time the hawks landed, Jig and Relka were surrounded by humans with spears. The king had kept at least some of his soldiers here. Why they needed so many weapons to capture two goblins was beyond Jig. After that ride, he could hardly stand, let alone fight.

"Sorry about this," Darnak muttered, dropping to the ground. He kept one hand on his war club.

Genevieve went a step farther, drawing her own sword and stepping in front of Jig. "We've come to speak with my father," she said. "You're welcome to try to stop us."

Darnak clucked his tongue. "I wouldn't envy you the job of explaining why you had to stick Wendel's daughter with your spears."

One of the guards lowered his spear. "But Your Highness, the goblins—"

"Have come to beg for mercy." Genevieve glanced at Jig, an apologetic expression on her face.

"The champion of Tymalous Shadowstar doesn't beg," said Relka.

Jig cleared his throat. "Actually—"

"He fought Billa the Bloody and single-handedly saved your father's army." Relka folded her arms. "Your king should be on his knees to thank Jig."

Genevieve rolled her eyes. "When you beg, don't let her say anything."

"The goblins will have to surrender their weapons," said another of the guards.

Jig handed his sword over to Darnak. Relka did the same with her own weapons.

"Darnak, what happened to Smudge?" Jig whispered.

The dwarf turned to show a metal box hanging from the side of his belt. Darnak had fashioned a light wire cage with a hinged top. Inside, Smudge sat happily munching the charred remains of an enormous moth.

"I used a bit of Earthmaker's magic to forge the bars," Darnak said. "Your pet's not the prettiest beast in the world, but he grows on you after a while. I imagine you could hang his cage by a lantern at night, and he'd do a nice job of clearing the insects from your tent."

Jig smiled and poked a finger through the bars to scratch Smudge's back. He squeezed his thumb against one of the bars, testing its strength. The cage was sturdier than it appeared. Not that this should have come as a surprise, given its creator. Dwarves probably even made their socks from plates of reinforced iron.

"You'd better hold on to him," Jig said.

"Aye." Darnak clapped Jig's shoulder. "Don't be giving up hope just yet, though."

Jig cocked his head, trying to hear the sounds of battle. By now Wendel's army had to be most of the way across the valley. The monsters would be fleeing in both directions, pinned between the elven forest and the charging soldiers. Which meant that any moment now—

The goblin drums changed from the panicked chaos of retreat to an even, three-beat rhythm. At the same time, the kobolds howled as one. The wolves joined in, their cries deeper and louder than the kobolds'.

"Sounds like they're rallying for one last attack," said one of the guards.

Darnak frowned and turned to Jig. Before he could say anything, Genevieve grabbed Jig by the arm and shoved him into the tent. "Say nothing until I signal," she whispered.

Large as the tent was, it felt as crowded as the goblin dining tables a year or so back, when Golaka was making ogre chitterlings. King Wendel practically had his own army crammed within these flapping walls. Jig could barely move without bumping into angry-looking men with big swords and heavy armor.

Grudgingly, the guards stepped back to clear a path.

The canvas walls turned the sun to twilight. In the center of the room, a long table sat to one side of a crackling fire. Smoke rose through a hole in the top of the tent.

Jig recognized more of Darnak's maps spread across the table. A heavyset man with short gray hair and a heavy cloak of black fur sat studying the maps. He wore a gold crown around his forehead. It looked terribly uncomfortable. The weight pushed his ears outward, making him look a bit like a goblin child.

Genevieve and Darnak pulled Jig toward the fire. He stumbled, nearly toppling headfirst into the flames before regaining his balance.

Genevieve sighed and said, “Father, I present to you the goblin who slew Billa the Bloody.”

Where your son failed. The words were unspoken, but Jig suspected everyone heard them just the same.

King Wendel’s pale, leathery face tightened. Jig heard unhappy mutters from the guards as well.

“He comes now to beg for mercy in exchange for that boon,” Genevieve continued. “To throw himself before you, a broken and—”

“Can I surrender yet?” Jig asked. He perked his ears, straining to follow the sounds of battle in the valley. He glanced over his shoulder, but the guards had closed their circle, blocking any escape.

“Cowards, all of them,” the king muttered. His voice was like a rusty sword being drawn from a too tight sheath. He stood, resting his hands on the edge of the table as he stared down at Jig. “What would you have me do, goblin? Allow thousands of monsters to roam freely through my land, slaughtering and eating my people? Turn Avery over to the orcs who even now assault its walls?”

“Your land?” Relka stepped up to stand beside Jig. One blue finger jabbed in Genevieve’s direction. “She and her brother came into *our* mountain, killing our warriors and dragging the rest off to serve as slaves! You’re lucky Jig doesn’t slay you all!”

Genevieve grabbed Relka’s ear and yanked her back. Darnak sighed and shook his head.

The king’s face turned dark. Jig remembered Barius’ face doing the same thing, generally right before he punched Jig. Would the king punch the goblins himself, or did kings order others to do their punching?

“We owe him, Father,” Genevieve said. The corner of her mouth quirked up. “Besides, he’s kind of cute, with those big spectacles and—”

"Cute?" The king stared at Jig, as if he wanted nothing more than to shove the table out of the way and snap Jig's neck with his bare hands.

"Oh, Genevieve," Darnak murmured. "Always having to tug the griffin's tail."

"They murdered your brothers," the king said.

"And they saved your daughter," Genevieve snapped. "Is that worth nothing to you?"

On the bright side, at least Wendel's fury was no longer directed at Jig. Were kings allowed to punch their own daughters? If they were anything like goblin leaders, they could probably do whatever they liked. Though Genevieve looked fully prepared to strike him in return.

"Tell me, Father," said Genevieve. "What do you think Mother will do if she learns you ordered her only daughter arrested?"

The king glanced away. "I meant only to keep you safe."

"*Safe?* If I hadn't escaped, I would be locked away in Avery, a city currently under siege by orcs." Genevieve bit her lip, and when she spoke again, her voice was cool. "You meant to keep me from interfering with your little war."

What were the chances of Jig sneaking away in the confusion, he wondered.

Outside the tent someone shouted, "The monsters are attacking!"

So much for sneaking away.

The guards moved aside as a panting soldier shoved through the door flaps. "Sire, the goblins charge through the valley, toward our camp."

"A move of desperation," said the king. He glanced at the map, adjusting several blocks with one hand. "Order the lancers to intercept."

"They're *past* the lancers."

The king froze. "How?"

Before anyone could answer, a second guard followed the first. "The kobolds. They've circled around our lines, and they're running this way."

Jig shrunk back. He knew exactly how it had happened. The wolf-riders had fled around to the far side of Avery before turning back. Wolves were faster than anything in Wendel's army. They would have raced past the lines, never slowing as they charged the camp. Then, as Wendel's army tried to pursue, the kobolds would have done the same from the opposite end of the monster line. Kobolds weren't as fast as wolves, but they were quick, and none of the monsters were stopping to fight Wendel's soldiers. No doubt some would be cut down by human archers, but most should reach the camp. A perfect flanking maneuver. Gratz should be thrilled.

Genevieve turned to stare at Jig. Her father followed her gaze.

The king's face got even wrinklier when he was angry. He drew a gleaming sword and stepped around the table. "Treachery! You beg for mercy in order to buy time for your army."

"I didn't mean to!" Jig squeaked.

"And you! You *helped* these creatures?" He pointed his sword at Genevieve. "Arrest my daughter. Darnak as well. And kill the goblins!"

Clearly stunned, Darnak didn't react fast enough as Relka snatched her sword from him. She leaped toward the king. "For Shadowstar!"

She made it only a single step before a crossbow bolt knocked her to the ground. The king walked forward and shoved his sword through her belly.

It happened so fast. Jig ran toward Relka, barely noticing the other guards closing in around him. The crossbow bolt had struck Relka in the shoulder. She could survive that wound. But as the king yanked his sword free, blood spurted from her stomach.

Jig covered the wound with both hands. *Help me.*

I don't have a lot of power to spare right now, Jig. I'm sorry.

Jig tightened his fingers, trying to hold the wound shut to slow the bleeding. The king's sword had pierced Relka's stomach just below the scar left by Jig's own blade the year before. *She's dying because she believed in you. Because she wanted to protect the goblins, like* you *told us to do. Now help her!*

Slowly, magic filled Jig's fingers. Always before, Shadowstar's power had heated Jig's hands like a fire. Now only his fingertips felt anything at all.

"Father, no!"

Jig glanced back, then yelped and dove out of the way. The king's sword tore through his cloak and sliced a shallow gash along his back. Jig rolled and crawled as fast as he could, nearly burning his hand in the fire.

He reached back to touch the cut, and his fingers came away bloody. Shadowstar must not be strong enough to keep Jig's cloak swordproof. That wasn't a good sign.

The king followed, stabbing at Jig's legs. At least none of the guards appeared willing to shoot their crossbows, not with the king so close to Jig. So all Jig had to do was stay close to the king without getting killed. Also, he had to finish healing Relka. And find a way out of here.

The guards moved to block his escape. Everywhere he looked, boots crowded together like trees.

Jig tried to crawl beneath the table, but Wendel stabbed his sword through the end of Jig's cloak, pinning him in place. Jig gagged and rolled over. A sharp tug tore the cloak free, but Wendel was already standing over him.

"Wait!" Jig said. "If you want to fight me, do it with honor. A duel."

The king was going to kill Jig anyway. At least this way he wouldn't have to worry about the guards interfering. If Wendel was as stupid about honor as his sons had been . . .

"Stabbing an unarmed prisoner is the sort of treacherous, dishonorable thing a goblin would do," Jig added.

Wendel's jaw clenched. "True."

Darnak grabbed the king's arm. "Wendel, don't be an—" He clenched his jaw. "Sorry, sire. What I was meaning to say is, that's an ill-advised choice. We need you leading our defense against their counterattack, not wasting your time with this goblin."

Wendel's sword shook. It was a large weapon, with ornate engravings all along the blade. The pommel held a ring of emeralds and diamonds, surrounding a carved animal head. "They murdered my boys, Darnak."

"And we've killed more goblin sons than I can count," Darnak said. "Both before and after they killed the princes. Your daughter promised to put an end to the slaughter in exchange for this goblin's help against Billa."

"Genevieve exceeded her authority."

"Aye," said Darnak. "And you'd have done the same thing in your youth."

"Enough, Darnak." Wendel picked up Relka's sword and threw it to Jig. Jig barely managed to grab the hilt, and then Wendel swung.

Jig rolled out of the way. Unfortunately, he rolled right into the fire pit. The searing pain in his hand was annoying, but his years with Smudge had accustomed him to such things. He scrambled back, brushing embers from his skin. The edges of his cloak began to burn. Some of the guards snickered.

He patted himself out, and something jabbed him in the side. He checked his pocket as he backed away. Perhaps Shadowstar had slipped an extra weapon into the cloak.

His fingers found the tiny goblin figurine Darnak had given him. Having no better ideas, he flung it at the king.

The metal goblin bounced off of the king's forehead, right beneath the crown. Wendel stepped back. A dot of blood formed on his skin, then dripped down over his nose.

Jig lunged.

Wendel was faster than he looked. He parried Jig's thrust down and to one side. The blade barely scratched the side of his leg. Then the king punched Jig's face with his other hand.

The sword slipped away, and Jig found himself on the dirt, staring up at the top of the tent. His mouth tasted like blood. Wendel punched *hard*. Jig tried to sit up, but movement made him want to vomit.

King Wendel filled his vision. Two of them, actually. Two Wendels and two big swords. As if one wasn't enough. Jig blinked, trying to clear his eyes and reconcile the two kings. Which sword should Jig try to avoid?

Wendel swung. Jig's panicked scream almost blocked out the simultaneous thud and clang that followed.

A slender sword blade crossed with a battered war club

over Jig's head. Both weapons held the king's sword away from Jig. "You dare to raise arms against your king?" Wendel asked.

"I raise arms to support your daughter," Darnak said. "To support the future queen of Adenkar."

"You swore an oath to me."

"To you and Jeneve, aye," Darnak said, showing no sign of strain as he held the king's sword at bay. None of the guards so much as breathed. "She's the one who'll be cursing my shade if I let the two of you get killed, and she'd have the right of it. I've been helping to raise your children from the time they were in diapers, and I've watched too many of them die. I'll not see Ginny lost to the same foolishness. We're about to be overrun. They've already reached the edge of our encampment. That goblin you're about to murder is the only one who might be able to stop them from slaughtering every last one of us."

Wendel turned toward Genevieve, who used her own sword to shove the king's weapon to the side. "Besides," she said, her voice light, "if you kill him, you'll never find out what poison he used."

He blinked. "Poison?"

Genevieve pointed to the cut on the king's leg. "When we attacked the goblin lair, I learned that goblins poison their blades."

"Pah. Darnak can heal the wound." Wendel shoved Genevieve back, then raised his sword again.

"Begging Your Majesty's pardon, but goblins have been known to use some nasty toxins," Darnak said. "Without knowing the actual poison, well, I might be able to save your life, but the side effects could be unpleasant."

Jig stared from Darnak to Genevieve and back, trying to understand. They both knew perfectly well that goblins didn't use poison on their weapons. Given the number of self-inflicted injuries Jig had healed over the years, poison would have wiped out half the lair.

They were bluffing. Like Grell had done. Only they were doing it to protect him.

Wendel spun to face Jig. "Was the blade poisoned?"

Jig managed to sit up without losing his last meal. "Well, I *am* a goblin."

"Tell Darnak what toxin you used, or—"

"You'll kill me?" Jig glanced at Relka. She was pale, but still breathing. "You'll do that anyway. And how many goblins can die knowing they killed a king?"

Slowly Wendel lowered his sword. "What do you want, goblin?"

"A treaty," Jig said. "Like you have with the elves." His lip was puffy and split, making his voice sound funny. "I want you to stop killing us."

Which was stronger, Jig wondered, the king's hatred of goblins or his desire to survive? From the fury on his face, it was a close thing.

More and more guards were glancing around, their expressions tense. Even Darnak jumped as a wolf howled nearby.

"As if these beasts would listen to you," Wendel said.

"They'll listen to him." Relka's voice was weak as a child's, and she drooled blood as she spoke. "He's Jig Dragonslayer."

Jig prayed she was right. *Have Braf get to the drummers and the orcs. Tell them to order a halt. Don't retreat, but wait for my signal.*

There was no answer. *Shadowstar?* Jig's chest tightened.

Then in the distance, the drumbeats changed to a slow, steady rhythm, like a heartbeat. The horns blew a moment later.

Jig was already moving toward Relka. He could barely feel Shadowstar's magic anymore, but he pressed what power he could into her wound.

"Sire, the goblins—" One of the guards stood in the open flap of the tent, gasping for breath. "They've stopped."

"How?" For the first time, the hatred had faded slightly from Wendel's voice, replaced by genuine curiosity.

"The power of Tymalous Shadowstar," Relka said, holding her necklace.

"Who?" asked Wendel.

Shadowstar, god of idiot goblins. Jig pinched the skin together, trying to physically force the wound to seal. *What had*

Relka been thinking? Every time Jig thought he had seen the limits of her madness, she proved him wrong. Leaping onto a hawk, attacking a king, all in the name of a god who—

Shadowstar's laughter, soft and strained, made Jig jump. *You think she did that for me?*

Ever since I stabbed her, she hasn't been able to shut up about the glory of Tymalous Shadowstar.

You're a smart one, Jig. For a goblin. Silence followed, long enough that Jig started to wonder if something had happened. Then Shadowstar said, *She could have stayed behind with her dying god. Instead she went with you. Why do you think she did that?*

Because she's crazy!

Another quiet chuckle. *Probably.*

"Order the men to withdraw, Father," said Genevieve. "Sign the goblin's treaty."

"Your sons are gone," Darnak said softly. "This won't bring them back. And losing you and Genevieve will destroy the queen."

Wendel's shoulders slumped. He wiped blood from his face and nodded. "The cure, goblin."

What cure? Oh, right. The poison.

"You *do* have an antidote, don't you?" Genevieve's glare rivaled Grell's.

Keeping one hand on Relka's wound, Jig used his other to fish through his cloak. "Swallow this, and you should be fine."

The king backed away. Rarely had Jig seen such an expression of horror from anyone, goblin or human. "It's a toe."

"It's been soaked in lizard-fish blood," Jig lied. "Something about their blood counters the poison."

"It's a *toe*," Wendel repeated.

Darnak handed a flask to the king. "Drink deep, sire. Dwarven ale's strong enough to mask most any taste."

Jig ignored them. He could feel Relka's muscle repairing itself one strand at a time as Shadowstar's magic trickled from Jig's fingertips. He hadn't even tried to pull the crossbow bolt from her shoulder yet, but if he could heal the worst of the damage to her stomach, she should survive.

Angry voices outside the tent made him cringe. At least

one belonged to a goblin. What were they doing here? Hadn't they heard the drums? If they attacked now, everything would fall apart.

Several of the humans readied their weapons. Both Genevieve and Darnak looked at Jig. He shook his head. This wasn't anything of his planning.

The voices drew closer, and then the tent flap was flung open. Two figures stood in the blinding sunlight.

"Jig?" Trok's voice.

The smaller figure shoved him aside. "See? Hessafa told you smelly goblin was here! Always trust scent!"

CHAPTER 17

JIG HAD NEVER REALIZED HOW MANY PEOPLE could fit onto the mountainside. He tried not to shiver as he glanced around. Kobolds and a few orcs covered the rocky ground. Many of the kobolds watched from the branches, shoved aside by a small delegation of orcs. Most of the orcs had already left, claiming the colder, treeless land higher up the mountainside. Apparently they *liked* the snow and wind. It gave them more opportunity to prove how tough they were. Rumor had it that a few of them had even taken to diving naked into the icy lake.

Orcs were weird. Or maybe the cold helped with the itching. During the attack at Avery, some of the orcs had circled around the town, searching for another way in that didn't involve being flung by a tree. In the process they had trampled through the vines the humans called poison ivy. They said regular poison ivy was bad enough, but these vines grew on elven soil. . . .

The hobgoblins were already discussing how best to bring the vines back and incorporate them into their traps.

Goblins crowded by the cave, packed together like pickles in a barrel. Jig grimaced and tried to force that image from his mind.

A smaller group of hobgoblins stood nearby, scowling and

testing their weapons. Apparently, with Jig gone and the goblin warriors all dragged away to Avery, the hobgoblins had run wild, looting the lair and slaughtering anyone who dared to challenge them. They had tried to do the same thing to Jig and his companions when they finally returned.

Oakbottom had tossed nine hobgoblins down the mountainside before the rest retreated. They retaliated by loosing some of their tunnel cats.

Bastard and the other wolves had solved that problem. Fortunately, Braf had managed to heal the stump of Bastard's leg, and the three-legged wolf was still as mean as ever. Jig just hoped they hadn't developed a taste for tunnel cats.

For now, the wolves were being kept at a smaller cave farther up the mountain. Jig still needed to figure out how to feed the beasts. Maybe the hobgoblin chief would donate a few of the warriors who had mocked Jig in the past.

Jig cocked his head, automatically silencing his thoughts while he waited for Tymalous Shadowstar to rebuke him for such a vindictive, goblinlike thought. There was no response. Jig had heard nothing from his god since leaving the king's tent four days ago.

With a sigh, he reached down to stroke Smudge, who sat happily in his cage on Jig's belt. At least the weather had improved since the battle the humans were calling "Billa's Fall." The snow was gone, and Jig could stand outside without shivering. Without shivering from the cold, at any rate. He pulled his cloak tighter, trying not to think about what was about to happen.

"They're coming," said Relka.

Directly ahead, Princess Genevieve approached on foot, followed by Darnak and her retinue of human soldiers. Her face was flushed from the hike, but she was grinning.

Beside Relka, Gratz was frantically paging through his notes. Dark blue scabs covered his face and arms from being trapped beneath Bastard. He was lucky the wolf hadn't killed him. Jig had worried that Gratz would try to punish Bastard for his injuries, but Gratz had been delighted. These days, the trick was to get him to stop showing off his "war scars."

"Do you remember your lines, sir?" Gratz asked. "Protocol dictates that you speak first."

Jig glanced at Trok, who made a half-hearted grab for his sword, as if offering to shut Gratz up. Jig shook his head, then turned his attention to Genevieve and Darnak.

The princess wore a new black tabard, this one trimmed with gold. A thin silver band circled her forehead. Jig could hear some of the kobolds admiring the crown.

Darnak had brushed his beard into twin braids. He carried a new war club of gleaming black wood. If the kobolds liked Genevieve's crown, they were practically falling out of the trees at the sight of Darnak's armor. Gleaming steel covered his chest, thighs, and shoulders. Heavy links of mail protected his arms and legs. Combined with the bulging pack on his back, Jig was amazed the dwarf could walk at all.

Genevieve stopped. Goblins, orcs, and kobolds all began to whisper.

Oh, right. Jig took a step forward. "Welcome, Princess Genevieve, to—" He swallowed. The other monsters weren't going to like this. "To Goblinshire."

Behind him, Braf whispered, "To where?"

There was a sharp thud, like a wooden cane smacking a goblin skull. Jig relaxed slightly. He had worried Grell wouldn't be able to make it.

"Well met, goblin," said Genevieve. With one hand, she slowly pulled her sword from its sheath.

Every monster went silent. Jig could see them reaching for their own weapons. Others searched the mountainside. Genevieve hadn't brought enough soldiers to fight, unless this was some sort of trap.

Indeed, looking at the stern expression on the princess' face, Jig was half tempted to draw his own weapon, even though they had warned him that this was coming.

Now was the part where Jig was supposed to kneel and let Genevieve finish a brief ceremony to seal the treaty. A ceremony that involved Genevieve resting her sword on Jig's shoulder. Right beside his neck. Where a slight tug would slit his throat.

Gratz coughed and waved his hand, urging Jig forward.

Jig stared at the sword. "Grell's the chief. Maybe she should be the one to—"

"Finish that sentence, and I'll have Golaka feed you to your wolves," Grell snapped.

Right. Jig dropped to one knee and held his breath. Genevieve had saved his life, back in the king's tent. She wouldn't kill him now.

The flat of the sword landed on his shoulder, hard enough to bruise.

"In the name of Wendel, King of Adenkar, in recognition for your—" Genevieve coughed. Her mouth was quivering, as if she were trying not to laugh. "Your service to the throne, I hereby grant thee the title of baron, Lord of Goblinshire and all who dwell in that land. Rise, Baron Jig of Goblinshire."

Jig waited until her sword was back in its scabbard to stand. As he did, Darnak stepped forward, holding a green ribbon with a silver medallion. As many times as he had mocked Relka's necklace, this one was worse. The medallion had the same ridiculous crest as Genevieve's armor. Darnak looped it over Jig's head like a noose.

In the silence that followed, everyone heard Grell's muttered, "If he thinks he can take my room, I'll strangle him with his own ribbon."

Jig turned the medallion over in his hand, studying the boar on the crest. Well, it had nice fangs, if nothing else.

A few of the human guards clapped their hands together. The noise startled the closest monsters into drawing weapons.

"They were applauding," Darnak said hastily. "To congratulate you. Genevieve ordered them to applaud, or else she'd be leaving them here to serve you."

From the look on the humans' faces, they were as unhappy about the whole process as Jig. In order for this treaty to be valid, apparently there had to be a baron to oversee the goblins' lands. Jig didn't know who had been more horrified, himself or the king. But according to the humans' laws, this was the only way.

Even now, Jig suspected the king was hard at work rewriting those laws. Just as, from the sound of it, the other goblins were hard at work fighting not to laugh.

Darnak unrolled a heavy scroll of lambskin. Wax seals and

ribbons decorated the bottom beside the king's signature. Darnak pulled out a blue quill and dipped it into the pot of ink lashed to the strap of his backpack, then handed the quill to Jig.

Ink splattered the bottom of the treaty as Jig scrawled his name. He returned the quill to Darnak, then turned to face the other monsters.

"That's it?" Braf asked.

"I think so," Jig said. He glanced at Genevieve, then added, "They've officially given us our own mountain."

Genevieve was clearly losing her struggle to avoid laughing in Jig's face. "I've convinced my father to forgo your first tax payment, so you won't have to worry about that until midsummer."

And Jig had thought his stomach couldn't hurt any worse. "Tax payment?"

"I'll let you explain that one to the hobgoblin chief," Grell said. She didn't bother to hide her amusement.

"You're also responsible for maintaining order here in . . . Goblinshire," Genevieve continued. "In the case of war, you can be summoned to lead your warriors to assist in the protection of Adenkar. A representative of my father's court will be by in the next few days to review your other obligations and duties."

From her wicked grin, she was already selecting which human to punish with goblin duty.

Darnak squeezed Jig's arm. "Good luck to you, Jig. Goblinshire has a fine protector. An unusual one, to be certain. But you've proven yourself a resourceful lad. Don't let your newfound title worry you. Having lived among goblins and their backstabbing, treacherous ways, you're far better prepared for politics than most."

Apparently that was the end of it. Genevieve pulled out her pipe as she turned to go.

Wheezing laughter turned to coughs behind him. Poor Grell was laughing so hard her canes barely supported her. Before Jig could say anything, Trok tugged his sleeve.

"Grell doesn't sound so good," he said, his voice eager. He sounded like a child about to get his first taste of Golaka's elf soufflé. "Remember what you promised me."

"I remember," Jig snapped. Already other monsters were closing in. Goblins, mostly. But there were hobgoblins, kobolds, even an orc, all shoving to be the first to talk to him. Jig had a sinking feeling that this would be his life for some time to come.

"Gratz!"

Gratz snapped to attention. "Yes, Lord General, sir?"

Jig rolled his eyes. "Deal with them." Before Gratz could answer, Jig scurried after Genevieve and Darnak. "Princess, wait!"

Genevieve stopped a short distance down the trail.

Jig moved uncomfortably close to the human and lowered his voice. "You haven't told your father the truth about Barius and Ryslind, have you?"

Genevieve shook her head. "What truth? That they were idiots who never should have come here? Even if I wanted to tell him, it's going to be a long time before he's willing to listen to me again."

"Don't worry yourself too much," said Darnak. "Once your mother goes to work, she'll bring him around. She got him to rescind my banishment, didn't she? The way I spoke to him, I half expected he'd be declaring war on all dwarfkind."

"There are those who would say yours was a harsher punishment," Genevieve said, pulling out her pipe. "Removed from the king's service and given to his daughter."

"A cruel sentence, to be sure," Darnak said, grinning.

She turned her attention back to Jig and smiled. "Besides, as long as I'm the only human who knows the truth, it means I have you as a friend."

"What do you mean?" Jig asked.

"My brothers are dead. That puts me directly in line for the throne, once my father passes on." Her fingers tightened. "If the people learn that the Baron of Goblinshire murdered two human princes, they'll go right back to hunting you goblins down. And that means you and I are going to be friends for a long time." She flashed a smile. "My family isn't terribly popular these days. I'll need a few friends."

That was reasoning a goblin could understand. Jig smiled back. "Thanks!"

Sure, she was manipulating him. But if she wanted to *keep* manipulating him, she also had to help keep him alive. What more could Jig ask?

He turned to Darnak and said, "Thanks for healing my tooth."

"Thank Earthmaker," Darnak said, touching his amulet.

Jig had tried and failed to heal the broken tooth himself, following his fight with the king. He was still adjusting to the everyday scrapes and cuts of life in the mountain. He hadn't realized how spoiled he had become over the past few years.

Darnak poked a finger through Smudge's cage. "You take care of your master now, you hear?"

Genevieve shuddered. Apparently humans simply couldn't appreciate a good spider. "Come, Darnak. We've a long ride home."

Jig waited among the trees and watched them leave. Partly he wanted to make sure none of the monsters tried to ambush them as they left. Mostly he simply wasn't ready to go back and be a baron. This was worse than being chief.

"You arranged all of this, didn't you?" he asked, staring at the sky. He took off his spectacles and wiped them on his shirt. "I don't know how, but this is all your fault."

"Is he speaking to you again?"

Jig yelled and fumbled for his sword. "Relka?"

She bent to retrieve his spectacles from the mud. "He's not dead, you know."

"Billa the Bloody stabbed him with a god-killing sword," Jig snapped, grabbing his spectacles. "And unlike you, Shadowstar didn't have a dwarf priest around to finish healing him."

According to Braf, Shadowstar had simply . . . disappeared. Braf wasn't sure, but he thought Shadowstar had said something like "It's good to see you again," before he died. Whatever that meant. Between the drums and the horns and the shouts, Jig suspected Braf had simply misheard.

"Tymalous Shadowstar was one of the Forgotten Gods," said Relka. "You saw how the humans and elves and other 'civilized' races couldn't even remember his name."

"So what?"

Relka pointed back toward the lair. "Kobolds and hobgoblins and orcs and goblins, all living together without killing each other. Not much, at any rate. A treaty with the humans. A goblin baron." She spread her arms. "Jig, Shadowstar was civilizing us. That's why he stopped talking to you. It's not enough that we've forgotten him. Not yet, anyway. But it's enough that we can't see or hear him anymore."

That was the dumbest theory Jig had ever heard. Though it did sound like something Shadowstar might do.

Could Shadowstar have somehow survived being run through with Isa's sword? "You really believe that?"

"I know it."

Relka was an idiot. Yet the knots in Jig's stomach eased a little. Shadowstar was a god, after all. Jig was only a goblin. Who was he to say what could or couldn't have happened?

"Relka, when Shadowstar was dying . . . or not dying. When he was back there in the valley. You could have stayed with him. Instead you came with me. Why—?" He hesitated, then decided he would need a few mugs of klak beer before he was ready to ask *that* question. "Never mind."

Jig stared at the medallion Genevieve had given him. Strange, to think that such an ugly little thing could stop the humans from killing them. From doing it openly, at least. This and his name on a piece of paper were all it took.

"Where is this so-called baron?" That sounded like the hobgoblin chief. Jig turned to see him making his way down the path, followed by a clearly agitated Gratz. "Your idiot goblins have ruined three of our hunting traps!"

"I'm sorry, Lord," Gratz shouted. "He didn't want to stand in line, and—"

The hobgoblin drew his sword, and Gratz shut up.

"What did they do to your traps?" Jig asked.

The hobgoblin's scarred, wrinkled face was a deep yellow, flushed with anger. "Well, one of them fell into our pit and broke his leg. Another tripped a rockslide Charak had been working on. The third . . . well, that wasn't a trap, exactly. By that time, my hobgoblins were a bit annoyed. Your goblin kind of stumbled onto Renlok's spear. Eleven times."

Before Jig could figure out how to respond, Trok came

running down to join them. A hobgoblin with a scar along his face was with him. Jig recognized Charak, a trapmaker better known to the goblins by his nickname, Slash.

Trok stepped so close to the hobgoblin chief that their chests nearly touched. "One of your tunnel cats got into the wolf pens again! Killed two of my goblins in the process."

Gratz cleared his throat.

"Right." Trok jabbed a thumb at Jig. "Two of *his* goblins."

Jig groaned. His stomach was bad enough, but now his head was beginning to hurt as well. If there was one thing the hobgoblins wouldn't tolerate, it was an attack against their trained tunnel cats. "Was there anything left of the cat?"

Slash grinned. "What makes you think they were fighting?"

Oh. Could tunnel cats and wolves interbreed? That was just what Jig needed, a litter of cross-breeds running loose in the mountain, eating anyone who got too close.

Jig grabbed Trok by the arm and shoved him toward Slash. "Go help the hobgoblins retrieve their tunnel cat." If he was lucky, maybe the wolf would eat Trok, and he would have one less problem to worry about. "Gratz, sit down with the hobgoblin chief and come up with some regulations about hunting and traps."

As Jig had hoped, the goblins and hobgoblins immediately began to argue with one another, instead of with him. Only after they had gone did he realize the rest of the monsters had disappeared. The mountainside was actually quiet! He turned back to Relka. "Where did everybody go?"

"Golaka and I were working in the kitchens earlier, preparing a few roast hobgoblins. I guess they must have finished roasting."

Jig's stomach rumbled at the thought. The hobgoblins might not be too happy about their dead warriors, but even they couldn't turn down Golaka's cooking. He wondered if barons were entitled to extra helpings.

He turned to head back, then hesitated.

"What is it?"

Jig perked his ears. The trees were empty. He heard nothing but the wind in the branches and the very distant sound of Trok and the hobgoblin chief shouting at one another.

"Nothing," he said. "I thought . . . nothing." He must have imagined the faint sound of bells in the distance.

He shook his head. "Come on, Relka. Let's go eat some hobgoblins."

Civilized, indeed.